CRITICAL ACCLAIM FOR

H. R. F. Keating and his Inspector Ghote Novels

'Few if any contemporary writers are as entertaining as the remarkable H. R. F. Keating.' **Len Deighton**

'H. R. F. Keating has created in Ganesh Ghote an enchanting and engaging inspector.' **P. D. James**

'The Indianness of it all is conveyed with utmost skill.' ***Evening Standard***

'H. R. F. Keating's Inspector Ghote is a man much like ourselves only more so: diffident, misdoubting his own powers, often sadly muddled by the unaccountable happenings assailing him . . . Comedy of the international situation such as might have won the admiration of Henry James himself.' ***Times Literary Supplement***

'Mr Keating has a long-established winner in his sympathetic and lively hero.' ***The Times***

'H. R. F. Keating breathes new life into the classic detective story.' **Reginald Hill**

'Inspector Ghote is one of the great characters of the contemporary mystery novel.' ***New York Times***

'One of the most engaging of all fictional detectives.' **Edmund Crispin, *Sunday Times***

'Mad, brilliant, touching . . . [*The Perfect Murder* is] a book of subtlety and great skill.' ***Evening Standard***

'A mixture of wit, gentleness and super storytelling.' ***Times of India***

'Surely the most likeable fictional sleuth.' ***Scotsman***

The Inspector Ghote Mysteries

H. R. F. Keating was the crime books reviewer for *The Times* for fifteen years. He has served as Chairman of the Crime Writers Association and the Society of Authors, and in 1987 was elected President of the Detection Club.

He has written numerous novels as well as non-fiction, but is best known for the Inspector Ghote series, the first of which, *The Perfect Murder*, was made into a film by Merchant Ivory and won a CWA Gold Dagger Award, as did *The Murder of the Maharajah.*

In 1996 H. R. F. Keating was awarded the CWA Cartier Diamond Dagger for outstanding services to crime literature.

He is married to the actress Sheila Mitchell and lives in London.

Also by H. R. F. Keating

The Inspector Ghote Series

The Perfect Murder
Inspector Ghote's Good Crusade
Inspector Ghote Caught in Meshes
Inspector Ghote Hunts the Peacock
Inspector Ghote Plays a Joker
Inspector Ghote Breaks an Egg
Inspector Ghote Goes by Train
Inspector Ghote Trusts the Heart
Bats Fly Up for Inspector Ghote
Filmi, Filmi, Inspector Ghote
Inspector Ghote Draws a Line
The Murder of the Maharajah
Go West, Inspector Ghote
The Sheriff of Bombay
Under a Monsoon Cloud
The Body in the Billiard Room
Dead on Time
Inspector Ghote, His Life and Crimes
The Iciest Sin
Cheating Death
Doing Wrong
Asking Questions

Fiction

Death and the Visiting Firemen
Zen there was Murder
A Rush on the Ultimate
The Dog it was that Died
Death of a Fat God
A Remarkable Case of Burglary
The Strong Man
The Underside
A Long Walk to Wimbledon
The Lucky Alphonse
The Rich Detective
The Good Detective
The Bad Detective

Non-fiction

Murder Must Appetize
Sherlock Holmes: The Man and His World
Great Crimes
Writing Crime Fiction
Crime and Mystery: The 100 Best Books
The Bedside Companion to Crime

H. R. F. Keating

The Inspector Ghote Mysteries

An Omnibus

The Perfect Murder

Inspector Ghote's Good Crusade

Inspector Ghote Caught in Meshes

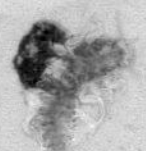

PAN BOOKS

The Perfect Murder first published by Collins & Co Ltd 1964
Inspector Ghote's Good Crusade first published by Collins & Co Ltd 1966
Inspector Ghote Caught in Meshes first published by Collins & Co Ltd 1967

This collection first published 1996 by Pan Books
an imprint of Macmillan Publishers Ltd
25 Eccleston Place, London, SW1W 9NF
and Basingstoke

Associated companies throughout the world

ISBN 0 330 34856 6

1 3 5 7 9 8 6 4 2

A CIP catalogue record for this book is available from
the British Library

Phototypeset by Intype London Ltd
Printed by Mackays of Chatham PLC, Chatham, Kent

Contents

The Perfect Murder

Winner of the CWA Gold Dagger Award

1

It was called the Perfect Murder right from the start. First the Bombay papers plastered it all the way across their pages. And then it was taken up by papers all over India.

The Perfect Murder: Police at House.

The Perfect Murder: New Police Moves.

The Perfect Murder: Police Baffled.

Every time Inspector Ghote saw the words he felt the sweat spring up all along the top of his shoulders. It was as if every one of India's four hundred million people were looking at him, challenging him to break it. The Perfect Murder.

Each time he had to pull himself together and remind himself of the cold facts. It was nothing like four hundred million people. Most of them would never hear of the Perfect Murder however many times it made the headlines in Bombay or elsewhere. Many of them were unable to read; some of them had never even heard of Bombay.

But still people kept calling it the Perfect Murder. And, though Inspector Ghote repeated to himself again and again that all that the case required was the proper procedure tirelessly applied, each time he heard the words the long patch of sweat came up right across his skinny shoulders.

Arun Varde himself had called it the Perfect Murder the night he had sent for the police with such urgency.

'The Perfect Murder,' he stormed, 'and in my house, the house of Lala Arun Varde. It must not be allowed. It shall not be allowed.'

Inspector Ghote knew what he meant. Arun Varde was a

man of immense wealth, a lala, a man with vast influence in the highest quarters. A murder in his house was a murder indeed.

The inspector swallowed nervously. He had a feeling that he ought not to let such a person tread all over him, otherwise his chances of ever applying the proper procedure would be slight.

'There are ten thousand murders in India every year, Mr Varde,' he began.

He was not allowed to finish. Lala Arun Varde swung his huge bulk round to face him, to tower over him.

'Ten thousand murders in India. What do I care about them? Are there ten thousand murders in my house? In the house of Lala Arun Varde? Are there one thousand? Are there a hundred only? Or fifty? Or ten? Or two. Are there two only?'

'No, but—'

'No. In my house there is one only. The Perfect Murder. They have dared to come into my house for that. Into my very house. They have come with their murderous knives, their guns, their pistols, their clubs, their cannons to strike me to the inmost middle of my heart.'

He came to a forcible halt for lack of air, sucked in a breath with a noise like the last great splurge of an elephant ingesting the entire contents of a river pool, and charged again.

'Yes,' he said, 'into my very house they have come. But do not think they will get away with it. Oh, the rotten, murdering, lying, robbing, fornicating devils, I will crush them. Blot them out, squeeze them to powder, crumble them to dust of dust.'

Looking at him as calmly as he could manage, Inspector Ghote thought that crushing and crumbling would come only too easily to such a massy, rolling mountain of a man.

'But, Mr Varde,' he said, 'the detection and apprehension—'

Lala Varde let loose an immense sob.

'Oh,' he moaned, 'they have struck me to the heart. They have entered my fortress. They have dared to do it. They have defied me, spat on me, rubbed me in the dirt. They have come into the very middle of my home and have defiled it. I am lost, lost. Helpless, hopeless, handless. Killed, murdered, dead.'

He flung himself down on a low couch, which groaned and buckled under the impact, and sat with his great pumpkin head lolling in abject dejection.

Inspector Ghote drew attention to himself with a neat little rat-tat of a cough.

'A murder has taken place, sahib,' he said. 'Very well. We will settle down to find out who is responsible. Just as we settle down to find out who killed all the other ten thousand people who are murdered every year.'

Lala Varde swung his head upwards and the inspector caught a glimpse of two sharp pig-eyes glinting.

'And how many murderers do you find? Ten only?'

'Nearly one third of murders reported result in convictions,' said Inspector Ghote stiffly.

Lala Varde laughed.

He laughed till his huge belly shook like a great steam engine pumping in and out.

'Oh, my poor Inspector,' he said, 'your police force is not very good.'

'It will be good enough to find out who committed this murder,' Inspector Ghote answered.

'So that is why to my house they send an inspector only,' Lala Varde countered.

Inspector Ghote smiled a little uneasily.

'I am not in charge of the case officially, Mr Varde,' he said. 'This is a DSP matter, definitely a DSP matter.'

'DSP one, two, three,' Lala Varde said. 'What do I know of your DSPs? All I see is inspector. A murder in my house and they send inspector.'

Inspector Ghote smiled again.

'DSP is Deputy Superintendent of Police,' he said. 'DSP Samant is personally in charge of the case, personally.'

'The Perfect Murder,' Lala Varde said with a great, gusty sigh, 'and a deputy only.'

Inspector Ghote did not succeed in smiling again.

He felt there was a due limit to the amount of such aspersion. It had been overstepped.

'Mr Varde,' he said with an edge of anger in his voice. 'I must remind you that this case is called the Perfect Murder for one reason only: the victim's name is Perfect, Mr Perfect, your Parsee secretary.'

He looked firmly at the huge man in front of him.

'There is no reason at all,' he added, 'why the crime should not be dealt with in a perfectly normal and easy manner. No reason at all.'

'Reason treason,' said Lala Varde. 'It is not a normal murder. It is my murder. They did it to me. Ah, the dirty ravishers of their own mothers, they thought that, without Mr Perfect, Lala Varde would be no good. Well, let them see. I'll show them, Perfect or no Perfect. They think I can't follow the details of my own business. I know what they say. They say I owe all my success to a Parsee secretary. Let me tell them that Lala Varde had made his lakhs and crores of rupees before he had ever heard of any secretary mekretary.'

He looked round for enemies.

'Ah,' he said, 'they struck right to the heart. What am I to do without Mr Perfect? Am I a clerk that I should have to add this figure to that? Am I a poke-and-pry little old dry-as-dust of a lawyer to go looking at deeds and land registers all day with my nose pushed down into old papers peepers?'

He creased his pot belly suddenly forward and peered down at some huge imaginary tome like a whale aping a tortoise.

Inspector Ghote drew himself up to a position of attention.

'Mr Varde,' he said, 'if you know the names of the murderers, I must request you to give them to me without delay.'

Lala Varde stopped peering into his imaginary register.

He plunged up and jabbed a podgy forefinger in the direction of the inspector.

'You must request me to give you the names of the murderers? This is a fine way to catch a criminal. You go to a poor man who has worries of his own and you say: tell me who I am to catch. Am I to be a policeman only now? All the State taxes that I pay, are they to go for nothing? Am I to do all the work of the Police Department when I have finished my day at the office? Is chasing after dacoits to be a hobby for me?'

Inspector Ghote remained at attention.

'Sahib,' he said, 'do I understand that you consider the murder has business motives?'

'Business badness,' Lala Varde replied. 'What other motive could it have? Nobody is going to kill that long stick of a Parsee because he has ravished their daughter, are they? Do you think he has been stabbed by a jealous mistress, so thin that he is she would have to want to be embraced by a basket of wires?'

'Sahib.'

Inspector Ghote took a short step forward.

His mouth felt dry and the thought of his little house in Government Quarters, his wife and his child came unexpectedly into his head.

But Lala Varde stopped ranting and looked at him.

'Sahib, you are making grave accusation. You must tell me the names of those you are accusing.'

Suddenly Lala Varde sat down again on the low couch against the wall.

'Inspector sahib,' he said, 'I am an old man. I have had a long life. Many enemies I have made. Always in business it is the same: it is each man for himself only. How can I tell which of them has done this to me? All my affairs are in ruin. All the facts and figures were in that man's head. And look at his head now. Broken to pieces. Inspector, what am I to do? Inspector sahib, come and sit here beside me and tell me as a friend what I am to do now.'

Inspector Ghote lowered himself till he just touched the edge of the couch.

'Well, sahib,' he said, 'a police officer cannot advise a private citizen about his business affairs.'

'No one can advise me any more,' said Lala Varde.

He shook his head mournfully. His fat chins rolled past each other. Smoothly working, fluidly soft parts of some mysterious machine.

'No one can advise me. No one can tell me what will pay and what will bring ruin. No one will know what to leave aside and what to take up to the finish. Ruined. Ruined. My cars I will have to sell. My sons I will no longer be able to support. My poor Dilip, what good will he be if he has to earn all he needs by himself only? Who will employ him to read mystery books all day? What will he do when he loses all his social position? What else does he care for?'

Inspector Ghote bobbed forward till he came into the fat old man's vision.

'Mr Dilip Varde?' he said. 'He is your elder son? Is he at present in the house? It would be necessary for me to take his evidence.'

Lala Arun Varde ignored him.

Instead he rocked from side to side in all-absorbing misery.

'And my Prem,' he said, 'he will have to leave college without his BA. He will never go to study abroad, never come back to his father's house MA- and American-returned.'

Suddenly he jerked his lolling head up.

'No,' he said. 'No, no, no. Wasting his father's money going to foreign countries, eating beef, forgetting his family, making love to white women. Never. Never. Never. I have told him so. I have told him so, Inspector sahib.'

He put his arm round Inspector Ghote's shoulders.

'This younger generation,' he went on, 'all they think of is to spend the money their fathers have earned. Never once do they think of taking their place beside the father, or working to keep him when he is old and too weak to fight the sharks that are infesting the business world, the dirty, lying, murdering thieves.'

'Ah, yes,' Inspector Ghote said quickly. 'You were saying, Lala Varde sahib, that you had reason to believe the murder of Mr Perfect was instigated by business rivals.'

'Ho,' said Lala Varde, 'you are a better fellow than you look, Inspector. You can see into the heart of things. Yes, you are right. They sent goondas by night to kill him.'

'I see,' the inspector said with renewing eagerness, 'and where is it such robbers would have made their entry?'

Lala Varde shook his head.

'How can I tell?' he said. 'I am a poor, ruined old man only.'

'In each case of housebreaking,' the inspector said, 'it is essential carefully to examine all traces which the thief or thieves may have left.'

He thought of his cherished copy of Gross's *Criminal Investigation*, adapted from the German by John Adam, MA, sometime Crown Prosecutor, Madras, and by J. Collyer Adam, sometime Public Prosecutor, Madras. He could see the exact place in his little office where the dark blue, cloth-bound volume reposed, the place of honour on top of his filing cabinet. He could see the very page he was referring to, with the patch at the left-hand bottom corner where the paper through much turning by sweaty finger and thumb had gone partially transparent.

Lala Varde heard the garnered wisdom in silence.

The Inspector jumped to his feet.

'First it would be necessary to conduct an examination of the entire premises,' he said.

Lala Varde did not move. His chins creased themselves more deeply as his head sunk despondently forward.

Inspector Ghote waited.

The fan in the middle of the ceiling clacked monotonously. The inspector coughed.

'Perhaps, sahib, if you are exhausted after this terrible happening, a servant could show me the house?'

'Servants.'

Lala Varde rose like a great black whale shooting to the surface of some calm sea.

'Servants. When you need them, what do they do? They hide. At the moment when a poor man needs all the help he can get, his servants at the first breath of disaster fly away.'

He strode to the doorway. An enraged elephant, truck extended like a battering ram forcing its way through the jungle.

'Bearer, bearer,' he bellowed.

From the far distance Inspector Ghote detected a clamour of incomprehensible jabbering voices.

'Bearer, bearer, bring whisky. Quickly, quickly.'

Lala Varde's voice boomed and echoed round the big house. But no one came.

'Bearer. Whisky for the inspector sahib. How can he catch murderers and lying fornicators with not a drop of whisky to strengthen his courage and invigorate his brain?'

Inspector Ghote coughed.

'Excuse me, Lala Varde sahib,' he said, 'but I have no permit for alcoholic liquor drinking. An inspector of police cannot defy the prohibition law.'

'Whisky. Whisky. Bring whisky.'

Lala Varde's voice rolled out into the darkness of the house.

But it drew no response, and at last he turned away and walked in the direction of the couch, wiping the sweat from his forehead with the back of his hand.

The distant clamour which the inspector had long ago noticed became more distinct. Voices were now distinguishable, intermingled with a steady rattling of iron against iron.

'Locked.' 'Locked, sahib.' 'Gate locked, master.' In English, in Hindi, in Marathi the clamour conveyed its message at last.

'A gate is locked, Mr Varde,' Inspector Ghote said.

'Gate, gate. What gate is this?'

Inspector Ghote smiled a little.

'There is perhaps some gate between the servants' quarters and the rest of the house,' he said. 'Perhaps from the days when the house was built for an Englishman? It is a very sensible precaution to lock such a gate at night; there are many burglaries in the city.'

'Gate hate. Locking knocking. What nonsense are you talking?' Lala Varde shouted. 'How am I to have a drink of orange juice only if I wake in the middle of the night with all the servants locked out by a gate? Besides, there is no gate.'

'There is certainly some disturbance,' Inspector Ghote observed. 'I will go and see what is happening.'

He turned to the doorway.

'No. Stay where you are.'

Lala Varde's shout rang through the room with totally unexpected ferocity.

The inspector looked at him: he smiled with haste.

'Ah, no, Inspector sahib,' he said. 'Do not be disturbing yourself. No doubt there is some little domestic matter. I would see to it myself. Sit down, Inspector. Take a rest. You should keep your energies for the tracking down of the murderer.'

As he spoke he waddled aimlessly about the room, making vague placatory gestures. But with the last words he turned and faced the inspector. He was standing squarely in front of the open doorway.

Bland, huge, and obscurely menacing.

2

Inspector Ghote did not hesitate. He took one quick look at the great, ominous figure in front of him, and then slipped quickly past and out of the open doorway. It did not take him more than a minute to find the cause of the multilingual clamour he had heard in the distance.

There was indeed a gate.

In a narrow archway leading from the body of the house out to the low range of buildings that constituted the servants' quarters a heavy, though deeply rusted, iron gate had been locked into place. Beyond it all the servants of the household were gathered in an excited phalanx.

'Ah, you have found the source of the trouble, Inspector.'

Lala Varde's fruity voice came from behind him.

He turned. The big, fat old man was serene and unconcerned.

'Yes, sahib,' the inspector said. 'But do I understand then that it is not customary for this gate to be locked?'

'Sometimes yes, sometimes no,' Lala Varde answered. 'But do not let it worry you, Inspector. I shall conduct you round the house myself.'

He looked over the inspector's bony shoulders at the servants, now reduced from clamouring to buzzing.

'Well,' he said, 'have you no beds to go to? Is this the middle of the day that you are all talking there as if you were standing waiting for a wedding procession to pass by?'

Sheepishly the servants began turning away from the rusted iron gate. Inspector Ghote looked at them anxiously.

'Is there no other way into the house for them?' he asked.

'Would they have stood there like pye-dogs when I was calling and calling for whisky if there was a way to get to me?' replied Lala Varde.

Unanswerably.

'Then I think I can leave questioning them till a later time,' Inspector Ghote said. 'But first I must put a constable to guard this gate.'

'Questioning pestioning,' Lala Varde said. 'Let me give you some advice, Inspector. Straight from the heart. Do not bother yourself with servants. Goondas it is who did the Perfect Murder. Goondas sent by those violators of their own sisters, the business community of Bombay.'

Inspector Ghote drew himself up.

'Lala Varde sahib,' he said. 'I would advise you not to make possibly slanderous statements about a respected section of the community. If your secretary was murdered by goondas, we shall easily enough find evidence of attempted break-in when we inspect the house.'

'Break-in, fake-in. How should they break into my house? All the latest American-imported grilles have I installed. Each window has one, best grade steel. You would not find it so easy to break into my house, Inspector sahib.'

'An officer of the CID does not break into the houses of private citizens,' Inspector Ghote said.

He squared his thin shoulders and set off round the house, leaving Lala Varde to follow or not as he pleased.

Starting at the massive front door he made a systematic tour in a clockwise direction, swiftly noting the details of each room he came to in his notebook. Quite soon it became clear that his task was going to be easier than he had thought. The main part of the house was built in a rough square facing inwards to a big courtyard. The majority of the dozens of rooms looked on to this compound. Here there were hundreds of windows – large and small, tall and squat, square and occasionally even round – but on the walls facing the outer world there was hardly an aperture and, without exception, each was protected by a steel grille of American manufacture.

Inspector Ghote grasped each grille firmly as he came to it and gave it a sharp jerk. None of them budged the least bit. Not content with this, he looked carefully at the surrounding woodwork in search of tell-tale scratches or other marks. He found nothing. As often as not a thin layer of city dust lay undisturbed on the sill.

In a much shorter time than he had expected he was back at the big front door, the only one to the house, leaving aside the iron-barred gate leading to the servants' quarters. He examined the door itself carefully, but remembering how long it had taken Lala Varde to admit him when he had first arrived, and the sound of three heavy bolts being dragged back one after the other, he was in no doubt that there was no way in here.

Next he sent one of his constables from the small squad waiting patiently near the door to guard the iron gate and two more to make a complete circuit of the outside of the house.

'Watch carefully for any sign of anything unusual and report at the double to Head Constable Sen,' he said.

'At the double,' shouted his burly head constable in dutiful imitation.

The two constables trotted off and returned in a few minutes with the air of men who had found it easy to complete a task in an unexceptionable manner. They reported that the outer walls right the way round the house were high and smooth. There was not even a water pipe or a nearby tree to make it possible to reach the distant roof.

Inspector Ghote turned to the hovering Lala Varde.

'Well, sahib,' he said, 'of course I must make my official report, but I can tell you now that no goonda could have got into this house. The outer windows are still securely fastened, the door is thick and was treble-bolted, the walls are high. There is no question of break-in.'

'These American grilles are excellent,' Lala Varde agreed. 'But expensive, Inspector sahib, expensive.'

He dug the inspector in the ribs.

Painfully.

'Mr Varde,' Ghote said, 'if no entry was effected to the house and if the servants were locked on the far side of that gate, there is only one conclusion that remains.' Lala Varde's eyes twinkled paternally.

'Excellent, Inspector. Excellent.'

'Mr Varde, I must ask you to furnish me with a list of the names of every member of your household.'

'My household, Inspector?'

'Yes, sahib. If the murder was not committed by an intruder or by a servant, then the members of your household come under grave suspicion. It is essential that I should be furnished with a list of them immediately.'

'But, Inspector sahib, you do not understand. It was not a member of my household that committed the Perfect Murder. It was a goonda. This is a crime of revenge, Inspector. A business rival is behind it.'

Inspector Ghote's eyes widened.

'But, sahib, it was impossible for a goonda to enter the house.'

There was a feverishly forlorn note in his declaration.

And, as he had expected, his words were entirely ignored.

'No,' Lala Varde went plangently on, 'if you want a list, Inspector, it is a list of my most dangerous business rivals I would give you. My secretary would . . . That is to say, I shall give it to you myself, personally.'

'Nevertheless,' said Inspector Ghote, 'I shall have to interview all members of the household. I should like to begin quite soon, if convenient. But I think that now the medical men will have finished examining the body, and so I had better make my own inspection. I would have liked to have done it before. It is most important to obtain evidence as quickly as possible. You say Mr Perfect was attacked in this room over here?'

He made his way towards the still closed door of a room near the front door but facing the inner courtyard.

'Yes,' said Lala Varde, 'it was in there that the Perfect Murder took place. But if you want to see the victim you are going the wrong way.'

Inspector Ghote wheeled around.

His face expressed simple amazement.

'The body has been moved?' he said. 'But express instructions were issued that nothing was to be touched. That is fundamental procedure. It is in Gross's *Criminal Investigation.* The position of the body must always be photographed.'

'Body, Inspector?' said Lala Varde. 'But there is no body. Who ever said Mr Perfect is dead only?'

3

There was nothing Inspector Ghote could do at first but gape at the tun-bellied figure in front of him.

'What did you say?' he asked.

'I said that Mr Perfect is not dead,' Lala Varde replied. 'That is why he has been taken away from where I found him. In that broken head of his are all my figures. You don't think I telephoned the police before I telephoned for my doctor, do you? I am not a fool, you know.'

His eyes gleamed.

'But the police surgeon?' said Ghote.

'My son Dilip took him up to see Mr Perfect,' Lala Varde replied. 'It is most important to have as many good doctors as possible. And a police surgeon would be a good man.'

Still Inspector Ghote stared.

'But the Perfect Murder,' he said. 'The DSP told me he was putting me on to the Perfect Murder. You talked about the Perfect Murder.'

'Yes, I talked about the Perfect Murder. Wasn't it murder?'

'No. It is murder only when the victim is killed. When the victim is not killed it may be attempted murder, assault occasioning grievous bodily harm, any one of a number of officially listed crimes.'

'If the murderer tried to murder him, it is murder,' Lala Varde declared. 'The Perfect Murder, Inspector. I am looking at you to solve it.'

Inspector Ghote swallowed.

'Then we had better go and see the victim,' he said.

There was nothing, he thought, that he had done to deserve this. He had conducted the whole investigation up to this point with complete adherence to the rules of Gross's *Criminal Investigation.* Admittedly, he might have tried to see the body earlier, and then he would not have been placed in this ridiculous situation. But, on the other hand, to have cut off Lala Varde in the middle of his description of the circumstances would have been tactless. And on the very first page of Gross it was laid down, 'That is indispensable, for many awkward situations will be circumvented by its use.' There was no getting past that.

He trudged up the wide stairway behind the weighty but indefatigable form of Lala Varde.

At the top Lala Varde turned to him.

'They will have put him in one of the guest bedrooms,' he said. 'He did not live in the house at all. Round the corner he had a room only.'

From a doorway off the far end of the corridor came the sound of muted voices.

'Ah,' said Lala Varde, 'that will be it. Well, Inspector, I will not detain you. There is much to be done.'

With a suddenness unexpected in so big a person he ducked round the corner leaving Inspector Ghote stranded.

But not for long.

Instead of moving towards the room where the unmurdered Mr Perfect lay, the inspector tiptoed rapidly back in the direction Lala Varde had taken.

He was just in time, as he put his head cautiously round the corner, to see the great fat man take from the folds of his dhoti an ancient rusty-looking iron key.

The inspector permitted himself a little smile of triumph as Lala Varde hurried away in the direction of the gate behind which his servants had so mysteriously got locked.

Then he turned back to Mr Perfect.

The room he had been put in was small and bare of furniture except for a rope bed. A naked electric light bulb and a small fan hung from the ceiling. The sluggishly revolving blades of the fan scarcely stirred the warm night air. A dozen agitated flies buzzing round the light were completely unalarmed by the ineffectual air currents generated less than a yard away.

The familiar police surgeon was standing rigidly upright at the foot of the bed listening with great intentness to a short, tubby little man with his wide mouth curved in a perpetual grin. A stethoscope bounced and jiggled on his chest as he jabbered away, and Inspector Ghote guessed he was the doctor Lala Varde had summoned. He was so busy making his points to the hawk-eyed, silent police surgeon that he completely failed to see the inspector standing quietly in the doorway.

Ghote decided to take advantage of the fact that the police surgeon was also not looking in his direction to acquire a little unedited information. The police surgeon he knew of old: he had never yet been induced to commit himself on a single subject no matter how insistent or direct his questioner. Even DSP Samant, on the rare occasions he had come into contact with him, had never succeeded in banging one entirely definite answer out of him.

'Yes, yes, it's a pretty clear case all in all,' the little frog-grinning doctor said. 'Pretty clear case, wouldn't you say?'

The police surgeon moved his head in an ingenious elliptical arc which could be held to signify either agreement or disagreement.

'Yes, exactly, exactly,' the frog doctor said. 'You have all the symptoms there. Weak pulse, but quite distinct at the brachial artery, and rapid and irregular. Wasn't that so?'

The police surgeon pursed his lips intently.

'Then we have pupillary reaction. A classical example. Reacting to light just like that. And no sign of inequality, no sign at all.'

He looked up at his tall and silent colleague in sudden anxiety.

'You didn't detect any irregularity, did you?' he asked.

The police surgeon grunted with razor-poised ambiguity.

'No, exactly. Not a sign. And no bleeding at the ears, no bleeding at the ears. No fluid either. Thankful for that, eh?'

The police surgeon lowered his eyelids till his eyes were almost shut and then opened them sharply.

'Ah, yes, yes, yes. Quite so. And respiration? What did you think of that?'

The police surgeon let a stern smile move the corners of his lips.

'Yes, just as one might expect. Slow and shallow. Very shallow, sighing almost. Would you say sighing?'

A barked cough.

'Yes. Classical case. Concussion, linear fracture of the back of the skull, no immediate sign of brain compression. I think that about sums it up. Hm?'

'Hm.'

'So, I tell you this as colleague to colleague: I intend to recommend home nursing. Day and night, of course, day and night. I can put Mr Varde on to a thoroughly reliable team. They know me, I know them. We've worked—'

Inspector Ghote, deciding he had learnt a reasonable amount, coughed delicately.

The little frog-faced doctor wheeled round.

'Good gracious,' he said. 'Policeman.'

He looked discountenanced.

'Good evening,' the inspector said. 'My name is Ghote, Inspector CID. I don't think we have met before.'

'Doctor Das, personal medical adviser to Mr Varde.'

A hand shot out to be shaken.

'It would be a great help,' Inspector Ghote said, 'to know whether the patient is likely to regain consciousness in the immediate future or not. In the case of the former eventuality a full and complete statement might be obtained.'

He looked at the police surgeon.

'That would undoubtedly be most valuable,' the answer came.

Luckily Doctor Das was prepared to embroider on the theme.

'Ah, yes,' he said, 'a difficulty indeed. You decide that the attack was carried out by, let us say, X. And promptly the victim regains consciousness and announces that he was attacked by Y. Most unfortunate, most unfortunate.'

He giggled happily.

'He may regain consciousness at any minute,' the police surgeon said abruptly.

Inspector Ghote looked at him as if he was a wild, matted-haired, dust-streaked sadhu who had suddenly offered him a cocktail.

The police surgeon coughed.

'On the other hand,' he said, 'unconsciousness may persist for some considerable time. Either is equally likely.'

Doctor Das clasped his little frog-paws together and popped in a new contribution.

'There's the nature of the wound, you know,' he said. 'At the very back of the cranium. He may recover completely and be quite unable to tell you who hit him. They may have come at him right from behind. Ah, yes, indeed.'

The police surgeon turned his stern face towards the inspector.

'We have also to take into account the possibility of amnesia,' he said. 'The victim may remember absolutely nothing of any events leading up to the attack. On the other hand, he may.'

Inspector Ghote felt that this line of inquiry had definitely come to an end. He tried something else.

'The nature of the wound,' he said, 'was it such that it could have been inflicted by a strong man only?'

'Difficult to say,' replied the police surgeon as promptly as a clock.

The inspector looked at Doctor Das. But this time he was to get no help.

He cleared his throat.

'May I look at the patient myself, Doctor?' he asked.

'Well, I see no reasonable objection to that,' Doctor Das said. 'After all, the poor chap is deeply unconscious. A careful examination, conducted with discretion, mind, is hardly likely to have any deleterious effect. Wouldn't you agree, Doctor?'

'Ha.'

Doctor Das evidently decided to interpret this as agreement. He beckoned Inspector Ghote towards the string bed.

Mr Perfect lay, it would appear, much as he had been found by Lala Varde. The high collar of the atchkan he wore had been opened, but nothing else had been disturbed. Three ballpoint pens were neatly clipped on to one of his pockets. The red one had leaked and a small pinkish stain was spreading over the white cotton of the atchkan. Neatly folded on the floor beside the bed were the injured man's metal-framed spectacles. One of the lenses was cracked and had been mended with transparent tape.

Doctor Das lifted the great pad of white bandages gently away from the back of the grey-haired skull.

The wound was curious in shape. It looked as if it had been inflicted, not with the traditional rounded blunt instrument, but with something long and knobby.

'Would a stick only inflict such injury?' the inspector asked.

'I shall bear the point in mind in my report to the DSP,' the police surgeon said.

It was a victory. Of a sort.

The inspector stayed standing at the head of the tattered charpoi looking down at the elongated form of Mr Perfect. He could just detect eventually the faint irregular movement of the white atchkan which was evidence of the unconscious man's light, shallow breathing.

He felt that every tremulous, sighing breath might be the last. The life before him hung on so slender a thread.

On one fitful exhalation hung the difference between murder and not-murder. If that breath ceased, then Mr Perfect would have been killed. The Perfect Murder would have truly taken place.

The inspector's mouth went suddenly dry and his heart began to beat thumpingly. He was possessed by an uncontrollable conviction that, if he found himself handling the Perfect Murder in actual fact, it would be exactly a perfect murder. Perfect, motiveless, never to be solved.

'Well, there he is,' Doctor Das broke in cheerfully. 'Not a sign of change as you can see for yourself. I dare say he'll be lying there just as he is this time three weeks; or three months.'

He began replacing the pad of bandages with neat, indifferent fingers.

'Of course,' he added, 'regular attention is indispensable, cost what it may.'

Inspector Ghote thought of the beggars lying day and night, fine or wet, on the pavements of the city in their hundreds.

'Well, gentlemen,' he said, 'I have to attend to the course of the investigation.'

He marched stiffly out of the room and made his way downstairs.

The house was much more animated now. The servants, freed from their unusual captivity, were scuttling to and fro ostensibly to see to Lala Varde's comfort, in reality to gossip and speculate over the dramatic event that had entered into the pattern of their lives.

The inspector caught one glimpse of Lala Varde himself, sitting in a big cane chair near a pair of French windows opened on to the cool of the inner courtyard of the big house. A large whisky stood by his side. His feet were being assiduously pressed by a kneeling woman servant. A tiny, erect little stick of a bearer was busy adding clove, cardamom and coconut to the chips of nut lying in a betel leaf, ready to present his master at the first sign of need with a neatly folded, deliciously luscious paan.

Inspector Ghote decided there was everything to be said for not disturbing the master of the house for the time being.

He made his way to the room where Mr Perfect had been found and shut the door behind him. Then in accordance with the rules as laid down in Gross he took out his notebook and starting at the door listed each object in a sweep following the same direction as the hands of a clock.

The very thought that he was carrying out a procedure in exactly the fashion recommended came as a considerable comfort to him. He did not hurry. And even this, he remembered, was to his credit. Doctor Hans Gross has some very scathing things to say about the 'expeditious investigator'.

There were a good many objects to describe although the room was small. Evidently it formed a convenient place near the door to the house for putting things for which no home could be found. There was a bookshelf, mostly filled with ageing newspapers, but containing on its top a tattered row of miscellaneous volumes. Inspector Ghote wrote down the name of each one.

Next to the bookcase was a small table on which there rested a bunch of long brass keys, evidently disused, an electric torch (without battery), a black umbrella with a brightly coloured plastic handle, and four empty matchboxes. Next in the circular tour came a tall display cabinet on the top of which, side by side, were an oil lamp in enamelled Benares work and a brass candlestick of European manufacture. On the other shelves were an assortment of glassware, a golf club and an air cushion, punctured.

On the floor up against the wall there was a clock without hands, a painting in the Moghul style, and a brass plate inscribed Varde Building Enterprises (Private) Ltd.

Inspector Ghote called a constable and instructed him in the method of storing large objects to avoid smudging fingerprints as recommended by Gross. Then he told him to apply it to the golf club.

He had the foresight to return to the room almost at once and was able to prevent the constable picking up the golf club in his bare hands.

Taking a careful note of the exact position of the small streak of blood on the floor, the sole evidence of the attack, the inspector went back to the courtyard to question Lala Varde again.

He found him fast asleep.

In repose his face bore a strong resemblance to that of a baby. Magnified.

The inspector looked at him. What should he do? There were a lot more things he ought to get to know. He had not even managed to learn what the old man's own movements had been during the hours before the attack was reported.

A spurt of honest anger swept through him. Lala Varde or no Lala Varde, no one had any right to fall fast asleep in the middle of a murder investigation.

He put out his hand towards the enormous, rounded, fat-padded shoulder in front of him.

And hesitated.

Behind him the noise of the servants chattering together rose to a sudden unexplained height. He wheeled round.

'Head Constable, Head Constable,' he shouted. 'Get those damned noisy servants together in their quarters. It's high time they answered a few questions.'

There were, certainly, matters which would be made a good deal clearer by finding out from the servants what they knew of events in the house during the evening before. But gathering everyone together for interrogation proved unexpectedly difficult.

No one was perfectly clear about how many servants there were meant to be. Even when the inspector had made it plain that wives and children who had reached the age of reason were to be included still new names were remembered and loud outcries started until the missing person had been found and stood in their proper place in the hierarchy of Lala Varde's domestic staff.

But at last everything was ready. At the head of the long vague queue – here thickly knotted where a large family clustered, there thin where enemies did their best to keep their distance – a small table was ceremoniously placed.

Before Inspector Ghote took his place at it he beckoned to Head Constable Sen.

'What we have got to find out,' he said, 'is when Mr Perfect was last seen alive. That is, was last seen before the attack.'

He frowned at himself angrily over his mistake.

'The servants were all meant to be in their quarters and that old gate had been shut and locked,' he went on. 'But we had better keep a sharp eye open for anybody who wasn't seen during the night. One of them may have hidden away somewhere. Make a note of every name and mark anything that you think suspicious.'

'Very good, Inspector,' said the big head constable.

He flourished his pencil two or three times in an impressive manner. The servants looked at each other apprehensively.

And then the questioning began.

'What is your name?'

'What are your duties?'

'Where were you earlier in the evening?'

'Did you see Mr Perfect?'

'When did you go to your quarters?'

And the answers were never as simple as they ought to have been. The timid ones refused to give their names, the sly ones gave false names and had to be recalled and shouted at when a member of their family accidentally betrayed the relationship or a jealous rival gave them blandly away. There were quarrels about whose task it was to do what, and age-old grievances were lengthily aired. Not one single person, it seemed at first, could say how they had spent the earlier part of the evening. Tirelessly Inspector Ghote sorted out the genuinely vague from the deliberately obscure, and applied the precepts of Doctor Gross to each of them.

Only on one point was everybody crystal clear: they had not seen Mr Perfect.

'I had not see Mr Perfect, sahib.'

Inspector Ghote slapped the table in front of him so sharply that a little cloud of dust rose up from it.

'When did you last see Mr Perfect? When did you last see him at all? If it wasn't today, when was it? Answer me that.'

'I had not see Mr Perfect, Inspector sahib.'

'Never? Have you never seen him?'

A frightened shake of the head. But still negative.

The inspector sighed.

'Next one.'

And patiently he plodded through them. He felt as if he could have filled in the comment against each name in his notebook in advance. 'Did not see victim.' It was as if Mr Perfect had never existed.

Twice even he left the little table and made his way alone to the small upstairs room where Mr Perfect, guarded now by a contemptuously wakeful Anglo-Indian nurse, lay with his grey head swathed in the white bandages. Each time he stayed by the tattered string bed until he could make out the sighing, wavering noise of the patient's breathing. Only then did he turn abruptly and go back to the endless questioning.

And at last there was only one left in the queue.

'Name?'

'Satyamurti.'

The head constable guffawed.

'Satyamurti, teller of truth,' he said. 'That will be a change.'

Inspector Ghote frowned. This was hardly the tact recommended by Doctor Gross. Insults of this sort were likely to produce awkward situations rather than to dissipate them.

The head constable, his heavy chin still wagging from enjoyment of his joke, caught the inspector's eye. The chin froze.

The inspector leaned forward across the table and smiled at Satyamurti, who was a boy of about sixteen, wearing only a dhoti, and so thin that each of his ribs was clearly visible.

'Well,' he said, 'and what do you do in this household?'

'I am sweeper, sahib.'

'I see. Well, I don't suppose you were cleaning up anywhere after it got dark this evening.'

'Oh, no, sahib.'

Inspector Ghote sat back in his chair.

The last witness and not even in a position to be helpful.

A final dreg of conscientiousness made him put one more question.

'Where were you in the evening then? In your quarters?'

'Oh, no, sahib. I was in hall.'

The inspector sat up with a jerk.

And promptly cursed himself. This might be a fish who had to be caught gently.

'In the hall of the house?' he asked.

'Yes, sahib.'

'I see. Where in the hall?'

'Just inside room by door, sahib.'

'By the door? The room where all the unwanted things are?'

Inspector Ghote held his breath.

'Yes, sahib, there.'

He waited for an instant. And then put his next question.

'What were you doing there, then?'

'I was waiting in case the master went out.'

'Oh, yes? Why was that?'

'Sometimes, sahib, when he is going out he is chewing paan. And he puts what he has not chewed in the brass bowl by the door. Then I can come out and take it.'

Out of the corner of his eye Inspector Ghote detected the head constable working himself up into a rage about such a deeply criminal act. He gave him a sharp glance and went back to the boy.

'While you were there in that room, could anyone see you?'

'Oh, no, sahib. It was dark.'

'I see. And did you see anyone? Did you see Mr Perfect? You know who he is?'

'Oh, yes, I know, sahib. He is the old Parsee who looks so tall and thin like a lathi. I knew him even though he had on atchkan.'

'I'll give you lathi,' growled the head constable, flexing his arm in the air as if he was about to bring a particularly thwacking lathi down on someone's back.

'Quiet,' snapped Inspector Ghote.

'You saw Mr Perfect then?' he asked the boy.

'Oh, yes, sahib, I saw him go out and then come in again. And then one time more.'

'When was this? Was it early or late?'

'It was twelve o'clock, sahib. He came into room and saw me then. He made me go back here.'

'Twelve o'clock?' the inspector said. 'You mean it was some time late in the night? Is that it?'

'No, sahib. Twelve o'clock really. I heard the clock in the Christian church. Twelve times it sounded.'

Inspector Ghote looked at the head constable with an air of triumph.

'Now,' he said, 'we are getting somewhere.'

He leaned towards the boy again with a friendly smile.

'Inspector Ghote. Inspector sahib.'

The urgent voice of a constable came from behind him.

'Go away. Don't interrupt, man.'

'Message from DSP, Inspector. Most urgent.'

Inspector Ghote turned round.

'Yes. What is it?'

'Please report at once to DSP, Inspector sahib.'

'To the DSP? At his house?'

'No, Inspector sahib, he has come into office.'

'Into the office? In the middle of the night?'

'It is morning, Inspector sahib.'

Inspector Ghote looked upwards.

It was indeed morning. The night had passed while he had so painstakingly questioned Lala Varde's army of servants and hangers-on. But it was still very early.

'You say the DSP has come into his office already?'

'Yes, Inspector sahib. And he sent me jildi jildi to fetch you.'

Inspector Ghote got up and buttoned up his uniform.

The DSP in his office at this hour. Something totally unprecedented must have happened.

4

Inspector Ghote got to the office in record time. His driver, a middle-aged stately fellow on the ground, invariably changed the moment he clambered into a police truck into a sort of impersonal, hectoring, hysterical onward force, all screeching tyres and squealing brakes. Having learned, well before the inspector, of the urgency of Deputy Superintendent Samant's summons, he excelled himself.

The inspector, impelled by the momentum of his breakneck trip, raced up the steps into the building and headed for DSP Samant's office door as fast as his legs could carry him. But, as his hand was raised to knock, a terrible, jovial shout from behind brought him to a full stop.

He turned round with misgiving to see, as he had known he would, the towering, blond-haired figure of Axel Svensson, his principal worry in the world until the moment the DSP had put him on to the Perfect Murder.

Axel Svensson was a Swede who had arrived in Bombay about a fortnight before during a tour of the Asian countries sponsored by Unesco, for whom he was writing an extensive study entitled *Police Force Prototypes for Emergent Nations.* DSP Samant had handed him over to Ghote with instructions that looking after him was to be his first priority. Axel Svensson had delightedly availed himself of the DSP's generosity.

And evidently had not yet finished.

'My dear Inspector,' he shouted.

His big voice boomed clangorously down the corridor

outside the DSP's office. It was probably the loudest noise that had ever been heard there.

Inspector Ghote ran quickly towards him.

'Good morning, Mr Svensson, good morning,' he said.

'Axel, my friend. You must always call me Axel. Don't stand on ceremony. I have told you before.'

Inspector Ghote bobbed a little acknowledgement at the tall, long-boned Swede.

'Yes, yes, of course. Axel sahib,' he said.

'Splendid to have caught you,' Svensson said.

Although the inspector was standing very close to him now, his voice sounded as loud as ever. The inspector glanced over his shoulder at DSP Samant's door, but it remained blessedly closed.

'Splendid to have caught you. I have a most urgent query I wish to put to you.'

'In just a moment, Mr Svensson, I—'

But the Swede battered remorselessly on.

'It it this, my dear Inspector. I have read that in your religious works gods are shown as taking bribes. Is that correct?'

Inspector Ghote flushed.

'The State police force has a department specially concerned with anti-corruption,' he said.

The Swede spread his big, bony hands wide.

'Ah, my dear Inspector, that I know. Already I have admired its work. It will form a most useful chapter in my book. But you haven't answered my question.'

'Examples of most excellent behaviour are shown in accounts of the deeds of the gods,' the inspector said. 'But, Mr Svensson – But Mr Axel, I have a most urgent summons by the DSP.'

'Oh, this won't take a moment,' the Swede said cheerfully. 'Just tell me: do the gods take bribes? Yes or no?'

He laid a widespread paw on the inspector's thin shoulder.

'There are stories where this appears to happen,' the inspector said.

'Excellent. Excellent. This will be most highly interesting. Because, you see, my friend, here is the point: if that is held up as admirable conduct, what effect does it have on the average policeman? That is it in a nutshell.'

'Yes, in a nutshell. You put it very well.'

He slipped out of the Swede's great red grasp.

But he lacked the brutal resolution to walk away sharply, and, before he had manoeuvred himself to the point where he could take a decent farewell, the Swede was standing toweringly between him and the DSP's door.

'Listen,' he said, 'if certain sections of the holy writings which do not conform with modern practices could be officially set aside, it would undoubtedly solve the problem.'

'But they are sacred. Sacred writings,' Ghote protested.

'Yes, but they advocate the offering and receiving of bribes.'

Inspector Ghote looked quietly firm.

'You cannot alter sacred writings,' he said.

The Swede shook his big head crowned with the short array of upright blond hair.

'On the one hand,' he said, 'you have an official campaign against bribery. On the other, respected religious writings condone and even encourage it. I do not understand.'

The inspector's face brightened.

'But it is perfectly simple,' he said. 'You have explained it yourself. On the one hand, on the other hand. The two things are quite separate.'

The Swede's pale blond eyebrows locked hard together.

And while they stayed locked Inspector Ghote at last slipped efficiently as a snake into the DSP's office.

He found DSP Samant sitting squarely at his desk attacking a report that lay in front of him. He was working with a red ballpoint and used it to make sudden, savage inroads on any part of the document which met with his disapproval.

Inspector Ghote saluted and gave his name in the sharp, military fashion he knew the DSP liked.

After some time, during which two or three more paragraphs were dispatched as cleanly as a terrier deals with a rat, Inspector Ghote abruptly found the DSP's keen grey eyes were focused on him.

'Well, Inspector? What is it? What is it, man?'

'You sent for me, DSP.'

'I did? I did?'

Hot surges of panic rushed through Inspector Ghote's brain. The constable had made a mistake. He had probably fetched the wrong inspector. The Perfect Murder had been abandoned at the very moment the scent was hottest. And, the DSP had been irritated.

'Ah, yes. Ghote. Just the man I want.'

The inspector's shoulders sank to their normal place.

'Yes,' the DSP said. 'A very important and urgent matter has come up and I'm going to put you on to it. Number one priority.'

Inspector Ghote felt himself assailed by a swarm of contradictory emotions. Pride, in being singled out in this way. Disappointment, at losing the Perfect Murder. Relief, that that was now going to be someone else's burden. Annoyance, at being switched so quickly from one thing to another.

Pride won.

'I'll do my best, DSP,' he said.

'I expect every officer to do that,' snapped the DSP.

'Yes, DSP.'

'But this is a matter requiring extreme tact. Extreme tact.'

The words of Doctor Hans Gross rolled sonorously through Inspector Ghote's brain.

'You may lack certain other qualities, Inspector, but at least I can rely on you to exercise tact. The utmost tact. I hope I can rely on you, Inspector.'

The cold threat of the last words made Inspector Ghote's mouth go so dry that he was unable to reply.

'Well, can I, man? Can I?'

'Yes, DSP.'

The croaking whisper was accepted.

'Very well, then. Now listen to me. There has been a serious crime, a very serious crime, in the personal office of the Minister for Police Affairs and the Arts. Now, I needn't tell you what that means: the matter has got to be cleared up. At once. Without fuss. With the maximum of efficiency. And the Minister is not to be in any way worried. Understood?'

'Yes, DSP.'

'Very well, then. I think you're the man to do it. Apply to me personally for any help you want. You've got my fullest backing in this, Ghote.'

'Thank you, DSP.'

DSP Samant picked up his red ballpoint again.

Inspector Ghote cleared his throat.

'Can you give me any further details, DSP? Or will they have them in Main Office?'

'Main Office? Main Office? Do you think this is a Main Office matter, man? Main Office know nothing about it. Nothing. The Minister was put through to me personally. And I'm giving you your orders direct.'

'Yes, DSP.'

Inspector Ghote waited.

'Well, what is it? What is it, man? What are you hanging about for? Get on with it, man. Get on with it.'

'Particulars, DSP sahib,' Inspector Ghote said.

He tried to make the word as quiet as possible.

'Particulars? Particulars? What particulars?'

'Particulars of the crime at the Minister's office, DSP. You said that he had informed you personally.'

'Of course he did, of course. You don't think that when the Minister of Police Affairs comes on the line he talks to any little whippersnapper, do you?'

'No, DSP. Of course not, DSP. And the details, DSP?'

The DSP drew a long breath.

Inspector Ghote tensed.

'A sum of money has disappeared from a drawer in the Minister's own desk,' the DSP said. 'That is virtually all you need to know.'

'Very good, DSP.'

Inspector Ghote saluted and began marching smartly out.

'The sum of one rupee, I believe,' the DSP said.

Inspector Ghote stopped in his tracks. He turned. The DSP's cold grey Maratha eyes stared at him fixedly.

'Well, Inspector, was there something else you had to ask?'

Inspector Ghote gulped.

'Well, was there, man? Out with it, out with it.'

Tact, thought the inspector. Tact, tact, tact. Many awkward situations circumvented by.

'Yes, DSP,' he said. 'The Perfect Murder. Who will be taking over on that case?'

'Taking over? Taking over? What do you mean, taking over? An officer of resource should be able to handle more than one matter at a time, Inspector.'

'Yes, DSP, but . . .'

'But what?'

'But you told me to give the Perfect Murder number one priority, DSP. And this new case too, DSP. Number one priority there, too.'

He looked into the chill grey eyes.

'And I was giving number one priority to the Swedish gentleman too, DSP. Anything he needed to know, number one priority. Anything he wanted to look at, number one priority.'

'Well, what are you coming yapping to me about, Inspector. Am I a mother that I have to nurse my officers day and night? It's a police officer's duty to get his right order of priorities. Think it out, man, think it out. Use your brains. Look at me. Do you think I don't have questions like that to deal with every moment of my life? Look at my desk now. Look at it, man.'

Inspector Ghote looked.

On the right-hand side of the desk was the 'In' basket. On the left hand was the 'Out' basket. Between them stood three other baskets, shoulder to shoulder. They were labelled 'Immediate', 'Urgent' and 'Top Priority'.

'You're not the only police officer who's ever had to make a decision, Inspector Ghote.'

'No, DSP.'

He saluted, turned, and this time marched straight out.

In the corridor Axel Svensson was waiting.

'Ah, Inspector,' he said, 'I hoped I would catch you. There is another important problem—'

'I am very sorry Mr Svensson,' Inspector Ghote said, 'but I have just been put on to a new enquiry. Number one priority.'

'Ah, excellent. I will come with you if I may. It would be a first-class opportunity to see the Bombay force in action.'

Inspector Ghote smiled. Palely.

'Of course, sahib,' he said.

'Axel. Axel, my friend.'

As they drove together over to the Ministry of Police Affairs and the Arts in Mayo Road Axel Svensson sought opinions on the effect of an arranged marriage on the ambitions of a typical police officer. Inspector Ghote felt it was altogether too much that he should be asked to cope with this as well as his other problems. He allowed himself to think just once of his wife, Protima, and what she would be feeling about the fact that at the end of his spell of night duty he had not returned home. And then he set to work on the desperately delicate task of weighing the demands of the attack on Mr Perfect against those of the theft of one rupee from under the very nose of the Minister of Police Affairs and the Arts.

He had done no more than miserably stare at the problem before they arrived at the Ministry.

And there he found that he had only one desire in all the world: to rush to a telephone and find out whether there had been any change in Mr Perfect. Firmly he pushed the impulse to the back of his mind. He was at the Ministry; he was on the missing rupee case; the only logical and proper thing was to proceed with his duty as it lay before him.

He left Axel Svensson and went up to the formidable-looking chaprassi standing magnificently turbaned in the very middle of the huge marbled and pillared entrance hall.

He coughed slightly.

'Police Inspector Ghote, CID,' he said. 'To see the Minister. Urgent business.'

The chaprassi looked at him.

He was a good deal taller than the inspector.

'Minister extremely busy today,' he said tersely.

'Naturally,' said the inspector, 'a man like the Minister must always be extremely busy. But on this occasion he has specially requested me to come as quickly as possible.'

The chaprassi shrugged his wide shoulders, tapering elegantly away to a slim but virile sashed waist.

'What name did you say it was?' he asked.

'Inspector Ghote, CID.'

The inspector said each of the last letters as forcefully as he could, but he was conscious that it was most unlikely to do any good. There was only one way to surmount this obstacle. Money would have to change hands.

Yet for an inspector of police to have to treat a doorman in this fashion was unthinkable. Especially as Axel Svensson was sitting sprawled over a stone bench at the edge of the great hall intently observing what was going on.

'Well,' said the chaprassi, 'I will pass in your name, but you will certainly have to wait a long time. The Minister is a very busy man.'

He put enormous significance into the last phrase. The inspector knew he was taking him for a fool. For a moment he was tempted to hint at the exact nature of his business, but the memory of Doctor Gross on the need for tact saved him.

'I think you will find that the Minister will be very glad to see me,' he said darkly.

But the chaprassi had heard similar expressions too often before and remained splendidly indifferent.

Inspector Ghote strolled, as airly as he could, back to Axel Svensson.

'I have sent up my name,' he said.

Axel Svensson leaned his big blond head forward close to the inspector's.

'Tell me,' he said, 'what exactly is the nature of the crime that has been committed in the Minister's office?'

'Theft.'

'Ah, theft.'

For a time this seemed to content the big Swede. Then he leant confidentially forward again.

'A big sum?'

'No.'

'Ah, a small sum.'

Inspector Ghote nodded.

'How much exactly, my friend?'

The inspector was suddenly conscious that he was sweating hard. It had been too much to hope that he could prevent this foreigner from getting to know the full details.

'One rupee,' he said.

'One rupee? But that is only one krona, and five krona go to the dollar, and—'

'Yes,' said the inspector spikily.

'Ah, I see. Yes. Yes, of course. But the theft of any amount from a Minister's office is an extremely important matter.'

Inspector Ghote looked at the Swede with open gratitude.

A peon, a pudgy-looking Goan, came down and started a whispered conversation with the chaprassi.

'I expect that is the Minister's peon,' Inspector Ghote said. 'It is strange though that he should be Goan. They do not often take that sort of job.'

He got up and walked across to the two whispering men. At an even pace and steadily.

The peon glanced at him and went on whispering.

'Are you from the Minister?' the inspector asked sharply.

'Minister's personal peon,' the chaprassi explained with befitting loftiness.

'Very well then, don't hang about,' the inspector said. 'The Minister is anxious to see me.'

'The Minister has a great many important duties this morning,' said the peon.

Inspector Ghote came to a decision. Principles for once could go hang. He put his hand into his uniform pocket and felt for some money.

It would be necessary now to redeem any unfortunate opinions that might have been formed. He did a little reckoning.

Suddenly the peon broke away. The inspector looked up to see what had happened.

Axel Svensson was striding across the great flagged floor towards them, enormous, distinguished, resolute.

'The Minister is ready for us?' he called across to Inspector Ghote.

The peon spoke first.

'Oh, yes, sahib,' he said. 'Minister waiting.'

They followed the peon up to the top floor of the great building, where it was at once evident from the hushed atmosphere and the opulence of the decor that only the most senior of all the employees of the Ministry were allowed.

Inspector Ghote found himself tiptoeing behind the chubby little Goan peon and angrily forced himself to bring the heels of his heavy brown shoes hard down on the cool stone floor. Only to discover that the approach of a very tall man in a white Gandhi cap, who looked at them coldly through an unexpectedly cheap-looking pair of spectacles, had made him creep more self-consciously than before.

He cast a glance behind at the thin figure now just stepping into the lift, half expecting that he would be summoning the turbaned chaprassi from the entrance hall to have them thrown out. But to his relief all he saw was a glimpse of disappearing white.

The little peon noticed his backward look.

'That was Minister,' he said ingratiatingly.

'What?' the inspector shouted.

And then, remembering where he was, he reduced his voice to a sibilant whisper.

'Why didn't you tell him who I was?' he hissed. 'The Minister wanted to see me on a very important matter. At once. Now.'

The fat little Goan shook his head.

'Everybody have to see Mr Jain, first,' he declared.

'Mr Jain? Who is Mr Jain?'

'Mr Jain Minister's personal assistant. Oh, my God.'

Inspector Ghote did not allow himself to be intimidated by this unforced expression of awe.

'Then take me to Mr Jain at once,' he said.

'Oh, yes, sahib,' said the peon.

Crouching a little before the inspector's wrath, he opened a door a few yards farther on and ushered them through.

Mr Jain got up from a desk which was entirely bare except for a single very small piece of paper on one corner of which he had written a few words in tiny, neat handwriting. He gave the impression of being pared down to the minimum in every possible way. His bones were covered with flesh, certainly, but not a fraction more than necessary to sustain life. His clothes were decent and not even particularly threadbare, yet they were so entirely without excess of any sort that they looked skimpier than a beggar's. His very movements were calculated to achieve their object with the least possible displacement.

But, to Inspector Ghote's secret relief, he realized at once who they were and what their business must be.

'Unfortunately the Minister has had to leave,' he said. 'A conference in connection with buying land for the new police training college. Rather an urgent matter. But if I can in any way help . . .'

He saved himself the rest of his sentence by employing a delicate gesture of the right hand, the fingers of which moved as much as an inch and a half.

'If you can give us the fullest possible details,' Inspector Ghote said, 'perhaps it will not be necessary to trouble the Minister after all.'

'The fullest details, yes.'

Mr Jain looked less happy.

'Yes, of course,' he added. 'We want this business cleared up as quickly as possible.'

He picked a tiny wisp of thread off his sleeve and carried it between finger and thumb to a waste-paper basket near the bare desk.

'On the other hand,' he said, 'I can only tell you what I know.'

'Of course, of course,' said Inspector Ghote.

He felt cautiously happy. There was much less opposition than he had expected.

'Very well then,' Mr Jain said. 'The situation as I understand it is this. The Minister came into his office very early this morning. As soon as he had arrived he took a ten-rupee note from his pocket and sent his peon to get it changed into singles. He said he wanted small change, you understand?'

Inspector Ghote felt pleased. Plainly he was going to be given a clear and courteous explanation of what had happened.

'I take it the Minister liked to have some small change always to hand,' he said helpfully.

Mr Jain's eyes suddenly went blank.

'I imagine so,' he said.

After a moment he recovered himself.

'But perhaps it would be easier if I took you into the Minister's own office,' he said.

They followed him into a great, airy room, quiet with rich carpeting, fresh with discreet air-conditioning and softly lighted from cane blinds that screened huge windows looking out over a jumble of roofs and the distant noise of scrambling traffic far below to the grey-green of the Arabian Sea on the horizon.

Mr Jain moved round till he was standing between the Minister's ornate chair and his enormous, glowing polished wood desk.

'This is the drawer,' he said.

'Stop,' said Inspector Ghote.

Mr Jain had been about to pull it open.

He looked up and then smiled.

'Ah,' he said, 'fingerprints. Of course. But you will already find my prints on the drawer, Inspector. The Minister asked me to close it for him when he had counted out the notes into it.'

'I see.'

'And he has asked Felix, his peon – you saw him, I believe – to open it,' Mr Jain continued. 'So you will find his prints too, and of course the Minister's.'

'It will be necessary for us to take your prints, sahib,' Inspector Ghote put in. 'Purely for purposes of elimination, you understand.'

'Of course.'

Mr Jain smiled again. Coolly.

'The elimination should be easy, Inspector,' he said. 'This room is thoroughly cleaned early every morning and the desk is polished. I inspect it myself before the Minister arrives.'

Inspector Ghote looked up.

'And you inspected it this morning?' he asked.

'I never do otherwise, Inspector. And I can promise you that the wood of the drawers was gleaming.'

'Then if we are lucky we shouldn't be very long,' Inspector Ghote said. 'We have records of all the sort of fellows who are likely to pick up sums of money from desk drawers.'

He felt an uprising of solid contentment. This was how police work ought to be. Theft reported, area of theft located, fingerprints taken, innocent parties eliminated, guilty party left, records compared, thief identified.

Mr Jain leaned forward and removed a speck of dust from the white telephone on the desk.

'But I very much doubt, Inspector,' he said, 'whether you will find any other fingerprints but mine, the Minister's and his peon's on that drawer.'

5

Inspector Ghote looked up in sudden desolation.

'What do you mean?' he said. 'Why should there not be other fingerprints on the drawer than the Minister's, yours and the peon's?'

'Because there is only one door to this room,' Mr Jain said. 'Because I myself was in the outer office from the time the money was put into the drawer until the theft was reported and no one else entered the room.'

He stared at Inspector Ghote with sudden arrogance.

The inspector's thoughts jumped and leaped about.

It seemed to him a long time before he was able to pin one of them down.

'You say you were in the outer office all the time,' he said at last, 'but how long was that?'

'An hour.'

Mr Jain slapped the words down.

'And in this hour,' the inspector said, 'no doubt you left the actual room next door for a few minutes once or twice?'

'Not for one single minute.'

'Wasn't that a little—'

But Axel Svensson interrupted excitedly.

'The peon,' he said, 'did he come and go into this room?'

'You must ask him,' said Mr Jain.

'One hour between the time the Minister put the notes in the drawer and the time he told you that one of them had been stolen,' Inspector Ghote said. 'Was the Minister in here for much of that hour?'

'No,' Mr Jain said. 'He told me he had some business to attend to and went out almost straight away. As soon as he came back he found the note was missing.'

The door of the outer office opened and the peon appeared carrying a tabbed file. He put it on Mr Jain's desk.

'Come in here,' Inspector Ghote called.

The man came in. He salaamed uneasily.

'What is your name?'

'Felix Sousa, sahib.'

'And you are the Minister's peon?'

Felix Sousa sighed.

'Yes, sahib. For five years I have been the Minister's peon.'

He made it sound like a prison sentence.

'You changed a note for the Minister this morning?'

'No – Yes, sahib, I did.'

'And you watched the Minister count the ten rupee notes you brought back into that drawer?'

The peon glanced at the drawer and groaned.

'Well, did you?'

'Yes, sahib.'

'You know that one of the notes is missing?'

'Oh, sahib, sahib, it wasn't me. I promise you that. Oh, my god, no. I never steal nothing, sahib.'

Tears began to well out of his eyes and mingle with the sweat on his pudgy cheeks.

'The office was empty. You came in here,' said Inspector Ghote sternly.

He tried to think of DSP Samant. There was nothing his superior liked better than breaking down a suspect. Especially one who, like the Goan, was ready to break at a touch.

'You came in here. The office was empty,' he repeated grimly.

The Goan gulped his tears.

'Oh, no, sahib. I never.'

'It is no use denying. The office was left empty and you were the only one with a chance to take the note.'

'But, no, sahib, no.'

'Stop that, I tell you. When it is plain that you were the only one that could have taken the money it is no use to go on and on denying.'

The man took a double-sized gulp.

'But, sahib, I never went in office. Never. Please ask Mr Jain. He will tell you I never went in. Once he stopped me. I was only going to empty the Minister's waste-paper basket, and he told me not to be a fool, sahib.'

Inspector Ghote looked at the spare-fleshed personal assistant.

'Is this true, Mr Jain?' he said.

'Yes,' said Mr Jain. 'He did not have occasion to go into the Minister's office.'

The Goan looked immensely relieved. But his troubles were not over for long.

'Oh, my God,' he burst out, 'and all the time there was something in the waste-paper basket.'

All eyes turned to the open canework basket in the corner of the big room. There reposing in simple solitude was a single crumpled sheet of paper.

The peon almost flung himself at Mr Jain's feet in abject apology.

'I would have empty, sahib,' he said. 'Honest to God, I would have empty if I had been in office.'

'It is one piece of paper only,' said Inspector Ghote.

He went across to the basket and pulled it out, uncrumpled it and looked at it. It contained a simple percentage sum ending with 'A.V. 20% – R.K. 30%'.

The peon went on protesting to Mr Jain about his good faith in the matter of emptying the basket. Mr Jain looked at him angrily.

'Oh, I know, sahib, you say basket must never be left in a disgusting state like that, but this time—'

'Be quiet,' snapped the inspector.

The peon shrank into silence and looked at him with wide, fearful eyes.

The inspector showed Mr Jain the sheet of paper.

'Is that the Minister's writing?' he said.

'Oh, yes. He often makes calculations of that sort.'

'Do you know what this one would be about?'

'Really, Inspector, I don't think I can discuss the contents of a note jotted down by the Minister in his private office.'

'No, no. Of course not. Please do not misunderstand. I wished simply to make sure that it was something that the Minister had put in the basket himself.'

'I think you can be certain that it was,' Mr Jain answered. 'No doubt it was some calculations he was making in preparation for the conference which he is attending at this moment.'

'No doubt.'

Inspector Ghote felt that a tricky passage had been negotiated. He walked across the big room and allowed the crumpled slip to fall back into the pristine basket.

'But if no one entered the room,' Axel Svensson burst out in his loud voice, 'how did the money get stolen from the Minister's drawer?'

Inspector Ghote wriggled his shoulders under his khaki uniform. He could have wished that the matter could have been put less uncompromisingly.

He looked at the lean form of Mr Jain.

'It is absolutely certain,' he asked, 'that no one entered the Minister's room from the time he put the notes in the drawer until the time he said that one of them had been stolen? You can vouch for that?'

Mr Jain looked at him calmly.

'Yes,' he said. 'As I told you, I was in the outer office myself, and for the whole time I was in full view of the clerks in the next office. You must check that with them, of course. But you will find it is true. I was there, and I tell you that no one came into this room.'

Inspector Ghote licked at his lips.

'Is it possible for the Minister to have made a mistake?' he asked.

Mr Jain shrugged discreetly.

'He counted the notes into the drawer while I was here, and Felix.'

There was a choking sound from Felix as if he would have denied his presence at the counting.

'You were there? You saw the Minister count?' Inspector Ghote asked him.

'Yes, sahib.'

The note of resignation.

Inspector Ghote looked round the airy room. The walls were smoothly unbroken except for the minuscule air-conditioning grilles and where the big windows, protected by their bamboo blinds, looked out to the distant sea.

He went across to one of them and pulled up the blind.

'You will be disappointed, Inspector,' said Mr Jain. 'The walls all round the windows in this part of the building are quite smooth.'

The inspector leaned out.

Mr Jain was quite right. To the left and the right, above and below great smooth blocks of massive stone stretched away into the distance unbroken by the faintest decorative mark that could give foothold to so much as a monkey.

He turned back into the room and walked over towards the big, smoothly shining desk with a frown.

'I have not had the honour of meeting the Minister,' he said. 'Can I speak frankly, Mr Jain?'

Mr Jain smiled very slightly.

'Did he forget that he had taken the money out already?' the inspector asked. 'Is it perhaps still there? Could he not have realized that it is possible for a note to fall down the back of the drawer?'

'I can see that you do not know the Minister,' Mr Jain said. 'None of those things are possible. The Minister . . .'

He paused.

And was saved from the necessity of framing a disloyal reply by the chubby Goan peon.

'He never gave no one quarter anna he could help,' he broke out. 'Oh, my God, no.'

'In any case,' said Mr Jain, 'he showed us the open drawer with the nine notes in it. He made us look down the back of the desk. There is no doubt the money is not here.'

Inspector Ghote sighed. He took a handkerchief from his pocket and, gently holding the corner of the drawer handle, repeated the actions Mr Jain had described.

But do what he might, in the end he had to admit that there were nine one-rupee notes in the drawer and that nowhere high or low in the big, luxurious room was there one single one more.

He looked round the room one last time. The white walls stared blankly back at him.

The others looked round.

Axel Svensson seemed especially unhappy.

He swayed slightly from side to side, and at last brought out the terrible thought that he had been so obviously wrestling with.

'In the East,' he said in an unexpectedly squeaky voice, 'mysterious things happen.'

'Oh, no, Mr Svensson. Sahib, no.'

Inspector Ghote was shocked, and hurt. This was treason to all his fought-for beliefs.

'Listen, Mr Svensson,' he said urgently, 'a rupee note is a piece of paper. It is a thing. You can touch it. It is put in a drawer, and later the drawer is opened and the note is not there. Very good. An object has been moved. That is all. We will simply have to examine the situation until we find in what way the object was moved, and who moved it. No more than that, Mr Svensson.'

For once the tall Swede did not ask to be called Axel.

'Oh, yes,' he said, 'it is easy to say that. If I had been in Sweden, if I had been in America, I would say that too. But I am in India.'

He looked round with patent bewilderment clouding his periwinkle blue eyes.

The big, airy room with its heavy carpeting, its big shiny

Ministerial desk, its neat white telephone, its discreetly humming air-conditioning, did not emanate an atmosphere of mystery.

'But all the same,' he said, 'I am in India. And a rupee note has disappeared from a room which no one has entered. Inspector Ghote, how did it happen?'

Inspector Ghote looked round in his turn.

The white walls were not broken by the faintest outline of any secret door, the air-conditioning grilles were tiny, the ceiling was as plain and unbroken as a single slab of stone, the carpet lay in one unpierced layer, the big windows stared out of the sheer cliff-face of the great building.

For an instant he shut his eyes.

'Why, Mr Svensson,' he said, 'it is very simple.'

6

Axel Svensson looked at Inspector Ghote with sudden astonishment. It was plain that he had not expected to be answered with such an air of confidence.

'All right,' he said a little truculently, 'if it is so simple, what happened?'

'Those windows, Mr Svensson,' answered the inspector.

'But they could not be reached by climbing.'

The Swede's eyes shone suddenly.

'Could it be,' he said, 'could it really be the rope trick? I always thought that was just a fable, but . . .'

Inspector Ghote shook his head.

'No, my friend,' he said. 'It's not a question of a rope up from the ground supported by a flute-playing showman. It's more simple. It is a rope, or probably four ropes, coming downstairs. At each corner of a platform, and on the platform a window cleaner.'

Even the ascetic Mr Jain looked impressed.

'I had not thought of that,' he said.

He went briskly over to the telephone on the shining desk and picked up the receiver.

'Works Department,' he said.

A rapid conversation took place. At the end of it Mr Jain looked up.

'Well, Inspector,' he said, 'you are quite right. The windows on this side of the building are cleaned on Monday mornings. This is Monday.'

He smiled widely.

'So very simple really,' he said. 'And I had thought . . . but never mind.'

Inspector Ghote smiled too.

But underneath he added a mental rider. Once already he had thought this business had been cleared up nice and easily. He was not going to be caught that way twice. Perhaps it was going to turn out to be merely a short distraction from his main task, but he would not let himself feel quite easy until he had heard a magistrate impose a sharp sentence on somebody or other for the temerity of stealing money from the very desk of the Minister for Police Affairs and the Arts.

Axel Svensson smiled in his turn. A little shamefacedly.

'Well,' he said, 'I know the rope trick is just something you read about really. But all the same I have been impressed, most impressed, with certain things I have heard and seen since I came to India.'

Felix Sousa smiled broadest of all.

'You, Sousa,' Mr Jain suddenly barked, 'what are you hanging about here for? Can't you see the Minister's waste-paper basket? It's in a disgusting state. Get it emptied, man, get it emptied.'

Deflated, Felix hurried across and bent obsequiously over the basket. He rescued the crumpled piece of jotting paper that Inspector Ghote had dropped back into it and bore his burden reverently away.

'Well,' said Inspector Ghote, 'I would put men on to getting the names of the window cleaners. When we know who they are, perhaps we shall be nearer an arrest. Thank you, Mr Jain, for your help. I shall hope to have good news for you before a great amount of time.'

He went down to the vehicle with Axel Svensson and snapped an order to get to headquarters as fast as possible. A telephone call to the Varde house had become an obsessive necessity, and there was also a report on the Ministry visit to compile. Mercifully the Swede was more subdued than usual. Ghote could hardly have spared him a thought. Like the mechanical display devices outside some cinemas, picture after picture flapped up into his mind, stayed a few seconds and flapped down to be replaced by another in an endless repetitive succession.

Mr Perfect lying on the tattered charpoi breathing so dangerously gently: Lala Arun Varde calling for whisky and arousing only the distant clamour of the locked-out servants: the thin line of the wound on the back of Mr Perfect's skull: the succession of steel-grilled windows looking out on to the streets round the house: Lala Varde hinting at his power and influence in distinguished quarters: and again and again and again, Mr Perfect's long, still, emaciated body hovering on the boundaries of death.

Ghote shook his head angrily. He must not allow this irrational fascination with the old Parsee to obsess him. It was wrong and illogical. Yet . . .

The driver, pot-bellied and impassive, brought the truck to a wild screaming halt, perfectly unnecessarily, in front of the CID building. Without bothering to do anything about looking after his Swedish charge, Inspector Ghote jumped out, pounded up steps and stairs and flung himself into his office. He grabbed the telephone with sweaty hands and shouted out the number of Arun Varde's house. He got put through with undeserved rapidity and as soon as a voice answered demanded to know how Mr Perfect was.

'Will go to ask the nurse-lady,' the voice said primly.

The Inspector waited, his fingers drumming away at the lined and blotched surface of his desk.

If he died, if he had died . . .

The thought hammered away to the rhythm of his restless fingers. He would not allow himself to complete the sentence.

There came a prolonged throat-clearing at the far end of the line.

'Yes, yes? Is he dead?'

'Nurse is saying patient just the same.'

Ghote dropped the receiver on to its rest without waiting for any more.

And when Axel Svensson came into the cramped office a few moments later he gave him a beaming smile.

'Just a few words of report to write,' he said, 'and then I would be going back to the case of the attack on Mr Arun Varde's secretary. I would be revisiting the house. Do you want to come?'

No sooner had he issued the invitation than he regretted his expansive optimism. But it was too late.

'Ah, the Perfect Murder,' said the Swede. 'Most interesting problem.'

'Not murder,' the inspector replied tersely.

'No, no, of course not. An attack only. I understand.'

The tall Swede nodded up and down good-humouredly, and the inspector set rapidly to work on his reports. The one headed 'Missing Rupee Case (Larceny from Office of Shri Ram Kamath, Minister for Police Affairs and the Arts) Most Confidential' presented no difficulties. The other, 'Attack on Mr Perfect, secretary to Mr Arun Varde', was decidedly trickier.

The truth of the matter was, the inspector told himself, that he had been taken off the case at a very awkward moment, for him. If only he had had a few more hours at Lala Varde's house all his preliminary work would have been completed. As it was, if the DSP came in and started asking questions, he would look a pretty fool.

He gave the door more and more frequent glances. But at last the second report was finished. He jumped up, and, pursued by the tireless Axel Svensson, set off once more for the Varde house.

He began to feel guardedly happy. After all, it was quite possible that the Missing Rupee Case was done with, and certainly he had dealt with it so far without fault.

He scouted back to make sure that he was not being too proud in saying that. But, no, he could not honestly see what else he could have done there. And, if things went well for a bit, he would soon be able to bring the case of the attack on Mr Perfect up to the same standard of efficient handling. The thing to do was to get hold of the remaining witnesses and get their stories out of them as quickly as possible. Then he could submit a new report, neatly laid out and with all the paragraphs numbered. Once the DSP had that he could hardly kick up one of his famous fusses. And with a good foundation laid there would be every chance of making some real progress with the case.

The only blemish was that he seemed to be stuck with Axel Svensson. And the effect of the setback inflicted over the rope trick was beginning to wear off. Bit by bit the Swede's remarks about Indian life were regaining their old decisiveness.

Inspector Ghote could have done without them.

'Mr Sven – Axel sahib,' he said as their vehicle roared up to the Varde house. 'There is one thing I should like you to understand. This case is rather different from the last. This is a private household. They may not be happy to find I have brought someone else with me, especially a European.'

Axel Svensson put his broad hand on the inspector's shoulder.

'That is all right, my friend. I perfectly understand. I shall be completely discreet, completely silent.'

Inspector Ghote felt it was the most he could have hoped for.

At the house he asked first for Lala Varde himself. He was taken by the erect little bearer he had seen before to the courtyard where the great man was sitting reading the advertisement columns of a newspaper.

'Good morning, Lala Varde sahib,' the inspector said. 'I was afraid you would have gone to your office.'

Lala Varde did not answer. Instead he leaned forward in his wide-seated cane chair and scratched with a great podgy fist at the side of his huge fat-covered ribs.

Inspector Ghote quelled a feeling of annoyance.

'Mr Varde,' he said in a voice which must have carried to every corner of the big compound, 'Mr Varde, may I introduce Mr Axel Svensson. Mr Svensson is working for Unesco. He is studying our police methods.'

Again Lala Varde seemed not to have heard, loud though the inspector's voice had been. But the inspector experienced a certain sense of relief this time: he had not looked forward to two such powerful personalities as Lala Varde and the tall Swede discussing any case he was meant to be in charge of.

He looked down at the massive sprawling form in the wide chair in front of him. Lala Varde's eyes were slowly closing.

'Mr Varde,' he said sharply.

Lala Varde's eyelids met.

'Mr Varde,' said the inspector again.

He put all the concentrated force he could muster into the words.

If they had no apparent effect on Lala Varde, they did not leave the little ramrod bearer untouched.

'Sssh, sahib. Oh, please to be quiet,' he said. 'Lala Varde is sleeping.'

Inspector Ghote turned on him.

'I cannot help whether he is sleeping,' he said, letting his pent anger rip out. 'I am police officer. I am investigating most serious case. I have to speak to Lala Varde here and now.'

'Oh, ho. So you think you can come trampling bampling into my house just because you are police officer.'

The inspector wheeled round. Lala Varde's great bloodshot eyes were open.

'I greatly regret to have disturbed you, sahib,' the inspector said with an air of rectitude, 'but I must remind you that Mr Perfect is still in a most serious condition as a result of the attack of last night. Rigorous investigation is essential.'

'But there was no attack. You are dreaming only, Inspector.'

Lala Varde gave a monstrous, unconcerned yawn.

Inspector Ghote seized his runaway temper and tethered it sharply back.

He took a deep, long, measured breath.

'Mr Varde,' he said, 'last night at 1.47 a.m. precisely you telephoned the Police Department. Is that not so?'

Squinting through half-closed eyelids, Lala Varde looked at him for a long while before replying.

'Oh, you policias,' he said at last, 'with your records of this and your records of that, your times that this occurred and your times that that occurred. I tell you, Inspector, if I ran my business by keeping notes of every little time that I stood up or I sat down, no money would I have, not one anna.'

The inspector took the veiled point.

'Exactly, sahib,' he said. 'You reported last night that your secretary, Mr Perfect, had been attacked. The report is entered in the appropriate log books.'

From behind his now definitively closed eyes Lala Varde emitted a gurgle of laughter.

'Not attack, Inspector,' he said, 'murder instead. I told that poor old Mr Perfect was murdered. In your record pecord you have written "the Perfect Murder".'

The words, with the unpleasant fact that it was almost certain that they were on official record somewhere, confronted the inspector. He felt them as the distinguishable outposts of a great cloud-wall that lay in front of him, shifting, advancing, retreating, but never doing more than give the delusion of penetration.

With an effort of will that almost hurt, he recalled the blue volume of Gross reposing in its place in his office. Doctor Gross would not permit a case to be handled in this way.

'Mr Varde,' he said, 'whatever the actual words used, it remains nevertheless that you reported an attack on Mr Perfect. Also it was not then a fatal attack, but even at this moment it may have become such. You cannot now say the attack never took place.'

He saw again the long prostrate figure of the old Parsee, lightly and delicately and dangerously breathing.

'What attack are you talking, Inspector? I know no attack.'

The voice was utterly bland, and thick with sleep.

'Very well, Mr Varde,' said Inspector Ghote, 'you leave me no alternative. I shall have to submit application to higher authority for permission to arrest you for obstructing a police officer in the course of his duty.'

The huge sleeping form in the wide cane chair spoke.

'And have you thought what higher authority will say when they learn how you treat Lala Arun Varde?'

Yet by the end of the sentence the bloodshot eyes were fully open and were regarding the inspector with wary respect.

'Mr Varde,' the inspector said, 'from enquiries to date we know that Mr Perfect was alive at midnight last night. At 1.47 a.m. you reported that he was dead, a statement subject to subsequent modification. It remains therefore to account for movements made by victim in the intervening period. Mr Varde, when did you last see Mr Perfect?'

'Inspector,' said Lala Varde in a tone of all-embracing reasonableness, 'what are you bothering your head with such matters? There is a lot of work for Police Department to do, Inspector. I know it. There is much disregarding of the prohibition laws in the city. People are obtaining medical certificates when they are quite unnecessary. The poorer classes are frequently making illicit brews. Such things must be stopped, Inspector. And then there is the whole matter of anti-corruption. It is needing the utmost attention.'

He heaved himself forward making the wide chair under him bend and shudder.

'Inspector,' he said, 'don't you think you ought to be doing this work?'

'Breaches of the prohibition law and anti-corruption activities come under different departments,' Inspector Ghote replied stolidly. 'Also my task is to investigate the criminal attack on Mr Perfect. I have been given it, and I will continue with it until it is finished.'

Lala Varde shook his head sadly.

'Oh, Inspector, Inspector,' he said, 'you are a foolish man.'

'No, sahib,' Inspector Ghote said with unshaken firmness. 'It is you who are foolish. It is always foolish not to answer questions put by a police officer in the course of his duties.'

'Very well, Inspector, I have said.'

'Very well, sahib. And now perhaps you will tell me when you last saw Mr Perfect before the attack?'

Lala Varde's eyes narrowed.

'At midnight you know he was alive?' he asked.

Inspector Ghote winced inwardly. If he had not been so irritated by the huge old man's obstinacy, he would probably have contrived to have kept this fact to himself.

'At midnight,' he admitted.

'Yes, that must be so,' Lala Varde said. 'Because at midnight I saw him also.'

'Mr Varde,' the inspector said, 'when Mr Perfect was attacked he was in the little room by the door to the house. Why should he have been in there?'

'Oh, Inspector, what questions you are asking. How should I know a thing like that? How should I know anything? I have too many things to think to be knowing why is this and why is that. It all falls on my shoulders. My son Dilip is no good. I have ordered him not to go to office today. He can think instead about what is the right thing to say and the right thing to do, and he can read his mysteries histories at home. If he went to office he would give orders, and then where would we be?'

'Your son is in the house, sahib?'

Inspector Ghote had come to the conclusion that he would get no more out of the father at the present moment.

'Yes, yes,' Lala Varde answered with eagerness. 'My Dilip is in house. I will call a servant to take you to him.'

He jerked forward in the chair and clapped his hands explosively.

'Come, come quickly,' he shouted. 'Is there nobody to show the inspector sahib where Mr Dilip is? Has everyone gone to sleep in this house?'

The erect little bearer, who had retreated indoors, came trotting back.

'Take the inspector to the tika sahib. Quick, quickly.'

Lala Varde leaned hastily back and closed his eyes.

'Lala Varde sahib,' the inspector said, 'where did you send Mr Perfect last night when he went out?'

'Oh, somewhere, somewhere. I really cannot be answering all these foolish questions.'

Lala Varde humped over away from the inspector and shut his eyes till the eyelids were squeezed together like two sets of rubber suction pads.

The inspector looked at him. He turned to Axel Svensson.

'Perhaps the answer will prove not to be necessary,' he said.

Apologetically.

He rounded on the little bearer.

'Show me where Mr Dilip Varde is,' he said. 'It is most urgent matter.'

He was glad to see the man set off loping rigidly ahead of him with a thoroughly harassed air.

Eventually he found Dilip Varde for them in one of the less used downstairs rooms. It was a sort of Number Two spare sitting room, heavily furnished in the Western style. Dilip was sprawled across a big puffy armchair covered in a dark moquette. It must have been very hot and uncomfortable for him. Large patches of sweat were spreading from each of his armpits across his once crisp white shirt. Under his dark jutting moustache his mouth was set in a down-turned sulky pout.

Signalling to Axel Svensson to delay a moment outside, the inspector entered the room with a brisk stride. As Dilip heard the unaccustomed step he quickly thrust the paperback he had been reading down into the crack between the back and the seat of his heavy armchair. But not before Inspector Ghote had caught sight of its lurid cover on which a square-jawed private eye was for ever menacing a busty blonde.

The little erect bearer bent in a stiff salaam.

'Inspector sahib ask to see you, sahib,' he said.

By this time Dilip was standing up. His hands flew to the knot of his thin-striped club tie and swiftly tightened it.

'Inspector?' he said. 'What sort of an inspector is this? Sanitary wallah, eh?'

'Inspector, Bombay CID,' Ghote said.

He looked Dilip up and down. The arrogant tilt of the head, the jutting moustache, the alien tie, the dark blue blazer with the brass buttons which he had left lying across the back of the heavy armchair, the dark flannel trousers immaculately creased.

'CID, eh?' Dilip said. 'Some trouble among the servants, I suppose. Why my father won't get hold of some decently trained chaps I shall never know.'

He strolled away in the direction of one of the windows looking out on to the central courtyard.

'Anyhow, old chap,' he said, 'you've come to the wrong place, you know. Servants are nothing to do with me. Thank goodness.'

He turned idly round again to look at the inspector, his hand toying with the bushy moustache.

'Servants' quarters not here,' he said with elaborate distinctness. 'Servants' quarters other way. Understand?'

'Sir,' said Inspector Ghote, 'officers of the Bombay police naturally have command of English. It is necessary to their work. Also I have not come about the servants.'

He felt his anger rising step by step, and had just enough power over himself to keep it in check. He cast his mind round. There ought to be some way of dealing with a person like this. Doctor Gross would not have been at a loss.

And in the nick of time inspiration came.

'Mr Varde,' he said, 'it is you yourself I wish to speak with, but may I first introduce my colleague? He is Axel Svensson, from Sweden, a visitor from Unesco.'

Axel Svensson, tall, blond, distinguished, academic, came in.

Dilip Varde's whole face betrayed the success of the inspector's stratagem. His eyes lit up and a crocodile smile appeared beneath his luxuriant moustache.

He advanced on the Swede with outstretched hand.

'My dear fellow,' he said, 'come in, come in. I had no idea you were hanging about out there. What on earth will you think of us?'

Axel Svensson put his huge pinky hand briefly round Dilip's slim brown one.

'So,' Dilip said, 'you're with Unesco, are you? I used to know some chaps with that outfit. Pretty good chaps. Though, mind you, that was some time ago.'

'The personnel change with great frequency,' Axel Svensson admitted. 'It is a problem we have yet to solve.'

'Yes,' said Dilip, 'it must be pretty awkward for you. Difficult to get hold of the right sort of chap, I suppose. We have just the same trouble here. Simply nobody fit to do most of the jobs that are going, when it comes to the point.'

'Oh, yes,' said the Swede politely.

'Well,' Dilip said, 'just what is it that you're doing here in Bombay? If there's anything we can do to make life a bit pleasanter, for God's sake let us know.'

'At present I am following the inquiry into the Perfect Murder,' Axel Svensson declared stolidly.

Inspector Ghote forgave him a lot for this, even down to calling the case once again the Perfect Murder.

Dilip took some considerable time to adjust.

'Oh, yes, of course, that,' he said at last. 'Shocking business.'

The inspector took his chance firmly in both hands.

'Yes, Mr Varde,' he said, 'it is precisely the attack on Mr Perfect that I have come to see you about.'

Dilip Varde turned reluctantly away from the Swede to look at him.

'Yes,' he said, 'I dare say you have. But I'm afraid I can't do anything to help you, old chap. Not a thing.'

But now that the inspector had got his teeth in he was not going to let go.

'You can answer some questions for me, Mr Varde,' he said. 'That at least will be most helpful.'

'But look here,' Dilip replied, 'you can't really want to question me. I mean, I know that somebody had a bash at that fearful old

Parsee, but beyond that I simply don't know a thing about it. Don't wish to know.'

'He is lying in this house most seriously ill,' the inspector said. 'Even at this instant he may be deceased.'

'Yes, yes, I'm sure you're right. As I said, it's a bad business, definitely.'

Dilip gave the ends of his moustache a revivifying tweak apiece.

'What you chaps have got to do, Inspector,' he said, 'is to see that the whole business is wrapped up and dealt with in the shortest possible time.'

'Yes, sir, that is certainly so,' Ghote answered. 'And for this reason I would be grateful to hear your answers to my questions.'

Dilip shook his head.

'But, no my dear fellow. You've got the whole thing the wrong way round.'

He turned to Axel Svensson again.

'I dare say you've noticed the wonderful facility of the average Indian for grasping the wrong end of the old stick,' he said.

'Sir,' said Inspector Ghote, 'I do not understand. What do you mean: I have got the business the wrong way round?'

'Perfectly simple,' Dilip answered. 'The object of the exercise is to dispose of the case as quickly as possible. Ek dum. Right?'

'Speed is essential,' Ghote agreed.

'Right. So you don't waste everybody's time by going round asking a lot of bloody silly questions. You go back to your little office, wherever it is, and you file a pretty swift report saying that everything's under control and can safely be forgotten about. Right?'

'But, Mr Varde . . .'

It was the outraged voice of the Swede.

Dilip turned to him.

'Not quite European practice?' he said. 'Well, no, I know it isn't. And let me tell you that in the old days it wouldn't have happened here. But as things are today, it's simply the only way.'

'But you cannot write a report to say a case is closed when nothing has been found out,' the Swede explained patiently.

'Ah, I know what you mean. Too well I know it. And in the British days I wouldn't for one moment have suggested it. No, no. If anything like this had happened then, it would have all been perfectly simple. Some decent chappie would have come round, we'd have given him a drink, he'd have asked anything that was necessary in a perfectly gentlemanly way and we'd have told him what he wanted to know. But, my dear chap, not today.'

He glanced significantly at Ghote.

The big Swede looked puzzled.

'This is a problem I do not wholly grasp,' he said.

'Well, the plain fact of the matter is,' Dilip said, 'that our policeman as he is today may be a good chap and all that, but he's simply had no experience of how civilized people live. He'd be totally out of his depth in a house like this. So there's only one thing to do: draw a decent veil over the whole thing.'

Inspector Ghote stepped forward.

'Mr Varde,' he said, 'I may be out of my depth but I am not out of my country. It will not help you now to be more English than the English. You will all the same have to answer questions. And I will point out that this is certainly what an Englishman from England would do.'

Dilip looked at him with a sudden total disappearance of geniality.

'Are you quite sure who you're talking to, Inspector?' he said. 'You don't have to remind me that this is India. I'm only too well aware of the fact. But however many drawbacks there are in that, there are also certain advantages. Advantages for me.'

'Mr Varde.'

Axel Svensson had got beyond outrage and into incomprehension. And certainly Dilip's unsubtlety was difficult to believe in.

Inspector Ghote decided that he must intervene quickly.

'When a crime has been committed,' he said sharply, 'it is neither India nor England nor America nor anywhere else. When it is a question of finding out who is to blame it is all the same world. No matter what place it is, first you must find the facts and then you must look at them to see what is the logic of them. That is why you must answer questions, Mr Varde.'

Dilip smiled.

'All this,' he said, 'for a ridiculous long stick of an old Parsee that no one cares tuppence for.'

'All this for a man who may be dying,' said the inspector.

Axel Svensson, calmer now, came to his assistance.

'Mr Varde,' he said, 'believe me, you must answer.'

Dilip shrugged.

'Very well,' he said, 'but be quick about it.'

'Then to begin,' said the inspector, 'where were you last night?'

'I was here in the house, if you must know.'

'Thank you, sir. And at what time did you last see Mr Perfect?'

'My dear chap, I really don't know.'

Inspector Ghote's mouth tightened.

'I am sorry, Mr Varde,' he said, 'but such an answer is quite unsatisfactory. It is possible for the servants not to be able to answer a question of this sort through ignorance, but you are an educated man. You must know when you last saw Mr Perfect.'

But already Dilip was regaining his initial truculence.

'I don't see why I should take any particular notice of one servant any more than any other,' he answered.

'Mr Perfect is not a servant, Mr Varde. He is your father's confidential secretary.'

Now Dilip's large eyes glowed with anger.

'You will permit me to know who is a servant in this household and who is not, Inspector.'

'Very good, if you wish to describe Mr Perfect in this manner. But that does not alter the facts. He is in a different class altogether from people like the sweeping boy. You must have noticed whether he was there or not.'

'And I tell you I didn't. I didn't ever take any particular notice of him. I knew he was a Parsee my father employed in the office and at home, on confidential matters if you like. But he was of no importance to me, Inspector. I didn't have to go through a Mr Perfect when I wished to speak to my own father, you know.'

Inspector Ghote found himself resenting the implication that he would know so little of life that he could make a mistake of this sort.'

'Of course not, Mr Varde,' he said. 'I never suggested such a thing.'

Dilip looked a little mollified. His hand went up to his moustache and he stroked it with affection.

'As a matter of fact,' he said, 'I hardly knew the fellow. My father took him on after I had gone to take charge of the firm's affairs in Delhi. I suppose he needed someone. And, in case you don't happen to know, I haven't been back in Bombay very long.'

'So you mean to say that you cannot tell me when you last saw Mr Perfect because you didn't notice him?' the inspector said with a trace of discouragement.

'Exactly.'

The inspector wearily braced himself for a new attack.

'Very well, Mr Varde,' he said, 'then I must now ask you what you were doing in detail during yesterday evening.'

Dilip responded with an access of sudden wild rage. It made his eyes pop wide and his mouth open convulsively.

'Are you accusing me of killing that ridiculous Parsee?' he spluttered.

'Mr Varde,' said the inspector, 'there is no need for anger. I am not accusing: I am asking only.'

Above all, he told himself, he would not give way to the jet of pure rage that he longed to shoot out in answer to the hot blast of Dilip Varde's fury. There would not be a shouting match. Investigations were not like that.

But Dilip interpreted his restraint in another fashion.

His fury turned to confident contempt.

'You are asking, are you, Inspector?' he said. 'Well, you can whistle for your answer.'

He turned and began walking towards the doorway.

The inspector felt himself in a ferment of contradiction. Was he right to keep so calm? Or was he really giving way to something deep in himself which feared Dilip and his like?

There was no time to resolve the conflict.

While Dilip was still in the room he let out an almost incoherent shout.

'Stop.'

Dilip did stop. He turned and looked at the inspector.

'Where are you going?' Ghote said, trembling with suppressed emotion.

'I am going to see my wife?'

'Your wife? Where is she?'

'I expect she is in the women's quarter. My mother is old-fashioned and prefers that. Do you intend to break in there, Inspector? I would have thought that was something even you would respect.'

Inspector Ghote hesitated.

And Dilip saw his hesitation.

He turned back to the doorway.

'When can I see you again?' the inspector stammered.

He knew that he had lost. An acute feeling of depression swept over him. He wanted just to sit down and let Dilip Varde do what he liked.

But Dilip gave him an answer.

'I really cannot say when you'll see me, Inspector. I have some important matters I wish to discuss with my wife. I may be a long time. And it is possible that I shall have to go back to Delhi quite soon. The firm cannot be left to run itself just because of an old Parsee.'

He walked out.

Inspector Ghote found he had not the moral energy even to point out that the firm had so far been left to run itself for less than half a day.

He stared at the doorway through which Dilip had departed, asking himself dully whether he would ever be able to get a clear picture of what went on in this house where Mr Perfect lay battered and perhaps dying.

There was nothing he could do, he felt. The old Parsee might be at this very moment breathing his tremulous last breath. If it was so, it would have to be so. The black darkness of obscurity would enfold the Perfect Murder in its every detail and he would be lost for ever.

7

Axel Svensson at last broke the long silence in the over-stuffed sitting room.

'This is a great problem,' he said. 'In countries where perhaps the police are associated with the former rulers, when independence comes there will be elements who are not willing to accept that they too must come under the same law as every other citizen.'

Inspector Ghote looked up at him gratefully.

'A policeman must not allow himself to be intimidated by the position of those he has to deal with,' he said.

'That is certainly correct,' the raw-boned Swede agreed.

Inspector Ghote rectified the droop of his shoulders.

'On the other hand,' he said, 'a police officer must not allow himself to bully a weak person. You will remember perhaps that Doctor Gross in his *Criminal Investigation* speaks of the danger of harassing a witness into making a false statement.'

'Yes,' said the Swede a little doubtfully.

Inspector Ghote brightened. This was a subject he had long wanted to talk about to such an expert as Mr Svensson. Much cherished though his copy of Gross was, there were sometimes moments when he wondered exactly how much authority the work carried. It was not an official issue; he had bought his own copy at a bazaar bookstall and, his eagerness to acquire it showing too plainly, had had to pay a stiff price. So occasionally he had traitorous doubts. This seemed to be an excellent moment to clear them up.

'Tell me, Axel sahib,' he said, 'is Gross a book much used in the police forces of Europe? What do you think of it yourself?'

Axel Svensson assumed a doubly serious expression.

'This is a very interesting subject,' he began. 'The book is, of course . . .'

His voice faded away.

Inspector Ghote looked at him. He in his turn was looking at the open doorway with his blue eyes widening every moment.

For an instant Inspector Ghote was puzzled.

What on earth was this mad foreigner? And then he understood. He took up the conversation where the Swede had left it.

'I think you will find that the methods of Doctor Gross which I am using in the present case will bring results,' he said. 'The key to the whole problem is using an efficient system. If an efficient system is used nothing slips through the net.'

As he spoke he crept quietly towards the doorway. His efforts to sound casual and at the same time deeply interested were only moderately successful.

'Yes,' he went on, 'method and order: those are the keys to success in any criminal matter. As I am sure you would—'

A sharp bound took him out into the corridor.

Pressed against the wall just beside the doorway was a young man of about seventeen, slim and still a bit gangly, dressed in a loud blue bush-shirt for which his chest frankly lacked the necessary development.

'Well,' said Inspector Ghote, 'and did you find our conversation interesting?'

'Conversation? I did not hear any conversation,' the young man said.

He began to slide away from the wall.

'I was just passing,' he said. 'I did not know there was anybody in there, as a matter of fact.'

He tried an insouciant smile.

'Just passing?' Inspector Ghote snapped. 'It was taking you a very long time to get past such a narrow doorway. What's your name and your business here?'

'My name is Prem. Prem Varde. I am a student, last year in college. Excuse me now, if you please, I have a great deal of work to do today.'

'You are Mr Arun Varde's second son?' Inspector Ghote asked without moving.

'That's right, Inspector.'

A feeble grin.

'Inspector. Inspector. Oh, so you know I am inspector in charge of the investigation into the attack on Mr Perfect. You heard nothing as you happened to pass by this room but you know that. Come in here, young man.'

He stood by until Prem had sidled into the room.

'Now,' he said, 'sit there and answer a few questions.'

Prem sat down cautiously on the very edge of a great overblown sofa and sucked at his full lower lip.'

'Your name?'

Prem looked up in sudden hostility.

'I have already said.'

'Your name, young man and quick about it.'

'My name is Prem Varde.'

'Age?'

'Eighteen, soon.'

'Seventeen. Occupation?'

'Student.'

'Student. And not at college. Why is that?'

'My father said I had better not go today. He said everyone was to stay in the house.'

'And did he tell you to spy on the police during their investigations? I suppose he did that, did he?'

The inspector refused to examine his motives in jumping so hard on the boy. If he was revenging himself for his defeat at the hands of Dilip, he was not going to admit it even to himself.

Prem swallowed and looked even more miserable.

'No, Inspector,' he said. 'Listening was my idea.'

'Ah, now we're beginning to get somewhere. You admit you were attempting to overhear a confidential conversation between two investigating officers on the subject of a criminal matter. You realize this could be a very serious offence?'

Prem's head sank till he was looking stonily at his shoes.

From behind the inspector came a cough from the big Swede.

'Luckily for this young man,' he said, 'we were simply discussing police methods in general. Otherwise he might really be in trouble.'

Prem looked up at him gratefully.

'Yes,' said Inspector Ghote, 'it is lucky for you. Otherwise you would find yourself behind bars pretty quick. Now, are you going to answer my questions, or are you not?'

'Yes, Inspector. If I can.'

'Let me tell you this, young man. It is your duty to answer. No "if I can" and "if I want to". You will answer and answer the truth.'

'But I only meant that I would tell you what I know. If I don't know, I can't answer.'

Fortified by this incontrovertible logic Prem looked a little happier.

'There are two possible meanings to my words,' he went on. 'They could be said to mean "I will answer if I feel that there is nothing to prevent me", or they could mean "I will answer if I know the answer". Now—'

'That's enough of that,' Inspector Ghote said. 'We haven't come here to listen to a lot of school lectures. We want the answers to a few straight questions. For example, when did you last see Mr Perfect? Or are you going to tell that you don't know who Mr Perfect is?'

'No,' said the boy. 'Of course I know him: he is my father's secretary. I see him every day. He always is in the house in the evenings after Daddyji comes back from office. In case there is anything he wishes to dictate or anything like that.'

'When I want to hear what the duties of your father's secretary are

I shall ask,' Inspector Ghote said. 'Now will you please tell me when you last saw Mr Perfect?'

'Yes,' said Prem.

'Good. When?'

'Half an hour ago, Inspector.'

'Half an hour ago? But—'

Inspector Ghote bit his lip in baffled fury.

'I did not mean when did you last see him,' he said. 'I meant when did you last see him before the attack.'

'I am sorry, Inspector,' Prem said. 'I thought you wanted to know if he was better. He is not. He is just the same. But I can tell you when I last saw him yesterday. I saw him leaving the house at about eight o'clock.'

'Eight o'clock. Where was he going? Was he going home?'

'Oh, no, Inspector. At least I don't think so. I met him by the door, and something made me wonder where he was going. It—'

'Did you wonder only? Why didn't you ask?'

'But I did, Inspector. I asked but he would not tell.'

'He would not tell?'

'No, Inspector. He just said it was on business for my father.'

'That's a likely story. On business. At that time of the evening.'

'But, Inspector, it is possible. Sometimes Daddyji does send Mr Perfect to talk business in the evenings. There are some things he says it is better to do then. Of course, often he does such things himself, but sometimes he sends Mr Perfect.'

'All right. But if you saw him go out at eight o'clock, when did he come in again?'

'I don't know, Inspector.'

'Don't know, is it? Or won't say?'

Prem gulped.

'Don't know, really, Inspector. I told you truth. The last time I had seen Mr Perfect last night was when he went out. I can't do more than tell you truth.'

Prem looked at him gloweringly.

'Very well, then, we'll leave that for the time being. Now, what did you do yourself after eight o'clock?'

'I had dinner with them all,' Prem answered, 'and then I went up to my room. I had to write essay. It was a very important subject. On the nature of beauty. I distinguished four kinds of beauty. There was—'

'We don't want your opinions on beauty: we want to know if you can prove what you say about being in your own room.'

'Oh, but Inspector, I can. I can prove. For part of the time at least. For part of the time Dilip was there.'

'Your brother? He said nothing of this.'

'But he was there, Inspector. He was. I did not want him to come in. I told him I was busy. I was very interested in my essay. I wanted just to finish. But he insisted on coming in.'

'And why was that?'

Prem looked up quickly.

'He just wanted to talk,' he said.

'He just wanted to talk. And how long did he want to just talk for?'

Inspector Ghote noticed Prem's tense calf muscles relax.

'Oh, for about half an hour,' the boy said.

The inspector saw his way ahead.

'I see,' he said less sharply. 'And this was from about what time? Just round about?'

'I do not remember exactly. It was late, I know. I was getting sleepy. It must have been about a quarter to twelve.'

'Quarter to twelve. Good, good.'

Inspector Ghote turned casually away.

'Well,' he said, 'we have made some progress.'

'Thank you, Inspector. May I go now?'

'Oh, yes, yes.'

The inspector gestured vaguely.

Prem hurried toward the doorway.

'Wait.'

Prem stopped as if an iron hand had clamped down on his shoulder.

'This talk with your brother,' Inspector Ghote snapped, 'what was it about?'

Prem turned round unwillingly.

'It was just talking,' he said wearily.

The inspector surmised that his tactics were going to work: the boy had felt the pressure was off and now that it was on again he was near to cracking.

'Just talking?' he said relentlessly. 'Just talking what about?'

Prem looked at the floor.

'Just one brother talking to another,' he muttered.

'And you can't remember what was said? I don't believe that talk took place at all.'

'But it did take place. It did, Inspector. It took place when I said. From about quarter to twelve till quarter past. No, till a bit later.'

'I see. You talked with your brother for nearly three quarters of an hour and you can't remember a word of the conversation. Come now, that just isn't good enough. What were you talking about?'

Suddenly Prem's head jerked up and he looked the inspector full in the face.

'I won't say.'

'You won't say? You won't say? What you mean is you can't say. You can't say because the conversation never took place.'

'It did. It did.'

'Then what was it about? One part of it only.'

'I refuse to say.'

'You refuse to answer my questions?'

'Yes.'

Prem glared sullenly in front of him.

'You realize that this may get you into serious trouble?'

'I don't care.'

'Come, I give you a last chance. What were you and your brother talking about?'

'I will not say. I refuse to answer any more questions.'

A cunning look came into the boy's eyes.

'I am under age,' he said defiantly. 'I refuse to speak until I have seen my father.'

He stared up into space.

Inspector Ghote went and sat on the sofa where he had placed Prem at the beginning of the interview.

For some time he looked at the boy, and when he spoke it was gently.

'Your essay,' he said, 'you were telling me what it was about.'

Prem flicked a suspicious glance towards him.

'Perhaps on second thoughts,' Inspector Ghote said, 'the essay could provide proof that you had been busy working in your room. Of course, it would be necessary to show that you had not begun it earlier, but that should not be impossible. What did you say the essay was about? The three kinds of beauty?'

'Four,' said Prem.

'Ah, four. And what are they?'

Little by little Prem recapitulated his essay. The inspector listened with profound attention though he did not follow a great deal of Prem's argument.

And in the middle of a most abstruse piece of explanation, in which the last of the four categories of beauty was divided into three subcategories and the third of these had five subsections, quite casually Prem left his theme.

'And that was where Dilip came in and insisted on telling me what he had just found out,' he said.

Inspector Ghote held his breath.

The boy looked at him.

'But I don't want to repeat it.'

'I do not want you to repeat out of curiosity only,' the inspector said.

He leaned towards the boy.

'Look,' he said, 'Mr Perfect was attacked in this house last night. It was a most serious attack. Even now he may be dying. At this moment. And, listen, that attack took place after midnight. We know that. And just at midnight all the servants went to their quarters and the iron gate was locked.'

He waited until he saw from the widening of Prem's serious eyes that his point had sunk fully in.

'You know that all the outside windows in the house are fitted with American steel grilles, don't you?' he asked.

Prem nodded.

'So what do we learn from this?' the inspector went on. 'It is simple. That the attack on Mr Perfect almost certainly came from someone inside the house. There are not so many. There is your father and mother. There is your brother and his wife and there is yourself. Now do you see why I must know just what you were doing?'

The inspector held Prem with his eyes, would not let him go. At last the boy dropped his gaze. The inspector saw the tip of his tongue come out and lick along the length of his upper lip.

When the boy spoke it was in a whisper.

'I think I will tell you,' he said.

8

Inspector Ghote leaned forward.

He felt as if little by little he had lured a wild monkey, sensitive and suspicious, to the very door of a cage. And he had a strong impression that this would be a monkey worth capturing. There was something odd about Prem Varde's refusing to say what it was that this brother had told him during the time that Mr Perfect might have been attacked. He had sensed this from the very first time the boy had mentioned the conversation.

What it was that had alerted him to the emotional charge Prem put on to the talk he could not exactly say. Perhaps it had been something to do with a tensing up of the muscles somewhere, or a slight overemphasis in speech, or the sudden appearance of a sheen of sweat on the forehead. Any or all of these signs might betray the difficulty of concealing something. This was a fact he had learned in response to the Teutonically severe behest of Doctor Gross. 'The smallest observation may some day be of decisive importance.' He knew the words by heart.

And now the wary monkey had put one paw right into the waiting cage.

'Oh ho, Inspector.'

Inspector Ghote whirled round as if a gunman had come at him from behind.

It was Lala Arun Varde.

'Oh, Inspector detector, what is this I hear? What is this about the way you have been treating my poor son?'

Inspector Ghote felt a quick flash of shame putting beads of sweat on his forehead. It was true: he had been guilty of bullying a witness for the sake of bullying.

'I hope I was not really too rough with him, Mr Varde,' he said. 'But you know what these young college boys sometimes are. They think that policemen are just there for them to make jokes at. You have to show them at first that you are talking serious matters.'

'College boys? What college boys is this?'

Lala Varde looked about in a puzzled way. His eye fell on Prem.

'What are you doing here?' he said. 'You do not know that this is a police inspector? He has important work to be doing. Now, off you go. Back to your books with their category pategories. Back to your studying while you can. Your father has something important to say to the inspector. This is not a time for little children only.'

Prem looked at him with blazing eyes.

'How often must I tell you,' he said, 'I am not a child. Soon I will be BA. I am college student. I am learning the fundamental principles of things. Then one day—'

Lala Varde broke into a deep belly roar of laughter.

'Then one day you will come into office and learn they were all wrong your fundamental principles,' he shouted. 'But until that day comes, off you go to your books. Shoo, shoo, shoo.'

He waddled towards Prem holding his arms wide and making slight pushing gestures as if he was an old woman chasing along a chicken.

Prem glared at him.

'I will never come in office,' he shouted. 'Never, never.'

He turned and ran from the room.

Lala Varde laughed.

'My sons, my sons. What trouble bubble they are, Inspector. Have you got children to trouble you?'

'I have one son,' the inspector said. 'But he is five only.'

'Not too young to be trouble,' said Lala Varde. 'These two they were trouble all their lives. First Dilip, then Prem. And after Prem, Dilip some more.'

'Well, in a way that is what you must expect from children,' the inspector said.

'Yes, yes, that is so. Have you got sons, Mr Svensson?'

The big Swede smiled.

'No,' he said, 'at present I am unmarried. I do not yet have those problems.'

'Ha. Well, you are a lucky man, Mr Svensson. A lucky man.'

'Well,' the Swede said, 'on the other hand, I have the problems of being a bachelor.'

Lala Varde rolled up to him and dug him four or five times in the ribs.

'Not very difficult problems, heh?' he said.

A delicate blush stole up the Swede's high-boned cheeks.

Lala Varde poked him in the ribs again and went on chuckling deep in his wide chest.

Till suddenly he stopped and turned to the inspector.

'But why did you treat my son so badly?' he asked.

'I explained, sahib. He is young and—'

'No, not that son. My son who is man.'

'Mr Dilip Varde?'

The inspector could not keep the surprise out of his voice.

'Yes, yes. What other sons have I got? And why will you not tell me why you treated Dilip so badly? He comes to me five minutes ago and tells me you insulted him, Inspector.'

'Insulted? Insulted a witness? I assure you, sahib, that is quite impossible.'

'But he told me you insisted on asking him what he did at each moment of last evening.'

'But, of course, sahib. I had to ask him that. Mr Perfect was attacked in this house last night. He is in danger of death. The door was bolted, the windows are fitted with grilles, the servants were locked away in their quarters, it is essential that I know where everybody in the house was.'

Inspector Ghote stood to attention. He was thinking about Mr Perfect. Was he in fact still alive? Was the case still one which he could hope to deal with successfully?

Lala Varde looked sombrely down at the shining leather of the inspector's belt.

'Yes. He has to know.'

It was Axel Svensson.

'You understand, Mr Varde,' he went on, 'a policeman has to know the whereabouts of every possible witness when a crime of this sort has been committed. When he knows that, he knows what can and cannot have happened. Inspector Ghote needed your son's statement as evidence.'

'Ah,' said Lala Varde.

A great smile spread across his face.

'Ah,' he said, 'now I am understanding. You must excuse an old man like me, Inspector. I am a silly old man only. I do not understand your timetable fables. But if you say it is important, then I will believe you.'

He shook his head sadly.

'You cannot expect a boy like Dilip to understand, though,' he said. 'It is all right for me, you know. I have a head on my shoulders good and hard.'

He grasped his huge head in between two widespread palms and shook it slightly from side to side.

'Yes,' he said, 'good and hard. But Dilip. My poor Dilip does not understand things, Inspector. He does not understand.'

He looked round with new belligerence.

'Why should he understand?' he went on. 'Why should a son of Lala Arun Varde understand? He does not need to understand. It is all right for his old father to have to understand things, and how the world is run. But Dilip does not need to worry his head with that. He can worry about better things. My Dilip has great worries about family honour. All the time he worries about his honour. When you have plenty of money punny behind you, Inspector, you can do that, you know.'

'I am afraid I do not—' the inspector began rather stiffly.

But there was no stopping Lala Varde.

'No, no, no,' he said, 'it is a good thing that Dilip does not have to understand business matters. I let him have an office of his own, of course. Best air-conditioning, direct import ex-US, carpets wall to wall, Coke machine, everything he wants. But I do not let him get in the way. I set him up in the Delhi branch, but, by God, I took care that all Delhi business was done from Bombay office. And when he tried to give orders I had to bring him back pretty damn quick, eh?'

Inspector Ghote looked politely interested.

'Ah,' Lala Varde said, 'I don't say he isn't a very useful person to have in the business though. I tell you he is worth every anna of what he is paid. Every anna. If I want to do business with an American firm or a British, is it any good them coming to me, Lala Varde? I ask you, is it?'

Axel Svensson gave a slight chuckle.

'I think you might be too smart for them, Mr Varde,' he said.

Lala Varde looked at him. He slapped his belly and roared with laughter.

'Oh, Mr Svensson, Mr Svensson,' he said, 'you are a great joker, I see.'

He wiped his eyes with the back of a podgy hand.

'But you are right,' he said. 'You are right. If I have to do business with an American firm they think I am cheating always. But with my Dilip they say "Ah, here is guy we can do business with." No? They think they can cheat him. Yes?'

A new gusher of laughter stopped him going on.

Inspector Ghote decided that it was time he took control. Each occasion he had had to deal with Lala Varde had been the same: events had got wrested out of his hands. He was a police officer in the course of his duties. There were matters he had to investigate. And investigate them he would. In the proper manner. No matter whom he was talking to.

'Mr Varde,' he said.

To his surprise he found that he had shouted.

But at least it had the effect of stopping Lala Varde's laugh.

'Mr Varde,' the inspector said more quietly, 'now that you have said you understand why certain questions must be asked, there is a matter I wish to put to you yourself.'

He gave a dry little cough.

'Mr Varde, what were your movements after you had had dinner last night?'

Lala Varde looked at him with astonishment like a great buffalo suddenly called on to dance a foxtrot.

'You,' he said. 'You are asking me what I was doing when they committed the Perfect Murder in my house? You are asking Lala Arun Varde to account for his movements? You are treating him like a dacoit? Have you gone mad, Inspector? Has a brainstorm come into your head? Do you know even what you are saying?'

Inspector Ghote backed a step.

'But, Mr Varde, but, sahib,' he said, 'already it has been explained to you by Mr Svensson, by my friend. It is necessary for the investigating officer to acquaint himself with the movements of everybody at the scene of the crime, irrespective of whether they are likely to have committed it or not. It is part of the official procedure as laid down.'

'Laid down, spade down. I am not going to be made part of your procedures, Mr Inspector. When you are dealing with Arun Varde you are dealing with somebody different. You can't go asking me your questions, and you can't go asking my son either. I will send him back to Delhi tomorrow. I will send him to England. I will send him to America. But you shall not ask him one bit of one single question.'

'Mr Varde,' said Inspector Ghote. 'You are attempting to interfere with a police officer in the course of his duties. I must warn you that that is a very serious matter.'

'You must warn me?'

Lala Varde's face took on an expression of concentrated explosiveness.

'You must warn me?' he repeated. 'Oh, no, Inspector. I must warn you. Oh, yes, indeed. I must warn you. One bit more of this and you will be out of inspector just like that. Back in constable you will be. Back walking the streets, and in the poorest quarter too. One, two. Just like that.'

Inspector Ghote listened to the tirade with little gushes of hot anger shooting out inside him till he felt on the point of bursting. Threatening a police officer. Who did he think he was? He needed to be shown pretty quick that that sort of thing didn't work in Ind—

And the trickle of cold doubt. Hadn't he heard gossip at the station? Perhaps he couldn't of his own knowledge pin down a case of an officer having been sent back to the ranks, dismissed the force even, because he had trodden on someone's toes. But he had heard stories. Most unpleasant stories.

The thought of his wife, of his boy Ved, of their neat new house in Government Quarters came into his mind with the suddenness of a clanging bell.

Methodically he pushed the thought down again. He was a police officer. All his life he had wanted this, and now he had achieved it. Inspector. And an inspector of police could not be threatened. No matter by whom. Lala Arun Varde or anyone else.

He drew himself up as erect as every muscle could make him. Under the thin khaki of his shirt his bony shoulders stood up in two sharp ridges.

'Mr Varde,' he said. 'It is my duty—'

The sound of booted feet running hard along the stone floor of the corridor outside made him stop in mid-sentence.

They all turned and looked at the doorway.

It was Head Constable Sen. He clattered to a halt and saluted Ghote.

'Message from DSP, Inspector sahib,' he said.

'Yes? What is it?'

Sen looked a little hurt at the unexpected sharpness in the inspector's voice.

'Result of check on window cleaners, Inspector.'

Inspector Ghote's eyes gleamed. This was just what he wanted. When Lala Varde saw for himself how an important case, a case at the Ministry itself, was solved he would realize that the Bombay CID was not to be trifled with.

'Good,' he said. 'They've got him, have they?'

He turned to Lala Varde.

'Nasty case of theft,' he said. 'From the Ministry of Police Affairs itself. But the fellow didn't get very far, thank goodness.'

Head Constable Sen coughed vigorously.

'DSP tell me to say windows were not cleaned this morning,' he announced. 'Schedule is behindhand. Cleaner wallahs cannot be guilty. DSP want to see you straight away, Inspector sahib.'

'A theft of one rupee and you cannot catch the thief,' bellowed Lala Varde happily, breaking into great peals of hooting laughter.

But Inspector Ghote did not stop to listen to them.

9

When Inspector Ghote arrived at the office, very hot and very bothered, he found that DSP Samant had packed up and gone home for the day. As all the other office workers of Bombay were thinking of doing the same thing this was to be expected. The DSP had however left orders. Very strict orders. And there had been another development.

It had been reported from the Ministry of Police Affairs and the Arts that when the Minister's peon, Felix Sousa, had been required to perform his last duties of the day no one could find him anywhere in the whole sprawling, spreading building. The DSP was inflexible in his attitude to this event: Sousa was to be located, without the least delay. Once found, Sousa was to be interrogated. The interrogation was to produce a complete and circumstantial confession. A report embodying this was to be on the DSP's desk first thing in the morning. Sousa was thought to live in the mill district. The DSP had obtained his address from the Ministry records section.

Inspector Ghote looked up at Axel Svensson, faithfully shadowing him still. The Swede, in spite of his size and weight, did not look as hot and sticky as the inspector felt.

'Well, Mr Svensson,' Ghote said, 'it looks as if my day is not over yet. I shall have to go and see if I can get hold of this fellow. So I'll say "good evening" to you.'

Finding one particular person in all the hundreds of thousands who lived in inextricable confusion in the poorer quarters of the city would not be made any easier by being interrupted at frequent intervals with requests for explanations of the Indian way of life.

But he knew that whatever he said was going to be useless.

As it was.

'But, my friend,' the big Swede said with boisterous enthusiasm, 'we will go together. I have not yet had an opportunity to see more of Bombay than the tourist parts. This is exactly what I wanted. The problem of policing areas of high population density is one which has never been sufficiently examined.'

'No, I suppose not,' said Inspector Ghote.

They climbed back into the police truck and set off at the dangerous speed which their impassive driver felt to be necessary if the status of the force was to be maintained.

But even he could not keep it up for long. Once past the main boulevards and properly into the mill district progress at anything much faster than a walk became impossible. Men, women, children, cows, dogs and various other forms of life so crowded the narrow streets that to have gone at even ten miles an hour would have caused a massacre.

After nosing their way through the indolent flood of living creatures for nearly an hour they came to the street they had been making for. It was a narrow alleyway by the side of a large decayed house once belonging to a prosperous cotton merchant and now a teeming tenement.

The alley was too narrow to take the police vehicle. So Inspector Ghote and Axel Svensson scrambled out. At once they were surrounded by a swarm of begging children shrilling at them at the tops of their voices.

Axel Svensson looked at them.

'It is getting late,' he said. 'You ought to be all in your beds.'

'You are our father and mother,' screamed one little boy of about eight with a brightly cunning face above sticking-out ribs and bloated stomach. 'You are our father and mother. Give us money to buy beds.'

Inspector Ghote felt irritated. It was getting late and this was the second night in succession he had been up. He felt that the Swede's reference to beds was at the least tactless.

'Children like these have no beds to go to,' he said. 'They have no homes for their beds. They go about the streets at night in bands like this to beg, and sleep where they can in the day.'

The Swede looked shocked.

The expression of bewilderment on his high-boned cheeks was so appealing that Inspector Ghote at once regretted his brusqueness. He made up his mind to protect him.

'Go away, get out, hut jao,' he shouted at the seething mass of children. He aimed a few blows towards them at random.

'But no, my friend,' Axel Svensson said. 'Look, I would like to give them something.'

He dug in his pocket for coins.

'No, sahib. That is not the way,' Inspector Ghote said. 'Give to one and you get a hundred. You must learn to accept them. Come on.'

He caught hold of the tall Swede's bare arm and with his fingers almost buried in its jungle of fair hairs he steered him up the narrow alley by now nearly in complete darkness.

'But . . . But a few cents, a few öre . . .' the Swede babbled.

Inspector Ghote tugged him forward.

They came at last to the house they were looking for. A fat man lay asleep just in the doorway, wheezing and panting.

The inspector knelt down and shook him awake. He raised himself on one elbow and was immediately caught by a fit of coughing that looked as if it would be his last act on earth.

They waited patiently and in the end his gigantic paroxysm subsided enough for the inspector to be able to convey that he was from the police. The man heaved himself up to a standing position.

'It was not my fault,' he said. 'I was not there. No one can prove—'

A new spasm of coughing assailed him. 'The fat on his bare chest slobbered and heaved as he rocked to and fro.

Inspector Ghote banged him heartily on his equally fat back. At last the man's anxieties subsided to the point where he was able to take in that he was being asked simply whether a Goan named Felix Sousa lived in the house.

He was obviously so puzzled by the question that the inspector believed him almost straight away when eventually he said that he had never heard of Sousa. They tramped dutifully through the ramshackle building but soon came to the conclusion that it was inhabited entirely by South Indians and that they had drawn a complete blank.

They stepped out again into the comparative freshness of the air of the alleyway.

'But this was the right address?' Axel Svensson asked.

'Oh, yes,' said Inspector Ghote. 'But Sousa doesn't live here.'

They went back to the vehicle and the inspector told the driver to make for the Dhobi Tulao district, explaining to the attentive Swede that this was one of the main Goanese areas of the city.

Again they pushed and shouted their way through narrow streets filled with people and animals while overhead a great coppery disc of a moon looked down on them.

'Doesn't anybody ever go to bed?' asked the Swede.

'Some people do,' the inspector said. 'Just before dawn it gets much quieter.'

After nearly an hour's tortuous journey across the packed suburbs they arrived. There were at least plenty of Goanese about and crowded among the tenements and mills were several dilapidated-looking Christian chapels.

They stopped the vehicle, got out and buttonholed the first Goan they could lay hands on.

'Do you know a man called Felix Sousa?' Inspector Ghote asked.

The man, a tall, incredibly serious-looking individual with a long, thin face, answered up promptly.

'Yes,' he said. 'I am Felix Sousa.'

'But no—' began the big Swede.

Inspector Ghote interrupted him before his wrath fully exploded.

'It is a very common name,' he explained. 'No doubt we shall find dozens of them before we get the one we want, if we ever do get him.'

He turned to the serious-looking Goan.

'The man we are looking for is a little different,' he said. 'He works for the Ministry of Police Affairs. He is the Minister's personal peon.'

The man looked impressed.

'He has got a good job,' he said.

'You know him?'

'No, sorry. I do not know him at all. But I do know another Felix Sousa, a shoemender.'

'No, thank you.'

Inspector Ghote still retained some politeness.

But before long the last of it had evaporated in the humid, richly smelly night air. They questioned almost a hundred people. They pursued a dozen false trails. And they were nowhere nearer finding their quarry.

Inspector Ghote's head was whirring with the inconsequent thoughts produced by lack of sleep. Occasionally a vision of Mr Perfect lying on the old string bed in Arun Varde's house troubled him for a little. But even this had to take second place to the ceaseless, plodding to and fro of their enquiries.

In spite of frequent visits to sellers of mysterious bottles of highly coloured, faintly sweet mineral waters his mouth felt as dry as cinders. His shoulders ached. His heavy belt seemed to hang from his waist like a leaden circlet. Every now and again he felt a fit of trembling make his legs quiver uncontrollably.

'We will try only the next place we get a clue about,' he said. 'And then we will give up.'

Once more they set out, buttonholing anyone who looked like a Goan and plying them with questions. Even the Swede conducted his own enquiries whenever he could find anyone whose English he could understand. And it was while the inspector was doing his best to extract some information from a small boy who was trying to protect his sister because he thought she was wanted for an immorality offence that he caught sight of his towering friend pushing his way excitedly down a nearby passageway.

He set off in pursuit.

Plainly Axel Svensson thought he had found the right trail at last. The inspector felt a wave of anger sweep through his weary brain. What did that great hulking foreign bear want to go rushing off on his own for? His arrival at any house in this area would be known at once. If Felix Sousa were really there he would take fright in an instant. After all, he had seen the stupid Swede that morning. He knew he was associated with the police. And if the DSP got to know that Sousa had been found and warned off . . .

Inspector Ghote broke into a run.

He pushed his way through the still plentiful number of people wandering about. He shouted abuse at anyone who got in his way. Far ahead of him he could see the Swede's fair hair high above the black heads, multicoloured turbans and white Gandhi caps of the passers-by.

Suddenly the blond coxcomb disappeared.

He's gone in somewhere, the inspector thought. Too late.

He rushed forward in the Swede's wake. But he had not been near enough to make out exactly which one of the many tiny dark entrances to the various houses the Swede had taken. He darted in here and there on chance. His breath started coming in long, groaning gasps. His legs trembled more violently than ever. His head felt like a giant gourd.

He plunged into yet another doorway. There were no sleeping figures in the entrance to kick awake and question. But quite unexpectedly from the pitch darkness above he heard voices.

'Hey, you there, chum.'

He recognized at once the English of an Anglo-Indian.

'Yes, what is it?'

Svensson's polite enquiry.

The inspector sighed with relief. He looked at the flight of steep stairs dimly visible by the light coming from the street. What was the hurry? He could rest a bit till Svensson had finished with whoever had accosted him.

He leaned against the wall, careless of whether the stains of red betel juice that splattered it would come off on to his uniform. Nothing mattered but two minutes' peace to get back his energies. He breathed long and deeply.

From above came another voice, also Anglo-Indian but higher pitched than the first. A youth, even a boy.

'Here, man, got any money?'

'Money?'

Svensson was still polite, the way he would be if he had been stopped in the street in Stockholm and asked by an old lady if he knew the right time.

'Yes, money,' came the older voice.

'Yes,' said Svensson cautiously, 'I have a little money.'

The stairwell of the tall chowl was strangely silent. And in the still, hot air Inspector Ghote heard the sound of a spring being released and the click of metal against metal.

He straightened up, forcing his tired limbs into readiness.

'Know what this is, chum?'

'It is a knife.'

The Swede's voice was steady.

Quietly Inspector Ghote began moving up the dark stairs. 'Well, do you want to give us your money, chum?' The boy had made the demand.

'No,' said Svensson.

'No?'

A moment's silence. Inspector Ghote froze to stillness on the stairs.

'Oh, well, if you don't, you don't.'

The clatter of feet coming down. The inspector slipped into the double shadow of a doorway. By the light coming up from below he was able to make out something of the two shapes that hurried by him. Anglo-Indians, as he had realized, one about eighteen and the other two or three years younger. Both wore black shirts with tattered white fringes at the pockets. The elder one held an open flick knife.

They went out of the house and were lost in the jostle of the streets.

'Mr Svensson,' the inspector called, 'Are you all right?'

'Oh, is that you, my friend. Yes, I am all right. There were a couple of what-do-you-call-them—'

'Teddy boys.'

'Yes, that's right. But they went.'

'Did you come here with some information?'

'Yes. I met Sousa's brother. He said he lived on the top floor here.'

Inspector Ghote made a face in the dark. If the Swede had met Felix Sousa's brother, no doubt he had been sent anywhere but in the right direction.

'I think he gave me the address before he knew what he had done,' Axel Svensson said. 'That is why I had to hurry, before he could give a warning.'

'Very good, sahib. Then let's see if you were right.'

The inspector managed to run up the rest of the stairs. At the top he flung open the rickety door on the landing without ceremony and felt about for a light switch. To his surprise he found one, and when he clicked it on a dim light from a single bulb weakly illuminated the room in front of him.

And there lying on a string bed fast asleep was Felix Sousa, with tired eyelashes drooping on chubby, innocent cheeks.

Inspector Ghote walked across to the bed, swung his right foot forward and planted it sharply in the Goan's well-padded ribs. The man sat up like a jack-in-the-box.

'Oh, my God, the police,' he said. 'It is not true. I have been here all the time. I swear it. Oh, my goodness, yes. I can prove it.'

'Stop it,' said Inspector Ghote.

The chubby Goan stopped it. He sat on the edge of the charpoi looking up fearfully at the inspector and behind him the immense spare-framed Swede.

'Now,' Inspector Ghote said, 'where is the rupee note you took from the Minister's desk this morning?'

'Oh, no, sahib. Honest to God, sahib, I never took no note. Good gracious me, no.'

'It's no use telling me you didn't take it. We know you took it. What we're asking is where you hid it.'

The chubby little peon looked fearfully round the small bare room as if he hoped that the hiding place was not too evident.

'It's not nowhere, sahib,' he said. 'I can prove it, sahib. I can prove every damn word of it.'

'If you took it, it must be somewhere,' Inspector Ghote said. 'What's the use of telling me you can prove you haven't got it? We know you stole it. We want to know just where it is. That's your only chance, man. Tell us that, and there's some hope for you.'

The tubby Goan licked his lips.

'Perhaps it is in the bed,' he said.

Inspector Ghote grabbed one end of the rope bed, tipped the peon off, and shook the whole thing out on to the bare floor. A number of different insects emerged, but it was soon evident that there was no rupee note.

'What do you mean by telling lies like that?' Ghote said viciously.

He looked down at the peon who had not attempted to move from the half-crouching position he had landed in after being tipped off the bed.

'Not lying, sahib. Oh, no, my God, not lying,' Sousa said. 'Just making suggestion, sahib. Oh, my gracious goodness, yes.'

'Well, we don't want your suggestions. We want the truth. We know you took the note. Where is it?'

Felix Sousa looked as if he was going to be sick.

And from the doorway Axel Svensson intervened.

'I myself would also very much like to know how you stole the note,' he said. 'We know you were not in the office from the time the ten new notes were left there until the time the Minister reported the loss. How did you get at that drawer? You can tell me, you know. I promise to respect your confidence.'

The peon listened to him open-mouthed.

'Where is that note?' Ghote said.

A tiny gleam came into Felix Sousa's eyes. Somewhere deep down, almost invisible.

'I was not in office,' he said. 'Oh, my God, no. I was not in office. Mr Jain will tell you that, sahib. I don't know nothing about who stole that note.'

Inspector Ghote looked at the Swede in exasperation.

'But all the same,' Axel Svensson said, 'that is to me the most interesting thing. If this man used some power which we in the West cannot conceive of, then that is what I want to know about.'

'There is no such power,' said Ghote testily. 'It is my duty to obtain a confession from this man. It is of no help at all if you point out that it is logically impossible for him to have committed the crime.'

'Oh, yes, by God, sahib,' Felix Sousa broke in enthusiastically. 'It's impossible I done it. Right away impossible. And I didn't do it too.'

'Mr Jain was too busy with his papers to see you go into that office,' Inspector Ghote said.

'Oh, no, sahib Inspector. You ask him. All morning he sat looking at that door. Didn't do no work with his papers, sahib. You ask clerks in outer office. They talk all the time about it. He just sat looking at the door, sahib.'

'You're lying again,' the inspector said.

He felt less conviction than before.

'You ask Mr Jain, sahib,' said the peon.

The gleam was very evident in his eyes now. He had a dazed expression as if he had suddenly been the subject of a miracle.

'Then why did you run away from the office?' Inspector Ghote snapped.

The light went out in the peon's eyes.

'Oh, sahib. I never.'

'No? Then why weren't you there when you were wanted? Why did they search the whole building and not find you?'

'Oh, sahib, it is true, yes. I ran off, sahib. I ran right off.'

'And why? I'll tell you why. You ran off because you had stolen the Minister's money. That's why you ran off.'

'Oh, no, sahib. I never stole that. I couldn't steal that, sahib. I wasn't in Minister's office, sahib.'

Felix was looking perkier again.

'Then why did you run off?'

Once more the tubby little peon looked woebegone.

'Oh, sahib,' he said. 'Oh, sahib, I knew what they were all thinking. They were all thinking Felix Sousa, the damn liar, stole that money.'

'But if you hadn't stolen it,' Ghote said, 'then you had nothing to fear.'

He realized he was making a concession, but he could see no way out now. Not unless he declined to admit the logic of the situation. And that he would not do.

'Oh, sahib, I couldn't have stole it, could I? Was never in that office, sahib.'

'Then why, why did you run away?'

'Everybody thought I stole it, sahib.'

Inspector Ghote blew out a long sigh of utter exasperation. He turned to Axel Svensson.

'That is the sort of difficulty you get in police work in this city,' he said. 'If people would only behave in a simple, reasonable, logical way.'

The Swede looked disappointed.

'You don't think he stole the money in a way which defied logic?' he asked.

Inspector Ghote was too tired to respond to the plaintive note.

'No,' he said. 'I do not.'

The Swede sighed.

'Come on,' Ghote said, 'let's get off to bed.'

He left the room without another glance at the podgy little peon and tramped heavily downstairs to where their driver was impassively waiting.

'The Taj Mahal Hotel for Mr Svensson,' he said, 'and then the office and home for me.'

The driver saluted with grave cheerfulness. He could afford to: he had not been on the go ever since the night before.

The inspector slumped in his seat beside the heavy Swede. For once the latter had no problems to discuss. Inspector Ghote thought about his home.

Protima would be asleep when he arrived. But she would wake at the sound of the car engine and she would be there to greet him. Together they would take a look at their son, sleeping peacefully in his bed at the foot of theirs. Then in a few minutes they themselves would be asleep.

The vehicle drew up with a screech of brakes outside the Taj Hotel. Svensson got out and stretched his huge limbs.

'My friend, I am tired,' he said. 'Tonight I will sleep like a log.'

Inspector Ghote smiled at him.

On the short trip back from the big hotel to the office he occupied himself in composing a brief factual report for the DSP. He stopped himself speculating on how it would be received.

As soon as he got to the office he wrote out the exact words he had decided on, and left the single sheet prominently on DSP Samant's desk. Then, rallying his last reserves of mental strength, he reached for the DSP's telephone. There was one thing more that had to be done before he could sleep. He dared not think how he would feel if at the other end of the line at Lala Varde's house he heard a voice say that Mr Perfect had died, but the question had to be asked.

It was a long time before anyone at the far end answered the call, but when they did Inspector Ghote recognized at once the voice of the Anglo-Indian nurse.

He took a breath.

'Mr Perfect,' he asked, 'how—'

'Oh, is it you, Inspector Ghote?'

'Yes, yes. But—'

'Well, there's still no change with us. No change at all.'

'Thank you, Nurse. Thank you.'

A few moments later the inspector was being whisked through the broad night streets where the flash and flicker of neon signs of every shape and size was almost the only sign of life. And then just ahead lay the neat house rows of the Government Staff Quarters where he lived.

He let himself relax at last.

The vehicle drew up with a sharp yelp of brakes outside his little house. He stumbled out, returned the driver's ponderous salute, stood for an instant in the warm darkness, yawned like a crocodile and went in.

As he had imagined earlier on, Protima had woken up at the sound of the truck. She was standing just inside the door in her white night sari. In a few moments, he thought, we will be asleep together.

Protima looked at him sharply in the faint light.

'Oh,' she said in a voice hard with bitterness, 'so at last you choose to come back home.'

10

Inspector Ghote felt his tiredness sweep back over him like a huge wave of thick black oil. The momentary lift in his spirits that had come at the thought of home and bed was washed away as if it had never been.

He shook his head dully.

'Well, where have you been all this time?' his wife demanded.

Her eyes were flashing with scalding fury.

'I am telephoning the office all the time,' she went on, 'and they are saying only that you are out on job. I am asking to speak directly to DSP and they tell me he has gone home. They say it is after office hours. It is office hours for him, and out all night and all day and all night again for you.'

Ghote shook his head in blunted negative.

'It's not so late,' he said. 'If you go back to bed now, there's plenty of the night left.'

'Oh, if I go back to bed. If I go back to bed and leave my son ill, sick, dying. What does his father—'

'What's that? Ved ill? What is it? What's happened?'

Protima's words magnified themselves in Ghote's weary brain and echoed and rebounded.

'It is what I say,' Protima replied. 'There is my Ved ill, and I am left all alone to worry.'

'But the doctor? Have you called Doctor Pramash? What is wrong with him?'

'Doctor Pramash? What good is Doctor Pramash?

Doesn't a mother know better what to do for her child than some doctor man only?'

A glimmer of light came to Ghote. A trace of hope in the whirling darkness.

'Ved,' he said, 'how ill is he? What were the symptoms?'

'Symptoms,' Protima exploded. 'Let you and that Doctor Pramash talk about symptoms and treatments and medication this and medication that. I know better. What the boy wants is his mother to comfort him.'

Ghote felt the chain of hope growing stronger. Link by link he hauled himself along it.

'So you were able to comfort him?' he said. 'He is asleep now?'

'Yes, I have got him to sleep at last.'

Protima's face was stern and ravaged by her task.

'Yes, at last now he is sleeping,' she went on. 'At last. When the father chooses to come home, he finds the sick child sleeping. He doesn't care. So long as he is not disturbed he doesn't care what agony the boy has had to endure.'

Ghote sighed.

'I did not know he was enduring any agony,' he said. 'I have hardly been back to the office to get any message. They gave me two cases at once to handle. Two number one priority. I have been chasing there, hurrying here for hours on end.'

He sighed again.

'I suppose it's just duty,' he said.

'Duty. Duty. Always it is duty. You and that police force of yours. Never do they think of the wife at home with the child sick and the worry beating at her brain. Oh, no, all they think of is duty. Inspector Ghote go there, Inspector Ghote come here. Never Inspector Ghote go home and see if your wife needs you. It is not your wife you are married to: it is the police force. Your wife is a toy only.'

'It is a way of earning a living,' Ghote said.

'A way of earning a living. You try that now, do you? What sort of a living do you earn for all your staying out night and day, for all your neglecting wife and child?'

She clicked her long, elegant fingers in a gesture of entire disdain.

'That,' she said. 'That only is what you get. A nothing. A mere nothing. Half of nothing.'

'But it is not so bad,' Ghote replied. 'At inspector rate I am in top all-India earning bracket.'

He looked at Protima. Her eyes, still darkened with kohl, darting fury, her full lips curved in scorn, her nostrils flared, and her body held in a taut defiance from which not even her crumpled sari could detract. There was no doubt she was beautiful. The astrologers whose horoscopes had decreed their marriage were right.

But at the moment it was apparent that she did not share this view of things.

'Inspector rate,' she said. 'Inspector rate. What good is inspector rate? What good is top all-India earning bracket if it takes in together first-class ministers and people like you? What good is inspector rate when I never get my refrigerator?'

'Oh, so we are back to that refrigerator now, are we?' Ghote said.

In an instant the picture had been turned over. If he saw her beauty at all now it was only as adding injury to her insults.

'So we are back at that refrigerator,' he went on as each angry phrase added fuel to his spreading fury. 'What do you want with a refrigerator? Did your mother have refrigerator? Did my mother have refrigerator? For hundreds and thousands of years people in India have got on without refrigerator, and now suddenly you can't live unless you have. Well, you'll have to manage all the same. Because there isn't going to be any refrigerator. There is no money for refrigerator, and there won't be any for many long days to come. So there.'

His voice had risen to a shout, on the edge of becoming altogether uncontrolled.

And suddenly Protima was transformed. Her erectness slipped instantly away, her eyes softened.

'Ssh,' she said pleadingly. 'Sssh, sssh. You will wake my little Ved. You will wake him in the first good sleep he has had.'

Ghote gathered himself up to jet out a reply.

And abandoned the idea.

'Let us sleep,' he said.

'I cannot sleep any more,' Protima answered.

She turned and walked away from him into the bedroom. Following her, he saw his son lying soundly asleep. He was breathing easily and did not seem in any way unwell. Ghote stood for a few moments looking down at him. Then Protima came and stood between him and the boy's bed. She darted him a look of contempt and turned away to sit on the floor beside the sleeping boy.

The limpid gracefulness with which she sank to the ground, even in the middle of this heavy display of sulkiness, melted Ghote's heart again.

'Come to bed soon,' he said.

He had hardly stretched his tense limbs out to their full length when she stood up and in one fluid movement was lying beside him.

She put out her hand and rested it on his chest.

And then with a single sigh she was asleep.

For a few moments he was able to contemplate the complications of his waking existence without the remotest trace of worry. The Minister's rupee and who had stolen it: the long, emaciated form of Mr Perfect lying unconscious in Lala Varde's house, carrying obscurely his own fate in each faint puff of breath. The two facts floated in front of him for a little while, and then he too was asleep.

To be woken after a very few hours by the shrilling of the telephone.

And at once all his preoccupations stood up in his mind like soldiers roused from brief slumber on the battlefield, in an instant alert, probing, restless. How had that rupee note disappeared from the drawer in the Minister's desk when no one had been into the room? What was it that young Prem Varde had been about to say when his father had come bursting in? Why really had the fat and timid Felix Sousa suddenly deserted his post at the Ministry? What was it that made Dilip Varde so touchy about anything to do with Mr Perfect? How could he convincingly explain to Axel Svensson that the Indian police forces were really divesting themselves of the spectre of corruption? Why had Lala Varde been so mysterious about the rusty iron locked gate that had shut off all his servants from the part of the house where the old Parsee secretary had been attacked? If Mr Perfect regained consciousness, what would he have to tell them? Or, would he never speak again? Would he die? Was he already dead?

One at least of his tumultuous questions was advanced, if not answered, when he hesitantly picked up the telephone.

The voice on the other end was the by no means hesitant one of DSP Samant.

'Ghote? Is that you, Ghote? Answer up, man. Answer up.'

The persistent voice with its almost perfect English accent buzzed and spluttered at him along the line.

'Yes, it's me, sir. Ghote here, DSP,' he answered. 'Is there anything I can do for you, sir?'

'Yes, there is. You can do what you're asked, if you please.'

'Yes, sir. Certainly, sir.'

Inspector Ghote waited for orders.

'Well, man? Well? I give you an order, and what do you do about it?'

'I'm sorry, sir. Didn't quite hear your order, sir. Must be a fault on the line, sir. These damned Post Office wallahs are always causing the utmost confusion, sir.'

'There is no fault on the line, Ghote. I did not give you an order this morning. I gave you one last night.'

'Oh, yes, sir. No, sir. No fault on the line, sir. Last night, sir?'

'Yes, man. I told you last night to find that chap, what's his name, that chap, Costa, the Goan peon at the Ministry. What they want with a Goan in a job like that I don't know. Bound to cause trouble. And I told you to bring him in, Ghote. So what do I find when I come to work this morning?'

Ghote assumed this question to be rhetorical. He waited patiently, listening hard at the receiver to a multitude of varying sounds – the faint jabber of two meaningless conversations in English and Gujarati, buzzings like the whine of a tribe of mosquitoes, sudden outbursts of angry clicking, the persistent rhythm of an unanswered phone in some other distant part of the city.

'Well, man?'

Ghote came out of a trance of misery with a thump.

'Yes, sir. Sorry, DSP.'

'I don't want to hear that you're sorry, man. I want to hear why you didn't obey your orders. When I was a young policeman I'd have been shot for that. Shot. The British may have been a race of imperialists, as we're so often told nowadays, but at least they understood the value of discipline.'

'Yes, sir.'

Another short pause. Enlivened only by the mournful voice of a telephone engineer intoning the words 'Testing, testing', as if he knew they would never be heard by an even more depressed distant colleague.

'Ghote,' came the DSP's sharp tones again. 'Ghote, I did not ask for your agreement on the merits of British rule: I asked why you hadn't arrested this man Costa.'

'Sousa, sir.'

'Damn this line. It's about time the Telephone Department had a charge of dynamite put under them.'

'Yes, sir.'

'Ah, you're there again. Well, what's your explanation, man? And you'd better be quick about it before that lunatic comes between us again.'

'Yes, sir. Well, sir, as I indicated in my memo of the twelfth inst., sir, I closely questioned the man Sous . . . That is, Costa, sir, and I formed the opinion that he could not possibly be responsible for the theft, sir.'

'I see. So you did nothing about him?'

'No, sir.'

'And you expected him to resume duty forthwith, eh?'

'Oh, yes, DSP. Definitely.'

There was a tiny pause at the far end of the line. A moment of gathering tension. Then came the terrier bark of the DSP again.

'Then I suppose it won't surprise you to hear that not only did he fail to report this morning, but that a special motorcycle messenger failed to find him at the address you told me he lived at?'

'Failed to report, sir?'

'Inspector Ghote, I do not wish to have to repeat every single thing I say to you.'

'No, sir. Of course not, sir. No, DSP.'

'Well, man?'

'Well, sir, it does look a little strange, sir, certainly.'

'No, Inspector, it does not look a little strange. It looks bloody strange. And what's more, Inspector, it is bloody strange. And furthermore again, Inspector, you're going to do something about it.'

'Yes, sir.'

'What are you going to do, Inspector?'

Ghote thought hard, and quickly.

'I'm going to get hold of the fellow, sir, if I have to turn the whole of Bombay upside down to do it.'

'That's a bit better, man. So get started. Move, man, move.'

'Yes—'

'Inspector. Inspector. Wait, Inspector.'

'Yes, sir? Yes, DSP?'

'The Minister, Inspector. I trust all this fine talk about turning the city upside down doesn't go as far as the Minister, Inspector. He is not to be disturbed. Is that understood? Not to be disturbed on any account.'

'Of course not, DSP. You can count on me for that. And I'll have this chap Costa inside in no time at all, sir.'

'You do. And, Inspector.'

'Yes, sir?'

'When you get hold of him this time, don't just talk to him, Inspector.'

The DSP's voice was patient, pleading.

'Don't just talk to him, Inspector. Get what you want out of him. Get a confession.'

'Very good, DSP.'

'Wait. Come back. Come back, Inspector. Are you there? Are you there, man?'

'Yes, sir. I'm here, sir.'

'Good. Well, listen, Inspector, how are you going to get this confession?'

'I shall press the prisoner very hard, sir. I'll keep at him, DSP.'

'No, you won't, Inspector. You'll do more than that. You'll stop the fellow getting any sleep, Inspector. You'll put a bit of treacle on his face, Inspector, and handcuff his hands behind his back till the flies come and do your work for you, Inspector. You'll give him plenty to eat, nice spicy, salty food, Inspector, and somehow or other his water bowl will be just out of reach the other side of his cell bars, Inspector. You'll take a nice red-hot chilli, Inspector—'

'But . . . But, DSP . . .'

'Yes, Inspector?'

'Gross's *Criminal Investigation*, DSP—'

'What's that? What's that, man? This line's going all to pieces again. What did you say?'

'Nothing, DSP. I'll catch this Costa chap for you, sir. Never worry.'

'Costa? The man's name is Sousa, Inspector. You'd better get that right for a start.'

'Yes, DSP.'

Ghote decided that this was a moment he could ring off, and did so before anything worse happened.

He waited for a few moments, in case when he picked up the phone again the DSP should prove to be still mysteriously connected up to him, and then cautiously and quickly he rang CID headquarters back and arranged for a vehicle to pick him up and take him to the place where the night before he had left the chubby and evasive Goan peon.

Again he replaced the receiver and waited for the line to clear. Waited with a sick feeling in the pit of his stomach. Waited to ring the Varde house.

A wrong number.

With deliberate, forced patience he dialled again. And got through. Only to have the call answered by an almost invincibly stupid servant.

At last his patience cracked.

'Get Mr Perfect's nurse,' he yelled down the instrument. 'Get Mr Perfect's nurse. Jildi, jildi, jildi.'

He tried to relax. At least the stupid idiot on the other end of the line had not put the receiver back on its rest.

The silence grew longer.

Then came a woman's voice he did not recognize.

'Is that Doctor Das on the line? Doctor, I am glad to hear. Patient is showing symptoms of deterioration, Doctor. Breathing is getting slow. Pulse is getting slow, too.'

'No, it is not Doctor Das,' Ghote shouted down the line. 'Get hold of him. Get hold of him quickly. What were you put there for, woman?'

'Who is that? Who is that?'

The voice at the other end buzzed peevishly.

Inspector Ghote took a long breath.

'Listen,' he said with great calmness, 'listen carefully. Your patient is showing poor symptoms: it is your duty to ring up Doctor Das at once and tell.'

'Yes. Certainly. I will ring.'

The voice was chastened, subdued.

In a sudden flash of sweat Inspector Ghote let the receiver fall back into place. With anxiety flicking and gnawing at him at every other instant, he got dressed as quickly as he could and tried to eat something.

The news of the DSP's attitude to the Sousa affair must have got round very quickly because he had scarcely swallowed any of his food when he heard a police vehicle draw up outside the house. He kissed his son hastily on the top of his head and was rewarded by a face looking up briefly from munching a crisp puri to smile at him, and then he rushed from the house.

It appeared that the news of the DSP's views had spread even farther than Ghote would have thought possible: sitting beside the driver, looking alert and formidable, was the huge form of Axel Svensson.

'Ah, good morning, my friend. I hear we misjudged our man last night,' he said jovially.

'Yes,' said Inspector Ghote.

'It begins to look as if some mysterious power will have to be considered after all,' the Swede went on cheerfully. 'You see, my friend, that would explain everything. This man, Sousa, would only have to—'

He stopped abruptly. Ghote had put his finger to his lips and was looking hard at the driver, the same impassive fellow he had had the day before.

Axel Svensson looked abashed.

'Oh, yes, of course,' he said. 'Of course. The details are confidential. Yes, quite so. Well, luckily, I did not say anything.'

His nearness to a gaffe seemed to silence him temporarily.

They reached the crowded mill district and plunged into the turbid streets. Patiently they wove, jostled and bullied their way forward. And suddenly a totally undeserved bonus fell into their laps.

The Swede abruptly clutched the inspector's bony arm in a grip like a steel claw. The inspector tried to slip away from him.

'There. There, my friend,' the Swede boomed excitedly. 'Look, there.'

Inspector Ghote could do nothing less than look.

And there was Felix Sousa.

The driver jammed on his brakes.

The chubby peon was standing on the edge of a small crowd gathered at a street corner. His back was towards them and he was completely absorbed by whatever it was he was watching. Inspector Ghote slipped from his seat and began quietly making his way forward. Axel Svensson followed.

'My friend,' he said in a reverberating whisper, made totally unnecessary by the unceasing din of city life going on all round them. 'My friend, what is it that the man is watching?'

Inspector Ghote looked.

At the centre of a knot of bystanders stood a huge milky white bull deformed by a large extra flap of flesh protruding from its hump. The creature was covered in a rich red cloth thickly covered in shells and edged with a variety of tinkling little bells and miscellaneous pieces of ornamentation. By its side stood a little man with sharp features and quickly darting bright eyes, dressed only in a not very clean dhoti.

Inspector Ghote turned to Axel Svensson.

'It is Bhole Nath,' he said, 'one of the holy bulls dedicated to Siva. Most deformed bulls are given to men of this community who spend their lives touring round with them. They answer questions that people ask.'

'Answer questions?'

'Yes. They are specially trained,' Inspector Ghote said. 'And as they are the bulls of Siva, who knows everything and everybody, their answers are greatly respected.'

Axel Svensson looked at the slight form of the inspector intently.

'But is it a trick like a circus dog, or is it something which we of the West cannot understand?' he said.

Inspector Ghote made no reply.

Instead he moved forward to a position nearly at the edge of the circle surrounding Bhole Nath and almost directly behind the absorbed back of Felix Sousa. The bull's performance was about to begin.

Its keeper darted his inquisitive, sharply pointed nose all round the crowd to make sure he had the proper degree of attention and then turned to the bull.

'Bhole Nath, Bhole Nath,' he said, 'tell me which of all the people that you see here has never told a lie?'

The bull regarded him gravely for a moment, snorted out a soft sigh and began looking over the crowd with calm thoughtfulness.

'If he chooses Felix Sousa we shall know,' Axel Svensson said quietly to the inspector.

'What shall we know?'

Axel Svensson looked surprised.

'Why,' he said, 'we shall know that what we were told by him last night was true.'

The bull went slowly round the circling crowd, every now and again looking with great luminous eyes into one person's face or another's. But it did not seem to be finding its task of picking out a perfect truth-teller at all easy.

At last it stopped.

It looked with glowing ardour at a young mother standing with her month-old baby in her arms looking on at the excitement with eyes wide in simple delight.

Slowly the bull lowered its head and advanced one of its horns towards the shyly smiling mother. The crowd sighed as one man with respect and wonder.

But the bull shook its head slightly.

There was a puzzled murmur. And the bull with breathtaking slowness advanced its horn inch by inch again. Lightly it came to rest against the baby in the mother's arms and paused.

For a moment the crowd did not understand. Then illumination came. 'The baby, the baby.' 'That's the one who has never told a lie.' 'That's the one of us all.' People looked at each other and nudged acknowledgment of the bull's cynical point.

'Now,' said the sharp-nosed keeper, 'does anyone wish to ask the bull any questions? A small sum as a token of respect to Lord Siva and he will answer with perfect truth.'

There was a polite moment of pause while all those in the crowd who would have liked to have a problem irrefutably solved waited for someone else to come forward first. But this sort of politeness did not enter into Axel Svensson's scheme of things. Before anyone else had stepped forward he strode to the inner edge of the circle, and bowed slightly – either to the bull or its keeper.

'Please,' he said, 'could the bull tell me whether this man here has stolen money from his master?'

And he extended a long, heavily muscled, deep pink, golden-haired arm in the direction of the unfortunate Felix Sousa.

At the edge of the crowd Inspector Ghote, inwardly cursing Axel Svensson like a madman, moved forward a pace so that the quaking, podgy peon could not escape.

'Oh, oh,' said the bull's keeper. 'Oh, oh, that is much to ask.'

'It is in the interests of justice,' Axel Svensson said.

'But a question like that, it will be very difficult for Bhole Nath to find answer,' said the keeper.

'But let him employ the ancient magic of the East,' Axel Svensson cried.

'Lord Siva knows everything,' said the keeper, 'but he does not always think it good for what he knows to be revealed.'

'But—'

From the far side of the now wildly curious crowd Inspector Ghote called sharply across to the big Swede.

'Money. He wants money.'

This streak of material consideration in a mystical matter momentarily discomposed Axel Svensson. But his inner struggle was mercifully brief and in a few instants he was pushing note after note into the keeper's hand. Bhole Nath could scarcely refuse to answer now.

The keeper turned to his charge and put Axel Svensson's question again.

'Bhole Nath, Bhole Nath, that man there, has he taken money from his master?'

Slowly the gaudily caparisoned bull advanced. Felix Sousa shrank back.

But the crowd was not going to be cheated of a sight like this. Inflexibly they pressed forward behind the tubby little Goan till he and Bhole Nath were face to face.

The bull with its great limpid peering eyes was unquestionably the more dignified of the two. Minute after minute it scrutinized the flabby cheeks and quivering lips of the peon.

And then unmistakably and with entire solemnity it nodded its great head to indicate the answer to Axel Svensson's question. Had Felix Sousa stolen from the Minister?

Yes.

And at once the prognostication received complex justification. Felix Sousa collapsed on to his knees and babbled out a confession.

'Yes, yes, it is true,' he blabbered. 'Yes, it is true. I have stolen. I have stolen from the Minister.'

11

Inspector Ghote and Axel Svensson leaped forward. Side by side they stood in front of the incoherently weeping Goan peon.

'You stole from the Minister?' Ghote said.

'Oh, yes, yes. By God, yes. I stole every damn thing I could. Oh, by God, yes, I am a wicked man.'

'Every damn thing?' Ghote said.

'Every damn thing, by God. I stole with the utmost damned rapidity.'

Axel Svensson's clear blue eyes shone with a pure excitement.

'The mysterious East, the mysterious East,' he said. 'I knew it.'

'You stole a one-rupee note from the Minister's desk yesterday?' Ghote asked implacably.

'Everything, everything. I damn well stole ever . . . No, no, no, no. I never took that bloody damned one-rupee note.'

Axel Svensson gripped Inspector Ghote's knobby elbow.

'Is he saying he didn't?' he asked passionately.

Inspector Ghote relaxed. He turned to the bear-like Swede.

'Yes,' he answered, 'that's just what he is saying.'

'But is it true?'

'Yes,' said Inspector Ghote, 'it's true. You heard him. He said "no" four times at least. That means "no". If he'd said it once it would have meant "yes". Twice would have meant “perhaps”. Three times “no”. And he said it four times or more.’

‘So it’s “no”,’ said the Swede. ‘We are back to the beginning once more. He didn’t steal the rupee.’

‘Oh, yes, sahib, by God, that’s right,’ Felix Sousa said from down on the filthy ground. ‘By God, that’s right. All the time I am stealing from the Minister. One, two, three, four. Just like that. But yesterday I couldn’t steal nothing. That damned Mr Jain he wouldn’t let me go into the Minister’s room. Not never, not damned once.’

Inspector Ghote looked round the busy streets running each way from the corner where Bhole Nath had put on his act. As he had hoped, watching the scene covertly from a distance was a police patrolman. The inspector beckoned to him. For a few seconds the constable tried to pretend he was looking the other way, but eventually he broke down and came over at the double.

He saluted.

‘Take this man to your nearest chowkey,’ Inspector Ghote said. ‘Lock him up there, and charge him with theft from Shri Ram Kamath, Minister for Police Affairs and the Arts.’

‘Yes, sir, Inspector sahib,’ said the constable.

He seized Felix Sousa and hauled him to his feet. Inspector Ghote watched them go and sighed.

He turned to Axel Svensson.

‘I think there would be a telephone in that big shop over there,’ he said. ‘I have to make a call.’

The big Swede tramped along beside him to the shop and waited until he asked for the sickeningly familiar Varde number. He wished he could have stopped himself. He knew it was wrong to have allowed this totally illogical link to spring up between his success with the case and the life or death of the old Parsee, but he could not suppress it, it was stronger than even the best of his intentions.

His anxiety was neither allayed nor worsened when he got through. The bearer who answered had just seen Doctor Das go up to Mr Perfect’s room. He had been hurrying, but looked cheerful.

So presumably Mr Perfect was at least still alive. But the doctor had been hurrying. Inspector Ghote felt suspended, waiting.

He paid for the call and looked at Axel Svensson.

'I don't know about you,' he said. 'But I am hot. Let's relax a moment and have a drink somewhere.'

The Swede unexpectedly groaned.

'That is something I cannot learn to tolerate,' he said. 'Always my Indian friends are suggesting a drink, and nine times out of ten it is sticky coloured water, or sherbet or buttermilk, or orange juice they are drinking.'

'This time it is sticky coloured water,' Inspector Ghote said. 'There's a halwa stall over there. Let's go.'

'To a sweetshop when one wants a drink,' said the Swede.

He groaned again.

A few people from the crowd round Bhole Nath had got to the stall before them, although during the bull's performance the enormously fat merchant who presided over the stall, aided by a pathetically thin boy, had been completely deprived of custom. It appeared that the merchant had not liked to desert his post in case of wholesale pillage, but he had made up for this by tormenting his young assistant. The two or three customers standing in front of the stall drinking buttermilk from tall brass tumblers did not keep him so busy that he was unable to continue this pleasurable activity.

It consisted of shouting an order to the emaciated brat to move one of the many trays of variegated sweetmeats, yellow, green, white, pink or prettily covered in silver foil, to a position on the stall supposed to be more advantageous to trade, and before the boy had had time to adjust the trays and dishes, to order him to move something else to somewhere else. Even before the inspector's arrival this had produced considerable confusion in the not noticeably well-ordered stall. Dishes of one sweet had been placed precariously on top of dishes of another. Trays had been left here and there on the ground round about while the xylophone-ribbed boy had dashed to the other end of the stall in obedience to a fresh bellow from its owner. Jars of buttermilk and jars of fruit juice had become inextricably confused.

The only beneficial result had been to keep the tribes of flies that beleaguered the stall in more than usual movement.

The inspector ordered a bottle of mineral water for himself.

'I might as well have one too,' said Axel Svensson resignedly.

'Yes, sahib. Certainly, sahib,' the merchant replied, bending obsequiously forward from the coil of fat that represented his waist. 'Pink mineral, sahib, or yellow mineral?'

'What are the flavours?' said the Swede.

'Very good flavours, sahib. Best flavours out.'

'Yes, but what—'

The inspector interrupted.

'It makes no difference,' he said. 'It is only coloured and sweetened water anyhow.'

The gross merchant smiled a sickly smile.

'Then pink,' said Axel Svensson. 'It looks less like real liquor than yellow.'

'Two pink,' the inspector said.

The merchant served them, puffing and panting as he leaned slightly forward from his sitting position behind the stall. And then while the inspector and his towering European companion looked on at the array of sweets – rasgullas, gulab jamuns, jelabis, chiwaras – with increasing moroseness, the fat old man turned back to his sport.

He stormed out another volley of commands at the poor emaciated boy, and hardly had the lad scuttled off to perform them than a contradictory series was bellowed after him. In the meanwhile the merchant put out an immensely podgy hand and let it hover meditatively over that section of his stock which he could reach without disturbing himself.

At last Inspector Ghote saw him pick on one particular sweetmeat, one so ravaged by the flies that no customer was likely to choose it. The merchant scooped the sticky green mass from out of its little earthenware container and conveyed it between fat-encased fingers towards his mouth. Even at this point he could scarcely bring himself wantonly to destroy some of his stock in trade. But at last greed overcame avarice, as to judge from the heavy rolls of flesh that spread downwards from his neck it must have often done before, and the great fat man took a tiny nibble.

Savouring it, his eyes fell on the scrabbling matchstick-legged boy. He smiled beatifically, and reaching forward as far as he could without toppling over he placed what was left of the green sweetmeat within the boy's field of vision. Then he turned away and began a jocular conversation with two of the customers spinning out their tumblers of buttermilk.

But all the while he kept the corner of his eye on the green, sticky, half-consumed bait.

And at last he was rewarded. The boy, who looked as hungry as a jackal in a famine, was unable to resist any longer. With trembling caution his thin fingers stretched out towards the sweet. And the great tub of fat pounced. His squabby hand closed like a swath of fat tentacles round the almost fleshless wrist of the boy and his mouth opened to pour out a compacted stream of abuse.

'Hey, there, halwa wallah,' snapped Inspector Ghote. 'Some more drink. And quick. The police force cannot be kept waiting all day.'

The merchant hastily let the boy go, heaved himself to his feet, brought two fresh bottles of his sticky concoction and poured them out into the already used glasses. While the inspector and Axel Svensson quickly drank down the slightly cooling liquid, the merchant carefully retrieved the first two bottles ready to fill them up again that evening and restore their labels to something like the state in which they had once emerged from the factory.

As the big Swede set down his glass he turned to the inspector.

'Well,' he said, 'I suppose it is back to the Perfect Murder now?'

'No, no, no,' Inspector Ghote snapped in sudden fury. 'No, it is not the Perfect Murder. It must not be that yet. It cannot be.'

'Very well,' Axel Svensson said soberly. 'Let us say "back to the Perfect case". I am sorry.'

'I am sorry too,' said the inspector. 'And you are right: it is important to get back. Too many things have been left for too long. But first there is one thing I must do: I must arrange to see Shri Ram Kamath.'

'See the Minister for Police Affairs?'

The Swede sounded disconcerted.

Inspector Ghote's small mouth set in a determined line.

'Yes,' he said, 'the Minister himself and no one else.'

'But, my friend,' said the Swede.

He laid a gentle restraining paw on the inspector's arm.

'But, my friend, is that wise? Did I not hear that the DSP himself had advised the utmost tact over this matter? I am sure he didn't intend you to see the Minister, and I am sure the Minister will not want to be disturbed by the enquiries of a simple inspector. If you don't mind my saying this.'

Inspector Ghote looked at him with hard eyes.

'All the same,' he said, 'I shall have to see the Minister. I have only just realized it, but I shall have to do it.'

The whole expression of his face was stonily glum.

'But why? Why, my friend? Please, please, think what it is you are going to do.'

'Can you not see?' Inspector Ghote said in a dreamily distant voice. 'There is only one course of action for me.'

'But, listen. That man, Felix Sousa, he may not have actually taken the missing note. But he has confessed to stealing from the Minister before. If you prosecute him, that will be enough. The case will be closed. Even, if you wish, you could bring up the matter of the note. No magistrate would find him Not Guilty over that, and Guilty on the other. You have no need to worry any more about the missing rupee, my friend.'

'No,' said Inspector Ghote, 'I must see the Minister himself.'

He marched back to the shop where he had telephoned to the Varde house. Axel Svensson went back to the vehicle and sat beside the impassive driver, who smelled powerfully of sweat, and waited. His face bore an expression almost of pity.

Quite soon Inspector Ghote came pushing back through the milling crowds.

'Well?' said the big Swede.

'I have an appointment for 9 a.m. tomorrow,' the inspector said.

For all the length of the journey to Lala Varde's house he remained quite silent.

As soon as they arrived he asked the bearer who opened the door, the erect little ramrod man, whether Doctor Das was still with Mr Perfect.

He did not dare to put the question he really wanted answered: whether Mr Perfect was still with the living, or whether his life had in ever slower breaths leaked at last away, leaving a black insoluble mystery as its only bequest.

But the little bearer's face split into a silent grin at his query.

'Doctor left, sahib,' he said. 'Told nurse-lady one or two nasty things. She made goddam mistake, Inspector sahib. Made doctor sahib come running for no need.'

He chuckled hoarsely, struggling to keep his utterly rigid back unquavering in spite of his mirth.

Inspector Ghote was possessed by a fierce desire to put the man to a probing examination about the exact state of Mr Perfect's health. He wanted to know to the last tenth of a symptom whether the nurse had had any reason or none to summon Doctor Das. But the dry little bearer laughed so long that by the end of it he had had time to realize that the man would know nothing.

'I have come to see Mr Prem,' he said when he thought he would be heard with attention.

'Yes, sahib. Very good, Inspector sahib.'

The little bearer, still occasionally letting out a hoarse steam-jet of dry laughter at the thought of the nurse-lady's discomfiture, led them into the house. Axel Svensson, trying comically to shorten his immense strides to the bearer's inflexible trot, leaned down to the inspector and put an enquiry in a circumspectly low voice.

'My friend,' he said, 'do you think it important, then, to find out what these two brothers were talking about on the night of the attack?'

'But you remember what Doctor Gross says?'

The Swede's clear blue eyes clouded in thought.

'I do not seem exactly to recall his observations,' he said at last.

'Surely you cannot be forgetting "Nothing comes about which is inexplicable, isolated, incoherent"?' said the inspector.

'No, no, of course not. I see what you mean now. Yes, yes. It is a very good point. This conversation is indeed unexplained, and isolated. It certainly ought to be investigated most closely.'

'And besides,' the inspector confessed, 'so far it is the nearest I have been able to get to anything which looks as if it should not be. Lala Varde and Dilip have denied and denied so often that I have not even begun to find out what they know.'

He walked along beside the tall Swede looking despondent. When they came to the second string sitting room where the inspector had caught Prem trying to overhear their conversation the little bearer pointed to the doorway, jerked out a stiff salaam, and left them.

The inspector stood and looked in to the quiet room with its overstuffed European furniture. Prem was standing by the window gazing out on to the deserted inner compound of the house. There did not seem to be anything much for him to be looking at.

At the sound of the inspector's steps on the stone floor he wheeled round.

'Oh,' he said, 'it's you, Inspector. I thought I would be seeing you again before long. Well, let me tell you straightaway. I have changed my mind. I refuse to tell one word of what Dilip said to me on the night of the murder.'

Inspector Ghote thought hard and quickly. Then he answered.

'Well,' he said, 'you have made decision, and you must stick to it. I respect it absolutely.'

Prem's head jerked forward and he gave the inspector a suspicious glance.

'But . . .' he said. 'But . . . But you must not do that. A police inspector has no right not to ask questions.'

The inspector smiled.

'Oh,' he said, 'you think it is my duty to get information out of you somehow, do you?'

'Yes. Yes, it is. And it is my duty not to let you have it.'

'This is a very hard view,' Inspector Ghote said.

'It is only possible view,' Prem answered.

He sounded passionate.

'It is only possible view,' he repeated. 'You are here to do what a policeman has to do: I am here to do what a murder suspect has to do.'

'Ah, I see,' said the inspector. 'Each has to play his part, is that what it is?'

Prem stared at him sullenly and said nothing.

'But, listen,' said the inspector, 'what must happen if you got hold of the wrong part?'

'The wrong part?'

'Yes. Suppose you are not murder suspect.'

'But I am. I must be.'

'You must be? I do not know why that is so.'

'Because a murder was committed in this house. No one could get in. Even the servants were locked in their quarters. And I was one of the people in the house. I have no alibi. I must be suspect.'

'You seem to think a great deal about this matter,' the inspector said tranquilly.

'But you don't think no one has said anything since you were last here, do you?' Prem answered. 'Everybody has been talking about it. There is nothing else but the murder all day long.'

'Is that so?'

The inspector walked across the room behind Prem and looked out of the window through which the boy had been staring as he had entered.

'Listen,' Prem said, 'you must suspect me. I was in my room alone working on my essay on the nature of beauty all evening. I was alone, except when Dilip came in and talked. And I cannot prove that he came in because he has said that he will not see you again, and I refuse even to hint at what it was we talked about.'

'That makes it difficult for us, doesn't it?' Inspector Ghote said across the room to the tall Swede who was still standing by the doorway.

'I am not going to tell you,' Prem said.

The inspector caught a flutter of movement at the corner of the courtyard. He craned forward to see what it was. Two of the maidservants had come out to sit and pod some peas.

'If my brother tells me something which is family secret,' Prem said, 'it is my duty not to tell a policeman who comes poking his nose in where he isn't wanted.'

Inspector Ghote moved slightly so that he could see the two girls in the compound without craning. They were both pretty.

'My brother says that he won't let a filthy policeman bully him,' said Prem. 'And I agree.'

A short silence followed.

'Mind you,' Prem said, 'he has had a shock. That's certain. I don't think he would always be as rude as that. Though of course he has been away in Delhi for some time and people change. Or, anyhow, some people change. You can divide people into two classes, as a matter of fact. Those who change and those who do not.'

'And which class do you come into yourself?' Inspector Ghote asked.

'I am not sure,' Prem said. 'Sometimes I think one, sometimes the other.'

'I see. And which do you think today?'

'I too have had a shock,' Prem said. 'Admittedly, Neena is not my wife, but she is my sister-in-law. And when you learn something like that, even about your sister-in-law, it's bound to affect you.'

'So you have changed?' said the inspector.

Prem glared at him.

'I suppose you think I oughtn't to have done,' he shouted. 'I suppose you wouldn't turn a single hair of your head if you were told your sister-in-law had been violated?'

Inspector Ghote did not leave the window. The girls were giggling together over their pea-podding.

'Violated?' he said.

'Yes. Violated. I suppose you know what that means?'

The inspector smiled to himself.

'And when did this . . . this act take place?' he asked.

'Oh, I don't know exactly.'

'Not exactly? You mean you don't know within an hour?'

'No,' Prem said. 'I do not know the year even. Perhaps I could work it out. Neena is not all that old now, and she has been married to Dilip for more than two years. It was before then, so it could have happened only during a certain time. Unless she was a victim of child rape, of course.'

'Yes,' the inspector agreed, 'it is important to consider all possibilities.'

'But in any case it is no business of yours,' Prem replied.

The inspector turned to face him.

'Who is supposed to have violated your sister-in-law?' he said.

Prem drew himself up.

'I refuse to say.'

'But you have told so much already. This is why your brother was speaking with you while you were writing your essay, isn't it?'

'Yes, as a matter of fact, it is.'

'And you told before that it was something he had learned only then.'

'I never said.'

The inspector smiled.

'I am afraid you did,' he said. 'So, you see, it is my business. If your brother really had learned this a few minutes before only, he may have taken certain actions. Now, who was the supposed violator?'

'I refuse to say. Absolutely.'

'I think it would be better if you told.'

'It is none of your business, none of your bloody business.'

Prem glared at him.

'Don't you see,' the inspector said, 'if your brother heard this just before Mr Perfect was attacked, then it is relevant to enquiries.'

'It is not,' Prem said. 'I swear to you that it is not.'

'It would be best if you told.'

'I can't. It was someone very important. Someone it is better not to talk about. It is a family secret.'

'Then it was not Mr Perfect?' said the inspector.

Suddenly Prem laughed.

'Mr Perfect,' he said, 'that dry old pea-stick couldn't have violated a fly.'

'All right. But you still won't tell me who this person is.'

'It is absolutely family secret.'

'Well,' answered the inspector, 'I said a few minutes ago that I would respect your decision to stay silent, and I will.'

He turned on his heel and left Prem, looking decidedly bewildered and a little apprehensive, standing in the middle of the stuffily furnished room. Axel Svensson, caught on the hop, stood there too for a few seconds and then hurried after the inspector.

'Well, congratulations, my friend,' he said. 'You certainly went the right way about getting information out of that young man.'

'Doctor Gross is most emphatic, as you will recall, about the necessity of correctly estimating the character of a witness,' the inspector replied.

'Ah, yes. Yes, of course,' said the Swede. 'But where does what we have just learned leave us?'

He spoke quickly, as if he was changing the subject.

'I mean,' he added, 'it is difficult to see how what happened to Dilip Varde's wife two or three years ago can be anything to do with the attack on Mr Perfect which has only just taken place.'

'If anything did happen to her,' said the inspector.

'If—'

'Doctor Gross has a whole section on the unreliability of young people as witnesses,' the inspector said.

He gave the Swede a searching look.

'So,' the Swede said hastily, 'you are going to check with Neena Varde herself. An excellent precaution. Shall we call a servant to show us to her?'

'No,' said the inspector, 'I think it would be a good idea not to. I think we will just go about the house looking for her. I am very interested in this house.'

'In this house?'

'Yes. In this house where one night quite suddenly an old gate is shut and locked so that the servants' quarters are cut off, and where a husband learns suddenly two years after his marriage that his wife did not come to him as maiden, and where attempted murder is committed.'

They walked along in silence for a little. But they were not destined to see much of Lala Arun Varde's house. Because Lala Arun Varde himself caught them prowling.

'Ho.'

They heard his enormous shout from somewhere behind them and both wheeled like sneak-thieves caught red-handed.

'Ho, policemen fleecemen,' Lala Varde shouted. 'What are you going creeping about my house like that? Ha, are you seeking out my womenfolk, you never-satisfied ravishers?'

His advance upon them had brought him within striking range. Like two darting pythons his left hand and right went out, and the pointing forefingers jabbed hard into the ribs of the inspector and the Swede.

Lala Varde roared with laughter.

'Oh, Inspector detector, forgive me,' he said, the tears beginning to stream down his generous cheeks, 'but you really both looked so like a pair of goondas that I had to say something. Oh, you robbers, you rapers, you ravishers.'

He rocked forward with laughter.

And suddenly stopped.

'What are you doing?' he said.

'We were looking for your daughter-in-law, Lala Varde sahib,' said Inspector Ghote.

'My Neena Peena. Ah, then I was right. You were seeking out my womenfolk.'

Lala Varde resumed his laughing. But the inspector and the Swede were unable to efface looks of considerable wariness.

'So,' Lala Varde said, when he had had his laugh out, 'so, and what do you want with my Neena?'

'It is necessary to interview all members of the household,' the inspector said.

'Interview? Yes. But what do you want to interview my Neena about?'

The inspector jumped in quickly in case his Swedish friend said anything he would prefer kept from Lala Varde.

'It is routine, sahib,' he said. 'It is necessary to ask every member of the household certain routine questions about their whereabouts at the time of the attack.'

'Attack? What attack?' Lala Varde said.

He looked at the inspector with sharply pig-like eyes.

'Of the attack on . . . That is, of the Perfect Murder, as they call it,' the inspector said.

'Ha, so you suspect my little Neena of killing that old long fool of a stick?' Lala Varde said. 'Well, you are right. She did it. That's certain. Certain sure. And look, she has just come into the compound. Now's your chance. Get her, Inspector sahib. Get her.'

The inspector darted a look out of the corridor window beside them. Sure enough a third person had joined the two maids and was evidently berating them for the slowness of their pea-podding. This would be Neena Varde. He decided he could leave her be for a few moments. She was obviously enjoying herself at her scolding and would be there for some time to come.

He turned back to Lala Varde.

'No, sir,' he said, 'I know your joking manner. But, really, you must be careful. You should not accuse lightly a member of your own family of such a grave crime.'

'Lightly rightly,' said Lala Varde. 'I tell you, Inspector, that woman is dangerous. She is a she-demon. No one is safe from her wiles. When I arranged for her to marry my poor Dilip, though there were good reasons, it was the greatest mistake I ever made in my life.'

His great cheeks drooped and his whole face took on an expression so woebegone that it looked as if it would never recover.

'The greatest mistake,' he repeated.

He sank to the ground where he was and sat cross-legged on the stone floor of the corridor.

Inspector Ghote coughed delicately.

'What exactly is it that makes you describe her as . . . Well, as a she-demon?' he said.

Lala Varde's head jerked up.

'Ah, you are poking prying now,' he said. 'Into the very heart of my family you go with your prying poking. But you won't do any good, I can tell you. Oh, no, my Inspector, if you want to find out about Miss Neena you must find out for yourself. But watch out. Watch out.'

Under his thin uniform Inspector Ghote's shoulders took on a straight line.

'Very well then, sahib,' he said. 'If you will excuse.'

He turned and walked quickly along to a doorway leading out into the courtyard. Neena Varde had her back to him and was still scolding the two maids, but he gained the impression that she was perfectly aware of his approach.

Three or four yards away he stopped and took a good look at her. Doctor Gross would have approved his caution.

Neena Varde was a short slight girl with something oddly elusive at first in the way she stood and in her gestures. Inspector Ghote found her hard to put into any category for all that both in the extravagant way she was lecturing the maids and in the clothes she had chosen to wear – a bright orange blouse with a sari in a red which clashed horribly – she seemed determined to assert her personality.

Under the lash of her tongue the two maids only giggled spasmodically, though had she meant everything she had said they ought to have been on their knees taking the dust from her feet and heaping it on their heads. And, as if to prove her lightning was without power to burn, in the middle of a towering denunciation she swung suddenly round and addressed the inspector.

'I know what you're here for,' she said. 'And I tell you it's no use.'

Inspector Ghote could not prevent himself blinking once at the unexpectedness of the attack. But he blinked once only.

'Good morning,' he replied. 'Am I right in thinking I'm addressing Mrs Neena Varde? My name is Ghote, Inspector Ghote, Bombay CID and this is Mr Axel Svensson, the distinguished criminologist.'

Neena's manner changed as suddenly as if a completely different person had been substituted for her in front of their eyes.

'A criminologist,' she breathed. 'Oh, how marvellous. Always I have wanted to meet a criminologist.'

She fluttered her eyelids a little in Svensson's direction. He licked his lips and found no reply.

'Then I am glad to have gratified your wish,' Inspector Ghote said. 'Mr Svensson is helping me with my enquiries into the attack on Mr Perfect, and he would very much like to know how you yourself spent the evening in question.

'Me?'

Neena looked up at the tall Swede.

'Yes, if you please,' he said in an unusually subdued voice.

'Oh,' she said, 'think of me interesting a great criminologist.'

She said no more, but looked modestly down at the ground.

'You would interest him more if you answered the question,' Inspector Ghote said.

'Oh, you don't want to know what a creature like myself was doing.'

'We do,' Inspector Ghote said.

Neena looked up intensely at the towering Swede.

'Yes, we do,' he said.

'Oh, but it's all so perfectly simple,' Neena said. 'I was in my room from the moment dinner was over. I had a terrible, terrible headache. I just lay there. On my bed. I was too weak even to move.'

All this was directed vehemently against Axel Svensson. And he, evidently picturing as vividly as was intended Neena lying helpless on her bed, was unable to prevent a dull blush marring the freshness of his Scandinavian cheek.

'And did you see anyone there?' Inspector Ghote asked placidly.

'Only my maid. I told her on no account to let a soul come near me,' said Neena. 'I just couldn't have borne it.'

'I see,' Inspector Ghote said. 'And now perhaps you could tell us something about Mr Perfect. Do you know him well?'

'That man. That man.'

Neena's voice rose abruptly almost to a scream.

'No, no, no, no,' she said. 'I cannot bear to think of that man. My head, my head. I must go.'

And whipping the corner of her sari across the lower half of her face she turned and ran in a series of curious little jabs of speed back into the house.

12

'Stop. Stop. Stop. I am not finishing.'

Inspector Ghote, shouting with increasing fury, set off in the direction Neena Varde had taken. He had her in sight for only the short time it took her to run across to the two servant girls sitting on the baked ground with the basin of podded peas between them, brush past them and disappear into a cool, dark doorway beyond.

As the inspector came up, just restraining himself from breaking into a run, the two maids with squeaky screams of excitement seized basin, peas and discarded pods and vanished in a wriggle of swirling saris the way Neena had gone.

Inspector Ghote halted, breathing fast, his uniform in disarray.

'But shouldn't we go after her?' Axel Svensson enquired, coming up in his wake.

A look of some embarrassment came over the inspector.

'It is probably the women's quarter,' he said.

He looked at the open doorway, mysterious, alluring, repelling.

And found a happy thought in his head.

'I think it would be better not to insist on interview,' he said.

With each word his tone grew more assured and thoughtful.

He looked up at the big Swede.

'No,' he said with new decisiveness, 'it would definitely be inadvisable to prolong questioning a person with obviously unreliable qualities like that young woman.'

Axel Svensson nodded energetically.

'A first-class decision, my friend,' he said.

Inspector Ghote turned smartly on his heel and set off across the compound for the distant French windows.

He found himself possessed of a strong impression that his every movement was watched, noted, stored as a subject for gossip. The many windows of all shapes and sizes that here, there and everywhere broke up the glaring white inner walls of the house with patches of soft black inscrutability could well have hidden twenty pairs of watchful eyes and he would have been no wiser. Above him in the sky now washed of its blueness by the harsh sunlight he noticed for the first time the monotonous cawing of the inevitable crows wheeling and gliding overhead.

Definitely, he told himself, the sound was not mocking laughter: it was the noise of stupid scavenging birds only.

He took a look back at the doorway through which he had allowed Neena to make her escape.

It was still black and blandly forbidding. He turned away.

But not before into the dark oblong had stepped the figure of someone he had not yet seen, a stately-looking woman of about sixty, wearing a dark sari of green silk. She plainly noticed at once that the inspector had seen her.

He turned back and began going across the compound towards her. She in her turn advanced on him, walking with stubbornly erect dignity, but without grace. Her hair was sternly grey and the features beneath it, strongly formed and well marked, were set unmovingly.

She reached the inspector, stopped and made the namaskar with hands placed decisively together.

'You are the police inspector,' she said.

'Yes, certainly,' he replied a little uneasily.

'I am Mrs Lakshmi Varde. Has my daughter-in-law refused to answer?'

Inspector Ghote licked his lips.

'I think she became upset,' he said. 'I hope you do not think my questions were in any way improper.'

A tiny glint of almost contemptuous humour came into Lakshmi Varde's sombre eyes.

'I said nothing,' she replied. 'Were questions improper?'

'Oh, no, no, no, no,' Inspector Ghote said quickly.

He looked round at a loss for words.

And saw Axel Svensson.

'May I introduce Mr Svensson?' he said. 'I should have done so already. Excuse me. He is Mr Svensson.'

'Mr Svensson,' said Lakshmi Varde. 'Good morning, Mr Svensson.'

'I should have explained Mr Svensson is a criminologist,' said the inspector. 'That is . . . That is, he is actually an expert employed by Unesco. He is making a study of our methods here in Bombay.'

'He will be very pleased.'

The inspector could not make up his mind whether this remark had been made at his expense or not. He talked to cover his growing confusion.

'You must answer my questions,' he said. 'I mean, that is, would you be good enough to try to see if you . . .'

'But, yes, Inspector. You must have questions. You should have come before.'

'I am very sorry,' Ghote said. 'I meant of course to come to you first. I realize that that is what I ought to have done, but various things—'

He stopped short.

'Inspector,' Arun Varde's wife said with inflexible patience, 'ask now.'

'Oh, yes. Yes, of course. First . . . No. That can come later. No. First I would like sincerely to know, that is, if at all possible, what were your movements . . . That is, your movements on the night of the murder.'

'Murder, Inspector? Has Mr Perfect died?'

Inspector Ghote felt the full force of the rebuke. What was he doing? Was he wishing Mr Perfect dead? Was he wanting to be faced with the Perfect Murder?

'No, no, no,' he stammered. 'I meant . . . That is—'

Lakshmi Varde cut him short.

'On evening of attack,' she said, 'first I saw that servants were cooking properly since we had guest. Then I saw meal was served. I ate myself. I went back to women's quarter. I went to bed.'

Inspector Ghote listened attentively. Axel Svensson seemed to think he could do with some assistance.

'Excuse me, madam,' he said to Lakshmi, 'but could you also tell us when you last saw Mr Perfect?'

'Yes,' she replied composedly, 'I saw early in evening when he came from office with my husband. After I was not where he should be.'

'I see,' said the Swede. 'That has been most help—'

Inspector Ghote suddenly interrupted.

'A guest,' he said. 'You told us there was a guest. Who is this? I have heard nothing of guest.'

Lakshmi gently ignored the rather hectoring tone of this. She smiled slightly, though without warmth.

'It was because guest was only my husband's brother-in-law,' she said. 'You know Mr Gautam Athalye, Neena's father?'

'Oh, yes. Certainly. That is, I know him by name, of course. A lawyer of such eminence. But of course I . . . Not personally, that is.'

The sweat was coursing down the inspector's face.

'I think it will be necessary to see him as soon as possible,' he blurted out. 'It seems likely attempts were made to prevent . . .'

He realized he was saying more than he wanted to.

Lakshmi Varde smiled again.

'Then if you are in hurry,' she said, 'I would go to my servants. They need to be watched.'

She began to leave but decided to add one more remark.

'You would find Gautamji very different from my husband, Inspector,' she said.

The inspector addressed her retreating back.

'No, wait. Wait.'

She turned with the faintest look of surprise at this peremptory request.

'Is there more I can tell?'

'Yes. I am sorry,' said Ghote. 'But will you say in what way Mr Athalye is different from your husband?'

'He is different. I just told it.'

'Yes, yes,' Ghote said. 'But I was surprised . . . That is—'

'You were surprised?'

Ghote drew a deep breath.

'Yes,' he said, 'I was surprised that you should have spoken about the difference.'

'And why?'

He looked straight into her unblinking eyes.

'It did not . . . does not seem to me that you are a person who would say a thing like that unless you were asked for your opinion.'

Lakshmi Varde regarded the inspector for a long time, unwaveringly.

'I must be careful,' she said at last.

'And the answer to my question?'

A swift blaze of anger came into her stern eyes.

'Gautam Athalye is a man of old school,' she said. 'He is not foolishly wishing to be great always. It would be better if it was his office my husband was putting into my Prem.'

And without ceremony she walked swiftly back into the house. This time Inspector Ghote did not attempt to keep her. Instead he made his way quickly over to the French windows.

Axel Svensson hurried after him, wiping a huge coloured handkerchief across his large pink features.

'Is it Mr . . . Mr Athalye you are going to?' he asked.

'It is,' said the inspector.

He sounded a little grim.

'I think I ought to have heard before this that he was in the house on the night of the attack,' he said. 'It may not be of great importance, but it is typical of how the whole matter has been treated. They think it is best to tell me nothing unless I force answers.'

He seized the heavy front door and began swinging it open without waiting for the obsequious, scuttering bearer to do it for him.

'Yes,' he said as he clattered down the steps to the street, 'they think they can do that. All of them.'

'Well, my friend,' said Axel Svensson, hurrying along beside him, 'you didn't let Mrs Varde put you off, once you had got a smell of the trail.'

At the waiting police vehicle Inspector Ghote stopped for a moment.

'She is a terrible woman,' he said. 'She gives me the feeling of being without my trousers.'

He clambered into the vehicle. The driver turned his rotund body a little, by way of asking for orders.

'The offices of Athalye and Co.,' said the inspector. 'And hurry.'

The latter instruction was unnecessary. As always their vehicle was flung at the traffic ahead with the maximum of reckless disregard for life, limb, property and road regulations. As always they arrived at their destination unscatched but with pounding hearts.

They jumped out and began to make their way across the crowded, broad and prosperous pavement towards the huge shining white concrete box towering up against the tired blue of the sky. From the deep shadow of the next doorway a Sikh fortune teller, with a huge, unkempt beard, ingeniously ragged clothes and a tattered notebook ready opened for immediate use, slunk up to Axel Svensson.

'Sahib,' he said, 'I see already that you would meet today a man who would tell you many things you most wish to know.'

Axel Svensson stopped in his tracks.

'What was that? What was that?' he said.

The Sikh salaamed.

'If I could cast the sahib's horoscope,' he said, 'I would tell him many things. Very cheap.'

A conflict visibly took place on the ox-like Swede's fresh-complexioned face. The ingrained scepticism of the cold North fought a battle against mysterious and exciting forces from the ancient East.

'Mr Svensson, please,' Inspector Ghote said a little pleadingly.

'But did you hear what he said?' Axel Svensson replied. 'How could he have told that we were going to ask someone to tell us things we want to know?'

'Most people going into offices want to learn something,' the inspector said sadly.

The big Swede looked at him and with a great shake of his huge shoulders turned away from the fortune teller and plunged into the up-to-the-minute austerities of the building in front of them. But even in the aluminium-walled lift sweeping them upwards to Gautam Athalye's offices he still wore a look of deeply thwarted curiosity.

The private office of the well-known lawyer, Gautam Athalye, was in sharp contrast with the international modernity of the building all around it. It was sombrely furnished in the style of a British bank of the early years of the century. Instead of the wall-to-wall carpeting in a contemporary colour which pervaded the rest of the building the room had a single large patterned square in shades of dark red and deep green. In place of the ubiquitous steel filing cabinets were two or three large wooden cupboards which might have been there for the best part of a century, except that the building had been in existence less than five years.

Gautam Athalye himself directed the inspector and Axel Svensson to two dark-wood cane-seated armchairs and then surveyed them benevolently from behind a wide mahogany desk.

He was a man of moderate height, conservatively dressed in European style, with a discreetly striped tie the only point of colour against the light grey suit and white shirt. His features were unemphatic; his hair was sparse and carefully brushed across his head to the best advantage; he had a moustache of modest dimensions.

'Well, gentlemen,' he said, 'in what way can I assist you?'

'We are investigating the attack on Mr Arun Varde's secretary,' Inspector Ghote replied.

'Ah,' said Gautam Athalye, 'what the Press likes to call the Perfect Murder. I prefer myself to think of it as the Perfect Incident.'

Inspector Ghote felt a sudden sympathy, and put his first question much less hostilely than he had intended.

'I understand you were visiting Mr Varde, as it so happened, on the evening in question,' he said.

'Yes, that is so,' the quiet lawyer answered without a flicker of embarrassment.

The inspector smiled.

'Would you be so good as to give me an account of your movements on the said occasion?' he asked.

'Yes. After all that is what you have come for.'

Gautam Athalye coughed, once.

'I entered Mr Arun Varde's house at approximately 7.20 p.m.,' he said. 'And I was shown into the main drawing room where I discussed business matters in general with my host and my son-in-law, Dilip. At approximately 8.30 p.m. we entered the dining room. The meal, at which all the family were present, lasted for some hour and a half, a little longer than I would have preferred. And then my host and Dilip and I returned to the drawing room while the others went about their business.'

He looked vaguely disapproving, though it was not clear why.

'And you left shortly after that?' the inspector asked.

'No,' said Gautam Athalye, 'unfortunately I did not.'

'Unfortunately?'

The modest-looking little lawyer stared hard at Inspector Ghote.

'You've met my brother-in-law, Inspector,' he said, 'so I don't need to tell you that affairs in that establishment are not always carried out in the most usual manner.'

The inspector leaned forward to signify that he understood what was meant without appearing to criticize Lala Arun Varde himself.

'Exactly,' said Gautam Athalye. 'So it will come as no surprise to you to learn that I was pressed to stay on in a fashion which frankly left me no alternative but to comply after I would have wished to leave. It is my habit to retire moderately early.'

The inspector nodded in sympathetic agreement, and gave a fleeting thought to his long nights on duty and the sleepless days that so often followed them.

'And not only that,' Gautam Athalye went on, 'but both my host and my son-in-law chose to desert me absolutely for a considerable time during that extensive period. It was extremely awkward.'

He frowned sharply.

The inspector's eyes lit up.

'Could you tell me when this absence was, sir?' he asked.

'Yes, of course.'

The inspector began to list times in his head, ready to fill in the blanks.

'They left me fairly soon after we had gone back into the drawing room,' the quiet lawyer said. 'At pretty well 10.15, I should say, and my host was away for a clear half-hour. I never saw young Dilip again the whole evening.'

The inspector felt a slow, puncturing disappointment.

'This wasn't after midnight?' he asked.

'Certainly not,' replied Gautam Athalye sharply. 'I am not accustomed to being nearly two hours out in my calculations, Inspector. And in any case I had left by midnight. Bundled out of the house and pushed into a taxi quite suddenly, as if I had overstayed my welcome.'

He shook his head disapprovingly.

'And Mr Perfect,' said the inspector, 'did you see him during the course of the evening?'

'Certainly I did,' Gautam Athalye said. 'And the fellow simply served to provide another excuse for Arun Varde's extraordinary behaviour.'

'What was that, sir?' Inspector Ghote dutifully enquired.

'It was just as we were going from the dining room back into the drawing room. Varde caught sight of this chap, and right in the middle of an observation of mine he walked over to him and began a long whispered conversation. Extraordinary way of going on. When I consider that I broke off another engagement at Varde's particular insistence to dine with him that night I simply cannot understand it. You can take it from me, I shan't be going there again in a hurry.'

'This was a special occasion then, sir?' Inspector Ghote asked, his interest perking up again.

'No, no,' Gautam Athalye said. 'Nothing particularly special. Dilip had just arrived back from Delhi. That was the supposed reason for the invitation. But as I see quite enough of the boy in the ordinary way at the club and so forth, I don't think there was any special need to make a great song and dance over him.'

With an effort the inspector prevented himself smiling at the notion of a family dinner for six being a great song and dance.

Dinner for six, he thought. These were the six from among whom he had in all probability to find Mr Perfect's attacker. He no longer felt like smiling.

'Mr Dilip Varde has only just come from Delhi then?' he said to keep the conversation going while he regained his equilibrium.

'Yes,' said Gautam Athalye, 'he has just been summoned back. I'm not sure he altogether welcomes it.'

The inspector wondered if he had not contrived to hit on a very useful line.

'Did he say anything about this, sir?' he asked. 'Did he suggest, for instance, that Mr Perfect might have something to do with it?'

Gautam Athalye considered the question solemnly.

'No,' he said at last, 'I can recollect nothing of that kind. Mind you, there would be some natural antagonism there, I dare say.

Perfect was, or rather is, a pretty industrious chap, and young Dilip appears to prefer to spend the greater part of his time reading a somewhat trashy sort of literature.'

'In the nature of pornographic matter?' Inspector Ghote asked.

'I really know very little about it,' Gautam Athalye said shortly. 'But I would say not specifically pornographic, more in the line of fictional representations of your own work, Inspector.'

'I see, sir. Now you mentioned that Mr Perfect was an industrious person. That means, I take it, that you know him well?'

'My brother-in-law and I have certain business matters in common,' Gautam Athalye replied calmly. 'So naturally I see something of his secretary, who does a great deal more than the average secretary is asked to undertake. Rather bad practice, I think.'

'Do you have any dealings with him other than for business matters?'

'No, no. Certainly not. It's always a mistake to use people of that sort other than solely in their proper capacities.'

The inspector got up as if he had no more to ask.

'It was very good of you to spare so much of your time, sir,' he said.

'Not at all. Not at all. We all have our duties as citizens.'

For a moment Gautam Athalye paused.

'Though some of us are rather remiss in carrying them out,' he added.

'That is true, sir,' Inspector Ghote agreed.

He shook hands with Gautam Athalye, and waited while the Swede did the same. Then he went towards the door. When he reached it he turned.

'Did you know Mr Perfect at the time that your daughter was married to Dilip Varde, Mr Athalye?' he said.

Gautam Athalye, standing beside his big mahogany desk smiling affably at his Swedish visitor, jerked suddenly straight.

13

'Inspector,' Gautam Athalye said levelly, 'if you think my daughter's marriage has anything to do with this deplorable Perfect business, then you are highly mistaken.'

He stood looking Inspector Ghote straight in the eyes and said no more.

The inspector thought quickly. His attempt to surprise an answer out of the lawyer had failed utterly. It was most unlikely that any other method would be more successful. Yet nevertheless his question had been sidestepped.

He looked over at the towering form of Axel Svensson. Should he invoke his aid in at least getting Gautam Athalye to admit or deny knowing Mr Perfect at the time of his daughter's coming into the Varde household? But instantly he rejected an appeal as being altogether too cowardly.

And still Gautam Athalye stood beside the old-fashioned European-style mahogany desk looking implacably at him and waiting for the next move.

'Mr Athalye,' he said, 'I shall accept your word that there is no connection. But I must tell you that if I learn anything to the contrary I shall have to insist.'

'Very well, Inspector,' Gautam Athalye replied. 'I do you the credit of assuming you know your business. If you wish to see me again, you know where you can find me.'

And the interview was over.

During the drive back to the CID Axel Svensson made only one remark.

'My friend,' he said, 'should I have told Mr Athalye that it was his duty to answer whatever question you put to him?'

Inspector Ghote smiled a little.

'I think Mr Athalye believes he knows what his duties are,' he said.

He relapsed into his previous state of deep, almost compulsorily melancholy thought.

A vision of the tall, old Parsee secretary lying in his confined upstairs room beneath the lazy, ineffective little fan seemed to haunt him. He could see as vividly as if he was really present the long form in the white atchkan with its tiny pink stain where the red ballpoint had leaked, and, laid neatly and safely on the floor by the charpoi, the pair of workaday spectacles with the one cracked lens.

No change. From what he had been able to gather this was the present verdict. For how many days, or weeks even, would it be the same? No change. Still teetering on the edge of death. Still able in one moment to make all the difference to his own life and prospects.

The thought drummed darkly in his head.

With Mr Perfect still alive, however tenuously, the possibility was still open of patiently working a way through the complexities and intricacies of the whole business till at last an answer emerged, till the facts yielded up, as they must, to logical and calm examination.

And, on the other side of the coin, Mr Perfect dead. The Perfect Murder weighing down on him and oppressing him. Dark and insoluble, dragging him and his whole career down to the depths. A continual reproach, a failure at the onset, a crippling disaster.

Firmly he tried to stop himself entertaining such notions. There could not be any real logical connection between the facts of the case and the old Parsee's physical state. Yet for all his efforts the sombre black thoughts rolled out.

Back in his office he could see only one refuge.

He raised his head and looked up at the heavy form of the tall, ever-shadowing Swede.

'Now I shall have to write a comprehensive report,' he said.

'Doctor Gross, you remember, is quite plain on the need to set down clearly and at length findings of preliminary interviews.'

'Oh, yes, of course.'

The big Swede sounded less enthusiastic than the inspector would have liked.

'So,' Ghote said with the firmness of desperation, 'I shall be busy for some hours, transcribing notes, you know, recollecting conversations, getting items in order, perhaps making out some timetables even.'

He began to feel a little less depressed.

'Ah, yes, good,' said Axel Svensson, making no move to leave. 'But what about conclusions?'

'Conclusions?'

'Yes. My friend, all your reports are of no use unless from them you draw conclusions. What is your opinion, for instance, of Mr Varde senior? That is obviously of crucial importance.'

'I know quite well how important it is,' said the inspector.

He sat down at his desk and opened its drawers rapidly one after another.

'I am sure you know that, my friend,' the big Swede replied cheerfully. 'And I am interested to hear your views. It is difficult for me, a European, to judge such a man as Mr Varde.'

The inspector looked round the little room with growing irritation. With the wide-shouldered form of the Swede towering in front of him the place no longer seemed a snug refuge from the difficulties of the outside world.

'It is all very well to be talking of conclusions,' he snapped, 'but you cannot make conclusions until you have set down data. Doctor Gross—'

He moved his head sharply to the left to try and see the familiar dark blue binding of the book with its tracery of faint white stains from successive eruptions of monsoon mildew. But the Swede's bulky frame came between him and the top of the filing cabinet where the book always reposed.

'Oh, I know that is what the textbooks say,' the Swede broke in boisterously. 'But all the same, my friend, you cannot meet a man like Mr Varde without coming to some conclusions.'

'Yes,' said Inspector Ghote, 'I suppose you are right.'

He got up from his desk and stood nonchalantly in a position where he could see Gross's manual and underneath it the set of shelves with the split bamboo decoration and the white plastic labels screwed neatly in a downwards row, "Songs" "Dance" "Piano" "Sacred" "Various". This relic of some departed British family with musical inclinations had been in the office when Inspector Ghote took it over. It was not listed on the Official Inventory and there had been attempts to remove it, but ever since he had placed on it the venerated copy of Gross he had resisted all such moves with quiet determination.

'Well?' said the Swede.

Inspector Ghote licked his lips.

'Lala Varde has already told me one serious lie, about the gate,' he said. 'And I think it possible he would tell more.'

'Ah, yes, good,' said the Swede, snapping up these flies like a voracious lizard. 'But do you think he lied about the attack itself?'

'Yes. No. Yes. I don't know,' Inspector Ghote answered.

'Well, what evidence have you got?' the Swede asked with dreadful briskness.

Inspector Ghote looked shyly down at the blue mildew-smirched surface of Gross.

'I have no evidence about the attack itself,' he said.

'But the locked gate to the servants' quarters, isn't that evidence?'

'Lala Varde lied about that, certainly. But that gate was locking people away from Mr Perfect.'

He looked at the Swede with triumph.

The Swede sighed.

'Yes,' he agreed, 'it would certainly seem as if that was protection for Mr Perfect, if anything.'

But this was not to be the end of his interrogation. In a moment he straightened his enormous shoulders.

'Very well then,' he resumed, 'what about Mr Dilip Varde?'

'Mr Dilip Varde,' the inspector repeated. 'He will be dealt with in my report.'

He looked wistfully at the blank surface of his desk.

'Yes,' said Axel Svensson, 'but what are you going to put in it about him?'

Inspector Ghote tried a little placating.

'Well, he should not have refused to answer my questions. That is definite. It is also suspicious. But on the other hand I do not think it ought to affect my judgement.'

'Yes, yes,' said the Swede testily, 'but has anything led you to believe he may have a reason for wanting to harm Mr Perfect?'

Inspector Ghote's mind flashed back to a certain intransigent Anglo-Indian schoolteacher under whom he had once come. She had had a way of relentlessly pressing on from question to question in this way until his mind had been bludgeoned into complete blankness.

But he had not quite reached that stage yet.

He looked up at the Swede.

'Yes,' he said, 'Dilip Varde perhaps fears that Mr Perfect has an undue influence over his father.'

'Good.'

Inspector Ghote drew a deep breath.

'And Prem Varde?' the Swede said implacably.

The inspector's mind raced again.

'If Prem thought that Mr Perfect was behind his father in making him go into the office . . .'

'Yes, yes,' said Axel Svensson. 'There was discord there. I sensed that.'

A flick of excited spittle appeared at the corner of his mouth. Inspector Ghote lowered his eyes.

'Now,' the Swede said, his voice almost at a shout, 'Dilip's wife, Neena, what about her?'

'She is not a stable person,' the inspector said slowly.

'I was right, I was right,' Axel Svensson shouted. 'I was afraid this was European prejudice, but you confirm me. Good, good, good. So her possible motive is, what?'

The Swede's voice reverberated round and round the small airless room.

'Oh, I don't know,' Inspector Ghote said.

'But you must, you must.'

'Then she may be supporting her husband.'

'Yes. Yes, that is it. Supporting him and intensifying perhaps his feelings of resentment.'

Inspector Ghote looked back at the Swede's great high-boned face thrust to within inches of his own.

'But what about Mrs Varde, Mrs Lakshmi Varde?' the Swede bellowed.

Inspector Ghote retreated till his back touched the wall behind him.

'Mrs Varde is a very dominating woman,' he said. 'At least, that is my personal—'

'Exactly. Exactly so. Yes, you have got it, my friend,' the big Swede trumpeted. 'She wishes to rule her husband with an iron rod. She fears he is getting too ambitious, too unlike her friend Gautam Athalye. And so, like a goddess she crushes this Mr Perfect who is encouraging the wildnesses.'

Beneath the crashing and roaring of the Swede's analysis a tiny notion crept into the inspector's head. That is utter nonsense, he thought. If Lakshmi Varde was that sort of woman she would have forced her husband to part with his secretary long ago.

He let the thought lie like a cool gem in his mind and said nothing.

'So,' Axel Svensson swirled on, 'we come at last to Gautam Athalye himself.'

Inspector Ghote found it almost easy to answer now.

'Mr Athalye was out of the house before midnight,' he said. 'And

Mr Perfect was seen at midnight. I will have the taxi driver who picked up a fare at Lala Varde's brought in and questioned, but I do not think we will find that Mr Athalye was lying.'

He looked up at the great Swede and smiled calmly.

'And now', he said, 'we have mentioned everybody, so it is time I began my report.'

The Swede seemed a little disconcerted. But he could not deny the logic of the inspector's remark. And, promising volubly to keep in touch, he left him at last in peace.

The inspector smiled to himself happily, opened the drawer in his desk where he kept clean paper and took out a substantial sheaf. He selected a sharpened pencil from a little brass tray with enamel decoration and began to write.

When he had finished he looked for the first time at his watch. And discovered that it was already late in the evening.

In an instant the balanced pyramids of thoughts which he had built up in the last hours tumbled to nothing. Their comforting solidity was swept away like morning mist. And the bleak realization of what he had just done to Protima confronted him: once more he had left her on her own without a word. Once more she had had to spend a long evening alone in the house while all around from the other homes in Government Quarters had come the cheerful sounds of family life, the calling voices, the homely clatter of cooking pots.

For a little he contemplated commandeering an office vehicle and driver to take him home as fast as could be. But he was no longer on duty. He thought with chill of what DSP Samant would have to say.

At a trot he set off to make his own way back.

And everything conspired to delay him. He just missed one bus. There was an interminable wait before another appeared. He failed to notice that it was not going the whole length of its route and he had to get out and wait for a following bus of the same number. A similar fate seemed to have befallen half the rest of Bombay and in the huge heaving crowd Ghote was totally unable to get near the next two buses that came along. The third he did catch, by now fuming with bad temper. And it turned out that his barely suppressed spite against the whole world was shared by most of the other passengers as well as the bus crew. There was a tremendous altercation between the latter and a bent-backed old woman carrying a squawking chicken upside down by its two legs. Neither side was willing to let the other have the last word. Epithets flew thick and fast. And the bus waited.

When at last Ghote passed the familiar board saying 'Government of India Staff Quarters. Class 2. No trespassers' he was choking with black rage, sweat-stained and thirsty, grimly tired and implacably conscious of the fact that, although he was in the wrong, he would be unable to keep calm if his wife even so much as hinted at reproach.

And when he came to the house he found it in complete darkness.

He went quietly in and put on the light. On the floor at his feet was a scrap of pink paper with some writing on it. He stooped and read the emphatic capitals:

AT LEAST DO NOT WAKE US.

He stood with hanging head for minute after minute, and then barely stirring himself he dropped off his heavy leather belt and after it the rest of his clothes. He flung himself down in the sitting room and slept where he had fallen.

He slept long, and with wild dreams of Mr Perfect hovering in the air over his head threatening at any instant to fall down and smother him.

And his wakening was sudden.

'Well, do you want to eat today or not?'

It was Protima.

He staggered to his feet, bleary-eyed and thick-headed.

'Well, answer,' Protima said sharply. 'Are you going to eat the food that your wife has cooked or are you going to pick up so-called meals in cheap eating places where you don't know what is being given you or who has touched it?'

'No, no,' he said, waving his hand feebly in front of him as if to ward off a blow. 'No, I will eat here. I – I am sorry. Last night I—'

He could not think of the right words.

He looked round. Through the open doorway he could see his son playing in the garden. Protima must have told him to creep out without making a noise. She must have given him other instructions too because the boy pretended not to see what was going on in the house although he must have heard the voices and have known his father was awake.

There was something unexplained too about the garden itself. He groped round in the heavy stickiness of his mind for a clue.

And then he realized what was the matter.

The sunlight. It was too strong. It ought to have had the clarity and sparkle of the very early morning, and instead it had already begun to blaze.

'The time,' he said. 'What time is it?'

He looked at his watch, holding his wrist close to his face to penetrate the blur in front of his eyes.

The watch had stopped at quarter to three. He must have forgotten to wind it the night before.

'Listen,' he said to Protima, 'what's the time?'

'Time,' she said. 'How should I know what time it is? Other women can tell the time easily enough: they have husbands who come home when they have finished at office and go out to get there again next morning. But I have to wait at home all day, all evening and all night. How should I know what time it is?'

A little flame of rage burned up through the thick fuzz in Ghote's head.

'I have to know the time,' he said. 'I have an appointment first thing this morning. At nine o'clock. With the Minister. With Shri Ram Kamath, Minister for Police Affairs and the Arts.'

He ought to have known that Protima was scarcely the person to be overawed by this honour.

'Minister, indeed,' she flashed. 'And what good do you think it will do you hobnobbing with a man like that?'

'Like what?' Ghote snapped. 'What are you saying about a Minister of the State Government?'

'I am saying the truth,' Protima shot back. 'The truth everyone knows about your precious Ram Kamath. He is just a no good. Bribes he takes, money and women, everything. And that is the man you are so proud to be going to see. Well, I hope you are too late. I hope you are too late by hours and hours.'

'Late. Too late.'

Blind waves of panic swept over and over him.

'The time, the time,' he yelled.

He ran into the bedroom as if he might find mysteriously there something to tell him what time it was. And then he thought of the wireless. He rushed back to the sitting room and snapped it on.

There emerged the devious, intricate, convoluted, intertwining sound of a softly sweet raga.

'Yes, that's right,' Protima said. 'Rush to leave your house once you are in it. Scorn the food that has been so carefully prepared for you and don't so much as look at your own son. Oh, for sins in my past life I am burdened with a policeman instead of a husband.'

'Stop. Stop. Stop. Please, stop,' Ghote shouted. 'Listen. I must know the time. Perhaps there is still a moment for me to eat, to talk to my little Ved, to talk to you. I want to. Believe me, I want to. But I must not be late for the Minister. I had so much trouble to get him to see me. If I am late he will straight away report it to DSP Samant. And then you will find yourself not married to inspector but married to constable.'

'Oh, that would be just fine,' Protima shouted back. 'That would be all I wanted. It is bad enough trying to live on inspector pay, and now you are going to do your best to get made back into constable. That will be very nice. That will be just what I expected. You make so many mistakes at your job that you get sent out on the street at—'

But the music had stopped. And the calm, limpid voice of the announcer was speaking.

Ghote flung himself across the room and pressed his ear carefully against the brown shiny cloth stretched across the loudspeaker.

'And the time is exactly eight-thirty a.m.'

'Eight-thirty. Eight-thirty. I shall never do it,' he shouted. 'It will take half that time to get from the office to the Ministry, even if we are lucky with the traffic. And I have got to get to office yet.'

He ran over to the telephone and dialled the office number.

The maddening noise of the engaged tone. Furiously he jigged at the rest.

Damn, he thought suddenly, I could have found out the time straight away. There's something you dial, 174, something like that and you hear the record of the hours and the minutes.

At last the voice of the operator came.

'Please, caller, show patience. The system is working at full—'

'Listen,' Ghote snapped. 'This is a police matter. Urgent. Put me through to 264456. I got engaged note. But that cannot be right. The number is CID. They cannot all be engaged.'

'I will try to put you through, caller,' said the operator. 'But there may be fault on the line.'

'But there mustn't be fault. Do you understand?'

'Service cannot always be responsible for all faults,' the operator said. 'They occur sometimes—'

'Quick,' Ghote said. 'Get me that number. Or I'll get you sacked if it's the last thing I do.'

The threat miraculously appeared to work.

In a few seconds he heard the voice of the CID switchboard man. He got himself transferred to the transport section.

A lot depended on who was in charge that morning.

And the inspector was in luck. It was Head Constable Chimanlal. A friend.

'Listen, Chimanlal bhai,' he said, 'this is Ghote here. I'm in a terrible jam. I've got to go and see the . . . Well, a very important person, and my appointment is for nine o'clock. Well, I'm at home, and—'

'But I have no transport left. Absolutely none.'

Chimanlal sounded genuinely sorry.

Ghote groaned.

'I had just one truck left, bhaiji,' Chimanlal explained, 'and then that big Swedish fellow, you know, the one—'

'Did he take it?' Ghote yelled.

'Yes, yes, I was saying.'

'And is he waiting in it?'

'Yes, yes, I was saying—'

'And is he waiting in it?'

'Yes. I can see him through the window. He is looking pretty impatient too. You know the way these Westerners—'

'Chimanlal. Do me a favour. Run out and tell him that I am here. He is waiting for me, Chimanlal. And he is right to be impatient.'

'OK, OK,' Chimanlal said. 'Right away, bhai.'

Inspector Ghote let the receiver drop on to the rest thankfully. He turned and snatched up his clothes from the floor where he had left them the night before and scrambled into them. They looked badly crumpled, but there was no time to do anything about that. He would have to try smoothing them out in the vehicle. Once the vehicle had arrived. And if all went well it could arrive in minutes.

Buckling on his belt he ran into the garden and looked up and down the service road. Amid all the noises of the city, the chatter and shouting of neighbouring houses, the wild cawing of crows, the tinny caterwauling of radio sets, the murmur of distant traffic, he thought he could make out the angry high-pitched note of a police truck.

He would have liked to have had a couple of minutes to ring up the Varde house. The thought of his dreams weighed heavily on him. But a luxury like that had to be relinquished.

He patted his pockets to make sure that he had got pencil and notebook and carefully reset his watch and wound it up.

He looked round for his son.

The boy was crouching in a corner pretending to be very absorbed in making a chain of marigold flowers.

'Hoi, little one,' Ghote said, 'aren't you going to speak to your father today?'

The boy said nothing. For a few moments he went on playing with the wilting marigolds and then Ghote saw him look slyly out of the corner of his eye up in his direction.

'So, you can hear me, Veddy,' he said.

The boy did not answer.

Inspector Ghote looked down at his rounded back and the frighteningly slight smooth neck. He frowned puzzledly.

Behind him came the sudden roar of a car engine and the squeak of brakes jammed on hard.

The boy glanced up.

'Ved,' Ghote said, 'Ved, don't you know what that is? It's the truck come to fetch me to work. Aren't you going to say goodbye even?'

The boy, still looking down at the dusty earth of the garden, shook his head.

Ghote crouched down beside him.

The truck driver, the same impassive speed maniac he had had the day before, gave a respectful but sharp toot on the horn.

'Listen, Ved,' Ghote said, 'what's the matter? Why won't you talk to me?'

The boy kept obstinately still. His fingers now had ceased to fiddle with the flower heads.

'Ved, what is it? Have I done something to you? Tell me if I have, my little boy, and I'll put it right.'

In a flash the boy wheeled round on his haunches till his face was within inches of his father's.

'You have gone away all the time,' he said. 'Don't go now, Pitaji. Stay here today.'

Ghote looked at his face, wide-eyed with pleading. From the road behind him he heard Axel Svensson calling.

'But, Ved,' Ghote said, 'but, Ved, you must understand. Look, you know what a policeman is, don't you?'

The boy looked at him and said nothing.

'Well, you do, don't you? I have often told you. What is a policeman for, Ved?'

'To put bad men in prison, Pitaji.'

'Yes. And if the policeman stays at home all day the bad men will not get put in prison.'

He rose to his feet but still kept looking down at the boy, waiting for a sign that he could go without rancour.

But no sign came. Instead from the truck Axel Svensson called with unconcealed impatience.

'Ved, if I stay at home the bad men will not be caught.'

'Bibiji says that you do not have to go,' Ved said.

'And your mother told you not to talk to me also?'

'Yes. And I don't want to talk to you if you always go away.'

Inspector Ghote drew in a long breath.

'Listen, Ved,' he said. 'I know it is not nice for you and Bibiji to have me away all the time. But there are a lot of bad men and if I did not help to catch them they would rob people and hurt them. So that is why I have to go. Do you see that?'

Slowly Ved lifted his head till he was looking straight at his father.

'Yes, Pitaji,' he whispered.

Ghote swooped down on him and hugged him hard. But not for long.

'Goodbye, Ved,' he shouted as he ran out of the garden. 'Goodbye and be good.'

He jumped into the truck.

Without waiting for an order the driver crashed into gear and shot off.

Inspector Ghote looked at his watch.

Nearly quarter to nine.

'My friend,' said Axel Svensson, 'you will be very lucky to be in time for your interview with Mr Ram Kamath.'

'Yes,' said Ghote miserably.

'But I expect he shares that general freedom from the trammels of time which is so admirable here.'

'No,' said Ghote, more miserably.

'No? How is that?'

'The Minister is well known for not liking to waste anything,' Ghote said. 'You understand I am speaking as friend to friend, but he is notorious for never wasting a single minute of time or a single pie of money.'

The truck had by now left the Government Quarters area and was beginning to meet the thicker traffic of morning Bombay. Their rate of progress got considerably slower.

'I think we shall be late,' said the Swede.

Inspector Ghote looked at his watch again.

Twelve minutes to nine.

As if to emphasize the slimness of their chances an immense traffic jam suddenly built up around them like a flowing stream turning in a single instant into ice. The root of the trouble lay in a dilapidated Victoria driven by a tall Muslim with a sprouting henna-dyed beard. His horse was so skinny that it looked as if it had reached its present place only by the triumph of spirit over flesh, and now at last sheer physical inanition had prevailed. Around it big cars and little cars, old cars and spanking new cars chafed and growled. A few bicycles contrived to slip slowly forward between the stationary vehicles, but before long they too congealed into their own private tangles, adding one by one to the number of minutes that must go by before the snarl could begin to unwind.

For as long as he could bear to Inspector Ghote prevented himself looking at his watch. When his nerve broke at last the hands said one minute to nine.

He groaned aloud.

'What is wrong, my friend?' Axel Svensson asked.

Inspector Ghote showed him the watch face.

'In exactly one minute from now,' he said, 'Shri Ram Kamath will ask our friend Mr Jain to bring me into his office. Mr Jain will tell him I am not there and—'

As suddenly as it had blocked the traffic began to move again.

'Hurry, hurry,' the big Swede shouted to the stately driver.

The driver needed no encouragement.

He slewed in front of taxis and cars, darted ahead of the big shiny buses, brutally frightened cyclists, terrified mooning pedestrians and made progress through the teeming streets at a speed which surpassed even the best of his previous tearaway plunges.

The Swede's face was glazed with fright as with a howl of brakes they drew up outside the Ministry. Inspector Ghote flung himself on to the pavement and bounded up the wide marble steps leading into the building. The chaprassi he had so nearly bribed on his previous visit was there in full splendour.

'The Minister,' Ghote gasped. 'Quick. I have an appointment for nine a.m.'

'Minister has gone out, sahib,' the chaprassi said with statuesque calm. 'It is past nine o'clock.'

Inspector Ghote looked at his watch.

Four minutes past nine.

14

Dejectedly Inspector Ghote tramped down the wide flight of shallow marble steps out of the Ministry. Axel Svensson was waiting for him at the bottom.

'We're too late?' he asked.

'Too late,' said Inspector Ghote.

The Swede consulted his watch.

'But it's only five past,' he said.

'I told you,' said the inspector. 'Not everybody in India has the habit of unpunctuality which you are kind enough to praise. The Minister has already left.'

They got back into the truck. Inspector Ghote told the driver, sitting more righteously upright than ever, to take them to Lala Varde's house, and with no more than his customary recklessness he screeched and swung them there.

No sooner had the heavy front door been swung open for them than Inspector Ghote saw Doctor Das standing in the hall.

He went cold in a moment.

Had Mr Perfect's crisis come after all?

'Doctor,' he said, hardly able to get the word out, 'how is he?'

Doctor Das bobbed and smiled.

'Ah,' he said, 'I don't think there can be any considerable objection to telling you that I have been visiting Mr Perfect. Yes. Mr Varde is deeply concerned and insists on frequent visits. Absolutely.'

'And his condition?' the inspector asked, unable to conceal his eagerness.

For a moment the wide-mouthed little doctor looked at him.

'There has been one minor change,' he said.

'Minor? What? What is it?'

Doctor Das shook a plump little frog-finger at the inspector.

'Now, you must remember this,' he said. 'Fundamentally, the situation is exactly the same as before. Exactly. The patient is still deeply unconscious. Yes, there can be no objection to telling you that.'

Inspector Ghote felt relief seeping slowly through him from head to foot.

'And his chances? What about them?' he said.

'My dear Inspector, now you are really asking too much. Not that I wouldn't tell you if I was able. I would certainly tell you that much. But, my dear good fellow, no one could. Mind you, some of these ayurvedic fellows might claim to tell you. They will tell you anything. I have had the greatest difficulty in persuading Lala Varde not to bring them in on this case. The greatest difficulty. I have had to threaten to give up myself. To give up.'

'You might tell me what chance he stood if you were able to,' Inspector Ghote said with quickening interest, 'but what is it that you won't tell me and could, Doctor?'

The doctor looked surprised for one second. Then he smiled broadly again.

'Yes, you are quite right, my dear chap,' he said. 'There is something I feel I shouldn't tell you. I really should not have let a hint of the matter slip. Most regrettably remiss of me. Most remiss.'

'Doctor,' said the inspector, 'Mr Perfect is the victim of a crime which I am investigating. I do not think you should withhold anything from me which might be relevant to that crime.'

'Ah,' said Doctor Das, 'now you are saying that in a manner of speaking Mr Perfect is not only a patient under Mr Varde's auspices but is also under the auspices of the Police Department?'

'What happens to Mr Perfect is very much the Police Department's concern,' said the inspector.

'Then I shall regard the department as having consulted me,' Doctor Das said briskly. 'And of course if I have been consulted I am perfectly right to give you an opinion, Inspector.'

'One moment,' the inspector said. 'What exactly do you mean by this talk of consultation, Doctor? Does a question of fees arise?'

Doctor Das looked shocked.

'My dear fellow,' he said, 'these things are really best not discussed in quite that way.'

'But nevertheless if you tell me this about Mr Perfect at some later date the Police Department will receive your bill?'

Doctor Das swept the whole business aside with an easy spreading gesture.

'These matters are dealt with by my secretary,' he said.

Inspector Ghote stood almost to attention.

'Doctor Das,' he said, 'I understand that in your capacity as a doctor something to do with Mr Perfect has come to your attention, and that you believe it would interest me. I require you to tell.'

Doctor Das abruptly bent forward half an inch as if he had had a sudden attack of painful dyspepsia.

'You think I should tell you?' he said.

'I insist.'

'Very well.'

He sighed.

'While I was with Mr Perfect just now,' he said, 'the level of unconsciousness rose a little and then fell back. The patient stirred and began to mutter something. You would like to know what it was he said?'

'Certainly.'

Doctor Das sighed again.

'All right then,' he said. 'The words were these: "Will not listen to good advice. He is fool to tell a fool. Secrecy best." And then he repeated that last phrase, "Secrecy best".'

'I see,' said Inspector Ghote. 'And that was all?'

'You want more?'

Doctor Das sounded outraged.

'If there is more, I want it.'

'Well, there was no more.'

'You are certain?'

'I have told you every word he said.'

'There is someone with him all the time?'

'Yes, of course. Lala Varde at least is paying.'

The doctor looked at Ghote more in sorrow than in anger and departed.

For a moment Ghote luxuriated in his feeling of relief. Surely all this must mean that Mr Perfect was no worse, perhaps even improving? Doctors always liked to make out that things were more serious than they were. It made the eventual cure more dramatic.

Axel Svensson turned from looking sombrely at the closed front door.

'Am I right in thinking he wanted to be paid for telling you that?' he asked.

'Almost everybody in India wants to be paid for everything,' the inspector answered with a trace of bitterness.

'But a doctor? Are you sure?'

The note of incredulity. The Swede had not shed any of his Nordic conceptions of professional integrity.

'Yes, I am sure,' the inspector replied rather shortly. 'Just because Doctor Das feels obliged to put his demands in a rather roundabout fashion it does not mean he is not making them.'

He gave a harsh bark of a laugh.

'He won't lose on the deal in any case,' he said. 'You wait till Lala Varde gets his bill.'

And, even as he spoke the words, he sensed behind him at the top of the flight of marble stairs the looming figure of Lala Arun Varde himself.

'Oh ho, so the policias are sending bills nowadays, are they?' Lala Varde boomed.

He descended the stairs like a monsoon cloud gradually approaching the parched earth as if borne down by the weight of water in it.

Standing on the bottom step, he pointed a pudgy finger at the inspector.

'I would pay all right,' he said, 'if I saw any sign of result. But you know Arun Varde: until he sees something he can touch he doesn't pay out, no, not a single rupee.'

Inspector Ghote chose to misunderstand this joking.

'You must be very well aware, sahib,' he said, 'that the police force is remunerated from properly levied State taxes. No member of it in any circumstances accepts money from a private citizen.'

Lala Varde's face at once assumed an expression of extravagant piety.

'Oh, no, no, no, no, Inspector detector,' he said. 'Oh, no, indeed. I know that well. Who should know it if not I? No policeman ever takes money from the public. Oh, dear me, no, no, no, no.'

Inspector Ghote looked at him stonily.

'I trust you have never had experience to the contrary in your business dealings,' he said. 'May I remind you that in bribery and corruption cases both parties to the transaction are equally to blame?'

'Oh, but, my poor Inspector, you know Lala Varde would never do a thing like that. Donations to police charities, yes. Many and often. I am thinking just now of making a donation for some nice furniture for that new police training college I hear they are going to build. But corruption poppuption. Never.'

He stood upright on the bottom stair, his huge fat chest puffed out under the thin kurta.

And then suddenly he plunged forward like a racing swimmer entering the water and strode up close to the inspector.

'A donation I am considering only,' he said. 'Considering, you understand. If I find policemen not being polite, considering I will stop. Yes, bang. Stop.'

Inspector Ghote looked him full in his many-chinned face.

'I hope you have had no cause for complaint over my conduct, sahib,' he said.

A huge splitting grin replied to him.

'Oh, no, Inspector. Politeness I have had from you in plenty twenty. But what I have not had is the murderer. The Perfect murderer. Where is he, Inspector? Oh, by God, yes, you ought to pull him out of this pretty damn quick.'

'Our investigations are proceeding,' Inspector Ghote answered.

'Proceeding misleading,' Lala Varde shouted back.

His face was three inches away from the inspector's.

'Oh, I know you fellows,' he went on. 'Only the other night was I betting that you fellows couldn't catch a thief on your own doorstep poorstep,' he said.

'Nevertheless, sahib,' Inspector Ghote said, with a flick of asperity, 'it is the crime on your own doorstep that we are concerned with now. I have certain questions I wish to put to you. Shall we go somewhere more private?'

Lala Varde laughed. Deeply and richly.

'Private, my good Inspector,' he bellowed. 'Do you think anywhere in this house of mine is private? Everywhere there are servants with their little ears wiggling piggling to catch any word I speak.'

He stopped, looked at them solemnly for a moment and then gave them an immense leering wink.

'And besides,' he said, 'how do you think I would find out what is going on in my own family if there was anywhere in this house private?'

'So that is why you locked the gate to the servants' quarters on the night of the attack on Mr Perfect,' Inspector Ghote said.

And he succeeded in sobering up the great snorting honking whale in front of him.

'Ah,' said Lala Varde, 'I think I have made a little mistake. Yes, I told you a lie about that, Inspector.'

He gave a gurgle of a laugh.

'But why did God give lies to mankind if not to use?' he said.

He looked at the almost puny form of the inspector like a visitor to a museum who finds in a display something he has always heard about and never seen.

He shook his head slowly and sadly.

'Yes, yes,' he said, 'I was missing my old Mr Perfect. I am missing his always saying I will not listen to good advice. He would have advised me to be more careful with you, Inspector. And from now on I will take his advice.'

Inspector Ghote cursed himself. It was something perhaps to have shown Lala Varde that he could not always get away with whatever he chose to say, but if it had been done at the cost of putting him more than ever on his guard it had been a bad bargain.

He collected himself for a new long struggle.

'Mr Varde,' he said, 'you yourself may not object to being heard by anybody who passes, but what I have to talk are police matters and I prefer to deal with them in private.'

An idea hovered for a moment near the edge of his mind, and without having time to weigh its merits he seized on it.

Wheeling quickly he walked the few steps to the doorway of the little room where Mr Perfect had been found lying in a trickle of his own blood.

'Would you come in here, please?' he said.

Lala Varde hesitated.

The inspector stood at the doorway waiting for him to enter, looking inwards as if any notion that Lala Varde should not do as he had been asked was inconceivable.

The clutter of derelict objects was just as he had seen it when he had inspected the scene the day after the attack on Mr Perfect. The bookshelf still held its piles of yellowed newspapers, the little table still bore its disused bunch of long brass keys, its unworkable torch, its umbrella and even the same four empty matchboxes. Side by side on the top of the display cabinet the oil lamp in Benares work and the European tall brass candlestick stood in exactly the same relation to each other as they had done when the inspector had meticulously recorded their existence in his notebook in the first hours of the investigation. Against the wall the Moghul painting still leaned beside the brass plate inscribed Varde Building Enterprises (Private) Ltd.

'No,' said Lala Varde.

The inspector jerked round and looked at him.

'No,' Lala Varde repeated. 'There is no reason why I should be going into that little pig of a room just to please you, Inspector. Oh, yes, I know it is the scene of the Perfect Murder, but you needn't think you are going to frighten me with that. No, no. If you have got anything to say, say it out loud here and now.'

It was the inspector's turn to hesitate.

Was this to lose a battle? If he gave way would he ever again be in a position of moral authority over the great fat business tycoon? Or was he being ridiculous in insisting on dragging a respectable citizen into a cluttered up disused lobby to ask him questions about a crime he himself had reported? And there was something else teasing away at the back of his mind, something else which he had to deal with.

The lack of a quick decision was fatal.

Lala Varde smiled comfortably, and the inspector knew that he had to concede the point. Was it more than just a point? He pushed the whole complex of thoughts brusquely away.

'Very well, Mr Varde,' he said, 'if that is the way you prefer it, I am perfectly willing to say what I have got to say just where we are.'

Arun Varde swept a leering glance over the big stone-floored hall.

'Well, Inspector,' he said, 'perhaps you will be lucky. At least I cannot see anyone listening to all these police matter patters you are going to talk.'

'They are also matters which concern yourself and your family,' Inspector Ghote said.

He spoke fiercely. And quickly wondered whether this was not the effect of hurt pride over having been worsted a moment before.

He plunged on.

'Yes, family matters,' he said. 'It has come to my notice, Mr Varde, that a very short time before the attack on Mr Perfect you decided to tell your elder son something you had concealed from him for years.'

Lala Varde's great moon-face remained utterly bland.

'But, no, Inspector,' he said, 'you have got some wrong idea into your head. What should I have to hide from my Dilip? Always I have told him everything. Perhaps too much even. If he had been a bad son he could have ruined me.'

Inspector Ghote looked stubbornly back.

'My information is that you revealed a domestic secret,' he said. 'That you revealed this secret a few hours only before the attack on Mr Perfect.'

Still Lala Varde was blandly calm.

'And where did you get such information, Inspector?' he said. 'From some paid informer perhaps? Oh, my dear Inspector, they should have put someone on this case with more experience. Don't you know that paid informers tell you what they think you want to hear only?'

'I cannot say what my source is,' Inspector Ghote said, keeping his voice as level as he could. 'But I have reason to believe this information is highly accurate.'

'Reason to believe, reason to believe. What good is your reason treason? How dare you come to me with such trash and try to get my secrets out of me? What's the idea behind it, eh? What's the idea of poking your nose in? I know what it is. I'll tell you what it is. It's just wanting to know things which are no concern of yours. It's trying to look in dirty books in the bazaars. I know what you do there. You try and get your filthy little thumb under the edge of the wrapping so that you can peek and pry and satisfy your nasty little mind. Well, I warn you: don't try lifting the paper that wraps up my family affairs. Because if I catch you at it I won't be like a bazaar book merchant and just call out against you. Oh, no, I'll do more than call out. Much more. A lot much more. I promise you that.'

As Inspector Ghote listened to Arun Varde working himself up moment by moment he succeeded in preventing his face showing the least trace of what he was thinking. And when Lala Varde had finished he spoke quietly.

'I will remind you of one thing only, sahib,' he said. 'Just one or two hours after you had told your son this thing Mr Perfect was attacked.'

Lala Varde's attitude changed much more swiftly than the sun breaks through after a storm.

'Inspector, Inspector,' he said, 'what are you thinking? That is what I ask myself. What is he thinking this man who has come so suddenly into the middle of my family? He knows so little. He will think such wrong things. I know what he is thinking. He is thinking my poor, good, kind, gentle Dilip is murderer. That is what he is thinking.'

'No question of a charge has arisen at the present time,' Inspector Ghote said.

But Lala Varde ignored this.

'But no,' he went on in a broodingly musing voice, 'but no, after all I do not believe he is thinking that. I know this man. I can see what sort of a man he is. He is not the sort of man who could make a mistake like that. He is a man who will go far in this police life of his. He is a man I must point out to his superiors as a man of far-sightedness, of understanding, of sympathy, of great sense.'

He looked at the slight form of the inspector in front of him with caressing kindness. And suddenly through the all-pervading haze a thin ray of light cut a plain signal.

'Because I am well acquainted with those in authority over you, Inspector.'

Inspector Ghote just moistened his lips.

'Oh, yes, sahib?' he said. 'May I enquire who it is in particular that you are thinking of?'

Lala Varde swelled up.

'I am thinking of your very—'

And he checked himself.

'Inspector,' he said soothingly, 'it is better if I do not mention. It would be wrong if anyone should think I was trying to influence you by mentioning such names. No, I prefer not to say.'

'Just as you wish, sahib,' said the inspector. 'And now, if you please, I would like answer to my question.'

'Question? Question? What question is that, Inspector? So many questions you are asking my poor old head is all whirling.'

Lala Varde put his large, astute-eyed head between his podgy palms and rocked it to and fro.

'Oh, Inspector, Inspector,' he said, 'I cannot do any more. Come tomorrow, my kind Inspector. Come tomorrow and I will try to answer.'

He began lumbering away, his head still held in his two vast chubby hands, his eyes looking here and there for the quickest escape route.

'Lala Varde sahib.'

The words shot out. Like an order.

Lala Varde shambling away. A cunning old bear.

'Mr Varde, I have some questions I must put to you as officer in charge of the investigations into the attack on Mr Perfect.'

The inspector issued the words.

And they impinged. Lala Varde, still with his back to the inspector and to the big silent Swede hovering awkwardly behind, raised his left arm.

With the fingers of the hand spread wide he made an impatient brushing away gesture.

Inspector Ghote closed in.

'Mr Varde, I would be most reluctant to raise question of failing to assist an officer of the law in the execution of his duty, but—'

Lala Arun Varde was facing him. Walking towards him, swaying slightly from side to side, an absorbed distant look on his broad face.

'What was that? What was that, Inspector?' he said in a vague friendly way from his distant station.

'Mr Varde, I have a question to which I insist on answer.'

'Good, good. You are acting like real policeman, Inspector. In the films I have seen them. "Answer up, buddy. Answer up, if you don't want to get hurt." '

Lala Varde bunched up a podgy fist into the semblance of a pointing gun.

He gurgled with laughter.

'Sir, this is not film,' Inspector Ghote said. 'I am acting like a policeman because I am a policeman. I am the investigating officer for a very serious case: it is my duty to put all necessary questions and obtain answers with minimum delay. That is what an investigating officer does.'

Lala Varde looked at him wide-eyed.

'He does that, Inspector?'

'That is his duty.'

Lala Varde's eyes went a shade wider even.

'Sometimes,' he said with an admixture of plaintiveness, 'sometimes a little bit he eats?'

'What is this?' Inspector Ghote snapped.

'Sometimes three or four minutes only he sleeps?' asked Lala Varde. 'Sometimes he drinks? Then there is the question of sexual matters. Oh, such a lot of things, such a lot of things.'

He drew himself up.

'Inspector,' he went on, 'sometimes you have to be man, not policeman. Inspector, this would be a very good time.'

'No,' said Inspector Ghote. 'No, no, no. This is not the time. Never is the time. Always until the case is solved I am the investigating officer. Till the end.'

He took one single step forward.

'Mr Varde,' he said. 'You told your son Dilip a few hours before the attack on Mr Perfect that his wife had had an affair with someone before her marriage. Mr Varde, who was that person?'

Lala Arun Varde sighed. Slowly he lifted his great round face and looked full at Inspector Ghote.

'Inspector,' he said, 'the man was Shri Ram Kamath, present Minister for Police Affairs and the Arts.'

15

The little sharp elephant eyes in Lala Arun Varde's big round many-chinned face glittered ferociously.

'Oh, yes, my Inspector,' he said. 'You have found out a secret. You have found out that when Neena Athalye was a girl she was unable to resist the well-known attractions of your present boss. You have found out something which Ram Kamath would prefer kept quiet. Let us hope for your sake, Inspector detector, that no one ever tells him that you know.'

Inspector Ghote fought down the chill he felt inside.

His mouth went suddenly very dry and he moved his lips to moisten them.

'If I have learnt anything of a confidential nature in the course of enquiries, you can be certain I know my duty to let it remain a confidential matter,' he said. 'Trust is an essential attribute for the detective officer. You will find it stated in the very best authorities.'

Lala Varde slapped him heartily on the back as he stood rigidly to attention.

'Oh, there is no need to worry,' he said. 'I am your friend, remember that. If there is ever anything I can do for you, you have only to say. And I know also, if ever I want anything done, I can come to you. There are always many things a policeman can do for his friends, thank goodness.'

'I think my enquiries at this point take me elsewhere, Mr Varde,' Inspector Ghote said.

He brought his head forward in a little nod and turned on his heel.

From the perimeter Axel Svensson smiled at Lala Varde. But the huge whale-like figure did not acknowledge it. He was standing looking at the inspector's back, and in his eyes was an unmistakable look of calculation.

The tall Swede strode out after the inspector.

He found him standing beside the police vehicle. The stately driver was nowhere in sight. The inspector marched back to the constable standing inconspicuously near the big front door of Lala Varde's house.

'Where is that man?' he snapped. 'Why isn't he waiting in the truck?'

'Don't know, sahib,' the constable said.

He looked uneasily from left to right and back again.

'What do you mean "Don't know"? It's your business to know. You're a policeman. A policeman. You're meant to have eyes in your head. Where is he?'

'He had gone that way, sahib,' the constable said.

The inspector was obviously not in a mood to be lied to.

'Damn him,' he said. 'Why isn't he here when he's wanted?'

'Perhaps he had to fetch something for car, sahib,' the constable suggested.

'He'll fetch more than something for car when he gets back,' said Inspector Ghote savagely.

'Listen, my friend,' Axel Svensson called from near the vehicle.

Inspector Ghote turned and walked back over to him.

'Listen, my friend, there is no hurry. Let us wait beside the car for a little. We can stand in the shade. I want very much to hear your comments on that last interview. I do not see how it advances matters to know now that it was Ram Kamath himself.'

Inspector Ghote stamped sulkily into the shade.

'What comment do you expect?' he said. 'That I have probably finished my police career whatever happens in the Perfect case?'

'But no.'

The Swede sounded shocked, incredulous, innocent.

'But surely,' he went on, 'because you have accidentally found out something to the discredit of a minister, something that has nothing to do with the case in hand, something that need never be mentioned again, that does not mean your career is in any danger? Is there anything I can do? I am perfectly willing to make recommendations. Anything.'

The inspector thought for a moment.

'Perhaps I am lucky,' he said. 'I had not taken into account what it might mean that you were there. Perhaps because of that nothing will happen.'

He heaved a long sigh.

'And after all,' he said, 'Ministers go in the end. They move departments.'

Unaccustomed lines of worry furrowed the Swede's wide deep-pink brow.

'It is certainly a problem for you, my friend,' he said. 'But remember this: if ever you have any reason to believe you are in trouble because of this, let me know. Wherever I am in the world I will do what I can to help.'

Inspector Ghote looked at him gratefully.

Axel Svensson raised a huge open hand to stop him speaking.

'My friend,' he said, 'no thanks are needed. I can recognize a good police officer when I see one. Something like this ought not to stop you getting in the end to where you deserve.'

Inspector Ghote hung his head.

He refused to let himself think about what the broad-shouldered Scandinavian standing beside him in the narrow patch of shade had said. Not now. Not at present. Later he would allow himself the luxury of taking out those words and fingering over each one lovingly. But for now they were safely stored away.

'There is one other problem,' the Swede said.

The inspector looked up.

'Yes?'

'There is the problem of the business of that missing rupee note. What you have just learned is going to complicate your handling of that, I am afraid.'

'No.'

Axel Svensson jerked his head round to look at the slight form of the inspector beside him.

'No,' said Inspector Ghote. 'I do not see that it makes a difference. A rupee missing from the Minister's desk this week cannot have a connection with the same Minister's sex life three years ago.'

'But all the same—'

'No. I know what I have to do there. I must see the Minister. It is ridiculous to attempt to deal with the case without doing that. What would Doctor Gross think?'

'But, my friend, what can you do?'

'I shall ask for another interview with the Minister.'

'But after being late last time?'

'I shall apologize. But if he wants to know who stole that rupee, he must see me.'

He craned his neck to discover if the driver was showing any sign of returning.

'What has happened to that fellow?' he said.

'But you oughtn't to be in a hurry, my friend,' Axel Svensson said. 'That is the lesson the East has for us today: the answer to the problem of unending rush.'

The inspector looked at him with an irrepressible dart of impatience.

'No,' he said sharply.

He paused and shook his head from side to side like an animal dodging the whine of an insect.

'But listen, Mr Svensson,' he said, 'you are really making a mistake there. I am a police officer, but if I always said "There is no hurry for that" or "Leave that till tomorrow" I would not deserve to be police officer very long.'

Axel Svensson looked at him.

'I suppose you are right, my friend,' he said, 'as far as police work is concerned. But all the same the Indian approach to the problem of hurry is decidedly of interest.'

Inspector Ghote decided to leave it at that. He looked out along the narrow street again for a sign of his impassive driver.

'It is a pity I did not bring my own car,' the Swede said. 'But to tell you the truth the problem of pedestrians in Bombay is sometimes too much for me. After I had nearly had two accidents on my first day in the car with people walking right into the way I decided to drive as little as possible.'

'But you must not give up like that,' Inspector Ghote said.

He forgot to keep the scandalized tone out of his voice.

'No,' he went on, 'that is to admit defeat. If we all left our cars at home the whole city would fall back fifty years, a hundred years.'

'Sometimes I think that would not be a bad thing,' the Swede said.

'No,' Inspector Ghote said with solemnity, 'I want you to promise not to have such ideas. Motor transport is a sign of progress: we need to make so much progress.'

The Swede looked down for a moment at his Indian friend's intense face.

'All right,' he said with matching solemnity, 'tomorrow I will come to the office in my car. I promise.'

After waiting beside the police truck a little longer Inspector Ghote had impatiently set off down the street in search of the missing driver. He had found him just round the corner soundly sleeping in an attitude of great respectability. In a sudden fury he had kicked him sharply awake with the toe of his brown shoe and had snapped orders at him all the way back to the office.

But once sitting at his own small desk with everything in its proper place all round him his bad temper had quickly melted away, and he had been able to make the intensive study of all the facts of both his cases recommended in the hallowed pages of Gross's *Criminal Investigation.* He had also written a careful report of his interview with Lala Varde, neatly omitting the actual details of his revelation and substituting equivalent details for the eyes of DSP Samant or anyone else who should come to read what he had written.

'Nevertheless,' his report concluded, 'although above disclosure would appear to have no direct connection with the attack, the above line of enquiry should be pursued as a most highly suspicious coincidence. To investigate movements of suspects further would prove most useless as none have offered alibis for period midnight to 1.47 a.m. (time of police receiving request for assistance). Of suspects as at present ascertained, Prem Varde may believe that victim was urging that he should be taken into office, to which he gravely objects. But no climax has arisen requiring sudden action by this suspect. Also Shrimati Lakshmi Varde, as before stated, has given occasion to believe she distrusts ambitious plans of her husband and may think victim was supporting these. However, in this case also no immediate cause for action has arisen. Lala Arun Varde himself is, of course, beyond suspicion since victim's indisposition is causing him severe trouble. Finally, Dilip Varde may believe victim was instrumental in regretted return from Delhi, which might provide reason for action. The foregoing reason also applies to Neena Varde. Proposed to proceed on these lines.'

He placed his neat signature at the bottom of the report and took up the telephone to make two calls.

The first was to Arun Varde's house. He made it with less anxiety than usual. What he had learnt from Doctor Das earlier in the day had given him a certain amount of confidence.

Nor did this prove to be unjustified. There was no change in Mr Perfect's condition. He succeeded in speaking to the reliable Anglo-Indian nurse, and she told him that her patient lay exactly as before. There had been no more muttered words, and no symptoms of damage to the brain.

With growing optimism the inspector put through his second call

– to Mr Jain, Ram Kamath's personal assistant. And again things fell into place neatly and smoothly. Mr Jain even seemed especially anxious that the inspector should see the Minister.

'I assured him that only the very gravest circumstances would have made you miss your appointment,' he said. 'And now I shall be able to repeat the assurance.'

He did not ask the inspector for an explanation. The inspector mentally withdrew his elaborate and not very convincing series of partially true reasons.

'Then we shall say at nine o'clock tomorrow morning,' Mr Jain said with warm finality.

'Nine o'clock,' said the inspector.

He felt no need to add 'I shall not be late again' or anything of that kind.

For once he left the office at the exact time he was due to finish. And in his comfortably optimistic mood he did not have the heart when he reached home to spoil the evening by saying anything to Protima about what she had persuaded little Ved to do that morning to tame his father.

And next day he was in no danger of being late for the office. He had slept well and had woken in good time to breakfast comfortably before leaving. The puris were cooked to perfection, the way he always liked them, thin and crisp.

When he had finished he went to the telephone and rang the Varde house to find out how Mr Perfect had spent the night. He was not surprised when he was told that the night had gone by completely without incident.

Things were going well, and going to go well.

He buckled on his belt, caught hold of Ved under each arm and swung him upwards until his softly gleaming hair all but touched the low ceiling of the room. Then he held him tight for a moment and kissed him.

'Kiss Bibiji too,' said Ved with authority.

He kissed Protima.

'Really,' she said, 'Mr Inspector. And what would DSP have to say?'

'I don't mind what DSP says,' he replied.

'Well, I do,' said Protima. 'I want you to keep in that man's good books, the way you are.'

'I won't stay there if I miss my appointment with the Minister a second time.'

She smiled.

'Oh, you won't be wrong twice, Mr Good Police Officer who is going to go where he deserves.'

'Now,' he said with a flicker of anxiety, half-felt half-feigned, 'you promised you wouldn't say a word about that to anyone. If Mr Svensson thought I had repeated that all over the place he would never speak to me again.'

She smiled, slowly. A fire of mischief running over the surface of a deep, fast-flowing stream.

'Now, go to office with you,' she said.

He went. And arrived in very good time. Even before Axel Svensson, who regularly presented himself well in advance of the official starting hour, a trick he had learned in the early days of his stay after Inspector Ghote had succeeded in giving him the slip for the whole morning on two days running.

The inspector sat down at his desk and took stock of the day ahead. First the meeting with Ram Kamath. Then anything that had to be done arising from that. And if just possibly he was able to put paid to the whole rupee business there and then, he could go straight off to Arun Varde's to deal with the Perfect Murder.

He stopped himself calling it that with a trace of impatience, and looked at his watch.

It was time his Swedish friend showed up. Otherwise they would be in danger of not arriving at the Ministry with plenty of time in hand.

He got up, padded quietly round his desk and went to the little set of bamboo-edged shelves. There in the shelf labelled *Sacred* was the file on the Missing Rupee Case, with its reports from the men who had interviewed the Ministry clerks and the Ministry window cleaners, with its plans of the rooms round Ram Kamath's office and of the floors above and below, with his own accounts of his interviews with the fussily neat Mr Jain and the deplorable Felix Sousa. And with the mystery still as mysterious as ever.

He let the file lie where it was. Until he had seen Ram Kamath there was nothing more he could do to it.

And in the shelf labelled *Dance* there was the file on the Perfect . . . No, not the Perfect Murder. The file on the attack carried out on Mr Perfect, Arun Varde's secretary.

He stretched out a hand to it, but instead looked at his watch. Axel Svensson would be arriving at any moment. Already he was more than a bit later than might have been expected.

The inspector straightened up, picked Gross's *Criminal Investigation* from its place on top of the set of shelves and opened it where he stood. He could start at any one of the familiar pages and know exactly where he was. The moment he heard the big Swede's long-stepping stride outside he could close the book and still know what came next.

Happily he read.

Through the thin partition between his room and the next he heard without paying attention to it the raucous noise of some of his colleagues talking to each other. They were swapping stories of how best to get confessions out of reluctant prisoners. Inspector Ghote knew it was only a sort of boasting match, and that more than half of what anyone said was made up. But he was uneasily conscious that Doctor Gross would not have felt able to join in.

Time passed.

Inspector Ghote rang the transport office and made sure that a truck was waiting for him. His friend Chimanlal was on duty again, and he felt reassured.

But Axel Svensson was cutting it pretty damn fine.

He read another paragraph of Gross.

The door opened slowly, hesitantly.

Inspector Ghote swung round. It was Axel Svensson. But there had been no loud strides along the corridor, and in an instant he understood why. The big Swede's normally rosily cheerful face was totally deprived of colour. His eyes looked sunken and his mouth was set in a hard streak of distress.

'Mr Svensson,' Ghote said. 'What's the matter? For God's sake, what's happened?'

'The car.'

The huge Swede could hardly get the two brief syllables out.

Inspector Ghote caught hold of his desk chair, dragged it to the middle of the room and guided the tall Scandinavian down into it.

The big Swede sat with his elbows on his knees, staring straight in front of him. In the small, fragile chair he looked like a great animal pretending to take part in human activities.

'The car?' Ghote said softly. 'What happened? Tell me.'

The Swede slowly shook his head.

'No,' he said, 'it's late. Your appointment with the Minister. If you don't go at once you will miss it again.'

The inspector flicked a look at the watch on his wrist. Axel Svensson was right.

'Listen,' Ghote said, 'just quickly tell me what happened. Are you all right? I can't go till I know that.'

'There was a boy,' the Swede said.

Each word jerked out.

'A boy,' he repeated. 'Not old . . . He ran out, right into . . . Just the way . . .'

Huge sobs suddenly shook his wide-shouldered frame under the white sweat-stained shirt. A moment later he was crying without restraint. A few broken sounds came from his jerking mouth.

Through the thin partition wall came the noise of a renewed burst of guffawing.

Inspector Ghote bent forward and put his arm on the huge Swede's shoulders.

'Now, just sit here and tell me everything,' he said.

The Swede attempted to shake his head.

'Listen,' said Ghote. 'Ram Kamath can wait. You sit here, and, when you feel you can, tell me all about it.'

16

After some five minutes Axel Svensson began to recover. Inspector Ghote put no more questions to him. Instead he patted him from time to time on the back and murmured almost wordless expressions of comfort.

And then the big Swede lifted up his head a little and started talking.

'I didn't kill him,' he said. 'Perhaps that was the most terrible thing. As soon as I went round to the front of the car I could see he was still alive. And then I knew what I must do. Already I had passed that big hospital near Victoria Terminus. I was going that way to avoid the traffic. I thought it would be safer.'

With an effort he prevented himself collapsing into tears again and went on.

'So I had to pick him up and drive him quickly back there. I had to do it. I knew.'

He turned for the first time and looked directly at Inspector Ghote.

'My friend,' he said, 'at that moment I nearly ran. I nearly ran off from it all.'

'But you didn't,' Ghote said quietly.

'No,' said the big Swede, 'in the end I picked him up and drove to the hospital. And then a police inspector came and questioned me.'

Again the big Swede looked up at Ghote. He peered up into his face as if his life depended on it.

'You know what that man said to me?' he asked. 'He said

it would be best for me if the boy was dead. He kept asking the hospital authorities if he had died yet, and all the time he did not bother to conceal that it would be good news if he had.'

'Yes,' said Inspector Ghote. 'That is the customary thing. If the accident victim does not live, he is not there to claim that the driver was at fault.'

'But—'

'No, I know what you are thinking. And, believe me, you are right. A life is at stake. But all the same you must remember that if that boy recovers, even if he recovers thanks to your prompt aid, then all the same he or his parents will almost certainly make out that you deliberately drove him down.'

'That is what the inspector said,' Axel Svensson admitted. 'He told me not to agree to anything, and above all not to offer any money to the boy's parents.'

He clutched Ghote's thin arm.

'But they will need money,' he said. 'People as poor as that will need money at a time like this.'

'I will see if something can be done without giving some slick little lawyer the chance of saying you admitted guilt by trying to pay them off,' the inspector replied.

'But listen,' said the Swede, 'I have not told you the worst thing yet. It was this, my friend. That inspector hardly bothered to ask me how the accident happened. Because I was a car driver – what is it you call them? a burra sahib – he just assumed I was in the right and that that poor boy was in the wrong.'

He looked at Ghote as if he would gouge out of him some reassurance.

But Ghote shook his head.

'That is not exceptional,' he said. 'But you must listen to me. Just because he took that attitude, you are not to do the opposite. Do you understand? You are not to go looking for reasons to blame yourself. You were not to blame. Isn't that so? The boy ran out right under you, didn't he? You told me that first of all. Before you recovered. Now, tell me that again.'

The big Swede breathed in slowly, a long deep breath.

'Yes,' he said. 'Yes, you are right. I cannot in all truth blame myself.'

'That is good,' said the inspector. 'Now you will have the right basis to work on. So, let us just see how things are at the hospital, shall we?'

He picked up the telephone and asked the switchboard for the number. While he was waiting he watched the big Swede. Bit by bit he was pulling himself together, looking round about him, wiping the stale sweat off his face, making his shirt more comfortable.

Once through to the hospital it did not take the inspector long to find out about the boy. He had been operated on. The operation had been a success, but it was too early to say if it had been too much of a strain. He thanked the nurse he had spoken to, rang off, and relayed his information to Axel Svensson.

'Then there is hope,' the Swede said. 'But, my friend, I have just thought. What about you? What about your appointment with the Minister?'

'Well,' said Ghote, 'I'll go off to that now, if you are feeling a bit better.'

The big Swede looked at him with pleading bright blue eyes.

'May I come?' he said.

'Of course.'

Inspector Ghote let the thought of his appointment and its consequences come properly back into his consciousness. He looked hastily at his watch. Five to nine. It would be impossible to get to the Ministry in time, but he did not consider abandoning the idea.

'Come on then,' he shouted.

With the tall Swede thundering along behind him he raced out to the waiting car and yelled an order to the driver. They scrambled in and started off with the forbidden horn going full blast.

Traffic melted away in front of them. Every light was in their favour. Their driver equalled his efforts of the time before.

But it was well after nine when they arrived at the Ministry. Inspector Ghote bounded up the wide flight of shallow marble steps. The same chaprassi was on duty. He recognized Ghote at once.

'Inspector. Inspector sahib,' he called out.

Ghote stopped and looked at him, panting.

'Message from Minister's PA, Inspector sahib,' said the chaprassi. 'Minister regrets he has had to answer urgent summons. You are please to come again this afternoon. Four o'clock.'

In the bright heat halfway back down the Ministry's sweeping marble steps the inspector told Axel Svensson what had happened.

'So,' said the big Swede, 'you are free to work on the Perfect Murder?'

Inspector Ghote looked at him.

'Even you call it that,' he said.

A shiver of premonition.

'Well,' said the Swede, 'the newspapers, everything. You get into the way of it. But murder or no murder, what's your plan?'

'I have been thinking about it quite a lot,' Ghote said. 'You know the one thing we have really learned still is that the attack took place shortly after Dilip Varde had heard that his wife had not come to him as maiden. Two such terrific events in one evening. I am not happy that that is pure coincidence even yet.'

The Swede shrugged enormously broad shoulders.

'Well,' he said, 'you may be right. But I cannot see how the gentleman you have just failed to see could be connected with a humble Parsee secretary.'

'No,' said Ghote. 'I admit it doesn't seem likely. But all the same I think a word with Dilip Varde about it might open up unexpected possibilities. And there is the chance also that he believes Mr Perfect persuaded his father to bring him back from Delhi.'

'However, that is not a very serious reason for murder,' Axel Svensson observed as they got into the truck.

At the Varde house the constable on duty at the door told them that Dilip Varde had gone out. For a long time it looked as if no one in the family knew where he was. He had taken no luggage, nor was he at his father's office.

At last Inspector Ghote thought of the sweeper boy, Satyamurti, with his habit of hanging about near the front door. He routed him out, and was at once rewarded. The boy had heard the tika sahib say he was going to the club. Some more enquiries and the name of the club was elicited. The inspector and Axel Svensson set off again.

The club – all clubs – constituted unknown territory for the inspector. He was glad, on the whole, that Axel Svensson still seemed to need his company; although, on the other hand, he had doubts about whether he would successfully manage to conduct himself as a man of the world with the big Swede's unclouded blue eyes fixed on him all the time.

He braced himself for difficulties ahead.

In the high darkness of the entrance hall, where they were left to wait while a bearer of appropriate status was found to take them to Dilip Varde, he looked round with as casual an air as he could contrive. He was not going to gawp, he told himself, but neither was he going to stand strictly to attention looking at the mere section of space that came immediately in front of him.

Idly he stared at the ample, dark-varnished portrait of an elderly Englishman in the unbending frock coat of the early nineteenth century presiding over the entrances and exits of members and their visitors. No doubt he was the founder of the institution. It was plain that he had a reputation as a traveller and pioneer: his right hand was resting squarely and solidly on a revolving terrestrial globe.

Inspector Ghote looked him full in the face.

Then he felt that a general casual survey would be permissible. He let his glance travel slowly, idly round, taking in the marshalled rank of elephant-foot umbrella stands, the faded green baize letter-rack with its criss-cross of pink tapes, the equally faded green baize noticeboard beside it.

There was no sign yet of the bearer. Axel Svensson was standing sombrely regarding the floor at his feet. Inspector Ghote counted the umbrellas in the elephants' feet. There were a good many of them, brought in anticipation of the shortly expected rains of the monsoon.

He sighed.

Still no bearer.

He strolled over to the noticeboard and cast a careless look at its rigidly compartmented sections, *General Notices, Social Functions, Sporting, Stabling and Kennels.* At this last he felt it would not be overstepping the bounds to peruse the single piece of neat white paper pinned to it.

He leaned forward and read, 'Six lovely Baby Bunnies for Sale to Good Homes.'

'Sahib.'

He started as if he had been caught stealing one of the heavy unornamented brass ashtrays on the dark wooden table close by.

It was the bearer.

Soundlessly they were led away to find Dilip. They passed along wide high carpeted corridors with here and there an open door giving a quick sight of the secret life being enacted all round them. Each door bore its wooden notice with elegant gold letters describing the mystery behind.

Through the one marked 'Ballroom' the inspector caught a fleeting glimpse of a wide gleaming floor surrounded by little alcoves with faded pink curtains, of a chain of unilluminated multicolour lights swooping irregularly above them, and at the far end he saw a squadron of tables and chairs drawn up preparatory to brisk sessions of bridge fours.

A glance into the smoking room showed deep armchairs in sternly regimented huddles of three with little dark oak tables and spindly chromium pillar ashtrays attendant on them, and beneath tall windows another table, large and leather-topped, almost completely covered by rank on rank of tattered-looking newspapers and magazines.

A last look through into the billiard room revealed rows of quiet, dark green snooker tables underneath long tin light shades and, beyond them, a bar, its shelves glinting with silver trophies.

The bearer opened a pair of French windows and took them outside. Inspector Ghote gave a quick look to left and right. He saw a series of grass tennis courts on one of which two boys of about sixteen were playing an inept game of singles with frequent stops for shouted exchanges of mock insults and laughter. In a rose garden, its spiky bushes burnt almost to nothing by the months of sun preceding the monsoon, a handful of children were playing under the supervision of three mothers. Standing still as statues half a dozen bearers with vivid sashes and turbans of blue and silver were scattered about waiting for the later rush of activity. On the terrace a couple of waiters were languidly laying tables for lunch with starched white linen tablecloths and heavy silver cutlery.

Dilip Varde was sitting at the far end of the long veranda diligently reading a brightly covered mystery story. A glass stood on the wickerwork table beside him. At the sound of approaching steps he turned round as if irritated that his solitude was being disturbed. When he saw who it was he jumped to his feet with an angry gesture.

'What the devil are you fellows doing here?' he said. 'Isn't a chap to have a bit of peace even in his own club?'

'Good morning, Mr Varde,' Inspector Ghote said.

'Now it's no use coming the soft soap with me,' Dilip replied. 'I tell you I will not be interrupted here. If you wish to see me, then you must apply in the proper way.'

'Mr Varde, the last time we met you threatened to do your best to prevent me seeing you ever again,' the inspector said.

He did not raise his voice.

'Well, what if I did? You chaps have far too high a notion of your own importance. It's time you learned that there are matters which are no particular bloody concern of yours.'

'Like Ram Kamath and your wife, Mr Varde?'

Ghote said it quickly, before he had time to think better of it.

And the effect was dramatic.

Slowly Dilip Varde sank back into his upright wicker armchair. His hand went up to his mouth like an automaton's and he stroked his too bushy moustache as if he hoped for comfort and found none.

Inspector Ghote was quick to keep up the pressure.

'Now then, sir,' he said, 'we know that you were informed about that matter during the evening of the attack on Mr Perfect. Also, scarcely had you heard, than this crime takes place. Well, what is the connection, Mr Varde? What is the connection between the Minister for Police Affairs and your father's secretary? We think you can tell us that.'

As he spoke he had been watching the figure in the wicker chair with all the concentration of a snake watching its victim.

At one moment Dilip's right fist had tightened convulsively, and then fraction by fraction he had relaxed it.

Now he turned and looked up at the inspector and the tall Swede hovering behind him.

And he smiled. The white teeth flashing under the dark moustache.

'That's the trouble with you chaps,' he said easily. 'If you go poking your noses into things you just don't understand, well then, you must expect not to know what goes on.'

Inwardly Inspector Ghote cursed himself. He had gone on talking too long. Dilip had had time to regain the initiative.

'You see, my dear chap,' Dilip continued, 'there's simply no connection there. Absolutely none. How could there be? Between a scrubby Parsee clerk and the Minister who, incidentally, has complete control over hundreds of chappies like you, Inspector.'

The flash of insolent white teeth.

'Mr Varde.'

It was Axel Svensson's voice coming from behind the spare form of the inspector. Axel Svensson's choked, indignant voice.

'Mr Varde, I wish to state that it is absolutely contemptible to threaten the inspector in that way.'

Dilip looked up. Inspector Ghote turned round and looked too. The great tall Swede stood glaring down, a heavy hot flush spreading awkwardly across his high-boned cheeks.

'Look—' Ghote began.

But Dilip cut across him.

'My dear chap,' he said, 'no need to get worked up, you know. I'm afraid you don't still quite understand the situation in this country of ours nowadays. We just have to do things a bit differently.'

'Then you should not,' the big Swede replied with increasing heat. 'You should not trample upon so fine a police officer as Inspector Ghote. It is intolerable.'

'No, Mr Svensson—' the inspector said.

But the amount of contradiction Dilip could take was limited, and Axel Svensson had come to the end of his quota. Before the inspector could finish his remonstrance Dilip had leapt up and placed himself facing the tall Swede.

'Look here,' he said, 'you can't come along in this way and tell me what's right and what's wrong. Just you keep well out of affairs that are no business of yours.'

'But yes. They are my business. Justice is the business of every honest man. You are threatening the inspector in a most unjust way. And I am telling you that you will not get away with it. No, sir.'

Inspector Ghote slipped between the two antagonists.

'Mr Varde, please understand,' he said. 'Mr Svensson is not quite himself. He has had an unfortunate experience this morning. He ought perhaps to be in bed.'

'No, no, my friend,' Axel Svensson boomed. 'No, too long I have been silent when such things are said to you. But this time I declare myself. If any trouble happens to you, then I shall make such – such—'

He looked from side to side as if the English word he could not lay his tongue to might be hovering somewhere near the air.

At last he found it.

'I shall make such stinkings you never heard of.'

Dilip's face paled with anger.

For a moment he said nothing, and when he spoke it was with ominous quietness.

'Are you threatening me, old chap?' he said.

Inspector Ghote almost jumped in the air to get up to the big Swede's level.

'No,' he said. 'No, you must not do this, Mr Svensson – Axel sahib – Axel, my friend, you are to come home now. At once.'

The Swede shook his head from side to side as if to clear away obstructions.

'It is time to speak,' he said. 'Too often I have let things go by. But now it is the time to speak. There is such a thing as a justice which is the same for all men, the same in Sweden, the same in India. And if I see that justice being trampled in the mud, then I will fight for it. Without stopping I will fight.'

'No, you are wrong,' Ghote shouted.

He knew his voice had got out of control. He knew he was beginning not to behave as a police officer ought in such surroundings. He saw the sashed bearers stir from their immobile poses.

'No, you are wrong,' he shouted again. 'That is not the way life is. It is too much to expect. Let things be as they are. My friend, you are trying to do too much.'

The pleading note in his almost incoherent tirade got through at last to the tall-framed Swede. His blue eyes lost their piercing anger and clouded over.

And Dilip, strung tautly, looking at him, saw the change.

'Yes,' he said with a sneer in his voice, 'you are trying to do too much. Your little friend here is quite right. You'd better go and lie down somewhere till you've cooled off.'

It was all Axel Svensson needed.

'You dare to tell me to cool off,' he roared. 'You have not the right to tell anybody anything. You perverter of justice, you should be silenced. Silenced for ever.'

'Are you threatening me?' Dilip said.

He was no longer quiet.

'I am not threatening you: I am telling you. It's time you and your like learned a few home truths. You dare to try and get a man like Ghote here into trouble, just because he uncovers a few miserable details of your private life. He's worth ten of you, twenty of you. I have waited and waited to say this, and now I will tell you all of it.'

'Oh, no, you won't,' Dilip shouted back. 'You'll leave this club immediately, or I'll have you thrown out.'

He leaned forward, the muscles in his neck twanging and vibrating with rage.

'Throw me out. You. You cheater and liar and traducer of justice. I'll see you damn boiled first.'

'Bearer, bearer, bearer.'

Dilip's shouts were on the edge of hysteria.

The turbaned bearers had to take notice. They looked at each other.

'Bearer,' Dilip shouted again.

He could not be ignored.

The bearers started to approach. Cautiously, slowly, keeping an eye on each other, no one going any faster than anyone else.

Dilip set his head at an arrogant tilt.

An actor's tilt.

'Bearer,' he said, see this gentleman out. And if he doesn't go pretty quickly, boot him out.'

The bearers, in spite of their imposing turbans, were small men. They looked at Axel Svensson. The towering Swede looked round him like a monster bear.

'Sahib,' said one of the bearers in a voice little above a whisper, 'please to go, please.'

'I haven't finished with this gentleman yet,' Axel Svensson replied.

'Right,' said Dilip with a fine show of having done with the whole business, 'throw him out then.'

He turned and dropped his pose of calm to glare furiously at Svensson.

'By the seat of the pants,' he said.
The little bearers hesitated.
Dilip turned to them.
'Ek dum,' he snapped. 'Ek dum.'
Slitheringly the bearers advanced.

17

'Well, Dilip, this isn't doing any good, you know.'

It was the dryly precise voice of Gautam Athalye.

As if all the participants in the scene – Inspector Ghote, Axel Svensson, Dilip Varde, the timid little bearers – were puppets with connected strings they swung round together in the direction of the French windows where, with a faint wrinkle of disapproval on his forehead, Gautam Athalye stood.

Nobody spoke.

'Well, Dilip, aren't you going to say good morning?' Athalye asked. 'I am your father-in-law, you know.'

Dilip's mouth under his luxuriant moustache contracted with suppressed fury.

'Yes,' he said, 'I have got something to say to you. Dealer in second-hand goods.'

One of the bearers, full of relief at having been saved from throwing the huge Swede out, incautiously moved half a step the better to watch what looked like a new quarrel beginning right in front of him.

The movement caught Dilip's eye.

'I have something to say to you,' he repeated, looking ferociously at his father-in-law, 'but I shall say it in my own good time.'

He swung on his heel in a gesture of high drama and strode off through the rose gardens, past a little English countryside-style summerhouse, and out through a narrow gate at the far end of the grounds.

Gautam Athalye cleared his throat.

'I heard some sort of row going on and I thought I'd better look out,' he said.

He patted his thigh three or four times with the rolled-up newspaper he was carrying and turned to go back indoors.

'One moment, sahib,' Inspector Ghote called out.

Gautam Athalye pulled out the half-hunter watch from his waistcoat pocket. He glanced at it in the palm of his hand and slipped it back.

'Yes, Inspector?' he said.

'I am sorry to have to take up your time,' Inspector Ghote said. 'But I must remind you that I am engaged on a very important enquiry.'

Gautam Athalye looked at him shrewdly.

'Very well,' he said. 'I hope I know my duty.'

He looked up and down the length of the veranda. The bearers scuttled back to their places under his apparently mild gaze. He glanced at the little wickerwork table Dilip had deserted.

'I suggest we settle ourselves here,' he said. 'I doubt if we shall be disturbed.'

Inspector Ghote hastily caught hold of two more of the upright wicker armchairs and placed them at the table. They all sat down.

'I won't go through the formalities of inviting you to take refreshments, gentlemen,' Gautam Athalye said.

'No,' said the inspector. 'I will come straight to the point. Did you hear what it was I asked that made your son-in-law so angry?'

For a moment or two Gautam Athalye did not reply. Then, having had all the time he needed to think out his answer, he looked up.

'Yes,' he replied, 'I did hear. And I can tell you straight away that there's a lot of truth in what you surmise.'

Inspector Ghote felt a little flame of pleasure break out into light somewhere inside himself.

'A lot of truth?' he asked.

Gautam Athalye sighed.

'Rightly or wrongly,' he answered, 'I had insisted that Neena, my only child, should be brought up largely in the Western manner. Times have changed since I was young, and perhaps I wouldn't do the same thing again today. Hard to tell.'

He paused and appeared to be conducting some often repeated inner debate. After a little he shook his head impatiently and went on.

'Well, in any case,' he said, 'there's no going back on what's been done. And in consequence of my decision about the girl's upbringing, which I am bound to say was not wholly agreed to by my wife, she mixed in all sorts of society from a comparatively early age.'

His hand slipped into his pocket and came out holding a pipe. He put it in his mouth and sucked at it without lighting it.

'Well,' he said, 'the upshot of the whole business was that she took up with this fellow Ram Kamath, who I'm sorry to say is a bit of a bad hat.'

He took the pipe out of his mouth and laid it on the wickerwork table.

'There was a child,' he said.

Inspector Ghote looked under the table at his polished brown shoes.

'I hardly need tell you,' Gautam Athalye continued, 'that, in the event, the girl's chances of a decent marriage were pretty seriously impaired. No use blinking the fact. Though of course we did our best to hush matters up to some extent. And so I was rather surprised when quite shortly afterwards Arun Varde, whom I'd never had very much to do with, came and made me an offer on behalf of his son, Dilip. Of course, that was not at all the way I had intended matters to be carried on. I think arranged marriages are rather out of keeping with some aspects of modern India. However, in the circumstances it was undoubtedly the best thing to do. Mind you, Varde's terms for a dowry were pretty stiff: he knows a bargain when he sees one. But I had to put up with that.'

He coughed slightly, brought a box of matches out of his pocket and began to light his already half-full pipe.

'Of course,' he added, 'I had one or two conditions of my own to make. No use jumping at a thing without thinking of the consequences.'

He sat looking reflective. Inspector Ghote leaned forward.

'You said Mr Varde came to you. I take it that in actual fact he sent his secretary, Mr Perfect?' he asked.

'Certainly not,' Gautam Athalye said sharply. 'Wouldn't have done at all to send a secretary on an affair of that sort. Certainly not. Why should you assume he would do a thing like that, Inspector?'

He looked severely across the little table.

Inspector Ghote licked his lips.

'I was thinking of a connection between what you have just been speaking about and the attack on Mr Perfect,' he said.

Gautam Athalye shook his head with brisk authority.

'No, no,' he said. 'You're highly mistaken if you think that, Inspector. Highly mistaken.'

His eyes twinkled reticently.

'Some of you fellows have a wonderful capacity for putting two and two together and making five,' he said.

Inspector Ghote heaved himself to his feet.

'Thank you very much for your help, sir,' he said. 'I hope we haven't taken up too much of your time.'

'Duty to help the police,' Gautam Athalye said.

He stood up and shook hands first with the inspector and then with Axel Svensson. Until they had left the veranda he remained on his feet watching them.

Outside the club Axel Svensson turned to the inspector.

'My friend,' he said, 'I wish to apologize for my behaviour.'

'No, no,' said the inspector. 'There is nothing to apologize. You were much distressed because of what happened first thing today with the car, but it did not matter.'

'But yes,' said the big Swede. 'I made statements which were incorrect. I let my difficulties in understanding the problems of your country betray me into saying harsh things.'

'No,' Inspector Ghote said, 'you have not misunderstood the problems. When you said what you did about justice, and obstacles being put in its way, you were quite correct.'

The Swede shook his head from side to side.

'I just don't know,' he said. 'I just don't know.'

'But it is plain,' said the inspector. 'A police inquiry is a police inquiry. Nothing must be allowed to obstruct it. We are dealing with a serious crime.'

Axel Svensson still looked bewildered.

'You appear down in the mouth,' the inspector said. 'Come, get in the truck. I will see you to the Taj Hotel.'

The Swede allowed himself to be led to the police vehicle. Only when he was seated beside the inspector did he raise an objection.

'But look,' he said, 'I must go back on my own. You have got work to do. Where would you be going now if it wasn't for me?'

'I don't know,' the inspector answered.

A wave of discouragement washed back at him. He thought of Mr Perfect. Yes, he might have had a good night. But what did that mean after all? Simply that his condition had not got worse. It left him still at death's edge. At any instant still he could breathe that last faltering sigh of a breath. And where would all those hopeful feelings of the early morning be then? Where would his whole career, his life, be?

'I don't know where to go,' he repeated. 'The more questions I ask the less I find out. What real motive had anybody got to attack Mr Perfect at just that moment?'

'Well,' said the Swede, 'it strikes me that Dilip Varde takes too much trouble to make out that Mr Perfect is of no importance. It is a pity you didn't get around to questioning him about his feelings at being brought back from Delhi.'

'Yes,' said the inspector.

He sounded so despondent that the big Swede, troubled though he was, immediately began trying to put matters in a better light.

'I do not think, all the same,' he said, 'that this is sufficient reason for murder. And especially as Dilip would have been in no hurry. He could have made plans and then acted.'

'Yes, that is so,' the inspector agreed. 'The attack shows every sign of unpremeditation.'

The tall Swede sighed.

'We seem always to be going round and round,' he said.

The inspector sat in silence.

'Where to, Inspector sahib?' the driver asked at last with his customary impassive gravity.

'Taj Hotel,' said Ghote.

'But what about you?' Axel Svensson asked.

The inspector sighed.

'I think I will just go back to office,' he said. 'In any case it is not long now till my appointment with Ram Kamath.'

'Do you mind me not coming to that?' said the Swede.

Inspector Ghote braced himself up.

'Listen, you must take a sleeping pill and lie down,' he said. 'That is the important thing.'

The big Swede turned his high-boned, pallid and sweaty face towards the inspector.

'You've been very kind,' he said. 'Good luck with your Minister.'

As Inspector Ghote followed a peon along the wide corridors of the Ministry of Police Affairs and the Arts towards the office of the Minister he repeated these last words of his Swedish friend over and over to himself. A mantra to put him on the side of the good.

The pared-away Mr Jain, waiting in the outer office, looked at him with patent curiosity. The inspector waited for him to say something, but he contrived to receive him and to usher him through right into the Minister's office without actually speaking a word and with the minimum even of controlled gestures.

Inspector Ghote felt as if he was a smallpox carrier. He wondered whether he was reading too much into Mr Jain's attitude or whether it was simply the effect of nerves. After all, he had never so much as spoken to the Minister before. He had seen him only in smudgy photographs in the papers and for the one swift glimpse of their passing in the corridor on his first visit to the Ministry.

He marched forward to the big desk and saluted.

Ram Kamath, crouched over the shiny surface like a querulous human question mark, peered through a cheap pair of tin spectacles at the document he was reading and did not look up. Inspector Ghote waited, staring down at the Minister's grey-haired skull and thin scraggy neck. After a while he coughed.

Slowly Ram Kamath uncurled. He looked up at the inspector, his long neck emerging from his skeleton-thin body like that of a suspicious tortoise.

'Hm,' he said.

'Inspector Ghote, CID, reporting, Minister sahib,' Ghote said.

The Minister said nothing. After a while he pushed his chair back from the desk with two emaciated hands and rose to his feet. He looked extraordinarily tall as he stood for a moment hovering over the inspector from the other side of the desk.

The inspector had to tilt back his head till the muscles at the back ached so as to look up at the Minister with the respect he felt proper. At last the thin figure moved away, and Inspector Ghote quickly tipped his head forward to relieve the pain in his muscles.

Ram Kamath paced silently up and down the huge room. The inspector, watching him nervously, noted the threadbare white atchkan drawn tightly round his spikily bony body and the bare feet with long jutting horny toes.

At last, without turning to face the inspector, Ram Kamath spoke in a reedy, dry croak.

'You wonder why I take into account one rupee only?' he said.

Inspector Ghote licked his dry lips. It was a difficult question to answer.

But apparently no answer was required. Ram Kamath, still pacing up and down the rich carpet which covered his office floor, looking like a gaunt bat that had accidentally forced its way into human surroundings, croaked out another bare ration of words.

'One rupee is one hundred naye paise,' he said. 'Each one of those naye paise is a most useful little bronze coin. There are many things it will purchase.'

Inspector Ghote waited, his head cocked slightly to one side.

'That is the great mistake people make,' Ram Kamath croaked on. 'They neglect what can be bought with even the smallest sum of money. They use such coins quite heedlessly. They even give them away.'

Inspector Ghote knew he had to assume the expression of a man who is hearing about a temple being defiled.

Ram Kamath continued to pace on silent bare feet round and about the large area of his office. It was a considerable time before he spoke again.

'You see me,' he said at last, 'in this great office with every sign of utmost ostentation. You cannot help wondering, when you think of the lakhs of rupees that have been spent on it, how I can talk of naye paise.'

The inspector decided that it would be wrong to voice the wonder that had been attributed to him, or even to express it in a polite look of enquiry. He kept his face sedulously blank. But it was true that he had wondered.

'The answer is simplicity in itself,' said Ram Kamath after another pause. 'Such furnishings are paid for from State taxes, and that is perfectly right. A minister is entitled to a degree of state in his surroundings: he is not bound to provide it out of his own pocket.'

Ram Kamath stopped his pacing, turned, and darted a look of intense suspicion at Inspector Ghote out of his crooked pair of tin spectacles.

Inspector Ghote was ready for him.

'Of course not, Minister,' he said.

'Hm,' said Ram Kamath.

But he resumed his vulture pacing of the rich carpet.

'That is what I can never understand,' he said. 'That people are so ready to spend out. They buy everything, they are quite thoughtless, reckless.'

He swirled round and again peered at the inspector as if he would anatomize him.

'You have a wife, Mr Inspector?' he said.

The unexpected question nearly caught Inspector Ghote completely off balance. He just managed to gasp out an answer.

'Yes, Minister, a wife and child. A boy, Minister.'

He let himself have one swift, comforting mental glimpse of Protima and Ved.

'Yes, exactly,' Ram Kamath spat out at him. 'You get yourself a wife. You buy things for her. Saris, bangles, sweetmeats. And you beget a child, and feed it and clothe it.'

Inspector Ghote tried to anaesthetize his mind.

With a shorter pause than before Ram Kamath went on.

'You spend money, Mr Inspector,' he said. 'You spend out good money.'

For a moment the thought of Protima's importunate demands for the refrigerator came into Ghote's mind, but he thrust the vision loyally away.

'You know I am not married?' Ram Kamath said, walking away now into a far corner of the big room.

The inspector hoped no answer was required again. And was right.

'Why marry? Why be put to such expense?' the Minister for Police Affairs and the Arts rasped out. 'There is no need for it.'

He swung round and advanced on the inspector down the full length of the room. His gaunt face under the sparse grey hair was set hard.

'Well,' he shot out, 'am I a physically attractive man, Inspector?'

Inspector Ghote gulped.

There was no doubt that this time an answer was expected. There was not even much doubt what the answer was expected to be. But the bald truth, the bald 'No' seemed impossible.

'You have more important things to do, Minister, than to concern yourself with such things,' he said at last.

'So I am physically unattractive, repulsive even?'

The burning eyes in the hollowed sockets again demanded a reply.

'Yes, in a—'

'Exactly.'

Ram Kamath swung on his bare heel.

'I am totally unattractive physically,' he said with dried-up precision. 'And yet, Mr Inspector, I do not find it necessary to go without the solace you and your like find in marriage.'

Inspector Ghote decided with relief that the questioning was over for the time being.

'You are thinking that I buy women,' Ram Kamath stated.

Another long perambulation of the thick carpet.

'I do not find it necessary. If a person has sufficient determination, sufficient resolve not to spend, he will find it perfectly possible to obtain what he wants without paying out so much as one naye paise, not even one.'

Inspector Ghote was suddenly assailed by an irrational conviction that he would not be able to stop himself blurting out something about Neena Varde. The unsolicited explanation of how a man as gaunt and mean-spirited as Ram Kamath could be responsible for Neena's downfall, a problem which had been obscurely puzzling him ever since he had set foot in the office, seemed to come so pat that he had an overwhelming feeling that it was up to him to add his piece of confirmation.

He took a deep breath and forced himself to concentrate on the matter of the missing rupee. He went over in his mind everything he had learned about it, and at the end of it all he found himself back where he had begun. The ten one-rupee notes put into the drawer in the empty office, the door watched and no other means of entry, and at the end of an hour one of the ten notes missing. Full circles, except for one possible line. The line that had come into his mind as he had watched the fat halwa merchant teasing his boy so cruelly.

And here something still felt unaccounted for. He reached into the back of his mind. Prying finger tips just touching a tiny neglected nugget of information.

And suddenly he had it. It had been given to him when his attention had been concentrated on the Perfect case and he had contrived for that reason to ignore it.

'So, Mr Inspector,' said Ram Kamath abruptly to the great area of plain wall in front of him, 'so you have learned what you came for, and you may go.'

'No.'

Inspector Ghote felt sweat spring from every pore of his body.

'No, Minister sahib. I am sorry,' he said.

Ram Kamath stood stock still staring at the white wall.

Inspector Ghote squared his small shoulders.

'I regret there is a question I must ask if the matter is to be cleared up,' he said. 'There is an important discrepancy. Only five people in the whole of Bombay are supposed to know the exact details of the theft from this office. They are myself, my superior DSP Samant, Mr Svensson, the Unesco expert who has been assisting me, your peon, Sousa, and your personal assistant, Mr Jain. Yet a prominent businessman in the city has asked me why I am so busy about the theft of one rupee only. How can that person have learned that the theft was of one rupee?'

For almost a minute there was no sound in the big room except for the buzzing of three mosquitoes. Then Ram Kamath spoke, very quietly and without turning round.

'Perhaps one of the people who knew told this businessman,' he said.

'Very well, sir,' said Inspector Ghote. 'But which of them was it? It was certainly not me. It was certainly not Mr Svensson because I know he has not had any contact with this person except when I was there. It was not DSP Samant. He is not the person to talk of an affair like this to anybody at all, let alone to someone who is a civilian. It could not be your peon. He is behind bars. That leaves only Mr Jain. May I question him straight away?'

'No,' said the Minister.

Inspector Ghote waited.

And soon enough the Minister broke croakingly into speech again.

'You know it was not five people only who knew about the rupee, don't you, Mr Inspector?'

'Yes, Minister sahib.'

'I congratulate you, Mr Inspector. Yes, I am the sixth person who knew. And it was I who took that note from the drawer. Almost as soon as I had put it in. It was suggested to me that my police force would fail this test. You did not fail.'

'If logical methods are logically applied in accordance with accepted worldwide practice, you can rely on them obtaining results, Minister,' Inspector Ghote said.

Ram Kamath stood looking at the same blank expanse of wall. In silence.

Inspector Ghote wondered whether he ought to salute into the air in front of him and go.

But it seemed that he was expected to stay a little longer. The Minister added one more thing.

'So, Mr Inspector,' he said, 'you know one of my little secrets.'

Slowly he turned round and looked at the inspector through the lenses of his tin spectacles.

'Do you think that is a good thing, Mr Inspector?' he asked.

He strode across to the door, opened it and held it wide.

Inspector Ghote realized that this question would be answered only with the passage of time.

He saluted and marched out.

18

Inspector Ghote did not telephone next morning to find out whether during the night there had been any change in Mr Perfect's state. Instead he got to the Varde house early, and before doing anything else made his way up to the little room where the old Parsee lay. Try as he might he could not rid himself of the obsessive notion that his personal success and Mr Perfect's state were bound up with one another. It was not as if he had not told himself a hundred times that such an idea was unworthy of his whole outlook. Yet it was there. Always at the back of his mind like a smooth, dense, black stone embedded at the very bottom of a deep pool. Immovable, adamantive, primeval.

He found the room intolerably hot and stuffy. The monsoon was due and overdue, and over the city there hung a heavy grey mass of cloud, penning in the heat and making even the sea for those who bathed in it tepid, warm and unpleasant.

The heaviness and the steamy heat were obviously having their effect on the still unconscious secretary, although the nurse, the competent Anglo-Indian girl, had assured him the moment he entered that there had been no real deterioration. But none the less the old man's light breathing seemed even more tentative and wavering. His hand, when the inspector gently touched it with his finger tips, was dry and hot as a lizard's back.

The inspector glanced up at the useless little fan limping round above him on the ceiling. If the rain of the monsoon did not come soon, he could not believe that Mr Perfect would survive.

With thoughts blackening moment by moment he went down to the hall where Axel Svensson was waiting for him.

The big Swede was not looking cheerful, even though he had heard that morning that the boy victim of his car accident had had a good night in the hospital and was now expected to recover.

'How do you find this weather?' Ghote asked. 'If you are not used to it, it can be very unpleasant. Myself even I have a little prickly heat at the back of my neck.'

The Swede nodded seriously.

'Yes,' he said, 'there is certainly a problem there.'

The little erect old bearer, who had gone to find Neena Varde at their request, returned.

He salaamed.

'Not at home, sahib,' he said.

'What do you mean, "Not at home"?' Ghote said.

'Gone out, sahib. Don't know where, sahib.'

'But she can't have gone out. There's a constable on the door and he tells me she's in. And that means she is in.'

The little bearer bent forward as much as his erectness would let him, but made no other acknowledgement.

'Very well then,' said Inspector Ghote, 'I shall have to search the house.'

He spoke the words bravely enough, but with every syllable he felt the optimism which he had brought from his triumph over the matter of the missing rupee oozing away. What was the good of logic if, when according to simple deduction a person who had not left a house and should therefore be available for interview by a police officer in the course of duty, was simply announced as not being there?

The prickly heat at the back of his neck, which he had been able to cite with scientific disinterestedness in trying to cheer up Axel Svensson, suddenly began to itch and plague him in earnest.

He swung irritably round and marched over to the little room off the hall where Mr Perfect had been found lying unconscious.

'Well,' he shouted, 'is she in here?'

She was not. The calm disarray of the little room stared back at him just as it had done on the morning he had taken his painstaking inventory of its contents. The old newspapers, the old books, the keys, the torch, the umbrella, the punctured air cushion, the oil lamp and the tall brass candlestick. Even the golf club which he had sent to the fingerprint bureau had been returned, after its examination had proved negative, almost to the exact place where he had first seen it. With an added jet of bitterness he recalled that the forensic scientists had been downright scathing of the notion that its rounded steel head could possibly have effected the curious long wound on the back of Mr Perfect's skull.

He stormed out and angrily began a systematic search of the rest of the house. For more than an hour he tramped round the insane juxtaposition of rooms piled one on top of the other, added to, subtracted from, multiplied indiscriminately. He rummaged through the dark caverns of the servants' quarters, he forced his way into curious little cellars that had been left for year upon year to the rats. He stared glumly into each of the eight marble bathrooms. He opened cupboards, chests, almirahs, wardrobes. He shouted and he swore.

The pre-monsoon heat was by this hour at its heaviest. The back of the inspector's neck felt like emery paper, sweat poured from him at every pore, his clothes stuck to his body and every time he moved tore away with a shimmer of pain. His mouth was parched dry and his throat ached. Inside the house it was not as glaring as it might have been, but the air was so utterly without freshness that breathing was a penance: outside in the compound, where the earth of the flowerbeds was cracked and hard as concrete, the air was a slight degree fresher, but the glare from the flat grey sky was so oppressive that even sunglasses seemed powerless to alleviate it.

If I suffer like this, thought the inspector, what about that poor old man upstairs? If the rain doesn't come by this evening, he will die. Murdered by the heat and by a person unknown. Never to be known. The Perfect Murderer.

At last the whole house had been searched with one exception. The inspector had sent frequent messages to the women's quarter but he had put off time and again making an actual visit there himself. On each occasion the women servants he had sent scurrying off to ask if Neena Varde was there had come back and had promised and sworn that she was not.

But nowhere else but the women's quarter remained.

Inspector Ghote looked round and spotted another of the women servants flitting towards the inexorably shut door.

'You. You there,' he called.

The girl hesitated and then began an undignified scutter towards the protection of the door.

But the inspector was too quick for her. He ran sharply forward and stood in front of the tall carved wooden door barring the way. A new wave of sweat sprang up on his body after this brief exertion and the prickly heat stung and smarted.

'What's your name?' he said to the girl.

He felt too tired and too sullenly angry to be anything other than bluntly direct.

'Chaya,' the girl said in a voice little above a whisper.

She looked down at her neat brown toes and gave a gentle wriggle of embarrassment.

'Very well, Chaya,' Inspector Ghote said, 'now listen to me. You are to go into the women's quarter and you are to say that in one minute I, Inspector Ghote, CID, am coming in after you. Do you understand that?'

The girl lifted up her face so that her eyes just rested on Inspector Ghote's for an instant.

He decided that it was acknowledgment enough.

He stepped aside from the tall wooden door and in a flash the girl had opened it a few inches and had slipped through.

The inspector stood outside waiting for the minute's grace he had given to go by. He wondered whether Chaya would have enough courage to speak up with his ultimatum.

The minute came to its end.

Inspector Ghote looked at the door. There was something definitely formidable about it.

He turned to Axel Svensson who had been following him with dog-like fidelity all through his search.

'I think it perhaps would be better if you did not come,' he said.

'Quite so,' said Axel Svensson. 'There is the problem of embarrassment. I perfectly understand.'

Inspector Ghote turned to the door again.

He jerked back his shoulders.

He turned the handle, pushed the door wide open and marched forward.

It was plain at once that the shy Chaya he had spoken to was a very different person on this side of the tall carved door. She had succeeded in a matter of seconds in rousing the whole garrison. They stood there in front of him shoulder to shoulder, all the various women servants, their saris pulled up over most of their faces and, at the head of the whole array, scorning the protection of so much as an inch of sari, was Lakshmi Varde.

But Neena was nowhere to be seen.

Inspector Ghote attempted to restrain himself from licking his upper lip.

'Good morning, Mrs Varde madam,' he said.

'Well, Inspector,' she replied, 'I see you have come into our private place.'

She looked like a stone goddess. Inspector Ghote invoked, with something like passionate devotion, the counter-forces of lucid rationalism.

'Yes,' he said with outward briskness, 'unfortunately the officer in charge of a serious case sometimes has to go to the most inner places.'

He looked steadily at the formidable figure in front of him.

'And sometimes it becomes necessary to ask most intimate questions,' he added.

A little to his surprise his firmness of tone won an instant victory. Lakshmi Varde said nothing. But she turned slowly round and looked at her supporters with such imperious coldness that no words were needed.

In a moment's soft swishing of saris, faint tinkling of bangles and rapid padding of bare or slippered feet the inspector and Lakshmi were facing each other alone.

'So, Inspector,' Lakshmi said, 'you had question to ask in private?'

Inspector Ghote fervently wished that the enormous blond shadow of Axel Svensson was standing behind him.

'Mrs Varde,' he said, 'I have already questioned all the people who were in this house at the time of the attack on Mr Perfect. None of them had alibi. Some of them had possible reasons for wishing to harm the victim. None of them had reason for carrying out the attack at the precise time it occurred. It showed no signs of what we call premeditation: yet who would suddenly wish to kill that old man?'

He saw Lakshmi Varde's grey eyebrows beginning to knit together impatiently at his long recital.

'But one fact of importance has however come to light,' he went on a little hurriedly. 'It has come to my attention that just before the attack your son Dilip had learned for the first time about the relations between his wife and a certain important figure.'

'I am knowing nothing of this, Inspector,' Lakshmi said.

But she spoke too quickly, she came in too suddenly.

Inspector Ghote needed only to register a look of disbelief.

'All right,' Lakshmi said, 'let me say this. I had been told nothing by my husband. The marriage arrangement was not in my hands.'

'Of course,' said the inspector. 'The negotiations, I take it, were conducted by your husband assisted by Mr Perfect.'

'Certainly no.'

Lakshmi Varde's eyes blazed with stern anger.

'I think you are not understanding,' she said. 'Although my

husband made arrangement himself, he would not take anybody from office into his mind for this. And also at that time Mr Perfect was not secretary but clerk only.'

Inspector Ghote decided that this dismissal of Mr Perfect was not put out simply for his own benefit. There had been something too habitual and unforced about it for him to have any doubts.

'So now we come to the question of Mrs Neena Varde,' he said.

'Of my daughter-in-law?'

Lakshmi looked at him haughtily. Too haughtily to be true.

'Yes,' he said, 'I sent message that I wished to see her. Where is she, please?'

'I do not know.'

The statement was plainly meant to put him off. Stonily he persisted.

'She has not left the house,' he said. 'The doors are watched. She is not to be found elsewhere in the house. I have searched myself. So she must be here.'

'Already I have said. I am not knowing where she is.'

'Then I must ask to search the women's quarter,' Inspector Ghote said.

Lakshmi Varde's eyes widened with anger. The sides of her mouth pulled sharply down.

But after a moment she gestured permission without speaking.

Inspector Ghote made a quick tour of the rooms, one leading into another. There were few places where Neena could be hiding. The inspector opened the three wardrobes he saw, looked at the string beds and lifted the lids of the few trunks he came across. But he found nothing. And he would not let himself be so illogical as to look behind the many pictures of gods and photographs of deceased relatives on the walls or under the grass mats on the floor.

He did go so far as to prod a huge heap of piled saris in cotton, in silk, in georgette, in chiffon, red, blue, green, orange, pink, yellow, purple, lavender and turquoise, with here and there a glimpse of an embroidered gold or silver border and the sparkle of sewn-on sequins. But his hand plunged down unobstructed to the carved top of the flat wooden chest beneath.

As the inspector entered each room the women servants scuttled out of it ahead of him. And a pace or two behind him Lakshmi Varde followed, silently regarding his progress.

A thin chill wind of disapproval.

Even in the sweltering heat the inspector felt it.

He completed his tour.

'Well, Inspector,' Lakshmi said, 'you have seen all.'

'Yes,' he said, 'I have.'

'Then you would leave us in peace now?'

'But first,' the inspector said, 'I must ask your daughter-in-law the questions she has run away to stop me putting to her.'

'Understand, Inspector, please,' Lakshmi replied, 'I do not perhaps agree with Neena keeping from you. I do not think such thing is necessary. But if she is wishing, it is her affair. If you want to question, you must find her first.'

'Certainly,' said Inspector Ghote. 'I will go and get her.'

19

'You know where is Neena?' said Lakshmi Varde. 'I am promising—'

Inspector Ghote raised his hand to stop her.

'Please,' he said, 'do not tell me that she is not here.'

He turned and walked back through the interconnecting rooms of the women's quarter.

For once defeated absolutely, Lakshmi let him go. Without hesitation he went back to the room where on the low carved chest the rainbow heap of saris lay piled. He swept them off on to the floor with a single gesture, stooped and lifted the richly decorated lid of the chest. And inside, crouching curled like a frightened rodent, was Neena Varde.

'It would be best if you stood up,' said the inspector.

Neena struggled out of the confined chest and got to her feet.

'I don't see why I shouldn't lie in there if I want to,' she said.

She glared defiantly at the inspector.

'Now,' he said sharply, 'I want to know what is the connection between Mr Perfect and your previous relations with Ram Kamath?'

Behind him he heard Lakshmi shoo away the servants. He paid no attention. Nothing was going to make him relax his scrutiny of every flicker of expression on Neena's face.

And emotion was certainly being shown there. A conflict of emotion, difficult to assess.

The inspector looked on, implacable as a camera.

Suddenly the conflict was resolved.

Neena burst into wild, broken trills of ringing laughter.

'My poor man,' she spluttered out at last, 'how on earth could you think that the two things had anything to do with each other? It's just ridiculous. That silly old stick of a Mr Perfect having anything to do with my private affairs.'

She was laughing so much she had to sit back on the lid of the rosewood chest.

'If it wasn't so funny,' she said, 'I'd be furious. What do you mean, you nasty policeman, poking your nose into my business?'

Inspector Ghote clung on to dignified silence.

Neena still went on laughing, though by now she had calmed down to the level of occasional bursts of giggles.

'Oh,' she said after one of these, 'if I had known you were so stupid I wouldn't have run away from you for one moment.'

'Then perhaps you would have answered my questions,' the inspector snapped.

'What questions? What other silly nonsense have you got into your head?'

'Where were you when you were pretending to be lying in your room at the time of the Perfect Murder?' the inspector shouted suddenly.

'The Perfect Murder.'

Neena exploded into laughter once more.

'How can you be so silly?' she said at last. 'That dreadful old Parsee is still lying up there as alive as can be. What a murder.'

Inspector Ghote felt a flush of irrational relief at the reminder, however humiliatingly put, that Mr Perfect was after all still alive, still just alive.

But the relief did not last long. Within instants it was swept away by a new anxiety coupled with fury at having been betrayed into thinking once again of the attack on the old Parsee as the Perfect Murder.

He stepped nearer the still-laughing Neena.

'Be quiet,' he hissed. 'Be quiet. Do you want the whole house to hear what is being said?'

Neena wiped the tears from her eyes. A streak of wet mascara was left smeared across the top of her cheek.

'Do you think I care who listens?' she said. 'Do you think I care? If you've got anything to say, say it out loud here and now.'

She looked at the inspector with contemptuous defiance.

And he stared back vacantly.

In his mind her last words echoed and re-echoed. And quite suddenly he realized where he had heard them before and who it was who had said them. And what it was they were linked with.

He turned and ran out of the room. He ran without stopping to glance at Lakshmi and the women servants hovering within earshot of the tumbled saris and the low rosewood chest. He flung open the tall carved door of the women's quarter.

Axel Svensson standing anxiously waiting outside was startled half out of his wits.

'What . . . What's happened?' he stammered. 'Have you . . . Have you insulted them?'

'Come on, this way,' the inspector shouted.

He ran forward. The tall Swede turned and hurried after him.

'What is it?' he called.

'The weapon,' Inspector Ghote shouted back. 'The weapon. It's been there all along in front of my eyes and I never saw it.'

He tore open the door of the little cluttered room where Mr Perfect had been found lying.

He half expected that the place would have been inexplicably swept clear in the short time since he had begun his search of the house there. But to his immense relief it still retained completely its air of an undisturbed museum of domestic trivia. The Moghul painting and the brass business plate, the four empty matchboxes and the broken electric torch, the piles of old newspapers and the ranks of unread books, the Benares lamp and the Birmingham candlestick.

Inspector Ghote darted forward and peered hard at this last item.

'Yes,' he called out, 'yes. Come and look at this. I was on the point of realizing about it when Lala Varde told me, "If you have got anything to say, say it out loud here and now." Only when I heard those same words again a moment ago did I recall. Look.'

He pointed an excitedly trembling finger at the brass candlestick.

Axel Svensson stepped nearer and peered hard at its base.

'But I see nothing,' he said.

'No,' said Inspector Ghote, 'not at the bottom. Look at the top. Just in that crack there.'

The Swede looked.

'But yes,' he said. 'A tiny piece of dried blood, definitely. The attacker must have failed to wipe it off in his hurry. But why should it be at this end of the candlestick? It ought to be on the base. If you use a candlestick like this as a weapon, you grasp it by the top, where the blood trace is now, and bring the heavy base down on your enemy's head.'

'That would be the logical thing,' Inspector Ghote agreed. 'But this time the attacker did not do the logical thing. He used the candlestick the wrong way up. Luckily for him in a way: if he had turned it round Mr Perfect would have been dead the moment he was hit.'

He pulled his handkerchief, clammy and sweat-stained, out of his pocket and used it to lift the candlestick down by two of its edges.

'Come on,' he said. 'Twenty minutes at the fingerprint bureau and this case will be solved. There is nothing like a little science.'

Holding the tall ugly brass candlestick well clear of his body he marched out of the house and down to his waiting vehicle.

The leatherette seat of the truck was burning hot after its wait in the oppressive heat. The inspector's skin pricked like fire as he sat holding the precious candlestick. Although the motion of the vehicle stirred to some extent the hot, leaden air, the extra heat from the engine in front of them entirely outweighed any benefit they might have felt.

The traffic was at its worst. Tempers were high and minor

accidents frequent all round, so that new, and even more irritating, jams developed every few minutes. Above the jangling turmoil the sky was like a closely hanging tent of greyish discoloured silk. The roads, the pavements, the buildings, even the people, all gave off a sullen shimmering glare which, sunglasses or no sunglasses, seemed to strike to the very centre of the brain.

The short trip felt interminable.

But at last they arrived. Sore, sweat-soaked and headachy, Inspector Ghote bore his booty into the offices of the fingerprint bureau in triumph.

He was a little disconcerted to find no inspector on duty. Sergeant Scroop, an Anglo-Indian, a small, bustling, bright-eyed man, was there together with another sergeant Ghote had never met.

'Who's in charge today?' he asked.

The second sergeant slid from his tall stool at the workbench and hesitantly advanced.

'Inspector's on leave,' he said. 'Deputy is sick. We're all that's left. You haven't got a job for us, have you?'

He sounded as if it was a prospect he did not much look forward to.

'Are you busy then?' Inspector Ghote asked.

'We could handle a job if we have to, Inspector. It isn't because we've got a lot on.'

'Don't be a fool, Desai, man,' Sergeant Scroop said. 'Do you want to get us a bad name in Mr Svensson's report to Unesco?'

'You've got prints for the principals in my case in your records?' Inspector Ghote asked. 'You should have. I had them taken and sent in.'

'We've got 'em all right,' said Sergeant Scroop. 'Somewhere.'

Inspector Ghote placed the candlestick on the workbench.

'Please examine the base only for prints,' he said. 'We think the weapon was used the wrong way round. You can see what looks like blood here in that crack near the top. Please be careful. We shall have to take it to the forensic scientists later.'

'Those boys,' said Sergeant Scroop. 'They're no good at all, man.'

Sergeant Desai nodded gravely.

'I can tell you one thing, Inspector,' he said, 'those chaps are absolutely incomparable.'

'Incomparable, incomparable,' Sergeant Scroop said. 'Here, tell us, Desai man, what that word means.'

Sergeant Desai shifted from foot to foot.

'Everybody knows that,' he said. 'Incompetent. That's a word everybody knows.'

'You,' said Sergeant Scroop, 'you'd mix up your best girl and your sister, you would.'

The inspector's eyes grew cold.

'Sergeant,' he said, 'I do not like to use my rank, but I tell you if you don't get a move on I will do so without hesitation.'

Sergeant Scroop swung away to face the workbench.

'They're all the same,' he muttered.

But nevertheless he set to work on the tall candlestick, though with maddening lackadaisicalness.

Above them the old-fashioned electric punkah with which the laboratory was furnished slowly groaned and creaked. It hardly seemed to stir the heavy air. Outside the lowering grey clouds had made it so dark that without the light over the workbench it would have been impossible to see.

Ghote could feel the thunder tension tingling on the surface of his skin, made doubly sensitive by its patches of prickly heat. The monsoon was already late. He wondered how much longer it would be delayed. Certainly by the feel of things it ought to come soon, but always at this time of year it felt as if the air could not go on one moment longer getting hotter and heavier. And often it did go on. On and on until nerves cracked. On much too long for someone as near to death as Mr Perfect.

He allowed himself to look at Sergeant Scroop. Some slight progress had been made.

'It looks as though it's coming on nicely,' he said.

And no sooner were the words out than he regretted them. Sergeant Scroop needed no loopholes to make himself a nuisance. He bounced round on his stool.

'Coming on nicely, is it?' he said. 'I suppose you think you know all about it, eh, Inspector? Just because you've got the rank, I suppose you think the knowledge comes to you from the sky?'

He jumped down and went across to Sergeant Desai.

'Hey, boy,' he said, 'tell the inspector just how long our course is before they think we're fit to so much as puff an insufflator. Tell him that.'

Sergeant Desai came and leaned on the workbench.

' "Insulator", that's another of those difficult words,' he said. 'I tell you all through that course I called it "insulator".'

He laughed lugubriously.

'Imagine that,' he said, 'calling it "insulator" instead of "insul—" '

He stopped and looked puzzled.

Sergeant Scroop swung leisurely round to him.

'Insufflator, man,' he said. 'Insufflator. That's the word you want. Not "insulator" but "insufflator".'

He looked up at the towering form of Axel Svensson.

'Honest,' he said, 'some of these damned Indians, they're so stupid you could laugh.'

Inspector Ghote longed and longed to reach out, grab the powder brush and rapidly deal with the candlestick. He clenched his fists hard. More sweat oozed out of his body. He thought he had sweated every drop he had.

Sergeant Scroop fished a half-smoked De Luxe Tenor out of his pocket, stuck it in his mouth, searched for a match, found one, lit it and held the flame to the end of the cigarette. He puffed a cloud of rank smoke out into the room. It swirled sluggishly under the punkah and stung the inside of the inspector's nose.

He bit his lower lip and kept silent.

At length Scroop got off his stool and went over to a cupboard, hissing a popular film tune from between his teeth. He found the

Varde family fingerprint record cards more quickly than Inspector Ghote dared hope. He remounted his stool, pulled the lamp lower and took up a magnifying glass. Slowly and elaborately he polished it.

Then at last he crouched down on the tall stool and began peering at the base of the candlestick.

After a few seconds he gave a long, low whistle.

'What is it?' said the inspector.

He held his breath.

Sergeant Scroop said nothing. Instead he leaned forward and looked at the scatter of fingerprint cards lying on the bench beside him.

'You got something?' Sergeant Desai asked.

'Yes,' said Sergeant Scroop, 'I've got something – a pain in the neck.'

They all stood round him waiting.

He puffed another cloud of sharp-smelling cigarette smoke out.

'Wait a bit,' he said, 'it could be—'

Without the least flicker of warning the lights went out and the electric punkah above them clacked to a slow halt.

'Another bloody power cut,' said Sergeant Scroop cheerfully into the dark.

'What had you found?' said the inspector.

He was unable to keep the impatience out of his voice.

'I found some prints,' Sergeant Scroop answered.

'But whose? Whose? Don't you realize the whole answer to the case depends on that?'

'Can't say, man.'

'You can't say? What do you mean?'

'What I tell you. I can't say whose prints I found till I can finish checking them against the cards.'

Inspector Ghote drew in a long breath in the darkness.

'But they might be those on one of the cards you're looking at?' he asked.

'Might be. Just depends on how soon I can start checking point by point. Got to get sixteen points agreeing before it counts as proof, you know, man.'

They waited in the dark. The minutes passed by. It grew even hotter and closer.

The inspector felt that at any moment he would tilt over in the enfolding darkness and flop to the floor in a daze of heat exhaustion.

He stopped himself swaying.

And if I feel like this, he thought, what about Mr Perfect? That little room up there in Lala Varde's house is every bit as small as this. The window is only a tiny slit, as useless for getting in air as the stupid little window here.

He knew what would happen. This delay would be fatal. While they waited in this damned unnecessary darkness the murderer would learn that the candlestick had been whipped off to the fingerprint bureau and would get away.

He twisted his sweat-mired hands together in an agony of impatience.

At this moment, he thought, at this very moment Mr Perfect is dying. He cannot go on any longer. An old man, in his condition, he could not live in this annihilating heaviness and heat. Now. At this instant the Perfect Murder had finally been comm—

As abruptly as the lights had gone out they came on again. The punkah groaned horribly and began working once more, though not as fast as before.

Sergeant Scroop took another puff at his evil-smelling cigarette.

'Please, Sergeant, go on,' said Axel Svensson.

He sounded as choked with fury as the inspector felt.

The sergeant got to work again. And within less than a minute he straightened his back and looked up at the ceiling.

'Yes,' he said, 'just what I told you: as clear a set as you could want. I brought 'em up a treat.'

20

'Whose? Whose? Whose?'

Inspector Ghote felt his careful layers of self-restraint whipping away under the double assault of the sweltering airless heat and Sergeant Scroop's maddening evasiveness.

'Whose are the prints on that candlestick?' he shouted.

Sergeant Scroop tucked his feet under his tall stool.

'Please, Inspector,' he said, 'if you'll only give me a minute to tell you.'

Ghote grabbed at the last shreds of his patience and clung silently and grimly on to them.

And at last Sergeant Scroop obliged with the reply.

'Mr Prem Varde,' he said. 'No doubt about it. They check on sixteen points at least. A clear set of the right hand. All alone on an unsmudged surface, only set there is. A lovely job I made of it.'

He turned and reached for the tall brass candlestick. Inspector Ghote leaped forward and intercepted him.

'Do not touch,' he said. 'It will be most needed as evidence, and especially when the forensic scientists show that the blood in that crack is that of the deceased.'

'My friend, we hope it won't come to that,' Axel Svensson said.

His words checked the inspector.

Yes, Mr Perfect might still be alive, must still be alive in spite of everything.

'You are right,' he said to the Swede. 'Mr Perfect is not

dead yet. But now we must go. Perhaps young Prem has decided to make escape.'

'Well, there is no reason for that,' the big Swede said. 'After all, he should not know we have found the weapon.'

But an uneasy look had come into his clear blue eyes, and he hurried along after the inspector down to the vehicle, hotter now than ever under the waves of heavy glare which had assaulted it all the time they had been in the laboratory.

In spite of the snarls of traffic they made surprisingly good time to the Varde house. From a sharp enquiry to the constable on duty outside they learned that Prem was at home. But this reassurance did not prevent the inspector snapping angrily at the little erect bearer who answered the door when he showed some slight hesitation about telling them where the boy was. And, even when the man remembered that he had seen him quietly reading in his own room not long before, the inspector took the wide stairs at a run and burst in without warning or apology.

Prem, dressed in an orange bush-shirt with a blue design on it, was sitting on the floor in front of a large picture or diagram that occupied most of one wall of the room. He seemed to be lost in ecstatic contemplation.

Sure at last of his quarry, Inspector Ghote allowed himself to pause and decide on the best approach. He looked at the diagram Prem was sitting in front of. It showed the relations between all the arts of the world in a series of little square boxes linked together by long black lines. No doubt it was Prem's masterpiece. It was a pity he would have to leave it.

Inspector Ghote stood to attention.

'Mr Prem Varde,' he said, 'I must inform you that the weapon used in the Perfect Murder has been discovered.'

Prem looked at him. An alert look, interested and acute.

'I think you know what that weapon was,' Inspector Ghote said.

'Yes, yes,' said Prem.

He seemed almost eager. His eyes shone.

'It was a candlestick,' he said.

'Exactly,' snapped the inspector. 'A brass candlestick of European manufacturing. And I must beg to inform you that the fingerprints of your right hand, and no others, were found on it.'

Prem's mouth opened wide.

'I know what you are thinking,' he said.

He glanced from side to side. A trapped animal.

The inspector coughed.

'I must ask you to accompany,' he said.

The window of Prem's room was one of those looking out on to the street. It was set high in the wall and covered with its American steel grille. Nevertheless he gave it a look of wild longing.

Inspector Ghote knew that there was no time to waste.

Like a tiger he sprang across the room and caught Prem's left arm in a locked grip.

'Now then,' he said, 'CID headquarters for you.'

He marched Prem swiftly out of the room ahead of him and down the wide flights of marble stairs. Behind them the big Swede, his white clothes crumpled and sweat-stained from the oppressiveness of the heat, followed like a perturbed ghost.

If I can just get him into the vehicle without any fuss, Inspector Ghote thought over and over again to himself.

His shoes, each a heavy penance in the enervating swelter, banged smartly on the stairs as they descended.

And then out of the corner of his eye he glimpsed Arun Varde himself hurrying along towards the entrance hall. In a flash he foresaw the hours of noisy protests and wild explanations that would occur the moment Lala Varde realized that his younger son was being taken into custody.

Savagely he pushed the boy down the stairs ahead of him at something approaching a run.

'Inspector?'

Lala Varde had seen him.

'Oh, ho, Mr Inspector detector. Hoi.'

Pretend he hadn't heard. That's the only way. Leave explanations for afterwards. Hurry. Hurry. Hurry.

'Hoi, Mr Inspector. A moment only.'

In the hall now. Only a few yards ahead, the big front door of the house. And beyond it the vehicle. Police territory.

'Hoi, Inspector, what's the hurry purry. Listen, I have got a good joke to tell you. A joke about the policias.'

Perhaps it would be better not to arouse the old man's suspicions by ignoring him when he was almost on top of them.

He turned.

'A little later, sahib,' he said.

A sop flung out behind.

'But, Inspector detector, it is a good joke.'

Inspector Ghote felt the old man's pudgy hand close on his elbow with unyielding insistence.

He turned round again.

The two little pig-eyes in the broad expanse of fat face gleamed.

Lala Varde put both hands on the inspector's arms.

'Such a good joke. Listen,' he said.

'No, I can't. I am—'

'Run, Prem, run. Run off from the dirty policias.'

The old man's bellowed order worked like a galvanizing shock on his son. In a moment the boy had slipped from the inspector's hold, had flung open the wide front door, was tearing down the steps to the street.

The inspector felt the two pudgy hands clamp like crab-claws on to his elbows.

With a ducking lunge he broke free.

'Stop him, stop him,' he yelled to the truck driver as helter-skelter he rushed down the steps after Prem.

The driver, hands folded across his pot-belly, took no notice. Inspector Ghote fixed his eyes on Prem's flying back and ran. Behind him, he heard with a flicker of relief the pounding steps of the big Swede.

In a few moments the Swede had caught up with him, and then he began drawing ahead, closing the gap between them and Prem. His long white-trousered legs reaching out over the ground.

With less than three yards to go, just as they reached the end of the street, a big shiny bus came by. It was not going fast because of a tangle of traffic ahead. Prem stretched out and caught hold of the rail by the door. He swung himself forward, and managed to get first a foot and then his whole body aboard.

Axel Svensson pounded after him.

A coolie with a big basket of building rubble on his head walked blindly into the Swede's path. Leaving them in a welter of legs and with the squeals of the unsuspecting coolie ringing through the air, Ghote hared on after the bus. But the traffic had untangled, and the bus driver seeing a chance to make up time put his foot down. The bus shot away. Inspector Ghote was left, winded till he thought he was going to be sick, bent almost double, watching the brightly painted shiny back of the bus vanishing into the crowded street.

He felt hot, dry tears in his eyes.

And then behind him came a voice. Axel Svensson's.

'Quick, my friend. Look, another bus.'

Sure enough, as is the way with public transport, a second bus of the same number was hot on the heels of the first. But it was not as yet going as fast. Inspector Ghote gathered himself together and darted forward. He caught hold of the rail. For a moment he thought it was going to slip out of his sweaty hand. But then he managed to grip it and haul himself up. He felt the big Swede's body come up behind his and glimpsed the huge pinkish hand with the covering of golden hairs wrapped round the rail above his head. He pushed his way further on board.

The bus was packed tight with passengers but Ghote managed to push and wriggle his way through them to a place where he could both see the bus ahead and be ready to jump off if he spotted Prem getting out.

He leaned at his lookout post thankful that for a few minutes at least he did not have to move any more. The heat was if anything heavier and more oppressive. It brought out every smell in the bus – people, diesel fumes, hot metal, spiced breath, rubber slowly cracking and perishing – and mixed them up and inflated them till they seemed to make such an assault on the nerves that screaming point could not be far off.

To the inspector's savage joy his bus was gradually catching up on the one in front. It was even possible that it would overtake it in some traffic jam and he could surprise Prem by getting off ahead of him and halting the escape bus.

At Kemp's Corner the traffic lights turned red just as the inspector's bus reached them. The driver came to a sharp and obedient halt. Inspector Ghote cursed him.

A moment later he felt Axel Svensson tapping him on the shoulder. The big Swede was too far away from him to be able to talk effectively but he had managed to reach his long arm out to attract attention. Now he turned and pointed back. The inspector looked in the direction indicated. A policeman was standing looking at the traffic, waiting to pounce on any offender.

Inspector Ghote swung himself half off the bus and shouted at the man.

If he could get a message to headquarters it would be a simple enough matter to arrange to intercept Prem.

The policeman peering intently at the waiting cars, taxis, buses, bicycles took no notice. The inspector shouted again. The constable was not far away, but he was so totally lost in his waiting game with some potential offender against the traffic laws that he might have been out on Elephanta Island in the bay beyond the city for all the help he was.

The bus jerked forward as the lights changed. Inspector Ghote looked ahead. Prem's bus had gained a considerable advantage.

But once more they slowly caught up. As Prem was on the leading bus there were longer delays for him at each stop as passengers pushed and fought to get aboard. Yard by yard the gap was reduced.

And then at Crawford Market the inspector saw Prem leap from the bus ahead and plunge into the shelter of the great iron-roofed edifice. He signalled to Axel Svensson to warn him. Their bus made reasonable progress and, less than a minute after Prem had got off, the inspector and the big Swede in turn entered the comparative cool of the great market.

Inspector Ghote looked up and down the long alleys of high-piled stalls on the great flagstones of the fruit section where Prem had entered. At first he could make out nothing but a jumble of soft-coloured fruits and the medley of sauntering buyers of every sort and kind strolling up and down choosing their purchases. And then a different sort of movement at the far end of one of the alleys caught his eye. It was the running figure of Prem Varde.

Hardly pausing to gesture to Svensson to follow, the inspector set off in pursuit, weaving his way through the leisurely shoppers, dodging and ducking. Past massive piles of bananas, yellow, pinkish, red, long and thick, short and stubby, past heaps of oranges, past mounds of grapes, past pyramids of luscious mangoes, past papayas and pineapples.

And then Prem suddenly chose to look back. The inspector skidded to a halt and crouched down by a stall replete with glossy figs, but the towering form of Axel Svensson could not be blotted out as easily. Prem must have spotted him at once because he dodged abruptly to one side and began running down a cross-alley with redoubled speed.

The inspector and Svensson set off in pursuit again. They were just in time to glimpse the boy leave the market for the bustle of Carmac Road again, and, with a new burst of speed, saw that he had plunged straight across the road and was making his way into the jumble of narrow streets and tortuous byways on the far side.

Straining and panting they followed. Luckily, Prem became involved almost straight away in a fracas with a couple of acrobats entertaining a small crowd in the middle of the alleyway he had chosen to plunge into. Just at the climax of their act the boy had burst through the surrounding onlookers and had tipped over the more delicately poised of the two entertainers. The other promptly seized him, held him close to his naked chest and subjected him to an intensive stream of incestuous abuse.

The inspector and the Swede were able to get well within sight before Prem gave a desperate wriggle, slipped from the acrobat's grasp, wheeled abruptly and flung himself into a small bazaar just off the narrow byway.

They tore after him.

The heat and the smells and the noise were utterly overpowering. Stallkeepers called and yelled, buyers jabbered and objected, each point of purchase was an explosion of shouting, expostulation and argument. Ancient gramophones wailed and clicked, brand-new radios pumped out speech and music in half a dozen different modes. Beggars, their painted sores treacle-dabbed to attract the flies, implored and commanded. Children fought and screamed, chickens running hither and thither squawked and screeched.

A score of opposing odours struggled for dominance. Cooking pots poured out the smells of richly luscious spices, little fires of dried cow dung added their acrid tang, other fires of wood strove to outdo them. Copra and drying fish sought to go yet one better than either. The very dust, puffing and eddying at the tramp of pair after pair of feet, shod and unshod, had its own penetrating aroma.

In the dense confusion of insane movement and wild hues it was no longer possible, as it had been in the staider aisles of the Crawford market, to pick out a running figure. Clash and colour assailed and blinded the eyes. Cloths of every bright shade imaginable swayed and dangled, brass and copper gleamed and glinted, bright balloons swung to and fro on their tugged strings, great chunks of raw and bloody meat hung glaring and motionless, hawkers with little barrows of multicolour towels or children's bright red slacks darted out into every eddy of the crowd, coloured and gilded pictures of gods and saints jostled each other for prominence, high-piled bottles of garish liquids tempted and repulsed.

And Prem was not to be seen.

Desperately the inspector plunged into the crowd, trying to progress on tiptoe so that he could crane over shoulders jerking and heaving ahead of him to catch a glimpse of his quarry. Unable to look where he was going, he failed to duck one of the dozens of burning tarry ropes hanging from the roofs of stalls for the convenience of passing smokers. Its red-hot tip drew a stinging line across his cheek. Tears came into his eyes. He halted for an instant to brush them away, and spotted Prem.

On the far side of a stall laden with a myriad of tiny bottles of scent the boy was creeping back in the direction he had come. Ghote darted looks on either side to see if there was a passageway between the scent stall and its neighbours. But both sides were immovably blocked by tall piles of packing cases.

He looked at Prem again. The boy was making good progress towards the street.

Taking a deep, hot, stinking breath the inspector dropped to his knees and pushed his way under the loaded trestle of scent bottles.

In front of him the astonished proprietor gave a loud scream, seized his hanging placard lauding the aphrodisiac qualities of his wares, and brought it down with a splintering crack on the inspector's skull just as he emerged from under the trestle.

Ghote, his head jabbing and darting with pain, staggered to his feet. And, with a noise like a high-pitched landslide, the hundreds of little bottles on the trestle cascaded to the ground and shattered into fragments. Their scents, their erotic stimulus guaranteed by the power of their aromas, sent up a great waft of smells so rich and sweet they brought tears to the eyes.

Inspector Ghote, careless of everything, flung himself out of the debris and pounded after Prem.

The boy had halted for a moment, distracted by the enormous noise of the crash and the immediately following explosion of every conceivable sort of sensuous odour – rose, Jasmine, Queen of the Night, khas, sandalwood, lilac. So Ghote was able to get to within four or five feet of him before, suddenly seeing his danger, he leaped forward again.

The inspector hurled himself grimly after him.

But he was dizzy from the blow with the scent placard and bit by bit Prem began pulling away from him. He risked a glance back. His faithful Axel Svensson was embroiled in a fearful argument with the scent stall man and was lost to him. Black despair coiled up and gripped at his heart.

And then Prem put his foot on a discarded strip of mango peel in the dirt and dust of the ground and fell headlong.

With a final painful effort Inspector Ghote dived forward, arms outstretched. A sense of dull joy came over him as he felt his hands close firmly on Prem's young flesh at last. He gripped and held.

21

For perhaps two minutes Inspector Ghote and Prem lay on the dirt-strewn ground of the bazaar without moving. Prem had tried once to wriggle out of the inspector's grasp, but when he had found that this was quite impossible had given up. He must have been almost as exhausted and out of breath as Ghote, and was quite content to lie inert and wait for what was to happen next.

At last the inspector was conscious of someone kneeling beside him. He looked up.

It was Axel Svensson.

'Are you all right, my friend?' the Swede said.

'Yes, I think so,' said Ghote.

'I have given some money to the man at the scent stall,' Svensson said. 'Rather a lot. I hope it was all right?'

'Yes. Yes, thank you,' said the inspector.

He let his head flop back on to the foul ground.

The Swede waited patiently. But at last he could be silent no longer.

'My friend,' he said, 'do you think you could stand now?'

'I suppose so,' said Ghote.

Still keeping a dug-in hold on Prem, he allowed the tall Swede to help them both up.

Then he faced the boy.

'Why did you do it?' he said. 'Was it just because you thought Mr Perfect was the one behind your father wanting you to go into office?'

Prem's frightened eyes took on a puzzled look.

'Mr Perfect was against office,' he said. 'He thought I would do harm if I went in.'

The inspector looked at him.

The quivering lower lip, the wide puzzled eyes, the bright blue and orange bush-shirt dirty and torn.

'But why then? Why?' he asked.

Prem looked even more bewildered.

'I went into the room by the house door,' he said slowly. 'I looked all round. I saw the candlestick.'

He stopped.

'And then,' said the inspector, 'you took it up and hit Mr Perfect. I know. But why?'

'No, no, no.'

Prem's head shook in violent disagreement.

'That wasn't on the night of the Perfect Murder,' he said. 'Then I was in my room as I told you. This was the next day only. I just held the candlestick because I thought this must be the murder weapon.'

Inspector Ghote turned and looked at the tall Swede. It was plain that, even through the wild jabber of the bazaar, he had heard what Prem had said.

'This would account for the fact that there was only one set of prints on the candlestick,' the inspector said. 'That had been worrying me a little. If the candlestick was the murder weapon, it ought to have had more than one set of prints and some smeared.'

'Quite so,' said the big Swede.

He sighed.

'So the problem remains,' he said. 'We are back where we started.'

Sitting later in his office, Inspector Ghote could hardly bear even to look across at the tall, bony form of Axel Svensson.

He sat at his familiar desk with his chin cupped in his hands. He had not bothered to switch the light on and the little office was so gloomy under the pall of heavy clouds that pressed down on the sweating city that the inspector could scarcely make out the familiar shape of the old blue volume of Gross's *Criminal Investigation* adapted from the German by John Adam, MA, sometime Crown Prosecutor, Madras, and J. Collyer Adam, sometime Public Prosecutor, Madras.

He felt that this was perhaps a good thing. In the full glare of the light overhead the book would have seemed to reproach him with his failure.

Or, he hardly dared formulate the thought, would he have to reproach Doctor Gross? After all, the case had been conducted strictly on the methods laid down . . .

Ghote groaned.

He knew he ought not to be just sitting like this, but he felt too depressed even to think of the possible steps he could take to get a fresh angle.

The air around him seemed thick as a heavy liquid. He lacked the vital force to fight his way through it. Outside everything was unnaturally still and tense, waiting for the sudden breaking relief that would come with the rain of the monsoon. Rolls of quickening thunder seemed to be the only sound able to penetrate the weight of the atmosphere.

But it could not be long now till the tension would break. Moving his dry tongue in his dry mouth, the inspector could taste the rain waiting to come like the tang of the brass of that cursed candlestick.

The thought of the candlestick with its shiny surface wiped clean of all clues to the identity of the person who had wielded it, almost as if they had stuck their tongue out at him and his doomed efforts, sent his mind back to Mr Perfect with the inevitability of a drug addict returning unresisting to his habit.

Once again he imagined the old Parsee lying on his sagging charpoi with the well-paid, indifferent nurse sitting in the room but scarcely giving him a glance. He saw the battered drained face under its heavy cap of gleaming white bandages and, spreading down from under the chin on which a grey stubble had slowly appeared, the less-than-white atchkan and its still untouched little pink stain of ballpoint ink.

How could those feeble breaths fight their way through the thin dried lips in this terrible heaviness all around them? How could the debilitated body resist the tension and the pressure of the hot airlessness under the great, grey, grumbling clouds above? How could Mr Perfect go on living, unless the rain came?

And the inspector knew, with iron-pressed certainty, that for all the taste of rain on his dry tongue, it might not come before nightfall. It might not even come for all the next long, tense, intolerable day. The experience of the past told its lesson. There had been other years when the monsoon had hovered and waited like this; the same thing could happen this time.

And if it did, it would kill Mr Perfect as surely as if at this moment he himself was putting his hands round the old man's scrawny neck and choking the flicker of life out of him. And then: black failure. The mark always pursuing him. Nothing to set against the weight of prejudice and distrust he had willy-nilly accumulated in the past few days. No progress, no reward for patient toil rigorously applied. Perhaps demotion, financial hardship, an embittered family life.

Inspector Ghote groaned blackly.

Opposite him the big Swede shifted restlessly but said nothing.

The silence grew and grew.

And then through the open window there came a stirring. A faint, premonitory shifting breeze. Watched and waited for so intently that its eventual arrival had seemed an impossibility, the rain really was coming at last.

Inspector Ghote pushed back his chair.

'This is it,' he said.

'It?'

'The monsoon. The rain. It's coming. At any—'

Like a sudden mad tattoo the first big drops of rain thudded down, explaining more vividly than any words what it was the inspector had meant. Within seconds the rain was falling in great swaths and sheets, plunging down with hysterical abandon as if it meant to penetrate to the depths of the parched earth that had been yearning for it.

Ghote leaped up.

'Come on,' he shouted. 'Come on, let's go out and see it.'

'Out? In this? But—'

Axel Svensson allowed himself to be swept out of the little office, whirled along the corridor and swished through the impressive portals of the headquarters out into the joyous rain-soaked street. Ahead of him the inspector looked up and let the rich, cooling, quenching rain pour down on to him. With a stare of bemused wonder the stiff Swede bit by bit allowed himself in his turn to surrender to the warm, sweet embrace of the tumbling water. All around them the great drops thundered on roof and pavement. The gutters gurgled and sang. The closed-in earth and the brittle foliage of the plants and trees breathed again in a sudden waft of released fragrance.

'Come on,' Inspector Ghote shouted again.

The hulking Swede, his bony face alive now with laughter, looked at him.

'Where to, for heaven's sake?' he said.

'To the Varde house, of course,' the inspector shouted. 'Let's go and solve this Perfect Murder.'

'But how? But why? But what has happened?' the bewildered Swede shouted back through the din of the rain.

'I'll tell you what has happened,' Ghote yelled. 'The monsoon has come.'

Their truck was standing where they had left it but their pot-bellied stolidity of a driver was nowhere in sight.

'Never mind, jump in,' Ghote shouted.

The big Swede sprawled in, and they were off.

At Lala Varde's they leaped out and, wading through the deep puddles that had already formed in the street, they clambered into the house. It stood empty and echoing to the drumming of the rain.

'Where is everybody? What has happened?' said Axel Svensson.

'The roof, the roof,' the inspector replied. 'When the monsoon starts everybody is liable to go out on the roof.'

He led the way up the stairs.

Sure enough when they emerged on to the flat black roof of the house the whole household was standing spread about in groups letting the water pour over them and stream away down the hungry waterpipes.

A little apart from the others, arms held high above his immense torso, was Lala Arun Varde.

He caught sight of the inspector as he came out onto the roof.

'Oh ho, policias,' he bellowed. 'I hear you have let go my son. Ho, ho, you have not solved the Perfect Murder yet.'

They went over to him.

'Is it the Perfect Murder?' shouted Inspector Ghote. 'Nobody ever dies when the monsoon comes. Don't say Mr Perfect is murdered now.'

'No, no,' Lala Varde yelled back. 'No, when the rain came at once the dry old stick looked better. He will live, Inspector detector, he will live and Lala Arun Varde will prosper.'

He shook the sheeting rain out of his eyes, and stuck out his fat pink tongue to gulp it up.

'Yes,' he bellowed on, 'the old stick will grow leaves in the rain. He will grow leaves and flourish. And that other old stick of a Ram Kamath, he too will grow leaves and he will agree to put his police college on the land I already bought. Now the monsoon has come even he will lose his caution and all his talking palking about wait and see what happens over the Perfect Murder.'

A wild idea began to grow, like the rain-restored plants, in the inspector's brain.

'Ram Kamath,' he bawled into Lala Varde's ear. 'You were doing a secret deal with Ram Kamath on the night of the murder?'

'Yes, yes, of course. Old Ram Kamath came to my house. What a night to choose, eh? What shaming naming. What trouble bubble.'

The inspector looked at him through the spearing, shimmering rain.

'But what about Gautam Athalye?' he shouted. 'Didn't he make you promise you would have nothing to do with Ram Kamath if his Neena became your son's wife? He told me he made conditions. Wasn't that one?'

Lala Varde blinked the rain away.

'You are cunning fox,' he said. 'You have guessed.'

He shook his head.

'But never mind, who cares?' he shouted. 'Who cares for dry old Gautam?'

He slapped time and again at his great rain-sodden sides with a noise resembling a volley of cannon fire.

The thoughts swam in the inspector's head like the debris twisting and whirling in the roaring runnels of the house. And the last piece fell into place.

Of course Ram Kamath's presence in the house had to be kept secret, especially from Gautam Athalye.

Of course the servants had to be locked out of the way.

Of course Athalye had to be made to stay where Lala Varde knew where he was and then had to be bundled into a taxi at the critical moment.

Of course Mr Perfect had to visit Ram Kamath to arrange the preliminaries and had to wear an atchkan instead of a baggy old cotton jacket and trousers. Only so would he be inconspicuous in the evening at the Minister's house.

Of course Lala Varde had wanted to put Dilip in the picture when his wife was involved.

Of course Mr Perfect would disagree and be so obsessed by his fears that they had broken through his unconsciousness into vague mutterings.

Of course Dilip, with his over-developed sense of the importance of the family, would be horrified to learn about Neena and Ram Kamath.

Of course, stupid as he was, he had burst out with the news to Prem and leaving him, still in a fury, he had seen the dim figure waiting by the front door.

Of course it had really been Mr Perfect, there to let Ram Kamath out.

Of course the two men were physically alike as two sticks – tall, thin, grey-haired, wearing tin spectacles.

Of course Dilip knew Mr Perfect only slightly.

Of course he had mistaken him for Ram Kamath, had seized the candlestick so hastily that he had got it the wrong way round, and had struck down the person he thought had ruined his honour.

And, of course, who but Dilip, the reader of mystery stories, would think in all the haste of wiping off fingerprints?

Inspector Ghote shook his head to clear the last doubts. The plummy raindrops flew all around.

But there could be no real doubts. The Perfect Murder had in fact been all a mistake, a simple mistake in the dark. He should have expected as much in this land of imperfections: to be confronted with a very imperfect murder, with a victim who was not meant to have been a victim at all and an attack that had, naturally, been bungled. He might have known it would be like this all along, a triumph of the incompetent.

Yet had he himself been so wonderfully competent? Hadn't all his cherished efficiency led only to a mad chase after the wrong person? Hadn't he in the end cleared up the mystery in a rush of wild, pointless enthusiasm brought on by the coming of the rain? There was nothing in Gross about the use of monsoon joy to solve murders.

And, now that he knew the answer, was he any better off? Mr Perfect would almost certainly live, but his own prospects looked worse than ever. If he hauled Dilip off as he had taken Prem, Lala Varde would be outraged to the point of taking every action, legal and illegal, that entered his fertile head. Things would not be pleasant, not pleasant at all.

He looked round about him. Dilip was standing conveniently in a corner by himself, looking moody. An arrest would present no problems.

No practical problems.

Axel Svensson leaned his big, blond head towards him.

'What is wrong, my friend?' he said. 'Suddenly you look most unhappy.'

'I have solved the Perfect Murder,' Inspector Ghote said. The big Swede's eyes broke into delighted wonder.

'But that is good,' he shouted.

'Is it?' said the inspector. 'I am going to arrest Dilip and he is the apple of his father's eye.'

He turned and looked at the great figure of Lala Arun Varde. The rain was beating and cascading over him, a wide smile of utter bliss was on his face, his powerful shoulders were spread to receive the blessing of the water, his pig-determined eyes were glinting now with purest pleasure.

He would not be like that for long.

Inspector Ghote shook his head sadly.

'It's all a great muddle,' he said. 'But perhaps after all muddle is the only possible thing.'

Inspector Ghote's Good Crusade

1

Inspector Ganesh Ghote came quickly down the wide, well-lit steps of Bombay CID headquarters. Quickly, but not too quickly. His business was urgent enough. It could hardly be more urgent. But he wanted time to think about it, to hold it in his mind and just a bit to gloat.

So he made himself pause on the bottom step and, before going over to the blue Dodge truck waiting with its engine throbbing, he dug his hand into his pocket, took out his loose change, selected with care the smallest coin and placed it in the ever-ready hand of the broken-legged beggar whose privilege it was even at this hour to occupy this post.

The beggar, without in the least altering his note of monotonous entreaty, darted his dirt-encrusted claw deep into the recesses of the seamy rag round his waist and then turned his head from side to side once more to assess the prospects around him.

Inspector Ghote crossed the broad pavement and clambered into the waiting truck.

'Go to the Masters Foundation, Wodehouse Road,' he said to the driver, a new and anxious-looking young constable he had not seen before.

'Very good, Inspector sahib.'

The young man let in his clutch with a joyous roar. He had been scared stiff at the possibility that he would be ordered to an address he did not know. But this was easy. Everyone had heard of the Frank Masters Foundation for the Care of Juvenile Vagrants. There had been no need for the inspector to say Wodehouse Road. He knew where it was all right.

He swung the Dodge roaringly towards a coolie crossing the wide road with a great bundle of firewood on his head. The man scuttled to safety in a satisfying scamper of long, bare legs under the light of the tall, craning street-lamps.

'Watch out, you fool,' Ghote said almost automatically.

He had hardly noticed what had happened. His thoughts were miles away. Seeing a succession of newspaper photographs of a young, serious-looking American, shaking ministers by the hand, peering down intently at foundation stones, purposefully snipping lengths of ribbon with large pairs of scissors. Frank Masters, the philanthropist. A long, thin-cheeked face with a jutting American jaw and heavy, dark-rimmed spectacles on either side of a long, enquiring nose.

Now dead.

Murdered, if what Deputy Superintendent Naik had told him turned out to be the true state of affairs. Symptoms of arsenic poisoning, the report had said.

Inspector Ghote bit the inside of his lower lip in momentary vexation. He wished he had had time to make a thorough check on arsenic and its effects. He remembered little enough of the single detective-school lecture devoted to poisons, various. And even his trusted Gross's *Criminal Investigation*, snatched up from its place of honour on top of his private filing cabinet, had for once let him down. Not a single index reference.

He frowned.

In the ordinary way it would hardly have mattered. If among the dozens of First Information Reports coming into the office on any one day there had been a suspected case of arsenic poisoning in any ordinary home, he would have been quite happy to let the local uniformed inspector keep an eye on things while he took a quiet half-hour or so to freshen up his store of knowledge. And then he would have descended on the scene and straight away snapped out those few questions that mark out the CID man.

But this was no ordinary home he was hurrying towards through the night streets. This was the Masters Foundation. And the victim of the arsenic was Frank Masters, the American millionaire every citizen of Bombay delighted to honour.

The case was going to attract a great deal of attention. The papers would be full of it. There might well be questions in the State Assembly. 'To ask the Minister for Police Affairs what steps are being taken in the case of . . .' 'One of the Department's most able inspectors is in charge and I can confidently . . .'

Ghote checked himself. He must not think such thoughts. The case would be far from easy. Days might pass with nothing to report, and the affair was the sort of thing that would be talked about at the Centre. The American Ambassador expressing anxiety. All Delhi buzzing with talk of loans being held up. The telephone lines down to Bombay hot with urgent enquiries. And every one of them coming back to him.

'Inspector Ghote, may I ask exactly what progress . . .?'

'Inspector Ghote, the Minister has requested . . .'

'Inspector Ghote, I give you just twenty-four hours . . .'

A sweat broke out on his forehead.

It was a warm night. The clear, brilliant weather of winter had ended with its accustomed abruptness more than a week before and now the sluggish day-heat persisted well into the hours of darkness.

The inspector pulled out a handkerchief and patted at his face.

As the truck was halted for a moment by a tangle of late traffic jockeying its way round the huge, dark, domed block of the Prince of Wales Musuem, he forced himself to think rationally about the case. Frank Masters. That was the starting point. What exactly did he know about him? What ought he to know?

He was a millionaire. Or was he? Certainly that was the impression left after reading in the papers about his innumerable benefactions all over the city. But was it exactly true? Was he still a millionaire? What was wanted now were the exact facts.

Well, the Masters Foundation was a fact. It was the crown of Frank Masters's charitable activities. The Frank Masters Foundation for the Care of Juvenile Vagrants.

Its founder could hardly have chosen a more pressing problem.

Ghote looked out into the garishly lighted streets. Sure enough, his glance fell at once on a pack of half a dozen boys, the eldest no more than ten, roaming up and down, clustering round any passer-by with arms held out for money, voices clamouring, eyes darting up and down looking for trouble.

And there were hundreds of them. Some homeless altogether, others who had run away or been chased out. All beggars, almost all petty thieves, many ready to turn to any other form of crime that came to hand.

Frank Masters had taken up a formidable challenge. But then he was the sort of person to do that, or so it seemed. A man determined to do good. Ready to spend all his millions, and himself, in doing it.

And now he was dead. Killed by arsenic poisoning. How had it happened? DSP Naik had had few facts to tell. Just that someone from the Masters Foundation had telephoned and had insisted on speaking to the most senior officer available. They had then reported that Frank Masters was dead, and the word 'arsenic' had been mentioned. That was all.

The DSP had summoned him almost at once. He had taken his orders. He had gone back to his office and rung down for a truck, had paused for just that moment to glance at the familiar, comforting, blue, mildew-stained volume of Gross and then had hurried out for the short trip through the still busy night streets.

Had hurried, but had not rushed. This was a case of such importance that he had felt entitled to savour a little the fact that he had been picked to handle it.

'You wanna know who killed him, mister?'

Ghote jumped in his seat.

He almost answered 'Yes.'

The challenge so exactly matched his very thoughts at the moment the Dodge had pulled up outside the tall front door of the Foundation building.

He looked in fury at the face thrust in at the truck's open window.

Only to be utterly disconcerted. The head at the window was the head of a twelve-year-old boy: the face was the face of a man of sixty.

The startling effect was due, he realized a moment later, to the spread of some sort of infection which had crinkled the skin of the boy's face into a thousand etched and tortuous lines. They gave him a look of extraordinary knowingness.

He was dressed in a ripped and tattered jacket of black plastic hanging open over a bare chest. Ghote could smell the sharp tang of his unwashed body.

'Get down, be off, get away,' he shouted.

He pushed hard at the truck door and the boy leaped lightly off the running board and stood dancing on the balls of his feet in the driveway. At the end of an indefinite blur of light coming from above the tall front door of the big, sprawling bungalow, two or three other shapes of children of about the same age loomed indistinctly up.

'Be off, the lot of you,' Ghote said sharply. 'What are you doing here? This is private house.'

The crinkle-faced boy in the tatterdemalion jacket bounced half a step nearer. His eyes were shining with bright malice.

'Live here, mister,' he said. 'This our private house. You come to visit, eh?'

Immediately Ghote realized who the boys must be. They were obviously some of the vagrants the Foundation catered for. A spurt of anger shot up in his mind at the thought that he had nearly let himself be caught out by that silly remark the boy in the jacket had shouted. He controlled himself sharply before he spoke again.

'You live here, do you?' he said to the wrinkle-faced urchin. 'And I suppose you are allowed to go prowling about at such an hour of the night?'

The boy grinned cheerfully back.

'Mister, if they had one half idea there'd be plenty trouble,' he said in a fantastic parody of an American accent.

'Then you had better get back to your beds before I am telling,' Ghote said.

The boy sidled swiftly up to him.

'You don't want to know who bumped off Masters sahib?' he asked.

And Ghote hesitated.

Such impudence ought to be dealt with by a quick cuff. Yet the boy knew already that Frank Masters had been murdered. And that was something which had only come through to the Police Department in the last quarter of an hour. It might well be worth getting hold of a possible witness like this before any interested parties found out what he knew and imposed their own views.

He leaned forward and looked hard at the boy dancing in the dim light from the window above the door.

'How are you knowing Mr Masters is dead?' he said.

The boy spat on the gravel of the driveway within inches of Ghote's well-polished brown shoes.

'We got ways of knowing things,' he said. 'We ain't gonna last very long if we don't know what goes on.'

Into the words he contrived to inject another slaughterously powerful dose of American accent.

Ghote decided that his claim was quite likely to be true. An urchin of this sort did indeed need to know everything that was going on in order to survive. There was nothing like gutter life for sharpening the wits.

Though there ought to be.

'All right,' Ghote said. 'You have been looking where you had no business. This time I would not take any action. But you must tell me what you saw. Everything.'

The boy grinned at him more widely than ever.

'Oh, mister,' he said. 'If we had been doing bad, maybe is better we are not saying anything.'

Ghote took a furious step towards him.

But the boy hopped back out of range. All the inspector could see now in the darkness beyond the light was the white of grinning teeth.

He stood still for a moment and worked things out. He could always call up some assistance, and perhaps with some difficulty catch this slippery customer. But that would reduce the boy to total silence. He could always simply turn away and ring at the bell beside the tall front door.

And yet . . .

After all, the boy at least knew that Frank Masters had been poisoned. A little advance information about the circumstances would make up for knowing so few facts about Masters himself and about the effects of arsenic poisoning. The trouble was worth taking.

He dug his hand into his pocket and pulled out a shining nickel twenty-five naye paise bit. He held it up between the tips of his fingers so that it caught the light.

As he had expected, in the pale area lit by the fanlight under the front porch the black-jacketed boy swiftly appeared.

'Now,' Ghote said, 'let us talk business. You told you knew why Masters sahib had been murdered. You say, and this is yours.'

'Oh, mister, mister.'

The wrinkled face shook sadly from side to side.

'Oh, mister. You don't think I would be telling for money?'

The boy stepped right up to Ghote and looked at him with an expression of total seriousness.

'Listen, mister,' he said, 'you know what Masters sahib done for us? You know what life we lived before he come along with his pick-up truck and bring us here? You know what is like being pavement sleeper in monsoon time? Oh, mister, if we tell who kill him, is not for money. Oh, never, no.'

Slowly Ghote let his hand fall to his side, still holding the despised coin.

'All right,' he said quietly, 'you just tell me everything you know.'

'Mister, it was all those women. All those gay girls.'

And in an instant the boy had snatched the coin from Ghote's limp hand and had danced back into the half-light.

'What women? What gay girls?' Ghote shouted.

He advanced a step and then thought better of it. Without help he would never catch a boy who so obviously knew his way about the garden, doubly dark under the shade of faintly seen trees, just as well as he knew his way round the crowded city streets in broad daylight.

'All right,' he said in a loud voice, 'I should have known better.'

He swung on his heel on the loose gravel of the drive and marched up to the front door.

His manoeuvre proved completely successful. Before he had even begun to put out his hand to the bell button the black-jacketed, crinkle-faced boy was standing beside him.

'Listen,' he said, a lop-sided grin sending the wrinkles twisting in a new direction, 'listen, Masters sahib is millionaire. Isn't it?'

Without turning from the door Ghote replied.

'All right, he is millionaire.'

'Then he must have gay girls. It stands to reason, isn't it?'

'That is all you have to tell?'

Ghote rang at the bell. Loud and long.

'No, sir. No, sir. That was just story. You wanna hear truth? Whole bag o' tricks? This time I tell. Honest, I tell.'

Ghote did not answer.

The boy was obviously an incurable liar. Not a word he said could be relied on. There was absolutely no point in . . . And yet. And yet he had known about Frank Masters being dead. And this time he had promised to tell the whole story.

Ghote turned and walked down the steps to the driveway again.

He waited in silence. One by one the whole gang came up. At last Ghote judged it the moment to speak.

'Listen to me, all of you,' he said. 'If any of you knows anything at all about the death of Mr Masters, it is your duty to tell. Your duty.'

He got a startling enough answer.

2

Out of the half-circle gathered in the patch of light from the house door one of the boys stepped suddenly forward. Without a word, he jumped high into the air, flung up his legs with a quick, strong jerk of his naked torso and stood in front of Inspector Ghote upside down.

It was a good comment on his exhortation to them to tell what they knew about Frank Masters. Perfectly clear, and dramatically expressed.

Do our duty? In our world this duty of yours looks pretty different.

And Ghote could not in his inmost mind deny it. It might be his job in life to see that citizens did their duty and to bring to justice those who failed to. But he had eyes in his head. He knew the sort of conditions the poorest people of the city lived in, the pavement dwellers, the beggars, the homeless like this boy. And he recognized that for them there was only one duty: to stay alive.

Behind him the big door of the bungalow opened abruptly. A swathe of sharp light spread out. The boys in the driveway vanished in front of it like so many sweepings.

Inspector Ghote turned. Standing on the threshold a stately, solemn bearer was waiting to take him inside to begin his investigation into the death of the house's master.

Quickly he climbed the steps.

*

A few minutes later the inspector was being ushered by the solemn, pear-shaped bearer into the doorway of a substantial wooden hut standing at the far end of a big garden partly hidden by a trellis on which Ghote had glimpsed in the soft darkness a gnarled wistaria tree thick with swags of blossom.

'Inspector Ghote, Criminal Investigation Department.'

Propped on a hard, white surgery couch, Frank Masters was in no condition to acknowledge any announcement.

His well-cut white shirt and trousers were splotched and stained with the terrible effects of the poison he had taken. The grave, intent face of all those newspaper photographs was limp and finished. The large-lensed, heavy spectacles had been dabbed down at the bottom corner of the couch, one side-piece askew, indispensable a few hours ago, junk now.

The bearer, his introduction performed, had quietly disappeared.

Standing in the far corner of the room, looking into the mirrored front of a white-painted cupboard, was a tall woman of about thirty-five dressed in a stiffly starched white overall. She had not turned when Ghote had been so solemnly introduced. He coughed apologetically towards her.

'I presume this is Mr Masters,' he said.

She swung round with a sharp bark of a laugh.

'Mr Masters, I presume,' she said. 'Yes, you're quite right, Mr Stanley.'

Ghote realized, with some uneasiness, that he had to deal with a Westerner. By her voice, an Englishwoman.

'My name is Ghote actually,' he said. 'Inspector Ghote of the CID.'

She made no reply but looked at him steadily.

'You are the doctor who attended the patient?' he asked.

'Dr Diana Upleigh,' she said.

She continued to look at him in silence with a faint smile on her big, pink-complexioned, strongly-featured face and a frankly appraising look in the wide-set eyes under the dark aggressive eyebrows. She was a good six inches taller than Ghote and was enabled to direct her stare sharply downwards.

When she spoke again it was in the cool, crisp English which sent a prickle of apprehensive irritation down Ghote's spine.

'It's hardly likely that anyone else would have "attended the patient", as you put it, is it?' she said.

'Well, no. No, it is not,' Ghote said.

He licked his top lip.

'Then you can answer the questions I need to ask,' he added.

'Why else do you think I hung about here?' she replied. 'I'd have left my dispenser to look after things if it hadn't been that someone responsible had to see you people.'

'Yes, yes, of course.'

He paused to collect his thoughts, a necessary process, and looked round the room. It was painted shiny white and was dazzlingly clean and firmly utilitarian. Besides the examination couch there were a white, square sink in one corner, a weighing machine with a height measure attached, two green-painted filing cabinets, some hard wooden chairs and a glass-topped table.

At the end of his survey Ghote came back to the surgery couch.

'This is the body of Mr Frank Masters Esquire?' he said.

'Who else?'

'And – and he is dead?'

The faint, cool smile came again.

'Do you want to make sure for yourself?'

'No, no, of course not. I perfectly trust your judgement. Please do not think I was making aspersion.'

'Well, I think I am just about capable of telling whether life is extinct or not. There wouldn't be much point in ten years' study otherwise.'

'No. No, I see that. Exactly so.'

Once again Ghote had to haul back his mind to the well-learned pattern of questioning.

'And he died here, in this room?' he asked.

'Certainly.'

He straightened his shoulders a little.

'It is essential, you understand, that I should get the whole circumstances perfectly clear. What is the purpose of this hut exactly?'

The doctor answered without any trace of amusement now.

'This is our dispensary. You probably saw as you came down through the compound: it stands all by itself here behind that trellis with the wistaria on it. There's this room, the examination room. And through there is the dispensing room itself.'

She jerked a glance at a door leading into the other half of the hut.

Ghote noted that there was no lock.

'Thank you,' he said. 'That makes it most plain. And now, what was the approximate time of death?'

'The approximate time? I take it you'd prefer the exact figure?'

A fraction of contempt had crept back into the cool voice.

'If you have it, I would prefer,' Ghote answered stoically.

'Eleven twenty-four precisely.'

'A very exact time.'

There was hardly a questioning note in his observation, but the doctor was quick to take it up.

'I happen to have a scientific training,' she said. 'I naturally realize the importance of exactness in these matters.'

'Yes, of course, I see that,' Ghote said.

He let his glance slip down and rest for an instant on the doctor's well-made, low-heeled brown suede shoes.

'We come now to the cause of death,' he said.

'Arsenic poisoning.'

The statement was abrupt and uncompromising. Hardly admitting the possibility of being questioned.

Though Ghote saw the need to put questions.

'You are certain of this?' he said. 'Has there been time for tests, etcetera?'

'No, there has not been time for tests etcetera. But you won't find I'm wrong.'

'A clinical diagnosis only,' said Ghote.

The doctor's heavy eyebrows rose a little at this use of the correct term.

'Yes,' she said. 'A clinical diagnosis. But you'll find I'm right. The symptoms were very clear.'

'There will have to be a check made at the laboratory of the Chemical Examiner,' Ghote said.

'Of course.'

A jet of abruptness.

'But in the meantime we can certainly proceed along the lines you have suggested.'

'Lines I suggested? Now, don't get this wrong. I haven't suggested anything. You've got your job, I've got mine. And, make no mistake, I'm going to leave you to get on with yours just as soon as I can.'

It sounded as if the doctor was hardly optimistic about the results.

'Very well,' said Ghote calmly. 'So will you please tell all the circumstances of the death that you know?'

The doctor considered for a moment.

'Yes,' she said. 'I think I can give you a pretty reasonable account.'

She strode over to the glass-topped table and perched on the edge, thrusting her hands deep into the patch pockets of her white overall.

'Frank – Mr Masters – started to feel ill, I believe, about a quarter past ten.'

She looked quickly across at Ghote.

'Oh, yes,' she said, 'only hearsay, I know. But I don't think you'll find it disputed. I asked him a few questions to get the picture. He managed to say that he'd begun to feel sick about a quarter of an hour before I saw him. The symptoms had developed pretty rapidly – abdominal pain, vomiting, you know the sort of thing.'

'Yes,' said Ghote.

He would certainly know from now on, anyhow.

'Well, by a stroke of luck I happened to be on the premises when it happened. I was having a talk to a couple of the boys, trying to get into their heads some sort of idea of decent behaviour. We've had a lot of trouble recently.'

'I see,' Ghote said. 'And who were these boys?'

'For heaven's sake, does it matter? You asked me what I knew of the circumstances of the death.'

'Where there has been a violent death almost anything may be relevant to the case,' Ghote said firmly. 'That is an accepted principle of police procedure.'

'Oh. Oh, all right then, I'll tell you who your boys were.'

But, quite unexpectedly, the doctor looked suddenly almost totally disconcerted.

'Well, that is . . .'

'Yes?' said Ghote.

She gave a short, barking laugh.

'As a matter of fact,' she said, 'I can't give you their names.'

Ghote lifted his head for battle.

'It's quite simple,' the doctor went on. 'I just don't know what their names are. I could find out, of course, but I just don't happen to know.'

Ghote looked at her steadily.

'You must call them something,' he said. 'You must have heard them call each other something. First names only would be quite adequate.'

'All right,' said the doctor, 'I'll give you them.'

Ghote slipped a notebook out of his pocket and waited with ballpoint poised.

'Their names, as far as I remember them, are Edward G. Robinson and Tarzan.'

Ghote lowered his notebook.

'Those are the names of film stars only,' he said accusingly.

The doctor smiled.

'That's exactly it,' she said. 'They choose to call themselves by those names: there's nothing we can do about it. It's quite a common thing. When they get any money they waste it at the pictures. And they talk of nothing else.'

'Tarzan,' said Ghote. 'Tell me something about him, please. He is a very acrobatical boy? About twelve years old?'

'That's him. He goes in for not speaking, for some reason or other.'

'I think I have met him, and the other boy you mentioned,' Ghote said.

'Met them?'

'Yes. They were waiting for the truck to arrive. Outside the front door.'

'What did they say to you?' the doctor asked abruptly.

'Say? What do you mean?'

'Oh, come, man. I meant what I said. What did those boys speak to you about?'

Ghote frowned sharply.

There were limits. A police officer in the course of his duties did not have to submit to cross-examination of this sort.

'They did not speak,' he said. 'I saw only. You told you were called to see Mr Masters at what time?'

The doctor shot him a quick glance.

'At the time I mentioned already,' she said.

'Ah, yes,' said Ghote, without acknowledging that he had set the little trap, or that it had been so scornfully leaped over. 'At ten-thirty, you said.'

'Exactly.'

'And what were your preliminary observations?'

'My preliminary observations? I didn't need anything as fancy as that, I assure you. One look and I saw that Frank was in a pretty bad way. For a bit I thought it might be severe food poisoning. But he kept muttering about a feeling of burning. That was when I began to suspect.'

'That it was poison, arsenic, you had to deal with?'

'That it was arsenic I had to deal with.'

Ghote ignored the elaborate mimicking of what he knew to be an over-preciseness in his use of English.

'You commenced the appropriate treatment then?' he asked. 'You administered an emetic or some such thing?'

'Don't be a bloody fool, man.'

Ghote was unable to prevent himself drawing back in sudden anger.

'Oh, don't get on your high horse now, for heaven's sake,' the doctor said. 'When you know me better you'll know I call anyone a bloody fool who says something bloody foolish.'

Ghote paused for a moment.

'You were describing the treatment of Mr Masters,' he said.

The doctor leaned backwards against the glass-topped table, her hands still pushed deep into the pockets of her white coat.

'I wasn't describing the treatment,' she said. 'You were. That was precisely what I was objecting to. Emetic. You've got a lot to learn. There wouldn't be much point, you know, in giving an emetic when the patient is sicking up his entire guts every two minutes, would there?'

'I am sorry. I am not very well acquainted with arsenic poisoning.'

'No, I can see that. It's a bit of a pity as this happens to be a case of exactly that. They might have sent someone who knew something about it.'

Ghote looked at her steadily.

'Such cases are extremely rare,' he said. 'The Police Department cannot provide special personnel in such circumstances.'

The doctor tilted up her chin.

'Then it won't be much use telling you what treatment I used, will it?' she said.

'Nevertheless I would like to hear,' said Ghote.

He turned to a fresh page in his notebook.

The doctor shrugged.

'Very well,' she said. 'As soon as I realized the likely cause of the trouble I ordered my dispenser to prepare a quantity of ferric hydrate. It's a question of adding alkali to tincture of ferric chloride – a damnably slow business but by far and away the best thing to do, even with only two of us here.'

'Did you have no ferric hydrate ready prepared?' Ghote said.

'Wouldn't have been any use if I had. It has to be fresh, you know.'

Ghote did not allow himself to be snubbed.

'I have already told,' he said. 'I am not highly acquainted with the procedures for arsenic poisoning.'

'No, evidently not.'

'This dispenser you mentioned. What is his name, please?'

The doctor bounced off the table.

'Are you intending to check up on me?' she snapped. 'Because if so, you can damned well whistle for his name.'

'Yes,' said Ghote. 'I would naturally ask the same questions to him as I have to you. What is his name, please?'

The tall, white-coated figure stood looking down at him, legs apart, feet planted firmly on the well-scrubbed floor.

At last she spoke.

'His name's Carstairs,' she said. 'He's an Anglo-Indian. He has a little room over in the bungalow, perched up on the roof. If you want him.'

'I will interview in due course. Please continue your account of events.'

The doctor slumped back on to the edge of the table.

'There's not a great deal more to tell,' she said. 'The fact of the matter was that we didn't get the ferric hydrate prepared in time. There's nothing you can do to hurry a scientific process, you know.'

'I suppose it is a case where shouting is of no avail,' said Ghote.

She darted him a furious look but made no reply.

'And at eleven twenty-four Mr Masters died,' Ghote said.

'Yes. At eleven twenty-four. The time I gave you before. As soon as I saw that death had occurred I left Sonny Carstairs here and went and got in touch with you people. Got hold of a man called Naik eventually. Seemed to understand what I said, more or less.'

Ghote decided to pass over such cavalier treatment of the Deputy Superintendent. It might perhaps be best for his own peace of mind if he forgot the remark had ever been made.

'Now,' he said, 'we come to the possible causes of poisoning.'

'Murder,' said the doctor.

She sat unmoving on the glass table top. Her hands were once again stuck into the patch pockets of her coat.

'That is obviously one possibility,' Ghote said. 'However, we must also consider the possibilities of suicide and accident.'

'There are plenty of easier ways of killing yourself than swallowing anything as unpleasant as that,' the doctor said brusquely. 'And besides, what would a man like Frank Masters want to kill himself for?'

Ghote pricked up his ears.

'A man like Frank Masters,' he said. 'What exactly then was Mr Frank Masters like?'

The doctor gave him a long, steady look.

She got up abruptly and strode across the room until she was standing beside the examination couch where Frank Masters's body lay uselessly propped.

She looked down.

'Frank was a good man,' she said. 'Simply that. A good man.'

She swung away, grasped for the door handle and in an instant was outside leaving the soft night air billowing in through the open doorway.

3

For some minutes Inspector Ghote stood quite still in the clinically harsh examination room alone with the broken body of Frank Masters. He forced himself to breathe deeply and slowly.

Calm, he told himself. That was the first thing. Calm to think out everything he had learned. He must not allow himself to be swept away by the attitude of this arrogant English doctor. Who was she—?

He stopped himself.

And by standing still in the middle of the room and concentrating hard he did at last succeed in getting calm enough to go over quietly and rationally all that he had heard and seen. He was just thinking how little the doctor had really said about Frank Masters himself when a curious faint scratching noise distracted him.

He checked an impulse to dart out into the darkness of the compound to investigate and made himself stand stock still apparently gazing into space.

Without having to exercise much patience he was rewarded. Down at the bottom corner of the open doorway he became aware of a slow, very stealthy movement. Without turning his head even a quarter of an inch he looked as far downwards as he could.

Second by second there crept into the range of his vision first a small brown hand, grimy and ill-kept, then a thin wrist and finally a section of a ripped-up, ragged black plastic jacket.

Ghote took a long, slow, deep breath.

And pounced.

Successfully.

He felt his fingers grip with satisfying hardness into the lean and stringy flesh of the leader of the boys' gang.

Unable to suppress a faint triumphant smile he hauled the urchin into the hut and on to his feet.

'Well,' he said, 'and what do you want?'

The boy twisted round in his grip.

'To find out what you are doing, Inspector sahib,' he said.

He grinned.

'Inspector sahib,' Ghote answered. 'So you have discovered that I am inspector. You have been listening at the window, have you?'

'Yes, Inspector,' the boy said, hanging his head a little.

Ghote tightened his hold on the thin arm. The boy winced and looked up at him.

'Dr Diana give you hell all right,' he said.

Ghote let the arm go.

'But she spoke truth, Inspector,' the boy said.

'Truth? Why shouldn't she?'

'When you were lying, Inspector sahib, she could lie also.'

'Me lying?'

But no sooner had he spoken than he remembered how he had denied that he had ever said anything to the gang outside the house.

He put his arms on his hips and faced the boy.

'Now listen to me,' he said. 'I am investigating the death of Mr Masters. This is a very important case: there are a lot of things I have got to do, and quickly. You will not watch over me while I do them. You understand that?'

'Oh, yes, Inspector sahib.'

'Very well. And if I catch you at it again I would make sure you are locked up where you would not trouble me any more. Do you understand again?'

'Oh yes, sir. Understand very good.'

Ghote stepped back. The boy slid gratefully towards the door. In the open doorway he paused for a moment.

'Understand okay,' he said. 'You don't worry. When Dr Diana make it hot for you, you don't want nobody to hear.'

Ghote raced out into the garden after him. He caught one glimpse of a swiftly moving shape beyond the wistaria of the trellis and set out in hot pursuit.

The roots of a tree caught his toe and an instant later he was flat on his face with the smell of dusty earth in his nostrils.

It was some three hours after this that he came to deal with the Foundation cook and got his next glimpse of real progress. Not that the intervening time had been idle. During it he worked his way steadily over the whole bungalow, finding out just who lived there and exactly where they had been earlier in the evening. With all the boys in the dormitories it was a formidable undertaking, but, aided by reinforcements from headquarters, Ghote got through it with speed.

He poked and pried into every cranny of the big, spartanly furnished house. He set the team with the ink-pad to work taking fingerprints wholesale; he supervised the departure of the body on its way to the laboratory; he directed the obedient but unimaginative police photographer in taking shots of every possible relevant scene.

He even went so far as to eliminate the possibility, suggested by the boy in the black jacket, that Frank Masters's death had anything to do with 'gay girls'. Certainly no one approaching that description had ever been seen at the Foundation.

When he had been at work for about two hours the reporters arrived. The pear-shaped bearer, looking somewhat crinkled at this late hour, came to tell him. He went and met them at the front door.

'No statement,' he said stiffly.

There were excited cries of protest.

'I have no time to be hobnobbing with pressmen,' he said sternly. 'I have investigation to carry out.'

'Yeah?' said one of the reporters, a tall, beaky-nosed man wearing a brightly-coloured picture tie. 'We got investigation to carry out too, you know.'

Ghote turned away.

But just as the bearer, with evident pleasure, was pushing the heavy front door closed he relented. After all, though there was something rather shocking about wearing such a tie, the man was right: he had his job to do.

Patiently Ghote allowed himself to be questioned. But when it came down to it he did not have much to tell. In spite of all he had done up to that point, he knew very little.

The reporters left, looking upset. And Ghote went back to see how the police surgeon was getting on. He conducted a casual conversation with him and succeeded in gathering that the arsenic had in all probability been taken about an hour and a half before Frank Masters had complained about feeling ill. He checked and cross-checked on the time this had happened and came once again to the question of the evening meal and its cooking and to the big gas-stove with its heavy butane cylinders, the gleaming refrigerator and the formidable array of pots and pans of the Foundation kitchen.

And there he tackled for the second time the Foundation cook.

'You cook all the meals in this house?' he asked once again.

The cook, a plumpish, short little man whose skin gleamed and glistened under the light of the single bulb hanging from the middle of the low ceiling, nodded silent acquiescence.

'Did Mr Masters eat the same food as everybody else?' Ghote asked.

'Oh, yes, sahib. Masters sahib very kind man. He say what good enough for boys from street good enough for him.'

'Was it good food?' Ghote asked.

The podgy little cook looked downwards.

'Not very good food, sahib,' he said. 'Not very good cook.'

For a moment Ghote thought about the picture of Frank Masters this evoked. The millionaire from America who was prepared to eat day in day out the indifferently cooked food he himself had provided for the vagrants he had rescued from the pavements of Bombay. The thought of the care and skill Protima, his wife, brought to his own meals rose up in his mind.

'What did you cook this evening?' he asked.

'Oh, very bad food this evening, sahib.'

Ghote felt a stab of impatience.

'I asked what food it was,' he said.

'Oh, yes, sahib. Very sorry, sahib.'

The cook bowed his head. Ghote could see the plump roll of fat on his neck shining as though it were polished.

'Well?' he said.

'This evening mixed vegetables and puris, sahib.'

'I see,' said Ghote.

Even with a meal sent in at the office, he reflected, he had eaten far better food than the wheat cakes and vegetables that this American millionaire had allowed himself.

'Did Masters sahib eat with the boys?' he asked.

'Oh, no, sahib. He eat own meal as per usual, sahib. In staff tiffin room, sahib.'

'His own meal? Then that was something different?'

'Oh, yes, sahib. It would not be right for the sahibs and memsahibs to eat vegetable only.'

'Then what did Masters sahib eat as well?' said Ghote.

'Beef curry, sahib, and fish curry. Good curry, sahib.'

'Ah,' said Ghote, 'so you can cook well enough when you want, eh?'

He looked down in triumph at the little cook, whose cringing attitude irritated him more and more from one moment to the next.

'Oh, no, sahib,' the little man replied promptly. 'Not good cook.'

'Then why do you say it was good curry?'

'Dr Diana come and watch me make, sahib.'

Ghote's ears pricked up.

'Does Dr Upleigh always do this?'

'Oh, no, sahib. Dr Diana got much more important things to do than make sure how I cook.'

Ghote's interest was totally gripped.

'So this was an unusual occasion, was it?' he said.

The podgy little cook looked up bewilderedly.

Ghote tried again.

'So it was special for her to come?'

'Oh, yes, sahib. Most special. Most extra special. Very kind. Very kind.'

He rubbed his hands together in writhing gratitude.

Ghote kept the pressure up. This was a piece of luck indeed. The unusual incident, the little difference in behaviour, this was what he had taught himself always to look out for. And now he had really got hold of something.

'Was this perhaps the only time Dr Diana had ever come to see you cooking?' he asked.

The cook looked up at him anxiously.

'Well, was it the only time?' Ghote said with a jet of impatience.

'Oh, yes, sahib. Only time she come.'

'You are sure?'

'Oh, yes, sahib. Indeed, yes, sahib. Only time. Most sure.'

Ghote breathed a sigh of relief. When the meal Frank Masters had eaten was being prepared, the doctor had been for the first time ever down in the kitchen pretending to be supervising the cook. And he had got firmly on to it.

'Good,' he said. 'Now, tell me exactly what happened to the food when it had been prepared. What sort of dishes was it put in? Are they still here? Have they been washed?'

'Oh, sahib, sahib,' the cook protested. 'Am only poor man, sahib. Not very much brain, sahib.'

He looked up at Ghote beseechingly.

Ghote took control of himself. The man's attitude filled him with a desire to march him off to the privacy of CID headquarters and there to get what he wanted out of him in the most unpleasant way he could. But he was not going to allow himself to think in such a way. The man was a man like any other and he would treat him reasonably, however creepingly obsequious he got.

'The dishes,' he said, 'they have been washed?'

'Oh, yes, sahib. Most thoroughly washed. Oh, yes, indeed. I know that I must see to that.'

Ghote felt a twinge of disappointment.

'That is a pity,' he sighed. 'However we cannot expect—'

'Sahib, sahib, you want see dishes before they wash?' the cook asked eagerly.

He turned and suddenly scuttled off by the door leading out of the house.

Ghote was after him in an instant.

And, just as he had expected, there outside the door he found the little cook busy picking morsels out of an open-ended oil drum that served as an extra dustbin. With delicate artistry he was placing them one by one in a clean dish.

Ghote felt near to tears. So much for getting hold of the unusual incident, the little difference in behaviour. He had slipped into the oldest pitfall of all: he had virtually told the cook what he had wanted him to say and the squirming creature had promptly obliged with a stream of pure invention.

Ghote stepped forward and with a well-aimed kick sent the half-filled dish spinning away in to the darkness.

'Come back inside,' he shouted.

The little cook trotted meekly into the kitchen in front of him.

And immediately Ghote regretted his violence. Just because he had been so pleased with himself over his discovery, he had taken out the subsequent disappointment on the person who happened to have provoked it. He made a resolution not to let this happen again, ever.

'The dishes were all cleaned already?' he asked the cook quietly.

'Yes, sahib.'

'And was this, or was this not, the only time Dr Diana had ever come and watched you cook?'

'She had come before, sahib,' said the cook.

He spoke humbly as ever, but without any sign of regret at having said exactly the opposite hardly two minutes earlier.

'When did she come?' Ghote said patiently.

'Oh, when Masters sahib was away, sahib.'

'When he was away? He has been away?'

'He has been back three weeks only, sahib,' the shiny-skinned cook said eagerly. 'He was away for three months, sahib. He was in the Punjab, sahib. He was very interested in refugees from Tibet, sahib. Very holy men, sahib.'

'Stop. Stop.'

By now, Ghote thought, the wretch had undoubtedly entered the realm of embroidery again, adding to this information piece by piece as it seemed to please or not.

'And it was while Masters sahib was away that Dr Diana came to see you cooking?' he asked.

'Oh, yes, sahib. Came to make sure I cook a little better. She say I was most appalling cook in whole of Bombay, sahib.'

The man looked up with something like pride on his plump features.

Ghote's toe itched. But he kept himself calm.

'Why did she not come at other times?' he asked.

'Oh, she was not in charge then, sahib. When Masters sahib go he put Dr Diana in full charge. She say at least she get some decent meals now, sahib. So she—'

'That's enough.'

'Yes, sahib. Certainly, sahib. I stay quite quiet, sahib. You want to think, sahib?'

'No, I do not,' Ghote snapped.

He seized on another question before his temper burst the limits he had set on it.

'So why did Dr Diana come to supervise you tonight? Mr Masters was here, wasn't he? Why did she come tonight?'

He waited anxiously for the answer. If there was nothing the fertilely anxious-to-please cook could suggest, this was perhaps after all a piece of behaviour well out of the ordinary.

'Oh, sahib,' the cook replied, giving him a sideways glance, 'that is easy to answer.'

He waited, hoping no doubt that Ghote would give him a clue about the reply he would prefer.

Ghote stayed silent, but decided he could let one shaft of angry impatience dart out.

'Well, sahib,' the cook said, 'it was like—'

Suddenly he stopped short and looked round Ghote as if he had at that moment seen the whole doorway behind the inspector turn into a sheet of flame or a roaring cascade of flood water.

'Will you tell?' Ghote snapped without taking his eyes off him. 'Why did Dr Diana choose tonight of all nights to come and watch you cooking?'

'I can answer that.'

Now Ghote did swing round.

He found himself face to face with a woman about sixty years old, dressed in an orange-toned sari, thin-faced with white hair drawn up on her head and the little mouth and quick eyes of a bird.

'I am Inspector Ghote, CID,' he said. 'May I ask what you are doing here?'

'It is rather I who should be asking what you are doing,' she replied.

She spoke English with an accent the likes of which Inspector Ghote had never heard before. He realized that in spite of her tanned complexion and workaday sari she was some sort of European.

'I am investigating the death of Mr Frank Masters,' he said cautiously.

There could be little doubt that his announcement came as a surprise to her. Of course it was strictly possible that she might have prepared the look of incomprehension and the quick flood of understanding which followed it. He did not know enough about her to tell. But if it was a performance, it was a faultless one.

'Herr Frank. Herr Frank,' she babbled now.

'Yes,' Ghote said, 'I regret to have to inform that he is dead, and that a police investigation is being carried out.'

'But Herr Frank. But what happened?'

Ghote kept watching her closely. He detected not a sign of calculation in the rapidly blinking bird-eyes.

'Mr Masters was poisoned,' he said carefully.

'Poisoned? But how? But what happened?'

She darted looks all round the kitchen. At the refrigerator, at the grimy burners of the gas-stove, at the ranks of pallid aluminium dekchis.

'There is no poison here,' she said.

It was a statement of fact.

She drew herself up.

'But that is a matter which I am bound to investigate,' Ghote answered.

'Then tell me how he came to take this poison.'

'You had better tell first who you are,' Ghote said.

She looked at him.

'Yes. Yes, of course. You would not know. My name is Glucklich. Fraulein Glucklich, citizen of the Republic of India.'

She gave a proud glance round. The cook at least seemed impressed. He salaamed deeply.

'Ah, Fraulein Glucklich,' Ghote said. 'Then you are the housekeeper, are you not?'

He mentally filled in a blank on a list.

'Exactly,' said Fraulein Glucklich. 'And that is why I am able to answer your question. Why did Dr Diana come into this kitchen tonight? Quite simple. Because she knew I would not be here. She knew I would be with the new swami.'

'The new swami?' Ghote said.

'Yes,' said Fraulein Glucklich with a little toss of her crown of white hair, 'you do not need to think that only Indians can benefit from the words of a wise man. I am happy to call myself sannyasini of Swami Dnyaneshwar.'

'And he was holding a meeting this evening?' Ghote asked.

'Of course,' Fraulein Glucklich answered. 'From five o'clock to midnight. It was advertised.'

'It was public meeting then?'

'Swami Dnyaneshwar would turn away no one, however unenlightened.'

Suspecting that he was himself one of the unenlightened Fraulein Glucklich had in mind, Ghote persisted.

'And there were a number of people present at the meeting this evening?'

'A number of people? I am happy to state that there must have been at least thirty. And great enthusiasm. We went long past the advertised time.'

'And you yourself were there from start to finish?'

Fraulein Glucklich looked at him sadly.

'Do you think I would miss one moment at the feet of such a swami?'

'You were at his feet the whole time?'

A faint blush came up in her withered cheeks.

'I think you misunderstand,' she said. 'I spoke of course metaphorically. I was not in fact kneeling at the swami's feet the whole evening.'

'You left for a little time?' Ghote said.

'No, no. I could not leave. I sat close to the swami every minute. On the ground, naturally.'

'Thank you,' Ghote said.

He supposed he would have to check with Swami Dnyaneshwar. It would not in all probability be an easy talk. Religious figures were apt to show little concern for things of this world. Which was excellent in its way: but difficult for a police officer.

In the meantime he could regard Fraulein Glucklich as having a total alibi as regarded putting arsenic that evening into anything Frank Masters had eaten.

'You were explaining that Dr Diana had perhaps come down to the kitchen for a particular reason,' he resumed.

'Certainly,' Fraulein Glucklich replied. 'She had come down to meddle. If I had been here, she would not have dared.'

Ghote reflected that seven hours and more with the swami did not seem to have made Fraulein Glucklich regard all her fellow human beings with unmixed love. Though it was certainly true, from what he had seen of Dr Diana, that she would indeed meddle whatever chance she got.

No doubt this after all was why she had come into the kitchen. There almost always was some equally simple explanation for what at first looked like suspicious departures from routine. Ghote felt abruptly tired.

'I tell you, Mr Inspector, such trouble I had when Herr Frank was away.' Fraulein Glucklich chirruped on, 'It is all very well for her to say she caught that man Amrit Singh, but she had no business to poke into everywhere like that.'

'Amrit Singh,' said the inspector.

Thoughts raced suddenly through his mind like racehorses crowding in a blaze of jockeys' silks towards a winning post.

Amrit Singh.

Amrit Singh was a personage well known to every man in the whole Bombay Police. If there was any organized crime happening anywhere at any time, it was safe to say that Amrit Singh, a huge, enormously tough, unshakeably cheerful yet plainly ruthless Sikh, was somewhere at the back of it. Burglaries, street robberies, brothel-keeping, bootlegging, trade in forged licences, smuggling, blackmail, protection rackets, anything and everything solidly illegal was meat and drink to Amrit Singh.

And he had never really been caught. From time to time certainly he had been pulled up and even convicted on some minor charge.

But even then, thanks to a battery of sharp advocates, he had never had to do more than pay a small fine.

On these occasions he invariably proffered in satisfaction the largest possible currency note. He had every reason to be cheerful.

And now he had turned up here.

It was difficult to pay any attention to Fraulein Glucklich, jabbing her little pointed nose in and out as she detailed her complaints against the formidable Dr Diana.

'Oh, yes, we had the notorious Mr Amrit Singh hanging about the Foundation. And, certainly, nobody realized it till Dr Diana took it into her head to question him. But she did not do anything so very clever. After all, he told her straight away who he was.'

The inspector ran over in his mind the information sheets he had seen recently. As far as he could remember there was nothing about Amrit Singh having been notified as causing trouble at the Masters Foundation. If there had been, half the men in the force would have been out looking for him.

'How long ago was this?' he asked.

'Oh, a month or more,' Fraulein Glucklich answered. 'In any case, it is of no importance.'

Ghote was undeterred.

'And since then?' he asked. 'Has anything been seen of Amrit Singh in the past few days?'

Fraulein Glucklich sniffed. Delicately.

'Of course not,' she said. 'He was told the police would be called if he ever showed himself here again, and I suppose he had the good sense to keep off.'

Ghote allowed himself a flicker of inward amusement at this withered-cheeked little European woman's notion that it was necessary only to mention the police to the huge Sikh thug to scare him off once and for all. But this was no time for jokes. If Amrit Singh was involved in something at the Foundation, he had to get after him just as quickly as possible.

One or two questions still must be asked, however.

He glanced at his watch.

'I would like to know more about what Mr Masters ate this evening,' he said. 'Your cook tells that he prepared on Dr Diana's instructions beef curry and fish. Can you tell—'

'Fish curry,' snapped Fraulein Glucklich. 'She ought to have known at least that Herr Frank did not eat that.'

'Oh, memsahib,' said the cook, 'that was special for Mr Chatterjee. You know how he like.'

Chatterjee, Krishna, resident social worker at the Foundation, Ghote noted automatically. He began looking for a way of cutting Fraulein Glucklich short without drying up a possibly useful source of information.

But Fraulein Glucklich's full attention was now turned on the plump cook.

'So Master Chatterjee likes fish curry, does he?' she said.

'Oh, yes, memsahib. All those Bengali fellows like fish.'

'And since when have his whims been pandered to in this house?' Fraulein Glucklich asked with a magnificently lofty toss of her little dried-up nut of a head.

'One moment,' Ghote said.

Fraulein Glucklich spared him a swift glance.

'Please,' he said, 'I wish to know with great urgency who exactly ate with Mr Masters this evening in the staff tiffin room.'

Fraulein Glucklich indicated graciously that the cook might reply.

'Yes, memsahib,' he said in something near a whisper. 'This evening only three in staff tiffin room, please. Masters sahib, Dr Diana and Chatterjee sahib.'

Ghote glanced at Fraulein Glucklich to see if this was likely. She appeared to accept it. He hurried on.

'Now,' he said, 'when the food is cooked, what happens to it?'

'Oh, sahib, it is taken to tiffin room by Vidur, the bearer.'

Ghote stored the name away. He remembered the man, a sullen-looking, pointed-nose Gujarati.

'And then?' he snapped.

'It is put on serving table, sahib, till Masters sahib ready to eat.'

'Till he is ready? It is there some time?'

'It is generally there a great deal too long,' Fraulein Glucklich broke in. 'Poor Herr Frank. So many things he has to do. Often I have to tell him several times that the food is waiting.'

Ghote decided that this was something he must pursue however anxious he was to get on to headquarters about Amrit Singh.

'And the food is often left in the tiffin room like that?' he asked.

'Much too often,' Fraulein Glucklich answered. 'More than once it has been stolen.'

'Stolen?'

'Certainly. The clients here, you must know, have no very high moral tone. On several occasions they have reached in through the window and stolen food from the serving table. In spite of the excellent supplies they get themselves.'

Ghote thought of the vegetables and puris the 'clients' had had that evening.

'So that it is most likely that Mr Masters ate the beef curry,' he said. 'And almost anyone could have put something in that if they had wanted to.'

'Put something in it?' Fraulein Glucklich said. 'But you cannot think seriously that anyone would have wished to kill Herr Frank.'

She tossed her head.

'That is ridiculous.'

It was an edict.

For a moment Ghote wished he could heed it. He was beginning to feel very tired now. If only it was impossible that Frank Masters had been murdered, then he would have done enough for one night. He could even go back home and get to bed.

But the desire lasted only a moment.

If Amrit Singh was involved, there was certainly no time for rest. And Amrit Singh must be involved. He had been on the spot not all that long before, and he was not going to be scared away by a warning about fetching a policeman.

Ghote's heart began to pound.

If he could not only solve the Masters murder but pull in the notorious Amrit Singh for it, then it would be such a triumph as there had never been before. And he would do it. If hard work and patience could piece together a case to stand up in court against the worst the Sikh's lawyers could do, then he was as good as hanged already.

There was a telephone in the stone-flagged entrance hall, he remembered. With scarcely an explanation, he left Fraulein Glucklich and the greasy little cook at a run.

Headquarters, it turned out, were not able to help much. Nobody knew where Amrit Singh was now. By no means for the first time he had thrown off the watch kept on him more or less permanently and had vanished into the blue. A number of rackets of various kinds were going on that he almost certainly had a hand in, but he could not be pinned down for certain anywhere.

Never mind, thought Ghote. He has been seen here, and that is enough.

He flung himself into a renewed whirlwind of activity, checking and double checking on every aspect of the affair. This time Amrit Singh was not going to slip out of the net through doubts over the evidence.

Tired though he was, he drove himself and his men steadily on. And all the while the thought of what it was all leading up to grew and blossomed in his head. Even the unpleasant business of emptying the dustbins into sealed containers for analysis was a delightful task. He sorted and picked at the mess of rubbish with his own hands.

'Hey, policeman,' a familiar voice suddenly called out. 'Don't you know that food belongs to the beggars?'

Ghote leaped to his feet.

That damned boy.

He peered all round in the before-dawn darkness out at the back of the house. But beyond the light of the lantern by which they had been working he could see nothing.

He felt his fury rising.

'If a beggar ate any of this,' he shouted into the darkness, 'he might find himself good and sick.'

'So what?' the boy called back at his most synthetically American. 'So what? Then you'd know where the poison was. And a good cheap way.'

Ghote found that he had no answer.

A wave of discouragement assailed him.

It had not abated when, having done everything at the Foundation he could possibly think of and made his way homewards at last, trudging across the patch of garden in front of his Government Quarters house he saw his wife standing just inside the open door. So, once again she had been unable to sleep while he had been away.

And Protima after a sleepless night was not an easy person.

A raucous cock suddenly crowed loudly from somewhere close by. Ghote shook his head from side to side trying to throw off the weariness.

'A bad case,' he said into the chilly, dawn-streaked air. 'A terrible business. I was lucky to get away as soon as this.'

Protima said nothing.

Ghote found he needed to make an effort to take the last step into the house. Behind him Protima closed the door and latched it.

And suddenly she put her arms round him.

'You would be tired,' she said. 'Come, there is tea nearly ready. I made it when I heard the truck coming into the Quarters.'

And, unusually, Ghote found himself telling every detail of the case to Protima. She was by no means the sort of person to appreciate the need for meticulous checking of samples from dustbins or accurate recording of exactly who was where at what time, and for this reason he never gave her more than an outline of what particular job he was on at any time. But the sudden relief of tension was too much for him now, and out it all came – the sense of bafflement he felt every time he tried to find out enough about Frank Masters to guess why he had been murdered, the almost frightening possibility of bringing in Amrit Singh, even the highly upsetting encounters with the boys' gang. He told her about everything, the samples he had collected, the fingerprints he had had taken, the hopes he put on what the laboratory tests would produce.

He even brought himself to admit how much he hated having to deal with Dr Diana.

'She was the worst of the whole night,' he said. 'The way she stood there, so tall and big, like a machine woman, and all the time making her judgements.'

He felt better for having brought it out. He tried a small joke.

'No wonder she is not married.'

Protima smiled back at him slyly.

He went over to her and took her in his arms. Through the thin cotton of her white night sari he could feel her body, warm, firm, protective.

'Oh, I am so tired,' he said.

'Come to bed then,' she answered. 'Come to bed and sleep.'

4

In the morning Inspector Ghote's hopes of the laboratory tests were answered. They showed that Frank Masters had taken arsenic in the form of arsenic trioxide. And when Ghote read the neatly compiled facts about this form of the poison he felt a growing sense of pleasure. Things were beginning to link up in a decidedly satisfying way.

Arsenic trioxide, he read, was a form of the substance moderately rare but often used as the basis of lotions for the treatment of certain severe skin diseases.

He did not need to dive into his notebook to remember the name of the man he wanted to see next. Sonny Carstairs. The dispenser at the Foundation. He jumped up from his desk.

And so it was with the irritating, but necessary, vision of the crinkled face of the boy in the black jacket in his mind's eye that Ghote began questioning the Anglo-Indian dispenser as he sat neatly on a high wooden stool in the back room of the dispensary hut.

'Tell me,' Ghote said, 'you must have a very big list of complaints to treat here. Is that so?'

'That certainly is so, man,' Sonny Carstairs said.

He pulled down the edge of his high-collared, trim white overall.

'Those boys,' he went on, 'you've no idea, man. They suffer from every disease there is. We have such a time with them. But worth it, worth every minute of it. For Frank's sake, you know.'

He looked up at Ghote with a quick smile. His brown eyes were luminous.

'I think I saw one boy with some terrible skin trouble,' Ghote said. 'Is that the sort of thing?'

'Oh, yes. Him I know well. That's a terrible case, man. We're doing our best for him, but it's hard work, hard work. That trouble has got so engrained.'

Sonny Carstairs sighed deeply. He took his left hand in his right, examined it for a moment and pushed down the cuticle on the neatly trimmed nail of his third finger.

'What treatment do you apply in such a case?' Ghote asked.

'Oh, that's quite simple. We use something called Fowler's Solution. It's a slow business, man, but we have to be patient, you know.'

'Fowler's Solution?' Ghote said. 'What's that?'

Sonny Carstairs looked up helpfully.

'It's just a solution that a chap called Fowler invented,' he said. 'It's basically arsenic trioxide.'

Suddenly his look of mild benevolence faded away.

'Arsenic,' he said. 'You don't think . . .?'

'Do you make the solution up yourselves?' Ghote said.

Sonny Carstairs slipped from his stool and went across to one of the big, white-painted cupboards hung all round the room. Ghote rapidly repeated in his mind the exact intonation the dispenser had used when he had said what Fowler's Solution consisted of. He could detect no falsity. Yet . . .

Sonny Carstairs opened the cupboard and selected one of a number of ranged brown glass jars with black screw-top lids and big white labels.

When he turned to face the inspector again his expression was even more uneasy. Ghote was quick to spot it.

'Something is wrong with the jar,' he said.

Sonny gave him a quick, worried glance and then looked down at the ribbed jar which he had put on the broad white shelf in front of him.

'Well? Come on.'

Sonny looked up from the jar as if reluctant to end a delicate scrutiny.

'I don't know,' he said.

'That will not do,' said Ghote. 'Something is wrong with the jar. What is it?'

He stepped up close to the white-overalled Anglo-Indian and looked at him hard.

Sonny Carstairs swallowed.

'For God's sake, Inspector,' he said. 'I tell you it may be nothing.'

'But it may not be,' Ghote said.

'I suppose so.'

It was a reluctant, shame-faced admission.

'So what is wrong?' Ghote said.

'Some may be missing. The jar feels emptier than when I stowed it away in the cupboard here.'

'And that was when?'

'It was only yesterday, man. When a lot of stuff arrived from the pharmacist's.'

Sonny was almost whispering.

'What time exactly?'

'In the afternoon.'

The neat little dispenser stared down glumly at his well-kept hands resting palm down on the edge of the shelf by the little, ribbed glass brown jar.

And quite suddenly he brightened up.

'It's OK,' he said.

'OK? You've made a mistake? There is none missing?'

Sonny looked up.

'Oh, no,' he said. 'I think it is missing all right, but I can tell you for certain. Just you wait a shake-o.'

He bobbed down and opened a big, flat drawer under the shelf.

Ghote, looking in over his shoulder, saw a handful of stiff-cover exercise books, a couple of chewed pencils and an old box which had once contained Flor de Dindigal cigars and now held three rusty razor blades.

Sonny took out the newest-looking of the exercise books.

'Here it is,' he said. 'Register of purchases.'

Ghote watched him open it. On the first page only there was a list of items, in precise, rather flowery handwriting, each with the day before's date against it and two bold initials in another hand, in red. 'D. U.'

That was easy: Diana Upleigh. Who else? Even if he had been unable to read, the totally unhesitant assertiveness of the big capitals would have told him.

'A new book has just been started,' he said. 'We are making up a lot of medicines we need now. For reasons of economy.'

'Ah,' said Ghote encouragingly. 'Your idea, I suppose?'

'Oh, no, no.'

Sonny seemed shocked.

'We owe this to Dr Diana,' he said. 'It takes someone of her calibre, you know, to institute real reforms. She saw that we could make a considerable saving.'

Ghote thought of the doctor's descents on the kitchen in the absence of Frank Masters and reflected that the actions of a person of such a calibre did not always receive the acknowledgement they got from Sonny Carstairs.

He watched Sonny's only faintly brown finger, with the neatly pared nail, skim down the column of the register.

'Ah, yes,' Sonny said, 'there we are. Just as I expected.'

Ghote read the entry.

'One 50-gram jar, arsenic trioxide.'

'Well,' he said, 'how much is left in the bottle?'

Sonny Carstairs rubbed his hands together smoothly.

'Just a jiffy,' he said.

He quickly brought out a weighing balance, set the position jar on one pan and a similar empty one on the other with a couple of tiny weights and adjusted the beam.

'Yes,' he said, as the indicator waved to a balance, 'you can take it definitely, Inspector, that a considerable quantity of this poisonous substance has disappeared.'

He put the balance back in its cupboard with an air of satisfaction.

Ghote flipped over a page in his notebook.

'I shall require that jar for the purposes of the police laboratory,' he said. 'I am making out receipt in due form.'

He wrote with diligence.

Without looking up, he let a question slip gently out.

'The keys to the hut,' he said, 'who else has them besides you and Dr Diana?'

It was not until later that he properly reconstructed the sequence of events in the next few seconds.

First there came a curious hissing gasp from the little Anglo-Indian. But this was almost immediately blotted out by the sharp crack of breaking glass as the jar of arsenic trioxide slid off the shiny top of the shelf and fell straight on to the cement floor below.

Ghote jumped back with the powder wafting up towards him in a venomous white cloud.

'It's all right, man,' Sonny Carstairs said. 'It won't do you any harm. It may be poison, but a small quantity on your shoes is not going to hurt.'

Ghote bit his lip with vexation.

'Destroying evidence is serious offence,' he snapped.

'Destroy – Oh. No.'

The neat little Anglo-Indian subsided on to the shelf and buried his face in his arms.

Ghote took a step forward, gripped him hard by the shoulder and jerked him up.

'Yes,' he said, 'destroying evidence.'

Sonny Carstairs shook his head.

'It was – It wasn't that – Look, man, it was the key,' he said.

'The key? What key?'

Sonny swallowed.

'The key of the dispensary.'

'What key is this? There are many keys. But there was only one jar of poison. And there it is.'

Ghote pointed dramatically to the chunky fragments of thick brown glass in the middle of the patch of exploded white powder.

'Do not tell me that you have not destroyed evidence,' he said.

The dispenser's smooth face was creased with conflicting anxieties.

Suddenly he darted forward and looked at Ghote with big, pleading brown eyes.

'Look, Inspector,' he said, 'I'll tell you. I must. I didn't knock that jar off the shelf on purpose. It was shock that made me do it.'

'Shock?'

Sonny licked his lips.

'Inspector,' he said, 'I just realized at that moment what it means. You see, there are not many keys to this hut: there is only one. And I am the one who keeps it.'

He thrust an anxious, sweaty hand into the pocket of the drill trousers he wore under his white overall and pulled out a flat key of unusual design with a neat piece of white tape through the hole in the top.

Ghote took it and looked at it.

'You are telling that this is the only key to the whole hut?' he said.

'Yes, Inspector. But listen.'

Sonny stepped half a pace nearer till his neat features were within inches of the inspector's face.

'Listen, Inspector, I swear by all that's holy that that key never left my possession.'

'There must be other keys,' Ghote said, turning irritatedly away.

'No, Inspector. That is a special American lock. It is very difficult to get keys for it. When we had it put on, just after Dr Diana first came, she said it was safest only to have two keys. One for her, one for me.'

Ghote went over to the windows. As he had recalled, they were fitted with heavy metal grilles well fixed to the surrounds.

'These windows cannot be forced as easily as all that,' he said. 'And not without leaving very plain marks.'

'No,' Sonny answered. 'That was Dr Diana too. When she came she insisted we improve security all round.'

Without replying, Ghote turned and went into the outer half of the hut, the examination room. As he had remembered, the windows there were exactly like the ones in the dispensing room, and equally plainly they had not been tampered with.

He came back.

'Well, what happened to the second key?' he said.

If this man was telling the truth about never having let the key out of his possession, then it was going to be hard to link the theft of the poison with Amrit Singh. And that was what had to be done.

'That key was crushed by a tram, Inspector,' Sonny said.

'A tram?'

Ghote took an outraged step forward. Sonny Carstairs stepped back.

'It was, it was, Inspector. Honest to God. It wasn't my fault. I'll tell you what happened.'

Ghote looked at him coldly.

'It was like this, Inspector. I had just locked up here one day just after we got the new keys and I was walking up to the bungalow holding my one in my hand when I happened to notice some of the clients in the road outside. I looked to see what they were doing and I found them throwing coins under the trams as they passed the house.'

Ghote waited impassively. Evidently Sonny felt that his narrative required some comment.

'Throwing coins, Inspector,' he said earnestly.

'Yes, I did the same sort of thing myself as a boy, only it was with trains on the railway.'

Sonny's neat features took on a look of faint disdain.

'Well then, Inspector,' he went on, 'naturally I went over and pointed out to the boys that they were committing a serious malpractice.'

'Oh, yes?'

'Well, first they uttered some obscene remarks, and then one of them ran up, snatched the key I was still holding and threw it under a tram that was just going by. It was the boy who insists on calling himself Edward G. Robinson.'

'I know him,' Ghote said, seeing the tattered black jacket and the crinkled old man's face.

'Well then, Inspector, you know that that is the sort of unbalanced action he would indulge in.'

Ghote did not answer directly.

'You are sure there were only two keys in the beginning?' he asked.

'If you don't believe me, go and see Dr Diana,' Sonny said. 'She will tell you all right, man.'

Ghote felt a sudden tightening of the muscles in his stomach.

'No,' he snapped. 'That will not be necessary. Not necessary at all.'

He swung round and looked at the neat figure of the Anglo-Indian.

'At the moment I have urgent work,' he said.

He hurried out, cursing himself for having shied away from an encounter with Dr Diana in such an obvious way. He knew he ought to check the keys story with her. If it was true, it was very important. There could be no doubt that the hut had not been broken into. The bars on the windows had plainly not been shifted, the lock on the door had not even been scratched. So that in the time between the afternoon when the arsenic trioxide had arrived and it having been put into Frank Masters's curry before the meal that evening someone must have used a key to enter the hut.

The most likely thing was that the dispenser was wrong about there being only one key. There must be another unknown one, or Sonny Carstairs had convicted himself out of his own mouth.

Ghote thought suddenly of his room at headquarters, of the familiar scored surface of his desk, the familiar walls and furniture. The very labels on his prized, non-issue filing cabinet, 'Songs', 'Dance', 'Piano', 'Sacred', 'Various', presented themselves vividly to his mind. Half an hour of peace there and he would be ready to tackle anybody.

He passed through one of the gaps in the heavy wistaria trellis and set off across the big lawn at something approaching a trot.

'Inspector.'

The voice rang confidently out in the hot air.

Ghote looked round knowing inescapably whom he would see. Sure enough, Dr Diana had just stepped out of a pair of French windows overlooking the big lawn.

'You called to me?' Ghote said.

'Of course I did,' Dr Diana declared, striding over the dark green grass towards him.

Ghote succumbed to the temptation to play for time. If I can just get away from her for the moment, he thought, until I have got a plan of campaign fully worked out. It is no use rushing into things without a proper plan of campaign . . .

'You have some information to give?' he asked as Dr Diana reached him.

'If I'd had any information, I'd have given it to you last night,' she said. 'I merely wanted to know whether you were making any progress. What you might call a friendly enquiry.'

She stood, her feet in flat brown brogues planted wide apart, looking down at him.

'Progress is satisfactory,' Ghote said.

No, he decided abruptly, to put off asking about the keys even one moment longer would be utterly ridiculous.

He coughed, putting his hand up to his mouth.

'There is one matter,' he said.

'All right then,' Dr Diana replied.

She glanced at the little gold watch fastened delicately to her strongly muscular pink wrist flecked with a down of golden hairs.

'But I warn you,' she added, 'I haven't got all day.'

This was a temptation Ghote resisted.

'What I have to ask may take some time,' he replied, feeling each word cutting off any means of flight, 'but it is a most important matter.'

'Out with it then,' Dr Diana said.

'Can you then tell, please, how many keys there are for the dispensary hut?'

For a moment Dr Diana did not answer. She glanced at Ghote with a look of calculation.

'So you've got on to that,' she said at last.

'I regret', Ghote replied, 'the course of the investigation cannot be disclosed to all and sundry.'

Dr Diana laughed.

'My dear man,' she said, 'I can think things out for myself, you know. You can't expect me to believe Frank Masters contracted arsenic poisoning from working in a smelter's shop or acting as assistant to an animal stuffer. Is he your idea of an under-gardener? Can you see him messing about with a fruit spray or something?'

'We admit that the case is being treated as one of murder.'

'Splendid. And how about admitting, while you're at it, that you were busy just a moment ago asking my dispenser about what arsenics we had in that hut. Well, we had some arsenic trioxide. It arrived just yesterday afternoon. Did he tell you that?'

'As a matter of fact, yes,' said Ghote sulkily.

'And is any missing?'

'That is impossible to say.'

Dr Diana put her arms akimbo on either side of her billowing white blouse.

'Listen,' she said, 'you can carry this reticence business too far. I'm a doctor, you know. I happen to be aware of what the lethal dose of that stuff is. And what's more, it's my stuff, or as good as. So cough up. Ek dum.'

'Madam,' Ghote said, 'you are not in position to give orders. It so happens that the jar of powder in question became accidentally spilt.'

Dr Diana burst out laughing.

She stood with the sun shining steadily down on her in the middle of the big back lawn and hooted with laughter.

'You Indians,' she said at last. 'How you manage it I'll never know. To get hold of the source of the poison and then to go and spill it all. I suppose it just slipped out of your fingers? You're wonderful, wonderful.'

'Please,' Ghote said, with an edge of sharpness, 'please, will you be so good as to tell whether you formed this opinion of Indians from the behaviour of your dispenser, Mr Carstairs?'

'Mr Carstairs? Mr Carstairs?'

Dr Diana seemed to find this as funny as anything else. She had to wipe away a tear before she could add to her reply.

'No,' she said, 'as a matter of fact the ever-obliging Sonny is moderately deft with his fingers. I wouldn't have him about the place if he weren't.'

'He is not in any way a clumsy individual?'

'No. I told you. Why do you ask?'

'Because,' Ghote said, 'Mr Carstairs was responsible for dropping the poison in evidence.'

Dr Diana suddenly paid attention.

'Was he indeed?' she said.

She thought for a moment.

'Tell me,' she went on, 'how do you think the arsenic got from my dispensary into Frank's stomach?'

'It is the police belief that he took it unsuspectingly,' Ghote said. 'But this is not the time to discuss.'

He turned resolutely and began to walk towards his waiting truck.

'For heaven's sake, stop waltzing away like that all the time,' Dr Diana said. 'And stop all this "police belief" nonsense. Everybody knows you took half the dustbins away with you, and a pretty fine mess you left behind too.'

Ghote stopped.

He turned back to face her.

'That is wrong,' he said. 'I personally supervised the dustbin operation. There was no mess.'

'Oh, wasn't there? Well, I'm surprised to hear it. There generally is when chaps like you have been around.'

'In this case not,' Ghote said furiously.

'All right, all right. I apologize. That's what you want, isn't it?'

'Apology was called for,' Ghote said.

'All right, you've had one. So now perhaps you'll tell me how you think the arsenic got out of my dispensary. I happen to be interested, you know. Especially as there's only one key and the place is meant to be pretty safe.'

'There is definitely only one key?' Ghote said.

Dr Diana blew out a sigh.

'Yes,' she replied. 'There's only one. We had two when we started, but that fool Sonny Carstairs went and let one of the boys snatch the second out of his hand and throw it under a bloody tram.'

'You had two keys only after the lock was changed?'

'You know all about it, don't you? Why ask me?'

'In a matter of this importance it is impossible to have too many checks,' Ghote replied.

He let his glance as he spoke wander back to the door of the dispensary hut. Sonny, he was certain, was still in there. If he suddenly came out and made his way off at speed, could he catch him?

He decided that he could, and gave his attention to what Dr Diana was saying again.

'All right then, if you're so keen on making checks you can see the correspondence we had with the firm that imported the new lock. They weren't very keen on supplying not more than two keys. I had to point out to them, pretty forcefully as I recall, that to go giving keys to every Tom, Dick and Harry simply defeated the object of the exercise.'

'Thank you,' Ghote said. 'I will send a sergeant to examine, if I may.'

He spoke a little absently.

If Sonny Carstairs had the only key during all the time between the arsenic trioxide arriving and the curry being left near the open tiffin room window, he kept thinking, then Sonny must be the only one who could have got hold of the poison. But if so, surely he could not have been so utterly stupid as to stand there and simply state the facts? No one who was guilty could possible be so senseless, and Sonny was a skilled technician, to say the very least.

He brought his thoughts sharply back to Dr Diana. She had been saying something in a very loud voice.

'I regret,' he said, 'I did not quite catch . . .'

'I said, "Who had the weak-kneed Sonny lent his key to then?" '

Why did I miss it? Ghote asked himself. Why did I miss that Sonny in spite of what he had said must have let the key out of his possession? And at once he knew the answer. Because at the moment he could have worked it out Sonny had suggested that it would be necessary for him to speak to Dr Diana again. And he had been ridiculously unwilling to face being taken for a fool once more.

'It was his habit to lend this key?' he asked sharply. 'I must point out that to allow the key of a building containing a number of poisonous substances to pass from hand to hand in this manner is a highly irresponsible proceeding.'

'Thank you,' said Dr Diana. 'But let me tell you that if I'd ever suspected he'd done this before, I'd have had him out in less time than it takes to tell. And, may I add, it's not particularly responsible to have missed asking him that question for yourself.'

'But if it was not his habit to lend the key,' Ghote answered, feeling himself growing hotter, 'then why do you say he did this? He may have kept it all the time.'

'And sat there and waited for you to find out he was the only one with access to the poison? Sonny may have his faults, but he's not that stupid.'

There was nothing else Ghote could do. It was no use claiming now that he had already thought of this. Dr Diana would simply not believe him.

'Very well,' he said, 'I would go and ask.'

He turned towards the gap in the laden trellis through which he could see the door of the dispensary.

'And you think he'll tell you?' Dr Diana said.

'He will tell,' Ghote replied.

'All right. All right. Don't sound so cross. I dare say you'll have the poor chap beaten up in some out of the way cell or other. He'll talk fast enough then.'

'He will talk when I want.'

'But will he tell you the truth?'

'I will see he does, however long it may take.'

'Even if there's another way of getting to know? A simple and easily made check?'

Ghote swung round. The doctor was standing looking towards him wearing an expression of amused tolerance like a placard round her neck. With an effort he conquered a desire to shout something, anything, at her.

'If you can suggest such a way,' he said, 'I would be delighted.'

'That's better.'

Dr Diana turned and began pacing sternly up and down the big lawn. Ghote walked beside her, adjusting his steps as well as he could to her formidable stride. But beyond that he would not let her get away with anything.

'You told you had something to help,' he said firmly.

Dr Diana looked at him.

'It's just this,' she said. 'It so happens the dispensary was being watched last evening. On my instructions.'

Her announcement, which was made with no little impressiveness, fell singularly flat.

Because, just as she produced it, the inspector became aware that at that very moment a watch was being kept on him.

All along the top of the wall which hid the house's dustbins discreetly from the garden he perceived a row of heads. Two of them he recognized at once. At one end was the boy who called himself Edward G. Robinson. At the other end was the young acrobat, Tarzan. Between were four other gang members.

And it was plain that every word of Dr Diana's clear English tones must have fallen sweetly and easily on those six pairs of pricked up ears even from down by the wistaria-laden trellis.

Inspector Ghote took hold of himself. One deep breath, two, three. Then he put a question without the least tremor of the mortified anger that had at first seized him.

'The dispensary was being watched on your instructions?'

He looked intently at the doctor.

'Why was that? Did you expect such a theft?'

Dr Diana laughed. The short bark of a well-trained English sporting dog.

'No, I didn't actually expect the theft of poison from my stocks. If I had, I can assure you I'd have done something about it, pretty quickly. But as a matter of fact the dispensary was only being watched as a sideline, so to speak.'

'Please explain,' Ghote said.

He tried by keeping his voice low to influence Dr Diana to drop her own tones to a point where every syllable at least would not come clearly to the listening boys.

But his quietness seemed only to make her louder.

'It's really perfectly simple,' she enunciated. 'It so happens I keep my car down in a little shed right at the bottom of the compound. You get into it from a lane at the back. Well, a couple of times recently someone, or some people have bloody well desecrated it.'

Her shocked tones rang through the big garden. From the quick flurry of movement up by the dustbin wall, Ghote deduced quickly enough that the 'desecration' had been the work of the listening gang, and that they were delighted with the reaction it had got.

'I see,' he said, in a properly impressed manner.

'Yes,' said Dr Diana, 'and I had a pretty good idea who was responsible. So, you know what I did?'

Ghote realized what she would have done: have told a couple of the gang to watch the car themselves to stop them interfering with it.

'What did you do?' he asked.

Dr Diana drew in a good breath.

'I told a couple of members of that particular gang to watch the car,' she said. 'Stop them interfering with it themselves.'

She glanced at Ghote with an air of triumph.

'A most ingenious manoeuvre,' he said. 'And who were these boys?'

Dr Diana's face hardened.

'The couple I mentioned last night,' she said. 'The ones they call Edward G. Robinson and Tarzan. The worst of the lot. I've some hopes for Tarzan sometimes, but I utterly despair of the other.'

Ghote was interested in this division.

'Why have you hopes for Tarzan?' he said.

They were getting nearer the dustbin wall. But perhaps it would do the boy good to hear something bright about himself.

'Oh well, we happen to have been able to trace his family,' Dr Diana proclaimed. 'Fisher folk, actually. They come from a little village up near Bassein. There's the usual history of a broken home. The father's taken up with another woman. But when we have a few facts to go on we can generally do something.'

'That is altogether encouraging to hear,' Ghote remarked. 'And did your device stop this desecration?'

'No, it didn't as a matter of fact,' the doctor said shortly. 'But that's not the point. The point is that anyone watching the garage shed would have been bound to see whoever tried to get into the dispensary. Look for yourself.'

She wheeled round and pointed down the long garden.

Ghote saw that she was right. The garage was tucked away in a corner of the compound and like the big dispensary was cut off by the wistaria trellis. To watch the garage it would be necessary to use this as cover and from that position anyone trying to approach the dispensary door, however stealthily, was bound to be seen.

'Yes, you are perfectly correct,' he said, turning to the doctor.

She took him by the elbow and propelled him swiftly and unexpectedly round.

'Then there's your answer,' she said.

She was staring straight at the row of heads along the wall over the dustbins.

5

The boys of the gang, confronted so suddenly with the combined glares of Inspector Ghote and Dr Diana, grinned fiercely back like so many monkeys.

Ghote turned to the doctor.

'I can find you in the house if I want?' he asked.

Evidently contented with the businesslike note in his voice, Dr Diana merely nodded briskly and set off indoors.

The inspector strode swiftly across to the boys.

Slightly to his surprise they made no attempt to scuttle away. When he rounded the wall he saw that they were standing in a row on tip-toe on the line of dustbins, which he had so painstakingly sorted through in the early hours of this same day. The boy in the black jacket, with the privilege of a leader, stood astride the open-topped oil-drum, one bare foot on either rim.

'Come down off there at once,' Ghote snapped.

Nonchalantly the boys jumped one by one and squatted happily on the grimy concrete of the little backyard. Only the one called Tarzan disobeyed. With one flick of his wiry wrists he simultaneously hoisted himself up and swung himself round until in a flash he was sitting perched on the top of the protective wall looking down at the inspector.

Ghote decided to leave him well alone.

He placed himself squarely in front of the black-jacketed, wrinkled-faced, squat form of the leader. He noticed with pleasure that, although the boy had risen to his feet, he had succeeded in almost transfixing him to the wall. Perhaps for once the conversation would not end in some atrocious impertinence followed by flight.

He gave him a long hard look.

'Before it was just talking,' he said, 'but now you have come right into the case. So it is answer up, and speak the truth.'

A wry grin worked its way through the boy's wrinkles.

'Oh, sahib,' he said, 'have you ever know when I not speak truth?'

'Yes, I have,' said Ghote. 'Now then, name?'

'Edward G., you can call me.'

'Edward G. I cannot call. What is your name?'

'OK, OK. You want my full name?'

'I certainly do.'

The boy looked up at him. His eyes were wide.

'Edward G. Robinson.'

It was all Ghote could do to stop his hand flashing out and landing smack on the crinkled cheek in front of him. Perhaps it was the very crinkles that saved the boy.

'You are speaking to police officer,' Ghote said, banging out each word. 'A police officer in the execution of his duty. You have been required to give your name. Your proper name. Are you going to obey?'

The boy's eyes stayed serenely wide.

'No,' he said.

Ghote gritted his teeth.

'Do you realize you are committing offence?' he shouted.

'So what?'

The words allowed the boy to give full play to his proudly acquired American. He took the opportunity for all it was worth.

'So you will find yourself in gaol,' Ghote shouted.

'For just not giving a name you like?'

The eyes in the crinkled face widened again.

'For obstructing a police officer in the execution of his duty.'

The boy abruptly held out his arms towards Ghote. His two thin wrists protruded far beyond the sleeves of the tattered black plastic jacket.

'OK,' he said, 'put on the bracelets.'

Ghote looked down at the pair of hands under his nose with baffled fury. It would be utterly ridiculous to lug a boy like this along to the station in handcuffs and solemnly charge him with an offence. But he was not going to let his authority be flouted. He was dealing with an important case, perhaps the most important case that would ever come his way. And this pipsqueak of a gutter urchin was holding him up.

He felt a wave of red rage come spurting up ready to burst in a deluge of frenzied action.

And suddenly in the middle of it the picture in front of his eyes registered. The two thin wrists held close together, looking as frail as the legs of a bird. Two stalks of grass almost that you could snap between your fingers.

This was only a boy.

What had he been himself at such an age? Nothing like as serious as he was now. The seriousness had come only when he had had to transform his desire to be a policeman into the slow slog of learning the job and taking its constant damping frustrations. He had been long enough sobering down, too. There had been the years at college when in the early days at least it had been touch and go whether he got through the course. And in his schooldays the teachers he had cheeked, the hours he had played truant.

He remembered himself running one day at the tail end of some political procession. He had had little idea of what it was all about. It had been enough that it was a chance to make all the noise he could. To run with his shirt tails flying and his bare feet shooting up the dust behind him, to wave a ragged piece of flag and to shout the worst insults he could think of at anyone who looked staid enough.

'Yah, ravisher of your own sister. Yah, imperialist dog.'

In a flash he pointed his finger straight out at the black-jacketed boy in front of him.

'Stick 'em up, wise guy,' he said.

And it worked.

A slow grin spread itself on the boy's wrinkled old man's face.

'So you wanna play it tough?' he answered.

'You tell me what I wanna know,' Ghote said, 'or I'll fill you so full o' lead you'll never know what hit you.'

All the lore of boyhood afternoons spent in the cinema came flooding back to him. Those long, hot, thirsty mornings of marching through the streets carrying an advertisement placard to earn a free ticket for later on were paying unexpected dividends.

'Now, talk, buddy,' he said, 'and talk fast. Were you watching that dame's car last night?'

'Sure was,' said the boy. 'Me and Tarzan.'

He looked over at his almost naked friend perched on top of the wall.

'OK,' Ghote said. 'And whaddya see?'

But this time the boy did not answer. A wary look flicked back into his eyes.

'What did you see?' Ghote said. 'Come on, this is important. I want to know just what you saw down there.'

'I tell you what I saw,' Edward G. answered suddenly.

'All right.'

'Saw a parakeet,' the boy said. 'Parakeet with green feathers.'

Ghote's fist tightened.

And then he realized his mistake.

'OK, kid,' he said. 'So you saw a boid. But what else did ya see? See any guy hanging around the dispensary?'

For a moment Edward G. calculated. Ghote could see it happening. Then the boy spoke.

'Yeah,' he said. 'I saw some guy.'

'You did?'

'Sure thing.'

'You knew this guy?'

'Sure I knew him.'

'He know you were watching?'

Ghote risked taking his eyes off Edward G. long enough for a quick look at Tarzan on the wall. He just noticed the boy glancing down at the ground on the far side. There was nothing he could do to stop him if he made a bolt for it, unless he wanted to lose Edward G. as well.

He decided to stick to what he had got and shifted a quarter of a pace to the side to be in the best possible position for a quick grab. Edward G. did not seem to take much account of the manoeuvre.

'Nah,' he said, 'when I keep watch on a fella he don't know there's nothing there.'

'Smart guy,' Ghote said. 'You gonna say what this fella did?'

'Maybe.'

'Fill you full o' lead if you don't.'

He bunched his fist into a gun shape again and crouched over it menacingly.

'OK, OK. I talk.'

'Go ahead, buddy, and make it good.'

'This guy he visit dispensary,' Edward G. said.

'Sounds a kinda clever guy get in there without a key.'

'This is a double clever kinda guy. He got a key.'

'Mister,' said Ghote, 'you kinda making things up. Only one key to that hut.'

'Sure thing,' said Edward G. with a professional shrug. 'And this guy got that key off the guy that keeps it.'

'Off Sonny Carstairs?'

'Off that two-timer. Just like we got the other key off him.'

'The one you threw under a tram?' Ghote asked.

The boys eyes went bright with delight.

'Guess he told you,' he said. 'He ain't gonna forget that in a hurry.'

Ghote's mind was cramming in the facts and assimilating them like a high-powered vacuum cleaner.

'OK, buddy,' he said, 'so who was this guy you saw go in the hut?'

But however American the question sounded, and Ghote fondly

believed it might have been concocted in Hollywood itself, it was one too much for Edward G.

Ghote saw the sparkle die out of the boy's eyes. The lips in the thickly wrinkled face closed hard. He shook his head.

'No dice?' Ghote said.

'No dice, mister.'

Ghote began making his fist gun again, but the boy shook his head before the forefinger had had time to point.

Ghote thought rapidly.

He had to know who had managed to get hold of that key at just the critical time. But obviously the limit of cajolery had been reached. And now a touch line was not going to help. The boy would deny everything. He could always be taken down to the station and handed over to a certain sergeant. But, although he would probably talk fast enough then, there was no knowing how much truth he would tell.

There must be some other way.

A bribe? Ghote's hand went to his pocket. He could not be sure. The boy would take the money all right. But would he—?

Then he relaxed.

'Say,' he said, still in his best American, 'you wanna come for a ride in the police wagon?'

There were two seconds while the success of his stratagem was in doubt. Ghote looked into the eyes in the crinkled face and tried to read what was going on there. A tiny upward flicker, as if seeking escape, indicated fear. But then there came a sparkle. Pure joy.

'Sure,' said Edward G., 'I could take a ride.'

He jerked a nod in the direction of Tarzan, still perched on the wall. Just.

'Can he come too?'

'All of you. So long as you spill the beans, and fast.'

There came a movement from the top of the wall. Ghote risked another glance. But Tarzan still lingered. The bait was powerful.

'OK,' Edward G. said lazily. 'I'll tell, mister. You know who I saw? I saw a big-time guy called Amrit Singh.'

Ghote's heart thundered in triumph. He had done it. He had got witnesses who had actually seen the big Sikh thug enter the place where the poison had been kept. And he had done it without in any way suggesting that this was what he wanted to hear.

Well, he thought, there are after all other ways of doing a policeman's job than twisting arms and landing out with kicks.

He looked down at Edward G. again.

'You ever work for Amrit Singh?' he asked with great casualness.

With too much casualness. He entirely forgot the Hollywood note and at once the gang in front of him froze into blankness.

He stood looking at the row of distant, incurious eyes and cursed himself. He had done it again. He had stopped to luxuriate in thoughts of his own cleverness, and he had lost touch at once.

He thought hard. And an idea came to him about what the boys' link with Amrit Singh might quite possibly be.

'Listen fellas,' he said, back in his broadest American, 'so you helped that guy out with something. A bit of smuggling maybe?'

He caught an instant of calculation in the wary eyes in front of him and hurried on.

'So what? Who cares? Smuggling's something the Customs guys can take care of. Smuggling never meant a thing to me.'

Edward G. grinned.

'OK,' he said, 'you win, I guess. That guy Amrit's working a big racket in gold. Could be we help him out sometimes.'

'Like last night?' Ghote said.

He held his breath.

'That's what he was here for,' Edward G. said. 'Heard some of his gold had been pick up. By Frank Masters. Came to look. Pronto.'

Ghote felt himself getting nearer and nearer the heart of the matter with every word he heard. Frank Masters. Here was the beginning of finding out how the good American was linked with the Bombay bad man.

'Amrit Singh was looking for gold?' he asked cautiously.

'Sure. The big boss locked the gold he found in the dispensary hut. Best place to lock anything. Is one place we can't get in. We tried, but we can't.'

Inwardly Ghote recorded with pleasure the advanced state his relations with the gang had reached. When Edward G. could happily admit to attempted theft in this way, things had certainly improved.

'So Amrit Singh was coming to get the gold back?' he asked.

'Guess so.'

'How did he hear it was there?' Ghote asked. 'From one of you? Who passed on a message? Was it you?'

He looked at the black-jacketed figure in front of him.

'Nope. Not me. Guess the news was all around the joint. Even they knew.'

'They?'

'The other big shots. Them.'

Ghote nodded.

'Why did the big shot himself hide the gold?' he asked, feeling his heart beat faster with every mention of Frank Masters.

Edward G. began to shrug this one off.

Then suddenly his attitude changed. He looked up at Ghote with eyes bright in his old man's face.

'You want me to tell?' he said. 'I could tell good.'

Ghote had control enough of himself to smile.

'Not interested in any more of those stories of yours,' he said.

Edward G. laughed.

'Was a honey,' he said. 'Went down a wow before.'

'Not for me,' Ghote said.

The boy looked up to the washed-out blue of the sky.

'We gonna hit the road yet?' he asked, nonchalantly flicking one of the many buzzing flies off his taper-thin thigh.

'Soon enough, soon enough,' Ghote replied. 'Maybe you'd care to tell where this Amrit guy is hanging out right now?'

Edward G. shrugged.

'Right now the guy's on the trail,' he said.

Ghote experienced a sudden vision, triggered off by this unlikely jumble of film talk, of the big Sikh loping along a dust track dressed in a ten-gallon hat, smoking a big cigar and with a sub-machine gun tucked under his arm.

'You wanna see the guy?' Edward G. asked.

'Sure thing.'

'Be right here tomorrow round about this time,' the boy said.

Ghote snatched a hungry glance at his watch. Ten o'clock. At ten tomorrow morning he would have Amrit Singh under his hand.

He took a deep breath.

This time he would not exult. He had been very lucky, and the luck might not hold. Besides could he really trust Edward G.?

He looked at the boy coolly.

'You're mighty ready to talk,' he said.

'Sure am,' said the boy.

The crinkled face looked up at him. The familiar twisted grin manifested itself.

'With all you policias around, you'd pick the guy up pretty quick. So why not spill the beans? And besides . . .'

A dangerously thin hand was held out.

Cupped.

Ghote knew better than to take his new friends completely on trust. Hardly had the police truck disappeared down Wodehouse Road in the direction of the Afghan Church with the gang clustered in the rear and the rigid back of the young driver signalling utter disapproval, than he had turned and sprinted for the telephone.

CID Records confirmed that Amrit Singh was still nowhere in sight. Yes, it was most likely he was out of Bombay.

So far so good.

He asked to be transferred to the Fingerprint Bureau. Yes, they had got a lot of prints from the dispensary at the Masters

Foundation, and a bloody waste of – Amrit Singh? The tone of the conversation changed rapidly. There was a remarkably short pause, and then an excited voice.

'Yes, sir. Definitely yes, Inspector. Prints of Amrit Singh's in the dispensary. Quite definitely. Thank you very much, Inspector.'

Ghote asked whether the Sikh's prints could also be found on the packet of broken brown glass or the black screw-top he had brought in later. They would check. It would take time but they would check. If it wasn't that the defence would insist on every precaution, they would find them there in five minutes.

No, all right. They would play it the inspector's way.

Ghote banged down the phone and stood for an instant thinking. What next? Yes, another of the facts he had stored away during his productive talk with Edward G.

The key. Amrit Singh had entered the dispensary with a key. A key he had got from 'the two-timer' Sonny Carstairs.

Ghote thought about Sonny for a few moments, and evolved a plan of action.

About an hour later, an hour spent mostly in allowing the reporters waiting at headquarters to extract a cautiously optimistic statement, Ghote watched two constables march into his little office in a great clatter of heavy boots and swinging brawny arms. Between them hung the neat figure of the little Anglo-Indian dispenser.

Ghote dismissed the constables and waited till the door had shut. Then he asked Sonny to sit down on the square-looking, heavy little wooden chair in front of his desk. Sonny sat with his knees close together and one hand clutching the other.

For an instant he looked down and flicked his fingers straight so that he could see the nails.

'I asked you to come to see me because a very serious matter has been brought to my notice,' Ghote said slowly.

Sonny looked at him across the lined and blotched surface of the desk.

For a little while Ghote kept silent.

After the hours of steadily burning sun the day was by now decidedly hot. Sonny began gently to sweat.

'In the course of enquiries,' Ghote began again at last, 'it has come to light that a certain person obtained unauthorized access to the dispensary at the Masters Foundation.'

He left it at that once more. Sonny clearly felt obliged to say something.

'How—? How did this person do – do that?'

'You know the answer perfectly well.'

'No, Inspector. Really I don't. I think perhaps you must have got a false impression. I'm afraid I can't help you on this. Yes, yes. I'm sorry, I can be of no help at all. If you'll excuse me. So, if you'll excuse me . . .'

Sonny stood up.

Ghote recalled once again how when he had begun to question Sonny sharply about the arsenic trioxide he had in a panicky gesture swept the jar to the ground. Perhaps that had been just acting so as to get rid of incriminating evidence. But he had not thought so then, and nor had he when he had decided to haul Sonny into the intimidating atmosphere of headquarters. Now was the time to prove it.

He glanced sharply up at Sonny.

'Sit down,' he shouted.

For half a second Sonny stood stock-still.

Then slowly he subsided on to the squat wooden chair.

'So you cannot help me on this,' Ghote went on. 'So you would like to be excused. I will bet you would. No wonder you cannot help me. You cannot help me because you are to blame.'

'No, no. Really, no. Honest to God, man, it isn't so.'

'What happened to the key of that hut?'

'Nothing did. Honestly, nothing.'

'It is the only key, is that not so?'

'I don't know.'

'Of course you do. You admitted it to me. It is the only key to that hut. Is that not so?'

'I – I suppose it is.'

'And someone else got hold of it. I want to know how.'

'I can't say. I can't say.'

'Can't you indeed?'

Ghote allowed a gleam of malice to come into his eyes.

'Can't you indeed?' he repeated slowly. 'Then we will have to see what we can do to help you, will we not?'

'No.'

He knew then that he had been right. The note of fear was too plain.

'Oh yes, we will,' he said, leaning forward across the desk till his face was only a couple of feet from Sonny's.

'You know that we have ways of helping people's memories in this department?'

'But – But it isn't allowed.'

'No, it is not allowed.'

He paused.

'But that does not mean it is not done. Now, that key. Who did you let take it? Answer now, or we will go downstairs.'

It was the last innocent enough phrase that did the trick. Sonny went grey under the sheen of sweat. He licked his lips.

'You know Amrit Singh, Inspector?' he said in a half-whisper.

Ghote nodded.

'He made me give it to him. You won't understand.'

Ghote thought he understood very well. Sonny was not a difficult man to make do what you wanted.

'When did he take it?' he said, not letting the pressure up.

'It was going on for eight o'clock last night, Inspector. I was just up in my little room on the roof. He suddenly came in. It was through the window. I knew him. He'd been consorting with the boys. I'd heard them talking about him. I knew what sort of man he was. Of low moral character. He demanded the key. What else could I do, Inspector?'

'So you handed it to him?'

'Yes.'

A total whisper now.

'And later he gave it back?'

'Yes. I begged him to. I said that, if he did, no one would ever know he'd had it. So after I'd given it to him I just sat there on the edge of my bed and waited. And after about quarter of an hour I heard a bit of noise out on the roof. And then suddenly the key came whizzing in. It hit me, Inspector. Look.'

Sonny quickly began tearing at the buttons of his jacket.

Ghote thought with amusement that it was exactly like Amrit Singh to have returned the key by throwing it good and hard at the poor dupe he had got it from.

'Undressing will not be necessary,' he said sharply.

Sonny fumbled for a bit trying to do the buttons up again. Then he stopped.

Ghote stood up.

'You can go now,' he said. 'Though I must warn you that you have not heard the last of this.'

He walked over to the door and held it wide.

He was longing to see the back of the wretched Anglo-Indian. Only then could he indulge for a few moments in pure exultation. This was enough. He was sure of it. Amrit Singh's fingerprints in the dispensary. Some evidence to come about a consignment of gold seized by Frank Masters. It should be easy enough to tie that up. And finally this plain, incredible statement that Amrit Singh had obtained the key of the dispensary where the poison was kept only a short time before Frank Masters had eaten the fatal meal. This time he had got the big Sikh. Good and proper.

Because this time the master thug had made one mistake. He had misjudged his catspaw. He might have guessed that Sonny would be as easy to break as a wisp of straw. But he must have relied on him keeping quiet at all costs about letting the key out of his possession. He ought to have known better than to trust such a soft creature for anything.

'Out you go,' Ghote said.

Sonny got up from the heavy little chair with reluctance. He approached the door Ghote was holding open as if what lay beyond was bound to be unpleasant.

For a moment he paused and looked at the inspector.

'Go on,' Ghote said impatiently. 'I have a great deal to do.'

'But don't you want me to tell you who else made me give them the key last night?' he said.

Ghote looked up at him.

6

Inspector Ghote's tower of exultant thoughts collapsed in an instant about his head. He could hardly believe that the despised Sonny Carstairs had said what he had. Yet the words had been clear enough. He had let the only key of the dispensary out of his keeping, not once but twice. The evidence against Amrit Singh was suddenly totally dubious.

Ghote stared at the neat figure of the Anglo-Indian dispenser. Perhaps if he had not treated him so contemptuously, he would have been alerted to the fact that there was more evidence to come. He sighed and resolved not to despise another witness ever again.

'You gave that key to two people?' he said.

Sonny Carstairs, smarting still from the treatment dealt out to him, evidently enjoyed Ghote's present discomfiture.

'Of course I gave it to two of them, man,' he said.

Ghote was not going to stand this.

'And who was this second person?' he snapped. 'It was bad enough to let Amrit Singh have it. Who else did you give it to?'

Sonny Carstairs gave him the hint of a smile, quiet and self-satisfied.

'I gave it to Mr Chatterjee,' he said.

'To Mr Chatterjee, the social worker at the Foundation?'

'Of course.'

'And what was this for? Does he have access to the dispensary? Was there some special need?'

Sonny Carstairs shrugged.

'He wouldn't tell me what it was for, man,' he replied. 'It was only a little while after Amrit Singh threw – after he gave me back the key. A knock came at my door. It was Krishna Chatterjee. He said he desired to speak to me urgently. I let him into my room and he asked me for the key.'

'And you just handed it over?'

The dispenser looked a little put out for the first time since he had produced his bombshell.

'Well, no. No, I didn't,' he said.

'But you told you let him have the key.'

'Yes. Yes, in the end I did.'

'He threatened you like Amrit Singh?'

Ghote thought of the social worker, whom he had seen on his tour of the Foundation the night before. He formed physically a complete contrast to the big, tough Sikh thug. He was a smallish, round-faced, slightly plump Bengali with a gentle, bubbling manner and big, soft almond-shaped eyes for ever flitting here and there. It was difficult to imagine him threatening to batter the life out of anybody at all, even the neat little Sonny Carstairs.

'No, Inspector, not threatened really,' Sonny said.

'What then? You gave him the key. He was not meant to have it. Did he give you reason?'

'No, Inspector. That was the hell of it. He refused absolutely to say why he wanted it. That was when he said he would tell . . . That was when I refused to let him have it.'

Sonny drew himself up with a touch of pride.

'You refused to let him have it,' Ghote said. 'Yet he went away with it all right. What happened?'

'I just sort of changed my mind, Inspector.'

'When he said he would do what? Come on, out with it. You are in trouble enough as it is.'

Any tendency to resistance in the dispenser had been well and truly rolled out of him in the earlier part of the interview. Now he simply swallowed once.

'He said he would tell Mr Masters about the drugs,' he muttered.

It did not take Ghote long to realize what this must mean.

'Oh,' he said, 'so we have the misapplication of drugs to take into account also.'

He took a longer look at Sonny.

'But you are not addict, I think,' he said.

'Honest to God, no, Inspector,' Sonny babbled. 'But just sometimes I used to take a sniff of ether or something. Till Mr Chatterjee caught me one day. And he said if he ever suspected I was doing it again he'd have me sacked – dismissed.'

'I see. And he threatened to have you sacked again if you did not hand over the key?'

'Yes, sir. Yes, Inspector.'

'But he did not tell you why he wanted it? Not at all? Not a hint even?'

'No, Inspector, honestly.'

'Then I will have to ask.'

But before Ghote put his question to Krishna Chatterjee he got a chance to ask another which had worried him perhaps even more. If the social worker had gone to the trouble of bullying the key out of Sonny Carstairs, surely he must have used it. After all, he had returned it in time for Sonny to open the dispensary up again when Frank Masters had had to receive treatment. So two people would have entered the hut that evening. But Edward G. and the gang had said nothing about a second visitor.

Ghote felt let down. After all that he had done to come down to the level of these boys, after all those silly games, they still had not been fair with him.

As soon as he had got rid of Sonny he had rushed down to his truck and told the driver to get round to the Masters Foundation as fast as possible. The Dodge drew up in the gravelly drive with a great screeching of brakes. As Ghote had half hoped, the noise and dust of their arrival immediately conjured up the familiar apparition in tattered and torn black plastic jacket.

The boy evidently believed that his relations with Ghote were still in the same comfortable state as when he had set off on the promised jaunt in the police truck. He sauntered carelessly up. Behind him the gang approached in an equally happy-go-lucky way.

'Hi,' said Edward G.

Ghote waited till he came right up close. Then his hand shot out and closed firmly round the battered black jacket.

'You,' he said. 'You are just the one I want.'

The boy blinked at him in utter astonishment. There could be no doubt that this time the inspector had the upper hand.

'No,' Ghote barked, 'just what do you mean by not telling that Mr Chatterjee went in the dispensary also?'

For an instant the question really worried the boy. Then the old, wry half-grin sent the deep wrinkles of his face off into new convolutions.

'You never ask,' he said. 'You wanna learn that, fella. Don't ask: don't get.'

'I'll teach you to fella me,' Ghote shouted suddenly.

All the rage of his disappointment over having had Amrit Singh so neatly trapped boiled up unexpectedly. He gathered up the tattered black jacket in his fist.

But Edward G. had enraged too many people in his short life not to know the signs to a hair's breadth. And in a moment Ghote found himself holding the filthy old jacket while its owner danced back to the edge of the gravel and stood on tiptoe looking at him, wearing only a grimy pair of shorts.

Ghote glowered.

'You knew it was important if anyone got into dispensary,' he said. 'I asked you specially about Amrit Singh, and you had the damned cheek to say nothing about Mr Chatterjee.'

His reply did not come from Edward G. himself. As if by some signal, he deputed the task to his lieutenant, the boy called Tarzan. And the reply was characteristic.

With a sudden wild whoop the boy launched himself high into the air and with the tips of his outstretched fingers caught hold of the edge of the beam supporting the roof of the front door porch. From there he swung forward without a break. His legs were extended, his bare toes pointed. He came flying towards Ghote before the inspector had time to realize what was happening. A long, sharp, extremely dirty, big toe nail just perceptibly flicked him on the nose. And then the boy was swinging back, and a moment later had dropped lightly to his feet and had darted off with the others out of sight round the back of the house.

Ghote stood forcing himself not to put up a hand and rub the place on his nose.

So when he had found Krishna Chatterjee, resident social worker at the Masters Foundation, it was with no very subtle method that he went to work.

The door of the office had a wooden nameplate on it with 'Krishna Chatterjee' painted in spidery black letters on a white background. Ghote gave the panel just underneath one perfunctory bang and opened the door.

The room was very narrow and long like a cupboard, except that at the far end there was a tall window. The cupboard-like look of the place was added to by the shelves along both walls running from the door down to the window. They were crammed with books, new and old, tall and squat, some fat and glossy, others thin, starved and paper-covered. They pushed and strained against each of the partitions fitted at intervals along the shelves.

For some reason the sight of them only inflamed Ghote the more.

What would anyone want with so many books? Spending a whole lifetime with their head buried in useless old tomes? What was the point of that? There were things to be done in this world. Frank Masters had not wasted his time reading books.

A figure stooping over an enormous sheet of paper spilling over the edges of a rickety typist's table looked up. In the dim light of the tall, narrow room Ghote could make out little more than a pair of enormous brown eyes glistening like some disturbed night animal's.

And as frightened.

So he began in a fashion that surprised even himself.

'All these tomes,' he said, 'all these tomes.'

He gestured towards either wall.

'What do you want with all these tomes?'

Krishna Chatterjee stood up, still stooping slightly as if the position was habitual.

'Well, it is Inspector Ghote,' he said.

He seemed relieved.

'Yes, it is Inspector Ghote. And Inspector Ghote is wanting words with you.'

Mr Chatterjee bustled round his desk, which in the confined space between the two book-lined walls was not an easy thing to do.

'Come in, come in, Inspector,' he said. 'Won't you sit down? The chair is not unsafe. I can guarantee that. Absolute, unconditional guarantee. You see, I have evidence. This chair is regularly sat upon by innumerable small boys while I talk to them in very imperfect Marathi or Gujarati. What better evidence of essential stability could you have than that? Eh?'

He held the chair in front of him with both hands and looked up at the inspector with his big eyes bigger than ever.

Certainly the chair did not look strong. It was a plain wooden one with a crude pattern of a lotus stamped on the seat. The rungs of the back were tilted slightly out of true.

'Never mind chairs,' Ghote snapped. 'We have more important matters than chairs to talk.'

Mr Chatterjee lowered the offensive chair to the ground, peered at it for an instant and shrugged his rounded shoulders.

'Yes,' he said, 'the books. All the books. The tomes. You want to discuss them. Well now, Inspector, I must confess that you strike me on the raw there. Yes, definitely on the raw. I do not need so many books. I realize it. And yet, you know, I cannot seem to help myself buying them. And really there is very little room left for new acquisitions. Very little indeed.'

He turned to examine anxiously the long rows of shelves.

'But I promise you one thing, Inspector,' he said, 'bibliophile that I am, I think I can say with perfect honesty that I do not let my passion interfere with my work. Indeed, it sustains it. Yes, sustains it, I think I can say. You see, Inspector, it is absolutely necessary in a profession like mine to have the widest possible grasp of human nature. And what can enlarge one's grasp of the infinite peculiarities of one's fellow creatures more than the study of the many and varied books that have been written about them? What indeed?'

Inspector Ghote caught hold of two words in all the spate.

'Perfect honesty,' he repeated. 'Perfect honesty. I do not think you can talk to me about that, Mr Chatterjee.'

The two big brown eyes in the round face in front of him suddenly were flooded with pain.

Mr Chatterjee held out his two hands wide.

'Inspector,' he said, 'that is an accusation I hoped never to hear. I am dishonest, of course, I recognize that. I talk of perfect honesty, but I recognize that there are states to which we can never attain. But, Inspector, I promise you, without one iota of unnecessary self-praise, that I do make an absolute point of keeping the ideal of honesty always in the forefront of my mind. It is not easy, you know, not easy at all. But dealing with the sort of young people who fall to my daily lot I believe it is absolutely essential. Absolutely.'

'So you practise honesty with the sweepings of the pavements,' Ghote said, 'and forget all about it when you are talking with a police inspector.'

'But no, my dear sir. Are you saying that I have been dishonest with you? Inspector, there has been some dreadful error.'

The big-eyed Bengali was every bit as voluble as before, but Ghote thought that somehow he was beginning to lack the full torrential flow of assurance.

'Nevertheless,' he said. 'I am accusing.'

Krishna Chatterjee looked round his book-lined retreat in plainly growing dismay. He reached up and pulled a tall volume from one of the higher shelves, peered at the title on its spine as if he expected it to have suddenly altered, put the book down on his little desk, trotted round to the far side, stooped and picked up a scrap of paper from the floor, examined it, shrugged, went to the window and lifted the catch, pushed at the two tall frames, realized after a little that they were held fast by the bottom bar, released it and eventually turned and faced the inspector again.

'It seems most appallingly hot all of a sudden,' he said.

Ghote marched up and stood in front of the desk.

'Mr Chatterjee,' he said, 'why did you lie to me in those few minutes that I saw you last night?'

The big brown eyes clouded over.

'Inspector, why should I lie?'

'Mr Chatterjee, your employer, the late Mr Frank Masters, has been murdered.'

'Inspector, I know it. I know it. Inspector, this is a very terrible thing. That man was an immense benefactor, Inspector. An immense benefactor. He poured out money into this city. I cannot begin to enumerate the causes that gained from his generosity. It is a totally terrible thing that he has been done to death in this appallingly violent way. Inspector, all my life I have striven to put into practice the principles of non-violence. To me, Inspector, this is catastrophe. Absolute catastrophe.'

'The principles of non-violence,' Ghote said. 'You seem very concerned to emphasize those. Can it be that you have ceased to obey them?'

A look of penetrating pain overwhelmed Krishna Chatterjee's roundly mild face.

For once he was deprived of speech.

'Now,' said Inspector Ghote sharply, 'I think it is time you told the whole truth. What did you want with the key of the dispensary yesterday evening?'

Krishna Chatterjee clasped his hands tightly together. He swallowed.

'Inspector, I do not know what you are saying. What key of the dispensary is this? I am a social worker, Inspector. That is a very different kettle of fish, I assure you, from a medical worker like my good friend Carstairs. Carstairs is the medical man here. And of course Dr Diana. Though not a man. Of course.'

'Your good friend Carstairs?' Ghote said.

'Well, that is of course only a manner of speaking. Yes, only what you might call a polite fiction. Not that I haven't the highest esteem for Carstairs. Don't misunderstand me, Inspector, I beg. No, I have the highest esteem for the good fellow, but I must admit in all honesty that he is not my friend. There are no common interests, Inspector. That is the whole trouble. And I do not think without some community of interest one can hope to achieve any really satisfactory relationship with a person. Except on a purely superficial plane, of course. Except purely superficially.'

'Then Carstairs is not a friend of yours?'

'Well, regretfully, I must admit it. No.'

'So that you had to use methods of blackmail to obtain that key from him?'

'Inspector, I do not know what you are saying.'

'Mr Chatterjee, you know very well. You obtained the sole key to the dispensary from Carstairs. You entered the hut and you took from it the poison that was subsequently found in the body of Frank Masters. You administered that poison.'

The round-shouldered Bengali glanced desperately from side to side. He opened his mouth to speak but no sound came. He clutched his stomach as if he were going to be violently ill.

'Inspector,' he said. 'Inspector, you must understand. I will make an admission.'

Having got the word out at last he seemed happier. He stood up straighter and let his hands fall to his sides.

'Yes, Inspector, I see that I can no longer attempt to hide the truth. I see, indeed, that it was foolish of me to contemplate doing so. I hope you will believe me when I say that I think it was truly the first time in my life I have ever attempted to practise flagrant deception. And I fear I was not particularly adept. Well no, I suppose I am grateful for that. In the long run.'

'The truth,' said Ghote implacably.

'Yes, the truth. I must tell it. Very well.'

Krishna Chatterjee stroked at his round cheeks with the tips of his fingers to brush away some of the beads of sweat that had collected there.

'Terrible humidity,' he said.

Ghote looked at him unblinkingly.

'Very well then, Inspector. I must confess that I did indeed obtain that key from the unfortunate Sonny Carstairs. I am afraid I took advantage of a piece of inform—'

'All right,' Ghote cut in. 'I know all about what you said to Carstairs. We need not go over all that.'

'Yes. Yes, I see that a person in your profession must avoid unnecessary and repetitious statements. Time is of the essence, doubtless.'

'It is. Come on.'

'Well then, you know that I had the key to the hut.'

'Yes.'

'And that in due course I returned it.'

'Yes.'

'Well then, I think that is all I can tell you, Inspector. Yes, with the greatest possible good will I do not think I have the right to add a word to that. No, not a word.'

'You took the key from Carstairs, and what did you do with it next? You went to that hut, did you not? And you took the poison. And then what?'

'No, Inspector. I can give you an assurance that I did no such thing. Though, of course, I realize that in the light of my past action you cannot be expected to extend any great degree of credence to my unsupported word. No, I realize that. But that is the most I can give you. Yes, definitely the very utmost.'

'Mr Chatterjee, I want to know what you did with the poison. Your exact course of action, Mr Chatterjee.'

'No.'

Krishna Chatterjee was sweating more profusely than ever now. He turned to the window and pushed it open wide.

'No,' he repeated, 'not another word.'

'The whole truth,' said Ghote.

He stepped sharply to the side of the desk.

And with a cumbersome, curious wriggling sideways lurch, little Mr Chatterjee was out of the window.

For a moment Ghote stood and gaped. The sudden physical action seemed so totally out of keeping with the scholarly Bengali's whole mode of existence that he could hardly believe that it had taken place.

For a moment only he stood and gaped.

And then he was after him. Three long strides took him to the window. In one vault he was through. He looked to left and right.

The window gave onto the side of the big bungalow. There was a narrow cement path running alongside the house wall and then a wide flowerbed full of big unkempt bushes, their leaves wilting a little in the hot sunshine. If Krishna Chatterjee had darted into these and then had stood quite still, it was going to be impossible to tell which way he had gone. And if Ghote happened to choose wrong, then before he could get back there would be nothing easier for Mr Chatterjee than to walk quietly away.

The sunlight glared down, too, just here and made it difficult to see anything more than the varied green masses of the bushes and the dense purple shadows under them.

Ghote blinked.

There was only one thing to do.

He began shouting.

'You there, come out.' 'Come out, you.' 'You'll pay for this.' 'Just wait till I get you down to the station.' 'Come out, you, I can see—'

And it worked.

Like a startled mouse Mr Chatterjee broke from cover not ten yards away. He ran ducking and blundering through the bushes with the dry earth under them sending up a wavy column of whitish dust. Ghote ran along the cement path until he had nearly drawn level and then plunged sideways.

'You stop,' he shouted once again.

Mr Chatterjee stopped.

'Run, sahib. Run away.'

A sudden shrill voice darted out from just behind Ghote. He turned in fury. Krishna Chatterjee began to run again, with little waddling steps hardly faster than a walk.

As Ghote had expected, standing at the corner of the house, once again clothed in the abominable black jacket, was Edward G. Robinson.

'You wait,' Ghote shouted at him.

He turned to pursue Krishna Chatterjee.

And suddenly went sprawling into a prickly, wiry-branched flowering shrub. He rolled, cursing, out of it and looked down to see what he had stumbled over.

A thin noose of rope was neatly caught round one brown shoe. He followed its length back. And there was Tarzan, grinning with great cheerfulness.

Ghote jumped to his feet.

In a flash Tarzan disappeared round the side of the building. Ghote tugged at the rope till it came off and set out in the direction Mr Chatterjee had bumblingly taken.

A few quick steps brought him to the driveway. The Dodge truck was standing there in a patch of shade. The driver was sitting at the wheel, bolt upright and quietly snoozing. Krishna Chatterjee, for all the ineffectiveness of his run, was just leaving the house gate.

In Wodehouse Road outside a bus was slowing to a stop. There was nothing to prevent the little Bengali jumping on board and then getting off again wherever it pleased him.

Ghote ran a pace or two forward. But it was hopeless.

'Stop,' he shouted.

And abruptly Krishna Chatterjee stopped.

He stopped, turned around, saw Ghote and began coming towards him. He was bending a little at the waist from the violence of his exertion.

Ghote did not have the strength of will even to go to meet him. He just stood, hoping the round-shouldered Bengali would not change his mind.

He did not.

In a few moments he was standing in front of the inspector.

'My dear sir,' he said. 'I owe you a most profound apology.'

7

Krishna Chatterjee apologized. He stated at length how wrong it had been for him to try to run off. He hinted that it was only the unusualness of his situation which had made him act in this way.

But he did not offer the least explanation of why he had persuaded Sonny Carstairs to hand over the key of the dispensary. Nothing Ghote could say would budge him.

'I am very sorry, Inspector, but I cannot divulge my reasons. I can only state as positively as possible that I did not in any way harm Mr Masters. It was the very last thing that I would wish to do.'

'But you took the poison?'

'Inspector, I did not.'

'But you went into the dispensary?'

Mr Chatterjee hesitated.

'Yes,' he said. 'I did.'

'Then, if it was not to take the poison, what was it for?'

'Inspector, I regret profoundly but I decline to say.'

'I could arrest you on the evidence I have.'

'Then you must arrest me, Inspector.'

'But if you say you did not kill Frank Masters.'

'I do say so. Most emphatically. But I realize that you cannot, in the nature of things, proceed to act on my unsupported word alone. You would be perfectly within your rights in carrying out my arrest.'

But, thought Ghote, I will not do it. Not however much I can see how, in spite of your strangely honest denials, you could really be the murderer of Frank Masters, a man of truth until the moment comes for the one lie. But I cannot bring myself to arrest you because I no more know for certain you are guilty than I know that Amrit Singh is. The evidence balances up. To a grain.

Amrit Singh forcing Sonny Carstairs to hand over the dispensary key. Krishna Chatterjee blackmailing him into doing the same thing. Amrit Singh hurling the key back after keeping it for just the time needed. Krishna Chatterjee returning the same key before it was wanted for the emergency of Frank Masters's illness. Amrit Singh's fingerprints discovered in the dispensary. Krishna Chatterjee confessing to having been there himself.

The balance was exact.

There remained one hope. The Fingerprint Bureau were still testing the mess of brown glass fragments that had been the arsenic trioxide jar. If they could definitely find one of Amrit Singh's prints on one fragment . . . Or one of Krishna Chatterjee's . . .

But not both. Not both, Ghote prayed.

Nor did a rare evening at home, spoilt only by four separate phone calls from newspapers, none of which Ghote now found easy to answer, do anything to resolve his dilemma. He arrived at the office next morning, Sunday, hoping passionately that the report from the Fingerprint Bureau might be there to provide the answer.

And as soon as he opened the door he saw it. A single sheet of foolscap paper in the familiar style with a dozen lines typewritten on it. And the heading 'For the attention of Inspector Ghote'. He crossed the little room in two strides, picked up the sheet, twirled it round, and read.

His spirits slumped.

Sonny Carstairs's prints had been identified on the glass fragments, and so had Dr Diana's. There was one other set, unidentified, doubtless belonging to someone at the pharmaceuticals factory. But not a trace of Amrit Singh's.

And equally not a trace of Krishna Chatterjee's, since the bureau had his prints along with all the others taken at the Foundation.

There was worse to come, a little. Underneath the bureau's report lay another one. It was from the sergeant detailed to check the key business, and it entirely confirmed what Dr Diana had said. The sergeant had seen her correspondence with the lock importers. Something of the awe with which she had come to be regarded by the firm seeped through even the formal words of the report. And the facts were clear: only two keys to the dispensary had ever existed. Only one did now.

So it would all depend on what could be got out of Amrit Singh at ten o'clock. There were a great many things Ghote wanted to ask him: details of his movements during and after the time the poison had been taken from the dispensary, what exactly he had been doing hanging around the Masters Foundation, and, above all, what his relations were with Frank Masters himself.

Nor did a third report, brought in a few minutes later, advance matters. It was on the check made to see whether Fraulein Glucklich had in fact spent Friday evening with Swami Dnyaneshwar. The swami had been unexpectedly precise. He was prepared to swear his sannyasini had been well and truly at his feet the whole time. Definitely.

Ghote looked at his watch. A long while to go yet before it got near ten o'clock.

He went over in his mind arrangements made the evening before to have the big bungalow in Wodehouse Road surrounded at the appropriate time. It would be a tricky business. Put too many men into the area before Amrit Singh was due, and it was almost certain he would spot something and be scared off; on the other hand, if it came to an arrest, there could never be too many hands waiting to grab a character like the big Sikh.

Resolutely Ghote set himself to tackle what routine work he could find to do. But it lasted all too short a time.

He picked up the telephone and spoke to Chavan, the uniformed inspector in charge of the ambush party. Chavan simply made it clear that he resented being fussed over, and Ghote put down the receiver with a sigh.

He looked at his watch again. It would still be absurdly early to set off.

He took out his copy of the *Times of India* Sunday edition. He had already read the meagre report of the case and the long obituary of Frank Masters. For all its length the latter had not helped him one little bit to understand the American. There had been the lists of charities which had benefited from his wealth. There was a reference to his education in America, but the names of the school and college he had attended meant nothing to Ghote. There was a more detailed account of the origins of the Masters fortune, but what use was it to know about how Frank Masters's grandfather had added acre to acre and oilwell to oilwell? There was a sonorous passage about India's poverty. It had not helped.

Ghote removed the paper's weekend supplement for women and children and put it in the top drawer of his desk to take home later. He closed the drawer firmly and with conscious virtue. He had resisted the lure of the colour comic page.

He turned to the political news.

> Pak. inhumanity to women. Even hard-boiled, old-time reactionaries burst into tears in the Lok Sabha today while referring to the plight of the large number of women who were recently abducted in East Pakistan.

Ghote shook his head. There was a limit to the amount of that that he was prepared to read. Something a little more down to earth would be needed to take his mind off Amrit Singh until the moment he could decently set off.

> Opposition Parties Accused. Stating that the Congress today was as strong as ever, a party spokesman said Opposition

members were magnifying small differences to vilify the organization. Party members should not be frightened by such tactics of the Opposition, but work with redoubled energy and in a selfless manner for the good of the people.

Ghote looked up. Was there something he should be doing with selfless energy at this moment to make certain of pinning that enemy of the people, Amrit Singh?

He looked all round his little office. A flicker of movement caught his eye down in the dark corner by the filing cabinet. He got up and went over.

Sure enough, at the bottom of the small glass-fronted bookcase in which he kept copies of current information circulars a tiny lizard had contrived to get itself trapped. As he approached, the little beast flung itself into a maniac whirl of activity trying to penetrate the thin sheet of glass that cut it off from escape. But within a few seconds it had fallen on its back on the bottom of the shelf, palpitating and exhausted.

Ghote took a sheet of paper from the top of his desk, rolled it into a tube, opened the drop-front of the bookcase and flicked the little creature out.

For an instant it lay on the floor, its beady eyes still. Then suddenly it appeared to realize what had so mysteriously happened to it. With a twist of its tail it righted itself, paused just long enough to gulp once, and darted straight into the safety of a small crack between the floor and the wall.

Ghote walked back to his chair, picked up the *Times of India* again and flipped over the pages. For a few seconds he lingered at an advertisement showing four women grinning frantically over a naked baby with a fifth looking soulfully away out of the picture with firmly shut mouth. 'A friendly tip to the fifth woman,' he read. 'Use our toothpaste and smile like the others: brush your teeth with it every night . . . and every morning, of course. More confidence in company . . . more fun!'

He found himself wondering whether his own breath was up to standard. He tried jutting out his lower lip into a sort of vent shape and puffing upwards. It seemed to be all right but it was hard to tell. And with a convenient neem tree at the bottom of the garden at home it was surely a waste not to use its twigs as he had always done.

He puffed upwards again.

His hand stretched out to the notebook lying on his desk ready to be slipped into his pocket when he left. He flicked through it until he came to the first blank sheet and scrawled a couple of words.

'Buy toothpaste.'

He looked at his watch again. Half an hour more and he could leave without upsetting Chavan's plans.

He made up his mind to settle down to the book reviews page. It was at least a way of catching up with all those things he wanted to know about, and should just occupy the right time.

He lowered his head and plunged in.

The door opened briskly.

It was Deputy Superintendent Naik. Hastily Ghote thrust the paper down behind his desk and stood up.

'Good morning, DSP,' he said.

The DSP came and stood on the other side of the little desk peering closely at Ghote.

The inspector tried to withdraw his eyes from the round, softly moustached face so close to his own. He could detect a slight asthmatic note in the DSP's breathing and it was evident too that here was someone who was thoroughly modern in the matter of dental care. A faint minty tang in the air was quite unmistakable.

'Now then,' the DSP said, 'are you making progress, my dear fellow?'

Ghote quickly debated the wisdom of telling the DSP his exact dilemma. He decided to say nothing. So much still depended on what he was able to get from Amrit Singh. If he could screw just one admission out of him, then he could justify pulling him in. But there was no point in handing the defence points on a plate by acting without enough evidence. And unless he had something concrete to put before the DSP, it would be much safer to say nothing. Rouse no expectations, bring no recriminations. You learned things like that after a while in the CID.

'I think we are doing well, DSP,' he said. 'There are several possible leads.'

He launched into an account of all the groundwork he had gone through at the Foundation.

After a little he gave up. It was obvious that the DSP was not listening.

Instead he was leaning forward over the narrow desk and peering with an extraordinary tenseness. For a few moments neither said anything. Then the DSP spoke.

'Inspector?'

'Yes, sir? Yes, DSP?'

'Inspector, there is a pimple on your neck. A small pimple, but distinct. I cannot make out whether it has come to a head yet.'

Ghote swallowed.

'No, sir,' he said. 'Thank you, sir.'

'You must watch such things, Inspector. I cannot have my officers being unhealthy. It won't do at all.'

'No, sir.'

'Are you taking plenty of exercise, Inspector? Exercise is very important. Are you playing hockey?'

'No, sir. Actually, no. I would like to, sir. But the work takes up a great deal of time, sir.'

'You must not let it interfere with proper precautions over your health, Inspector. And one more thing.'

'Yes, sir?'

'All these men Inspector Chavan is sending out for you. What is that about?'

Caught.

Ghote drew a deep breath.

'I came across a lead up at the Foundation on Amrit Singh, sir.'

'Amrit Singh. Amrit Singh. Those men are for Amrit Singh?'

'Yes, sir. I thought it best to take pretty full precautions. You cannot be too careful with a fellow like that, sir. I had this tip from some of the young boys up at the Foundation. They said he would be there again at 10 a.m., sir. So I shall tackle him myself then, and Chavan will give me backing.'

'You will go up there at 10 a.m. and tackle him, eh?'

'Yes, DSP. I managed to get the confidence of those boys, sir. They are a bit mixed up in Singh's smuggling activities, I think. But I will sort it all out at 10 o'clock.'

'You will not, Inspector. You certainly will not. A pack of pavement sleepers choose to tell you that Amrit Singh will be up at the Foundation at 10 a.m., and you sit on your backside here and wait for him. He'll be there and gone this moment, Inspector. Get after him. Get after him, you damned fool.'

Ghote felt the sweat spring up from every pore in his body. What if the DSP was right? Amrit Singh warned and . . .

His heart thumping, his mouth dry, forebodings of disaster screeching like sirens in his brain, he tore from the room and flung himself down the stairs.

8

The blue Dodge truck skidded to a halt on the loose gravel of the drive at the Masters Foundation. Inspector Ghote leaped out. He took one look at the big, slightly shabby bungalow. Nothing different as far as he could tell. Still, silent and asleep in the hot sun.

But Amrit Singh would hardly be in the house itself. The compound was the place.

Ghote ran.

There was nothing for it but a frontal approach. To go round to the lane at the back would take too much time now. And help him no more. Amrit Singh could go out this way just as easily as by the back.

Darting glances to left and right, the inspector pelted over the dark green of the big lawn, dodging trees and flowerbeds and all the time searching along the line of the trellis ahead for the least sign of tell-tale movement.

Nothing.

The garden, the dispensary hut, the garage shed, the whole place seemed to be asleep. Ghote conscientiously examined every corner, but with growing despair. He ought not to have relied on what that boy had said, even though at the time they seemed to be getting on so well. Obviously since the incident of Krishna Chatterjee's panic flight they had found a way of warning Amrit Singh. If he had come here at all, it had been earlier. And now he was safely away again. Lost somewhere in the teeming vastness of the city.

He came to a dispirited halt. Hot, sweaty and profoundly

miserable. Why, oh why, had he been so self-confident in front of the DSP? It was all very well to feel he had done everything possible on the case so far, but there was no need to have boasted like that.

'You looking for someone?'

As he might have guessed, it was Edward G. Robinson. He chose moments like this to appear from nowhere. Ghote hardly looked up from the matted grass at his feet.

'You looking for a guy called Amrit Singh?'

'You know that.'

'You think a guy like Amrit Singh going to be caught by a policeman only?'

Ghote's eyes flashed in anger.

'Not when he has friends like you to warn.'

But the boy simply grinned.

'Look,' he said softly.

Ghote turned and followed the line of his glance.

And there, happily swinging over the tall, barbed-wire-topped wall in the far corner of the compound, was the burly figure of the Sikh himself. He landed lightly enough, for all his size, on the balls of his feet on the soft, dusty ground. Ghote could see his great, black beard shining lustrously under a heavy blue and red turban.

With one quick look at the black-jacketed boy at his side, Ghote stepped forward.

'You, Amrit Singh,' he said in a loud, clear voice. 'Stay where you are. This is the police.'

He saw the brawny figure stop and look towards him. Then there came a quick second of calculation. A glance back to the tall wall behind him, a look forward to the big empty garden.

'Hallo, Inspector Ghote.'

Amrit Singh strode forward to meet the inspector, his hand outstretched, a smile showing the white teeth in the depths of the luxuriant black beard.

Ghote found that the boy by his side was no longer there. He took the big Sikh's outstretched hand. His grasp was as steely as the quietly glinting bangle that circled his wrist.

'And why would as great a man as Inspector Ghote want to see a poor travelling salesman?' Amrit Singh said.

'There are some questions to ask,' Ghote said.

He felt that he had been a little more rushed into his interrogation than he would have liked. But there was something to be said for holding it here in the deserted garden. If the big Sikh tried to get away there was plenty of time to shout a warning. And Chavan's men, with any luck, would soon be taking up their positions round the house.

'Questions?' Amrit Singh said. 'It is sad that I can never talk to my friends in the police just like two men talking. Always they want the talk to be questions and answers. Their questions, my answers.'

'If you had less to hide, perhaps there would be less to ask,' Ghote replied.

The big, thickset Sikh laughed till his beard shook.

'How can you think that I have things to hide?' he said. 'You know me. I travel about selling here, buying there, making a poor living.'

'And what were you selling or buying in this compound on Friday evening?' Ghote said suddenly.

'In this compound? You are joking only, Inspector. This is no bazaar. How should I be buying and selling here?'

'You do not deny that you were here?'

Amrit Singh opened his great hands wide in a gesture of simple amazement.

'Why should I deny? You have seen me here now. You know how I know my way here. And what is there to deny after all?'

'Then you admit trespassing on private property?'

'Oh yes, I admit.'

The big Sikh laughed.

'Oh, I have committed very terrible crime,' he said. 'No wonder it is a CID inspector himself they have sent to arrest me. Trespassing. Will it be hanging matter, do you think, or seven years' RI only?'

Ghote felt the sting of a defeat.

'It is not rigorous imprisonment matters only that I am wanting to talk,' he said. 'How did you get the key to the dispensary hut there?'

He glanced over at the long, low hut with its criss-cross of heavy wires at the windows and stout wooden walls.

The Sikh laughed again.

'Hanging matter, is it?' he said. 'To have a key to an old hut. Oh, you policias, you are getting more strict every day. Once they did not want to hang you for every little mistake. But now the least thing you do and already a policeman is there with a rope ready to put round your neck.'

'You have not answered my question,' Ghote said. 'How did you get that key?'

'There are so many keys,' Amrit Singh said with a shrug of his broad shoulders. 'How can I remember each one?'

'There are not so many keys. There is one only. The lock on that door is no ordinary one. It is American-type. There is one key only for that, and you had it.'

'Perhaps it was given to me,' Amrit Singh replied.

His eyes were bright and dancing under the jutting black eyebrows.

'And who should give you the key to the dispensary at the Masters Foundation, you a notorious thug?'

'Who knows who might give it?' the Sikh said. 'Masters sahib himself it could have been.'

Ghote felt his blood begin to race. Was there really some link between the Sikh and the mysterious American millionaire? Or was it, after all, only the big thug's particular brand of humour?

'Masters sahib,' Ghote said cautiously. 'What do you know of Masters sahib?'

'Oh, he is a very generous man,' the Sikh replied.

'Everybody knows that,' Ghote said. 'You have to read the papers only to see that.'

'Then if he is so generous, why should he not give me key?'

Amrit Singh leaned back on his heels delighted with this simple piece of wit.

'What did Frank Masters know about you so that you had to make sure he could not speak?' Ghote snapped suddenly.

But Amrit Singh was too old a hand to be caught this way.

'How should I know a man like the great Masters sahib?' he asked. 'I, a poor travelling salesman?'

'What were you doing so near his house on Friday then?' Ghote said.

A dark glint of humour came into the Sikh's eyes.

'I suppose you have witness who saw me, Inspector sahib?' he said.

'It is not for me to tell you of the nature of the evidence that the police department has,' Ghote replied.

'Perhaps you are not sure yet that your witness will say the right things?' Amrit Singh answered quickly. 'Perhaps he has not yet had enough teaching in his part?'

'I do not find it necessary to use evidence of that sort,' Ghote replied stiffly.

'Ah, no, I beg your forgiveness,' said the Sikh. 'I forgot I was speaking to the great Inspector Ghote, the one who never bribes his witnesses, the one who can never be bribed himself.'

Infuriated as he was by the big thug's cheerful contempt, the inspector could not help feeling at the same time a quick-running vein of pleasure. So he had got a reputation for not rigging the evidence, for not taking any sort of bribes. It was a tribute.

The Sikh laughed.

'Though it is pity that you will always be so poor,' he said.

'If it is necessary to be poor I am happy to be so,' Ghote said, the words tumbling out before he had time to check them. 'My rate of pay is enough to live on. There is no need for luxuries and refrigerators and air-conditioning and all those sort of things.'

The Sikh inclined his head in solemn agreement.

'Oh no,' he said, 'no need, no need at all. But it is pleasant to be cool, and to drink beer from the ice and to have your own car to ride in.'

'That is nothing to do with it,' Ghote stormed. 'I am asking you questions. Important questions. What food did Mr Masters have to eat on Friday?'

'Iced beer he had to drink, that I will bet,' the Sikh replied.

'I asked what he had to eat.'

The Sikh shook his head from side to side till his big beard wagged.

'Oh, Inspector,' he said. 'I have heard the news, you know. Masters sahib is dead. They say he was poisoned. Am I going to tell you what food he had, even if I knew?'

'Then you do know?'

Amrit Singh stepped a pace back and held up his right hand as if he was taking an oath.

'I am not knowing one thing,' he said.

'I think you are. Tell me, did you have to open the window, or was it open already?'

The Sikh's eyes widened enormously.

'What window is this, Inspector sahib? I know of no windows.'

'The curries on the serving table,' Ghote said, 'how many were there?'

'What table, Inspector? What curries?'

'You refuse to answer?'

'Inspector, how can I answer? I am knowing nothing of all this.'

'Then what were you doing in the compound on Friday?'

The Sikh bowed his great turbaned head.

'Inspector, I was trespassing.'

'But I asked why. Why were you trespassing?'

'Inspector, I am a very bad fellow. A deplorable fellow, Inspector.'

'Why were you in the garden?'

'Such a bad fellow, Inspector.'

Ghote looked at him in silence for a moment.

'There are ways of making you answer,' he said.

'Oh yes,' said the Sikh promptly. 'Very terrible ways. I know. Many have been tried on me.'

He leaned forward a little and winked. Hard.

'But not by the good Inspector Ghote,' he said. 'Inspector Ghote does not do such things.'

And again Ghote felt the little quicksilver dart of pleasure. But he did not let it deter him from his object.

'Did Dr Diana eat the fish curry or the beef?' he snapped.

'Ah now,' said the Sikh, 'that Dr Diana I am knowing. A very fearful person, Inspector. Is it not? Most terrible. Enough to make the heart of a man tremble.'

He filled his lungs with air, letting the big muscles swell.

'But with the curries,' he added, 'I cannot help. You would have to ask the memsahib herself, Inspector. Though I can feel for you if you do not want. Even I am a little afraid of Dr Diana.'

Inwardly Ghote fumed. Had Amrit Singh really divined his own timidity about Dr Diana? Or was he just striking at a venture?

'There is nothing to be afraid,' he snapped out. 'Dr Diana is just resident medical officer at Masters Foundation. What is there to be afraid in that?'

Under the tangle of bushy black eyebrows the thickset Sikh's eyes gleamed with sudden dark lights.

'Oh, there is nothing, nothing at all,' he said. 'Only it is not given to everyone to be as brave as a police inspector. It is not everyone who would face a gun and think nothing of it.'

His hand slipped down towards the heavy sash round his waist. Ghote calculated that he almost certainly did have a gun concealed there.

'What is this facing of guns?' he demanded. 'Do you think Dr Diana threatens me with gun?'

Amrit Singh laughed.

The picture of Dr Diana as a gunman seemed to amuse him a

great deal. He laughed with a deep, rich chuckle that shook his entire brawny frame.

At last he wiped the back of his hand across his eyes.

'Oh, Inspector,' he said, 'that Dr Diana does not need gun. But it was not her I was talking.'

He was no longer laughing now.

'No,' he said, 'it is not her who would be threatening the good Inspector Ghote with a gun. Not her at all.'

He looked steadily at the inspector and quietly patted the folds of his cummerbund. The motionless, intent eyes.

Ghote felt a flicker of pure apprehension down in his stomach. An uncontrollable flicker of apprehension.

'Enough of this,' he said with sudden briskness. 'Amrit Singh. I am asking what you were doing in this compound on the evening of Friday last?'

'Inspector,' said Amrit Singh, 'I am not telling.'

'What were you doing in that hut?'

Ghote pointed at the long dark brown shape of the dispensary.

'Inspector, you would have to prove for yourself.'

'Why did you kill Frank Masters?'

'Inspector, are you going to arrest? I am quite ready, Inspector. I am quite happy to go to your station and be locked up in one of your little cells.'

A faint smile curled the wide mouth hidden in the luxuriant beard.

'But watch out, Inspector. Watch out when we come to court.'

Ghote knew that he had to let him go. If he was going to get him in the end, he must not rush in and spoil everything. No doubt, Amrit Singh had realized from the drift of his questioning that there was still something needed to make a reasonable case. Otherwise he would have more likely made a bolt for it than have offered himself so happily for arrest.

It would be a bad moment when he got to know about Krishna Chatterjee. His defence team would make a terrible amount out of that.

Ghote resolved that, come what may, he would get at the truth quickly. But until he had got out of his dilemma he was hamstrung. And the balance was still exact: on one scale the quiet little man who could so easily have been pushed by his own virtues into murder, and on the other scale the big bad man, a real killer for all his joviality.

Ghote went home for something to eat rather than face Inspector Chavan and explanations about why the careful net of uniformed men had not been called into play.

He was still thinking about what he would say eventually as he stepped into the little square of garden in front of his small white house. The smell of cooking tickled his nostrils. He hurried in, suddenly devouringly hungry.

Protima was busy kneading dough for chapattis, her bangles jingling rhythmically.

'Have you made enough for a husband to have some?' he said.

She did not look up from the soft, whitish slack piece of dough.

'Oh,' she said, 'you thought I would not know you were back, you policeman with your thumping shoes. Already I have put in more flour.'

Ghote smiled.

'I am ready to eat all you have made,' he said. 'What a terrible morning I have had.'

'And so I am going to hear all about it,' Protima said. 'All about how this old fingerprint matched that one and that there was some dirt of a most interesting colour under the toenails of some poor man you have hauled into your big headquarters.'

From where he stood Ghote could just see the smile lifting the corner of her cheek. He stooped and put his arm round the curve of her bending back.

'Oh, stop your nonsense,' she said. 'You see I have work to do.'

Ghote stepped back.

He thrust his arms out in a great stretch.

'Well,' he said, 'some fingerprints have been useful to me today.'

And he told Protima what hopes had been dashed by the lack of Amrit Singh's prints on the ribbed brown glass of the broken jar.

This time she did turn away from her dough.

'But my clever Mr Policeman,' she said. 'So near to catching a man like that Amrit Singh. In no time at all they will have to be thinking of promotion for Inspector Ghote.'

'No, no,' said Ghote hastily. 'I tell you I am far away from catching Amrit Singh. And besides I am very low in seniority. There is no question of promotion for a long time.'

'But they do promote out of turn,' Protima replied. 'You were telling only three days ago of all the talk because that Inspector Nimbalkar has been made Acting-DSP, you know that.'

'But Nimbalkar is quite a senior man,' Ghote protested. 'That is not the same thing at all.'

'We shall just see,' Protima said, with a slight, secretive smile.

She began to cook the chapattis with great concentration.

Ghote sat on the edge of the gas cylinder and watched her in silence. Suddenly he sighed breathily.

'If only I could get into my mind a clear picture of him,' he said.

'Oh, but you have a very good brain,' Protima replied a little absently.

'But he is so far from anything I have ever known. It is so difficult with a man like him,' Ghote said.

Protima looked round from the whining flame of the gas-burner for an instant.

'What man is this?' she asked.

'But Frank Masters,' Ghote said. 'Who else could it be but Frank Masters? If I had a clear picture of him, then perhaps I could see why either Amrit Singh or Krishna Chatterjee wanted to poison him, whether it was the bad man because he stood in his way or the good man from some twist in his goodness.'

'Oh, Frank Masters is only rich,' Protima said. 'Rich people are like all the others underneath.'

'But it is not that he is rich,' Ghote said. 'If it was that only . . . But, you see, that man was good too. All that money he gave up, to live on just the same food as he provided for those vagrant boys he took from the pavements.'

He checked himself.

'Or nearly the same food,' he added.

'Well, if it pleased him to do such things.'

Under her dark blue and green sari Protima shrugged her invariably elegant shoulders as she rose from the gas-rings.

'Come along with you,' she said. 'The meal is ready now.'

'But do you understand such a man?' Ghote said.

Protima looked him full in the face and smiled a slightly mocking, provocative smile above the wide brass dish she had put the food on.

'I understand the man I have got,' she said. 'And I would rather have him than all your millionairing, vagrant-rescuing ones put together.'

In spite of his anxieties Ghote smiled back.

'Then you do not want more money, little Hindu wife,' he said. 'You do not want, for instance, refrigerator?'

Before she could set down the dish and get at him he dodged nimbly away out of the kitchen, giggling like a schoolgirl after a mild reference to the difference between the sexes.

Not a minute later than his due time, Inspector Ghote was back at headquarters. He felt he owned that to himself.

But he waited till he heard voices in Inspector Chavan's room and went past the glass-panelled door in a swift glide.

When he was seated at his own familiarly blotched little desk a sudden wave of discouragement swept up on him. He thought over the whole Frank Masters affair. And whichever way his thoughts turned, they seemed in no time at all to run up against a blank wall.

The fact of the matter was that he had done everything there was to be done. He had been utterly conscientious. He knew it. And all that his every effort had been able to turn up was this appalling balance between the possibility that Krishna Chatterjee, a man whose very goodness might have turned somehow sour, was the one he was looking for and the simple desire to fix the business fairly and squarely on Amrit Singh, who had already got away with murder more than once.

There must be something he had forgotten.

He pulled open the lowest drawer in the right-hand side of his desk where he kept his supply of paper and took out a hefty wad. From the little enamelled brass tray he took a pencil. And with the utmost care he set himself to write an account of the whole business from start to finish.

It must show some new line somewhere.

About an hour later, just as he was getting to the end, the door opened.

Ghote looked up quickly. It might be Chavan.

But it was Deputy Superintendent Naik. Hastily Ghote put the sheet he was writing face downwards on the pile in front of him and stood up.

'Sit down, sit down, Inspector. I am just looking in to see what progress you are making. You are letting him cool off a bit?'

Ghote felt he had no time to think. If it had been Chavan, he knew some reasonable excuse for not picking up Amrit Singh would have come to him in time. But the very sight of the DSP, entering so unexpectedly, had driven every coherent thought from his head. He only knew that his careful account of the case, so nearly finished, had not done a thing to give him a new lead.

The DSP plumped down on the squat little chair in front of the desk, puffing heavily. He cocked an eye up at Ghote.

'Cool off, DSP?' Ghote stammered. 'Well, that is . . . In a manner of speaking, yes. Sir.'

The DSP leaned slowly forward.

'That pimple,' he said. 'It does not seem to be getting any better. It is larger than when I saw it before.'

Ghote smiled uneasily.

'You are not having digestive troubles?' the DSP asked. 'That is often the root cause of blood disorders, you know.'

'No. No, thank you, sir. Really my digestion is very good, considering.'

'Considering?'

The DSP slewed round in the heavy little wooden chair and gave Ghote redoubled attention.

'Considering what?' he said. 'You have some chronic complaint? A duodenal, perhaps? I have often thought you were underweight, Inspector.'

'No, no. No, it is nothing like that, DSP. It was just a joke really.'

Ghote swallowed.

'It was just a joke, sir,' he said. 'I meant I have a very good digestion considering how often a detective officer has to snatch what food he can from all sorts of eating places.'

The DSP looked grave.

'Yes, that is a very serious consideration,' he said. 'Very serious.'

His hand strayed out to the papers on Ghote's desk. For an instant Ghote contemplated putting something down quickly on top of the pile, something heavy. But it was too late.

DSP Naik picked up the top sheet, turned it over and began reading. He made no comment. He picked up another sheet, and another and read through them rapidly.

'Inspector,' he said thoughtfully, still reading, 'you have checked on other possible sources for arsenic trioxide?'

Ghote breathed a sigh of relief. This was a question he could answer with a good conscience.

'Yes, sir,' he said. 'I have had most thorough checks made. And I can trace no leakages. And think of this, sir: you have a man poisoned with a substance like that in one place, and enough of that substance to kill him is stolen not a hundred yards away. Well, sir, the chances of the two being unconnected are most remote.'

The DSP looked up at the ceiling fan for a moment.

'Yes, Inspector,' he said, 'I think we can dismiss the possibility altogether.'

Ghote let a feeling of relief begin to creep over him. Perhaps the DSP would be satisfied with having made one cogent observation.

But, no, he returned to his reading with renewed vigour.

Suddenly he jumped up.

'What was that about leaving Amrit Singh to cool off?' he said. 'It looks from this as if you even think he may not be guilty.'

Hot surges of blood ran up and down Ghote's back. Did the DSP realize he had not actually arrested Amrit Singh?

'But, sir,' he managed to say, 'there is Krishna Chatterjee. Sir, it might just as easily have been him.'

The DSP put his hands on the front of the desk and leaned over towards Ghote.

'Inspector,' he said, 'I am surprised any officer working under me could be so ridiculous.'

'But, sir, it is fact that Chatterjee went into the dispensary at just the crucial time. Sir, social workers can be killers too.'

'I dare say they can,' said the DSP. 'So you must just take very good care to see no one ever finds out about your Mr Chatterjee. That is all.'

Ghote made no reply. He was not shocked. No one could have been in the service as long as he without realizing that at times likely evidence was suppressed. But one way and another he had drunk too deeply at the springs of different approaches to crime and justice to feel that the DSP's attitude was one that, when it came to it, he could ever copy himself.

Up till now he had always succeeded in letting his acquiescence be taken for granted and had avoided compromising himself. But now, thanks to this silly business of allowing the DSP to think he had actually brought in Amrit Singh, he had let himself get caught fast.

The DSP wheezed more loudly.

'Inspector?' he said.

'Yes, sir?'

'You don't seem to agree, Inspector.'

'But, sir,' Ghote said, 'I am as keen as anybody to see Amrit Singh on the end of a rope.'

'I should hope you are, Inspector.'

The DSP looked at Ghote with an unexpected twinkle of kindness in his eyes.

'Listen, my good fellow,' he said, 'just because everything points to Amrit Singh don't start trying to convince yourself he is somehow or other not the man you are looking for. It is a terrible temptation to be too clever, you know. In time you will learn that.'

Ghote suddenly saw how it was that a man like the DSP had got to where he was in the force. He was right. The obvious answer did often somehow look too easy.

'Come on now, man,' the DSP said. 'Get down to that cell and beat it out of him.'

Ghote sat upright in his desk chair.

'DSP,' he said, 'Amrit Singh is not in a cell.'

For three wheezes out and two wheezes in DSP Naik was silent. But under his cheeks the colour gradually spread and darkened.

And at last the pent-up feelings splurged out.

'Inspector Ghote. I have just been sitting here reading your account of this most important case. You have summed up the situation with admirable clarity. Every word you have written points to only one thing. For the first time in the history of this department we have got that bastard Amrit Singh just exactly where we want him. And now I hear from your own lips, from your own bloody lips, that you have let him go.'

His tautly spread right hand swept round and clutched in agony at his solar plexus.

'Let him go. Let him go.'

He moaned the words over again as if they were too completely awful to be assimilated at one swallow.

Slowly he crossed to the door and held it open.

'Inspector,' he said, 'you will go out now and first of all get hold of those damned urchins at the Foundation. Then you will drill into each and every one of them such facts as we need to make sure that Amrit Singh hangs. And when you have done that you will stay out of this office until you have brought that unutterable Sikh back here on the end of a pair of handcuffs. Do you understand that?'

'Yes, DSP,' said Inspector Ghote.

9

Inspector Ghote was too sensible to defy DSP Naik's orders then and there where he had been given them. He at once grabbed his telephone and with a great deal of shouting ordered a truck to take him round to Wodehouse Road.

The DSP stood beside the open door, still wheezing hard, and stared at him in silence.

Ghote wished he would go.

He wanted a few moments to think. He had had to say he would obey orders, but there must still be a way round. Only, unless he had a little time to himself, he would not be able to sort things out. And now he had been pressured into calling for transport to take him to the Foundation. He could always stop the truck outside and sit and think on the spot, but if he did the driver would begin to wonder why he had been sent out at a moment's notice and now was being made to hang about at the kerbside. And nothing must distract him from thinking this through properly.

There must be a way out.

Ghote collected a notebook and put it in his pocket. Still the DSP said nothing, and still he remained exactly where he was, leaning a little bit forward and wheezing ever more slowly with each breath.

Ghote turned towards the doorway.

And down in the corner where he kept his filed information sheets he saw that the same little lizard had contrived once again to imprison itself in the glass-fronted bookshelf. If he left it in there in the shut-up office it might die. He might be away all the rest of the day if he did have to try and pull in Amrit Singh.

He hesitated.

And then he quickly picked up one of the sheets of paper on which he had so painfully written out his account of the case and rolled it into a cylinder.

As he did so, his eye fell on the words he had written at the top of the page. 'From information received from Dr Diana Upleigh, resident medical . . .' And suddenly he knew that there was after all something that he had left undone in his investigation. He had not got all that he should have done out of Dr Diana. She, more than anyone in the Foundation, knew Frank Masters. And it was in the character of the young American that the reason for his death must lie. Once he had a firm idea of what that was, then it should surely be obvious whether he had died at the hands of a stop-at-nothing thug or at those of a talkative, pedantic, over-the-edge little Bengali intellectual.

Ignoring the still expectant figure of DSP Naik, Ghote stepped swiftly over to the glass-fronted bookcase, opened it, flicked up the little lizard with his paper cylinder, slid it off near to the crack at the edge of the floor and tossed the paper into the wastepaper basket.

'I am going now, DSP,' he said.

The DSP made no reply. He was staring at the empty patch of floor where an instant before a tiny lizard had blinked its two beads of eyes twice and had darted incredulously to safety once again.

The stately, pear-shaped bearer at the Masters Foundation showed Ghote, when he asked for Dr Diana, into the doctor's private sitting room. Ghote had glanced into the room when he had made his first tour of the bungalow just after the crime, but now he stood in the doorway and looked with care.

It was cool and quiet for all the unrelenting brightness of the sun outside. At each of the windows a heavy split cane blind hung, letting in only broken and jumbled bars of light. They caught the flowered pattern on the material of the soft armchair in which Dr Diana sat. They caught too the real flowers in a blue pottery bowl on a low table of dark wood, carved with heavy scoops in a curious rough pattern. Ghote had seen such work in the homes of other Britons: it always made him feel it came from somewhere very distant, where the people were as brutally decided as the thick strokes of the carving.

He looked up from the low table with its bowl of soft-bloomed flowers. On the walls there were a mirror and two photographs. Each was in a dark frame carved in the same fierce style. He looked away.

Dr Diana, who had been reading an illustrated magazine sent from England, laid it down. Ghote registered the smell of the thick, shiny paper and the sepia brown squares of the photographs of clumps of Englishmen and women standing about in ungainly but determined poses.

'Well,' Dr Diana said, 'and what can I do for you?'

She looked up at him from the billowing mass of her flower-covered armchair. She was wearing a frock in much the same pattern as the chair material though the flowers were smaller and more tightly bunched. Her face was aggressively pink and white. The rather coarse eyebrows were raised in an attitude of direct enquiry.

Ghote braced himself.

'I have come to you,' he said, 'because I think you are the one who can most help me in the next stage of my investigation.'

'Oh,' said Dr Diana, 'then your investigation has got past one stage, has it? I'm glad to hear that.'

'My enquiries have revealed a great deal,' Ghote said.

'But not anything on which you can actually take action?'

Ghote made himself ignore the rebuke.

'My problem is otherwise,' he said. 'I have discovered too much in many ways. Too much about what has been going on at the Foundation here, and too little about the person who suffered from it.'

Dr Diana sat up straighter in the billowing, flower-covered armchair.

'What nonsense,' she said. 'If you've discovered anything that's been going on here, it can't have any bearing on Frank's death. And you don't need to go poking your nose into his whole life history to find out who killed him either.'

'Excuse me,' said Ghote, 'but I think the opposite is the case. I have found that there were people in a position to obtain the arsenic trioxide, but until I know more of their relations with Mr Masters, I cannot decide whether they would want to administer.'

'Well, there isn't any mystery about Frank's relations with anybody,' Dr Diana declared, flopping back in the big chair. 'Frank was as open and straight as anyone in this world.'

'That is something to have learned,' Ghote replied. 'But I would like to learn more.'

'All right, learn more if you want to. But don't come bothering me for it. I've got the whole of this place to run now, and I really haven't got time to attend to inessentials.'

'Of course I understand that you are very busy, but—'

'I'm more than very busy. If the Foundation's to go on without Frank it's absolutely essential that I should take hold of the reins firmly right from the start. Otherwise the whole place'll go to pot. I know, I've seen it happen to other places before.'

'Then you are taking over permanently?' Ghote asked, seeing how he could discuss what Frank Masters had done in a way acceptable to Dr Diana.

'Yes, yes, of course. That was always understood,' she said brusquely.

'And you are to carry on with the same policy?'

'Naturally. Frank Masters set the pattern. We shall always honour his memory. His plans will be carried through to the last detail. Except where circumstances alter, needless to say.'

'Of course,' Ghote agreed. 'And how would you describe these principles?'

'My dear man, I should have thought they would have been obvious to anybody.'

Ghote said nothing. And, as he had hoped, Dr Diana after a short pause did go on to explain the self-explanatory principles on which the Masters Foundation had run during the lifetime of Frank Masters himself.

'Frank was a very rich man,' she said. 'He had had great advantages. But he knew that he must share them with those less fortunate than himself. You've got to give sometimes in this world, you know.'

She looked at Ghote challengingly.

The thought came into his head that he himself gave very little. He remembered the beggar on the office steps. The last time he had given him anything was when he had wanted a few moments to think about the Masters case the night he had come out here for the first time.

But Dr Diana was continuing with her exposition of the principles behind the Foundation. She rose like a lioness from the big chintz-covered armchair and strode up and down the cool, dark room.

'We in the West have got to give to those countries that need help,' she said. 'We have all the advantages: we have got to share them.'

She swung round.

'Of course, you have your own way of life,' she went on. 'We respect that. Frank respected that. He went up to the Punjab, you know, a month or two ago and did a lot of work studying the religious outlook of the Tibetans, and all that sort of thing.'

'Yes,' said Ghote, 'I had heard.'

Dr Diana looked at him briefly.

'Yes,' she said. 'Well, that was all very well, but of course there were a great many practical things that needed doing here too.'

'It was then that you discovered that Amrit Singh was making a nuisance of himself in the Foundation?' Ghote put in quickly.

He was delighted that a chance to introduce the Sikh's name had come up so easily. Perhaps he could get on to mentioning his possible links with Frank Masters.

'Oh, him,' Dr Diana said shortly. 'Yes, I dealt with him. But, as I was saying, Frank did more than simply give money. He could have stayed at home in America and done that. Or, I could have stayed back in the UK and organized a few raffles and things for the Church Missionary Society. But Frank was not just a giver: he was a doer. He came out here and got down to a spot of good hard work.'

Ghote bowed his head slightly.

'That's the trouble out here,' Dr Diana went on.

Her pacing of the cold darkness of the room had grown swifter now. She covered its length in a few long strides, came up against a wall, halted as if affronted, swung round, and set off again.

'That's the trouble with so many of you,' she said. 'You haven't got the simple bloody guts to get on with the job. That's all that's needed, you know. Roll up your sleeves and get down to it.'

She came to a full halt again in front of the mirror in its dark coarsely carved frame. She looked at her reflection in it for a few seconds. Her muscular pinky white arms were bare to the elbow.

'Yes,' she said, 'people out here are mostly in a damned appalling muddle. What they need is a swift leg-up. Over the stile.'

She swung round sharply and marched up to the inspector.

'But don't you go thinking that we aim to help them every inch of the way,' she said. 'That's not it at all. Help them to help themselves. That's what Frank believed in.'

'A most excellent principle,' Ghote observed.

He felt he was at last beginning to get a grasp of the hitherto totally enigmatic figure of Frank Masters. It was not helping him to see why he had been killed yet. But it was filling him with a certain awe. He himself was so much below this.

'Well, there it is,' Dr Diana said tersely. 'That's what Frank believed. Heaven knows, I don't want to be a nursemaid to anybody myself. It just so happens I've a good clear mind, and I can see what has to be done. And when I do, I go ahead and do it.'

She had come up against the mirror again. She swung away from it after a few instants.

'And that was what Frank was like too,' she said. 'He had a clear mind. He saw what was to be done and did it. And this city has a lot to be thankful for because of that.'

Ghote could only agree.

'That is most true,' he said. 'Most true.'

A niggling thought reared up.

'But Amrit Singh,' he added. 'Mr Masters did not realize that Amrit Singh was bad influence?'

Dr Diana looked shocked.

'Now, just you listen to me,' she said. 'Frank Masters had the widest open eyes of anybody I ever met. He was no sloppy, sentimental fool, all think beautiful thoughts and do nothing. When he saw that something was wrong he got up on his two feet and darn well did something about it.'

'Yes,' said Ghote.

He left Dr Diana seated once more in her billowing chair turning over again the thick, odoriferous leaves of the English magazine. He felt doubly oppressed now. To begin with nothing that she had said seemed to indicate clearly one way or the other whether Krishna Chatterjee or Amrit Singh was most likely to have poisoned Frank Masters.

But, more than this, the thought of Frank Masters himself was oppressive. The picture of someone with so much, not only giving and giving abundantly of what he had, but getting up, in Dr Diana's expressive phrase, 'on his own two feet' and doing what needed to be done in this world, made him feel simply inadequate.

He decided, in spite of DSP Naik, to seek refuge in his office and try to pull himself together and decide what to do. As the truck approached the headquarters building he leaned forward and told the driver he would get out where they were. The man shrugged and stopped for him. Ghote waited on the pavement till the Dodge was well out of sight and then set off towards the office on foot. It had occurred to him that he stood a much better chance of reaching the sanctuary of his own little room if he went in by the back way.

He made his way through the jostling crowds on the pavements thinking over and over the details of Frank Masters's life as Dr Diana had recounted them to him. And suddenly he stopped in his tracks.

A thought had struck him. By going round this back way he was once more avoiding the beggar on the front steps.

He turned and marched back the way he had come and round to the front of the building. At the steps he stopped, took out all the coins in his pocket and selected the largest. He went up to the monotonously whining figure crouched at the edge of the wide steps. And then he stopped again. He plunged his hand into his pocket and brought out a second coin. Quickly he thrust them both into the beggar's grimy paw. The man swept them away out of sight even more quickly.

He did not look at the inspector. His begging whine continued unchanged and unabated.

Ghote crept into the building and up to his room. Although the DSP was nowhere to be seen, he still did not feel very happy. He sat at his desk, but he could not bring himself even to contemplate the complications of his life. He knew that in fact once he did begin to think there was only one thing to work out. DSP Naik had ordered him in the clearest possible terms to prepare a number of witnesses with false statements as a preliminary to getting up the case against Amrit Singh. Well, Amrit Singh might well be guilty. He probably was. But equally—

He stopped himself going on. He must not think about the dilemma. The two equal blank walls would oppress him to desperation.

Almost stealthily he fished the newspaper out from behind his desk. It was at least a way of preventing himself thinking of anything else.

West Silent on Pak. Guilt. Many members of the Lok Sabha referred today to the sad fact that the world had displayed an incredible indifference to the sufferings of the East Pakistan minorities. There had been some stirrings only when it became known that Christians were also being persecuted by the Pakistanis.

He lowered the paper.

This did not seem to be in the spirit of Frank Masters. On anybody's part. He wondered what he would do about it if he was actually faced with the problem. Ought he perhaps to face himself with it? He could give up his job, give up everything, go to the Pakistan border and by example and exhortation . . .

He thought of Protima and little Ved at home. How would they live if he went off? And were there not problems enough in Bombay? Perhaps having a proper police force in the city was a help even.

Except that the police force was not being at all successful in the case of the wanton murder of Frank Masters.

He tried the paper again.

Guerrillas Active in China. Reports reaching Western capitals speak of serious anti-Government unrest in China. Trouble has broken out in various parts of the country.

If only it was as easy as that. If only your problems really did solve themselves. If only something would happen in the mysterious land on the far side of the Masters case which would solve his problem.

But that was not the way things went.

He skimmed indifferently down the rest of the column.

A group of 400 guerillas has been causing trouble in Yunnan, according to . . . Corroborating reports of unrest in Canton the *Hongkong Tiger Standard* said . . . According to an eye-witness report a special meeting was held.

'Inspector.'

He looked up.

DSP Naik was standing right up close to his desk, looking down at him coldly. Slowly he lowered the paper and tried to stuff it away under his chair.

'Inspector, I do not expect to find my officers idling with the papers and such trash in working hours. A policeman must be a dedicated individual, Inspector. He should be above such trivial nonsense.'

Ghote slowly stood up with head bowed.

The DSP regarded him in silence.

Now comes the moment when he asks why I am back here, Ghote thought.

His stomach muscles tightened. He felt sick.

'And Inspector.'

'Yes, sir. Yes, DSP?'

'You do not look at all well. There is a distinctly greenish tinge to your complexion. I spoke to you before about the need to take regular exercise. Have you made any arrangements yet? Have you asked the Sports Officer when he can find you a place in a hockey team?'

'No, sir. Not yet, sir.'

'Then see to it, Inspector, see to it. There is one thing I will not stand and that is unfitness among my officers. That I will not stand.'

And to Ghote's amazement, with those words DSP Naik turned and, wheezing like a dynamo, stumped out of the room.

Ghote straightened his shoulders as the door shut. There was nothing else for it now. He would have to go and see those boys.

He hoped he would not find them. The Foundation's clients were supposed to take jobs when they could, and Ghote hoped that this would be a day when all the boys of the gang would be employed somewhere in the city, and that no one would know where. It was possible. It was possible even that they would all choose just this day to drift mysteriously away from the temporary security the

Foundation offered. This was something that could happen. He knew that much from his first long, patient night of investigation.

But it had not happened today.

The pear-shaped bearer took him with great solemnity round to the boys' dormitory. He did not throw open the door and announce him, but not being able to do so obviously left him feeling uneasy. He salaamed to Ghote with extra deepness as if to put the situation to rights.

The dormitory was simply a large room in the big, rather old, bare bungalow. It may once have been a drawing room. It would have needed a large, very expensive carpet to cover the big area of floor. Now the heavy tiles were bare, with here and there a black crack snaking jaggedly across them. The only furniture was two ranks of serviceable string beds running down the two long walls. Once there must have been a lot of chairs, sofas, tables to fill the empty echoing space.

On the bed in the farthest corner the whole gang was assembled. At the head, squatting smoking a stub of cigarette, was Edward G. Robinson in the dignity of his tattered black jacket. At the foot, comfortably upside down, was Tarzan, resting on the nape of his neck with his bare legs running up the wall. The others lounged between them, half on the floor, half on the creaking bed.

Before Ghote said anything he held a quick debate with himself. Should he or should he not talk in the film American he had used before? It had worked then, but he had a strong feeling that he had overrated its success. After all, Edward G. had behaved very badly over helping Krishna Chatterjee when he had attempted to get away. It was no thanks to the boy that he had not disappeared entirely.

On the other hand, there was the fact that Amrit Singh had not been warned off. Edward G., with his mysterious appearance when the big Sikh had entered the compound, had even seemed to be on Ghote's side.

Ghote abruptly came to a decision.

It was not good enough. He was a police officer. He was not

going to hang on every whim of a dirty, cheeky little street urchin like that.

'Yes,' he said sharply, 'you are the boys I wanted to see.'

Edward G. removed the butt from between his crinkled lips with finicking care and blew out a cloud of rank smoke.

'Now, you listen to me carefully,' Ghote said. 'It seems you do not realize what has happened in this house where you are treated so well. Mr Masters has been murdered. That is no joking matter.'

He looked at them severely.

It was difficult to be sure whether Edward G. did or did not make some tiny movement of command. Possibly Tarzan simply took it into his head himself. But whichever way it was, he lazily but with plain intent swung his wiry legs round and moved them pointedly apart in a gesture which could only indicate the lewdest contempt for the inspector and everything he had to say.

Ghote ran forward and delivered a stinging blow with his open palm on the boy's lean thigh.

Tarzan took absolutely no notice.

'Now, look—' Ghote began to shout.

And then he pulled himself together. After all, what he wanted from these boys was cooperation. And this was certainly the wrong way to go about it. Whether he really did want them to cooperate as fully as DSP Naik had ordered, he did not know. But he was at least going to do everything he ought.

He decided to approach the matter obliquely.

'You must tell more about the message to Amrit Singh,' he said. 'It is not clear how he came to know that Mr Masters had found the smuggled gold and locked it in the dispensary.'

He reflected that this was true enough. That whole part of the business, he had hoped, would have made itself clear after Amrit Singh had been arrested. Now it would form a very useful introduction to the subject of 'witnessing' the big Sikh actually taking the poison from the dispensary.

He glanced at the boys. For the most part their faces were

stony. He might as well have not been there. Only Tarzan appeared to react at all. He slowly lowered his legs and swung himself round till he was sitting upright with his back to the inspector. That was something.

'Come on,' Ghote said sharply. 'I want answer.'

Still the boys said nothing. Edward G. puffed intently at the stub of cigarette. Ghote addressed him directly.

'And from you,' he said, 'I want explanation. Your behaviour when I was questioning Mr Chatterjee was deplorable.'

'I had to give the sucker a chance,' Edward G. said casually. 'Guess I had my fun with him. So now I help.'

'What do you mean "sucker"?' Ghote said. 'Mr Chatterjee is a very important person. He is charged with great responsibilities for your welfare. How dare you speak of him in such terms?'

'If the guy's a sucker, he's a sucker,' Edward G. explained with tired patience.

'He is social worker.'

'Brother, you said it.'

Ghote tried another tack.

'When I have gone to great trouble for you boys,' he said, 'that is hardly the reward I expect.'

Edward G. slipped off the bed and walked across the room. Ghote turned to watch him. The boy kept silent. He crouched on the floor in the opposite corner and began scuffling at the broad tiles. Ghote could not quite make out what he was doing. He spoke sharply.

'Well, I am waiting for explanation.'

Edward G. answered without turning round.

'Listen, fella, you are a cop. You don't get treated nice. Get it?'

'But I have been better to you than a policeman might be,' Ghote argued.

For a little Edward G. did not bother to reply. Ghote saw that he had succeeded in prising up one of the tiles. Now he dipped his hand into a hole under it. Only when he had secured a crisp and shiny packet of American cigarettes did he say anything.

'Listen, fella, when the cops have got something to give, they get something too. When it's nix, it's nix.'

'In this world it should not be get, get, get only,' Ghote said fiercely. 'Sometimes it should be give. I am going to ask you to give.'

Edward G. replaced the tile and tapped it into place with the heel of his bare foot.

'Mister,' he said, 'for give you have come to the wrong guy.'

He dropped his hands to his sides and stood in front of the inspector. Ghote looked at him. The bare feet, the bare thin legs, streaked with dirt, the battered and filthy pair of shorts hardly kept up round the desperately thin waist, the bare chest with the remains of the black plastic jacket hanging from the shoulders above, the diseased and wrinkled old man's face on the boy's head. No, he had indeed come to the wrong guy for giving.

He felt confused.

All he could do was to plough on. He was a policeman. He had received clear and categorical orders from his superior officer. All he could do was to carry them out to the very best of his ability.

'I have come to discuss your evidence when we make arrest for the murder of Frank Masters,' he said.

The boy could not prevent a quick dart of interest.

'You must know who it is we are going to arrest,' Ghote went on.

'It would take more policemen than you have got to get Amrit Singh out of the Morton Road place,' Edward G. said.

'We shall see about that,' Ghote answered quickly. 'You boys need not think that the police come out worst every time. Your friend Amrit Singh may be pretty tough, but we are not so weak.'

He puffed out his chest a bit. It was important that the gang should be taken in by this boast. Otherwise they would realize they had let slip where Amrit Singh was hiding.

'Oh,' said Edward G., his crinkled face splitting with delight, 'I would like to see Amrit Singh taking you apart, Inspectorji. Oh, that would be good to see.'

'But you will not,' said Ghote. 'You will see your friend Amrit

Singh in handcuffs before too long. We shall find him all right wherever he is.'

The boy was after all only a boy. Ghote had no difficulty in detecting the faint look of relief in the wrinkled face at the thought that he had not really given away the Sikh thug's hiding place.

'Now,' Ghote went on, 'it is when we have arrested that you boys will come into the picture. It is a question of evidence.'

He saw them look at one another with open uneasiness.

'Well,' he said sharply to Edward G., 'you have important evidence to give. You were the one who saw Amrit Singh go into the dispensary where the poison was kept. It will be your duty to state that fact in court.'

'Mister,' said Edward G., casually taking out one of the American cigarettes, 'I ain't going to court.'

'You are,' Ghote said. 'You will be called as witness. It is too late now.'

'You call away, mister.'

'We would do more than call. If you did not come by yourself, you would come in handcuffs.'

Ghote thought again of how he had threatened to use handcuffs before and how ridiculous he had felt when the boy had held out his stick-like wrists. But perhaps he had been wrong to have allowed himself to be influenced by the thought of the ridiculousness of the situation. After all, DSP Naik expected him to get his witnesses and if this was the only way . . .

'You would have to find first,' Edward G. said.

'We would find,' said Ghote. 'But now it is a question of just what you would say in court.'

'I would say nothing, mister.'

Ghote decided to ignore this persistent line.

'You know,' he said, sitting down on the edge of the string bed next to the one the boys were lounging on, 'you know, we have to be very careful about the way we tell the truth when it comes to court. This is one of the difficulties a policeman faces.'

The boys received this insight into another kind of life with stoicism.

'Yes,' Ghote went on, 'it is all very well to come out with the simple truth. But the defence employs lawyers. Very clever lawyers. If we are not careful, they can make the simple truth look like simple lies.'

'That is bad,' Edward G. stated.

Ghote began to wonder if after all he was not beginning to make contact again. Perhaps all that was needed was to show that even a policeman had his difficulties.

He sighed.

'It is hard for us,' he said. 'Very hard. We would like to tell the truth just as it happened. But if that will not be believed, what are we to do? That is why sometimes we have to—'

He stopped and searched for an analogy which might make it clearer to his audience.

'Sometimes we have to polish up the truth a bit,' he said. 'You know, like you polish up a brass ornament so that it shines and everybody can see that it is what it is.'

Edward G. Robinson puffed out a long conical cloud of tobacco smoke. The rich smell of best American tobacco.

'Hey, Tarzan,' he said, 'go and polish the ornaments, boy. They ain't shining too good.'

The joke was extremely successful with the other members of the gang. They lay on their backs, kicked their legs in the air, and roared with laughter.

Ghote frowned.

'That was to give you a general idea of what I meant,' he said. 'You do not have to have ornaments to understand.'

But the boys went on laughing. Only when they had stopped did Edward G. answer.

'You want me to fake some evidence?' he said. 'How much you going to pay, copper?'

Ghote's heart sank.

He had not expected this. Somehow it had been in his head all along that he would have the greatest difficulty in persuading Edward G. to agree with the Deputy Superintendent's plan. And now it looked as if he had known from the start what Ghote would be bound to ask and would be only too pleased to agree, if the price was right.

'It is only a question of stating what we know to be true,' Ghote said. 'We know Amrit Singh poisoned Mr Masters. You yourself saw him go into that dispensary. You were too far away to see him take the jar of poison down and take some of the powder out, but if you had been looking through the window you would have seen.'

'Oh, but I did see, mister,' Edward G. said.

10

Inspector Ghote stood on the bare tiles of the client's dormitory of the Masters Foundation and gaped. On the string bed in front of him the boy called Edward G. Robinson sat with his legs tucked underneath him and his half-smoked, fat American cigarette dangling from the puckered lips of his raddled and diseased face. There was a look of utter candour in his eyes.

'You saw Amrit Singh take the poison?' Ghote said incredulously. 'You actually saw in the dispensary hut and Amrit Singh went over to a cupboard and took some of the poison?'

His thoughts were wild. Shooting through them all was the feeling of maddening irony. He had contemplated disobeying the orders of a superior officer so as to avoid persuading this boy to say falsely he had seen the Sikh thug steal the poison. And all along the boy had actually watched him do it and had chosen to keep silent.

Mixed with this were surges of plain fury. Why had the little devil taken it into his stupid head to say nothing about going up to the window of the dispensary hut when he had been on watch at the bottom of the compound?

The fury might have overridden everything else, except for one thing. Amid all the inconsequent jumble in his head, Ghote could not entirely suppress a strain of growing triumph. Never matter how it had come out, the fact remained that he had now got his evidence against Amrit Singh. And he had got it without cheating. Here was something he could put up in court without the least hesitation, and it was something which by all the laws of reason and justice should hang Amrit Singh. At one stroke he would have ended the career of the biggest thorn in the side of the Police Department and at the same time have solved the murder of the biggest foreign benefactor in the whole city of Bombay.

But under the whirl and tumble of these thoughts another strain lay.

Ghote took a step nearer the boys on the bed and looked hard down at Edward G.

'You saw him take the poison,' he said, 'the poison in the little blue jar?'

Edward G. looked up at him, candid-eyed as ever.

'Oh yes, Inspector sahib,' he said, 'from the little blue jar. I saw with my own eyes.'

Ghote stepped back.

The smashed fragments of the brown glass jar on which the Fingerprint Bureau had failed to find a single print belonging to Amrit Singh formed a picture in his mind as clearly as if they were laid out at that moment on the cracked tiles of the dormitory.

Ghote might have persisted. Edward G.'s evasion had not solved his dilemma. If anything it had sharpened it. It was plain that, if the boy was happy to invent a story about seeing Amrit Singh steal the poison just to annoy, then in fact he certainly had not crept up to the window of the dispensary when the big Sikh had been in there.

So DSP Naik's orders to secure witnesses who would swear to seeing this happen were all the more difficult to obey.

Ghote had just reached this conclusion when the stately bearer who had escorted him to the dormitory reappeared.

'Inspector sahib,' he said, with a salaam worthy of the bare room's days of former glory.

'What is it?' Ghote snapped at him.

The man's unvarying solemnity invited insults.

'Telephone, Inspector sahib. If you would be so good as to step this way.'

Unpuncturable, it seemed.

As the inspector followed him through the bungalow, he turned to hoping it was so.

He picked up the telephone.

A fearful wheezing could be heard on the other end of the line. DSP Naik. Ghote's heart sank. If I was unpleasant to that bearer, he reflected wryly, I have been punished for it soon enough.

'Inspector Ghote here,' he said into the telephone.

'Ah, Inspector. You have got the boys all right?'

Ghote hesitated an instant.

'I have just been interviewing, DSP,' he said.

Two prolonged wheezes. And then the DSP spoke again.

'Interviewing, yes. But making sure of evidence, what about that?'

It was at this moment that Ghote took a decision.

'I do not think you would have to worry about that, DSP,' he said.

He spoke the words with every ounce of conviction that he could muster.

'Good man. Good. Then get after Amrit Singh and bring him in.'

'I am seeing to that, DSP.'

'And, Inspector.'

'Yes, sir?'

'Do not forget I would like to hear you are getting some decent exercise. Hockey, Inspector.'

'Yes, DSP.'

Ghote put down the receiver.

There was nothing else for it now. He would have to find out who had murdered Frank Masters before DSP Naik realized that the boys were not going to provide doctored evidence. And his next step in that event was clear. Thanks to what Edward G. had let slip he could at least get hold of Amrit Singh.

And he now had a weapon to use, of a sort. If DSP Naik was

prepared to have the Sikh arrested on the evidence as it stood, then at least the threat of using that arrest was ready at hand.

Ghote straightened his shoulders.

It was late that day, however, before the inspector came face to face with Amrit Singh again, and when he did so it was in circumstances that he would have preferred to have been different.

He had the name Morton Road to go by and nothing else. He could have asked around at headquarters to find out whether Amrit Singh had a known hideaway there. But he had learned his lesson from DSP Naik discovering his proposed plans over the ambush at the Masters Foundation. It was no use talking: he had to act on his own.

Morton Road, for all its solid English name, proved to be a very ramshackle thoroughfare in North Bombay. It ran in fits and starts for nearly half a mile north from Foras Road. Ghote set off to walk its whole length, keeping an eye wide open for any sign of Amrit Singh's presence. One trip along its length convinced him that he had set himself a hard task. There were dozens of tall, narrow houses with dark uninviting doorways and little open-fronted shops on the ground floors, their high shelves crammed with a huge miscellany of cheap goods and little boys scrambling up monkey-fashion to serve the customers. Here and there were courtyards, which could reasonably come under the description of 'the Morton Road place', even if they were not strictly on the street. Amrit Singh could be anywhere. It was all disreputable enough.

From decaying balconies from which fluttered long strips of many-coloured drying saris, street-girls looked down calling to likely customers. At doors here and there stood heavily muscled men idly swinging hefty sticks and interrogating the occasional hangdog visitor.

When he got to the far end Ghote almost decided to give up and go and see what was known about Amrit Singh's Morton Road place at headquarters. But the thought of how easily the DSP might get to know that his orders had not been carried out finally persuaded him to try again.

There was a small hotel on the top corner of the street, an uninviting place smelling of South Indian food and stale coffee, obviously designed to catch the unwary arrival at the nearby Central Station. The proprietress, a big, shapeless, very dark woman with bright betel-stained lips, made no objection to him taking a room for the rest of the day. As she shut the flimsy door and left him he heard her chuckling hoarsely as she waddled downstairs. He quickly took off all his clothes except for a cotton vest and his trousers. It was easy enough to find plenty of dust to smear over these two garments to make them look inconspicuous enough for the area.

He located a back way out and a minute later was idling down the crowded and dirty street with the acrid smell of smoke, spices and ordure in his nostrils and in his ears the clashing sounds of shouted conversations in half a dozen languages, blaring radios and assorted musical instruments.

He stopped at a small eating stall and ordered tea. Sitting on the creaky wooden bench, nursing his brass tumbler between his two hands, he listened to the talk of other customers. And sure enough he had not been there much more than twenty minutes when he heard the name Amrit Singh.

He turned slowly and looked at the stall owner, a tall bald-headed man with the predatory nose of a vulture. It was evident from the glitter in his close-set eyes that he knew who was being talked about and was following the conversation with interest.

The two customers who had mentioned the Sikh were at the far end of the stall from Ghote and he could not, without drawing more attention to himself than he would have liked, get near enough to hear more than a murmur of what they were saying. But he was happy enough to have got a smell of the trail as quickly as this.

Some ten minutes later he called the stall holder over and asked for something to eat. When the man came back he beckoned him close.

'I have heard that this street is a good place for certain things,' he said.

The bald head ducked a little nearer him.

'I have a friend who has a friend somewhere near here called Amrit Singh,' Ghote went on.

Into the close-set eyes came a look of calculation. Ghote put his hand into the pocket where he had put all his money and other possessions before leaving the corner-hotel. He took out two rupees.

'I would very much like to see Amrit Singh,' he said. 'I hear he would have something for me. But unfortunately my friend is away and I do not know where to go.'

The bald-headed, bird-of-prey stallholder shook his head. Ghote tried a little more money.

'Amrit Singh is a very dangerous man,' the stallholder said.

Ghote shrugged his shoulders.

'Perhaps I shall find what I want somewhere else,' he said.

'It is very likely,' said the man.

But in the several hours that followed Ghote got no further clues. Then as he was leaving a paan shop, where he had spent a good deal of time negotiating over a twist of black tobacco before bringing Amrit Singh's name into the conversation, a beggar reclining propped on the shop's stacked wooden shutters with a great balloon of swollen leg laid out in front of him plucked at his trouser leg.

Ghote nearly went straight past. But the memory of Frank Masters and his new resolves stopped him. He felt for a coin small enough not to attract attention and put it in the man's hand.

'You want Amrit Singh?' the beggar said, a meandering grin appearing on his puffy and blotched face.

Ghote's heart thumped.

'You know where he is?' he said. 'I have been sent with a very important message, but I cannot find him.'

The beggar laughed for a little bit.

'Many messages for Amrit Singh,' he said.

A trickle of saliva escaped from his loose lips.

'Where can he be found?' Ghote asked.

He was beginning to be afraid that the man was not intelligent enough to give him a clear answer.

But his fears were unjustified.

The beggar pointed with the length of gnarled stick he had to act as a crutch.

'In that courtyard just past the street tap.'

Ghote looked in the direction the wavering stick was pointing. The courtyard entrance was dark as pitch although the sky, or what could be seen of it in the gap between the tall houses, was still filled with light.

Ghote gave the beggar another coin, a large one, and hurried off. The man's hiccuppy chuckles followed him.

At the entrance to the courtyard Ghote stopped. He was in something of a quandary. It was a good bet that Amrit Singh was there to be found, and he very much wanted to be sure of him. But when he had him he wanted to have the upper hand, and, dressed the way he was, by now a good deal grubbier and sweatier than when he had left the little hotel, he could not see himself playing the assured police inspector. Yet if he went back and got his clothes the beggar, or someone else, might warn the big Sikh. And even approaching a house in such a district looking like a policeman was liable to send all the inhabitants scuttling out by a back way.

It was this last thought which decided him. He plunged forward into the thick darkness of the courtyard entrance.

Beyond, the place was lighter again. The pale blue sky looked down into the yard and it was easy to see the several doorways that led into it. Ghote chose the first and made his way over to it. There was a narrow hallway with the slumped figure of a man wrapped in a whitish cloth fast asleep on the floor. Ghote pushed at him with his foot till he stirred. Then he crouched down beside him and spoke sharply.

'Amrit Singh? Where is Amrit Singh?'

'What do you want with Amrit Singh?'

It was not the stirring figure wrapped in the sheet that spoke. The voice came from behind Ghote and at the same time he felt a hard hand clamp firmly down on the nape of his neck.

He slipped forward over the half-sleeping figure and attempted to wriggle to the side.

An instant later he was dangling upright, his feet off the ground and a pair of locked arms tightly round his waist.

But for all his slightness of build, Ghote was not the sort to be caught like this. One sharp, well-judged backwards kick and he was free. He wheeled sharply round, crouching lightly on the balls of his feet ready for a throw.

And without the least warning felt another pair of arms clamp round his chest.

He was lifted up and suddenly jabbed hard down. The force of the unexpected jerk sent a spasm of pain shooting up from his left heel. For an instant he lost consciousness.

When he came to it was to find that the sleeping man at the foot of the stairs had disappeared. In his place stood his first attacker, a huge creature wearing only a loincloth and a turban. Ghote could see his bare chest gleaming in the dim light, with the muscles standing out like great coils.

The man thrust his face close up to the inspector's in a wave of bad breath and garlic.

'What do you want with Amrit Singh?'

'I have business with him,' Ghote said. 'Private business.'

Behind him the man who was pinioning him gave him a sudden sharp shake.

'What business?' said the big, bare-chested man.

'I want to see Amrit Singh,' Ghote repeated.

The big man drew back his clenched fist. His eyes, sunk in the heavy flesh of his face, were shining with sharp excitement.

'What is this? Why, it is my old friend, Ghote.'

Behind the heavy face and glittering eyes there appeared the luxuriantly curling beard, the jutting eyebrows, the bulky turban of Amrit Singh himself.

'Hallo, Inspector,' he said. 'This is most pleasant. You have come to visit only? I did not know you knew my poor home.'

He gave a little flick of his head and Ghote found himself standing on his own feet again. A dull pain spread up from his left heel.

'But I have found you out,' he said to the big Sikh.

Amrit Singh laughed.

'Come up, come up, Inspector,' he said.

He turned and marched easily up the stairs. Ghote followed. He was limping badly, and at the turn of the stairs when he put his foot down awkwardly an involuntary groan escaped him.

'I hope those fellows did not treat you badly,' Amrit Singh said. 'They are rough men only. But good-hearted.'

He chuckled to himself in the ever-increasing gloom of the stairway.

Below Ghote could hear the two good-hearted fellows grumbling to each other in mutters.

Amrit Singh opened a rickety door. A beam of light came out. Ghote blinked.

'Come in, come in,' Amrit Singh said.

Ghote entered. He saw at once that the place was a speakeasy. The room was bare except for two hard wooden chairs placed almost in the middle of the floor and a sagging bed in one corner. Protecting an inner doorway was a crude wooden counter on which stood half a dozen thick, dirty glasses and a hair-oil bottle half full of heavy brown liquid. Behind the counter was a weary-looking man with a thick growth of beard and a little bright blue Christian medal hanging from a thin chain in the gap where his stained red check shirt was open to the navel. Sitting on the floor beside the two chairs were three young men. They looked a good deal cleaner than their surroundings. Two of them wore kurtas of fine white cloth and the third had a bush-shirt of dull blue silk and a gold chain round his neck. As

Ghote entered he was leaning forward towards his two companions with a dreamy, ecstatic look on his face reciting poetry.

None of the three took any notice as Amrit Singh strode round behind the rough counter, shouldered the bartender aside and led Ghote through a jangling glass-beaded curtain into the inner room.

This was as bare as the outer one, furnished only with two beds facing each other on opposite walls about six feet apart. A small electric light bulb dangled from the ceiling. There was no fan. By way of decoration there was a religious motto in a wooden frame painted silver.

Amrit Singh flung himself back on one of the beds and lay resting his thickset frame against the damp-patched wall. He said nothing, but rested there uttering an occasional grunted chuckle. Ghote sat on the edge of the bed opposite. He decided to leave the Sikh to make the first move.

He read the motto on the wall. 'Love thy neighbour as thyself.' The frame hung askew.

Eventually Ghote came to the conclusion that there was no point in not speaking after all the difficulties he had had in getting there.

'Why did you poison Frank Masters?' he said.

Amrit Singh did not stir a muscle.

'Inspector,' he answered, 'I hoped you would have decided not to speak more about that.'

'You were in the compound of the Masters Foundation the night Mr Masters died,' Ghote said.

The Sikh's eyes twinkled.

'But will your witnesses say that in court?' he asked.

Ghote paused for an instant. The time had come.

'They will say more,' he replied. 'They will say they watched you enter the dispensary hut. They will say they crept up to the window and saw you go to the cupboard where the poison was kept, open the jar and take out enough to kill Frank Masters.'

The Sikh's eyes ceased to twinkle.

'And who will say that?' he demanded.

Ghote smiled a little.

'Do you think I will tell and let you threaten them into silence?'

'There would be no need. They would be lying. In court they would break down.'

'We will see.'

Ghote felt a flicker of the hunter's excitement. Amrit Singh was coming up with the predictable responses. He would hardly expect him to go down on his knees and babble out a confession straight away. But along this path lay what might amount in the end to an admission. Certainly enough of one to let Ghote feel that the Sikh was being arrested with good cause.

He stayed silent. And as he had expected Amrit Singh was unable to let the conversation drop.

'So you have witnesses that I was seen to go into that hut?' he said.

'One of them you know,' said Ghote. 'We will take steps to see Sonny Carstairs gives evidence that you made him hand over the key.'

The Sikh gave a single grunt of a laugh.

'Sonny Carstairs,' he said. 'I would like to see him in court.'

'You will.'

'But evidence I had the key is not evidence that I went into the hut.'

'We have that.'

'And evidence that I went into the hut is not evidence that I took the poison.'

Ghote could not stop himself hesitating fractionally. But it was fractionally only.

'We have that evidence also,' he said.

A faint smile lifted the Sikh's full lips in the deep jungle of his beard.

'That is strange,' he said. 'Because that at least I did not do.'

Ghote pounced.

'You entered the hut then?' he said.

Amrit Singh's eyebrows rose.

'You had evidence?'

'We have evidence for more than that.'

The Sikh shook his head.

'Not for me taking the poison,' he said.

Suddenly he swung to his feet. Ghote instinctively tautened up.

The Sikh laughed.

'Oh, Inspector, if it was going to be like that, would I have told my man downstairs to let you go?'

He paced up and down the little room a few times.

Then he stopped and looked down at Ghote.

'I will tell you what happened,' he said.

He shrugged.

'Why not? You can be sure later I will deny.'

He sat down on the bed opposite the inspector again. This time crouching eagerly forward.

'Last Friday afternoon,' he said, 'I came back here from some business in Hyderabad and there was a message waiting. It said that that Frank Masters of yours had found some gold in his bungalow and that he had taken it and locked it in the dispensary hut.'

Ghote leaned forward another inch.

'I knew Frank Masters,' the Sikh went on. 'I knew he might lock away the gold while he thought whether to tell that his favourite boys were smugglers only. So, although I did not expect gold there that day, I went.'

Ghote's brain was seizing on each driblet of this story, especially these hints about Frank Masters himself, and pounding at them like a hammer.

The Sikh shrugged his massive shoulders.

'It was possible,' he said. 'That boy may be very good at standing on his head but he is not very sensible. No matter. I went to the Masters Foundation. I knew all about that hut and that it was the one safe place to lock away anything. So I slipped up to the house, climbed a drainpipe, went along the roof and had a little talk with your good Sonny Carstairs in that room of his.'

He found the recollection very amusing.

At last he went on.

'Then I went back and went into the hut. I did not think I was seen, but it is never possible to be sure. That is why it is important to have good lawyers, even though it is expensive.'

He laughed again.

And suddenly sobered up. He got to his feet and stood towering over the inspector.

'I went into that hut,' he said. 'I looked everywhere for the gold. There was nothing there. I went out of the hut.'

His deep-set eyes were glowing fiercely.

He turned away.

'I thought the message must have been a mistake,' he said. 'Such things happen. And when I asked it was indeed too hard to find who had sent it first.'

Ghote felt a gradually spreading sense of depression. Why had the Sikh told him all this, unless it was actually the truth? Or was it just some of the truth? Some, but not the vital last piece? Had Amrit Singh detected that hesitation before he claimed that the police had evidence for the actual theft of the poison? And then had he invented this plausible tale?

'That was a very interesting story,' he said slowly.

'Oh, Inspector,' said the big Sikh, 'you are not going to arrest me, a confessed gold smuggler?'

'A confessed smuggler and not a confessed murderer,' Ghote said.

'You want a lot, my little inspector.'

Ghote urged himself on a step.

'I have got good evidence,' he said.

The Sikh smiled.

'No evidence is good that is made for the occasion,' he replied. 'It may look good now, but after it has been dragged through the courts it will look different, I can tell you.'

'We will see,' said Ghote levelly.

Suddenly a deep glint of malicious humour appeared in the Sikh's eyes.

'And we will see how Krishna Chatterjee looks in the witness box,' he said.

Ghote's heart felt filled with lead. So Amrit Singh had somehow found out that shortly after his own visit to the dispensary the little Bengali had followed in his footsteps. And it was easy to imagine what a poor showing someone as timid, scrupulous and suggestible as Mr Chatterjee would make at the hands of the sort of lawyers Amrit Singh used.

In no time at all they would have him plainly labelled as a murderer. And they might well be right. After what the inspector had just heard from Amrit Singh he really believed at this moment that the almost painfully good social worker had for some reason seen Frank Masters's death as a lesser evil and had put him out of this world from sheer excess of kindness. If only some clue to what that reason was would appear.

And yet, he said to himself, the man standing in front of me here is in real fact a killer. Jovial, happy-go-lucky, but proven in all but the processes of law a murderer.

Ghote let the waves of gloom roll over him.

And, quite unheralded, a flash of light appeared. One single, incautious phrase that the thickset Sikh had used came back into the inspector's head. There might be a way out yet.

11

It took Inspector Ghote some time to get away from Amrit Singh. The big Sikh offered him the pleasures of an evening at his speakeasy. Ghote found them easy enough to refuse. Amrit Singh suggested his house of ill-fame farther along the street. Ghote pretended to be shocked. At last he consented to take one drink, not from the bar room next door, but from Amrit Singh's personal supply of guaranteed American bourbon.

He endured patiently a number of jokes about policemen drinking smuggled liquor in an illegal drinking den. And at last he got away.

By consent, nothing more was said about the murder of Frank Masters.

Ghote took a risk as soon as he got out of the Sikh's house. He had an unpleasant feeling that the moment his back was turned Amrit Singh would slip out and disappear once more. So he went into the first likely shop he saw and asked if they had a telephone. He rang headquarters and in the most discreetly garbled way he arranged for a new watch to be put on the Sikh. As he had expected, the duty telephonist was incredibly slow to understand, and before the talk was finished it must have been plain to the listening shop man that Ghote was not the grubby passer-by he seemed.

Growing more anxious with every minute, he waited outside the shop till he saw a pair of constables, looking distinctly apprehensive, appear some way down the ill-lit street. Then he hurried back to the seedy corner-hotel, so tired now that he could hardly stand. Luckily the place also ran to a telephone. He called Protima and said briefly that he would not be home that night. She sounded sleepy. But before the latent anger in her voice had had time to spark out he rang off.

Something more to attend to when he had time. There was the matter of DSP Naik's game of hockey, too, if it came to that. He flopped down on the grimy bed, felt the pain in his left heel ease a bit and fell fast asleep.

He woke early next morning. As he had expected, he was pretty badly bitten by bugs. But nothing worse had happened. His clothes were still there. His pockets had not been rifled. His heel hurt much less. He bathed and dressed and went out.

He made his way as quickly as he could to the Masters Foundation and presented himself once more at Krishna Chatterjee's little narrow book-lined office.

The Bengali social worker had his head studiously bent over a hectically jacketed American work. He looked up as Ghote came in and at once grew very serious.

'Inspector,' he said.

His face got steadily more sombre.

'Yes,' he said. 'I am ready to come.'

He stood up. For a second or two he searched over the cluttered surface of his desk and then he picked up a piece of white card closely covered with notes in black ink, underlined here and there in red. He put it down carefully on the open page of the wide-margined American book. Then he took it up again.

'I suppose it will be no use marking the place after all,' he said. 'A gross superfluity.'

He looked down at the card with its close lines of neat handwriting. His big, almond-shaped eyes seemed to fill with tears.

Ghote suddenly felt wretched.

'It may be a long time before – before this whole affair is over,' he said. 'These things often take years even. Put in your bookmark.'

He coughed.

'But nevertheless I must do my duty.'

'Yes,' said Krishna Chatterjee.

He stood silently by the crowded desk. After a moment or two he picked up the card of notes, slipped it hurriedly into place and slammed the book closed. Then he stood silent again, looking at the book-crammed larder shelves of his cubbyhole almost caressingly.

Ghote cleared his throat.

'Perhaps you would prefer to tell here,' he said.

'Tell?' said Mr Chatterjee. 'What is there to tell?'

Ghote looked at him.

'But it is necessary to make a full statement,' he said. 'If you want to confess.'

It was Mr Chatterjee's turn to look surprised.

'To confess?'

'Yes. You said you were ready to come.'

Suddenly the round-cheeked Bengali's face was transformed. From a picture of utter dolefulness it changed in an instant to one of helplessly lost, giggling merriment.

'Good gracious me,' he said. 'Oh, my dear fellow, what a mistake I have made. A most comical error, most truly comical.'

Ghote felt a surge of irritation.

'What error is this?' he said sharply.

Krishna Chatterjee wiped his eyes with the back of a plumpish hand.

'A quite simple error,' he said, 'but of major proportions, I assure you. You see, I was not offering to make a confession: I was saying simply that I thought you had come to arrest me, and that if I had to go I was ready.'

The simple misunderstanding appeared to break in on him again in its full ludicrousness. A new fit of high-pitched giggles assailed him.

Ghote looked at him.

And bit by bit his irritation succumbed. Abruptly a giggling laugh welled up in his chest. A moment or two later he had his arm round the Bengali's bent shoulders laughing almost as heartily.

'You were quite right,' he said, drawing breath hard. 'Quite right. A ridiculous misunderstanding. I came for quite another reason too.'

'You did not come about the murder even?' Mr Chatterjee asked.

'Not directly about the murder,' Ghote said.

'Oh no, this is too much.'

Once more the plump little Bengali was reduced to helpless tittering.

'What was it then?' he asked, looking up at Ghote expectantly, as if whatever he said was bound to be even more ridiculously amusing.

'Oh, it was nothing. A small thing only.'

Mr Chatterjee managed to subdue his giggles almost to silence.

'Inspector, if there is anything I can do to help, you have to ask only.'

Ghote pulled himself together.

'It is a small thing,' he said. 'But it is to a certain extent important.'

Into his mind came the line of hard thought that had led him here. The casual remark made by Dr Diana that she had hopes of reforming the boy Tarzan because they knew his home background, that he was from a fishing family. Adding to this Amrit Singh's presence here at the Masters Foundation, and Amrit Singh's interest among many other illicit occupations in smuggling. Tack on to this that Ghote knew, as every Bombay policeman did, that the city was one of the big routes for bringing gold from the Middle East, where a little tola ingot might be worth fifteen American dollars, into currency-starved India, where the same tola would be worth the equivalent of forty dollars. Then add one thing more. The incautious word that Amrit Singh had let slip the day before. The phrase about it being possible that gold had been brought into the Foundation without his own knowledge because the boy who was good at standing on his head was not also very sensible.

And now had come the time to play for all it was worth this hunch that Tarzan and his fishing family were a key link in the gold smuggling chain.

'Just a small thing,' he said. 'I happened to hear that you know where the boy they call Tarzan lives. You know the boy? It would be most helpful if I could have his address.'

Krishna Chatterjee had stopped laughing too.

'Certainly we have his address, Inspector,' he said. 'There is rather an unfortunate family situation there. The boy's mother died and the father took—'

Mr Chatterjee looked the Inspector full in the face.

'Well,' he said bravely, 'there is no point in mincing words. He took a paramour.'

He sighed.

'There was considerable ill-feeling, of course,' he said. 'But at least we have the facts to work on. Facts which I know on this occasion to be true. Yes, on this occasion.'

Again he sighed heavily and contemplated the difficulty of arriving at facts which would in the end prove true when dealing with the half-world of young vagrants.

Ghote coughed and looked pointedly at a cluster of card-indexes on one of the long shelves. Mr Chatterjee followed his glance.

'Yes, quite so,' he said.

He sat down at his desk.

'Unfortunately, however, Inspector,' he said, 'I cannot let you have the address.'

'But you said you had it.'

'Quite so, yes. Yes, we have it. It is there in that index. Under "T". We have been reduced to filing it under the name the boy prefers to use. Lamentably unscientific.'

'Yes, yes,' Ghote said. 'But did you say I could not have the address?'

'But of course I did.'

'But why? Why?'

Krishna Chatterjee drew himself up on the little hard chair behind the cluttered desk.

'Inspector, it is professional ethics.'

Ghote gaped.

'But I must have that address,' he said.

'I am sorry, Inspector. But absolute confidentiality is the core of the social worker's code.'

'But I need that address. It will almost certainly result in the arrest of a major criminal.'

'Inspector, I think you do not understand.'

'I most certainly do not understand.'

'Inspector, it is like this. We have to establish a relationship with our clients. It is of the utmost importance. Crucial, I might say. And to do this it is essential that they can give us their entire and complete trust. So, they must believe that we would not in any circumstances betray anything we have learned from them.'

'All right,' Ghote said. 'Let this boy believe that. Let him believe anything you choose to tell. But give me that address.'

'No. Most regretfully, no.'

Ghote felt a pure, burning rage sweeping a clear path before it.

He turned without another word and strode along the narrow book-lined room towards the square of dull red cardboard indexes with their neat rows of little brass handles waiting to be jerked open. He could see the single letter 'T' down towards the bottom right-hand corner of the array.

As he reached out to it, the little Bengali's plump hand banged hard across the front panel.

'Inspector, I will not let you.'

Mr Chatterjee wriggled round till he was between Ghote and the wall. He stood upright. The sweat was gleaming on his forehead.

Ghote stood looking at him.

Then he abruptly turned away.

'Very well, Mr Chatterjee,' he said, 'if you wish to impede a criminal investigation.'

'Inspector, it is a matter of the utmost regret. But, I am sure you will appreciate that a principle is, alas, a principle.'

He stayed standing in front of the square of red indexes. Ghote, without another word, stamped out.

And, no sooner had the door of the little office swung to behind him than he took to his heels. On tiptoe he ran out of the big front door, past the corner of the house, through the wilting bushes of the shrubbery and round to the place where Mr Chatterjee's narrow window looked out on to a prospect of greenery.

There he waited in the deep shadows, with the broad leaves of a hibiscus dappling the sunlight on his face.

He did not have long to wait. A bell sounded fiercely from inside the house. Mr Chatterjee, whose studiously bent back Ghote had been watching as if mesmerized, pushed himself back from his desk. He looked at his watch. Through the small opening between the two frames of the window Ghote could even hear him say to himself 'Tut, tut.'

Then he got up and with complete unconcern waddled happily away.

Ghote let one whole minute pass while he considered the strain of almost wild determination Mr Chatterjee had so unexpectedly shown himself capable of. That and the ease with which the little Bengali could be deceived.

Then he strolled out of the bushes, put his nails into the crack between the two window frames and prised them easily apart. He swung his leg across the sill, ducked his head through and stood up.

He crossed to the set of indexes, reached out for the handle of the one marked 'T,' flipped through the cards and came across the neatly written name 'Tarzan' in no time at all. He read rapidly through the notes written underneath, keeping an ear cocked for noises on the far side of the door, and found that they told him nothing new. Except for the last item. The scrupulously printed address, the simple name of a coastal village and its nearest little town and the terse instruction. 'Hut nearest sea.' He read this twice over and had it by heart. He closed the index, crossed to the window, slipped out, turned and pushed the two frames gently together again and dusted off his hands.

'Nice work, Inspector.'

It was the voice of Edward G. Robinson. It could be none other.

Ghote wheeled round. The boy was standing among the bushes in much the same place that he himself had stood to watch Mr Chatterjee. He must have seen everything.

'What – what are you doing here?' he shouted.

The boy had the grace to look put out.

'I can explain, Inspector. I can explain everything.'

Ghote breathed a secret sigh of relief. Perhaps the boy had not understood what he had seen. With luck he had even succeeded in putting the boot on the other foot. The boy was going to be the one to do the explaining.

Ghote advanced towards him with heavy tread.

'Well?' he said. 'Let me hear it, and it had better be good.'

'I was making sure you didn't steal anything, Inspector.'

Ghote dived forward, his hands reaching out.

And it was all he could do to save himself from falling head foremost into the soft earth clutching at nothing. From round the corner of the bungalow came a happy laugh.

'And you did not steal.'

'I would hope not,' Ghote muttered.

'When you could have had a good haul. Not very clever, Mr Inspector.'

Yet, some four hours later, approaching the place where the boy Tarzan had his home, Ghote reflected that perhaps after all he had not had such a bad haul. He had got the link he needed in the chain which might well in the end put Amrit Singh behind bars for a good long time on a gold smuggling charge. And that was more than a little.

With a faint frown of uneasiness, he recalled a certain Inspector Patel, a preventive officer of the Customs. He had met him some time ago at a conference on the very subject of gold smuggling, and he had a distinct feeling that he ought to have informed him of what he had learned about Amrit Singh. This was the sort of thing that made for a lot of bad blood between a State service like the police and a Central one like the Customs.

He shrugged.

After all, it was vitally important to him to be the actual person who put the big Sikh away. Unless he could get him on a major smuggling charge, DSP Naik would want to know why he had not charged him with the murder of the always enigmatic figure of Frank Masters. And doing that was something Ghote was still determined to avoid.

He looked round.

He had come a good distance, some twenty-five miles or more from the centre of Bombay, first by a slow, crowded suburban train and then in an aged tonga drawn by an aged horse. In front of him lay the sea, the wide sweep of the Arabian Sea stretching out into the far, hazy blue distance. Between him and the water's edge was a length of muddy sand littered here and there with the debris of the ocean, shells, sea-smooth stones, the skeletons of fish. Directly behind him was a deep green tangle of lush vegetation, sucking rich life from the low swampy ground.

Ahead he had just made out the dark mounds of a number of huts clustered at the point where the sand gave way to the matted vegetation. They must be what he was looking for. In one of them Tarzan's family would live, the oldish father, the woman Mr Chatterjee had called the paramour and one other son, a young man of eighteen.

Ghote advanced carefully, keeping under the shade of the ragged palms at the top of the grey beach. A big bird with long trailing legs and widespread white wings suddenly rose up in front of him and lazily ascended into the pale blue sky.

He felt out of place. His shoes were thick with mud and his legs dragged.

He looked at the little village with its scatter of beached boats again. Beyond it the shore curved to form a wide creek. In the distance he could see an immense, low railway viaduct cutting across the soft, muddy landscape. He wished he was on a train there, heading steadily and directly back to the city.

But ahead of him lay his only hope of gaining enough time to break the dilemma of whether Krishna Chatterjee or Amrit Singh had been the one to open with a protective piece of cloth the jar of arsenic trioxide in the dispensary hut and tip out some of the contents. If he could only get enough here to hold the Sikh on that major smuggling charge, he would have bought himself just so much extra time. And then he would press and press until at last something cracked and down went one side of the balance once and for all.

He saw now the value of the terse instruction 'Hut nearest sea' on Mr Chatterjee's precious index card. In all the collection of huts, each constructed in almost exactly the same way out of mud bricks slimed over with a greenish growth and precariously roofed with palm leaves, one stood out by being built a good ten yards nearer the wide expanse of the sea than any of the others. And, sure enough, just outside it stood two figures corresponding to two of Tarzan's family, a small wiry man of about fifty and his sturdy young son. They were methodically at work repairing a net hanging between a pair of tall bamboo poles. From time to time the young man straightened his back and turned to gaze out to sea. Once he caught hold of his father by the elbow and pointed to the far horizon where a small smudge of dark smoke showed a distant steamship heading south for Bombay Harbour.

The old man looked at the smoke impassively, glanced up at the sun as if to tell the time and went purposefully back to his net-mending. Ghote wondered whether the paramour was inside the hut. The old man must have hidden qualities, he thought, to have acquired a mistress when his own appearance and demeanour were so unpromising.

He looked round at the rest of the village, noting everywhere the signs of poverty. A youngish woman emerged from one of the huts and came over towards the old fisherman. Ghote looked at her closely. Would she be the paramour? She wore her sari tucked up hard between her legs in the fisherwoman's fashion so that it showed every outline of her whipcord body. She walked with a decided sway. Ghote found his thoughts beginning to wander.

The woman said nothing to the two men at their net but went through the gap in the tumbledown little fence surrounding the hut, stooped and entered. The inspector wondered whether the time had not come to approach.

Suddenly from inside the thin-walled hut there came a deep burst of laughter. The young woman came hurriedly out clutching a wooden bowl and an instant later another woman followed her. She was enormous. A great round, shiny face presided over a pyramid of contented chins, which in turn capped a huge wobbling torso culminating in a vast rounded belly and huge shaking hips. And it was immediately apparent from the comfortable way she looked about her that it was she who was the mistress of all she surveyed, the paramour.

She went over to Tarzan's brother and said something which evidently she found colossally amusing. She jabbed the young man in the ribs to emphasize the humour of the situation. His ribs were well-covered: they needed to be.

At last she decided that her joke had been well and truly dealt with. Still chuckling subterraneously she turned back towards the hut. Ghote broke from cover and approached.

They watched him coming with frank stares. He stopped and asked if they had a young son who had run off to Bombay.

'Oh, that boy, that boy,' said the paramour, lifting her great pudgy arms in a gesture of despair. 'What has he done now? There is a devil in him. I know that. A devil, a real devil.'

She clasped her thickly fat hands to her massive sides and snorted with laughter.

'Well,' Ghote said, 'I will not hide from you that he is causing us a lot of worry. I have come from Bombay to see if I can find the cause.'

The paramour was still laughing at intervals.

'Oh, the cause is easy enough to know,' she said. 'It is that devil in him. I tell you when first I came to this man—'

She halted herself, waddled heavily over to Tarzan's father and slapped him tremendously on the back. The little wiry fisherman took no notice at all, simply making use of the interruption in his twisting and tying of the threads of his big hanging net to glance once again at the position of the sun in the sky and then at the little lapping waves of the sea as they advanced slowly up the muddy beach.

'When I first came to this man,' the paramour went on, 'I took that boy to my heart. Everything of the best I gave him. Milk he had to drink, meat to eat. Never once did I beat him. And you know what he did?'

She swung round on Ghote.

'He tried to run off.'

Ghote looked serious. But seriousness was foreign to the paramour. Abruptly she burst into new guffaws of laughter.

'To run away he tried,' she shouted. 'And his brother I had to send after him to bring him back, holding his ear.'

The thought convulsed her. Her massive sides shook like jelly, her enormous thighs wobbled, her immense bosom heaved in and out.

The brother turned from the net-mending to confirm her story.

'Yes,' he said with laboured earnestness, 'he ran away from a good home. Of course, I had to bring him back.'

He stood thinking for a little.

'I held his ear very hard,' he said.

This was a new and delightful matter of amusement to the paramour. She positively stamped on the loose, greyish sand under her feet in an ecstasy of mirth.

Her little spouse turned and looked at her without moving a muscle of his face. Then he glanced once more at the thin scummy line of the advancing tide and from that to the long curving black craft that lay pulled up on the beach in front of their hut.

'But later the boy ran off again?' Ghote asked.

'Oh, he ran off,' said the paramour, grinning hard. 'This time he had reason. After being good to him had been so badly repaid, I started to beat him.'

She looked down at her massive forearm.

'I beat good,' she said.

She began to titter again.

Unexpectedly Tarzan's father left the half-mended net and came up to Ghote.

'You go,' he said.

Ghote looked at him. His face was so unmoving that he could hardly believe he had spoken the two abrupt words.

He did not repeat them, but the jerk he gave to his head was eloquent enough.

'Soon I will have to be off,' Ghote said easily. 'But first I must learn some more about this boy. Did he have friends in the village, for instance?'

The fisherman turned away and went over to his son. He muttered something that Ghote could not catch and both of them looked out to sea with shaded eyes.

Ghote turned to the paramour.

'What about the friends?' he said.

She shrugged her huge, well-padded shoulders.

'It is easy to have friends,' she said. 'You make a joke. They laugh. You laugh. You have friends.'

She gave Ghote a hearty slap on his back and burst into a fountain of deep chuckles.

Ghote forced a smile to his lips.

'Does the boy ever come home nowadays?' he asked.

Before the massive paramour had time to reply, the fisherman again came up to Ghote. This time he pointed in a totally unmistakable way.

'Go. Now.'

Ghote nodded and smiled.

'In a minute. In a minute I go. But first it is most important for me to know whether the boy ever comes back here. You know, that is a very important sign to us. Whether the runaway still feels a liking for his old home at times.'

The fisherman turned to the paramour.

'Tell,' he said, and jerked his head towards the lean black shape of his boat.

The paramour raised her two hands in the air.

'He is going fishing again today,' she said. 'Oh, ho, the poor man. Twice in one day sometimes he has to go out on that terrible sea to support his family. And the day after tomorrow is Holi. He will not go to sea on such a holiday, so there is a day lost. And we need money to buy the things for the feast. That is why he must go out today again. The poor man, the poor man.'

She cascaded into a shower of deep, guttural giggling.

'Ah, it is a hard life,' Ghote said.

'Oh, hard, hard, very hard. Before daylight they go out and now they must go again. The catch this morning was so poor, so poor.'

She turned a happy smiling face towards the vast spread of the ocean.

Out of politeness, Ghote looked too. And then something distinctly odd caught his eye. The whole beach in front of the little village was littered, he saw, with dozens of tiny fish. Here and there a big seagull would fly up from the sea, sweep gently down and pick one up in its beak. But it was obvious that the birds, bobbing contentedly on the little chopping waves, had had their fill that day. And the litter of fry round Tarzan's father's boat was every bit as noticeable as elsewhere. He had had no poor catch that morning. That was certain.

'Perhaps,' Ghote said, 'you could tell me the names of the boy's friends in the village here. Often, you know, a boy will tell his friends more than he will tell anyone else.'

He slipped a notebook from his pocket, turned over the pages, perched on a post in the tumbledown fence and sat looking up expectantly.

The fisherman gave his son one short glance of baffled fury and then resumed his habitually dour expression.

The boy came heavily up to Ghote.

'It is not right to come asking questions of poor people,' he announced.

Ghote looked up at him.

'But this is in the interests of your brother,' he said. 'Do you not want to help? I think you could tell me a great deal of what I want to know.'

'He ran away,' the young man said. 'He left his good home. He ought to be put in prison.'

He turned on his heel.

His father glanced at him and then looked over at the boat. They went down to it across the soft, unwetted sand of the higher shore and began making sure they had everything they needed to put to sea. Ghote turned to the paramour again.

'Now,' he said, 'there is no hurry. You think about that boy. Think who used to play with him on the shore. And then one by one tell me the names as they come into your mind.'

She grinned and shook her head.

'Oh, I have better things to do,' she said. 'There is the meal to get for these men. They are always hungry, always eating.'

She laughed.

'Then they will not be at sea long?' Ghote asked.

'Long? Long? Who can tell? Who can ever tell with a fisherman? He sets sail when the sea is calm and in a moment the sky darkens and the wind blows, the whirlpools come and he is drowned.'

This thought was too much for her composure. She roared with elephantine laughter, bent forward and doubled up as far as her vast bulk would allow.

Ghote waited.

The two men by the boat, without exchanging a word, began suddenly to push the narrow craft through the sand towards the lapping wavelets. Ghote kept his eyes on the great laughing woman.

'Now you must tell me the names,' he said loudly.

The boat had grated its way to the edge of the sea. The fisherman and his son ran round to the stern and bent low to shove it harder.

Ghote leaped to his feet. Still clutching his notebook, he sprinted over the loose, slippery sand.

The boat was afloat now. The fisherman scrambled in over the side. His son stayed at the stern pushing with all his might, the dark greenish water up to the backs of his knees.

Ghote reached the water's edge. He plunged in, shoes and all.

The boy gave a final, wild shove and flung himself into the boat at the back. It glided easily forward over the little chopping waves. Ghote waded on, leaning against the heaviness of the water all around his legs.

He flung himself almost full length. One outstretched hand just made contact with the rough edge of the little vessel at the side somewhere near the prow. He flung his notebook in with the other hand and heaved with all his strength.

The fisherman came towards him along the length of the narrow, swaying craft. Ghote managed to get his other hand on to the boat's side. The fisherman stooped and lifted up a heavy wooden gaff. He leaned over Ghote's tightly clutching hands and brought the wooden handle chopping hard down on Ghote's fingers.

Ghote tightened his grip.

His legs were clear of the bottom now. He gave a terrific jerk with them and felt himself shoot through the water. He heaved hard and got his head up to the edge of the little boat, which leaned deeply over towards him.

'Let go, let go,' the young man shouted. 'You will sink the boat. It is wrong to do that.'

'I am coming with you,' Ghote gasped out.

'No,' said the fisherman.

'I am coming. Help me in or I will upset the boat.'

He tugged down on the edge of the frail craft as hard as he could. Underneath him he felt the water slipping past his soaking trousers, tugging and pulling.

12

Suddenly Ghote felt the tugging strain on his arms cease. The unsmiling fisherman and his tubby, self-righteous son had grasped him under the armpits and were carefully easing him over the side of their frail craft. He had won.

Once he was aboard and the danger to the narrow little boat had been averted, the two fishermen let him flop like a sodden sack down near the prow and turned their backs on him. For some minutes he was content that they should do so. He wanted only to be left alone. If he could just have time to ease the wrenched muscles of his arms and sides, he felt, nothing else mattered.

But soon he began to feel better and started to look about him. The fisherman had by now hoisted their tall, thinly triangular white sail, patched here and there with old flour sacks. The wind was beginning to fill it out and send the little boat skimming through the slightly choppy sea, heading out away from the creek and the fishing village towards the distant blue line of the horizon.

Ghote noticed his notebook lying in the bottom of the boat near three plump pomfret left there after the morning's catch. He gently pushed himself off the hard beams of the thin gunwale and reached for it. It was soaked with cold, salty water but looked as if it would be salvageable. He pressed the covers together so that a thin stream of water, slightly blue from ink that had run, trickled out. Then he pushed the wet mass into his pocket, where it thumped heavily against his side.

He lay back and thought.

At least he had achieved his first object. He had stuck close to the two fishermen at what was obviously the start of a trip to pick up something smuggled. The signs had been too plain to be anything else. The trip out to sea at this time of day when the routine was to leave before dawn and come back on the wind that could be relied on to sweep in from the sea during the morning. The two men's obvious keenness to leave at a certain time and to have got rid of him before they went. No doubt some sort of rendezvous had to be kept. The patent excuse of needing extra money because the morning's catch had been poor when these three plump evidently eatable fish had been actually left in the boat.

So now the task was to watch the two of them like a cat to see what it was they had come out to sea to do. One thing was in his favour already. Evidently the old fisherman had decided that in spite of his presence the rendezvous must be kept.

Ghote stretched forward and began trying to wring the heavy sea water out of his trouser legs. In the stern of the narrow boat, cleaving its way swiftly through the little waves, the two fishermen talked together in muttered voices over the long steering oar. Ghote pretended not to notice. It would be hopeless to try to overhear them. The thing to do was to lull their suspicions.

He sat up straighter. The fresh wind, laced with spray, chilled his face. He envied the close-fitting caps the other two wore.

'Well,' he said in a loud voice, 'I think it is most important to have an idea how a boy like your son would earn his living.'

From the other end of the long, narrow boat the old fisherman looked at him sourly.

'Yes,' Ghote went on, shouting a little in case his words were being whipped away by the breeze even before they reached the stern of the skiff, 'Yes, someone like me has to know just what it feels like to work the way the boys we help will have to.'

He warmed to his theme.

'When I saw the very hut the boy lived in,' he said, 'I realized already much more about him. The damp walls, the palm leaves on the roof. Do they let in the rain?'

For a little he thought his question was going to go unanswered. But the lure of all this pity was too much for Tarzan's brother.

'Yes,' he said at last, making his way forward a bit, 'always the rain comes in when it is heavy. But we have no money for a better roof. We work so hard. We get up while it is still dark and set out to sea, and then the merchants give us so little for our catch. It is not fair.'

Ghote edged along the boat towards him. At the stern his father, taking no notice, threw out a long baited line and watched it unblinkingly.

'This is what I want to hear,' Ghote said. 'I want to know the way you live. To see how to help your brother. That is why it was so important for me to come out to sea with you.'

The young man nodded gravely.

'That boy,' he said. 'He must not be helped. He has run away from home when he should be working with us. He should be sent to prison.'

'But no,' said Ghote loudly, carried away by his role as social worker. 'That is not the way. When a boy runs off from home, we have to ask what made him do it. To see if we can put that right.'

The runaway's brother looked at him solemnly.

'The boy is bad,' he pronounced. 'He left us. We have to do the work. And we have so little money. Even this boat may be taken from us for the money we have borrowed. He should be locked up.'

He tilted his chubby chin and looked away out to the far horizon. In the distance the faint blur of the smoke from the steamer Ghote had noticed before was still visible. The old man hauled in his line. A pomfret was jerking and wriggling on the end of it. He tugged it off the hook and flung it forward.

'Or he should be well beaten,' the young man added.

Ghote found nothing more to say.

For some while Tarzan's brother sat where he was, evidently waiting for some further understanding comments on his lot from this heaven-sent professional sympathizer. Ghote let him wait.

Eventually the youngster seemed to realize that the source had dried up. He gave Ghote a sudden glare and made his way, swaying slightly to the narrow boat's motion, to throw out a second line beside his father's in the stern.

He put his head close to the old man's and indulged in a long muttered tirade.

The old man turned and looked at Ghote along the length of the frail boat. He seemed to be weighing him up.

Ghote looked down at the sea slipping past the sides of the craft. A big patch of yellow, sun-bleached seaweed slid up, swept by a yard or two away and slowly disappeared.

The choppy waves began to grow higher and the boat dipped and rose with an unpleasant, regular motion.

The boy put his head near the old man's again and added something to what he had been saying before. It was obviously a forceful plea. The old man shrugged his shoulders and seemed unable to make up his mind. He brought in another flopping, fat pomfret.

The boy added one more sentence. And then brought his clenched fist sharply upwards in an unmistakable punching gesture.

Ghote was unable to prevent himself looking hastily all round. They were far out to sea now. The low coast was barely visible behind them. Beyond it the distant, jagged outline of the Western Ghats could be seen dark grey against the blue of the sky. Ahead and to each side the sea stretched blankly and ominously out, flecked here and there now by a white cap of a wave. Only on the far distant horizon was there a sign of human life, the last tiny smudge of smoke from the rapidly disappearing steamship.

Ghote looked along the length of the skiff at the two fishermen squatting together in the stern. The boy was fattish, but hefty. His father, though lean, was wiry and had a decidedly ugly look to him. If it came to a struggle, the odds would be very much on their side. And, even if he won, he would still be left with two prisoners to keep subdued, miles out to sea in a boat he had no notion how to sail. He felt sick.

The son had caught a fish now. As soon as he had dealt with it and baited his line again he once more urged some action. The old man took another searching look at Ghote. The inspector felt very sick. The sweat rose up on his brow in spite of the salt spray which was coming more heavily off the bobbing waves with every moment that passed.

Suddenly Ghote realized that he felt sick for a very good reason. The little boat was bouncing on the waves with altogether too much speed. Much though he wanted to outstare the two fishermen in the stern he had to let himself look downwards into the sea for a moment's respite.

A bladdery, iridescent Portuguese man-of-war sailed by right under his nose, its evil purple filaments trailing out behind. Ghote closed his eyes. But the image remained. He was sick.

He forced himself up and glared down the boat at the two others. Only to see in the eye of the impassive old man a glint which was purely and unmistakably sardonic. He nudged the boy and said something terse. The boy looked down the skiff at Ghote. He burst out laughing. The old man said something more. Suddenly he leaned his whole weight against the long steering oar. The little craft veered swoopingly. Ghote felt burning hot all over. The boy roared with laughter. His father swung the boat back to its former course.

But only for a moment. For what seemed after this an eternity to Ghote he swung the tiny vessel to and fro so that it dipped and plunged like a wild thing. Soon Ghote had to lean over the side again and be even more sick. By the end of it he hardly knew or cared where or what he was. And all the while the old man went on impassively fishing, cynically, it seemed, tossing the gaping-mouthed catch up the boat towards Ghote.

He stared dully at their great, staring cold and horrid eyes. In the rigging of the slim mast the freshening wind whined and sang.

Suddenly the boy grabbed his father's arm and pointed away to his left. The old man stopped swinging the boat. He stared in the direction the boy had pointed, shading his eyes with a lean hand. The easing of the tossing motion revived Ghote a little. He looked at the two of them in the stern with the dispassionateness of an extremely distant observer.

And then at the very back of his mind a tiny signal started up. This was what he was here for. Not simply to fight against the overwhelming sickness and misery that had invaded every part of him. But to pursue a police investigation.

With an effort that brought the sweat back to his forehead in huge drops he forced himself round to follow the line of the old man's concentrated gaze.

At first he could see only the hateful dark sea with its ominous lacing of white crests. Then suddenly for a second's glimpse he made out something else. A tiny orange speck.

He let himself slump back on to the bottom of the boat again.

Under his veil of misery he forced himself to think. There could be no doubt that the orange speck he had seen was what the two of them in the stern had been looking at. What would it be? The orange was the colour of rescue dinghies he had seen being used as swimming rafts up at Juhu Beach sometimes. The colour was one that could be seen from the maximum distance.

And then he had it. The steamer he had noticed before. Someone on board had dropped the gold to be smuggled off it attached to a float in that bright orange. It was the task of the old man and his son to pick it up.

No wonder the Customs people had not had much success rummaging ships when they had rounded Colaba Point to the south and come up into Bombay Harbour.

Abruptly the little boat began to swing and swerve again. Ghote looked up. In the stern the two fishermen were looking at him intently. And he could not look back. He let his head sway forward and was terribly sick once more.

It was about this time, he later worked out, that they had picked up the orange float. He had had a glimpse of it, in fact. Or had he imagined it? An oddly-shaped balloon of tough orange cloth, like a huge drop of liquid the wrong way up. He certainly had not simply imagined the length of thin cord and the quite small package tied to it. They had dropped the incriminating orange bag over the side and the sea had sucked it down, but the fine line they had kept. It would be useful for catching fish. And might have come from anywhere.

What had happened to the package? He had not seen it being undone. Tacking their way shorewards again with the bobbing little craft dipping and swinging if anything even more wildly than before, he had done his utmost to watch this part of the process. But the odds were against him. He had to fight the drain on his strength. He had to see, if he was to see, without letting them realize that he had. It would still be quite easy for them to attack him in this state of weakness.

So he had missed getting even a glimpse of the little bars of gold. He just had to assume their existence.

As they neared the shore the wind backed and they got a good run in. In the little boat's stern they seemed to have decided that Ghote was no longer a danger. They let him lie in the prow, looking backwards to the wide sky and the dark sea. They made no further attempt to swing and sway the boat.

He began trying to work out how to catch the two of them red-handed. It was obvious that on his own like this he was not going to be able to impound the whole vessel when they touched the beach. He would have to rely simply on keeping his eyes wide open. But he reckoned that he had the advantage of surprise on his side. The fisherman and his son thought they had been too clever for him. Well, they would see.

He sat trying to regain his strength.

Above him the narrow white triangular sail was stretched taut to the wind. The boy got up and untwisted a rope. The sail quivered and a series of horizontal rucks slid down it. Then, quite quickly, it collapsed into the boat. The momentum carried them smoothly forward. It was a neat piece of seamanship. The skiff came up to the low slope of the beach with its speed dying gently away and touched bottom as softly as a falling leaf reaches the ground.

The boy jumped out. He caught hold of the worn wood of the bow beside Ghote and ran sharply forward. Underneath them the sand grated harshly. Then the skiff stuck fast. From the family hut the paramour came waddling hastily to meet them, laughing contentedly to herself. On her head she carried a big, flat basket wider at the bottom than the top.

'Did you like your trip to sea?' she greeted Ghote as he scrambled out on to the warm, blessedly firm sand. 'I am glad to see you back safely.'

She dropped the basket on the sand and laughed with her head thrown back.

Ghote looked at her angrily.

'Oh, there are many whirlpools out there, and dangers,' she said.

Her stepson picked up the basket and held it in his outstretched arms just at the edge of the boat. His father caught hold of a couple of the fish lying in the bottom of the boat and lobbed them neatly by their tails one after the other into the basket. Ghote watched, his eyes darting from the man stooping down to pick up the fish to the boy standing holding the broad basket. One by one the fish swung gleaming through the air and landed with a smack on the others already in the basket. Not one seemed any different from the next.

At last the old man straightened up. The boy put the basket on his head and set off across the sand with its litter of broken white shells, ribbons of seaweed and little humps of worm-casts. He was heading for the curing yard at the far end of the cluster of shacks that made up the village.

Ghote watched him go.

13

When Tarzan's unsympathetic brother had carried his flat basket of plump fish past the palisade of the curing yard and out of sight, Inspector Ghote swung round to the old man sitting impassively on the edge of his beached boat, beginning to gather up the stiff folds of the sail into neat coils.

Ghote let him finish the task. Then he moved in confidently.

'I would like to see the three fish still at the bottom of the boat,' he said with quiet triumph.

For a moment the old man crouched in front of the fish braced for combat. But Ghote knew he could not lose now.

'They are my fish,' the old man said.

'I want to see them,' Ghote replied implacably.

'They are for us to eat only.'

'You can eat them after I have seen them.'

'Who are you that you should see my fish?'

The stony-faced old man began looking up towards the huts as if he might summon his neighbours to help defend his private property. Ghote darted forward, dipping agilely into the boat and seized one of the fish.

He squeezed it hard.

And felt nothing.

He pushed the old man back and grabbed the other two fish. He thrust his fingers down their gullets.

Nothing.

He stepped back. The old man took a short knife from

his loincloth and in a single jerk ripped open the first fish from mouth to tail.

Mockingly he presented the two pieces for Ghote's inspection.

Ghote hung his head. Cheated, and so easily. He looked over at the curing yard. Villagers were coming and going from it in a regular procession. Some carried bundles of dried fish on their heads. Others swung baskets by their sides. Tarzan's brother strolled back to the family hut, empty-handed.

He could always arrest them still. He could swear to having seen them behaving suspiciously at sea. But with no actual gold to prove his claims he would have a hard time getting a conviction, let alone being able to touch Amrit Singh. With such a doubtful case against them, the old man and his son would never even consider turning approvers and giving evidence against the big Sikh.

He had failed. He would be unable to get the Sikh on a smuggling charge. His orders to arrest him for murder and work up the evidence afterwards stood.

No, he thought obstinately, he would at least see Krishna Chatterjee once again. He would try his squeezing process at least once. He would give himself twenty-four hours more. Not a minute above that. And then he would go the whole hog, pull in Amrit Singh, bring every pressure to bear on the boys to say the right things in court. Be a complete DSP Naik man.

Ghote decided to play it tough.

He had Krishna Chatterjee brought down to headquarters. After all, the social worker was no Amrit Singh. He would hardly stand up to rough treatment. The threat of it, or even the hint of it, might still change everything.

Before his victim was due to arrive he set about making a few preparations. He pulled his squat, little spare chair out from its place against the wall and set it very carefully in front of his desk. He went round to the other side and sat down. He leaned forward to judge the distance between himself and anybody sitting on the little chair.

He came to the conclusion that the gap was a bit too wide and went round the desk to make a final adjustment.

There was no harm in a policeman having finer feelings, he told himself, but that did not mean he had to be soft. Far from it. Real softness was as much going too far with witnesses as not going far enough. The right thing, the truly tough thing, was to judge the amount to a nicety. This was the real world where people acted. They did things. It was necessary to do things back to them to set the balance right again. But the whole art was to do just what was necessary and no more.

He turned the heavy, squat chair a few degrees round so that it would be a strain on anyone sitting on it to look directly at the occupant of the desk.

After all, if Krishna Chatterjee had indeed been driven by some inner urge to poison Frank Masters, then he laid himself open to whatever sort of treatment he might get. He had put himself in the wrong. And if that meant being pretty tough to himself, it was the kindest thing in the end.

A scutter of movement caught the inspector's eye.

He turned round. The little lizard had once again got itself caught in the glass-fronted bookcase. Ghote shrugged. Some creatures would never learn. He went round to his own side of the desk again, sat down, opened the bottom drawer and took out a wad of clean paper. He looked at the pencils in the enamelled brass tray in front of him. Some of them seemed a bit blunt. He took a little bright purple plastic pencil sharpener from the deepest corner of the bottom drawer, where he kept it to stop it being pinched, and set to work.

A few minutes later he heard the tread of heavy boots on the corridor floor outside. A sharp but respectful knock sounded on the door.

'In,' he called.

It was Krishna Chatterjee, escorted by two constables.

'Wait outside,' Ghote said to them briskly. 'You may be needed.'

The two big men with their shining brass buttons and heavy highly polished boots saluted smartly.

Ghote watched them go and then turned back to his pencil sharpening. Krishna Chatterjee, round-faced, round-shouldered, stayed where he was by the door watching him. In the bookcase down in the corner the little lizard flung itself wildly at the unyielding glass.

At last Ghote glanced up.

'Sit down,' he said. 'Please.'

Krishna Chatterjee came forward and sat on the heavy chair, having tried unsuccessfully to shift it slightly first.

'Good after—' he began.

Seeing that Ghote was busy down behind his desk restoring the plastic pencil sharpener to its hiding place, he stopped. Ghote took a long time tucking the little purple object safely away. It would do the talkative Bengali the world of good to have to sit for a little with no one to speak to.

At last the inspector swung suddenly up.

'Well,' he barked, 'have you thought better of this ridiculous nonsense?'

Mr Chatterjee leaned forward, twisting round uncomfortably.

'Inspector,' he said, 'I very much regret, but I have nothing more to tell you. I admit that for reasons I thought good I entered the dispensary on the evening Frank Masters died. I admit I obtained the key from Mr Carstairs by using what amounted to threats. But I must insist on keeping the reasons for that visit strictly confidential.'

'You must insist?' Ghote said, leaning back so that Mr Chatterjee had to twist forward even more to keep his face in view, 'you must insist, and what right have you to insist on anything at all?'

Mr Chatterjee looked very pained. His big, almond-shaped brown eyes went liquid with hurt.

'Inspector, I had hoped you would respect my decision. I assure you it is one that is totally inevitable. Totally.'

'Nothing is inevitable when it gets in the way of a police inquiry,'

Ghote said. 'We have ways of removing inevitabilities, Mr Chatterjee.'

He glanced over the little Bengali's head at the door of the office where he had ordered the two enormous constables to wait.

Mr Chatterjee wriggled round in the heavy little chair to follow the direction of his glance. The big, brown eyes widened in fear.

'Yes,' Ghote said, 'we have ways. So I suggest you think again, Mr Chatterjee. Do some very hard thinking. And very quick thinking.'

He swung himself suddenly forward across the narrow, lined and ink-blotched desk, bringing the legs of his tilted chair down on to the floor with a jarring bang.

'Now,' he said, 'when you took the poison from the jar what did you keep it in on the way up to the house?'

Opposite him, not eighteen inches away, the round face of the little social worker went suddenly flabby.

He stammered for an answer but could find nothing to say.

Ghote never for half a second took his eyes off him.

At last the little Bengali managed to stutter out a reply.

'Inspector, you must understand this. I am not telling you any lies. Perhaps it would have been altogether less distressing if I had. But I have a constitutional objection to falsehood. So, when because of Frank Masters I am obliged not to inform you of certain matters, there is nothing I can do but fall back on silence.'

He twisted round even farther in the squat, heavy chair. His eyes shone with trepidation.

'Inspector, spare me,' he murmured in a voice that could be scarcely heard.

Ghote knew that this was the moment he should act. Even the reference to never telling lies alerted him. That way lay thoughts of doing evil that good might come. Now was the moment to leap up and stand over the fundamentally timid Bengali and shout and shout until he got a confession.

But something else Mr Chatterjee had said had set up a sudden long echo in his mind.

He leaned a little more forward.

'For Frank Masters?' he asked. 'You are keeping silence for him? Tell me what it is about him that makes you do that?'

Mr Chatterjee looked up. His big eyes had a faint gleam of hope in them. Reprieved.

'Yes,' he said, 'it would have been more satisfactory perhaps not to have referred to this. But it is the strict truth.'

Ghote pressed the palms of his hands down on the blotched surface of his desk.

'All right,' he said, 'but what was it about Frank Masters that made you do that? What was his secret?'

A look of staring dismay suddenly appeared on Mr Chatterjee's face.

'His secret—' he stammered.

'Yes,' Ghote said, his voice almost at a shout, 'what is this secret of his personality that made him so different from all of us?'

The dismayed look faded from the Bengali's round face. He coughed a little primly.

'Oh yes, that,' he said. 'Well, you might put it that it existed only to a certain extent. Frank Masters was unlike us, certainly. We are not all immensely wealthy men, and we do not give up all that wealth in a crusade in a foreign country. That is true. But on the other hand, Frank Masters was in many ways all too like us. That is to say, all too human.'

He came to an end and sat contemplating the humanness of Frank Masters with a woebegone expression.

'All to human?' Ghote said at last. 'Please explain that a little more.'

Mr Chatterjee looked up.

'In certain ways his very wealth was a disadvantage,' he said. 'He was apt to prefer to be kind rather than to be strictly useful, and his money frequently gave him the opportunity to smother up any unfortunate results of too much kindness by the exercise of further acts of generosity. And at this stage on many occasions a certain lack of interest would manifest itself. He failed to follow through.'

Mr Chatterjee pronounced these last words with great sadness. Ghote nodded sagely.

'Yes,' he said, 'you can often do more harm than good that way. People like that should not really be allowed to interfere in other people's lives.'

'No. You are wrong. Quite wrong.'

Ghote jerked back in astonishment. In the big, almond eyes of the little Bengali there shone fire.

'No,' he repeated, 'you are quite wrong. Frank Masters did good. That we must never forget. He set out to use his wealth to do good to others, and this he did. Whatever else we reproach him for, this blots out everything.'

He breathed rapidly.

'After all,' he went on, 'he had no need to spend his money on us, and live a life that was relatively austere. Decidedly a life that was relatively austere.'

He sat looking straight forward at the wall to Ghote's side. His big eyes were moist.

Ghote puffed out a long breath.

'I dare say there is something in all that,' he conceded.

He pulled himself together.

'However that is not the point. We are not here to discuss the charitable activities of Mr Masters. We are here to discuss his sudden death.'

He glared fiercely at Mr Chatterjee.

'His sudden death and the part you played in it.'

Mr Chatterjee slid round again to the uncomfortable position in which he could look Ghote straight in the eye.

'Inspector,' he said, 'I must repeat that I played no part at all in Mr Masters's death. It was the last thing in the world I would have wished to have occurred. The absolutely last thing.'

'That will not do,' Ghote shouted.

But it was too late.

Mr Chatterjee sat serenely now on the heavy chair. During his summoning up of the spirit of his former chief Ghote's threats had lost their power over him.

'That will not do at all,' Ghote repeated. 'I must have answer.'

'I regret that you have had such answer as is in my power to provide.'

The little social worker looked modestly down.

And Ghote let him go.

When the door had been softly shut he sat there contemplating bitterly the course of the interview. To begin with, he had puffed himself up with all those thoughts about being tough. And little Krishna Chatterjee had shown him what real mental toughness was.

For a moment he speculated on whether this display of inner unshakeable resolution put the little Bengali more definitely into the murderer class. He decided that it did not. Certainly, this was the sort of force that could have led him to an altogether unlikely ruthlessness. But the mere possession of it did not necessarily mean that he was bound to have killed Frank Masters. Amrit Singh, if it came to that, possessed beyond question the ability to kill.

The scales were still level.

The thought of Frank Masters plunged Ghote into deeper gloom. He had actually been so foolish as to abuse him, to sit there and utter statements about preventing people like him interfering in other people's lives. How could he have done it? In face of an example of real goodness like that? Mr Chatterjee was right to have snubbed him.

He bunched up his fist and banged it down on the pile of untouched white paper in front of him. The dull, padded sound of the blow reverberated quietly through the small room. Down in the glass-fronted bookcase the lizard was stirred to a fresh frenzy of ineffectual scuttling.

Wearily Ghote got up, took a piece of the paper, went over to the corner and hoicked the little beast to freedom once more.

*

Shortly afterwards he went home. There was no point in staying in the office. At any moment DSP Naik might come in and start asking awkward questions. Home was safe.

Home was delightful. He found Protima in a very good humour. His son was being extremely serious and well behaved, which in a replica of a man only a quarter lifesize he found always so absorbing that for a time nothing else seemed to matter.

He relaxed. Frank Masters might have been murdered in circumstances which were still almost as mysterious as when he had been assigned to the case, but that could wait. The impression he had at last begun to gain of the murdered American as a human being, and one whose very existence posed problems in behaviour almost too big to deal with, might be still heavily present in his mind, but at least it could for a few minutes be pushed into the background. To be a father and a husband and nothing else was important and right. Ghote watched his son and talked in a low voice to Protima about the events of her day at home.

'But you,' she said at last, 'what have you been doing? Your clothes? How did you get them into that terrible state? When you came in they looked as if you had been wading through the sea in them.'

So Ghote was gently urged back into being a policeman. He told Protima, in brief outline, about how he had hoped to catch Amrit Singh as a smuggler and about how he had failed, leaving himself faced as inexorably as ever with his dilemma about Amrit Singh and Krishna Chatterjee and the DSP's almost inescapable order.

Protima promptly justified his former reluctance to tell her about his work by getting the situation typically wrong.

'But why cannot you arrest Amrit Singh? she said. 'He was the one who poisoned your Frank Masters,'

'But he did not,' Ghote replied, 'Not necessarily. I explained to you. Both he and Krishna Chatterjee admit going into the dispensary where the poison was. Both swear they did not take it. Either could be telling the truth. And while I know for a fact that Amrit Singh has killed three people himself at least, I am also sure that someone like Krishna Chatterjee could push himself to the extreme of murder. It balances up.'

'Then you do not want to believe Amrit Singh killed Frank Masters?'

'It is not a question of what I want to believe. It is a question of simple logic.'

An unexpected stain of dark anger appeared momentarily on the smooth stream of his tranquillity.

'Logic,' Protima laughed. 'It is no good talking your logic this and your logic that. You know I never understand such things.'

She made them sound as if they were all right for little Ved, solemnly bringing dishes of pickle in from the kitchen for their evening meal, but not really worth considering above that level.

'But you cannot escape logic,' Ghote said, his voice suddenly rising.

Ved looked up but said nothing.

'Oh, I can escape it very well,' said Protima, undisturbed. 'You must not let such things worry you.'

'But I have failed to find who killed Frank Masters.'

'All right. You must ask yourself who killed him. Was it Amrit Singh, was it Krishna Chatterjee, was it that Dr Diana?'

Ghote's fury boiled over.

'How can you be so stupid?' he shouted. 'I tell you it could not possibly be Dr Diana. She does not come into it at all.'

Protima gave a little toss of her fine, long head.

'Well,' she said, 'from what I have heard about the way she talks to you, I think it must be her. But enough of this nonsense. If I do not go to the kitchen now, we will have no food tonight.'

And she went.

Ghote stood in the living room looking at the empty doorway, oblivious of Ved arranging the pickle dishes with great exactitude.

'Dr Diana has absolute alibi,' he said into space. 'For all the time when the poison was stolen she did not have a key to the dispensary. That is a fact.'

From the kitchen came the sound of a pan being put on the gas-ring and its contents being stirred briskly. Ved went back in to fetch another pickle dish to complete his display.

Ghote marched up and down. He began to feel hot and uncomfortable even in his fresh clothes. He slumped down on a rattan stool in the corner and fanned at himself furiously.

Protima came back in calmly carrying the food with Ved and his final pickle dish in the rear. Ghote glowered at them and stayed where he was.

'Well,' Protima said, 'the meal is ready. Are you going to eat?'

Ghote did not reply.

'Come, why are you sitting like that?'

'It is hot.'

'Then take some water to drink. It has been standing in the big clay jar. It is quite cool.'

Ghote got up and helped himself, dipping a brass tumbler into the big pot. He drank.

'Cool,' he said contemptuously.

'Well, it is cool as water can be kept without refrigerator.'

'Refrigerator, refrigerator. There you go again. Always dragging it in. Always nagging about it. Always hinting.'

It was the signal for battle.

But Protima with that contrariness that was both the bane and delight of her make-up, refused to fight. Instead she was all sweetness.

'No, you are wrong,' she said. 'Really, I do not always go on about the refrigerator. Or if I do, it is joking only. Yes, I would like, I admit. But if we have not got the money, then we cannot have one. I know that.'

And, as was always the case, she melted Ghote completely.

'But you will get one one day, soon even,' he burst out. 'I meant to keep it secret. I have been saving.'

It was true. He had been saving in secret. Whenever Protima had talked about how wonderful it would be to have a refrigerator he had taken good care to laugh at her, to ask how Indian women had survived so many centuries without such objects, to say that at his present rate of pay such luxuries were unthinkable. But some time before he had been unable to resist setting aside a lump sum in back Dearness Allowance that had unexpectedly been paid him. It had made a start and bit by bit he had added to it. Now, although the refrigerator was still a good distance away, the sum in the post office account he kept for it, his refrigerator fund, was of a respectable size.

Protima came running up.

'You have been saving? In secret? Oh, my husband, such a deceiver he is. Oh, you funny man, you good man. How much have you saved?'

'Nearly five hundred rupees.'

'Five hundred rupees. Five hundred rupees. But that is wonderful. How clever to get so much together and never hint at it to me.'

Never, thought Ghote a little wryly.

Protima laughed tenderly.

'And you are so silly, too,' she said. 'When you have saved that much money there is no need to go any longer without refrigerator. It can be bought on easy terms.'

She came up to him and stroked the back of his head with a long, slim, fine-boned hand.

'Oh, Mr Practical,' she said. 'With his logic here and his logic there. Sometimes you must think of how things really are in the world. Tomorrow you can get the money and we will go to the Hiro Music House shop and make the arrangements. We can have proper cold drinks tomorrow night even.'

'I will see,' Ghote said.

He felt suddenly shy about the whole transaction.

'But the next day is Holi. It would be nice to have cold drinks for the holiday.'

'I may be too busy,' Ghote said with a trace of irritation.

'Then we will wait. We have waited so long, two days more will not matter. Straight after Holi we will go.'

'Yes.'

14

Next morning as soon as the big post office in Frere Road was open Ghote drew out the whole sum in his refrigerator fund. He found that it actually just exceeded the five hundred rupee mark.

'With accrued interest,' the elderly, delicately-spectacled clerk explained gravely.

Ghote waited while his passbook was ceremoniously ruled up.

He sighed. He had wanted to let the money grow and grow till he had accumulated every one of the 1,090 rupees which the refrigerator he had his eye on would cost, excise duty and taxes apart. But these he generally contrived to leave out of his calculations.

Carefully he fitted the crisp new notes away in an inner pocket. And as he did so an alarming diminuendo of thoughts spiralled through his head. That it was wonderful to have actually got hold of so much money; that life with a refrigerator in the house would be like them having a whole series of gifts; that there were many people much less lucky than this, like the gang over at the Masters Foundation, saved from the misery of the gutters only by chance, or the people of the fishing village, always on the edge of disaster. Then the thought came that Frank Masters would have gone to the aid of the village if it had happened to come to his notice; and then that to a villager five hundred rupees would seem unattainable wealth; then that Protima did not know exactly how much he had saved; and next that he ought to devote at least some of this wealth to helping the wretchedly poor people he had been brought into contact with; and finally that he should go out to the village as soon as possible and give Tarzan's family a generous present.

He had meant to decide on the way exactly what the appropriate sum was, whether it should be as much as fifty rupees or whether less would be fair. But instead he found he could think of nothing but that by going off on this jaunt he was avoiding doing his duty over Amrit Singh.

All the way through the flat, dreary, crowded stretches of North Bombay, past the tall mill chimneys and the squalid shacks between them, he cursed himself for not simply arresting the big Sikh. He might not be the toughest man in the force, or the cleverest, or the biggest pusher, but at least he did his duty. Always. As laid down. Until this business.

It was the thought of Frank Masters, the good man, that had done it, he reflected. If this investigation had been into anybody else's death, perhaps he would have felt able to accept his orders and carry them out to the end. Afterwards someone else, someone senior, could take the responsibility if the orders had created more harm than good. And if improving the evidence like that put Amrit Singh in a cell for a really long time, well, that was where Amrit Singh ought to be, and everybody knew it.

The stations along the way were slowly ticked off – Matunga Road, Santa Cruz, Ville Parle, Andheri, Goregaon, Malad, Kandivlee, Borivli. He found the same old tonga and weary horse as he had used the day before and made the same uncomfortable trip to the point where the road to the sea became a mere path. Blackly he ploughed along the muddy strip of sand towards the village, keeping just in the shade of the matted tangle of vegetation springing from the marshy land at the highest point the tide reached.

Because there could be no doubt about one thing. If ever anybody was a bad person, a man content to live well at the expense of anyone he could bully or bang money out of, it was Amrit Singh. And he was a proven killer, too.

Ghote stopped.

Ahead of him, standing casually behind a thick sprout of growth at the foot of an old, leaning, battered palm, there was a figure in a heavy red and blue turban with a white shirt and tight whitish trousers kept up by a broad sash. A Sikh. You could tell a mile off. But more than any Sikh, surely.

Over the soft, grey sand Ghote advanced carefully, noiselessly.

Yes, there in front of him, spying over the village in much the same way that he himself had done the day before, was Amrit Singh. In the flesh.

Ghote glanced round. There ought to be a police shadow somewhere in sight.

He could see no one. He decided to plunge into the dank vegetation behind and try to work round Amrit Singh in a half-circle to see whether he had been properly followed or not. If he had been let off the hook, someone ought to pay for it. It was not so often that they had the big Sikh where they wanted him, and after that long afternoon tracking him down in Morton Road no one should have let him get away.

When he got back to the office he would . . .

He pulled himself up. Surely this was just the result of thinking that Amrit Singh's shadow would see Inspector Ghote miles from his proper territory at a time when he should be answering his DSP's queries back at headquarters.

But there was no one to observe such curious behaviour as it turned out. Almost an hour later when he had emerged on to the grey sands again after completing his slow, careful half-circle he was convinced that if anyone had been tailing Amrit Singh they had let him get right out of sight.

He quickly looked along the beach to the tongue of jutting vegetation where he had left the sturdy Sikh. He had had glimpses of him often enough while he was manoeuvring round, but he had not seen him for the last few minutes. He was still there, only sitting comfortably at the foot of the tree now.

The inspector drew a deep breath of relief.

He looked over at the scatter of palm-leaf thatched huts and the palisaded curing yard. Outside most of the huts the women sat or stood in little groups. Many of them were preparing food. Children ran about on the greyish sand, except for a group of girls busy stringing flags on lengths of cord in preparation for the Holi holiday next day. Evidently the men were still at sea. Was Amrit Singh waiting for their return? He certainly seemed in no hurry to move.

Quite suddenly Ghote decided to tackle him. This time the advantage of surprise would be on his side. He smiled quietly.

A few steps along the soft, yielding sand and he was within easy speaking distance. Amrit Singh was looking out to sea. Plainly he had no idea that anyone was so near to him.

Ghote spoke softly in a voice which would just reach the big Sikh.

'Amrit Singh, why did you kill Frank Masters?'

Amrit Singh leaped up. His right hand reached swiftly down to the bulge in his cummerbund.

'No,' said Ghote. 'No guns. You do not think I would come out here without saying where I had gone, do you?'

'A gun, Inspector?'

The tall Sikh laughed. But for once without conviction.

'No,' said Ghote, 'this is not the time for shooting. This is the time for answering only. Why did you kill Frank Masters?'

'Inspector, you know that I did not,' Amrit Singh said.

The words were delivered flatly, as a matter of mere form.

'I know that you did,' Ghote said. 'You took the powder from that green glass jar. You put it in the curry on the serving table by the open window of the tiffin room at the Foundation. Why did you do it, Amrit Singh?'

But he had overplayed his hand.

'Inspector, I did not take any poison. I did not know it was powder even. Or that it was kept in a green glass jar.'

Ghote thought of the smashed fragments of the little brown jar the arsenic trioxide had been in. If the jar had not been broken, would they after all have got a trace of one of Amrit Singh's prints off it somewhere? Or would it have been a latent impression from Krishna Chatterjee?

He felt the initiative was slipping away.

'Inspector.'

Ghote looked quickly up at the big Sikh. Unexpectedly, his voice did not contain the familiar broad hints of irony. For once he did not seem to be playing with his interrogator like a jungle cat. He seemed ill at ease.

'Well,' Ghote snapped, seizing on the first thing that came into his head to gain himself the upper hand again, 'well, what exactly are you doing here? Is this a bazaar for a poor travelling salesman to display his goods?'

And he seemed to have made a lucky hit.

Amrit Singh looked nervously at the collection of patched, dank, greenish huts with the women in their tightly wrapped saris squatting outside them.

'Inspector,' he said, 'we are friends. are we not? And it is strange for friends to meet here.'

'Never mind about friends,' Ghote said. 'What are you doing here?'

'A man may travel where he wants,' Amrit Singh said.

Again he lacked real conviction.

'He may travel where he wants, but he should be able to say why he is there, Ghote stated.

'Look, Inspector, between friends,' Amrit Singh began again.

'Between a policeman and Amrit Singh,' Ghote said.

The Sikh ploughed on.

'Inspector, I am a poor man. You are a poor man. Between poor men there is always friendship.'

Suddenly Ghote remembered the five hundred rupees in his pocket, and why it was that he had come out to the village. To see whether there was something someone not really poor could do for people in real danger of having just nothing to eat if precarious luck turned only a little against them.

He looked past the Sikh's broad frame down towards the cluster of flimsy huts. The group of girls rose to their feet at just that moment and carried a long string of pathetic little flags towards the curing yard.

Amrit Singh, who had been looking at Ghote trying to assess his reaction to the general propositions he had been putting out, gave up and launched into a more direct approach.

'Inspector sahib,' he said. 'I am poor. I know it. You know it. Poor as can be. But just today, as it happens, I have a little money. I have been lucky in selling some things. I know I ought to use the money to pay off the heavy debts I have, but I am ready not to. For a friend.'

'What about the huge sum you made at the Masters Foundation?' Ghote said, trying for another lucky shot.

'Inspector, no huge sums have I made. I am a poor man, the poorest of the poor. But today I have a few rupees, perhaps even a few hundred rupees, and if you like I will share them with another poor man who is my friend.'

'Are you trying to bribe a police officer, Amrit Singh?'

'Inspector, that I should do such a thing. I am trying to share my luck only. And I am remembering a friend who only two days ago was talking about such a thing as a refrigerator.'

The Sikh decided that he had advanced enough counters for the time being. He waited to see if they were taken up.

And Ghote, standing in front of him, his eyes unmoving, keeping the questioning firmly in his own hands, felt his heart patter hard.

A refrigerator. How had the Sikh happened to hit on that, of all things, to propose as a bribe?

Perhaps he had let something of his private life appear when

Amrit Singh had been talking to him in the compound at the Masters Foundation. He must watch himself.

His silence had the happy effect of forcing the Sikh to go yet another stage onwards.

'Ah,' he said, 'there are many refrigerators, but why should not poor men like you and I have one? It would cost not very much money. I saw yesterday only a fine refrigerator in the paper. And it would cost only one thousand and ninety rupees.'

Again he waited, with so much more bait economically laid out.

'If you are offering me the price of a refrigerator to forget I have seen you here,' said Ghote levelly, 'then you can stop right away. I will take no bribes.'

'Inspector, think of your wife when you go home and say a refrigerator is coming by the next delivery. Or when you show her the very notes that will buy one. One thousand rupees, Inspector.'

The Sikh's hand slipped between the folds of his broad sash. Ghote had little doubt that somewhere there he had notes to the value of a thousand rupees, and beyond. He thought of the notes in his own pocket, and of what they were intended for.

'You are generous,' he said to Amrit Singh. 'But then when your money has been taken from other people only, you can afford to be generous. If it had been truly your own, would you give it to others? And out of true kindness, like Frank Masters? Or would you keep every anna?'

The Sikh evidently understood that this was a really final answer. His dark eyes suddenly glowered with rage.

Ghote tensed slightly, expecting violent action.

But he got only violent words.

'Give? Kindness?' said the tall Sikh with deep contempt. 'What man would look on you as a man if for no reason you gave? Money is not a plaything to be handed to children only. If a man has got money for himself, then he knows it is worth something. He does not go here and there giving.'

From the emphasis he put on this last word, it was plain that

Amrit Singh had a very different outlook on life from that of Frank Masters.

'You would be twice the man you are if you had given a tenth only of what Frank Masters gave,' Ghote said sharply.

'Frank Masters.'

The Sikh spat into the slimy earth at his feet.

'I know all about Frank Masters,' he said. 'Why did he have to come all the way to Bombay to rule other people's lives? Are there not poor people in America for him to play with? But, no, he has to come here to make himself feel good. Only in India can he find the very poor and get the most for his money. For a few annas here he can make a poor boy do just what he tells him, and can say to himself that he has changed a life.'

Ghote felt that he wanted to protest but could find nothing to say.

'Oh yes,' the Sikh went on, 'if you want to find a really bad man, look there. There is someone who, just to feel happy himself, will make someone else change his whole life, will make him go where he thinks it is best for him to go, do what he thinks is best. And not even to get money. But just so that he feels good with himself. If I had my way Frank Masters and all his sort would be dropped into the harbour with a good rock tied to their legs.'

'So that was why you killed him?' Ghote said.

But he knew that the question was only a hasty jibe. His real answer was going to be in deeds not words: he was going to give every anna of the five hundred rupees to the fisherman's family. To make it up, in a way, to Frank Masters.

Only one thing stopped him from running down straight away to the huts and shouting for the great fat paramour.

That was that he did not want to let Amrit Singh go. More than ever now he wanted to make sure he could have him pulled in at any moment. An idea occurred to him. Swallowing his anger, he made himself speak casually.

'Well, perhaps you are right,' he said. 'Frank Masters was certainly very rich.'

'And very bad,' said Amrit Singh determinedly.

'And yet you and I are far from having his money,' Ghote went on.

He positively saw the spark of hope light up again in the Sikh's dark eyes.

'Yes,' the tall man said, 'we are poor.'

Ghote sighed.

'But we can be friends,' Amrit Singh said. 'And what money we have we can share with friends as friends. And friends can help each other. They can keep quiet about some things sometimes.'

'Perhaps,' said Ghote.

Amrit Singh dug his hand into his sash again.

'No,' Ghote said. 'I will think. It is wrong.'

Amrit Singh shrugged his broad shoulders.

'Can I see you somewhere later? Tomorrow?' Ghote said.

Amrit Singh calculated for a moment.

Then apparently he decided to make the best of a difficult situation.

'I shall be at Morton Road early tomorrow,' he said.

'Then perhaps I shall see you,' said Ghote.

The tall Sikh did not wait to exchange pleasantries a moment longer. He had got as good a bargain as he could hope for, and in an instant the thick swamp vegetation swallowed him up. Ghote caught one quick sight of the red and blue turban, and no more.

He turned towards the huts of the village.

Outside Tarzan's family hut now the paramour was sitting cross-legged. Between her enormous rounded knees, straining tight the cloth of her sari, there was a big bowl in the bottom of which she was pounding something. Her great forearms, whose flesh pressed hard against the dozen thin glass bangles she wore, were working rhythmically bringing a pestle down and down with terrible heaviness.

When Ghote's shadow fell across her she looked up. The moment she saw who it was she laughed till she shook.

'Have you come looking for that bad son again?' she said.

'I have come because of what I saw yesterday,' Ghote replied.

The remark evidently seemed to her even richer in humour than her own question. She roared and gasped with laughter.

'What you saw yesterday,' she got out at last. 'Or was it what you did not see?'

Ghote ignored all this.

'Yesterday,' he said, when he thought she would hear him, 'yesterday I saw how difficult it was for you to live without being a prey to evil men. And that is why I have come back: to offer help.'

'Oh, it is difficult to live,' the paramour agreed. 'In a few days we have to pay money back on the boat, and it is not there. We save nothing. The men will not do it. You know what they say? That because a fisherman lives by robbing the sea he cannot save what he makes.'

She giggled softly, almost to herself.

'But you see how foolish this is,' Ghote said. 'You are a woman of authority. You must make them put away a little when the catches are good.'

The giggling became a frank laugh again.

'All right,' Ghote said, 'I understand your difficulties. And I am prepared to help you start again. This is what I will do.'

He put his hand into his pocket and pulled out the tight bundle of notes. For an instant the fat woman stopped laughing completely. Her eyes went wide.

Then she lowered them to look at the handful of pounded spices in the big bowl and giggled modestly a little.

'I want you to take this money,' said Ghote. 'It will pay off much of the debt on your boat. Then your catches will bring you a proper livelihood, you and both your stepsons. But you must promise you will make them save when they do well, so that they can last over a poor catch without borrowing again.'

A podgy hand reached upwards towards the roll of notes he held.

'Will you promise?' he asked.

'Oh, sahib, I will promise. Such wealth. Such goodness. Sahib, I kiss your feet.'

Ghote thrust the money into her fist.

But he could not help noticing that she made no move to kiss his feet in actuality. Instead she shoved the notes down into her enormous bosom and stayed with her head lowered.

Ghote decided that it would be best to leave at once. He turned and marched off through the yielding grey sand along the top of the beach. He tried to analyse his feelings. They were confused, but seemed mostly to be stirrings of disappointment. He had certainly not felt a great surge of happiness at the moment the notes had left his hand. But there had been something in the way the big podgy fist had enveloped them that had disconcerted him.

He turned and looked back.

It came as no real surprise to see that the enormous paramour was sitting there visibly quivering, even at this distance, with great tides of irrepressible laughter.

The journey back to Bombay was terrible. To begin with, Ghote found when he got to the end of the muddy path through the swamps that there was no tonga waiting at the start of the road. Amrit Singh had commandeered it. The extra walk to the railway station took him hours. The sun beat down. The dust rose up. His left heel began to throb where it had been so jolted at the Morton Road place. He felt abominably tired.

Then he had an interminable wait for a train, and, once it had come, progress was hardly faster. The stations crept by – Borivli, Kandivlee, Malad, Goregaon, Andheri, Ville Parle, Santa Cruz, Matunga Road. At last they pulled into Churchgate Station. It was by now late in the afternoon.

Standing in the station concourse, buffeted by people hurrying by in all directions, mostly carrying, it seemed, huge bedding rolls, Ghote stood and tried to make up his mind what to do. A red-shirted coolie with three battered cardboard suitcases under each arm banged into his back.

Should he go to the office even at this late hour? What would he say if the chaprassi on duty in the entrance gave him a message that DSP Naik had been asking for him all day? How could he possibly tell him that he had spoken to Amrit Singh and had not arrested him? There would be certainly no point in confronting the DSP with the question that reared up in his own mind at any and every opportunity. If he said to him 'Which of them did it? Which?' he would be told pretty sharply not to talk such nonsense.

And it was possible the DSP was really right.

A man wheeling a low barrow neatly piled with dozen upon dozen of sticky-looking cream horns scraped its edge all the way across Ghote's shin bones. Ghote stepped sharply back and banged into an elderly, bespectacled traveller nursing a big earthenware drinking water jug. Some of the water spilt. The eyes that looked at Ghote through the spectacles were infinitely reproachful.

Ghote strode away.

There was no point in going home. Although he hardly dared put the thought into words the suspicion was beginning to lurk somewhere in his mind that he had been a colossal fool to give all that money away. It would need a great deal of explaining.

He tried thinking about Frank Masters to counteract these thoughts. After all, when Frank Masters gave huge sums away nobody put it in the papers that he was a fool.

And with the memory of Frank Masters back again came the question: Which of the two? Which?

Ghote decided to go to the Foundation once more. There was nothing to be done there, but at least he would be near the source of it all.

Before he got to the big, old bungalow in Wodehouse Road he became involved in another incident of the sort which, it seemed, had dogged him ever since he had first been put on the case.

His bus stopped a little north of the Foundation and he was

walking abstractedly along towards it, past the Catholic cathedral, past Stranger's Guest House, past the YMCA, when an abrupt contortion in the traffic stream beside him caught his eye. He looked round.

Standing half in the deep storm gutter, half in the roadway itself, were the boys of Edward G. Robinson's gang. Their heads were bent in a tight circle and evidently some deeply secret negotiation was going forward. The passing traffic was swerving sharply to avoid them and an occasional driver with an unusually tender social conscience broke the silence-zone rule by giving a quick toot of his horn as he passed. But the boys ignored it all, even the rackety van Ghote saw at that moment positively brushing the back of Edward G. Robinson's tattered black jacket.

With a sigh Ghote walked over. He caught a glimpse of a couple of old fruit juice bottles half filled with reddish brown liquid. He did not need to ask what this was: too much bhang processed from hemp leaves into a sweet drink had come under his eyes in the past for there to be any doubt. However, in the quantity the boys had, though illegal, it was much less dangerous than standing in a busy roadway.

'Hey, you,' Ghote shouted.

The boys looked up. Edward G. stuffed in a leisurely way the bottle he had been holding into the one remaining practical pocket of his battered jacket.

'Hi,' he said.

Ghote looked at him sternly.

'That is no way to behave,' he said. 'You are causing traffic congestion and also risking injury.'

The boys looked at him in silence, all except Edward G. himself, who showed true leadership by taking absolutely no notice whatsoever.

But Ghote was in no mood to appreciate such qualities. He felt a spasm of sharp irritation and stepping forward caught hold of the boy's arm and shook it hard.

Edward G.'s appallingly crinkled face remained eloquent with total boredom.

'Listen to me,' Ghote said with all the emphasis he could put into the words, 'listen to me. This is dangerous. Do you want to see one of you getting killed?'

Edward G. turned right round to face the inspector and put a friendly arm round Tarzan's bare shoulders.

'This one's pretty dumb,' he said. 'He could go all right.'

15

To Inspector Ghote's surprise, in spite of Edward G. Robinson's limited attitude to road safety, a minute or so later the boys began to drift back into the half-heartedly cared for front garden of the Masters Foundation. But beyond this concession they ignored him and wandered over to settle down contentedly under the shade of a peepul tree. Tarzan swung easily up into the branches and hung upside down above the others like a half-naked, wiry bat and the two bhang bottles appeared again.

Ghote looked at the group for a moment and then turned and faced the steps of the Foundation and the tall front door.

Faced them without pleasure. The fact was that he was still entirely undecided about what he would do. Whom should he ask to see? There was really no point in questioning anybody. He had asked everything long before. He had seen every cranny in the big bungalow. He had made every test he could think of, taken every measurement.

As much to force himself to come to a decision as for any other reason, he went up to the wide steps at a run and put his forefinger firmly and definitely on the bell push.

But he still had time to make his decision and unmake it. The die was cast, but the dice was still toppling over and with its number yet to come up. He seized on the notion of asking to see Krishna Chatterjee again. It was all that was left: battering away at an unyielding surface in the mere hope that in spite of all the signs something would crack, that little Mr Chatterjee would let something slip and settle it one way or the other. Either the killer, or the innocent one.

The bell remained unanswered. Ghote decided not to press it again. There might still come to him a last-minute flash of inspiration for some other way of breaking the dilemma.

'Hey, mister, what you going to do?'

He recognized the voice without needing to turn around. Edward G. Robinson again. As usual hitting the nail exactly on the head and driving it painfully home.

'Come on, mister, what you going to do in there? Who you going to see? Going to make the big arrest?'

Ghote decided to turn around.

From the slight height of the doorstep he looked over at the group under the peepul tree. They were happily and completely at ease. One of the bhang bottles was just finishing its round. It had come to Tarzan. Ghote watched fascinated for a moment as the boy contrived to take a long, cool swig of the sticky liquid while still remaining hanging from his branch. Then he turned to Edward G. Robinson's wrinkle-interlaced face. It semaphored an expression of simple, impudent questioning.

'What a police officer is going to do at a private institution can be of no possible concern to you,' Ghote said in a loud and clear voice.

'If the police officer is going to bully poor old swallow-all Chatterjee it is of concern,' came the reply.

Edward G., expert in film American, had also caught the inspector's tone, to a nicety.

Ghote bit his lip.

'If I wish to question, I shall question,' he said. 'Mr Chatterjee, or anyone else I like.'

He saw that Tarzan was flapping his arms up and down in a highly agitated way. Another comment. And, true enough, it was the way he felt.

Edward G. took a lazy swig of bhang. He was lying on his back with his left knee raised and his bare right leg swinging idly across it.

'Listen, mister,' he said, 'why you bothering about this case any more? So you ain't cracked it? So what?'

'So the death of the great benefactor of the children of Bombay is still a mystery,' Ghote answered. 'Does that mean nothing to you? You would not be here at this moment if it was not for Frank Masters coming from America and spending his money to help you. You.'

He came down two of the steps and glared over at the reclining form of Edward G. Robinson across the hot afternoon sunshine.

'Mister, did you ever think I might like not to be here?' Edward G. said, gently twirling the bhang bottle. 'Did you ever think I might want to sleep on the pavement instead of in that great, big, warm and dry house?'

He squinted through half-closed eyes in his wrinkled old man's face at the solid whiteness of the bungalow behind Ghote.

'What nonsense is this?' Ghote replied.

He came right down the steps and strode across to the idle group under the peepul.

'What nonsense is this?' he repeated, facing them. 'Are you hungry? No. Are you wondering every day whether you will starve to death before long? Or catch some illness? No, you know you will get treatment here from the money that good man did not hesitate to give.'

'You know what he felt when we got better?' Edward G. said.

He drained the last of the bhang. There was a rustle of protest at this from the other members of the gang. Edward G. ignored it.

'You know what good Frank Masters felt when his good money had saved our lives?' he asked Ghote. 'He felt "I have got another boy to be mine for ever." He felt mighty fine.'

The cowboy drawl might have come from the lips of the Lone Ranger himself.

Ghote drew breath to reply. What infernal impudence, he thought. What gratitude. The man who had come from America to look after these boys, and had got killed for his pains. And now this. All right, he would tell them a thing or two. It was all very well for a thug like Amrit Singh to put out opinions like that, but for a boy, a mere boy, and one who had actually benefited from Frank Masters's great kindness. It was appalling, truly—

He stopped himself.

What was he doing? Dictating what someone else should think.

Just because the boy had expressed an opinion that did not echo the respectability of every schoolmaster that had ever lectured a delinquent, he was accusing him of all the crimes in the book. And it was not even as if the picture of Frank Masters he had put before the boy was a true one. It did not square up really with what he had learned from Krishna Chatterjee. It was almost as distorted as Amrit Singh's view of him. Or, come to that, as the view Dr Diana had put when he had questioned her about Frank Masters in her English-looking room in this very house.

No, he would stop it.

He looked down at the boys.

'If you go on drinking bhang,' he said, 'in the end you will suffer worse than any pleasure you get. But perhaps you knew that.'

He turned and walked back to the front door. His ring on the bell had remained unanswered. He climbed the steps and rang again.

'Well, mister, what you going to do?' Edward G. sang out.

Ghote turned round.

'I am going to investigate a most curious discrepancy,' he said.

As Inspector Ghote approached the dispensary hut, where he had been taken by the solemn, weighty bearer who had eventually opened the door to him, he found that the burst of courage and curiosity that had sprung up in him at the moment he had realized there was a curious discrepancy to investigate was oozing fast away.

Dr Diana, he said to himself, Dr Diana. Was he really going to tackle her successfully? Would he actually manage to make her account for the fact that she had praised Frank Masters to the skies while Krishna Chatterjee, apparently with the best of intentions, had painted a very different picture when he had been questioned at headquarters?

He licked his lips and contrasted the two portraits that had been given to him.

Little Mr Chatterjee had convincingly spoken of the man whose immense wealth was a disadvantage leading him all too often to be kind rather than useful, a fallible mortal subject to mortal failings such as gradually declining interest in the face of unsuccess. Dr Diana, on the other hand, had talked about a man who saw what was to be done and did it. She had said Frank Masters was no sloppy sentimental fool.

And somehow, Ghote realized now, what she had said had not rung true. It had been too much delivered as a challenge. While Mr Chatterjee had seemed to speak with instances in mind.

Ghote was aware that he had failed to answer Dr Diana's challenge. Probably he had not realized earlier that the two views of Frank Masters were in such contrast because he had been hiding from himself this very failure.

The bearer threw open the door of the hut, the rough wood hardly measuring up to the treatment.

'Inspector Ghote, Bombay CID,' he announced, apparently unconscious of the fact that the last time he had used such words had been to usher in Ghote to the dead body of Frank Masters.

Ghote, well remembering the first occasion, stepped inside. Once again Dr Diana had her back to him. But this time she was not standing looking fixedly into the mirror on the cupboard face. She was bending over the sink in the corner with a whimpering eight-year-old boy propped up on one knee.

She glanced round for an instant.

'Oh,' she said, 'you again. Well, you can see I'm busy.'

'I regret,' Ghote said. 'I was not informed you were engaged.'

Dr Diana turned the high chromium tap of the sink on full blast.

'When one of the kids gets bitten by a pye-dog,' she said, her voice for all its clarity hard to hear above the spluttering of the water, 'I don't get time to go round warning everybody. I'm too busy to bother with trifles.'

'I perfectly understand,' Ghote said. 'I will return when you are free.'

'Oh, no, stay now you're here,' Dr Diana answered. 'You can talk to me while I see to this chappie. I dare say I'll be able to spare you enough attention.'

She turned back to the boy.

'Here, let me look again,' she said. 'Now. Steady on.'

The boy's whimpering became louder.

'What do you want anyhow?' Dr Diana called over her shoulder.

Ghote hesitated. Was he really going to let her get away with giving him the fag end of her attention like this? And then he decided that he was. He would not let a sense of his own dignity interfere on this case.

'I want to talk to you about Mr Masters,' he said.

'No,' said Dr Diana. 'That doesn't look too good to me.'

Ghote realized that she was not talking to him. He waited.

'Here,' the doctor went on, 'let me see the finger.'

She glanced round at Ghote.

'Thought we'd been into all that,' she said.

She took hold of the boy's hand, bent low over it and put the blood-covered finger to her lips. She sucked hard.

'Yes,' Ghote said. 'I thought that also. But a certain discrepancy has come to light.'

Dr Diana took her mouth away from the boy's finger, and spat slappingly into the sink.

'Discrepancy?' she said contemptuously, as she put her lips to the small brown hand again.

'Yes, discrepancy,' Ghote replied firmly.

The single note of contempt had done its work. In a moment all the courage that had seeped away, and the curiosity, sprang up again. He went on.

'You told that Frank Masters was never kind only. You told that he saw what had to be done and did it. I think that was not true.'

Dr Diana spat out another mouthful of the boy's blood. She spared time to give Ghote a steady, appraising look before she bent to her work once more.

Ghote waited.

At last Dr Diana took her mouth off the boy's finger again. She examined the wound.

'Yes,' she said, 'that looks a bit more like it. Now, come over here.'

She led the boy, moaning quietly to himself and shaking a little, over to the glass-topped table.

'Stand there a moment,' she said, turning to the cupboard with the mirror front.

As she opened it and ranged over the rows of bottles, jars and packets inside, she gave Ghote her answer.

'All right. I dare say I did gloss over one or two things. I can't see that it matters.'

She found the bottle she was looking for and put it on the table. She turned back to the cupboard.

Ghote ignored the fact that he was having to speak to her white-coated back.

'I am investigating Mr Masters's death,' he said, with an edge of controlled anger. 'And when I ask questions about him I expect to get told the truth.'

Dr Diana turned slowly back. She was holding a blue paper packet of cotton wool. She looked at Ghote expressionlessly.

'Yes,' she said at last, 'yes, I see that I shouldn't have done that.'

She pulled a lump of cotton wool off the roll from the packet. Then she went over to the table and tipped a plentiful quantity of Mercurochrome on to the neat wad she had made.

'Now, laddie,' she said, 'I'm afraid this is going to hurt.'

She reached down and picked up his hand.

The boy looked up at her with wide eyes. His teeth were chattering hard.

'Then I would like to hear from you what Mr Masters was truly like,' Ghote said.

The boy screamed as Dr Diana firmly pressed the red-soaked pad on the wound.

'Frank?' she said when the boy was quieter.

She took a dressing from the cupboard and began strapping it round the boy's finger. Ghote watched. And waited.

But for some time Dr Diana was too occupied to add anything more. She finished tying the dressing into place, took a hypodermic from the cupboard and went quickly into the inner part of the hut.

For an instant Ghote wondered whether he should follow her. But he recollected the grilles on the windows and the fact that there was no other door to the whole hut and decided to stay put. Dr Diana returned a second or two later. The hypodermic was half full. She went up to the boy.

'Now, nearly finished,' she said.

Ghote could not help noticing that, though brusque, her voice was clearly comforting. The boy looked up at her, still shaking.

'Have to get an anti-rabies shot into him as quickly as possible,' Dr Diana said.

She addressed her remarks to the top of the glass-covered table but Ghote interpreted them as a sort of apology for not answering more quickly.

He stood looking at the fine, gleaming needle held steadily in the thin flesh of the boy's arm while Dr Diana firmly squeezed the shot home.

'There,' she said, taking the needle out, 'now we'll just put you down somewhere comfortably and then you'll begin to feel better.'

With one swoop she picked the feather-light boy up and deposited him on the hard, white examination couch. Ghote wondered if it had been used since Frank Masters's body had been removed from it. Dr Diana took up a coarse, red blanket from the foot of the couch, shook it out and placed it over the boy.

'That'll warm you up,' she said.

She turned to Ghote.

'Well now, Frank. As he really was. I suppose you have a right to know.'

She went over to the sink, stooped, picked up a small kettle from underneath it and filled it with water. Not until she had taken it to the electric boiling ring in the inner half of the hut did she give Ghote her full attention.

'I've a notion,' she said, 'that you got your picture of Frank from that credulous idiot Krishna Chatterjee.'

Ghote kept his face blank.

Dr Diana grunted a half-laugh.

'All right, protect your sources of information. I don't mind. But let me tell you one thing. Chatterjee is a nice fellow and all that, but he's simply too good. It isn't that he won't see people's faults, but by the time he's finished finding excuses for them he's forgotten the faults are still there.'

Again Ghote made no comment. Dr Diana, hands thrust into the patch pockets of her white coat, went on.

'Did he tell you that Frank was a damned bad administrator?' she asked. 'If he did, I bet he found so many excuses for not doing administration that in the end you thought it was a positive virtue to go about wasting what resources we have.'

'Being a bad administrator is hardly a grave fault,' Ghote said. 'I am not going to be satisfied so easily, you know.'

Dr Diana's eyes flashed.

'I wasn't trying to fob you off, as a matter of fact,' she said. 'When I make up my mind to tell someone something, I tell them. So you can just listen.'

Ghote made no reply.

'No,' Dr Diana went on, 'I'm not making out a lack of administrative talent is a crippling moral defect. What I am saying is that Frank was not only a bad administrator, but that he wouldn't realize it. He thought that whatever way he tackled something was the right way.'

'And you found this out when he left you in charge and went to the Punjab?' Ghote asked.

'I'd suspected it for years. But, yes, when he went sidling off to his mystics I realized just what a mess he had made. He was a poor judge of character for one thing. The way he let himself be deceived by that rogue Amrit Singh was a positive scandal.'

'Amrit Singh?' Ghote said.

Dr Diana looked at him.

'Oh, don't get so excited,' she said. 'Everybody knows you'd like to pull in Amrit Singh for this. But if you do his lawyers will have him out in no time. And well you know it. After all, you haven't got cast-iron proof, have you?'

'Where did you hear this?' Ghote snapped.

Minute by minute he felt himself being pushed back on to the defensive, and he resented it.

'My dear man, surely you realize everything you've done and said here has been watched over and talked over till we're sick of it?'

Ghote knew it only too well. With the eyes and ears of the clients everywhere he could expect nothing less.

'Whether we shall take action against Amrit Singh is a matter for us,' he said. 'What I want to know is what were Mr Masters's relations with him.'

'Practically non-existent,' Dr Diana answered. 'What could they be? Amrit Singh hung around here because he had dealings with some of the boys, as you'd expect. And Frank saw him, and let himself be charmed. Typical of him. But I put all that right when I found out what was happening.'

'So,' Ghote said, 'this is a very different Frank Masters I am hearing about.'

Dr Diana gave him a still scornful look.

'Well,' she said, 'you didn't think I was going to let Frank down if I could help it, did you?'

'No, perhaps not,' Ghote replied. 'But now you cannot help it.'

'No. Very well then. What else can I say to blacken him? That he was selfish? Well, that's certainly true.'

'Are you saying that he did all this just for his own sake?'

Ghote gestured round at the walls of the hut in their dazzling white paint, the medicines in the cupboard, the boy quietly lying on the hard couch.

Dr Diana puffed out a sigh.

'To tell you the truth,' she said, 'I honestly don't know. Who does? About someone else? On the whole I think his motives were mixed. Some days whatever he did was to make Frank Masters feel good. At other times, well, I can't say.'

She treated Ghote to a sort of grin.

'It made life pretty difficult, you know,' she said.

Ghote hardly heard. A terrible thought had struck him. He had been building up in his mind an ideal of Frank Masters. Dr Diana's words had shown him that it was not at all like the truth. And yet, on the strength of this ideal, he had been so stupid as to give away five hundred precious rupees. How could he have been so utterly foolish? Krishna Chatterjee had spoken of Frank Masters as a man who did good, certainly, but he had at the same time painted him as human. It was only hearing him abused by someone as calmly unscrupulous as Amrit Singh that had turned the balance in the end.

Ghote saw now that it had been a gesture of sudden revulsion to thrust all that money into the podgy hand of the paramour, a silly and impulsive gesture. And in making it he had given away every anna he had scraped together to get his own wife something she had wanted for years.

'I – I have to go,' he said abruptly. 'Yes, I must go now. Thank you for your help. But I must go.'

Dr Diana was looking at him wonderingly as he hurried out.

'You could have had some of the coffee I was making for the boy,' she said.

16

One thought tapped away inside Inspector Ghote's head as he ran off through the big garden of the Masters Foundation. Perhaps it was not too late. He had given the paramour the five hundred rupees only that morning. She would hardly go hurrying round to the moneylender to pay off the debt on the boat right away. Moneylenders were not that popular.

So she would still have the rupees.

And from the way she had taken them, he would have every right to demand them back. She had shown no gratitude. All right, she would lose the money.

It was with this idea lodged solidly in his mind that he arrived in the hurly-burly of Churchgate Station again and set about finding a train to take him back. As he scanned the timetable and ran to make enquiries here and there the same thought kept hammering away in his head. It is not too late: she deserves to have to pay the money back.

And there was no train.

He could hardly believe it. He repeated his round of enquiries but had no more success. While he had been talking to the boys outside the Foundation and seeing Dr Diana in the dispensary time had passed. Then the trip across the city, though short, had been more than usually bedevilled with traffic hold-ups. And there it was. No train going out that far till early next day.

He thought of hiring a car but then remembered that after all the following day was Holi. There was even less chance of the paramour handing the five hundred rupees over to a moneylender in the middle of all the festivities. He decided to get out to the village as early as possible next morning.

He spent a miserable evening. He did not dare go home till late in case there was talk about the refrigerator. He dared even less go to the office in case orders were waiting for him to get in touch with DSP Naik. In the end he went to a cinema. The amorous intrigues of the film failed to grip. The music grated on his nerves. He left before it was over.

Next morning when he arrived, hot, sweaty and unoptimistic, at the village he found it looking very different from his previous visits. The overlying atmosphere of poverty had been temporarily swamped in an uprush of holiday gaiety. On the greenish, decaying walls of the huts bright, crudely coloured banners reflected the equal brightness of the sunshine and rippled happily in a strong breeze coming saltily off the sea. From the masts of the village boats, beached high and dry today on the soft sand, fluttered gay pennants, long and twisting, or stubby and forcefully patterned. More streamers and banners decorated the tall net-drying poles.

On the beach in front of the huts a positively enormous bonfire had been built. Ghote wondered for a moment how a community of such poverty could have gathered together the great pile of broken wood, discarded household objects, substantial pieces of furniture and even boat oars that made up the bulk of the merrily crackling blaze with its attendant circle of children, now excitedly jigging up and down, now suddenly solemn in front of the glowing heart of the fire.

But he had no time for idle speculation.

In all the stirring jubilation he was faced with the awkward business of broaching the reason for his visit to Tarzan's family. The evening before, during the slow unwinding of the colourful love epic in the cinema, the notion that the paramour had somehow forfeited any rights to the five hundred rupees had finally faded away in the harsh light of reality. He had handed the money over: he wanted it back. That was what it amounted to. He wanted it back because he had parted with it under a false impression. Frank Masters was not the person he had thought. The family had not been entitled to the money.

Even the very altered atmosphere of the village could not rob him of this cast-iron resolution. Even the sight of the family themselves standing outside their hut, on the verge of entering into the general jubilation, could not kill this.

One glance at the paramour however was enough to make Ghote dismiss her as the best one to approach straight away. Her natural jollity had already so blended with the gaiety all around her that he doubted whether it would be possible to communicate at all. Tarzan's brother, standing jigging a little in time to the rhythmical drumming coming from the far side of the great fire as if he knew his duty in times of merriment, he reserved as a last hope.

He concentrated on the father. Certainly the old man seemed impervious to the increasing noise and excitement. His face was as absolutely impassive as ever. His arms were folded indomitably across his ribby chest and he stood, legs just a little apart, still as a statue.

Ghote went up to him.

'Good morning, good morning,' he said cheerfully.

He looked back over his shoulder at the revelry behind him.

'Happy holiday,' he added.

Tarzan's father moved his eyes. He looked at Ghote. But his expression did not alter.

'Well,' Ghote said, 'how are things with you today? The village seems to be very happy. I hope you feel your troubles are a little less?'

He thought he had succeeded in bringing the subject of the five hundred rupees neatly to the fore.

Tarzan's father looked away.

Ghote tried again.

'This is not a day for the moneylender to come round, is it?' he said.

He laughed.

The laugh ended up on a cracked note he did not like. And Tarzan's father ignored it all.

'So you have not had to pay off your debt yet?' Ghote said, feeling the time for delicacy had come to an abrupt end.

'Our debt?'

The paramour had evidently been more attentive to the conversation than her lolloping half-dance to the drumming rhythm had indicated. She turned round now to Ghote, still dancing and still smiling with as much all-embracing benevolence as ever, and put out a podgy finger to dig him in the ribs.

'You have come to see us paying our debt with that money?' she asked.

'Yes. No.'

'Tomorrow. Tomorrow. Perhaps later. This is no day for debt paying. Holi hai.'

Ghote felt obliged to smile and even essay a slight dance step. And, in fact, he did already feel suddenly much more light-hearted.

So the debt was unpaid. Then the five hundred rupees were still safely tucked away somewhere. Though it was not going to be easy in the middle of dancing, smiling and shouting 'Holi hai' to broach the delicate core of the problem.

Ghote tried.

'No, no,' he said. 'I did not come to watch such a thing. I would not do that.'

'You came for Holi?'

The paramour seized him with two solid, chunky hands and swung him three times round to the beat of the drums.

'No, no, no.'

Ghote managed to break free. He thrust his face close to the paramour's bouncing, jiggling fat orb. He spoke sharply and clearly, and with a touch of desperation.

'I came to take back the money, some of the money,' he said. 'For a little while. I find I need – I must have it. I must have the money back. Now.'

The grin across the paramour's huge face split into an enormous crease, deep pink, dotted and littered with stumps of white tooth, wide as a crater.

'You want the money back now?'

'Yes, yes. I am sorry. I do. It is most urgent. I will talk about it later. After this . . .'

He looked past the great wobbling bulk of the paramour at the festivities on the sand in front of the village. They were really beginning to warm up now. The drums were beating madly and almost everybody had joined in the dance.

'It is gone. All gone. Gone.'

'Gone?'

Ghote felt a great cold wedge of ice descending crushingly down on to him.

'What do you mean gone?' he said. 'Where has it gone?'

It was the paramour's turn to wave at the rising tide of celebration on the sands. The high-piled blazing fire, the teams of musicians, the flags and banners everywhere, the fireworks screaming up into the blue sky, the food clutched in happy hands, the bottles waving high above heads.

'It has gone for Holi,' she said. 'Such a Holi the village has never known. It has gone to honour the great Krishna. Every anna.'

Ghote turned slowly away.

The sight of that huge face, stupidly happy, reasonlessly gay, maddened him. She had spent every anna of his five hundred rupees in treating the whole village to a wildly extravagant fiesta. Every one of the rupees that at least ought to have gone to make the family's whole life easier by lifting the crushing burden of their debt. Gone. Spent. Going up in smoke.

No wonder the big fire had been blazing so merry on such a fine assortment of rubbish. When money was being thrown about in that way, anyone would be willing to sacrifice a dilapidated piece of furniture or even an oar past its prime.

Waves of pure rage swept through and through him as he marched away.

And quite suddenly, approaching the swirling crowd of merry-makers on the sand, his mood changed. The rage fell apart to leave a hard residue of bitter determination. Never again was he going to set himself up to help or judge other people. They had their lives to lead: he had his. And he knew too what the life he had to lead was. The life of a policeman. Doing his duty as he should. All right, so DSP Naik was prepared to tell plain lies to improve the case against Amrit Singh. Well, he was probably correct. After all, this was the formed opinion of a respected and senior police officer. Who was Ganesh Ghote to go getting himself up against that? No, from now on he would do his duty as it was put to him. And first of all he would go and pull in Amrit Singh. On the murder charge. And the moment he had seen him safely behind bars he would go out to the Masters Foundation, get hold of those damned boys and see that they came into line. He would get up such a case against Amrit Singh that the DSP himself would not be able to better it.

Round him the excited holidaymakers suddenly whirled.

He found himself in an instant surrounded by smiling, smiling faces. Everywhere bodies jerked and swayed in dance. In his ears shout after shout, 'Holi hai, Holi hai, Holi hai' rang and echoed. Fireworks fizzed and banged right, left and centre. Their smell mingled dramatically with that of a hundred sweaty bodies. For a few moments a broad-shouldered fisherman stood pressed close to him, his head thrown back and his mouth opening and shutting rhythmically in the words of a song of consistent and remarkable lewdness.

Krishna and the milkmaids, Ghote thought sourly, hemmed in and pressed upon from every side.

And then the real business of the day began. With a multitude of high, screaming whoops the saturnalian colour throwers came roaring into the fray. With big, crude syringes they sprayed long, drenching streams of coloured water, red, yellow, blue, high into the air and down on to one and all. Other swooping troops puffed huge clouds of pink and purple powder at anyone and everyone, but especially at anybody in the least way high and mighty.

And in all the simple village throng, who looked higher or mightier or more worthy of drenching and powdering than Inspector Ganesh Ghote, CID? Tossing powder by the handful, squirting ink by the bicycle pumpful, they came at him from every side. In seconds he was wet through, red wet, blue wet, yellow wet. And on to the wetness the coloured powders, pink, turquoise and orange, clung and smeared. He put his head glumly down and pushed forward. Dancing bodies bumped him, hands seized him and whirled him bouncing round. The drums beat in his ears, and everywhere the faces were smiling, smiling like maniacs.

I have deserved this, he thought. This is a fit punishment for coming here with my money and telling people how to live their lives. Exactly fit. They have taken my money and used it to buy all these pots of powder and buckets of dye and they have jumped on me and put me down to the lowest level of the low. Well, there it is.

Buffeted and banged, swung and tossed, he endured it till at last he found himself quite suddenly ejected from the whirling crowd.

He staggered a few paces clear and stopped to draw breath. He flapped at his multi-coloured clothes in an ineffectual attempt to get them looking a little more presentable. Then he gave up. He would have to go home looking like this, and that would be the crowning blow of his punishment. He looked round to see where he was and how he could get to the inland path without going through the crowd again.

And just twenty yards away he saw Amrit Singh.

This time the big Sikh was doing more than spy over the village. He was down on his hands and knees round at the back of the palisaded curing yard scraping up the soft muddy earth with his bare hands like a dog.

An energetic and extremely purposeful dog.

At once Ghote realized what it was that he must be doing. The patch of earth he was working at was clearly marked out by lying in the exact centre of a triangle formed by three singularly ugly, stunted and battered banana palms. If ever there was a place to bury something in the sure hope of digging it up again, this was it. And what had anyone here to bury that Amrit Singh would want to dig up but gold?

He had caught him in the very act.

Ghote stood where he was, poised. Surely this must be it? He would get Amrit Singh now, get him for smuggling. Fair and square. And after that he could see once more what he could make of the mystery of Krishna Chatterjee.

The big Sikh's broad back lifted and from behind the heap of dark earth he picked up a small but heavy bundle wrapped in a piece of dirty coarse gunny. This was the moment.

Ghote ran forward silently across the soft, dry sand.

And something – a scatter of little sharp-beaked paddy birds, a fleeting shadow – warned the Sikh. With half a glance behind he was up and off, his long legs striding out, heading down the gentle slope of the seashore, out and away by the quickest route that came.

Ghote ran. He felt his legs moving swiftly under him. He would do it. In spite of whatever unlucky accident had warned the Sikh he would catch him.

But one thing he had forgotten.

His own appearance. The multi-coloured fool. Flashing down towards the distant sea, covered from head to foot in a dazzling array of the brightest shades, with the strong sun catching every colour and the breeze sending every loose end flying, he was a sight to catch the eye of even the most absorbed Holi reveller.

There was a sudden, sharp, directed roar of laughter, and then the crowd closed in on him again.

He was caught by both hands, flung round in circles, jumped high, swung low, sluiced once more from chunky syringe and venomous bicycle pump, sloshed and soaked from bucket and jug, puffed and dusted again, green, blue, yellow and above all red. The very air he breathed was smoking with colour.

There was nothing he could do. All the while he kept thinking of the big Sikh, striding out across the beach with the heavy package in the dirty, earth-stained sacking clutched firmly to his chest. And taking with him that sudden, last delusive hope.

As abruptly as he had been caught up the capricious crowd let him go.

Dazed and half-blinded he took a few drunken steps clear of the noise and wild movement. One idea he had kept in his head. Amrit Singh had been running towards the sea. Hardly looking where he was going he set off at a loping run down the gentle slope of the grey sand.

At last he found himself well clear of the revellers, dodging through the scattered groups of narrow beached fishing craft lying careened over to one side or the other. He stopped for a moment and looked both ways along the shore.

Amrit Singh was there.

His tall figure, a single lone presence on this day of mass celebration, could be distinctly seen making its way along the edge of the sea over to where the sluggish creek broke the low coastline. And he was walking. He thought he was safe.

Ghote set out in pursuit, cutting straight across the grey sands to head off the Sikh following the shore line. He wondered why Amrit Singh had not taken the same short cut.

And then he knew. Abruptly his feet began to sink in soft, wet, rippled sucking sand. Should he go back? To retrace his steps and then go round the long way would mean that he would almost certainly lose sight of Amrit Singh. And above all he must stay where he could see him. If the Sikh stopped to bury the heavy little package again while he was unobserved all would be lost.

Ghote decided to plunge on. A little crab scuttled across the wet sand in front of him.

He cursed himself for not having noted that wet gleam as the Sikh must have done. But there was nothing he could do now. Supposing the water-saturated patch got suddenly deeper? People were sucked to death in places like this.

And then he was out.

The sand under his soaked and heavy shoes was suddenly firm. Wet still, but hard now, almost like a cement floor. He began to run.

He found himself moving easily forward and smiled a little to himself, thinking he was not as out of training as DSP Naik had supposed. Tramping the hot, crowded and hard streets of the city was probably every bit as good for the stamina as playing games of hockey. Even if it lacked the same touch of glamour.

He moved swiftly forward, almost as if in a dream. And everything began to take on a matching dreamlike quality. Behind him the sound of the Holi revellers was faint now, shrill, musical and distant. The pounding, brutal noise of reality had simply been left far behind. Above the solid black smudge that represented the dancing crowd he saw, when he glanced for a moment over his shoulder, a light, fabulous and unlikely cloud of pinkish red, the dazing, dazzling powder of a short time before. And, turning back, ahead of him walking with his head down and arms still clutching tight the heavy little bundle, was Amrit Singh. On the smooth, caked sand Ghote's heavy shoes were making no noise. As if still in a dream he let his legs stretch out in a quiet increase of pace and a second later launched himself almost gently through the air.

His arms closed hard round the tall Sikh's legs. And he had him. Gold-handed.

But he never got Amrit Singh safely behind the locked door of a CID headquarters cell. At the railway station he enlisted the help of the local police to make sure his hard-won captive, for all that by then he was being held at his own gunpoint, did not succeed in making a break for it. It was a sensible precaution. But it was Ghote's undoing.

As he stepped out of the train at Churchgate Station he was

greeted by the immaculately white-clad form of Inspector Patel of the Customs. In the sudden realization of the contrast between his own clothes after the Holi assault on them and the Customs man's spotless appearance he even almost forgot the existence of Amrit Singh, handcuffed firmly to his wrist. But Inspector Patel could plainly think of nothing else.

'Well, well,' he said, giving Ghote a quick, piercing look from his thin, chopping blade face. 'This is a very unfortunate business indeed.'

Ghote looked at him. His bewilderment must have been all too obvious.

'This business of arresting the man yourself for a purely smuggling offence,' Inspector Patel explained painstakingly.

'I had the gold put into the safe at the chowkey where I took him first,' Ghote said.

'Yes, yes,' said Inspector Patel. 'I dare say that can be put right. But you cannot expect this other business to be forgotten just like that. You had no right to do it, you know. No right. Not for a purely smuggling offence.'

And so it was that Ghote, stained and spattered from his encounter with the celebrating villagers, had to stand mutely among the noisy crowds at Churchgate Station and watch Inspector Patel, in the full glory of a properly entitled Customs officer, lead away the faintly sardonic figure of the notorious Amrit Singh.

Suddenly he thought of the refrigerator fund and what it had been spent on. His world looked very flat.

He waited till late that night to make his apology to Protima. Longer than this he felt he could not put it off. It must be done that day.

But the day could be prolonged.

They were sitting outside in the yard at the back of the house. Already it was beginning to feel a little cooler.

'We could sleep now,' Protima said.

'Just a few minutes more. It is only now that it is pleasant.'

'And tomorrow? Are you going to be fresh tomorrow if you have such a short night when for once you do not need to?'

'Tomorrow will be different,' Ghote said.

Tomorrow you will know that your cherished plans for the refrigerator have fallen to pieces, he thought.

He said nothing more.

From the neatly shaped, heavy bulk of the neem tree nearby came the muffled cheep of a sleepy bird. Ghote sighed.

It was true, it was pleasant out here at this time of day. It was cool. It was calm. Everything was peaceful. You could put everything finally into its place, if you wanted to. Except, perhaps, that some things would have to be looked at before they were put away, and . . .

So in the end it was Protima who brought up the subject of the refrigerator fund.

'Tomorrow,' she said. 'Tomorrow will be a great day for me. Can you get the money out early?'

Ghote took a breath. One. Two. Three.

'There is no money,' he said.

'No money? But you told—'

'There was. There was. I did. But – But I have done a very silly thing. I have given the money away.'

'You have given away five hundred rupees?'

Protima was too astounded, it was obvious, to keep the sheer incredulity out of her voice.

'Yes,' Ghote said.

His disappointment at not having the confession received with more understanding put an edge on his voice.

'Yes,' he repeated with a touch of bravado, 'I have given away five hundred rupees.'

Protima rose to her feet like a sudden whirlwind.

'Who have you given it to? How could you give away so much? Have you no thought of your family even?'

'Whose money was it?' Ghote shouted, suddenly swept right away.

'Who earned the money? Who saved it up? If I had said nothing you would never have even known there was five hundred rupees.'

'That has nothing to do with it. There were five hundred rupees. Five hundred rupees. And you gave them away. Gave them.'

'What do you mean that has nothing to do with it? It has everything to do with it. I have just explained. As far as you are concerned the money simply does not exist.'

'Oh, I know that. It does not exist indeed. You have given it away.'

'That is not what I meant at all. Not at all. Why can you never understand a simple piece of logic? If I had given the money away, of course it would exist. But I was saying that it does not exist. As far as you are concerned.'

'Have you or have you not given the money away?'

'I told you I had given it away.'

'Then what do you mean about "if you had given it away"? You have. You have given away the money that was to buy me a refrigerator. After all the years when I needed one so much, when it is the day before we get it, you give the money away. My money.'

'Your—'

And he stopped himself. He took a deep breath and told himself that he was in the wrong. He had given the money away. Protima was right to be angry. But how to tell her what had happened to the money after he had given it away?

'Listen, my little one,' he said.

This was almost his last card. The special term of endearment he kept for her. The expression that meant so much because it was so plainly not really true. The tall, invariably elegant Protima, fine, chiselled, fiery, was never anyone's 'little one'. Except his. It was his right.

'Listen, my little one.'

She stopped. She stood looking at him, even though it was with smouldering, guarded eyes.

'I can explain everything. It was all the fault of this damned case.'

She seemed restive at this and he hurried on.

'Look. It was. I tell you it was having to think all the time about such a person as Frank Masters. I saw him as a man of such generosity, coming to this country from the luxuries of America, devoting his time to caring for the vagrants that most of us do nothing about. I began to think about what sort of person he must be, and what sort of person I was.'

'And so you set up as a little Frank Masters of your own and gave away my refrigerator money?'

He would not be roused.

'Yes, I did. That is what I did. And only afterwards did I begin to find out what Frank Masters was really like.'

'What?' she exclaimed. 'His death was caused by something bad he had done? Underneath all the while he was—'

'No, no, no. It was not that. Frank Masters was not a bad man. But he was not the all-good man that I thought either. I found that out in the end. He had his faults. And one of them was even giving away too much.'

Protima was looking doubtful now. He stared at her intently.

'Listen,' he said, 'that is what my mistake was. I tried to be like him, and instead of doing my work I began thinking about whether I was a good man or a bad man. And – And there is worse.'

'What worse?'

'What happened to the money after I had given it to the poor family of fishing people who needed it to pay off the debt on their boat.'

He was whispering now.

'They took the money,' he went on, 'and they spent every anna on celebrating Holi. It all went up in smoke. Down to the last pie.'

And Protima threw back her head and laughed.

He sat where he was on the rattan chair with the sagging arm and looked up at her. In the faint light he could see her neck, smooth and columnar, as she laughed and laughed with her head back and her whole body shaking.

'Oh, Mr Policeman,' she gasped at last. 'Mr Policeman, what a judge of character you are.'

'If it comes to a criminal . . .'

He had begun stiffly, but he could not keep it up. In a moment he too was shaking with mad outbursts of laughter.

From the open window of the house behind them came a plaintive voice.

'What is it? Why are you laughing?'

Ved.

'It is all right,' Protima called. 'It is just your father. He is such a funny man.'

No reply came. After they had stood in silence for a little Protima walked softly into the house. She came out again almost at once.

'Asleep,' she said.

She looked at Ghote down her nose, her eyes sparkling a little.

'You with your difficult case,' she said.

'But it is difficult,' Ghote said.

'When you have arrested Amrit Singh with smuggled gold on him?'

'Yes. I know that. But still I am just in the same position as before over the Masters affair. Certainly Amrit Singh would say nothing more to me all the way back in the train. And I suppose he will never say anything.'

'Does it matter now?'

'But of course it does. The situation is exactly the same as before. Frank Masters started to be sick soon after he ate a beef curry. He was poisoned by arsenic trioxide. Arsenic trioxide was stolen from the dispensary at the Masters Foundation just before the meal. Only two people went into that dispensary, both of them without any right to, Amrit Singh and Krishna Chatterjee. It rests exactly equally between them.'

'But just because Frank Masters was sick,' Protima said, 'why should it be poison? I think you are quite wrong about that. Little Ved is sick sometimes, and no one says it is poison then.'

Ghote sighed deeply.

He knew there was never any point in going over such details with Protima. She might be wonderful when you had made a terrible mistake, but she lacked any powers of logical reasoning.

'Well?' she said in face of his sigh and silence. 'Well, is that not right?'

Ghote shook his head.

'No, I am afraid it cannot be that,' he said.

'But why not? Are you saying that Ved has been poisoned so many times? I think you policemen need to come and do a woman's work in the house.'

'No,' Ghote said. 'I have explained everything.'

'But I have told you that children get sick for all sorts of reasons. That was something you forgot.'

Suddenly Ghote felt nettled.

'I did not forget,' he said sharply. 'Just, please, leave police work to me and I will leave house matters to you.'

He saw that Protima was ready with a reply. As she invariably was. And he made up his mind that he would not hear it. This was his business.

He jumped up and walked quickly into the house, his head tilted up proudly.

But, once out of Protima's sight, he checked himself. His old fault again. And it was at that moment that he solved the Masters case.

17

Inspector Ghote's first action was to go as fast as he could through the city centre and out to the Masters Foundation. There he found that he had arrived in the middle of a serious crisis. As he stood just inside the tall front door, pausing for a moment to set in his mind the final details of his plan of campaign, there came hurrying past the obsequiously bent form of the podgy, shiny-skinned cook. He went at a half-run, bare feet pattering on the floor, towards the door of the staff tiffin room. At it he stopped, groaned heart-rendingly, ducked his well-greased head even lower and entered.

A waft of cooked-food smell, rich and spicy but with a tang of the burnt about it, came out. Ghote realized that he had arrived at the time of the evening meal. He thought for a moment and decided that this suited him pretty well.

He saw that the cook, in his worried haste, had neglected to close the door completely. Quietly he walked across and stood listening.

It was not difficult to make out what was going on. Just as he approached, Dr Diana's clear English tones rang out.

'You know what I've had you called in here for?' she was demanding.

'Oh, yes, memsahib. Know very well,' came the cook's soft reply.

'All right, my lad. Let's just hear what. If you know so well.'

'Oh, memsahib, is my disgraceful cooking.'

'Yes, it is your disgraceful cooking. But don't think you're going to get away with all those apologies this time. I want to know just why your cooking's so disgraceful.'

'Very bad cook, memsahib.'

'Come on, that won't do at all. Why are you bad? Tell me first exactly what was bad about the food tonight.'

'Don't know, memsahib. Just appalling all round, memsahib.'

'No, it was not.'

'No, memsahib?'

'No.'

'Cooking good, memsahib?'

'No.'

'Oh yes then, cooking very bad. Sorry, memsahib.'

'I asked you just what it was you had done wrong tonight. I am not interested in how bad you want to make yourself out to be. I simply want to know what you did wrong with the food we are attempting to eat now.'

'Yes, memsahib.'

'Well?'

The cook evidently could think of no way of abasing himself in a manner that would please Dr Diana. He remained silent.

After an ominous pause Dr Diana's voice floated coldly out again.

'You know that this cannot be allowed to go on, don't you?'

But it was not the cook who answered. Instead Ghote recognized Fraulein Glucklich's curiously accented English.

'Dr Diana,' she said sharply, 'I think you are forgetting something.'

'I tell you one thing I cannot forget. I cannot forget the interminable series of utterly disgusting meals I have had to put up with here. And nor do I think the whole blame should be put on the cook.'

'No, indeed it should not. That is precisely what you are forgetting. If the cook is bad, I would remind you, it is because the late Herr Frank, whose purusha has passed on in the great samsara, deliberately chose a bad cook.'

'All right,' Dr Diana came back icily, 'he did choose the cook. But then it's simply time you and everybody learned that Frank's choices are no longer binding in this establishment.'

Even from where he stood in the quiet hall Ghote could hear Fraulein Glucklich's gasp.

'That is certainly a very true observation.'

It was Krishna Chatterjee intervening now.

'Certainly a most true observation,' he repeated. 'But on the other hand, there can be no doubt that an institution that bears the name of Frank Masters is bound, at least temporarily, to pay due attention to the practices observed in his lifetime. Perhaps, however, there is a solution to the problem that would heed the wishes of all parties to this unfortunate occurrence. What I mean to say is, is it not possible to arrange for some instruction for this poor fellow?'

Ghote waited in some apprehension for Dr Diana's answer to this. But the reply when it came arrived from elsewhere. From the unexpected voice of Sonny Carstairs.

'I think Dr Diana's right,' he said. 'It's all very well remembering Mr Frank and all that. But we know who's in charge now, and a jolly good job she's making of it.'

Now it was that Dr Diana spoke.

'Yes,' she said, 'it's obvious some people know who's in charge now. But don't think fulsome praise is going to do you any good, Sonny, my lad. One slip in the dispensary, and you're out. I promise you that.'

Sonny Carstairs laughed.

In spite of everything Ghote felt sorry for him.

But Dr Diana had not finished.

'Come on,' she said to the still silent cook, 'I asked you for an explanation of what went wrong with your vindaloo tonight. I am still waiting for it. And I warn you that I shall not wait long.'

Ghote decided that the moment had come. He stepped into the open doorway.

'But I must ask you to wait at least a little, Doctor,' he said.

His entrance certainly created its sensation. The podgy, glistening cook, crouching hypnotized almost under Dr Diana's wrath, positively jumped. Sonny and Krishna Chatterjee sent their chairs scraping back. Fraulein Glucklich violated her studious sannyasini's calm with a little squeak. And even Dr Diana looked distinctly surprised.

'What the hell are you doing here?' she said abruptly. 'Can't you see we're in the middle of a meal. Really, we must be given a bit of peace sometimes, you know.'

'I regret,' Ghote said quietly. 'But I have come on very important business.'

'That's as may be,' Dr Diana replied. 'But I can't see that any business of yours can be so important that you have to come barging in here without so much as being announced.'

'Perhaps not,' Ghote said. 'But my business is important. You see, I know now who killed Frank Masters.'

'Do you indeed?' Dr Diana said. 'Well, you'd better get on and arrest them.'

She turned her chair slightly so that she was facing squarely in the direction of Krishna Chatterjee.

Ghote did not pretend to be ignorant of what she meant by the move.

'You think I have come to arrest Mr Chatterjee?' he said.

'Well, you'd hardly come to our tiffin room to arrest Amrit Singh,' Dr Diana replied.

'And supposing I want to arrest neither of the gentlemen?'

'Don't be a fool, man. We all know what the situation is. Vague threats like that will get you nowhere. The poison that killed Frank was put into the curry he ate in this very room. It was stolen from the dispensary not an hour before. Two unauthorized persons entered the dispensary, Amrit Singh and Chatterjee here. You have come to us, so I suppose it's for Chatterjee.'

'Certainly I have succeeded in working out why Mr Chatterjee went into the dispensary,' Ghote said.

Sitting in front of his neglected plate, Krishna Chatterjee stirred uneasily.

'If I had listened to everything I had heard with an open mind,' Ghote went on, 'I would have known long ago.'

Dr Diana glared at him. He hastily continued.

'It was just a matter of connecting three things. That Mr Chatterjee greatly respected the late Mr Masters in spite of what he knew were faults in his character, that the boy Edward G. Robinson boasted to me that he could tell a good story about why Mr Masters was supposed to have hidden some gold in the dispensary, and thirdly that he cheekily referred to Shri Chatterjee as a "sucker".'

The little Bengali's big eyes looked up at Ghote with dawning realization, and a sudden tinge of laughter.

'Yes,' Ghote said, 'I believe Edward G. must have told you Frank Masters had lost his money and was smuggling gold, and you believed it and tried to hide the fact from the world.'

'My dear sir,' said Mr Chatterjee. 'And you are telling me that the whole business was a pure fabrication? I am most extremely relieved. Something like that could do incalculable harm.'

He blinked two or three times.

'Of course, I very much doubt whether I would have gone through with it,' he added. 'To the bitter end, you know.'

'Well, Inspector, what are you doing here, then?' Dr Diana said abruptly. 'Why aren't you rounding up Amrit Singh?'

'We have him in prison awaiting trial already,' Ghote answered.

'Then it was him?'

'No.'

'But—'

'Dr Diana, you said just now that the poison that killed Mr Masters was put in the curry he ate. How can you be sure of that, may I ask?'

'Because on your own admission he was proved scientifically to have eaten that curry shortly before he died,' Dr Diana answered carefully. 'Because he was full of arsenic trioxide. Because the symptoms set in at just the right time.'

She looked at Ghote with all the certainties of science itself behind her.

'The symptoms appeared,' Ghote answered calmly. 'But what caused them? Was it arsenic trioxide? Or was it just an ordinary emetic, Doctor?'

Dr Diana's eyes went wide.

'What do you mean?' she said.

'I mean that, if the curry had contained not poison but a simple emetic which anyone could obtain, then Mr Masters need not have been poisoned at dinner when he had the beef curry you ordered for him. He could have been poisoned afterwards. At a time when there was nothing to stop you getting hold of the arsenic, Doctor. When you had sent Mr Carstairs here away to call the police. Then it was quite simple to take the powder from the dispensing room next door and to offer poor Mr Masters a drink. From a doctor's hands.'

Ghote kept his eyes firmly on her. There could be no doubt she was hearing the truth.

She stood up slowly.

'Yes,' she said, 'it seems I wasn't as clever as I thought. My congratulations, Inspector. But you do see that I had to do it, don't you? He was going to take his money, lock, stock and barrel, and spend it on a pack of mystical Tibetans. All this was going to be allowed to drop. Just like that.'

She looked round, seeing through tear-blotched eyes the workings of the big house beyond the four walls of the tiffin room, the steady rescuing of the almost hopeless flotsam of the big city's pavements, the doing good.

'I could have made something of this place,' she said.

Just as the blue Dodge truck took Dr Diana off to headquarters dusk fell. Ghote stood on the Foundation steps enjoying for a few moments the ending of the day's glare. He breathed deeply. There was nothing to stop him relaxing now. The rest was routine.

'So you finally got her,' a familiar voice said in his ear.

He noticed the shapes of the thin, wiry bodies emerging once more from the darkness.

'Yes,' he said, without looking round, 'she has been arrested.'

'Just the sort of dirty trick you get with a policeman,' Edward G. said.

'Dirty trick?'

Ghote wheeled round and glared furiously into the upturned, crinkled face.

'She fought to keep all that money from going to those stinking holy men,' Edward G. explained.

Ghote looked at him in astonishment.

'You knew that?' he said.

The boy sighed in the darkness like an exasperated schoolmaster.

'I told you,' he said, 'we need to know what goes on. We need to.'

'And you knew that she was the one who sent the message to bring Amrit Singh down to the dispensary at the right time?'

Edward G. laughed.

'She reckoned he was safe to get off at the trial,' he said. 'She reckoned all those lawyers would do it.'

'She was probably right,' Ghote said.

The boy grunted contemptuously.

'Just like a social worker that idea,' he said. 'You ever think what would have happened if we'd said we did see him steal the poison?'

Ghote peered down at him. In the gloom it was difficult to make out the expression on the wrinkled, wry, old man's face.

'Still,' the boy added, 'you were pretty clever to catch her.'

Ghote felt a ridiculous sense of having received an accolade.

'Thank you,' he said. 'But you should never forget that the police are not always stupid. Sometimes by sheer hard—'

He pulled himself up sharp.

'Or at least,' he said, 'we have wives who cannot be tricked.'

Inspector Ghote Caught in Meshes

Author's Note

The nature of this story has made it necessary to venture here and there into fantasy. There is no such thing as the Special Investigations Agency (though there is a Federal Bureau of Investigation, but that is in another country). There is no India First Group, and the secret that it protects is equally imaginary. There is certainly no such person as my Inspector Phadke and his behaviour is dictated entirely by the demands of the story. There is not even a Queen's Imperial Grand Hotel.

H. R. F. K.

Prologue

The three men had been sprawled there in the shade of the big Flame of the Forest for nearly two hours, but although it was very hot and almost intolerably muggy they had not slept. There was a feeling of tension behind their air of easy-going relaxedness. It showed in the way every now and again one of them would check over his gun.

The Sikh in the orange turban had an American self-loading Garand rifle and the other two had revolvers, one a British Army officer's issue Webley and the other a much abused Smith and Wesson dating from the early years of the century. This last was hardly reliable at a range over five yards, but none of the three expected to use it at even this distance.

The people of the village just below the slight hill on which the solitary Flame of the Forest stood had taken some time to get used to their visitors, but an hour after their arrival they were left almost completely to themselves. The old women squatting outside the huts gossiped away as they pounded the corn and hardly so much as glanced across at the three of them in the shade of the big tree. The little children tumbled and played unconcernedly in the dirt. Over in the fields, still muddy from the monsoon rains which had hardly yet finished, the men, naked all but for a cloth round their waists, and the women, with their harsh red and green saris tucked between their legs, bent low over their work as they had done all their lives and would go on doing. Afterwards.

*

Nor did any of the villagers pay much attention to the bullock cart that had lumbered past about the same time that the three strangers had settled down under the Flame of the Forest. It came from the next village south and its driver was known to them all, a notorious ne'er-do-well, Bholu, much gossiped about because once a year or so he would make his way right up to Poona, toiling over the sharp ascent of the great Ghats, and there he would lose every anna he had been able to lay his hands on in whatever gambling games he could find.

With a man like Bholu it was not in the least surprising that he should drive his lumbering beasts through the village, going this time north away from Poona on the road which led eventually to the distant, teeming city of Bombay, and then abruptly seem to lose interest and stop. He had halted in the shade of a small banyan tree by the roadside. He had had at least that much sense. And there he had stayed, letting his great, heavy-horned beasts lower their heads and tug discontentedly at the few tufts of grass growing there.

A hundred yards or so down the road a gang of men, some of them recruited from the village, were at work mending the embankment where it had fallen away during the first heavy monsoon rains. But Bholu paid them no attention. Instead he sat on the boards of his big, awkwardly constructed cart and looked backwards to where under the wide-spreading Flame of the Forest tree the Sikh stranger's orange turban shone like a gaudy jewel.

If anyone spared Bholu a thought they would have believed he was sleeping away the heat of the day. But he was not. In spite of everything he was awake, wide awake.

The three men waiting under the Flame of the Forest had already passed through the village earlier in the day. They had come from the direction of Poona in a battered old Buick painted for the most part a bright blue. But they had not stopped and no one had taken any notice of them. Dozens of vehicles went rattling by along the road between Poona and Bombay at every hour of the day.

In the car then there had been five of them. They had driven past, negotiated the place where there was single-lane traffic only by the roadworks and had gone on to a village about ten miles away. Here two of the party had been let out of the car, rather unceremoniously. No sooner had the battered blue Buick swirled round and left again, heading back in the Poona direction now, than the pair had begun conducting a search of the immediate area. Whatever it was they were looking for they appeared not to find, because after a little a short and rather angry consultation had taken place between them. Then they had approached the villagers.

With a good deal of truculence they had asked for fuel to build a fire, and when they paid they had done so too generously, which did nothing to appease the feelings of resentment they had aroused. The blacksmith, from whom they had bought a can of kerosene at a grossly inflated price, was most vocal in expressing this general annoyance. As a man of substance, the possessor of a petrol pump strategically situated at a point where the straight road from Bombay made a small accountable twist and traffic conveniently slowed up, he naturally exercised certain rights of leadership. He was expected to set the tone in questions both moral and practical. And he enjoyed exercising this right to the full.

So he was the first to express open doubts about the intentions of the two interlopers. Why did they want to build a fire? They had brought nothing to cook. And even when the fire was ready, a neat heap of dried dung-cakes and pieces of brushwood, they had done nothing about lighting it.

The blacksmith did not actually put these doubts to the two men sitting beside the unlit fire taking advantage of the shade made by the road embankment. Every time anyone had asked them a friendly question they had bristled aggressively. It was quite likely that if they were pressed too far they would start an ugly incident of some sort.

But in the shelter of his tumbledown little shop the blacksmith put the case against them in no uncertain terms.

'And why do they jump up to look at every car coming from Bombay direction?' he demanded in conclusion. 'They are cars only. There is nothing to look.'

His hearers nodded gravely. That clinched the matter.

The elegant dark green hired Chevrolet, not long out of Bombay, was moving fast down the straight length of the trunk road to distant Poona. Already it was covered with dust, although there was nothing like so much of it on the surface of the concrete as there would be later in the year. But then the car was being driven a good deal faster than it should be.

Leaving the city not long before it had acquired a long black scratch on the rear nearside wing where the driver, a tall, beige-suited young American with a crest of extraordinary flaming red hair and an equally unmistakable streak of flaming red beard, had grazed a lamp standard. But this experience had apparently done nothing to warn him to take it less hectically. The car, headed firmly south now, was shooting along the road every bit as fast as it was safe to go, and faster.

The two truculent men beside the unlit fire leaped to their feet for the twentieth time. The car coming towards them slowed. The driver, a harassed Mysore civil servant taking his family back to Belgaum after a wedding, negotiated the double bend by the blacksmith's petrol pump with care. The two men craning over the top of the embankment slumped down again and sat waiting.

Bholu, the bullock driver, sitting in his cart in the shade of the small banyan by the roadside, shook himself to make sure he had not dropped off. Above him the sky was brazen with heavily massing clouds.

Under the Flame of the Forest on its gently moulded hillock the Sikh pulled two cigarettes from a packet of Cavander's and tossed them over to his companions. Then he pushed himself up from the rope bed they had hired from the people in the village. It was not a very good bed. The wooden end-bars were too thin and in consequence the long cords were slacker than the cross ones. The Sikh had been contemptuous when it had first been carried over to them, but a chorus of voices had sworn that it was the best in the village. He had paid less to borrow it than had been hoped.

With his face crinkled to protect his eyes from the glare he looked away north in the direction of Bombay. The road stretched straight and long into the far distance cutting through the patterned squares and strips of the caramel-coloured fields. Here and there a tree broke the straightness of the line for a moment, like the little banyan in the shade of which the bullock cart still rested. Farther on the line was more effectively interrupted by the gang at work on the fallen embankment. Piles of stones lay half across the concrete, and ant-like figures could be seen moving slowly from one heap to the next or clambering painfully down the side of the embankment itself.

Beneath the wide sweep of the metallic sky, with the sun almost directly above them now, the sounds of the gang's labours were too faint to be heard. The Sikh slumped down on the creaky bed and picked up the Garand rifle once again.

When they had first arrived, parking their battered blue Buick in the shade of a straw-rick and facing it carefully towards Poona, their weapons had evoked a flurry of questions from the curious villagers. Eventually and grudgingly the Sikh had said that they had come to shoot 'some mad dogs'. The reply had appeased the villagers, more or less. It was the most informative answer they could persuade the party to make on any subject, and so they had been shruggingly abandoned as a source of entertainment. Back at their laborious daily round, nobody thought to wonder why it was that the strangers never made any attempt to find mad dogs to shoot.

The red-haired, red-bearded American was still pushing the elegant green hired Chevrolet along for all it was worth. Penetrating dust had settled everywhere round him and his taut features were covered with a fine layer of it, streaked once or twice where a path had been traced by a heavy drop of perspiration.

Suddenly on the long straight road ahead he spotted a man in a check shirt and jeans standing beside a small, overloaded family car waving energetically. The little car, a Fiat, was halted far enough out on the road to make it necessary to slow down drastically.

The red-bearded American was unable to avoid looking the stranded driver full in the face. The appeal made to him was blatant.

He braked abruptly.

'Hell,' he said.

The man in the check shirt hurried over.

'Gee,' he said, 'you from the States too?'

'Guess so.'

'That's just great. You see what's happened to us? Back axle gone.'

He turned and glanced at his car. Back axle trouble might have been expected. From its heaped-up roof rack to its cluttered floor the little vehicle was almost all load. Spare tyres, a pushchair and rolls of bulging bedding made up the roof baggage. In the open boot there was a Primus stove, petrol cans, a formidable tool kit, two buckets and a shovel. In the back three T-shirted children sat cross-legged on top of a mound of suitcases. Each spare space held a box of Kleenex. A determinedly cheerful young mother wearing a faded Aertex shirt sat in front nursing an enormous string bag of fruit. She looked very, very hot.

The father of the family had become even more cheerful.

'This is great,' he said again. 'We saw a kinda garage about ten miles back. I think someone from there could fix this. They're pretty good at breakdowns, the Indians.'

The red-bearded driver of the big, hired Chevrolet looked at him in silence.

'So if you could just give me a lift back there,' he went on, unabashed, 'then maybe they could come out here with some kind of a mechanic.'

He looked expectantly at his compatriot.

'Ten miles back,' the red-bearded man said. 'I saw that place. It's fifteen miles there if it's a yard. I'm sorry but I have to get to Poona and quick.'

He looked at the watch strapped to the inside of his dust-covered wrist.

'Hell,' he said, 'I've wasted too much time as it is.'

'But – but, gee. I can't ask just anybody to go back, and if I have to walk all that way in this heat . . .'

The young family man looked up into the brazen dome of the sky. But already his fellow countryman was jerking the hired Chevrolet savagely into gear.

It took the blacksmith a good while to stir up his fellow villagers to the point of action. But at last they moved in a body out of the comforting shade at the back of the shop. The blacksmith followed them. He had picked up a rusted length of iron drainpipe that had been lying in a corner for years waiting for a use to be found for it.

Three or four of the stouter-hearted villagers looked around for other weapons. It took them a few minutes to find anything suitable. But at last they were ready, one armed with a length of chain, another with a big vegetable-chopping knife, a third with a long piece of bamboo which had been half holding up a corner of the blacksmith's veranda.

'We'll teach them,' the blacksmith said. 'Coming here like that.'

There was a satisfying, angry mutter of agreement.

'Get them running,' the blacksmith shouted.

They advanced in a knot to the edge of the road opposite the point where the two interlopers had built their unlit fire. The sound of a car approaching fast from the Bombay direction caused the posse to halt. They might perhaps have got across the road before it arrived, but they were prudent men and waited.

The car slowed with a squeal of brakes at the unexpected kink where the petrol pump was. On the far side the faces of the two intruders appeared on the top of the embankment like two dusty boulders with wide, white staring eyes.

They both registered the fact that the driver of the car was red-haired and red-bearded at exactly the same instant. Simultaneously they let go their holds and slithered down the slope of the embankment. As if carrying out a well-practised routine, one seized the kerosene tin, screwed off its cap in a series of swift jerks and upended it. The liquid golloped out on to the little pile of sticks and dung-cakes. The other watcher had already opened a box of matches. With shaking fingers he pulled one out and, without closing the box, attempted to strike it.

The dark green Chevrolet pulled smoothly away. The blacksmith and his men took heart from the suddenness with which the intruders had vanished the moment they themselves had appeared at the other side of the road. They set out to cross now with new resoluteness.

The fumbler dropped his match.

From the top of the embankment the blacksmith and his men looked down.

'What do you want here?' the blacksmith shouted. 'You have no right. Do you think you own the place?'

The man who had poured the kerosene grabbed the matchbox.

The blacksmith's supporters were applauding.

This time the new match was struck without trouble. In the silence that had followed the blacksmith's speech the tiny spluttering sound as the flame burst could be distinctly heard. The man holding the match stooped swiftly.

From the heap of sticks and dung-cakes a twirl of thick, sooty black smoke went up.

The two interlopers turned at once and ran. With a ragged cheer the villagers set out after them. None of them paid the least attention to the fire. But its smoke, despite its coming into being so haphazardly, rose steadily into the sullen stillness of the midday air.

Under the shade of the big Flame of the Forest the Sikh leaped up from the creaky bed. He grabbed hold of the arm of the man nearer him and pointed.

To the north perhaps some ten miles away a thin, soft black streak of smoke was slowly mounting into the brazen sky.

Quickly the Sikh unknotted the grimy white sweat cloth from round his neck. He took a couple of paces forward out into the sunlight. He lifted his right arm and slowly waved the dirty cloth. It spread out and fluttered a little. The others, intent on giving their guns one last, unnecessary check, paid no attention.

Down by the banyan tree Bholu, who had succeeded in staying awake for all the oppressiveness of the heat, staggered to his feet. He shook his head a little to gather himself together and, standing astride the clumsy frame of the cart, waved his bare arm once or twice in the air. Then he turned, scrambled to his place on the butt-end of the cart's heavy shaft, and leaning down first to the right then to the left, he seized the tails of his great, lanky bullocks and gave each a vicious twist. The huge animals, jerked out of a heat-induced doze, started suddenly forward. The cumbersome wooden wheels of the cart grated sharply out. Heavily it progressed down the road in the direction of the single-lane section where the embankment labourers were sleeping through the worst of the heat.

*

The man in the dark green hired Chevrolet was pushing the car along at maximum pace once more. Irritatedly he glanced down at his watch, then took a new grip of the wheel and tensed forward in his seat. Ahead of him the dusty concrete lay in an unbroken ribbon. Never for an instant did he take his eyes off it.

The lumbering bullock cart ceased to move just as it reached the roadworks. The squeaking of its wheels had caused two of the sleeping labourers down at the foot of the half-reconstructed embankment to stir. But when the sound stopped they went back to sleep again without having moved.

The huge cart was still in place a few minutes later when the dark green dust-covered car came up. The driver was in plenty of time to halt when his insistently-sounded horn failed to clear the way.

At the far end of the single lane he leaned his flaming red-bearded head out of the car window.

'Will you get the hell out of the way?' he shouted.

Bholu, perched on the heavy shaft between his two whitish beasts, looked at him blankly.

'Hell, I don't speak your damned language, whatever it is,' the red-haired American yelled.

He opened the car door and got out. He marched along towards Bholu pointing with great forcefulness in the direction he wanted to go. He glared at the bullock cart. He made it utterly plain that with its two great pointed-horned animals it was blocking his way.

He hardly noticed the three figures who stepped out from the shade of the banyan a little farther along the road and advanced towards him. In the soft dust their flapping sandals made scarcely any sound. The Sikh pushed the safety catch off on the Garand rifle with his thumb.

The bullock on Bholu's left lowered its green-tinted horns with the little glinting brass tips and the bobbing coloured thread balls round them. Softly he pawed at the ground. A long trail of heavy saliva dripped slowly down his loose dewlap. Both beasts steadily flailed their much-twisted tails, stirring the flies to motion on their dirty white flanks.

When the American noticed the three advancing men he did not appear to take in the fact that the Sikh carried a rifle and the other two had revolvers, one British Army issue Webley and the other an extremely old Smith and Wesson.

'Hey, you fellows,' he called. 'You speak English? Can you tell this sonofabitch to get his stinking, crummy wagon out of my way?'

The three men did speak a certain amount of English. But they did not reply to the American's request. Instead they walked steadily and silently forward.

The sound of the strident New World voice caused a good many of the labourers at the foot of the embankment to stir in their sleep. But not one of them thought it worthwhile to get to his feet and investigate. For a few moments the midday quiet returned.

Then came the sound of shots in the hot stillness.

1

Inspector Ganesh Ghote sighed for his native land. Things had come to a pretty pass. A visiting American shot down in the crudest sort of highway robbery. A dacoity taking place within fifty miles of Bombay, on a main trunk road. And that this should happen to the brother of a world figure like Professor Gregory Strongbow. Here was the world's famous hydrodynamics expert, a man who had conferred immense benefits on the human race, on holiday in India, and his brother is brutally murdered.

It did not bear thinking about.

The blue Dodge police truck went thundering along the dusty Poona road. The pattern of the fields whirled past, broken only by the occasional deeply-cut, wandering nullah or the clustered huts of a village. Ghote looked steadily ahead.

It should not be far now. And the moment he arrived he must get his teeth into the case. It would not be an easy affair. Dacoits were notoriously difficult to track down. No doubt these had carried out their robbery quite openly and had relied as usual on going into hiding until the trouble had blown over. But for once they had miscalculated. They had contrived to pick on someone too important, and they had killed him. At least for once there would be maximum backing at all levels.

Ghote vowed not to rest till he had identified the culprits and step by step had tracked them down. He owed that much to the national reputation.

They approached a fantastically overloaded little Fiat which had broken down by the roadside. An American family by the look of it, the children in bright T-shirts, both father and mother in jeans. Luckily there was a mechanic lying on his back under the vehicle. This was no time to have to stop and offer assistance.

And now a momentary slow-down where the road took a sudden twist round a blacksmith's shop and its rusty old petrol pump, and it should be about another ten miles.

Yes, the deputy superintendent had said the dacoity had occurred where the traffic was held up by roadworks and there ahead was a place where the embankment had crumbled away. And yes, there was a dark green car stopped in the full glare of the heat. That should be it.

His driver brought the over-heated Dodge to a screaming halt worthy of the best traditions of the Bombay Police. Ghote jumped lightly down and took in the scene with a quick glance.

A harassed and sweaty but stolid-looking constable was keeping back a small crowd of gaping villagers and workers from the road-mending gang. The empty car, a Chevrolet, unusually enough, stood at the point where the road narrowed to one lane. At the other end of the single lane there was a bullock-cart. Its two bullocks with their coloured horns down were dragging at the last remains of some roadside tufts of grass. A couple of paces from the car there was crudely traced in the dust the outline of a man's body. Beside it the surface of the concrete had been darkened by a dried-up pool of blood over which buzzed some fat flies.

Ghote went over towards the constable to get his report.

And was suddenly startled to hear a loud shout from a little way down the road.

'Hey, you.'

He turned. But immediately regretted having done so. The shout might not have been directed at him. It should not have been directed at him, an inspector of the Maharashtra State Police.

Only he knew perfectly well that it was.

There was no doubt either about who the shouter was. Striding along the dusty-layered surface of the road was a tall, broad-shouldered Westerner. Everything from the well-hung cut of his crisp, beige-coloured suit to his broad-brimmed straw hat with the coloured band round the crown proclaimed him a American.

'You,' he called again, as he strode forward. 'You, are you the inspector from the police they said was coming from Bombay?'

Ghote squared his thin shoulders.

'I am inspector in charge of case, certainly,' he said.

'Well, I'm glad to see you finally got here,' the American replied.

The thought flashed into Ghote's mind that this was a pressman. He found the notion a little daunting. Indian journalists he could cope with, though he never much liked even their brashness. But an American reporter. A tough, remorseless conductor of special investigations. How had this one got on to the murder so quickly? It was typical of them. And what would he not make of it? The sort of reports he would file would knock crores of rupees off tourist revenue.

Ghote licked his upper lip.

He would be asked all sorts of details about his personal affairs. There would be uncomplimentary physical descriptions of himself in each day's story, of his lack of height and his thinness. He had heard about American-style papers. They would want to mention his wife, his child. Perhaps they would say that Protima spoke English badly, that she distrusted Western furniture and clothes.

'Now, I'd like to know right away just what you intend doing,' the American said.

Ghote looked up at him. He seemed to be in his late forties, broad and still slim. He had a markedly handsome face with a long, straight nose, and a crisp darkening of beard-shadow along the sides of the wide jaw. Undoubtedly he was tough. And there was an angry glint in his eyes.

'I have no time for Press affairs now,' Ghote said loudly. 'I have a great deal of work ahead in the conduct of the investigation. Kindly wait until afterwards.'

'Press affairs?' the big American said. 'What the hell do you mean, Press affairs?'

He glared down at Ghote.

'Look,' he said, 'it's my brother who's been murdered here. My brother. And I want to know just what you're going to do to pin down the men responsible.'

A hugely unsettling wave of astonishment swept over Ghote. Was this really Professor Gregory Strongbow, the world-famous scientist? If the man himself had not said so, it would have been almost impossible to believe. He did not look old enough. He looked much too active. Why didn't he stoop? And the tously hair under that hat with the bright, coloured band, that was hardly academic. Then there was the way he had shot out those questions in that reporter's style. But perhaps this was due to the shock of his brother's death.

'Professor Strongbow,' Ghote stammered. 'I beg your pardon. Please accept my profound regrets. Allow me to introduce myself. Yes. Yes, of course. I am Inspector Ghote, of Bombay CID. Specially detailed to investigate this case. Yes, Ghote. My name is Ghote.'

In an onrush of desire to make up to Professor Strongbow for his original attitude, Ghote wondered whether he ought perhaps to tell him more about himself. To bring out his wife's name and his boy's, to state his own qualifications in full, even to explain that although he was married to someone who did not speak English well she was still an intelligent and characterful woman.

But the professor gave him no opportunity.

He shot out a broad, tanned hand for Ghote to shake. His grip was impressively firm.

'Glad to meet you,' he said. 'I guess I may have been a little abrupt. To tell you the truth, I'm pretty on edge.'

Ghote's eye went involuntarily to the crudely traced outline in the dust. He saw too for the first time that in the door panel of the dark green Chevrolet there was a dented round hole where it must have been struck by a bullet.

'Perhaps we should go over to the shade to talk the matter over,' he said.

Professor Strongbow seemed glad to fall in with the suggestion. He turned quickly away and took out a handkerchief to wipe his face.

'It certainly is hot,' he said. 'And humid.'

They set off towards the shade of a small banyan tree between the roadworks and the village. Ghote saw that a small car was parked under it.

'You were not with your brother?' he asked the professor. 'You were travelling in another car?'

'No, I wasn't with him. I was staying overnight at Poona, visiting the hydraulics laboratory there. I'm in that line myself.'

'But you are the foremost world authority,' Ghote said. 'When I was given my instructions for the case this was specifically stated.'

The professor smiled slightly. Ghote noticed that in spite of the determined line of his jaw and the uncompromising straightness of his nose the eyes were deep-set and understanding. He wondered suddenly whether he had embarrassed him.

'But why was your brother not with you in Poona?' he said quickly.

Almost at once he regretted the question. He should not be drawing the bereaved man's attention to such things in such a tactless manner.

But the professor seemed only too anxious to explain.

'It's like this,' he said. 'My brother and I decided to come to India together. I had some vacation due and I thought he ought to get away for a bit. But we don't have all that many interests in common. We didn't have, that is.'

He took a few paces in silence, and then resumed with a jerk.

'Yes, that's how it was. We split up. We decided to split up for a while. He went out yesterday to see some things that primarily interested him, and I went over to Poona to see the hydraulics lab there. A pretty fine set-up too.'

'Thank you,' said Ghote, 'thank you.'

He coughed a little.

'And you had arranged to meet today in Poona?' he asked.

'No,' said the professor.

A trace of a frown appeared on his wide forehead.

'No, to tell you the truth, I wasn't exactly expecting Hector to come on to Poona. The arrangement was I would see him tomorrow when I got back to Bombay.'

'But he changed his mind?'

For a little Professor Strongbow did not answer.

'I guess he must have,' he said at last. 'Hector was somewhat impulsive, you know.'

He fell silent again.

From something in his tone Ghote deduced that impulsiveness was not part of the professor's make-up. And the professor himself seemed to realize the implications of what he had said almost at once.

'Not that impulsiveness isn't a fine thing,' he added. 'I sometimes think a good many of us are liable to think so long we finally don't act at all.'

'There is a great deal to be said on both sides,' Ghote observed, feeling torn between supporting the professor in his eulogy of his dead brother and not appearing to criticize the man himself.

The professor grunted.

'Your tourist people in Poona were certainly very nice to me when the news came through,' he went on. 'They put this girl, this Miss Brown, in touch with me right away. And she fixed up a car and got us out here.'

Ghote noticed that in the car parked in the shade of the banyan a girl was sitting. She appeared to be wearing a sari.

'Miss Brown?' he asked.

'Yes,' said the professor. 'I guess she must be some kind of a

Eurasian, though she looks pretty British and talks that way. But she told me her first name was something Indian.'

He laid a hand on Ghote's elbow and halted him a moment.

'As a matter of fact,' he said, 'I didn't exactly catch what she said when she told me. It sounded like Shack— something. Is that possible?'

'Was it perhaps Shakuntala?' Ghote suggested.

'Yes. Yes, that's it. Shakuntala, you say? Thanks, Inspector. I didn't want to have to hurt the girl's feelings by calling her Miss Brown all the time.'

Sitting sedately at the wheel of the little grey Hindustan she had provided for the professor, Shakuntala Brown smiled a little when she saw the two of them approach. Ghote noticed that, in spite of her sari, her hair was a light brown and her complexion distinctly pink and white. He wondered for a moment where she could come from. But he had no time for much speculation. As soon as the professor had introduced them, bringing out the 'Shakuntala' with noticeable clarity, he felt obliged to start putting all the right questions. It was important to give this foreigner the correct impression of Indian police-work.

'Please tell,' he said, 'something of your brother's habits. Was he for example a great free spender? Was he accustomed to pull out his wallet and offer to pay in notes for the least service?'

The professor considered gravely for a moment.

'No,' he answered. 'No, I don't think you could say that about Hector. He might have got excited some place and waved a lot of money about, but he certainly didn't give the impression of being loaded.'

He gave Ghote a quick, appraising look.

'You're wondering why anyone should have picked on him to rob?' he asked. 'Did you know that those guys had been waiting over there by that tree all morning?'

'All morning? Waiting?' Ghote said, with a sharp frown.

'That's what your patrolman told me,' said the professor.

He looked steadily at Ghote.

'Is that what you'd have expected?' he asked.

But, unexpectedly, it was Shakuntala Brown who answered.

'Mr Strongbow,' she said, 'you will have to get used to the idea that India is a very different country from the United States. People have a different timescale here. They are prepared to wait hours for the very slightest of reasons. You couldn't be expected to understand that.'

She spoke with vehemence. Ghote once more wondered about her. Was this her usual manner? Or did this unexplained behaviour on the part of the killers cause her to feel furious for some reason?

But there was no time for side issues. He turned back to the American.

'The car your brother was driving,' he said. 'It is an expensive model and unusual. Had you bought it for the length of your stay in India?'

'No,' Professor Strongbow answered thoughtfully. 'No, I don't know anything about the car. I guess Hector must have rented it just today.'

'To go to Poona to see you?'

'That I can't say for a fact.'

'But it is likely? He was driving on the Poona road. You were in Poona.'

'It looks like a reasonable assumption certainly.'

'But you told you did not know why exactly he should come to meet you?'

Ghote noticed a sudden blankness in the cool eyes opposite him.

'No, I don't know that,' the professor said. 'I guess he suddenly wanted company or something.'

Ghote shrugged his shoulders slightly.

'Perhaps he told someone in Bombay,' he said. 'You are staying at the Taj Mahal, or perhaps you prefer the Nataraj?'

'No,' said the professor. 'As a matter of fact we settled for a place called the Queen's Imperial Grand.'

'Surely that is a very old-fashioned hotel for Americans?' Ghote said.

Professor Strongbow smiled just a little.

'That's more or less the point,' he said. 'We weren't all that anxious to find ourselves with a crowd of people from the States.'

Ghote, who was beginning to think of the next stage in his inquiry, added one more question out of mere politeness.

'You preferred to see more of our country?'

Busy with his thoughts it was an instant or two before he realized that the professor had not answered. He looked across at him.

After a moment the American spoke.

'The truth of the matter is,' he said, 'that Hector had become somewhat notorious just recently back home. He had expressed certain vigorous political views, and had been forced out of his post at the university we both teach in. So I persuaded him to keep out of the limelight for a while.'

It was plain that he was reluctant to say this of a brother so recently killed. Ghote stepped quickly out of the shade of the little banyan and signalled to the constable.

The man, who had been waiting patiently just out of earshot, came over at a trot and crashed thunderingly to attention.

'Inspector sahib?'

'You were the man who reported the dacoity?' Ghote asked.

'Yes, Inspector sahib. I am stationed five miles away only. As soon as one of the men from road repair gang informed I proceeded here by bicycle immediately.'

'Good man. The body was still where it fell then?'

'Yes, Inspector sahib. But owing to the great number of flies and the presence of vultures I ordered it to be taken under shelter, having first made outline in road dust.'

'Excellent. And what signs of dacoity did you observe?'

'The body had been robbed, Inspector sahib. But the thieves had failed to notice passport in back trouser pocket. It was through this that I made preliminary identification. When the burra sahib here arrived he carried out confirmation.'

The constable dipped his head respectfully towards Professor Strongbow.

'Yes,' said the American. 'It was Hector all right. And the men who killed him must be found.'

The angry glint had come back into his eyes. Ghote hurried on with his interrogation of the constable.

'I hear the men in question waited all morning up there under that Flame of the Forest tree,' he said. 'Is that correct?'

'It is what the villagers say, Inspector sahib.'

'How many men were there?'

'Three, Inspector.'

'And you obtained full descriptions?'

The constable sighed.

'These village people,' he said. 'They see nothing. They make no methodical observations. They told only that one was a Sikh and that they smoked a great many cigarettes.'

'I will question myself later, but you seem to have done well.'

'They were right about quantity of cigarettes smoked, Inspector,' the constable said. 'I examined ground under tree myself. There were forty-eight stubs present. Cavander's brand.'

'Common enough,' Ghote said, 'but good work all the same.'

He felt some pleasure that the constable was giving a good impression to the American. Certainly the latter was missing nothing. His eyes never lost their grave alertness for an instant.

'How did the men get here?' Ghote asked the constable next.

'They came by car, Inspector.'

'Did any of the village people take its number?'

'None who saw it can read, Inspector sahib. They said it was a blue car and old only.'

Ghote grimaced. But it was the sort of thing that might be expected.

The American beside him took half a pace forward.

'Inspector,' he said, 'I'd like to know something.'

'Certainly,' said Ghote.

'Now that you've established those guys waited all day just till Hector's car came along, does that alter your opinion at all of the nature of the crime?'

'That it was a dacoity?' Ghote said.

'If that means highway robbery, yes.'

'A dacoity is technically a robbery carried out by five or more persons,' Ghote said.

'All right, allowing for the fact that there seem to have been only three in this case, do you still think it is just a matter of straight robbery?'

'It is unusual for dacoits to wait so long,' Ghote agreed.

He saw a look of acute interest flick into the American's eyes, to be replaced at once by his habitual cautious watchfulness.

'It is unusual,' Ghote repeated, 'but no more. It is probable that your brother's car was the first to stop at the roadworks. You see that the bullock-cart there blocked the way.'

He turned to the constable.

'The cart was there at the time of the accident?' he asked.

'Yes, Inspector sahib. I gave orders for no one to move.'

'Good man.'

'There is one thing, Inspector, also.'

'Yes?'

'Some of the village women report having seen a small fire of black smoke start from a point down the road shortly before the dacoits left their waiting place. They believe it was a signal fire, Inspector.'

Ghote heard the American catch his breath beside him.

'These women,' he asked the constable, 'are they to be trusted? Or are they foolish gossips only?'

'I think they may be right, Inspector. Certainly, it is strange for anyone to start a fire like that. But I could not leave the scene of the crime to carry out investigation.'

'No,' said Ghote. 'But I will investigate just as soon as I have finished here.'

'Then you think this may not be a simple robbery?' the American said eagerly.

Ghote turned to him.

'Please,' he said. 'There are certain things which appear a little unusual. But it is people we are dealing with, even though they are criminals. You cannot expect people always to do things according to the pattern of the textbooks.'

'So you are going to claim this was just robbery?' Professor Strongbow said.

He sounded disappointed.

Ghote looked up at him squarely.

'Professor,' he said, 'it is perhaps hard for you to understand that someone as close to you as your brother has been killed in a most ordinary way. But this is almost certainly what has happened. He has been victim of accident, if you like. The accident of these men choosing this day to commit dacoity. It is natural to look for signs of something special. But it is a mistake to try to read special meaning into the slight differences this case has from one tomorrow.'

For some moments the American did not reply. Then he sighed deeply.

'You could be right,' he said.

Ghote looked round more briskly.

'It is necessary now for me to examine the body,' he said. 'I imagine you would prefer to stay here by the car with Miss Brown?'

'No,' said the American, 'I'll come with you.'

'But it is not necessary for me to hear your identification,' Ghote said.

'All the same I'd like to come.'

'As you wish.'

They walked back along the road to the village in silence. The constable marched just ahead of them to show Ghote the way to the hut where he had had the body carried. His feet thumped steadily and evenly on the dusty surface of the road and then squelched through the mire of the shady village.

They stooped and entered the hut.

Already there was a sharp, unpleasant smell and the flies were buzzing hard. Ghote looked down at the rather thin figure in the beige, silk suit with the ugly rips in the chest and the dark, dried stains of blood. The face bore only the slightest resemblance to the professor's by the hut entrance. Above all, the crest of flaming red hair and the streak of beard of the same intense colour made the dead man look different.

Behind him the American spoke.

'He was not the sort of man you could mistake,' he said.

'No,' Ghote said. 'A fine man, Professor.'

'A distinctive man,' the professor answered.

Ghote felt that the comment was hardly the proper one in the circumstances. It was not what ought to have been said about a brother so recently killed. It was not a correct tribute.

But after all the professor was an American, and perhaps they were different about such things.

To change the subject a little he pointed to a small black and white metal disc the dead man had in the buttonhole of his left lapel.

'What is this, please?' he said. 'It is some sort of badge?'

'Yes,' Professor Strongbow answered. 'It's a badge all right. A CND button. The Campaign for Nuclear Disarmament. Hector was a great one for that. As a matter of fact it was that that caused all the trouble back home, the reason why I persuaded him to come over here really.'

He watched silently as Ghote continued with his examination.

'Yes,' he said after a little, 'I persuaded him to come. To keep him out of trouble.'

He gave a short, unmirthful laugh.

Ghote finished doing what he had to do and straightened up.

'There's one thing,' the American said. 'That button. Can I take it?'

Ghote knew it was not strictly allowable.

'Please to have it,' he said.

The American bent forward, twisted the button out of its place on the lapel of the beige-coloured suit and slipped it into his pocket. They went out into the oppressive heat.

Ghote was relieved to be able to walk briskly back to the scene of the shooting, and as soon as they arrived he fired a stream of questions at the patient constable, who dutifully pointed out the few material factors there were to show. Ghote checked the name of the car-hire firm that owned the dark green Chevrolet. He inspected the vague scuffled patches in the dust where the killers must have stood. He gauged the distance between the car and the bullock-cart at the far end of the roadworks.

The police breakdown truck coming to haul away the Chevrolet for examination arrived in a great swirl of dust. It stopped with a howl from its brakes, slewing dramatically across the road. Ghote bit his lip in vexation. Behaviour of that sort did not really give an impression of efficiency. It simply made the Police Department look like a lot of children.

A cheerful head constable jumped out of the truck swinging a driving wheel fitted with clamps to go over that of the car to be fingerprinted.

'OK to take, Inspector?' he shouted.

Ghote noticed that the American had turned and was walking slowly back towards Shakuntala Brown under the little banyan. He turned back to the head constable.

'You be damned careful with that car,' he snapped.

The head constable executed a pantomime of being extremely chastened. He approached the dark green Chevrolet on tiptoe.

Ghote hoped that the professor had not seen this display. It was difficult to make out.

'Inspector sahib,' the local constable said respectfully at his elbow.

He turned to him with relief. At least here was somebody who did what he had to do sensibly and properly.

'Yes?'

'If the car is going, Inspector, shall I tell this bullock-cart wallah to be on his way?'

Ghote looked across at the squatting figure of the driver on the big, unwieldy cart.

'No,' he said, 'you will not tell him to go. That man set up a fine road block at just the right time. I want to know why.'

2

Inspector Ghote strode determinedly towards the patient, squatting figure of the bare-backed bullock-cart driver. If there was anything more to the attack on the red-haired American than a simple dacoity, then this was in all probability going to be his chance to find out.

But something in the sharp forcefulness of his stride must have signalled a warning to the man perched on the clumsy shaft of the big cart. Because with a sudden leap into the air he flung himself down on to the road, staggered once and hared off along the dusty concrete surface with his long, bare legs scissoring out like a champion runner's.

Ghote went after him in an instant.

The constable was scarcely slower off the mark. But both of them had to negotiate the bulk of the heavy cart and by the time they had a clear run the bullock driver was well ahead. His skinny body looked as if it ought not to have the stamina to keep going at this pace for more than twenty yards, but plainly his looks were deceptive. It was all Ghote could do not to fall behind, and the constable, pounding along in his heavy boots, seemed to be even less well able to keep in the chase.

Ghote swore to himself. The fellow would not have to go far before he got some chance to get out of sight. And once he had done that he could disappear into the vast stretch of the countryside with its hundreds and hundreds of anonymous, almost unidentifiable people and be lost perhaps for ever more. There were thousands of homeless men wandering up and down the length of India, and it was beyond the scope of the possible to check on more than a handful of them.

Already the almost naked runner ahead of them was nearing the professor, slowly making his way towards the banyan tree. A hundred yards or so further on and the village would be reached. And there in a dodging game among the cluster of huts their quarry would be almost certain to get away.

And then the man stumbled. Perhaps in passing the tall form of the American he had taken his eyes off the road at his feet for an instant. But whatever the cause, he had stumbled badly. And Ghote and the constable had their chance. Within moments Ghote had closed up to the point where he was ready to fling himself forward in a final lunge.

He felt a sense of pounding joy as he took a deep breath and launched himself into the air.

Something heavy struck him a tremendous blow on the left shoulder, sending him sprawling away off target. His reaching fingers almost touched the bullock driver's earth-stained loincloth but the impact of the blow was too strong. With a jarring crash he landed flat on his face on the hard concrete.

It was the big American. He had taken it into his head to hurl himself at the bullock driver at just the instant Ghote had launched himself forward. And he too had landed every bit as awkwardly in the dust. Above them the constable came to a teetering halt, his way totally blocked by their outstretched bodies.

Ahead, the fugitive gave one quick glance round and then turned, leaped helter-skelter down the road embankment and was off across the wide spread of the fields.

'Damnation,' said Ghote.

The American heaved himself up till he was on all fours on the dusty road.

'Inspector, I'm sorry,' he said. 'I've let him get away.'

He pushed himself upright.

'I don't know what came over me,' he said. 'I don't usually act like that. I guess it was just that I suddenly realized that here was someone who could lead us to the men who killed my brother. I guess I suddenly thought I could avenge Hector that way.'

He looked at the figure of the bullock driver, already getting smaller as he headed stubbornly across the pattern of the little fields. A long way behind, the constable, who had in his turn jumped down the embankment, was toiling conscientiously on.

'And all I did was to make sure the guy got away,' the professor said.

Ghote reflected that this was probably true.

'Kindly do not worry,' he said. 'It was good of you to try to stop the fellow.'

And suddenly he saw that all was not yet lost.

He turned to the professor.

'Your car,' he said, 'can I use same?'

'Sure thing.'

The American swung round at once and began running towards the little grey Hindustan by the banyan. Following, Ghote noted that he ran well, taking long economical strides over the dusty surface of the road.

And he thought fast too, for all his generally cautious approach to things. Already he was shouting to Shakuntala Brown at the wheel of the little car to move over.

By the time Ghote had got there she was in the front passenger seat. The professor scrambled into the back. Ghote jumped in, banged the door to and tugged at the starter. The engine broke into life and Ghote swung the little vehicle round and set off along the road in a storm of fresh dust.

Within a minute they had reached the narrow cart track which Ghote had suddenly spotted as they had watched the fugitive gradually getting smaller and smaller as he ran from field to field. Ghote swung the little Hindustan off the road and set it bucketing and swaying down the narrow, crumbly track as fast as he dared.

'You know,' said Professor Strongbow from the back, 'with any luck we're going to cut the guy off.'

He leaned forward with an elbow on the top of each seat. And suddenly the little car gave a violent lurch to the right as its front offside wheel dipped into a deep rut and its engine stopped dead.

They were hanging perilously over the banked edge of the path, with below them in the shade a miry patch of caramel-coloured earth waiting for their fall. The professor flung himself back with a groan.

'I just should never have said that.'

And the shift in weight did the trick. The little car rose an inch or two in the front, Ghote leaned backwards as much as he could and restarted the engine. Cautiously he slipped into reverse and put in the clutch. The car crept back on to the path again.

Half a minute later they were off once more. And within another two minutes Ghote and the professor were sliding down the bank from the path into the fields. Ahead of them, not fifty yards away, the bullock driver plunged on unaware of his danger.

'This time I'll leave him to you,' the American said as they set off across the soft earth of the recently flooded fields.

He dropped back a yard or two and left Ghote to make the running. Quite soon the bullock driver heard them. He looked up startled almost out of his wits, and began to go off in a new direction. But it was too late. A pace or two more and Ghote was within striking distance again.

This time, with his quarry plainly exhausted to dropping point, he did not attempt to fling himself forward. He ran on a little, closing the gap between them with every stride. Then he reached forward and grabbed.

The hunt was up.

Ghote swung his captive round to face him. And found that he had misjudged his man. A sharp, well-pointed blow hit him hard in the pit of the stomach and he sat down abruptly in the soft earth, cursing himself all the way. The bullock driver appeared to be filled with new life at his success. He tore off again while Ghote, feeling sick, looked round.

It was hardly possible that the constable would catch him. He had stopped when he saw the fugitive had been cut off and was now much too far behind. Ghote heaved himself to his feet. He felt totally winded. It looked as if he had lost his quarry after all.

But he had reckoned without the professor. He came past at that moment, going like the wind. Somewhere in the chase he had slipped off his jacket and the hat with the gay, coloured band had been snatched off long before. Now his shirt was puffing out behind him and a heavy lock of his dark hair was biffing and battering at his eyes. But nothing was putting him off, and in a moment he shot himself forward in a low tackle that brought the bullock driver down with such a thump that the crows in every field around rose up in the air cawing like a whole congregation of startled old ladies.

Ghote quickly stumbled over and caught hold of his thin wrist before he had a chance to lash out a second time.

'Thank you very much,' he said to the professor.

'I was the one who nearly let him get away in the beginning,' the American said.

'You certainly made up for it,' said Ghote. 'I hope this fellow will turn out to be worth all the chasing.'

Ghote waited to begin questioning his prisoner till they were all back at the scene of the killing. With the driver of his own truck, who had made it clear that his business was driving and not chasing people over fields, and the stolid local constable each holding the man by one arm, Ghote stood in front of him looking him straight in the face. He was rather gaunt in appearance with a wide moustache covering the whole of his upper lip and defeated, downward-looking eyes.

'Well,' Ghote snapped, 'what is your name?'

No answer.

'Your name?'

'Bholu.'

Very sulkily delivered, without looking up.

'All right, Bholu,' Ghote said, 'you blocked the road with your cart so that those dacoits could rob the car when it stopped. But your friends made the mistake of killing the driver. You were helping them. That means you are as guilty of murder as they are. So you would certainly be hanged.'

He waited for this to sink in.

Bholu could not have looked any more miserable. But Ghote assumed that after perhaps half a minute the full unpleasantness of his position would have become quite clear to him.

'Now,' he went on, 'there is just one chance for you. If you give me every bit of help you can, then I would see if something can be done. But it is see only, you understand.'

Bholu gave a short moan.

'Come on,' Ghote shouted suddenly, 'talk.'

Bholu stole a glance to the ground at his side but said not a word.

'Very well,' Ghote said, turning away, 'put him in the truck. We will take to Bombay, charge him straight away, and in no time at all we will have him hanged.'

He noticed Professor Strongbow, standing a little way apart, begin a movement of protest. Quickly he walked off before the American could say anything.

Bholu broke into a sudden clamour of speech.

'Sahib, sahib. I cannot tell. Sahib, if I tell they would shoot me. Sahib, I know it. They would shoot me, sahib.'

Ghote turned round comfortably.

'And if you do not tell,' he said, 'we would hang you.'

Bholu darted quick glances from side to side. The constable at his back gave his right arm a quick twist.

Then, in a very quiet voice which Ghote had to lean forward to hear, Bholu began to talk.

'Sahib, they are not dacoits at all,' he said. 'It was not to rob the

American that they made me stop his car. It was for them to kill him. Sahib, they were paid to do that. They were paid a great sum to kill the American with the red hair and the red beard.'

Professor Strongbow stepped quickly forward. He gave Ghote a long, questioning look.

Ghote concentrated on the bullock driver.

'These men who were paid all this,' he said, 'who are they?'

'Oh, sahib, I do not know.'

'Yes, you know. How could they come to you for help if you did not know? Who are they?'

'Sahib, sahib, I owed one of them money. I had great losses, sahib.'

'Who did you owe? Why did you owe him?'

'It was the cards, sahib. Sahib, I could not help. I had to do what they told, sahib. So much money I am owing.'

'Who did you owe the money to?' Ghote said. 'I want the name.'

'To Lal Mahsi, sahib.'

'Lal Mahsi? What Lal Mahsi is this?'

'Lal Mahsi who keeps a house for playing cards at Poona, sahib.'

'Ah, him,' Ghote said, though the gamblers of Poona were altogether unknown to him. 'You went to which house to lose so much money at cards?'

'To the one in the Sadashiv Peth, sahib.'

The gaunt-faced bullock driver gave a dry sob.

'The number of the house?' Ghote said.

He knew Poona well enough to remember that the houses in the crowded old city were numbered right through each quarter, with figures running up to thousands.

'What number in the Sadashiv Peth?' he asked.

And Bholu told him.

'All right,' Ghote snapped. 'And the others? The names of the other men with Lal Mahsi?'

'Sahib, I had never seen before. It is true, sahib.'

'But they came here to kill an American with red hair?'

'Yes, sahib, yes. They knew when he would be coming, sahib. By a signal.'

Bholu's eyes were blank with misery.

'Look, Inspector,' Professor Strongbow said, 'I told you before I wasn't sure my brother was killed during a straight robbery, didn't I?'

'Yes,' said Ghote, 'several things are beginning to fit into place now.'

The American looked at him speculatively.

But before he had decided to say anything more Shakuntala Brown, who had been listening with disturbing intentness to every word that had been spoken, intervened.

'All the same, Professor,' she said, with more urgency than seemed called for, 'I'm sure the inspector will tell you that people in this country will invent any story to get themselves out of trouble. Don't forget, on the face of it it still looks most likely that your brother was killed in an ordinary dacoity. He was robbed, remember.'

The American said nothing. But he looked at Ghote.

'Thank you, Miss Brown,' Ghote said. 'But what Professor Strongbow has noticed is enough to make me have damnable doubts about this being simple dacoity. Damnable doubts.'

'One thing there can be no doubt about at all,' Deputy Superintendent Samant barked, 'is that what you have got to deal with, Inspector, is the nastiest case of dacoity we have had for years.'

'But, DSP,' Ghote said, 'I think it is possible that—'

'Yes,' said DSP Samant sharply, 'the fact that the victim was the brother of a very distinguished foreign visitor does not really alter the nature of the crime at all. Dacoity, Inspector, pure and simple dacoity within fifty miles of Bombay.'

Oppressed by the severe neatness of the DSP's office with its walls covered in many-coloured charts each completely up-to-date to that morning's entry, Ghote sat wondering when and how he was going to say what he had to. Because, cost what it might, respect for his own deductions coupled with a strong feeling that he must not let his new American acquaintance down, were going to make him contradict every word the Deputy Superintendent was saying.

He listened respectfully while the DSP vented his irritation that such an event should happen within his jurisdiction, and, worse, on his duty day.

Then at last there came a pause.

'Sir,' Ghote said, 'I beg to state I am not convinced this is a case of dacoity. Sir, I believe it was assassination.'

'Nonsense, man, just because the victim was important, don't get it into your head that the crime has to be something special too. Dacoity, man, plain dacoity. Now, what are you going to do about it?'

'But sir, the red-haired American's arrival at the point where he was ambushed was clearly signalled by means of a fire. I questioned the people at the village where it was lit, DSP. And they had no doubts that the fire was a signal.'

The DSP's hands gripped the arms of his heavy cane-seated chair decisively.

'Just because some stranger chooses to light a fire in their village a lot of ignorant country people get all excited,' he said. 'But that doesn't mean that one of my officers has to fall in with them. I want to hear no more about it, Inspector.'

'DSP,' said Ghote with a trace of desperation, 'Professor Strongbow, who is most determined his brother's murderers shall be brought to book, himself supports my view.'

The DSP sighed. Sharply, like a little shunting locomotive.

'Inspector, Professor Strongbow is a most distinguished scientist. He is the brother of the murdered man. He is a guest in our country. But none of these things means that you are obliged to adopt his every passing opinion and slavishly copy it. Pull yourself together, man.'

'Yes, DSP. But there is the question of why the killers waited all morning near the place in question, sir.'

'All right, Inspector, let me hear you out to the bitter end. Now, just why does Professor Strongbow think his brother should have been assassinated? Assassinated!'

The DSP gave a laugh that sounded much more like a bark.

'Sir, he would not say. He simply stated, sir, that the circumstances seemed to him to indicate his brother had not been killed in the course of a robbery only.'

'He would not say?'

'No, sir. I pressed him as far as I could, sir. But he is a distinguished visitor, sir.'

'And he would not say?'

'No, sir.'

DSP Samant's greyish Maratha eyes glared.

'But you, Inspector, you feel obliged none the less—'

The telephone, which had begun to ring a few moments earlier, brought his tirade to a stop. He picked up the receiver.

'Samant. What is it? What is it? Mehta? Mehta? Never heard—'

A sharp voice uttered two syllables at the far end of the line.

The DSP coughed.

'Colonel Mehta,' he said, 'good evening, sir.'

The voice at the other end of the line began a long discourse of sharply broken up phrases. The DSP listened.

Ghote, standing to attention in front of the big desk with its neatly ranged wire baskets, tried not to listen. He concentrated his attention on the wall behind the DSP where a large street map of Bombay hung. He set out to trace the route between the office and his home.

'But, Colonel, if Mr Strongbow was on an official—'

The distant voice cut in sharply.

But the word Strongbow had caught Ghote's attention. He considered himself absolved from the duty of being only physically present in the DSP's office. If this conversation was anything to do with his case, he owed it to himself to hear every word he could.

But he tried to keep the expression on his face as distant and respectful as it had been before.

'Yes, yes, I see, Colonel,' the DSP said, 'that puts quite a different complexion on the matter. An unofficial visit is definitely snooping. Definitely. And Trombay is the Atomic Energy Establishment. We cannot tolerate snooping there.'

The voice at the other end of the line made a brisk observation.

'Yes, I see, Colonel. But all the same, surely he could not have learned very much. After all—'

A very short pause.

'Oh, I did not realize that, Colonel. He is— He was a physicist, eh? Nasty business.'

Ghote thought he caught something about Colonel Mehta knowing it was a nasty business. But he could not be sure that he had heard properly. There was something else too which he did not catch at all.

Whatever it was it made the DSP start glancing here, there and everywhere round the room as if he was looking for something with the utmost urgency. Ghote, handicapped by not knowing what this object was, began looking too.

'Briefcase, man, briefcase,' snapped the DSP.

A cold feeling swept through Ghote's mind. The briefcase was on the DSP's desk. It had been almost under his nose. If he pointed this out, it would make his superior officer look a fool. On the other hand, he obviously wanted his briefcase, and quick. He was looking plainly frantic, holding the telephone receiver at the full length of the wire, uttering placatory noises and trying to peer round the corner of the desk at the floor in front of it.

Taking advantage of this, Ghote nipped forward, grabbed the initial-stamped case, and proffered it in silence.

The DSP dropped the receiver, yanked furiously at the straps of the case, opened it at last, dragged out the evening paper of the day before and began wildly threshing it apart.

He grabbed up the receiver again.

'Yes, Colonel, I have it now. Damn fool hid my briefcase. Gossip column, third item. Yes. I see it.'

He began to read, muttering out a word or two every few seconds to indicate to Colonel Mehta on the far end of the line that he was still with him. Ghote, leaning fractionally forward to get a better view, was able to see that the item the DSP was reading was accompanied by a small, blurred-looking photograph surrounded by sharp black lines. After a few seconds he connected it with the dead body he had looked down at in the foul-smelling hut out on the Poona road.

The voice at the far end of the telephone line crackled impatiently.

'Yes, Colonel, I have read it now,' the Deputy Superintendent said. 'But it seems to me, you know, that the fellow was some sort of a crank. All this nonsense about joining the "Hands Off Cuba" movement and leaving his job over nuclear tests. Whatever any of us may feel about whether this country should make a bomb, I hardly think one is called on to leave one's job over it.'

The DSP spoke with a certain easy blandness. Colonel Mehta, whoever he was, replied with a plain crackle of fury.

'Oh, yes, yes,' the DSP said quickly. 'Yes, indeed, Colonel, I do see that. A convinced nuclear disarmer and a qualified physicist. The combination, exactly, Colonel.'

Another burst of jabbered words.

'Yes. Well, thank you, Colonel. I will do as you suggest. It will be most helpful. But one more thing, Colonel.'

Squawk.

'It would be most useful if you could tell me just what it is that Mr Hector Strongbow could have discovered out at the Atomic Energy place at Trombay.'

The telephone receiver in the DSP's hand crackled and spat so violently that he was forced to hold the earpiece a few inches away from his head. Ghote distinctly heard the words 'ridiculous and impertinent curiosity'. But he decided to erase them for ever from his memory.

The DSP put his ear back to the receiver again and listened attentively.

'Yes, Colonel,' he said at last. 'I give you my personal undertaking.

Except for the inspector in charge of the case and myself not one word about the matter will be mentioned here. Not one single word.'

A final fierce crackle from the far end and the DSP replaced the receiver in its cradle with a long whistle of a sigh.

'Inspector Ghote,' he said, 'it seems that your dead man visited the Trombay Atomic Energy Establishment the day before his death. That is a fact you are to keep completely to yourself.'

'Yes, sir, I would—'

'And, Inspector.'

'Yes, DSP?'

'It further appears that this case is no longer a matter for this department.'

'Oh. Then I revert to roster duties as heretofore, sir?'

'No, Inspector, you do not. You report at once to Colonel Mehta of Special Investigations Agency. You continue your activities working alongside him. And heaven help you, Inspector.'

3

The address Ghote was given for the Special Investigations Agency proved to be that of an enormous and ancient office block in the Fort area. The big, many-pinnacled, hundred-year-old building, redolent of the days when mighty British interests built alien, aggressive citadels in Bombay to remind themselves of distant, different and impregnable castles, was not at all the sort of place the inspector had imagined as the headquarters of the mysterious body that had intervened so unexpectedly in his affairs.

If ever the block had been devoted to one particular purpose those days had long gone. Now it was divided and subdivided into a hundred little sets of different offices fitting complexly together inside the great dark red honeycomb of a building. The Special Investigations Agency must be only one among them. In the tall entrance hall with its high walls broken into long rectangular panels by long rows of projecting pillars, Ghote found a huge black noticeboard split up into dozens of tiny compartments. Each had a name on it written in white paint yellowed to a lesser or greater degree according to the age of the firm in question.

It took Ghote a long time to spot at the top right-hand corner of this massive directory, in letters still almost completely white, the simple words, 'Special Investigations Agency'.

He had hoped at first that the board might give him some indication of the nature of the agency. The larger firms in the building had several compartments of the noticeboard to themselves and indicated where their various branches were located and sometimes even announced the names of heads of departments. But the Special Investigations Agency provided no such clues. The only fact to be deduced about it was that it occupied one of the offices at the very top of the building.

He set out to climb flight after flight of stairs to see what more was to be discovered.

He did not feel at all happy. Not only was he venturing into unknown territory where all his familiar and trusted links with his fellow policemen would no longer hold, but the whole business of Hector Strongbow's death had now taken on dimensions entirely beyond him. DSP Samant had not helped. Beyond giving Ghote the address he was to go to, he had done no more than extend a vague assurance of providing any help needed. When Ghote had ventured a question he had told him that he would find out all he needed to know from Colonel Mehta.

Ghote paused for a moment at the turn of the stairs and wondered how long it would be before he even got up to where the colonel was supposed to work. Resignedly he set off again. Ten stairs up, turn, ten stairs up, another turn.

His feelings of dissatisfaction crystallized into the thought that he was going somehow to be prevented from probing the American's death to the bottom. This business of his having paid that unofficial visit to the Atomic Energy Establishment out at Trombay smelt plainly nasty. Was it all going to end with an order to let the case simply drop? When someone was murdered he wanted to know who had done it and to get them firmly behind bars just as quickly as possible. That was what he was for. It was his job. And now it might be pulled from under his feet.

The walls beside him grew progressively shabbier as he climbed. The patches where the distemper had peeled away got larger. The stains where passers-by had spat out bright red betel juice grew older and dustier. His doubts about what lay ahead increased.

What sort of an organization could possibly have its offices in such sad and petty surroundings?

And at last, right at the top of the interminable stairs, there was the door he was looking for. It did nothing to relieve his pessimism. Its last coat of paint had been applied long ago. A layer of dust lay undisturbed along the bottom of each of its panels. The only thing that indicated life of any sort was a small black-painted board on which the words 'Special Investigations Agency' had been superimposed on the half-obliterated traces of innumerable former tenants.

Ghote stepped up to the door and briskly knocked.

'Come,' a voice called.

Cautiously the inspector opened the dusty door. He found himself in a small outer office. It was totally bare. A large, smooth-surfaced, faceless safe was embedded in one of the walls, but otherwise there was no furniture of any sort. Even the ubiquitous trade calendars, which have to be hung somewhere, were entirely absent. There was only another door facing him, every bit as dusty as the first and standing slightly ajar.

'Inspector Ghote,' the sharp voice said from behind it. 'Come in, man, when you're told.'

Ghote felt a sudden inward sinking. His name already known. His arrival expected.

He pushed at the second door. The office that he now found himself in was furnished to some extent. Bang in the middle of the bare floor there was a table with a telephone on it. Placed at it was a small, hard chair. Sitting in a slightly larger chair on the far side of the table was a man of about forty-five, whom Ghote supposed must be Colonel Mehta. But otherwise the room was as bare as the outer office. Not a cupboard, not a filing cabinet, not even a scrap of paper.

'At ease, Inspector, at ease,' said Colonel Mehta. 'Take a pew.'

With a brief economical gesture he indicated the hard chair in front of his table. Ghote pulled it out and sat down with his knees neatly together.

He looked at Colonel Mehta.

The soldier in mufti. It was written all over him: his neat, discreetly checked suit and firmly knotted striped tie; the hard-trimmed, vigorously bristling moustache above the stern line of an unsmiling mouth; the square set of the shoulders and the habitual, utter straightness of the back.

Ghote prickled. Soldiers were people he had had little to do with, creatures from an alien, different world with other and different standards.

'Well, Inspector,' the colonel said, 'no doubt you're wondering just what the bloody set-up is.'

'DSP Samant said you would inform, sir.'

'Did he indeed? Well, don't you be too sure. The less anyone knows about me and my work the better I'm pleased. Never forget that.'

He glanced sharply round the bare room.

'That's why I sit in a place like this all day,' he went on. 'I don't surround myself with clerks and orderlies and all the rest of it. I don't go filling in yards and yards of bumpf. Too many people are full of an appalling urge to make out reports on everything in sight. And what happens next, eh? They have to stick by what they've written. Slows 'em up, bogs 'em down. Damn bad idea.'

'Yes, sir,' Ghote said shortly.

'Ha,' said Colonel Mehta. 'All this isn't telling you what the Special Investigations Agency is, is it?'

'No, sir.'

'Yes. Saw you thinking just that. Not all that much gets past me, you know.'

'No, sir.'

'All right then. What shall we say about Special Investigations?'

Abruptly the colonel got to his feet and began pacing up and down the bare floor of his cramped office.

'In every modern country, Inspector,' he said, 'whether it likes it or not there has to be an organization like mine. Every country has secrets. And when you've got secrets you have to have someone to make damn sure they stay secret.'

He swung round and stared hard at Ghote, sitting neatly on his hard chair.

'Now I know there are all sorts of bloody organizations that might be called on to deal with protecting secrets,' he went on. 'There's the Intelligence Bureau up in Delhi for organized, major crime. Or there's the Special Police Establishment wallahs. They might have a finger in the pie if corruption was involved, as it almost always is. But people like that are too big. They're open to pressure. They're in danger from leaks. No, what you've got to have is a small, highly efficient outfit that reports straight to the top and keeps itself pretty much to itself. Well, you can give it what name you like. We happen to call ourselves Special Investigations Agency.'

He stood for a moment tautly considering whether he had said all he had meant to.

'Let me tell you one thing more,' he added at last. 'And that's this: the Special Investigations Agency has never lacked work.'

He strode abruptly back to his bare table, pulled out his chair and sat down.

'Now,' he said, 'about this particular matter.'

Ghote leaned forward.

'You may have thought, Inspector, that you were dealing with nothing more than a piece of damned dacoity. Let me assure you that you couldn't be more wrong. Hector Strongbow was shot dead as a deliberate act. And I can tell you precisely who ordered that act.'

A fierce jet of satisfaction went through Ghote. So he was going to find out after all who had killed the American.

'I can tell you who ordered the death,' Colonel Mehta said. 'But I cannot give you one single name.'

With an effort Ghote kept his face impassive. But his thoughts were bitter. He was going to be cheated. He was going to be prevented from doing the thing he existed for.

'I said just now that my outfit was kept pretty busy,' Colonel

Mehta went on. 'Well, a good many of our activities are concerned with one organization. They're a body you won't ever have heard of. And yet one day, if things go their way, every man jack of them will have their names in the papers week in week out as rulers of this country.'

For an instant Ghote wondered whether the trim figure sitting in front of him, elbows on the table, might not be someone he was dreaming about. Every word seemed to be leading more and more rapidly away from reality.

'Inspector.'

Colonel Mehta barked it out like an order.

'Inspector, you think all this is a lot of ruddy fantasy, don't you?'

'No, sir. That is, sir . . . Sir, it is hard to believe.'

'Yes, Inspector, it's hard to believe. Though I should have thought the body of Hector Strongbow would have convinced you. That was real enough, wasn't it?'

'Yes, sir, it was real. But all the same, a group that may one day rule this country and yet no one has heard of it . . .'

'Exactly, Inspector. That's precisely its strength. It has a name but scarcely anything else that you can lay your hands on. It's called "India First" and it consists of one small group of leaders plus a considerable number of agents. Now, hardly one of those agents knows more than two of the others, just the chap he gets his orders from and the chap he passes orders to. So there's nowhere you can get at them. And yet, when India First thinks its time has come, it will spring into life and, in a couple of hours even, you won't be able to move an inch without bumping up against one of its men.'

He leaned back a little in his heavy chair.

'You know what I sometimes call India First, Inspector? I call it a revolution in embryo. It's there. It's tiny. But given the right conditions it will change overnight from a little group of outcasts into the lawful government of this country. And who'll be the traitors then, eh?'

He sat looking at the inspector in silence. It was a good while before Ghote ventured to speak.

'And it is India First that you suspect of killing Mr Hector Strongbow?' he said.

'I bloody well don't suspect them. I know. It's stamped with their hallmark, sheer bloody efficiency. I've thought for a long time that they had a man inside at Trombay. With the boys there producing plutonium as all the world knows they do, they were bound to try to infiltrate. You can see what happened. This chappie spotted Hector Strongbow sneaking around, realized a little later from the bloody paper that he was a trained physicist and a nuclear disarming fanatic and put in a report, pretty sharp. Then his masters acted.'

The colonel paused to let Ghote absorb this train of events. But a very different thought had entered the inspector's head. He sat rigidly on his hard chair and voiced it.

'Sir,' he said, 'if Mr Hector Strongbow had found out something at Trombay that was meant to be secret, was it not just as much in the interests of Special Investigations Agency that he should not broadcast it to all the world?'

Colonel Mehta's neat eyebrows rose.

'Yes, Inspector,' he said, 'it was. Our interests are identical. India First wants India's secrets to stay secret just as much as we do.'

'Sir,' Ghote said, 'I read the newspapers. I know what goes on in other countries. In some places, sir, if a foreigner came across a secret to do with atomic energy their Secret Service would not let him live.'

Colonel Mehta grunted.

'You're quite right, Inspector,' he said. 'I can't pretend I'm crying any tears for Mr Strongbow. But there are strict orders for a case like that. We have to bring the chappie in for trial. For trial in camera if necessary, but fair and honest trial.'

'Sir, if you are not crying tears for Mr Strongbow, I am. He was killed, Colonel. You say it was on the orders of the leaders of India First. Very well, it becomes my duty to find those men and charge them with conspiracy to murder.'

Colonel Mehta laughed.

'If they ever let us catch them alive,' he said, 'we'll charge them with a sight more than the murder of one American tourist. But your brief is rather different, Inspector. It isn't concerned with Hector Strongbow. It's concerned with his brother.'

'His brother? With Professor Gregory Strongbow?'

'Yes, Inspector. You see, the situation there is rather tricky. According to my information, the professor had left for a visit to Poona before his brother got back from Trombay. It looks as if Hector was hurrying over to Poona to consult his brother when he was killed. But the question arises: had he in the twenty-four hours between his visit to Trombay and his death managed to give his brother just a hint of what he knew?'

'You mean he might have telephoned him?' Ghote asked.

'Telephoned? Don't be a bloody fool, man. You don't put information like that on an open telephone wire in any circumstances. Even Hector would want to keep it strictly to himself till he blew the gaff. That's just first principles.'

Ghote sat in silence. The colonel's reasoning, now he came to look at it, was perfectly correct. In this new world he had stumbled into, a world of distrust in every direction, everyday reactions no longer applied.

But he would have preferred not to have been called a bloody fool to his face.

'Right,' said the colonel. 'Now, if it turns out that Professor Strongbow did get a message of some sort from his brother, India First is going to get to know. You can bet your boots they're working full out on that this very minute.'

Ghote risked a question.

'How would they do this, sir?'

'Oh, a dozen ways. They'll have men making casual enquiries at his hotel. I dare say they'll contrive to search his baggage. It wouldn't be too difficult.'

'No, sir.'

'They won't want to kill a second American visitor unless they have to. But if they do find out he knows something, they'll risk raising double hell all right to stop him talking. And double hell they'll get. I hear your professor saw the American Consul this afternoon. If there's a second death, we'll be forced to kick up such a shindy nothing else will matter. So, if only for that, I need to know just what the situation is before India First does. And that's where you come in.'

'Me, sir?'

'You, Inspector. If the professor does know something, he'll very likely decide to play his cards pretty close to his chest till he gets back to America. So it's up to you to gain his confidence. You'll have every opportunity. You can go on carrying out your investigation, outwardly. But remember, your real objective is quite different. You're there for one thing: to find out just how much Professor Strongbow knows.'

Inspector Ghote approached the Queen's Imperial Grand Hotel in a state of inner tempestuousness echoed ironically by the churning anger of the sea in the great sweep of the bay on to which the hotel looked. A strong wind, which had sprung up with the suddenness usual at this time of year, was sweeping across the broad boulevard of Marine Drive. Even in the darkness of early evening the crashing of the waves beyond was disturbingly evident.

The Inspector felt his worst forebodings had been fulfilled. He had been violently uprooted from the familiar network of his everyday activities. He had been deprived of the sense of support they gave him in whatever difficulties he might encounter. And he had been abruptly left to float in a stormy darkness.

A task had been imposed on him which he knew he had to carry out however much it went against the grain. He had to discover from this American in the hour of his bereavement whether his brother had succeeded in confiding anything to him before he had been killed, and what it was that had been said. And one thing was plain. The American would not be ready to tell him. If he had been the sort of person to pour out his troubles to any sympathetic listener, everything would have come out already.

But now confidences would have to be prised out of him. It was a hateful duty. In the short time he had known Gregory Strongbow he had come to have a strong feeling of respect for him. And together they had joined in the chase of the bullock driver and had brought it to a successful conclusion. They had shared that and it had made them, if only a little, friends.

And now it had become a duty to use that friendship to extract from the American something he would prefer to keep secret. Worse, he would have to pass on what he had learned without letting the American know he was doing it.

It might not have been so bad, if he was not feeling so strongly the tug of his proper calling. He ought not to be tricking secrets out of innocent foreigners. He ought to be finding out who had killed Hector Strongbow. And, to add to it, he had been ordered to pretend he was doing exactly this. He would have to carry out all the stages of a murder investigation, and yet stop himself thinking of it as the thing he was doing. The temptation would be there all the time. The familiar procedures would have to be merely gone through, a series of meaningless rituals. And at every moment they would tempt him to give them his full allegiance.

But he would not succumb. If worming a secret out of Gregory Strongbow was to be his task, he would do it.

He climbed the spread of marble steps, traced over by a web of black cracks, and entered the huge, ultra-decorated pile of the hotel.

He was not, however, to have his unwanted meeting with Gregory Strongbow as soon as he had expected.

In the hotel foyer, a deserted area of chequered tiles where four or five isolated groups of wicker chairs clustered round stumpy, dust-covered palms in squat wooden tubs, a tall figure hastened towards him. He wore a dark, flapping European-style suit, much creased and ink-stained, and walked with curious, erratic, over-long strides. Ghote had recognized him at once. He was a journalist, writer of a daily column, a man called Dharmadhikar, known to everybody by his initials, V. V.

'Inspector, Inspector.'

V. V. began to speak, in a loud, insistent voice, well before he had reached his target. Although the big foyer was temporarily deserted except for the hotel receptionist distantly at work behind her big counter, Ghote experienced a violent desire to put a finger to his lips and shush down this strident noise.

'Inspector Ghote, the very fellow I was wanting to see.'

'Good evening,' Ghote said. 'But I regret I have important business.'

V. V. caught hold of his elbow with a large, bony hand.

'Ah ha,' he said. 'It is no doubt business with Professor Gregory Strongbow?'

Ghote had half-admitted it before his sense of discretion caught up with him.

'It is police matters,' he eventually said with a jerk of stiffness.

'Yes, yes, indeed,' V. V. replied. 'Police matters, of course. The killing of Hector Strongbow is a police matter most certainly. But, Inspector Ghote, ask yourself whether it is not more. Ask yourself whether it is not a public matter also.'

'I did not say it was the murder of Mr Strongbow.'

'You did not, Inspector Ghote. But that is the business I have to talk with you. The murder of Mr Hector Strongbow, brother of a most distinguished foreign visitor, whom I have had the honour this moment to see.'

'Professor Strongbow?' Ghote said. 'Where is he, please?'

The gangling journalist's eyelids drooped for a moment over his prominent eyes.

'I make note that it is Professor Strongbow you are wishing to see,' he said.

'Well, what if it is so? His brother has been killed. Is it so extraordinary that someone from the police should wish to talk with him?'

V. V.'s eyes were wide open now.

'But what will Professor Gregory Strongbow say?' he asked. 'Will he wish to state complaints about the conduct of investigation, Inspector Ghote?'

Ghote was filled suddenly with the thought that Gregory Strongbow would be quite right to complain. The investigation was taking place only as a front for something quite different.

'I cannot discuss,' he said.

'But, Inspector, the public has a right to know that this investigation is being conducted full steam ahead. That is something you must agree, isn't it?'

'I have no time for Press questioning now,' Ghote replied.

'Then you do not agree? You consider this is a matter to hush up? Remember, Inspector Ghote, please, that there have been other attempts to hush up cases considered inconvenient by the Police Department.'

'It is not question of hushing up.'

V. V. leaned his bony face down over Ghote's.

'Then be so kind as to give me main outline of police activity to date,' he said.

Brusquely Ghote tugged his elbow from the journalist's grip.

'I regret,' he said, 'I have urgent business.'

Business, he thought to himself, which I would much rather put off and put off till at last it is all forgotten.

'Very well, Inspector Ghote, then may I say that the inspector in charge of the Strongbow case refused to comment when asked whether the police were not totally baffled?'

Ghote felt as if a huge, leather-winged insect was battering and buzzing at him without prospect of abatement. With a spasm of pure irritation he plunged out of the journalist's reach. Only when he was at the far end of the big chequer-tiled foyer did he turn round defiantly.

'You may say nothing, nothing,' he shouted.

Coldly furious, he set out to find Professor Strongbow. It took him some time, but at last he ran him to earth in the hotel's Bulbul Permit Room. The remains of his anger flared in a last bitter thought. He should have guessed, he said to himself, that an American would be found in the sole place in the building where it was permitted to consume alcohol in public.

And then the bitterness evaporated. He went across the room to the high-backed cane sofa where the unacademic-looking Professor Strongbow was sitting, feeling that he was calm enough to set about his unpleasant task with some subtlety. He noticed with relief that Shakuntala Brown was not there. Perhaps after all the professor would be willing to say more about his brother when he was sure of not being interrupted.

But the moment the big, broad-shouldered American spotted Ghote he leaped to his feet.

'Ah, it's you, Inspector,' he said. 'At last.'

To Ghote's complete surprise there was an unmistakable note of anger in his voice.

4

Ghote felt a sense of painful shock. Of all the things that might happen he had not expected that Gregory Strongbow would turn on him. And the American had made no attempt to keep his voice low. At the sound of his biting words the barman had looked up from behind his high, dark-wood barricade and the knot of bearers standing in a far corner had moved as one man to stare in his direction.

'Yes, at last,' the American repeated, no less angrily and no less noisily. 'I'm delighted to find that someone's going to bother to tell me something after all. I thought I was going to be left here for ever hearing not a damned thing. It's only my brother who's been killed, you know.'

'Professor, please,' Ghote said. 'I have been doing my best.'

'Naturally you've been doing your best. Damn it, that's your pure duty.'

'But what more can I do?'

'I'll tell you what more you can do. You can come out with the truth. I've been doing some thinking since we got back to Bombay. And I'm not sure that I haven't been soft-soaped all the way along the line.'

'Sir, I assure you—'

And abruptly Ghote realized that if the American had not been soft-soaped up till now, the process was about to begin. He himself had come into the permit room, with its new wall paintings of lovers, nightingales and winebibbers all around, with just that intention. He found he could not go on.

He hung his head.

When Gregory Strongbow started speaking again, Ghote did not at first even listen. Then suddenly he awoke to the fact that the American's voice was no longer rasping and angry. He paid attention.

'Believe me,' the American was saying, 'I don't ordinarily behave like that. But I guess I'm all to pieces. Look at it my way. I'm kind of disorientated. It's partly that it's all so different out here, but I just don't know any longer what's the truth and what isn't.'

Ghote felt a flood of sympathy for the big American, looking at this moment so very foreign with a lock of brown, curly hair flopping down on to his forehead and the blue eyes underneath clouded and pained.

He sat down opposite him on the edge of a big, low armchair and leaned forward. Only to realize that he was not able to say the things that had sprung to his mind. He would have liked to have burst out that he shared the American's sense of having his familiar ties suddenly sheared away. He would have liked to have told him that the two of them were in the same situation. And instead he was going to have to sever yet one more link that the American had with reality. He was going to have to give him, in place of the reassurance he was entitled to, a string of half-truths about his brother's death and its investigation.

'Professor Strongbow,' he said cautiously, 'I do not think you need to have these feelings. I was about to assure you that police methods in this country are not so different from police methods anywhere else. We are devoting full resources to our enquiries.'

He saw in the American's handsome face the effect his words were having. There was a closing-up, a withdrawal. It was unmistakably plain.

'Okay, so you're doing fine,' the American said. 'But you still aren't telling me too much about it.'

'That has been simply due to lack of proper opportunity,' Ghote replied. 'But I would tell you now. There is, to begin with, a most thorough search going on in Poona for the men whom Bholu, the bullock driver, betrayed.'

'A good many hours have passed since you got that information out of Bholu,' Gregory Strongbow said mulishly.

'Of course. But kindly do not think those men will be seated at home awaiting arrival of police. It would take a great deal of time to establish where they may be in concealment.'

'And that is all being left to the Poona police?'

'Naturally I am putting faith in the men on the spot,' Ghote answered. 'In due course if results fail to eventuate I would go to Poona myself. But in the meantime I am trusting them to do their work in a proper manner.'

'But what if they don't do their work in a proper manner? My brother's killers get clear away, I suppose. Well, I don't intend to let that happen. I brought Hector over here, and I mean to see the whole matter of his death finally cleared up.'

'Be certain the Police Department is not lacking in efficiency,' Ghote replied. 'But are you yourself even giving fill cooperation? Already it seems to me that you have been unwilling to tell all you could about your brother.'

The American, who had just picked up his glass of faintly sizzling whisky and soda, set it down sharply on the dark, polished table with the big brass ashtray dead in its centre.

'Just what do you mean by that?' he snapped.

Ghote was a little surprised at the vigour of his reaction. But, having at last brought the conversation to the point he had been manoeuvring towards, he decided he must press forward.

'I mean, for example,' he said, 'that you have never told where your brother went when you each decided to make a different expedition yesterday morning.'

Watching the American closely, he saw a new wariness come into the blue eyes.

'Well, if I didn't tell you, it was pure oversight,' Gregory Strongbow answered after a moment. 'Hector went over to Trombay, to the Atomic Energy place. That was his field, you know.'

'It was an official visit?' Ghote asked.

The American shrugged with noticeable carelessness.

'I don't think so. Hector just said he'd take off for Trombay when I told him I wanted to see the hydraulics labs out at Poona. I guess he hoped they'd show him around if he just checked in there.'

'I see. And is this what happened?'

'I don't exactly know. He spent the whole morning away, so I guess he must at least have gotten inside the place.'

'But, since you did not see him again after this visit, you naturally do not know about it?' Ghote asked.

'That's not exactly so,' the American replied. 'If we're going to put so much emphasis on me telling you everything, then I'd better dot all the i's and cross all the t's. I did as a matter of fact see Hector after he'd been to Trombay.'

Ghote felt his heart pounding. He knew he had to be icily careful at this point. He leaned even further forward. The faint bitterish smell of the American's whisky impinged on his nostrils.

'And now please,' he said, 'I want you to think very carefully. Did your brother say anything to you, when you saw him, to give a clue as to why he should go out to Poona?'

But Gregory Strongbow answered sharply.

'I already said I have no idea why Hector was going out to Poona. I just suppose he changed his mind and thought he'd join me.'

'What was it he said to you when he met you after going to Trombay then?'

'He didn't say very much about anything,' the American answered.

'But, please, he may have said something which would give a clue to help investigation.'

'I tell you he did not. We just happened to meet for a few minutes, a few seconds even, outside this Victoria Terminus you have. I had my train to catch. I just saw him and called to him and we exchanged a few words.'

'This was outside V. T. Station? You did not go to a restaurant for a cup of tea, perhaps?'

'Certainly we did not. I already said: it was just a few words spoken right there on the sidewalk with half a million people milling all around.'

'I beg your pardon then.'

Gregory Strongbow looked a little mollified.

'These few words,' Ghote went on. 'Can you remember exactly what your brother said?'

And abruptly the American's anger returned.

'No, I cannot,' he said. 'And if I could, I don't think I would repeat them to you. We had a short, private conversation between two brothers. That's all.'

'But it would be of great practical value to know what was in your brother's mind at that point.'

'No, it would not.'

'Please, I think you are obstructing my investigation with this attitude. You seem totally unwilling to tell things I need to know. And yet you are free enough with giving out Press interviews.'

'I have not given out Press interviews.'

'Excuse me, I met a journalist as I entered the hotel who told me he had come from seeing you only that moment.'

And suddenly Professor Strongbow grinned.

'I've done it again,' he said. 'I've let myself get all worked up. You're perfectly right: I did give a Press interview. Or at least when this guy came up and said he'd written a piece about Hector in his column I just told him that I hadn't really anything to add. He asked me a couple more questions and I simply replied "No comment." I certainly told him nothing I haven't told you.'

And Ghote decided he would have to leave it at that. It was more than obvious that Gregory Strongbow had not the least intention of telling him what the talk with his brother outside V. T. Station had been about. Or at least not at this time. He would simply have to report what he had found out to Colonel Mehta and try again later.

The thought was not pleasant.

Within an hour Ghote was back at the Queen's Imperial Grand Hotel. The hour had been every bit as hateful as he had expected. Colonel Mehta, sitting as upright as ever in his scoured bare room, had done nothing to conceal his anger that his orders had been baulked. This, his expression implied as clearly as if he had written it out under Ghote's very nose, this is what comes of working with damned inefficient civilian police.

Ghote left feeling that he had let down the whole force from the commissioner to the newest constable. And his outlook was not improved by the thought that the task in which he had partially failed was not what he should have been doing in any case. He ought to be at this moment sitting in his office urging on the people at Poona, and instead he was going back to Professor Strongbow to see how quickly he could persuade him to change his mind and tell him in full what his brother had said on the crowded pavement outside V. T. Station.

All the way to the hotel he scolded the driver of his truck for not going fast enough. And the driver, a dried-up, nutty-faced long-service constable whose whole life lay in nurturing this particular blue Dodge, had dourly listened and had got through the jostling traffic at exactly his usual speed.

At the Queen's Imperial Grand Ghote went straight back to the Bulbul Permit Room. But Gregory Strongbow was no longer there. A quick tour of the public rooms failed to produce either the American or even his Tourist Department guide, Miss Shakuntala Brown. Ghote went back to the big chequer-tiled foyer and over to the reception desk.

Behind its glossy teak rampart the receptionist he had noticed earlier on was still sitting, perched on a heavy, high stool and busy sorting through a pile of cards from a wooden index file behind her. Ghote saw now that she was a Parsee. She appeared to be about forty-five or so, though it was difficult to tell as she plainly spent a lot of time contriving the sprightlier manner of someone ten or more years younger. But tell-tale lines of anxiety round her eyes betrayed her and her cheeks were a little hollower than they should have been.

On the narrow top of the teak counter, around which there ran a little brass rail giving it a faintly nautical touch, there was a fretwork stand about six inches high bearing a strip of white card on which there was written in purple ink the words 'Miss Mira Jehangir'. Evidently the Queen's Imperial Grand did what it could to emulate the practices of the glossy new Nataraj and the newer Shalimar.

'Miss Jehangir?' Ghote enquired.

It had occurred to him that it was more than likely that the person behind the desk would not correspond to the name on the notice. But his pessimism was unfounded. The receptionist swiftly spread a thin, bejewelled hand across the cards she was sorting over and looked up.

'Can I help you?' she said.

'I am looking for Professor Gregory Strongbow.'

'What name is it, please?' Mira Jehangir asked.

Ghote was a little surprised to receive this counterquestion but he gave his name without demur.

Mira Jehangir picked up a pencil from the shelf beneath the gleaming deck of the mildly nautical counter and carefully wrote Ghote's name down.

'And the nature of your business?' she enquired blandly.

'Professor Strongbow is expecting me,' Ghote replied stiffly.

'I see. Then I shall have to find out whether we have a Professor Strongbow on our register.'

'But he is guest at the hotel. I am wishing to know simply whether he is in or not.'

But Mira Jehangir slipped down from her tall, heavy stool and without another word turned to the wooden index on the wall behind her. She began opening and shutting the drawers with a great parade of business efficiency.

'Yes,' she said, after some little while, 'I can put you in touch with Professor Strongbow.'

'He is in his room? What number please? I will go up.'

'He is most probably in the Bulbul Permit Room,' Mira Jehangir replied, turning back to the inspector. 'Like many foreign guests he spends much of his time there.'

Ghote noted calmly that only an instant before she had denied knowledge whether Professor Strongbow was staying at the hotel at all.

'I have just come from the permit room,' he said sharply. 'I know very well that Professor Strongbow is not there. Is he in his room, please?'

'I will make enquiries,' Mira Jehangir replied.

Her eyes flitted round the big foyer as if she hoped that something would happen to prevent her taking this unequivocal step. But evidently she found nothing. She moved along to a house telephone, of a pattern obsolete enough not to belie her desk's air of belonging to the early age of steam navigation.

She asked for the professor. A voice at the other end spoke, but Ghote was unable to hear what it said. Miss Jehangir replied with a guarded 'Yes' and listened again. At last she put the ridged tube of the receiver back on its curling hooks.

'Professor Strongbow is not able to receive visitors,' she said.

Ghote frowned.

'You did not tell who was asking for him,' he said. 'Inspector Ghote.'

'I have your name,' Mira Jehangir replied, tapping her notepad with a long, pointed, deep pink nail.

A suspicion came into Ghote's mind.

'You spoke with Professor Strongbow in person?' he demanded.

'Professor Strongbow is not in his room.'

'But you told you had rung him.'

'I think there must have been a misunderstanding. I rang only the bearers outside the professor's suite. They informed me that he was not there.'

'And you do not know where he is?'

Ghote stood in front of the elegant, evasive Parsee and put his question with force.

'I cannot help you,' she replied, her eyes flicking into the background.

Ghote turned away. He felt furious. He ought to have made arrangements to keep in touch with the professor. He might be gone for hours now and there would be no chance of making any progress with his distasteful task and perhaps getting back to his proper work.

He stood disconsolately beside one of the five potted palms islanded in the cold sea of the foyer.

Suddenly a voice whispered from the other side of the dusty, drooping spines of leaves.

'Excuse, sahib.'

Ghote swung round.

Standing discreetly behind the palm so as to be almost invisible from the reception desk was one of the hotel bearers, an elderly man with sad eyes wearing a much-darned white uniform. When Ghote looked at him he salaamed deeply.

'Sahib, you ask for Strongbow sahib?' the man said.

'Yes,' Ghote said. 'Yes, yes, I did.'

'I am Strongbow sahib's room bearer, sahib.'

'Do you know where he is?'

'No, sahib.'

'Then what—?'

'But, sahib, he ask me if he shall take coat to wait for friend out in Marine Drive. And, sahib, I told most definitely coat would be necessary. I told immense great waves at this time of year. Sahib might get very badly wetted to the skin. Most definitely coat, I told.'

'Quite right, quite right,' Ghote said heartily. 'But did Strongbow sahib say where in Marine Drive he was going to wait for his friend?'

'Oh, no, sahib. If Strongbow sahib wanted to wait there, I would not be asking anything about that. Only telling coat is most definitely necessary.'

'Yes, yes. A coat would be very necessary,' Ghote agreed, cursing inwardly that the bearer's devotion did not extend beyond recommending appropriate clothing for the prevailing weather.

He gave the man a small tip and hurried outside.

What he had learned was disquieting. Why should a respectable American visitor choose to meet someone in the open air on a night like this? The wind was whipping across the broad span of Marine Drive outside and down in the sea the waves were crashing and thundering against the sea wall.

Going down the sweeping marble steps of the old hotel he could not prevent himself breaking into a trot, though it was hardly the dignified behaviour the police force might expect from one of its officers. Luckily, his driver had not deserted the truck. He had its bonnet-flap back and was wiping the top of the engine with a small piece of greasy rag.

'Good man,' Ghote said. 'Now listen, I want to see if I can find someone waiting somewhere along Marine Drive. He should not be too hard to spot, a tall American. He would be wearing a coat.'

The driver gave his engine one more careful wipe.

'Yes,' he said, 'he would need a coat. Along there waves have been breaking right across road.'

He pointed into the middle distance like a conscientious guide showing a visitor a cherished view.

'Hurry, man, hurry,' Ghote snapped. 'We will not find him by standing here talking about waves.'

'Very good, very good, Inspector sahib,' the driver replied patiently.

He gave one final, obsessional flick at his engine with the rag, clamped down the bonnet and climbed into his seat.

'Which way, Inspector? Left towards Colaba first?'

He nosed the truck to the edge of the long sweep of the boulevard and waited.

'No,' Ghote said perversely, 'go the other way, right, up towards Chaupati.'

The driver shrugged and swung out into the broad road.

It had begun to rain and there was scarcely anybody about. Away ahead of them an earnest citizen was marching along with an umbrella held almost horizontally to one side in an effort to keep at least a quarter of himself dry. As they drew up to him a sharp cross-gust turned the umbrella almost instantaneously inside-out. Ghote saw him gather the spiky remains together and stride away bare-headed and resigned.

But this was the only sign of life. Hard though Ghote peered into the squally darkness, he could not see the least trace of a tall coated American waiting in this unlikely place for an unknown friend. Certainly the sea side of the road was totally bare. No one in their senses would walk there, exposed to the wild swirls of spray that were flung at intervals over the protecting wall as the great waves hurled themselves against it.

Even such traffic as there was went at speed. Driving slowly along on the sea side as they made their way up to Chaupati, it was easy to understand why everyone else was hurrying. The biggest of the waves looked as if they were bound to crash over the narrow top of the sea-wall, and each looked powerful enough to catch the truck up and sweep it into the wind-tossed hedge dividing the two carriageways.

'Switch on the headlights,' Ghote said.

The alternate glare and shadow from the big blocks of flats made peering into the darkness doubly difficult.

The driver obeyed, and with this help it was more possible to be sure that even on the far side of the road, in the comparative shelter, no one was lingering about.

They reached the tall statue of Lokmanya Tilak presiding forlornly over the deserted stretch of Chaupati Beach where in less happy times he had exhorted great crowds to rebellion. And still there was not the least sign of the big American.

'We had better go the other way,' Ghote said grumpily.

He realized that it would have been much more sensible to have taken that direction first. A rendezvous was plainly more likely down near the busy streets of the Fort than up at this end of Marine Drive, with its respectable, pastel-coloured blocks of expensive flats.

'Get a move on,' he muttered half to himself as the truck swung across the road in a wide U-turn.

'Better not go too fast, Inspector sahib,' the driver said. 'It is hard to see, and we may have missed him already.'

In deference to the fact that the man had been right about which direction they ought to have taken in the first place Ghote let this pass in silence.

The truck headed back along the wide sweep of the bay, its headlights picking out every now and again a heavy plume of white spray whirling far across the road.

'My wife's cousin's son was drowned just here four or five years ago,' the driver said. 'He was out playing just at the end of the monsoon like this, and a wave swept him right over the wall. In one second he was gone.'

Ghote refused to let himself take this remark at more than its face value. But he edged forward on the worn seat of the truck and peered even harder into the tricky darkness surrounding them.

5

The headlights of the slowly moving police truck picked out the high, looming walls of the Brabourne Stadium nearly at the far end of the long sweep of Marine Drive. Inspector Ghote sighed.

'If Professor Strongbow was ever here at all,' he said, 'we have certainly missed—'

His driver must have caught sight of what had stopped him in mid-sentence at the same instant as he had. Jammed-hard brakes sent the truck skewing wildly round on the wave-wetted surface of the wide road. Before it had come to rest Ghote was out and running forward with every ounce of his strength.

'Stop,' he shouted. 'Stop. Police.'

His cry must have reached the group of struggling figures on the far side of the road close up against the low top of the sea wall. Three of them turned for an instant and looked over in his direction. But it was for an instant only. Then they swung back to the fourth figure, the tall man in the light coat already down on the ground. With one concerted heave they raised him like a log above their shoulder level.

'Stop,' Ghote shouted again.

But he knew it was useless. Long before he could reach them the three attackers with a last lunge would send the prone figure in the flapping coat swinging over the low top of the sea wall. And with the great waves hurling themselves eagerly forward he would have no chance after that.

The three dark shapes ducked a little as they gathered themselves for the throw.

And with total suddenness there came the huge roar of a giant wave swinging high over the top of the wall. The solid block of water hit the struggling group and swept all four figures tumbling before it.

Ghote stopped and stood with staring eyes.

Several moments passed before he was able at all to make out what had happened. But when he did so he saw the scene with extraordinary clarity. The huge wave had collapsed into a mere sheet of swirling water as it spread across the wide road, and behind it the four figures it had tumbled down were outlined like statues. The three attackers, having been on their feet, had been hurled farther into the roadway than their victim. As Ghote watched they crouched or knelt in the rushing sea water, their faces still turned towards the point where they had intended to hurl their victim to his death.

It was clear that they must have dropped Gregory Strongbow the moment the wave hit them. He was a good deal nearer the low sea wall, already on his feet and staring wildly around as if looking for some new danger.

After the screaming roar of the wave at its highest there was now by comparison almost complete silence. In this point of lull even the swirling water on the road seemed still.

And then Ghote heard something new.

He swung round towards the sea. A second wave, out-topping the first, like a full-grown brother overshadowing the stripling, was progressing towards them with a silent speed that belied its size.

The three attackers must have seen the mass of dark water at the same moment. They put their heads down into their arms and braced themselves for the impact. The American, looking in their direction, had not yet realized what was happening.

Ghote put his head down and pelted forward.

He reached the American before the water hit the sea wall beneath them. He seized him round the chest and actually lifted him off his feet with the force of his dash forward.

Then the water came over the wall. For a long minute everything was chaos. Breath-crushing, choking salt sea was everywhere, first hurling itself forward, then whirling back in an undertow almost as powerful.

And, after what seemed a time too long to measure, at last there came something approaching peace.

From the foot of the inner side of the sea wall where he had calculated that a narrow strip of safety might lie Ganesh Ghote struggled to his feet. Beside him the big American groaned loudly in the darkness. Ghote reached out to him.

'Can you run?' he said.

'Yes. Yes, I can run.'

'This way.'

He took the American by the hand and together they dashed across the wide area of the road in the direction of the police truck. Water, inches deep, tugged at their feet.

But it seemed that there was to be no third wave. The sequence had altered. Away in the distance Ghote heard a comparatively puny mass of water break harmlessly to pieces against the protective concrete blocks in the darkness below. And equally, it appeared, the human danger had vanished. Hardly had they reached the truck when the driver hurried up.

'Inspector, are you OK?'

'Yes, yes. We managed to get into the shelter of the top of the wall.'

'The others have gone, Inspector. When the water had gone I saw them running. I tried to chase. But it was no good.'

'All right,' Ghote said. 'It does not matter. But we must take Professor Strongbow back to his hotel. He is soaked to the skin at least.'

He was no drier himself. The two of them sat in the back of the truck with the cold sea water seeping down on to the floor all round.

After a little Ghote put a question.

'What happened, Professor, please?'

The American lifted his head.

'I got a call at the hotel,' he said. 'It was someone who said they could tell me more about Hector if I met them on my own. He said to wait on Marine Drive by this Brabourne Stadium. Is that the name?'

'Yes, yes. But who was this person?'

The American groaned a little.

'He wouldn't give his name,' he answered. 'Or at least that's what Shakuntala said. She took the call.'

'I see. Then you went to the place indicated?'

'Yeah. I waited around a while, and then these guys came up. I expected there would be only one, but it didn't seem to matter. They seemed to want me to go over to the far side of the street with them. I thought it was to go where there was no one around. So we crossed over. And then they went for me. I did what I could, but it was three against one.'

He looked out into the darkness as the truck hummed its way steadily along the wide sweep of the boulevard. The waves were beating rhythmically against the masonry of the sea wall sending high towers of spray flaunting into night air. He shivered and turned to Ghote as if for reassurance.

But Ghote was lost in thought. And for all the rest of the short trip back to the hotel he remained silent. Silent and worried.

The American put no questions. It seemed he too had plenty to think about.

Ghote had stayed in Gregory Strongbow's suite at the hotel only long enough to make sure he was comfortable and to extract a promise from him not to go out again in any circumstances. Then, wet and cold though he was, he had hurried down to the hotel foyer where he remembered having seen a public telephone.

Quickly he slid the heavy door of the booth to behind him and rang the number Colonel Mehta had given him. It was supposed to reach him at any hour of the day or night. Listening to the sound of ringing at the far end, Ghote hoped that for once one of the colonel's arrangements might have broken down.

But abruptly the ringing ceased and a voice he recognized at once as Colonel Mehta's asked sharply who was calling. Briefly Ghote gave him the bare facts about the attack on Gregory Strongbow.

'I suppose you didn't catch any of the damned fellows.'

Ghote felt obliged to defend himself. After all, for a mere policeman he had done well enough.

'No, Colonel, we did not catch. My driver gave chase but they had too much start. Otherwise we might have got it out of one of them who ordered this attack.'

What reply Colonel Mehta made to this counter-thrust Ghote never knew. His voice suddenly receded so far into the distance that it was impossible to make out even one word.

'Colonel. I am sorry, Colonel, but you have gone very faint.'

At the far end Ghote could make out that the colonel was shouting.

'Something seems to have gone wrong with the line, Colonel,' he said.

'Listen, man, listen.'

'Yes, Colonel.'

Ghote listened with fierce intentness. He saw that his damp clothes were making a small puddle on the floor of the telephone booth.

'You will not get far along those lines, Inspector.'

'You believe this attack was not connected with the killing of Mr Hector Strongbow?' Ghote asked.

'Don't shout, man, don't shout. I can hear you perfectly well. And of course our friends are out to get the professor now. But they're too bloody clever to let you catch them through one of their strong-arm men. Chaps like that just work for money and no questions asked.'

'Yes, Colonel, but—'

The far, far, tinny voice at the other end broke in. Ghote stopped and strained to hear.

'No, Inspector, what you forget is that you're up against some very good chaps. Don't you believe all this nonsense about the Indian inability to carry out any plan with a modicum of simple efficiency. It just isn't bloody well true. I know. I knew it in the Army. We didn't stand for inefficiency there, I can tell you.'

In Ghote's right ear, sensitized now to a high point, picking out the faint crackle of this lecture, there came suddenly a single click. The noise was as effective as a pistol shot.

Ghote involuntarily jerked the receiver away from his head. When he gingerly listened again the colonel was still talking, but his voice had returned to normal strength. Ghote decided to pretend he had missed nothing.

'The finest fighting force in the world,' the colonel was saying. 'You can't beat the simple Indian jaiwan as a fighting man, Inspector, and don't you forget it. It may have pleased certain people at certain times to make out that nothing Indian was any good. But that doesn't accord with the bloody facts. Who was the first man to discover the laws of gravity, eh?'

Ghote realized with a hot flush of embarrassment that this was a question he was expected to answer. An enamel-bright recollection of himself at the age of eleven sitting in a long desk cramped against half a dozen school mates came into his mind. He could see, as if it was this moment, Mr Merryweather, their implacable Anglo-Indian teacher, standing in front of the dusty whitish blackboard and rapping out the story of Newton and the apple.

But he knew that, of all the answers to give, the name Isaac Newton would be the least acceptable.

'I don't know his name,' Colonel Mehta snapped out at the other end of the line. 'But I can tell you this much, man. He was an Indian, an Indian. And atomic theory. What about that? All buttoned up by Indian sages hundreds of years ago. And we even had a perfectly adequate flying machine in those days, so they tell me. And cotton cloth. Where was the earliest known sample in the world found? In the Sind Desert, man. In the Sind Desert.'

Ghote's eyes focused on a short message some vandal had scratched on the sacred dark wood of one of the panels at the back of the booth. 'I love Gracie,' it stated. He wondered how long ago the desecration had taken place. No doubt the lover had long since transferred his affections to some other Betty, Milly or Rosie.

With a start he realized that the voice at the far end of the line had ceased to speak.

'Yes, sir,' he said hastily. 'But this is what I have been wondering, sir. Can I now cease attempts to find out what the professor heard from his brother? It seems India First has decided he learned something, does it not, sir?'

'No, Inspector, you cannot cease your attempts.'

Ghote thought for a few seconds.

'Please,' he said at last, 'I would like to know why.'

'Because orders are orders, man.'

'Sir, I am not army officer.'

'I don't care what you are, or who you are. You're under my command now and you do what you're bloody well told.'

'Sir, can I go to higher authority?'

'No, Inspector, you cannot. Understand this: there is no higher authority for you to go to. You've been entrusted with State secrets. Secrets no one under Prime Minister level has any right to know. So you keep them right under your hat. Now and for ever. Do you get that?'

'Yes, Colonel,' Ghote said.

It was an admission of defeat. What the colonel had said was, after all, perfectly true. In this world of darkness into which he had been plunged there were no lifelines.

'And you definitely wish me to continue to seek the professor's confidence, sir?' he said bleakly into the telephone mouthpiece.

'I most certainly do, Inspector. I have to find out what the leakage point is at Trombay. Just remember that.'

'Yes, sir. But then, sir, may I tell the professor about the existence of the India First group? Sir, already he suspects his brother's death is not simple dacoity. So I will never gain his trust if I continue to pretend the death in question was a straightforward matter, sir.'

There was a long pause at the other end. Ghote began to think he had lost the connection. But at last the Colonel answered.

'Very well. You may tell him India First exists. But not one single word about us, do you understand? As far as Professor Gregory Strongbow is concerned there is no such thing as the Special Investigations Agency.'

'Yes, sir. And thank you.'

'You may tell him that you have been charged with his personal safety, Inspector. That's so as to give you everything you need to stick close to him. And if you can't learn about that conversation outside V. T. Station under those conditions, then you'll be making a pretty poor show of things, Inspector.'

This time there was no mistaking that the phone had clicked dead. With a feeling of dull heaviness Ghote pushed open the sliding door of the dark booth.

Gregory Strongbow was alone in his suite when the inspector knocked. He came to the door, led Ghote through the curious anteroom devoted to housing a single heavy ironing board for the use of the visitor's bearer, and on into the sitting room. This was a vast, airy chamber with a number of pieces of heavy furniture all grouped round a rather small wicker table placed in the exact centre of the big, somewhat threadbare Kashmir carpet. Dominating the whole was a tall decorated mirror fixed to the wall opposite the windows. As a looking-glass the mirror had disadvantages. The chief of them was that under the glass there had been ingeniously inserted a full-length coloured picture of George, King-Emperor of India. But large areas of tarnish also detracted not a little from the mirror's usefulness.

The professor appeared to have got used to its looming presence and no longer paid it any attention. Ghote found himself constantly turning back to it.

But he made himself pay attention to business.

'Miss Brown?' he asked first. 'Is she here in your suite?'

Shakuntala Brown had been causing him a good deal of anxiety. On the way up from his conversation with Colonel Mehta he had begun thinking about the close knowledge India First seemed to have of the professor's whereabouts. And he had come to the conclusion at once that it was more than likely they had a spy close at hand. Shakuntala Brown filled the bill. He had to admit that she was not the only possibility. Two others were clearly suspect. There was V. V. Dharmadhikar for one. He certainly seemed to be taking a very keen interest in all the professor did. And then there was Miss Mira Jehangir at the reception desk downstairs. There could hardly have been a less satisfactory encounter than his brush with her earlier on.

Nevertheless Shakuntala Brown remained the most likely candidate.

'Shakuntala?' Gregory Strongbow answered. 'No, she isn't here. She was. But she went out. She'll be back though. Did you want her for something?'

'I would need to see her,' Ghote said. 'I need to hear about the telephone call she took.'

'Yes, I guess you would. Have you any idea who that caller could have been?'

'Yes,' said Ghote. 'I have.'

Gregory Strongbow looked startled.

'Already?' he said.

'There is something I ought to have told you before,' Ghote replied.

He saw the look of hope growing in the American's face and quickly continued.

'I believe you already think there is more to your brother's death than a simple killing. Well, I can tell you now that I think this also. Your brother was victim of a terrorist group, a group called India First.'

Gregory Strongbow frowned.

'A terrorist group?'

'What else?'

The American kept silent. Then he took a pace towards Ghote and looked down at him almost angrily.

'I'll tell you who else,' he said. 'By the Indian Government, or some outfit of theirs. Damn it, Trombay is an Indian Government affair, isn't it? So if Hector was killed because he went there, it stands to reason he was put out of the way by Indian Government agents.

'But it is not so,' Ghote almost shouted.

He felt a sense of outrage that anyone should make such suggestions about his country.

And the feeling must have communicated itself to the big American. At once his aggressive look softened. He put out a hand and vaguely waved Ghote down into one of the sprawling armchairs surrounding the pathetic little central wicker table, and then squatted on the edge of the next chair in the circle.

'Listen,' he said, 'I'm not claiming that India is the only country in the world that would do a thing like that. Hell, if you'd asked me three days ago I'd have said India was one of the few countries that wouldn't. But my brother is dead. I brought him over here and he's dead. Look, I'm not saying that there aren't guys working for the US who wouldn't kill someone to stop a security leak.'

'Please,' Ghote said, 'I assure you in India it is not so. It must not be so. There are orders not to deal with things in that way. I can reveal that much to you. And kindly consider this: there is such an organization as India First. It exists to make India seize an important place in the world. I assure you of this on authority I trust.'

'All right, all right,' Gregory Strongbow said.

A look of hurt was crinkling the lines round his eyes.

'Then if such an organization exists,' Ghote argued, 'is it not more likely that they killed your brother?'

Gregory Strongbow leaped to his feet.

'OK,' he said, 'I hand it to you. It is more likely. We'll go on that—'

Someone knocked at the door.

For a moment Ghote and the professor looked at each other as if this was the first move in a concerted attack. Then the American smiled.

'Relax,' he said. 'It'll be Shakuntala.'

He went to the door and opened it. Shakuntala Brown was there.

Ghote looked at her with care. She had changed her sari since the afternoon. Indeed, she looked so fresh now that this was probably where she had been while he had been talking to Gregory Strongbow. The sari she was wearing now was silk, a deep red patterned with cream circle shapes. For a moment Ghote thought it would look well on his wife, but then he decided that it was a little too restrained to reflect her personality properly. But it suited this girl's fair complexion.

'I think the inspector here wants to ask you a few questions,' the professor said to her.

She crossed the room and sat in a corner of one of the big chairs. Ghote went and sat next to her. Gregory Strongbow tactfully went over to a chair on the far side of the circle.

'It was you who took the telephone call for Professor Strongbow?' Ghote asked.

'Yes, it was me,' Shakuntala Brown said.

She spoke guardedly, with a hint of being anxious to say only the minimum necessary.

'How did that happen? That you took the call? Was it for you? Did the caller know Professor Strongbow had you as guide?'

'No, I was in here and the professor was out. I think he was down in the permit room.'

'I see. And what exactly was said?'

'Just that if Professor Strongbow wanted to know who killed his brother he should wait down by the Brabourne Stadium, on the Marine Drive side.'

'That only?'

'Yes. That was all.'

Ghote pounced.

'I thought there were instructions the professor should be alone? If that was not said, why did you leave him? You would have been useful. Perhaps his informant would not speak English.'

'They did say something about him having to be alone,' Shakuntala Brown answered in a sulky voice.

'Then why did you not tell? I asked carefully for exact particulars. Why did you say nothing of this?'

'I happened to forget that,' she said with rising sharpness.

'Miss Brown,' Ghote said, 'what exactly is your position in this business? Who sent you to work for Professor Strongbow?'

'I am employed by the State Tourism Department.'

'But you are not Indian national?'

Her back straightened as if on a spring.

'How dare you say that? How do you know? Do you want to see my passport?'

Ghote blinked.

'All right,' Shakuntala Brown said, 'I admit my father was born English. But he was an Indian citizen for five years before he died. And when he became one I became one.'

'I am sorry,' Ghote said.

He felt apologies had been called for. But he still had questions to put.

'Now,' he said, 'would you kindly tell me if anything more was said by that telephone caller?'

Shakuntala Brown's eyes ceased to flash. The wary look Ghote thought he had seen in them before returned.

'I have told you everything,' she replied.

'You said that once before. I proved that was wrong. Was there anything more?'

'Hey.'

It was Gregory Strongbow.

'Hey, listen, Inspector,' he said, 'you're questioning Shakuntala as if she was some sort of criminal. All she did was take the call.'

Inwardly Ghote could not refrain from cursing him. He wanted to do all he could for him, but if there were going to be protective, chivalrous interruptions of this sort the stock of goodwill he had for him would rapidly run out.

He turned to him now.

'Kindly understand,' he said, 'that it is most necessary to establish full particulars. I was doing that only.'

He went back to Shakuntala Brown. But the interruption had given her time to reconsider.

'Inspector,' she said, leaning earnestly forward in the big chair, 'believe me, I only want to help too. I genuinely forgot the bit about letting Professor Strongbow go to the appointment alone.'

'Very well,' Ghote said. 'But please to remember it is important to tell everything.'

He decided to seize a chance and swung round to Gregory Strongbow again.

'Is that not so, Professor?' he said. 'Is it not important to tell everything?'

He gave him a long look. From the momentary hardening of the blue eyes in the handsome face he knew his meaning had been taken. Shakuntala Brown had not been the only one to withhold information.

He waited with anxiety.

'Certainly,' Gregory Strongbow said coolly, 'certainly it's important to keep nothing back. Unless it happens to be a matter which has no concern with police enquiries.'

6

Early next morning Inspector Ghote hurried straight to the Queen's Imperial Grand Hotel. The weather had improved with its usual abruptness. But he did not let himself linger to enjoy the freshness of the light breeze coming in from the sea and the sparkle of the first sun. He knew that, had anything gone wrong at the hotel during the night, he ought to have been informed. And he had posted men enough round about both outside and in. But nevertheless he realized he would not feel happy till he had seen Gregory Strongbow with his own eyes.

He felt a strong, quite irrational attachment to the tall American with the unacademically tough set to his jaw and the eyes with the tell-tale wrinkles of concern puckering the tanned skin. This man was in a way his only point of contact with reality in the different world he had so suddenly found himself in. Colonel Mehta was no use: he was too much from another world himself. And every other contact seemed barred by the terms of his orders.

On the shallow marble steps of the ornate pile of the hotel Ghote did allow himself to pause for an instant.

He needed just one second to overcome the ugly thought that it would be his duty for the next sixteen hours or more to watch Gregory Strongbow and wait for the one moment at which he might say what it was that he had learned from his brother. And in exchange he would be feeding out half-truths about an investigation he was only pretending to control.

He ran into the hotel and made his way to the dining room.

And there was the American, sitting equably opposite Shakuntala Brown at a big table spread with a heavy white cloth and covered with complicated silver cutlery. He looked utterly at ease. The very sight of him seemed to send Ghote's anxieties sliding away off his back.

He went over.

'Good morning, Inspector,' Gregory Strongbow said, smiling. 'It's a better day. Have you had breakfast? Will you join us?'

He gestured at the laden table. In front of him two small greasy-looking eggs lay in the middle of a huge white plate surrounded by small and dark slivers of hard bacon. A large coffee cup stood to the right. Towards the centre of the table there was a toast rack containing sixteen small pieces of toast somehow suspiciously limp. Three pots for various sorts of marmalade lay beyond and to the left-hand side was an enormous silver cruet.

'I don't exactly recommend the porridge,' Gregory Strongbow said. 'There seemed to be lumps in it here and there.'

He smiled up at Ghote.

'In fact,' he said, 'I don't altogether recommend the breakfast at all. I have a feeling it's a British legacy I ought to avoid.'

'Thank you,' Ghote said, smiling too now, 'luckily perhaps, I have already eaten – fried vegetables, pickle, crisp wheat cakes, tea.'

The professor looked thoughtful.

'I guess there must be a middle way,' he said. 'Even if I have to make it just a cup of coffee like Shakuntala here.'

He looked across at Shakuntala Brown with a grin.

'Mind you,' he added, 'I'm improving the situation bit by bit. The first morning they tried to bring me something called bed tea. I don't like tea much any time, but to have to cope with it before I'd really woken up. Wow.'

But suddenly the smile left his face.

'What is it?' Shakuntala asked quickly.

Gregory Strongbow shook his head slowly from side to side.

'It's nothing really. Just that I remembered joking over bed tea with Hector the morning he went off to Trombay. He told me he'd tipped his on to the floor.'

He sighed.

'It was somehow because of that, because of my attitude to that, we decided to go our different ways a bit,' he said.

'But you mustn't let that worry you,' said Shakuntala. 'You shouldn't reproach yourself over what would have only been a tiny disagreement if your brother had lived. That's attaching too much importance to just a few words. Really it is.'

She leaned forward so earnestly that the American smiled.

'I guess you're right at that,' he said. 'It's not that I should be worrying about. It's squaring it with Hector for getting him into that trap at all.'

He swung round to Ghote.

'Inspector, what is happening? What kind of progress are you making?'

Ghote felt as if he had been slapped.

'We are doing everything possible,' he said sulkily. 'But it is not just a question of arresting a gangster with a tommy-gun. If it was that only, we would do it in no time whatsoever.'

Curiously, this hardly-concealed jibe at the America of films about Chicago seemed to mollify Gregory Strongbow. He leaned back and took an immense swig of coffee. Ghote felt more than ever obliged to persist in his justifications.

'You must remember,' he said, 'the man whose name we know in Poona and his associates would have fled their domiciles. This we now have confirmed. And it is bound to take time to track them down. We may have to wait for the advent of an informant. But be assured we are waiting and watching.'

The American began tackling some toast. It resisted his knife with rubbery stubbornness.

'I can appreciate all this,' he said. 'But it doesn't make it any easier for me. I have a duty to Hector. And I don't feel I'm doing it by just sitting around all day.'

Shakuntala Brown, up till now sitting quietly sipping at her coffee, leaned forward over the massed array of china.

'But there is no need for you to sit,' she said. 'We can arrange some activity for you that will take your mind off this business.'

'I'm sorry,' Gregory Strongbow said, 'but I don't want my mind taken off this business.'

Shakuntala's eagerness was unabated.

'But listen,' she said, 'what could you do yourself to find out who killed your brother?'

The American shifted uneasily in his chair.

'I know, I know,' he said. 'But all the same I must do something. I could go around with the inspector here. Keep my eyes open.'

'No,' said Ghote.

They looked at him.

'I regret, no,' he repeated. 'Professor Strongbow has been seriously assaulted. It is most likely another attempt will be made. I cannot undertake his safety if he goes here and there about the country, even if he is with me.'

Shakuntala answered this with direct indignation.

'But you can't keep him shut up in the hotel here. You can't make him a prisoner like that.'

'That's certainly so,' Gregory Strongbow agreed.

He gave Shakuntala a glance of appreciation, which emboldened her to go on.

'Listen,' she said, 'if we were to make an expedition somewhere, say over to Elephanta Island, if we did it without warning, no one would know where the professor was. He would be quite safe then.'

'But I don't want to make any expeditions,' the American objected.

'You must,' said Shakuntala with decision.

She looked at him straight in the eye with all the directness of a schoolgirl discovering the things that need to be put right in the world.

'You must get out and see the beauties of our country,' she declared. 'You owe that much to yourself. It's what you came here to do. You ought to go on with it.'

And the simple vigour of her attack won him over.

'OK,' Gregory Strongbow said. 'You could be right, I guess. I'll take this one trip anyhow. Where did you say we'd go?'

'To Elephanta Island. It's out in the harbour. It takes an hour and a half or so by boat.'

'Sounds OK. When do we start?'

'You do not start,' said Ghote abruptly.

He was annoyed with himself for not having squashed this idea more quickly. But he had not counted on Shakuntala being able to sway a man as quietly determined as Professor Strongbow.

'You do not start,' he repeated, 'because if you go running here and there all over the place I cannot guarantee your safety.'

'But Inspector,' Shakuntala said quickly, 'he will not be running about all over the place. He will be simply making one expedition. I would be very careless in my duty if I had suggested anything else.'

'In any case,' Gregory Strongbow said with decision, 'I am going. Shakuntala, what time will we get back? We'll give Inspector Ghote a detailed itinerary and he can make all the checks he wants.'

Shakuntala looked at the delicate gold watch on her wrist.

'It is now eight o'clock,' she said. 'We could go down to Apollo Bunder almost at once and hire a boat. I will arrange for a lunch basket and we could spend all day on the island and get back by, say, six this evening. Is that all right?'

She looked at Ghote with an air of challenge.

'I think in any case,' he said obstinately, 'you are forgetting the weather. It may look calm now, but only yesterday the sea was most high.'

'But that was unusual,' Shakuntala said.

She turned to Gregory Strongbow.

'Professor,' she said, 'I have heard the forecast for today. I promise you there is no chance of a storm. And I think Inspector Ghote knows that as well as I do.'

She turned her intense gaze on Ghote. And, since in deference to the truth he had to admit another big storm was unlikely, his glance fell.

'I guess I'll go then,' Gregory Strongbow said.

'In that case I must insist on accompanying,' Ghote snapped out in a sudden squall of bad temper.

'Glad to have you,' Gregory Strongbow replied placidly.

Ghote's feeling of resentment lasted until they were well out into the harbour on their way to Elephanta in a battered old whaler, discarded no doubt in years long past by the Royal Indian Navy. It had been the best craft Shakuntala had been able to hire at this late monsoon period when no regular outings took place, but its shortcomings only added to Ghote's inner anger.

There were also the doubts that had arisen over their departure from the hotel. Ghote had gone to considerable pains to arrange for the professor to slip out without fuss. But at the last moment he had caught sight of Mira Jehangir behind her brass and teak reception desk taking a close interest in their activities. He had told himself that she obviously took a close interest in everybody who set foot in the big foyer and that it was doubtful in the extreme that she could have worked out that the professor was leaving for a whole day away. But an uneasiness remained.

It had been doubled at least by an incident that took place on the Apollo Bunder just as their decrepit craft had been leaving.

Ghote had been the last to climb down the iron ladder from the low wall at the quay edge down to the waiting boat. As he had begun his descent a rattly old car had drawn up on the far side of the Bunder. He had taken one look at it as he felt down with his foot for the rung below. And just as his head had ducked beneath the low wall at the quay edge a tall, gangling figure in a flapping European-style suit had stepped out on to the rough grey stones of the pavement.

He had been almost sure it was V. V. Dharmadhikar, the journalist. He cursed himself now for not having obeyed his instinct and climbed two rungs back up again to make sure. But the others had been waiting and he had felt he ought not to detain them.

And, after all, he told himself, even if it had been V. V., what of it? He had a right to stop his car wherever he wanted. The Apollo Bunder was a reasonable place for a gossip writer to park his car. A liner might be docking at Ballard Pier soon with some celebrity or other on board. In any case it was more than likely V. V. had not seen their party at all.

But he had got into the old whaler feeling unreasonably put out. And matters had not been improved by Gregory Strongbow.

No sooner had Ghote settled himself on one of the sea-smoothed thwarts of the boat than the American had begun expressing doubts about the craft's engine. Certainly there was something pretty pathetic about this piece of machinery. It was an outboard motor from some much smaller vessel and it dangled over the whaler's stern with its little propeller only just below the surface of the water. But Ghote felt that the professor was in some sense a guest and should not have made disparaging remarks about the arrangements. He felt glad that their boatman, a ribby-chested, inward-looking old fellow, apparently understood only Marathi.

'Please do not feel concerned,' he had said sharply in reply. 'That engine may perhaps stop but if it does it will not be a disaster. No doubt this chap would get it going again in absolutely no time at all. In India we have a great ability for improvisation in the most unlikely circumstances.'

For some reason this had seemed to disconcert the American. He had suddenly looked extremely thoughtful. Ghote even wondered whether he could have heard about the village mechanic who had repaired the car of an American family on the Poona road at the time of Hector Strongbow's death. But the report had only come in late the night before. The family had read about the killing and had told the police in Poona that they had unsuccessfully asked a red-bearded American to help them out. Had Hector Strongbow stopped, Ghote reflected, the men who had lit the signal fire might have been chased away by the local villagers before the young American had come through.

In the meanwhile the old whaler's pathetic little engine spluttered on. With every cough it gave, Ghote was convinced that it was going to stop altogether and this anxiety did nothing to improve his resentment of the whole expedition.

But Shakuntala obviously was delighted with the venture. She kept up a continuous, enthusiastic commentary on everything that came in sight.

'Look. Look at that boat there. They have been using dugouts like that for thousands of years in these waters.'

Gregory Strongbow laughed. He pointed away from the long log being laboriously paddled inch by inch through the heavy, pea-soup water over to a distant speedboat cutting its way purposefully along with a wide white wake spuming out behind it.

'That may not be so romantic,' he said, 'but it takes a lot less out of you.'

'All right,' Shakuntala replied cheerfully, 'if you want modernness, how about those? Indian Navy frigates.'

Her pride was naïvely evident.

Ghote looked at the two grey warships moored in the distance with their ominous guns pointing forwards. He found that he too was feeling a similar pride. But he made up his mind that not a hint of it would get out.

'I know America has a much bigger fleet,' Shakuntala went eagerly on, 'but I bet all those aircraft carriers and things are not one bit more efficient than our frigates.'

'I wouldn't be surprised if the frigates weren't a whole lot smarter,' Gregory Strongbow conceded gravely.

Ghote felt uneasy. The talk reminded him of Colonel Mehta and his assertions about the efficiency of the Indian Army.

'That's Cross Island over there,' Shakuntala chattered on. 'And behind it you can see freighters waiting to get into the docks.'

Ghote found he could not resist introducing a note of sourness, although it would hardly enhance the tourist attractions of India.

'I hear there is a new strike of dockers,' he said. 'That is why the freighters are waiting still.'

'You should try New York's dockland for strikes,' Gregory Strongbow said. 'We can certainly beat India there.'

But a short silence fell. It was not long however before Shakuntala had perked up again.

'You can see Elephanta quite clearly now,' she said. 'To the right of Butcher Island where that big tanker is just coming to its moorings. The oil is for the refineries at Trombay, over there, where you can see the sun on that marvellous white dome. That's the Atomic Energy . . .'

Her voice trailed away.

'I guess that's another field where the US is ahead of India,' Gregory Strongbow declared.

There was a much longer silence.

'There is that speedboat again,' Ghote said, for want of anything else to break the awkwardness with.

'She's certainly making a hell of a racket,' said Gregory Strongbow.

And it was true that the engine of the launch, a big but battered-looking craft, was as noisy as it was possible to be without actually blasting itself to a seizure.

Shakuntala bounced back into the conversation with a display of real interest.

'Oh, I would love to go out in a boat like that,' she said. 'I never have, you know. All I've ever done is to chug out to Elephanta on the old launches. It must be marvellous to go cutting through the waves in a real speedboat.'

They watched the launch's frenzied plume of white wake.

'I dare say you have often been in boats like that,' Shakuntala said to the American.

'Why no. Such little sea-going as I've done has been in fishing boats not so much different from those over there.'

He pointed to half a dozen high-prowed, lateen-sailed craft winging along on the freshening wind.

'Those are called eagles,' Ghote contributed dutifully.

'It's an appropriate name all right. They look light as birds.'

'Oh, watch there,' exclaimed Shakuntala. 'The speedboat's coming right towards us. I do hope it holds its course. I'd love to see it close to.'

The old launch had turned towards them and was noisily approaching now in a straight line so that its long frothed-up white wake was no longer visible. They watched it without talking for a little. A large blotch of rust could be clearly seen near the bows. Ghote felt abruptly depressed that what had once been plainly a beautiful boat should have been so neglected. Beauty deserved care.

And suddenly an unaccountable notion entered his head.

He looked quickly round them. They were almost half-way to their destination and there was not another vessel of any sort nearer than a mile away. He glanced back at the speedboat. It was still heading straight towards them. He shaded his eyes and peered hard at the battered craft. He thought he could make out that the man standing beside the helmsman was holding a pair of binoculars to his eyes and looking dead ahead.

He decided he had to speak.

'I regret,' he said, 'I do not like the look of that boat. I do not like it one little bit.'

Gregory Strongbow whipped round and stared at him. It was plain that he had understood. He turned back and concentrated his gaze on the speedboat still heading towards them in a dead straight line, its engine racketing hard.

'What do you mean?' Shakuntala asked.

'I mean that I think this is another attempt on Professor Strongbow's life,' Ghote said. 'And I think this time it would not fail.'

He looked round again at the empty sea, with the wind breaking its mud-brown surface into small choppy waves.

'But that isn't possible,' Shakuntala said, with curious definiteness. 'It's quite impossible. I tell you it's just not so. It's totally impossible.'

Gregory Strongbow turned towards her.

'How well can you swim?' he asked.

'I can swim quite well, but—'

'I think it will be no use however well we swim,' Ghote said. 'If they are going to run us down, they will not leave it to chance whether we drown.'

Gregory Strongbow's face set hard.

'I guess you're right,' he said quietly.

He looked round at the chill, dirty, vacant and unfriendly sea. Then he looked up and down the length of their small boat from the pathetic little engine choking and spluttering as if every cough would be its last to the worn bow-post pushing its way through the water as it had done for years and years past. There was no help there.

There could be no doubt any more about the intentions of the oncoming speedboat. The three men on board could be clearly seen, the helmsman standing concentratedly over the small wheel, the man beside him who had now let his binoculars fall on the strap round his neck, and nearer the stern a squat figure wearing a singlet crouched anxiously over the engine-well with beside him a long formidable boat-hook.

Gregory Strongbow leaned towards Ghote and held his elbow. He jerked a nod towards their boatman sitting contentedly beside his little engine.

'Can you talk to that guy?' he said. 'Can't he get some more speed out of that engine?'

Ghote turned and shouted in Marathi.

'Can we go faster?'

The boatman looked across at him as if he thought he must be mad and then dropped his chin on to his chest and resumed his reverie.

Turning away, Ghote saw that the American and Shakuntala were staring as if transfixed at the thundering craft not twenty-five yards away. And their faces were appalled.

7

The roaring engine of the battered old speedboat choked once only. And then it died. The man near the stern in the white singlet dropped his boat-hook. The clatter as it hit the deck sounded oddly clear in the hush that had come with the cessation of the engine's strident note.

The speedboat continued to slide forward in silence through the muddy brown water towards the little whaler. But it was steadily losing speed. A few moments later it was obvious that it was going to drift past the stern of the steadily chugging whaler eight or ten feet too far away. The man in the singlet was already working frantically at the engine. In the whaler they heard him curse quite clearly as he put his hand on some part of it that was still hot.

His two companions stood by the wheel looking blackly at the whaler ploughing through the oily water away from them. The man with the dangling binoculars had a heavy, oval-shaped head with slightly greying hair, close-cropped. His chest was like a barrel under his dirt-smeared khaki shirt. The muscles of his arms stretched the short sleeves tight. The steersman was younger, not much over twenty. He wore a bright red check shirt and his stained white trousers were kept up by a length of lighting flex. His dark, thin face was marked by a long scar running from above the level of his eyes right down his left cheek to the chin in a broad gash noticeably lighter in colour than the rest of his face.

'When we get back,' Ghote said to Gregory Strongbow, 'I

would go to the Records Department and see what we know about those three.'

'Should we turn around and make for the city right now?' the American asked.

'I think we had better keep straight on to the island,' Ghote said. 'It is nearer. And if they get their engine to start again . . .'

They continued to watch the speedboat. It had ceased to have any way on it at all now and was drifting broadside on. The boatman too turned to look.

'Sahib,' he said to Ghote in Marathi, 'shall I turn and take them in tow?'

With a feeling of total unreality, Ghote realized that the man had all along been completely unaware of what had been going to happen. He must have thought the speedboat, though coming carelessly near, intended to pass just astern of them. No doubt he was used to such unthinking behaviour from the owners of fast craft and had endured feeling his old boat dip and plunge often enough in the heavy wash of vessels higher up the social scale.

'Leave them,' Ghote said to him. 'They will be all right.'

The man shrugged his bony shoulders as much as to say that with mad foreigners on board anything could be demanded. He sunk into his habitual dreamy state, contenting himself with one muttered comment. Ghote only just caught it.

'But to leave a craft at the mercy of the sea: that brings bad luck always.'

Bad luck, if bad luck there was to be, did not appear to have followed them to Elephanta. Everything there seemed to go well from the moment they negotiated the slippery separate concrete blocks of the little pier where the sea swirled and lapped between each one in a mildly dangerous way that Ghote felt he could easily cope with. Surrounded by a noisy band of begging children they routed out an old custodian from his bungalow and set off with him to see the famous caves.

The weather was much more bearable out here, with a little breeze to temper some of the mugginess. They wandered slowly up the spaced steps of the stiffish climb to the open-sided caves. Round a jagged crag of rock, and there they were: an unenclosed forecourt, a flight of smaller steps and the first massive columns rising from the living rock.

The custodian began delivering his set-piece description in a meanderingly quavering voice. His performance filled Gregory Strongbow with continuous amusement. Ghote had expected that Shakuntala would be shocked at this. He had thought she would insist that the looming, impressive beauty of many of the honey-coloured sculptures came first. But evidently the American had more influence on her than might have seemed likely. She abandoned herself completely to the innocent joyfulness of his mood. And before long Ghote too felt himself being infected.

He knew that he ought to be preoccupied with the professor's safety. In whatever way India First had learned that they were out in the exposed stretches of the harbour in an open, defenceless boat they had certainly been quick to take advantage of the situation. The sudden presence of that powerful speedboat certainly underlined the efficiency of their underground opponents. But somehow in the light-heartedness of the atmosphere on the island it was difficult to remember that any menace lurked for them anywhere.

The guide's vintage electric torch sent its goldeny yellow beam feebly out towards a new group of sculpture.

'This relief represents Siva and Parvati, his consort, seated together, with groups of male and female inferior divinities showering down flowers from above. Behind is a female figure carrying a child on her hip. This makes it clear that the scene represents the birth of Skanda, the war-god. Other authorities state that what is represented is Parvati, the consort of Siva, in a temper.'

Gregory Strongbow laughed out loud.

The guide abruptly extinguished his ancient torch, perhaps by way of rebuke. In the suddenly darker gloom Ghote darted quick, nervous glances to left and right. But the big, open rocky cave would have echoed and re-echoed the slightest noise from any intruder and he relaxed once more.

'I guess it's nice not to have to decide between the two theories on that scene,' Gregory Strongbow said. 'Any technique for holding two contrary beliefs simultaneously gets my vote all right.'

The guide laboriously switched his torch on again, having been apparently more economical than offended. At the same instant he picked up his unvarying discourse with a minute description of the next group of statuary 'unfortunately mutilated by the Portuguese soldiery about the year 1582'.

The professor leaned towards Shakuntala and spoke in a voice a little more subdued than before.

'Those soldiery. No wonder India invaded Goa.'

Ghote thought he saw the girl straighten a little in the dim light. For a moment he wondered whether she was going to deliver the defence of India's action which had flashed through his own mind. But she simply laughed a little and they moved on.

Before long Ghote felt obliged to inject into the holiday atmosphere one note of warning. He insisted that the tour of the caves should finish as soon as it reasonably could and that immediately afterwards they should eat the lunch Shakuntala had provided and be ready to set out again for the city. His plan, evolved even before they reached the landing-stage, was to wait till some large vessel was passing down the harbour and to make their way back within sight of it. In this way, he thought, they ought to be reasonably safe from a second attack.

They ate their meal on the top of one of the twin linked hills of the island, looking out across the water, which appeared from this height deceptively easy to cross, at the huge, dark sprawl of Bombay city. Ghote methodically scanned the whole expanse of the harbour from the distant spire of the Afghan Church near the tip of Colaba Point to the white dome and chimney of the not-to-be-mentioned Atomic Establishment at Trombay. But he did not see the least sign of the drifting speedboat. He decided that its crew must have got the engine started again and made for the sanctuary of the crowded city.

He peeled another of the little Nagpur oranges that topped their hamper and put aside his troubles.

When they had finished the meal they decided to indulge themselves with a final stroll by going back to the pier along the coast of the little island. It was still tolerably pleasant with the light wind coming off the sea tangy with salt and they spun out the last minutes of freedom from care as long as they could. Every now and again they halted to look down from the top of the little cliff along which the path ran at the sea breaking in small plumes of spray on the rim of black rocks below.

Behind them a tangled mass of trees, creepers and bushes made a green background alive with the flitting movement of white-faced monkeys, brilliantly coloured birds and darting, gem-like insects.

'The tide's certainly ripping past those rocks,' Gregory Strongbow said. 'I suppose we'll get away from that pier OK?'

'Oh, yes,' Ghote answered. 'What concerns me more is to make sure we set out at a time when some suitable vessel is coming into sight.'

The professor smiled with some shyness.

'Hell,' he said, 'I feel like a fool having to be protected like a consignment of bullion or something.'

'You don't think they'll try again really?' Shakuntala asked. 'I was never so frightened in my life when they were coming down at us like that.'

'We'll be all right,' Gregory Strongbow said quickly.

He stopped and picked up a short piece of stick from the path at his feet.

'Look,' he said, 'we can see how strong the tide is.'

He strolled over to the edge of the short drop down to the rocks and with a dexterity Ghote envied tossed the stick neatly into the gap between the cliff-edge and the spine of sharp rocks. The water, boiling and bubbling along the narrow channel, seized the fragment of stick and swept it bouncing and twirling out of sight.

Shakuntala clapped her hands.

'Wait,' she said, 'we must have a race.'

'OK,' said Gregory Strongbow, 'it's a bet.'

They searched the path for a few moments and each returned with the stick of their choice.

'Now, are you ready?' the American called out, standing waiting to launch his craft into the boiling torrent.

And, as if in answer, three figures shot from the thick vegetation behind them as though fired from giant springs.

Ghote had hardly time to register that they were the three men from the speedboat before the scar-ripped young steersman had knocked him to the ground. Struggling to get his hands free to grip the youth, he saw that the squat engineer had swept Shakuntala aside and was crouching in front of the American. Evidently Gregory Strongbow had not been taken quite as much by surprise as the attackers had intended. The barrel-chested, bullet-headed man who had had the binoculars was already on the retreat with a trickle of blood showing under his nose.

But the odds were too great. Just as Ghote succeeded in freeing his hands and getting a grip on the young steersman's long hair, the two others simultaneously hurled themselves back at the American. Ghote twisted his fingers fiercely round the oiled strands of hair and jerked. But suddenly a voice called out sharply.

'Finish. He finished.'

Ghote saw the tense mouth beside the long scar just above his own face open wide. Then he felt sharp teeth biting his nose. He gasped with pain. And in an instant the youth was clear, his oiled hair whipping through Ghote's loosened fingers, and his knee coming pounding down into his stomach.

For a moment he was unable to move. Then his senses flowed

back and he staggered to his feet. He drew a deep breath to fight off the nausea that almost overwhelmed him and looked round.

Gregory Strongbow was nowhere in sight. And only the sound of rending branches deep in the tangled, luminously green vegetation on the far side of the path indicated that not a minute earlier three violent men had been at work.

Shakuntala Brown, lying where she had fallen on the stony surface of the path, suddenly began to sob.

Ghote forced himself to go to the cliff-edge. At its foot he saw at once the inert shape of the American. He was lying face downwards across a jagged peak of rock with the boiling sea tugging at his feet. Already spray had soaked his light, well-cut suit from head to foot. In the still sunlight it glittered dazzlingly.

Shakuntala came and stood at the cliff-edge.

'We must bring him up,' she said.

Ghote looked down at the broken figure.

'Yes,' he said, 'something must be done. I suppose his relatives will want to have him buried like a Christian. One of us ought to watch here while the other goes and gets a boat round.'

'But the tide,' Shakuntala said. 'It will sweep him away.'

Ghote looked down again.

'Yes, it may certainly rise high enough,' he said. 'But fetching a boat is the only way. To try and climb down would be simply ridiculous. Look at the steepness of the cliff and the spray is constantly wetting it rendering it doubly dangerous.'

'But—'

Shakuntala left it at that. Looking down at the broken shape on the rock below, it was only too plain that there was nothing more to be said.

At that moment Gregory Strongbow distinctly moved. For one instant he raised his head, only to let it fall again as inertly as ever back on to the hard, black, gleaming wet surface of the rock. But the single movement had been perfectly plain. Ghote did not doubt that it had happened for all the apparent lifelessness of the body both before and afterwards.

Shakuntala said nothing but dropped down to her knees and peered over the edge of the cliff with passionate intensity.

I shall have to climb down, Ghote thought.

The speed at which the tide was rising was plain to see. Already the brown suede shoe, which had been only half submerged when he had first looked over the cliff, was permanently below the surface of the racing water. At any moment Gregory Strongbow might have another fleeting return of consciousness. He would need only to raise his head a little higher and he would slip on the treacherous wet surface of the black rock and slide down into the vicious sea. And then he would have no chance at all.

But getting down the cliff would be almost suicidally dangerous. The drop, though of only some twenty feet, was practically sheer. Hardly a single handhold, it seemed, jutted out of the iron face of the rock. And the whole lower third of its surface glittered and gleamed with the spray tossed up from the waves breaking on the spine of rocks below.

Suddenly into his head came the thought of his wife and son in the neat security of their little Government Quarters home across the harbour in the comfortable, crowded city. Surely this was where his duty lay? He had married Protima, entered into a contract with her. They had brought little Ved into the world. Could he go back on claims as strong as these? A running glimpse of Protima's life as a widow shot erratically before him: hanging on in the house of whichever relative tolerated her, without possessions, without position, without anything in her future but a long succession of featureless days.

And all that lay between her and such a life was one tiny slip on these twenty feet of sheerly falling rock which separated him from the huddled body of an American stranger.

He looked downwards once again. Gregory Strongbow's body lay just as it had when he had first seen it.

Only there was a difference.

He knew now that inside that case of flesh a heart was beating, however irregularly. Down there, not ten yards away in a straight line, a man lay in danger of being swept to certain death. He could see him: he would have to go.

He knelt down and slowly took off his shoes. He felt a desolate sadness sweeping over him. Neatly and carefully he placed his shoes side by side on the path.

'Please run down to the boatman,' he said to Shakuntala, 'and get him to bring the boat round here as quickly as possible.'

'You are going down?'

'I must.'

'Then I will stay.'

'No,' Ghote said, 'you can do nothing by standing here watching. Kindly go immediately.'

Although it was true enough that she could not give him any practical assistance, it was not mere arguments of commonsense that made him wish passionately that she would leave. He felt acutely that if he was to risk himself in this way he must do so completely on his own. The girl's presence, her fears for him as she followed his progress, would be an added burden. He felt he was entitled to thrust it away as rudely as he liked.

'Please hurry,' he said, biting off the words in case they exploded into rage. 'Please hurry, time is important.'

And to his immense relief she turned and began half-running, half-stumbling away along the stony path. He turned back to the cliff.

By the time he had lowered himself over the edge, he calculated, there would be little more than twelve feet of rock to negotiate. At the bottom, given a certain amount of luck, he ought to be able to get astride the same black jagged spur as Gregory Strongbow. He ought to be able to hold him there till help came. But it would be on the twelve feet of sheer, slippery cliff-face that the end could all too easily come. One slip, one mistake and nothing could stop him tumbling helplessly down into the boiling cataract fanged with black rocks below. He could not escape injury, and dazed and disabled he would be swept within seconds far beyond his limited range as a swimmer. And he did not see how he was to avoid making that one slip.

He lay on his face beside the edge and heaved himself over. Soon his wriggling toes encountered two almost imperceptible projections. Pushing against them with all his force, he lowered himself slowly clear of the top edge of the cliff. He pressed clingingly to the hard surface of the rock and groped about with outstretched fingers. First his left hand then his right found holds of a sort at about the level of his chest. They were mere tiny protuberances, but he set his fingers round them like claws and felt he might trust his weight on them for a little. He took a breath and moved his right leg from its perch. He slithered it downwards searchingly.

Down it went and down on the smooth surface of the rock. But at last just as it was extended as far as it would go his toes encountered a minute ridge. He explored it carefully. It proved to be about six inches long and at its widest point a little more than half an inch deep. He twisted his leg till all five toes were resting squarely on the tiny flat surface. Then he swung his weight over and took his left leg off its first hold.

The moment he did so he felt the little ridge under his toes begin to move. He knew the whole thing must be slowly coming away in a single big flake. Sweat sprang up all down his front. He felt it salty on his tongue as he licked his upper lip. He felt it where his chest was pressing hard into the rock, and he felt it all the way along the length of his thighs as he fought to stop them trembling.

Forcing himself not to hurry, he brought his free left foot back on to its former hold. Then equally slowly he withdrew his right foot from the flaking ridge and brought it back up again. When at last he had got it securely on the protuberance where it had rested at first, the sense of relief that invaded him was so relaxing that he almost let go of everything.

Then he realized that all he had achieved so far was to get back to exactly the position he had started from.

Why not give up? The thought presented itself to him insidiously. After all, he had tried. Shakuntala Brown was witness to that. He had set off to climb down there, and he had simply found that it was impossible. Surely this was a moment for other claims to be heard? There was a certain value to his life, when all was said and done. He was a trained police officer. He had accumulated a fund of experience over the years that could bring many a wrong-doer to justice, if he were there to do it. At some time in the future it was more than possible that his skill and knowledge, and his alone, would save someone from murder. He owed something to the future too.

But the line of his thoughts carried him on.

If he were to creep back over the top of the cliff now and lie face downwards in the hot sun not looking at what he had left behind, then he would be letting those three men who had leaped so suddenly out of the trees get away with their crime. He would be cashing in the measure of luck he had been handed when the engine of their launch had stopped at that critical moment. He would be letting India First attain its objective without a fight.

He came to a decision. He must force himself to push away from the comforting face of the rock so that he could see what he was doing on the climb down. Feeling his way blindly was plainly not going to get him to Gregory Strongbow's side.

He counted to three and he forced himself away from the cliff-face.

To his surprise he found that he felt a great deal safer. His sense of balance had begun to assert itself. He was able to look downwards without having to fight back waves of pure terror.

And almost at once he spotted something that looked as if it might solve half his problem. Invisible from the top of the cliff because of the way the shadows fell, there was a long, thin crack running vertically down the face a little way to his right. It occurred to him that if he could jam his toes and the ball of his foot into this, it would give him a hold infinitely more efficient than a crumbly little ridge.

He swung his right leg far out, still keeping himself as clear of the rock as he dared. He just reached the crack. Cautiously he wriggled his toes into it and then his instep. In a moment the foot jammed fast. It was uncomfortable but it seemed to be totally reliable.

He looked down for a moment at his objective, the boiling line of broken foam interspersed with jagged black teeth of rock. And quite suddenly the waves of pure fear came back. He forced his head up till he was confronting the rock an arm's length away and took three deep breaths.

It was enough.

He swung his other foot off its hold and over towards the crack. He found he was able to observe the wriggling toes below him with clinical detachment as he manoeuvred them into the crack in their turn.

It struck him that if the fissure made as good a hold as this for his feet, it might serve equally well for his hands. He would have to put his fingers in as far as they would go and then press them hard outwards against the sides of the crack with his elbows stuck out. He reached across.

Half a minute later he had discovered that he was right. He was crouching in front of the narrow crack feeling almost as safe as if he was standing on the familiar pavements of the city. He began lowering himself neatly down. If he was able to make this much speed, he was almost certain to get to Gregory Strongbow before the tide reached high enough to drag him off his perch and even, with luck, before another bout of returning consciousness made him lift his head again, shift his weight and slide into the angry sea.

After a while he found that, not without unexpected minor complications, he had reached the end of the crack. The cliff on either side was already wet from spray and cold to touch. There were perhaps six feet to go. He began to search around for other holds.

And there was nothing.

This time the cliff really was sheer. A blank surface polished, it seemed, by the constant beating of the waves, glistening and unyielding. He searched it again. And again. But there could be no doubt. There was not the faintest possibility of climbing down any farther from this point. Could he risk jumping? He could not conceivably see what might await him in the bubbling mass of foam at the water's edge. It would be launching himself into the unknown.

There was only one thing to do: to go up again.

Grimly he set out. But going up proved a good deal harder than coming down had been. Not only did he have to tug his weight up, but each danger that he had overcome had to be overcome again, every carefully negotiated passage had to be carefully negotiated once more.

And when he had done it, he reflected, he would be back at the beginning for the second time.

Was this the moment he could abandon it all? Was he being given a second chance to take the sensible way out? Because now he had really tried. He had risked his life in no uncertain way for this stranger. What about those near and dear to him? It was their turn now.

A seagull came screaming up to the cliff near his head. He closed his eyes in a sudden new access of fear. The sound of the bird's harsh, taunting voice dinned in his ears and then seemed to fade. He found he preferred knowing what was happening to the comfort of darkness and opened his eyes again.

He looked round. The bird had flown over the top of the cliff. Below him he saw the shining white patch on the black rock that was the American's inert body.

He began looking for another route downwards.

It was not long before he found it. His eye travelled from a single tuft of tussocky grass to a knob of stone which looked as if he could get a couple of fingers round it, and on to another crack, shorter than the first but useful now that he had learned the trick. Then there was a whole series of tiny protuberances leading well into the spray zone and finally something that looked like a ridge big enough to plant a whole foot on.

He swung himself off. And almost at once his right foot slid sharply on a tiny area of bird-droppings. His leg shot off the hold together. The weight of his whole body tugged at his hands gripping two little rough patches on the rock-face. Inexorably his right hand was pulled away. He tried to gain some support by twisting his left leg round and thrusting upwards. The force of the manoeuvre suddenly sent a piece of stone shooting away beneath him and his leg dropped sharply down.

He hung on hard with his left hand, the fingers biting into the hard surface of the cliff-face. Desperately he clutched out for some support with his other hand. But millimetre by millimetre he felt his sweaty fingers sliding from their hold. He registered the moment when the index finger slipped away.

And then came the fall.

8

An agonizing jab of pain shot up Inspector Ghote's right leg as his foot hit a submerged rock in the boiling torrent at the foot of the cliff. For a moment he remained upright. Then the force of the water swept him stumbling forward. A sharp edge of black rock seemed to come chopping up towards his face. It struck him on the left shoulder, flinging him sideways.

And suddenly the tug of the racing water ceased to pull at him. His face was clear of the surface, though drenched by successive lashing bursts of spray. He was mercifully jammed hard between two rocks. And safe.

He tried to heave himself up a little and found that he could manage it. Slowly he worked his way round till he was facing in the direction of Gregory Strongbow.

The American was still spreadeagled across the black spine of rock. The distance between them was about three yards. But those three yards were one ominous mass of boiling, bubbling, frothing sea. Each of them could be on separate tiny islands with a deep torrent cutting them off from each other. Or it might be that Gregory Strongbow was only half a dozen paces away.

Ghote began to push himself upright. His right knee darted spasms of pain all the way up his leg. But it seemed to support his weight. Gritting his teeth he tried a step forward. His foot slipped on the awkward angle of the rock underneath it but the rock was there. If all went well, he had only to go forward step by step now and he would reach the American at last. A second pace brought his painful right leg up to his left. Then another advance. Once more forward with the right foot, enduring the dart of pain that this meant. Then another advance with the left foot.

And in an instant he was down.

The water was over his head, beating at him, blotting everything to black confusion. He flung out his arms and felt the peak of rock he had been jammed against before. He scrabbled wildly and his head came out of the water. His brain cleared. He fought his way upright again.

It took him minutes to push against the swirl of the torrent enough to regain his former position. But at last he managed it. He paused to consider, holding his left thumb in his right hand, a superstitious trick that had always brought him luck as a schoolboy.

There was, after all, a deep gap between himself and Gregory Strongbow. He had found out that much. Was it going to prevent him getting to the American? Was he going to be this near and be baulked at the last minute?

Cautiously he set out towards the spine of black rock with the inert, white-suited body flung against it. He calculated that he could take two more paces with each foot before he reached the edge of the deep channel between them. One with the left, one with the right. A pause to let the pain ebb away a little. Then one more with the left and another with the right. A longer pause and at last the fiery agony was bearable. He took a deep breath.

And flung himself full length down into the sea. He reckoned that it was the only way. If the deep channel went right up as far as the American's rock, then he would be swept away. If it was a little less wide, he might find something to hold on to on the far side.

He felt his outflung arms slowly going down through the bubbling water. And then there was something solid. He clutched desperately. His fingers made contact. His grip held. He hauled himself forward.

He had made it.

*

He had had to lie across the unconscious body of Gregory Strongbow on the spine of black rock for nearly an hour. The tide had reached as high as the American's knees and had then slowly subsided. Rescue, when it came, had been comparatively easy. It seemed that deep water went quite close to the foot of the cliff and the boatman was able to bring the old whaler to within a few feet of them. He had been extremely phlegmatic about the whole operation, tossing a rope over to Ghote as if such things happened every time he took a party across to Elephanta.

Between them they had hauled the heavy body of the American into the boat and Ghote had wearily dragged himself on board after. Then he had let go. He had felt that his share was over. He was vaguely aware that Shakuntala was busy with Gregory but what exactly she was doing seemed to be of little concern to him.

Even when she had called out triumphantly that he was beginning to regain consciousness he had hardly stirred. But a short rest at the landing stage and tea provided by the custodian of the caves, who had seemed almost bereft of speech without his monologue to recite, had restored him enough to think what had to be done. He had come to the conclusion that the American was fit enough to get back to the city and see a doctor there, and they had made the journey across the harbour easily enough.

Then it had been merely a matter of getting the boatman to take them to a less conspicuous landing point than Apollo Bunder and bundling into a taxi back to the Queen's Imperial Grand Hotel.

He told the taxi driver to go round to the back of the hotel when they arrived. From his inspection of the building the evening before when he had placed a discreet watch over the American, he knew that there was a back entrance with a short flight of service stairs to the first floor where Gregory Strongbow's suite was.

Leaving Shakuntala to settle the bill, he took the American by the elbow and piloted him in. Less than two minutes later the door of his bedroom was safely closed behind them. And Mira Jehangir, sharp-eyed at the reception desk, would have no idea that he was back and in reasonably good shape. Nor would V. V., if he should happen to be sitting waiting somewhere in the big foyer, be any better informed. If either of them was feeding India First with information, at least a short respite had been gained.

He helped Gregory Strongbow over to the high bed with its heavily flounced counterpane and high mounded pillows.

'Lie here for a little,' he said. 'Then when you are feeling better we will think where we should hide you.'

'I am feeling better,' the American declared in rather too loud a voice.

Nevertheless he flopped down on to the big bed and lay quietly.

'Now what's all this about hiding me?' he said. 'I don't get it.'

'It is quite simple,' Ghote explained, fighting against a feeling of weariness. 'The India First people do not know their attack failed. If we can hide you safely away somewhere and get you proper medical attention, they will never learn.'

The American thrust himself up off the soft bedding.

'And I'm nice and tidily kept a prisoner?' he said.

'No, no. Not in any sense a prisoner. But it would be best for your own safety.'

'I'm not doing it.'

The American still kept himself up on his elbows and glared at Ghote.

'I'm not doing it, I tell you. I might as well go scuttling back to the States. But I'm not going to do that either. I'm going to stay here and stay a free agent. No one's going to order me around and keep me cooped up. That's for sure.'

Ghote sighed.

'You are a free agent,' he said. 'You can do what you want.'

'Then I stay right where I am.'

Gregory Strongbow flopped back on to the pillows and closed his eyes.

'But one thing I insist,' Ghote said.

'What's that?'

'That you see a doctor without further delay.'

There was a short silence.

'OK,' Gregory Strongbow said at last. 'I guess I do feel a little beat.'

This admission alarmed Ghote after the American's toughness of a moment before. He felt a new flood of energy and hurried into the suite sitting room to the telephone. He found that the hotel regularly used a Dr Udeshi who lived only a few minutes away.

When he got back to the bedroom Gregory Strongbow seemed to be asleep. He sat down on a little cane-seated chair by the foot of the huge bed and waited. After about five minutes the American spoke.

'I don't feel so bad after all,' he said cheerfully. 'You know, all I need is a drink. Let's take a stroll down to that Bulbul Permit Room and see what a little whisky can do for us.'

'No,' said Ghote.

'Hell, why not?'

'To begin with you are plainly not really well. And in the second place, though the India First people are bound to find out you are back here before very long, I wish to keep it secret while I can.'

'Very sound reasoning,' the American replied.

Ghote registered that the oddly forced tone he spoke in must mean that he was by no means well. There was more than a hint of delirium in it.

'I tell you what though,' Gregory Strongbow continued in the same hectic tone. 'I tell you what. We can have a drink up here. It's legal. It says so on that little notice by the door. Drinking's allowed by permit-holders of the following classes, one, visiting Sovereigns, two, foreign visitors. And I'm a foreigner in these parts.'

He began heaving himself up from the downy plumpness of the bed and groping round for the bell push. Ghote wondered if he ought to restrain him by force.

Mercifully a loud knock came on the outer door. Ghote hurried away to answer it. It was Dr Udeshi. Ghote led him in without stopping for formalities.

And Dr Udeshi, portly, solemn, with an immense, stubbly, grave jaw, would not hear of any alcohol being taken in any circumstances.

'My dear sir,' he boomed after examining the American, 'one week in bed, one week, nothing less. I cannot undertake to avoid complications unless strict rest is enforced for at least that period. I cannot undertake it.'

And the relentless pressure of such a personality was too much for the American. He lay back on the huge plateau of the bed and looked up at the high ceiling, where no fewer than seven long-bladed fans twirled rhythmically.

'If that's what you say, Doctor,' he murmured.

'I absolutely insist. Absolutely. Already you are showing decided symptoms of fatigue. Decided symptoms.'

'I guess I do feel tired.'

Dr Udeshi rose from his little chair beside the bed and administered an injection.

'I will leave you now,' he said. 'I advise a short, refreshing sleep and afterwards a light meal. There is nothing you need particularly avoid. Choose whatever will stimulate the appetite.'

His head inclined in a grave, permissive bow. He replaced his hypodermic in its appointed place in his black leather Gladstone bag.

'I will return tomorrow morning at approximately ten a.m.,' he said. 'But if you should need me before that time, do not hesitate to telephone. I am always available.'

Wafting a dense aroma of reassurance in every direction, he made his way out.

Ghote turned to Gregory Strongbow.

'I too will leave when I have seen Miss Brown,' he said. 'But before I go I want you to promise me one thing.'

The American turned his head and looked at him. He seemed less feverish after Dr Udeshi's ministrations.

'What is it?' he asked quietly.

'Not to leave this room under any circumstances without telling me,' Ghote said.

The American's eyes were wide open.

'All right,' he said. 'It's a promise.'

His eyes closed. He was asleep.

Ghote encountered Shakuntala in the broad corridor outside Gregory Strongbow's suite. Three bearers squatting together a little farther along looked at them curiously.

He told her briefly what Dr Udeshi's findings had been. She looked serious but relieved.

'He has ordered a week's complete rest,' Ghote said. 'Kindly make certain Professor Strongbow obeys those orders. I must be sure he does not leave his rooms.'

Shakuntala nodded solemnly.

'You can trust me for that,' she said.

Ghote gave her one sharp, critical look.

'Can I?' he asked.

She looked back at him earnestly.

'I give you my word.'

Ghote decided not to report to Colonel Mehta till the next day.

When he did so, toiling once more up the interminable flights of neglected stairs to the little office in the topmost cranny of the big building in the Fort area, he felt much better able to cope with whatever the colonel might have to say. A long night's sleep had restored him, and only an occasional twinge of pain in his right knee remained as a tangible sign of his buffeting in the torrent at the foot of the Elephanta cliff.

Colonel Mehta, sitting upright at the totally bare little table in the bare office, heard in silence his account of the two further attempts the India First thugs had made on Gregory Strongbow. When Ghote had finished he looked up at him under his bushy eyebrows.

'And the professor,' he said, 'did he express his gratitude for you saving his life?'

Ghote thought for an instant.

'He was very tired last night, sir,' he said. 'Almost in a state of delirium until the doctor saw him.'

'Hm. Have you seen him today?'

'No, sir. I came straight here. But I telephoned the hotel. He is well.'

'Then you'd better get round there and receive his thanks, hadn't you?'

'I do not expect to be thanked,' Ghote said stiffly.

'On the contrary, Inspector. You will put yourself in the way of being bloody well thanked.'

'But—'

'And in the aftermath of that gratitude, Inspector, you will take the opportunity of asking your man what it was his brother said to him when they met after that appalling visit to Trombay.'

Ghote considered this in silence for a few seconds. Was he going to take advantage of the American's natural feelings in this way? Was this the sort of order he was bound to obey?

'Well, man?'

'I will do what I can, Colonel.'

'I should bloody well hope so, Inspector.'

'Colonel.'

The colonel's hard eyes looked up at Ghote standing in front of him. There was an expression of incredulity in them at the prospect of an order about to be questioned. But Ghote had no intention of doing that.

'Colonel,' he said, 'may I ask what progress you yourself are making?'

Colonel Mehta's mouth snapped to under the line of his bristling moustache.

'I will remind you, Inspector,' he said, 'that the activities of the Special Investigations Agency are top security matters.'

'Sir, it had occurred to me only that it might be possible to get at the controller of the India First through whoever is spying on Professor Strongbow. I was wondering only if such a step will be necessary.'

Colonel Mehta permitted himself a token smile.

'Such a step is still necessary, Inspector. India First is not the sort of organization that can be broken in a couple of days. But don't deceive yourself into thinking you're going to get at their Number One in that way. There is such a thing as the chain-of-command system, man.'

'Yes, sir. But it is the only way I can do anything. And unless something is done the murder of Hector Strongbow will go unsolved.'

The colonel looked up at Ghote speculatively.

'There's still plenty of the policeman about you, isn't there, Inspector?'

'I hope there is always, Colonel.'

The colonel shrugged.

'Carry on if you want then,' he said. 'But don't think you'll advance matters one little bit.'

'Thank you, sir.'

So before Ghote went to call on Gregory Strongbow he permitted himself the luxury of setting in train a few police enquiries. The familiar routine lapped briefly and comfortingly round him.

He sent to Records for anything they had on the three thugs from the launch. He got in touch with the inspector in charge of harbour crime about the launch itself.

He telephoned Poona and checked on Shakuntala Brown.

Yes, she was the daughter of a British forest officer who had eventually taken Indian nationality. And, yes, she was employed by the State Tourist Department.

He made a few enquiries among his headquarters colleagues and unearthed the history of Mira Jehangir, receptionist at the Queen's Imperial Grand Hotel. She was, it appeared, the sort of person about whom his colleagues were likely to have a good deal of information, even though she had never come under their professional notice. Her father had been a jewel merchant, who from over-ambitiousness had run himself into bankruptcy and then had promptly died. His penniless sixteen-year-old daughter had become the mistress of a whole series of businessmen, but had reached the end of each association no better off than at the beginning. Until at last she had thrown in her lot with Mr Wadia, the widower manager of the Queen's Imperial Grand. If the gossip was true, she was doing her best to induce him to marry her. But once again she seemed to be getting the worst of it. Instead of being the exigent adored one, she had become a more than usually hard-worked employee, without pay.

About V. V. he had little need to make enquiries. He was known to everyone as a journalist, always poking into anything that looked at all unsavoury. He could be expected to be sniffing around the Hector Strongbow case, but what his motives were only he himself could say.

Happier for this short interlude back in his proper harness, he went to see Gregory Strongbow. Almost at once he found that, like it or not, he was carrying out Colonel Mehta's plan for him.

Gregory Strongbow lifted himself up from the heaped mound of his pillows the moment he came in.

'Inspector,' he said, 'I've been hearing from Shakuntala more about what you did for me. You saved my life.'

An instinct to thrust this aside overwhelmed Ghote. He smiled down at the tall American.

'Well,' he said, 'please to take care of that life then. Do not let me hear of you getting out of bed one moment before Dr Udeshi gives permission.'

Gregory Strongbow grunted.

'That guy,' he said. 'He was in here already. He's not going to let me out of his clutches if he can help.'

'That is an excellent thing. After concussion it is necessary to take great care. Doctor's orders should be scrupulously obeyed.'

'I'll do that. But in any case I gave you my word not to go gadding out, remember. That'll keep me in here more effectively than any doctor.'

Ghote relaxed. The danger seemed to be averted. And it looked as if he was not going to be able to obey Colonel Mehta's instructions. If it was not in him, it was not in him.

'But you are looking much better,' he said cheerfully to the professor.

'Yes, I'm feeling much better. I guess last night I was pretty well delirious. But I'm in my right mind now all right. In one way that's why I'm glad I didn't do anything about thanking you then. I'd rather you didn't think it was just delirious ravings.'

'But – but there was no need.'

'Yes, there is a need. You saved my life. You did more. You climbed down that cliff when anyone could see it was beyond the line of duty. And I'm going to say straight out that I'm never going to forget that. Never.'

A warm rush of emotion swelled up in Ghote's heart. He darted up to the big, high bed and seized the American's broad hand where it lay on the deep fold of the white sheet.

The American shifted about a little.

'Hell,' he said, 'I can't go on calling you Inspector all the time. I want to call you by your first name from now on.'

He grinned a little.

'I only hope it's something I can pronounce,' he said.

Ghote smiled.

'It is Ganesh. Ganesh. Quite easy.'

'Ganesh. Thank you, Ganesh, for saving my life.'

Into the rosy flow of feeling in Ghote's head a tiny hard thought surfaced like a blue-black spike of rock in a wide river.

This is the moment, he found himself thinking. This is the moment that I have got to ask him, to ask Gregory, what it was that his brother said to him as he waited to catch the Poona train.

'Gregory,' he said, 'if your life has been saved, it is true also that your brother's was lost. I would prefer not to mention, but this is not the time to be ruled by fear of hurting another person's feelings.'

The American reached across to the tall, polished teak bedside table. From it he picked up a small black and white object, his brother's CND badge.

'I got Shakuntala to fetch me this first thing today,' he said. 'I'm not forgetting what happened to Hector.'

'No,' said Ghote. 'I see you are not. That badge shows me. Does it mean that you are going to take up where Hector could not go on? Gregory, what did he tell you in that talk outside V. T. Station?'

Gregory continued to look at the thin disc in his hand.

'We had a talk,' he said. 'I don't think any purpose would be served by going into it all.'

'Please, Gregory, I need to know what your brother said.'

The American glanced up at him briefly. Ghote caught one glimpse of cautious, appraising blue eyes.

'Do you really need to know, Ganesh?'

'Yes, Gregory, I need to.'

He put all the conviction he could contrive into the words.

'I don't think so, Ganesh. Ganesh, I'm going to ask you a favour, friend to friend. Just don't ask me that any more. All right?'

Ghote looked down at him. His head had flopped back on the immense mound of bluey-white pillows at the top of the bed. He was staring expressionlessly up at one of the seven long-bladed fans swinging whiningly round from the ceiling.

'I regret,' he said, 'it may be necessary at some stage of my enquiries to ask you that question again. I am a police officer.'

He felt a sudden burning fury at having used just those words at this moment. He was a police officer. But if ever there was work a police officer should not have to do this was it.

'All right,' Gregory said slowly. 'If you have to, you have to.'

The big fan swung round and round above him at the end of its long shaft.

*

Ghote left the American as soon as he felt he decently could. Outside the suite he checked and double-checked his security arrangements. A major hotel in a fashionable part of Bombay ought not to be a place where a murder can be committed. The organized forces of society had a right to expect something. But he was going to take no chances.

He had personally selected the constable stationed by the internal telephone at the end of the corridor outside the suite. He was a moon-faced fellow, not over intelligent but trustworthy as a trained dog. He looked up at Ghote now, his eyes wide with determination to absorb every minutest particular of his orders.

'Now,' Ghote said, 'your duty here is very simple. You are guarding Professor Strongbow, the big American. You know him?'

'Yes, yes, Inspector sahib, I know well. He is American. He is tall. He has the face of a lion and kind eyes.'

'And if anyone except his room bearer goes to the door of his suite, what do you do?' he asked.

'Ring, ring, ring on this telephone, Inspector sahib. Double quick time.'

'Good man.'

Ghote went outside and looked up at the windows of the professor's suite and the long wooden balcony with the dark area of greenish monsoon mould below it. He studied the whole surroundings hard, but simply confirmed his earlier finding that the balcony was accessible only to the half dozen grey crows that perched along its hand-rail.

Finally he decided that he could go back to his office and safely pursue his enquiries into the three possible India First spies.

Shakuntala was his main object. The promptness with which she had arrived at the professor's side after his brother's death was a fact that had itched obscurely just under the surface of his mind ever since he had realized why Hector Strongbow had been killed. So far his enquiries on the telephone to Poona had produced only the answers that might have been expected. But there was a lot more that could be asked, given time to ask it.

He pulled his chair into his little scored and scratched desk, picked up the telephone and got through to Poona. He felt comfortable. This was his work. Patiently unearthing facts, comparing them, checking for the inconsistencies. The sheets of scrap paper piled in front of him began to be covered page by page with scrawled notes. He shuffled through them, marked words here and there, thought for a little, put in yet another call.

He forgot about getting anything to eat.

Some time in the afternoon he rang the Poona police again. It was only to check one tiny point. But to do so he had to explain at length who he was and what case it was that he was investigating.

No wonder the crime rate is so bad, he thought. When everything takes so much time.

'Inspector Ghote?'

A new voice at the end of the crackling, buzzing, appallingly bad line.

'Inspector Ghote speaking.'

'Good afternoon, Inspector. It is Inspector Phadke speaking. I think I have something to interest you.'

'Yes? Yes, what is it?'

His thoughts raced round the subject of Shakuntala Brown, the too-Indian English girl.

'I am holding a certain Kartar Singh, Inspector. He is a cousin of Harjeet Singh.'

He had almost asked who Harjeet Singh was. But he stopped himself in time. Harjeet Singh, the man Poona had provisionally identified as the Sikh leader of the ambush party. Not to have known about him would have been to give this Inspector Phadke a very low opinion of Bombay efficiency. He owed more than that to his colleagues here.

'A cousin of Harjeet Singh,' he said thoughtfully into the telephone. 'And is he talking?'

Inspector Phadke laughed cosily.

'Soon he will be talking, Inspector.'

'Then I will have a report when you have something to state,' Ghote said.

He had not liked the sound of Inspector Phadke's laugh. No doubt often a policeman owed it to the forces of law and order to extract information from a suspect. But he owed it to himself not to enjoy that sort of thing.

'Goodbye, Inspector,' he said, putting down the receiver.

He stopped and thought. Kartar Singh was something Gregory should be told about. Pulling him in represented a real advance in the hunt for the actual killers of Hector Strongbow. It would be a pleasure to have something to tell Gregory that reflected nothing but credit on Indian police-work.

Carefully he gathered up his notes, Shakuntala Brown, Mira Jehangir, V. V. Dharmadhikar. He clipped them in three separate bundles and put them in the top drawer of his desk, the one he could lock.

There was no answer when he knocked on the tall, dark door of Gregory Strongbow's suite.

He frowned sharply. Even if Gregory was dozing, Shakuntala Brown ought to be there.

He knocked again. A noisy tattoo.

And still no answer. He tried the door. It was unlocked. A sudden fury swept into his head. Surely they could at least have taken the simple precaution of keeping the door locked? Was it up to him to think of everything?

And all the time the possibility that the suite might prove empty had to be thrust down. It could not be empty. Gregory had promised. Shakuntala Brown had declared he could trust her for that.

He shouted.

He ran through the deserted sitting room into the bedroom. On the big, high, flounced bed the huge mound of bluey-white pillows was deeply dented where Gregory had been lying. But of Gregory there was not the least sign.

Ghote tore over to the door of the bathroom, his last hope. He flung it wide. The huge, slightly rust-stained bath stood solidly in the middle of the bare, white-tiled, narrow room under the high ceiling. There seemed to be dozens of mirrors, large and small, mostly a little blotched. He saw himself reflected and re-reflected. But nothing else.

No one.

9

Inspector Ghote ran out of Gregory Strongbow's empty suite. The thought which he had thrust away so hard was simple reality now: Gregory had gone. He really had broken the promise he had made not to leave without giving warning. And Shakuntala Brown had done nothing to stop him. Surely this meant she was working for India First? And if this was so, then Gregory was heading for danger once again.

At the end of the long tan-carpeted corridor he saw his carefully selected constable, sitting almost to attention on a small gilt-painted chair.

'What happened? What happened, man?' he called out.

The constable jumped to his feet.

'Is all right, Inspector sahib,' he said. 'Professor Strongbow is outside as of now.'

'Outside? Outside?'

'Yes, Inspector. The party left thirty-five minutes ago, accompanied by other party.'

'Other party? You mean Miss Brown?'

The man's expression of patent anxiety to please wilted.

'I am not knowing her name, Inspector. Please, I am very sorry.'

'Never mind her name. An English-looking girl, but wearing a sari.'

The woebegone moon-face brightened.

'Yes, Inspector. That is quite right. A green sari. It was dark green.'

'But why did you let them go?'

The constable's face was solemn again.

'Inspector, I had orders.'

'Yes, orders to protect Professor Strongbow at all costs. He cannot be protected if we do not know where he is.'

'No, Inspector. Not those orders. Orders to telephone pretty damn quick if anyone tried to get into professor's room.'

Ghote sighed.

His sense of justice compelled him to recognize that the man had indeed obeyed orders. Only too faithfully.

He swung away and hurried down to the public rooms. But as he expected there was no sign of Gregory or Shakuntala in any of them. In the foyer at the reception desk he saw the familiar, watchful form of Mira Jehangir.

He went quickly over.

'Professor Strongbow?' he snapped out. 'Did you see him leave?'

But as he might have expected he did not get a straight answer.

'Professor Strongbow leave?' Mira Jehangir said, looking down at the long, painted nails of her elegant, jewel-covered hands.

'I know Professor Strongbow has left,' he said. 'What I am asking is when he went, and whether he told where he was going.'

'You want to see the professor then?'

'I asked if you knew where he has gone.'

Mira Jehangir's flickering eyes at last came to rest looking at him.

'Perhaps he just went to buy something,' she said. 'There is the American Express in Dadabhai Naoroji Road also.'

'Did he say that was where he was going?'

Ghote tried to induce her to continue looking at him but in vain.

'Inspector, he tells me nothing,' Mira Jehangir said with a hint of bitterness. 'He hides in his room and I do not know whether he is dead or alive.'

For a moment Ghote was tempted to pursue this answer. But he foresaw the great quagmire of evasiveness that any such questioning would produce.

'But you saw him go out,' he said. 'Did you see which way he went?'

'Through the swing-doors it is not possible,' Mira Jehangir replied regretfully.

Ghote glanced across at the tall doors. It was certainly true that their tinted glass blurred all figures outside them.

'How long ago was it that he left then?' he asked.

'Professor Strongbow?'

'Look,' Ghote shouted. 'Already you have been told that he left. I am asking how long. How long?'

Mira Jehangir shrugged her elegantly thin shoulders.

'Ten minutes perhaps,' she suggested.

'As little as that?'

'No. No, perhaps it was a little more. Perhaps it was nearer half an hour, or an hour. It was probably about an hour ago.'

Ghote found his hand was gripping the little brass rail of the faintly nautical counter with such force that the fragile tube was in danger of breaking. He took a deep breath and turned away.

After a moment's thought he hurried back up to Gregory's suite again. Perhaps he could tell from what clothes the American had taken where he was likely to be heading for. He worked his way through the rooms systematically. But as far as he could tell nothing had gone. A lot of clothes still hung in the two tall wardrobes. There was a faint mouldy smell when he opened them, but that was almost certainly just the time of year. The sitting room was exactly as he had last seen it with the heavy chairs grouped round the small central wicker table. There was no sign of a note.

It was just as he was leaving the bathroom that he saw it. He had dealt with the bathroom in a few seconds. There was little to see. The rust smears on the bath and the blotches on the mirrors could tell him nothing. Except that on the small mirror fastened to the back of the door there was a message. Just five words scrawled in lipstick.

Gone to Sewri – Launch there.

He understood immediately. The launch. That must be the launch that had come bearing hard down on them in the harbour. Somehow Gregory must have learned that it was up at Sewri. There were plenty of berths along the waterfront there where a boat such as the launch could be tucked away out of public notice. So the stupid idiot had rushed off at once to see if the three men who had gone for him on Elephanta were waiting there.

But the message in lipstick must surely have been left by Shakuntala? What could that mean?

There was no time to think.

He bounded down the wide sweep of the main staircase two steps at a time. What a piece of luck that he had come over in the truck.

He skated across the chequered desert of the foyer, barged through the heavy, tinted swing doors and shot across the wide, startlingly hot pavement towards the truck. The driver, the same nutty-faced fanatic perpetually in love with his internal combustion engine, was standing by the open bonnet, tinkering as usual.

Thank goodness for some loyalty to something.

'Quick,' he shouted to him. 'Up to Sewri. Somewhere there we must find a launch. A big one, painted white.'

The man turned to him, his eyes shining at the prospect of putting his truck over a fast obstacle course through the buffeting traffic from the crowded southern tip of the city all the way to the Sewri dockland on the north-east shore. For an instant he turned back to the opened engine, unable to resist the temptation of a last, lingering wipe with his bundle of cotton waste. Then he slammed the bonnet back home, nipped like a monkey into his seat and a moment later they were jockeying out into the traffic stream.

And at that second a contrary thought jumped into Ghote's head. For all his eagerness to be pushing on, something that he had half-noticed in the foyer of the Queen's Imperial Grand sirened obscurely for his attention.

The truck jerked to a sharp halt as a flock of pedestrians waiting to make the broad crossing coming up to Flora Fountain suddenly decided it was now or never.

The abruptness of the stop seemed to shake the realization of what he had seen in the foyer to the forefront of his brain. It had been the tall, gangling figure of V. V. Or had it?

Ghote found that he could not be sure. He had gone through the lobby at such a speed. He had the clear impression of the tall, dark-suited form of the journalist in his mind's eye now. But was it simply the result of an over-worked imagination. Or had he really been there? Spying once again at a critical point, with that uncanny knowingness that seemed to be the hallmark of India First?

They were edging their way round Flora Fountain itself now, the impassive portly nymph looking down on them from a swirl of frozen draperies as cars, bicycles, lorries and buses bullied and banged in a fume-heavy tangle of shouted obscenities, racing engines and squealing brakes. Ghote decided he would never know the answer to his questions for sure. He tried to sit back and conserve his energies.

But progress was maddeningly slow. For all his driver's pouncing concentration and the smooth reliability of the vehicle, they were still only in Dadabhai Naoroji Road. Drifting slowly past on the right was the mass of the Municipal Offices, its domed tower loftily clear of everyday preoccupations against the metallic sky. He remembered the capricious fact that the statue in front was of Sir Phrozeshah Mehta.

The name presented him with the image of Colonel Mehta. He would be sitting at this instant in that bare, pared-down office, waiting to receive the information he had ordered so confidently. Ghote moved his shoulders uneasily. Would he ever match that military standard of efficiency?

Another Parsee honoured in statuary by a grateful city, Sir Dinshaw Petit, surrounded by his little oasis of greenery, slipped behind them. But the enormous, red-brick bulk of V. T. Station seemed to be taking hours to float by. Ghote looked out at the pavement. It had been somewhere here that Gregory had had that short conversation with his brother which he was so unwilling to talk about. Could it really be that they had simply discussed some deeply private family matter? It was possible. There were things that one owed it to all the history of one's childhood days not to chaffer in the public eye. But would he ever manage to find out whether it was something like this now? A few minutes before he and Gregory had been sworn friends. Gregory had acknowledged the saving of his life in the most solemn way. But now he had wantonly broken an equally solemn promise not to go anywhere without giving full information. So what chance was there of learning his inner feelings now?

Ghote glared at a dirty, bright blue truck ahead of them. It was loaded high with roped crates coming away from the Government Dockyard and it was progressing, with all the deliberateness it owed to such an important load, to some distant destination beyond the city. At the back was a small notice saying 'Horn Please'. And using the horn was forbidden.

'Get a move on, damn you,' he shouted suddenly at the square rear of the vehicle.

'I will cut past before we get to Crawford Market,' his driver said philosophically. 'Paltan Road would be best.'

Ghote sat back. It was terribly sticky and close.

Sure enough, just as they passed the *Times of India* office on the left they slipped round the outer side of the truck and slid neatly into the stream of traffic intending to fork right into Paltan Road. But the sight of the newspaper office plunged Ghote back into depressing thoughts about V. V. once more and he got no pleasure from the success of the manoeuvre.

If V. V. was an India First spy and had been there in the foyer, then already they would know he was heading this way. They would make sure Gregory had been dealt with before he stood a chance of getting anywhere near. It had been the merest luck they had been defeated up to now. It could not go on.

And progress through the traffic was still infuriatingly slow. Away on the left as they crept jerkingly along the narrower width of Paltan Road the clock tower of the Crawford Market stayed in sight far longer than seemed possible. At the complex junction where Carnac Road crossed their path it took hours to cut their way inch by inch round to the right. And even when they reached the point, just before the bridge over the railway, when they were able to head directly north again into Dongri Road there were still miles to go.

Ghote groaned out loud.

Gregory and Shakuntala knew where they were heading for. It might be the India First thugs' launch or it might be simply another false rendezvous but they knew where to go. While he himself had to search the whole waterfront at Sewri when he did get up there.

He cursed the note on the mirror for being so short. The lipstick surely meant Shakuntala had written it, but why had she said so little? Perhaps it had been because Gregory had insisted that they should go without leaving him any message, and this had been all she dared say out of a sense of loyalty. Always provided that she was not India First's spy, planted on Gregory with businesslike calm before he even knew his brother's death was anything more than an accident.

They were making quite reasonable progress now alongside the noisy railway lines of Dongri Road. But he remained wrapped in gloom.

They passed Masjid Station. Perhaps Gregory and Shakuntala had not used a taxi. Perhaps they had simply caught a suburban train to Cotton Green? It might be a quicker way to get to Sewri, if you were lucky. But a taxi seemed more likely. If Shakuntala were really wanting to help him follow, she would probably have insisted on a taxi. It would give her more chances of getting another message back to him. Only was she on his side?

He cursed.

She was out there in front of him somewhere. She and Gregory hurrying to some point on the waterfront. The answer to the whole enigma was there. But maddeningly stretches of road, infuriating conglomerations of traffic lay ahead.

At the big crossroads where Sardar Patel Road cut at right angles across their route they were held up for a clear five minutes. They broke through at last and shot away at a good speed but still not fast enough to obliterate the sheer space cutting him off from all he wanted to know.

Sandhurst High Level Station flitted past. They swung left and turned sharply into Mazagon Road with barely a glimpse of the massive outline of the J.J. Hospital a quarter of a mile away to the west.

And, for all that he knew it was ridiculous, Ghote could not stop himself sitting forward in his seat and peering at each car ahead. Something might have delayed them, and making progress like this, they might catch them up.

He spotted the yellow and black of a taxi.

'Do you see it?'

'What do I see, Inspector?'

'The taxi, you fool. The taxi. Can you go any faster than this?'

'Going as fast as possible, Inspector,' the driver replied, with a touch of sulkiness.

Ghote forced himself to say nothing more.

At the crossroads with Nesbit Road a heavy stream of lorries was rolling across their route from the left going in the direction of the P. and O. dockyard. The taxi ahead was forced to stop and they drew up alongside. Ghote whipped round and peered into its dark interior.

A fat lady in a very pale pink sari sat in deep communion with a large sticky sweetmeat, holding it in front of her between a finger and a thumb and nibbling reverently.

Ghote flopped back against the hard, hot seat.

At this very instant, he thought, Gregory may be teetering on the very edge of the trap.

The truck jerked sharply forward as his driver tried to cut ahead of the other vehicles lined up waiting to move on. Ghote noted that he was trying to get over to the centre of the road so as not to be held up by cars forking off down Love Lane a hundred yards or so ahead.

I should have had a man waiting outside the hotel day and night, he thought. I should have had someone there to follow Gregory the moment he showed his nose outside those tinted swingdoors. That was what a really efficient police officer would have done. He would have trusted no one. He would have put his whole reliance on the system, and nothing else. The simple facts dictated that if a police guard was being kept on someone then that person must never be allowed to get out of police surveillance. It was as simple as that.

And he had failed: he had let himself be ruled by his feelings about Gregory. He had simply trusted him to keep his word. It was ridiculous. And in an hour's time, or at the end of a search lasting till far into the night, he was going to find Gregory's body with a knife in it, or half a dozen bullets, in some out-of-the-way corner of the water-front.

He looked up. His surroundings were now as depressed-looking as he felt himself. Big, grimy-walled mills arrogantly squatted wherever they pleased, leaving only narrow, black passages between for the tumbledown shacks of little human ants. Solid, tall chimneys exuded serpents of thick smoke. Behind the high, dirty blank walls the clank and roar of remorseless machinery could be heard even above the noise of the truck engine.

The driver began to swing to the right.

'What the hell are you doing?' Ghote snapped. 'Straight ahead. Straight ahead.'

'Quicker to cut down into Reay Road, Inspector,' the man said placidly.

Ghote drew breath to shout him down.

But it would be quicker, he realized. Once into the straight run of Reay Road, in these more outlying parts of the city they would really be able to shift.

'All right then,' he said.

But the truck had made the turn well before he had given his agreement.

At Reay Road Station they did indeed begin to move. Ghote sat forward again, intent on the chase. In no time they were snaking into Sewri New Road and ahead of them were the grounds of the European Cemetery.

'Turn right, Inspector?'

'Yes. And fast as you can till we get to the docks. Then as soon as we do, dead slow and keep your eyes open.'

The truck hummed and whined as they took the clear road along beside the cemetery at top speed. In less than a minute they were at the docks.

Now, thought Ghote, just one bit of luck and we will find them.

'Go left or right, Inspector?'

Ghote took a long look to the right, towards the great area of the Grain Depot. The launch could be there. But equally it might not. One thing was certain: there was no black and yellow of a taxi.

'Go left. And take it dead—'

He stopped.

From the far side of the junction a figure had come suddenly running from the narrow passage between two towering godowns. A figure in police uniform, a sergeant. And it was plain that something was wrong.

The sergeant, a tough-looking veteran with a bar of grey moustache across his upper lip, came to a halt on Ghote's side of the truck breathing heavily, his face streaked with runnels of sweat.

He saluted.

'Inspector,' he said, 'seeing the blue of your Dodge was like a miracle. I have got Pal Bedekar trapped in there.'

He looked over towards the black slit of the passage between the two huge godowns. Obviously he expected Ghote to know who Pal Bedekar was.

'Good man,' Ghote said, trying to sound as enthusiastic as he could.

It was clear that this was an event of importance for the sergeant, who probably had spent twenty years in this particular, crime-ridden section of dockland. But the thought of Gregory Strongbow somewhere ahead of them, perhaps not fifty yards and in mortal danger was hammering incessantly at Ghote's brain and he could give his attention to nothing else.

'Only one thing, Inspector,' the sergeant went on gravely.

'Yes? Yes?'

'He is carrying knife, Inspector. On my own I cannot be sure to get him out. And if I am waiting too long he can climb out.'

The claim was blatantly staked.

A red fury seized Ghote. Why should this idiot stand there so seriously doling out the history of some petty dockside thief? Of all the times to have chosen to make his great capture, why had he picked on this, the moment that Gregory Strongbow was there, so near, waiting for help?

He forced himself to speak casually.

'Sorry, Sergeant. You are out of luck. I have an important . . .'

He saw the look of sheer incredulity spreading up from the grey bar of the man's moustache.

Damn him, he thought, I cannot do this to him. The climax of a long career. To throw away all those patient years.

'Well, I can give you five minutes. You want me to come after him with you?'

'Three minutes only, Inspector sahib. With someone to help, I can deal with Pal Bedekar in three minutes only.'

He turned at once and made for the narrow passage between the two tall, windowless godowns. Without hesitating for a moment he marched in.

There was not room for Ghote to walk beside him. He followed a pace behind, peering hard into the deep shadow ahead. When they had gone about fifteen yards down the passage he saw the sergeant's Pal Bedekar. He certainly looked as if he would take some dealing with. He was a heavily built man of perhaps forty, naked all but for a cloth round his middle, crouching at the end of the passage, his hands held in front of him ready for action. And he had only one eye.

Ghote felt a snicker of apprehension go through him in spite of himself. A one-eyed man: the traditional figure of ill omen.

'All right, Bedekar,' the sergeant shouted. 'You are coming out now.'

The heavy, crouching figure at the end of the passage grunted contemptuously. Ghote saw the glint of a knife as his right hand moved a little.

'Do you want me to take him, Sergeant?' he asked.

'Oh, no, please, Inspector. For this I have waited a long time. Just as long as you are there in case I make mistake.'

He advanced steadily towards the heavy, crouching figure. Ghote followed two paces behind, ready to jump the moment he saw how their opponent had reacted.

Suddenly the sergeant dived. The smack of two bodies coming into collision was like a thunderclap in the narrow passage. There was a swift manoeuvring of arms and legs in the gloom. Ghote saw the glint of the knife as it moved jabbingly twice. For an instant he lost it. Then he saw it again.

He darted in. With a jet of animal pleasure he felt his fingers digging hard into a muscular forearm. He heaved his full weight to one side and twisted for all he was worth. The knife fell to the flagged ground with a clatter. It was all over.

A minute later the sergeant was marching a glowering, defeated criminal out into the harsh light of the road. Ghote, who had stopped to retrieve the knife, came after. He noticed a patch of dark blood spreading over the sergeant's shirt.

'Are you all right?' he said to him.

'Is nothing, Inspector. A dog like this could do nothing to me.'

The sergeant gave a savage jerk to the arm he had doubled up behind his captive's back.

'We can handcuff him to some building for a few minutes,' Ghote said. 'I have a missing American visitor to go after.'

'An American?' the sergeant said.

He turned round to address Ghote directly.

'An American got out of a taxi here just before I spotted Bedekar,' he said. 'Would he have a girl with him? American too perhaps, but wearing a sari?'

'That is him,' Ghote said. 'Almost certainly. How long ago was this?'

'Only twenty minutes, Inspector. They hurried down that way.'

He pointed to a gap between two godowns a little further along the road. Ghote did not wait to hear any more. He ran full tilt into the dense shadow.

For a moment the comparative darkness forced him to check his pace. But without waiting to accustom his eyes to the gloom again he plunged on. A discarded piece of mango peel or something equally slippery suddenly sent his right foot skating along under him. He thought he was bound to fall. His flailing arms encountered the walls of the godowns on either side of the narrow passage. He spread his hands wide and saved himself. And then he was out in the light again.

The passage had led on to the quayside itself. Almost directly in front of him a small steamer was being loaded with cotton. A pair of derricks swung the big, bursting, white bales from a great square stack up through the air and down into the ship's holds. There was a knot of dockers round the stack, absorbed in their task, moving with unhurried skill, occasionally calling out some comfortable intimate joke.

Little use asking them whether they had seen an American with a white girl wearing a sari.

He looked along the quay the other way.

And at once he saw the old launch with the rust blotch near the bows. It was tied up at the foot of a flight of slimy, broken-down steps. None of the India First thugs was to be seen.

Moving fast but with caution, he made his way along under the shade of a row of godowns towards the top of the steps. No one was working up at this end of the quay and everything was curiously silent. He took care not to bring the heels of his heavy shoes down hard on the stone surface for fear that any purposeful sound would give a warning to whoever might be down in the launch cabin. The donkey engine working the two derricks behind him chugged muffledly away and occasionally the dockers could be heard making one of their loud, almost meaningless, jokes. But as he approached the tumbledown flight of slimed-over stone steps there was not the least noise and nothing seemed even to be moving.

A single brooding kite was perched totally motionless on the top corner of a high blank square of wall just at the point where the steps began.

As Ghote reached the pair of dark-rusted bollards marking the head of the steps he took one last cautious look behind him and to either side. Nothing. Nobody.

And suddenly at his feet the launch engine broke into violent life.

10

The noise of the launch's heavy engine shattering the silence of the deserted quay went through Inspector Ghote numbingly. Gregory, he thought. If Gregory Strongbow is in that boat, I have got here just in time to see him disappear.

He took one despairing look round. Away from the wall of the quay the dirty brown water stretched into the far distance with nothing breaking its surface. A craft like the launch could roar out into the wide reaches of the harbour and head away straight down south into the limitless stretches of the Arabian Sea.

The powerful engine settled down from its first crashing roar into a deep throb of contained power. It was ready to send the boat surging through the water at the flick of a lever. All that was needed was for someone to come out of the cabin, unwind the rope at the stern and toss it away. Then nothing could detain them.

Ghote took four steps along the quay and hurled himself outwards.

He landed by pure luck on a part of the launch's deck near the stern where there was nothing to injure him as he sprawled forward. Under him the boat canted sharply over and swayed heavily back. He began pushing himself up.

With a crack like a pistol shot the door of the cabin immediately in front of him banged back. The barrel-chested man who had hurled Gregory Strongbow over the cliff on Elephanta stood there.

Ghote, swaying slightly from side to side with the rocking of the boat, looked at him blankly.

What shall I do, he thought. I have made things no better, charging blindly out here like this. Why did I set myself up all alone against people like India First? This man will be too much for me by himself. And the other two are probably there behind him.

All I can do is to make it hard for them.

In the open doorway the barrel-chested thug let his jaw drop wide. Ghote registered the fang-like yellow teeth.

Then suddenly the man shouted.

'Police. The police. Quick.'

He bounded forward. Ghote could not prevent himself glancing into the darkness behind him. The other two thugs were there. And that instant of missed concentration was all the barrel-chested man needed. He hurled himself at Ghote like a battering-ram.

Ghote felt himself go down with a thud that knocked the breath out of his whole body.

This is the finish, he thought. I have let the whole police force down for ever.

It was a moment of overwhelming despair.

And then he realized that nothing more had happened. The big thug had not flung himself down with hands searching for his throat. The others had not rushed to help.

He jerked up his head.

The three of them were already at the top of the slimy stone steps. They were making off as fast as they could. He guessed then what must have happened. They could not have believed he was on his own. They were trying to get away before the rest of his men were on to them, the forces of justice always at his command.

He scrambled to his feet.

In the black space of the cabin doorway Gregory Strongbow appeared. His face looked very white under the locks of curly brown hair. He stared up at Ghote.

'How did you find us?' he said. 'How did you? You were just in time.'

The sound of his voice unlocked a torrent of emotion in Ghote's mind.

'It is not question of how I found you,' he shouted. 'It is question of how you came out to here.'

He took an impulsive pace forward so that the boat swung and swayed again.

'Yes,' he said, 'that is what you have to answer: why, when you gave your word to me you would not leave the hotel without telling, did you go all the same? What is the good of giving trust when straight away it is broken? What is the good at all?'

Gregory blinked at him.

'Hell,' he said, 'I have to sit down somewhere.'

He looked round him with the hasty selfishness of someone taken unexpectedly ill. By the craft's low rail there was a coil of rope deep enough to sit in. He took a couple of swaying paces towards it and sank down.

'You are well?' Ghote asked with sudden concern. 'They have not done something to you? And Miss Shakuntala Brown? Where is she?'

The American smiled wanly.

'She's OK,' he said. 'Come out, Shakuntala.'

Shakuntala appeared at the cabin doorway. She too looked pale, but seemed otherwise all right.

'No,' Gregory said, 'all those guys had done so far was sneak up on us and keep us in there. What they were fixing to do was scheduled for later, I guess. When we were well out to sea.'

'You are all right, Gregory?' Shakuntala said, looking down at him anxiously.

'I'm OK, more or less. It's just that I should never have got out of bed. Your Doctor Udeshi was quite right.'

'And why did you get out of bed?' Ghote asked. 'Why did you come out here? That is what I want to know. That is what I think I have a right to know.'

For some time Gregory did not answer. Then he looked slowly over towards Ghote.

'Yes,' he said, 'you have a right. I feel bad about this. A fine time to feel bad too, I suppose, when I've got myself into a hell of a jam and you've got me out of it.'

He grinned, and then immediately looked totally serious again.

'I want you to believe this,' he said. 'I felt badly about all this before ever those guys sneaked up on us. I really did. Before we even saw the launch I wanted to call you and tell you what was happening. But, damn it, you never see a call-box in this city.'

'You have to go into a shop and make request,' Ghote said.

'You do? I'll know next time. But that doesn't make it any better, me taking off like that in the first place.'

Again he looked at Ghote with honest, serious eyes. Ghote looked coldly back.

'Well, damn it,' the American said, 'I was lying there in that fantastic fluffed-up bed with nothing to do but think. And I reckoned you didn't seem to be interested in anything except what I had happened to say to Hector. So I thought I should try and do something for myself. I owed it to Hector, didn't I? Didn't I?'

But Ghote was prickling.

'I am not interested in anything?' he said. 'But a great deal was being done.'

'It was?' Gregory answered with abruptly rising sarcasm. 'I didn't see too much of it.'

Suddenly he rubbed his hand across his face.

'No,' he said, 'I didn't mean that. I'll tell you the truth. I did think it. Cooped up there, I thought Indians couldn't run a police force in Paradise. But that was only a kind of patriotic nightmare. Honestly it was.'

'A full-scale hunt was taking place for this very launch,' Ghote replied stiffly. 'Men were proceeding northwards, both along the beaches on the east side and along the docks this side. Here they had already reached the P. and O. dockyard at Mazagon.'

'Where's that?' Gregory asked.

Shakuntala answered.

'It's about a mile south of us. They would have reached this place quite soon. Our Mr Batliwala sounds a bit unnecessary now.'

She smiled at Gregory with a hint of conspiracy.

'Mr Batliwala?' Ghote said sharply.

'A terrible private eye I hired,' Gregory explained. 'I used the telephone and went on asking till I got hold of a detective agency that specialized in docks security. That was Mr Batliwala.'

'And you told him everything?'

Ghote did nothing to keep the outrage from his tones. Although Gregory knew nothing of Colonel Mehta and the Special Investigations Agency, the thought that he had chosen to tell some nasty little private detective all about India First and the real reason for Hector Strongbow's death made him feel black with betrayed despair.

'I told Mr Batliwala one whole heap of fantastic nonsense,' Gregory said. 'I owe Hector at least that. I can still be trusted for something, you know.'

'And so can the Bombay Police be trusted,' Ghote answered quickly. 'Do you think we had done nothing? Not only had we nearly found this boat, but we knew the names of those thugs. They had records. They were willing to do any dirty work round the harbour for a hundred rupees among them. And if we had been left in peace we would have had them behind bars.'

Gregory shut his eyes.

'You can't make it any hotter for me than I'm making it for myself,' he said. 'And you got me out of it all too. You still haven't told me how you got here just in time.'

'I can explain that,' Shakuntala said. 'I left a message for the inspector,' she said. 'I scrawled it in lipstick on a mirror in the bathroom just as we left. I am sorry. You believed I'd stick by you.'

Gregory shook his head.

'You weren't under any obligation to me,' he said. 'And I'm the one who ought to be doing the apologizing. Apologizing all round.'

He pushed himself to his feet and came across to Ghote holding out his hand. Ghote took it.

'No more helping me without telling?' he said.

Gregory grinned.

'No more,' he said. 'Not ever.'

He pumped Ghote's hand again.

'And how about you?' he went on. 'No more bothering over what Hector did or did not say, eh?'

Ghote dropped his hand.

'I regret,' he said, 'I must keep freedom of action in all cases.'

The American looked as if he had been suddenly jabbed viciously in the ribs. After a moment he shrugged.

'As you like,' he said.

That night Ghote looked in on Gregory just before he made his final security arrangements at the Queen's Imperial Grand. He found him alone in pyjamas and a thin, red silk dressing gown drinking a final whisky-and-soda in his sitting room.

'I wanted only to tell you that I am making full arrangements for your protection tonight,' Ghote said.

He began backing out into the suite's little vestibule still occupied solely by the heavy, antiquated ironing board.

'No, no,' Gregory said hurriedly. 'Listen, Ganesh, come in a minute, will you. There's something I want to say.'

Ghote closed the heavy teak door behind him with reluctance and stepped into the sitting room. He felt that relations between himself and Gregory had fallen back into a state of chill neutrality. And, since he was pledged to discover something Gregory plainly did not wish to make known, he preferred on the whole that this state of affairs should continue. And now with this invitation to 'Ganesh' it looked as if Gregory had other ideas.

'Sit down, sit down,' the American said. 'Look, what about a drink?'

'No thank you,' Ghote said.

But he placed himself compliantly on the chair next to Gregory's.

The American sat in silence. He picked up his glass, looked at it, leaned forward and replaced it on the little central wicker table.

Ghote felt obliged to say something.

'You wish to hear more about the activities of the police in clearing up the matter of your brother's death?'

Gregory shook his head wearily.

'No, I trust you for—'

He broke off and swung round in his heavy chair to look directly at Ghote.

'It's Shakuntala,' he said.

'Shakuntala?'

'Yes, don't you see? When we went out to Sewri she was the only one who knew where I was going. And no sooner had we got there than those thugs of yours blew in.'

'But you are forgetting she left message for me,' Ghote said.

Gregory's revelation of what was worrying him had taken him by surprise. He was not concerned to pretend that Shakuntala could not be an India First agent. It was something he had even wanted to talk over at length with Gregory. But finding the American suddenly so keen to make out a case against her, he felt constrained to come to her defence. He felt he was obliged to say what he guessed Gregory really wanted to hear.

But a look of obstinacy settled on the American's openly handsome face.

'No,' he said, 'I'm not forgetting that message. But that could have been to draw suspicion away from her. I've been weighing this thing up.'

His hands were twisting nervously together on his lap as if they were fighting one another.

'Look,' he burst out, 'I like that girl. It so happens I liked her the moment I saw her. She's darned sympathetic.'

He looked over at Ghote as if he was relying on him to understand more than he had been willing to say.

Ghote felt the responsibility, and resented it a little. Gregory was too distant from him to have a right to expect such a degree of understanding. He was a foreigner. If he wanted to tell him something, then he ought to say it straight out and in plain terms.

Yet he felt that he ought to take up the challenge since it had been made. If there could ever be real sympathy between people of such different backgrounds, then this was the test.

He coughed a little primly.

'There is something I have to ask,' he said.

'Yes?' Gregory said hopefully.

'At home, are you a married man, Gregory?'

The American smiled slowly.

'I guess you took my point,' he said. 'Well, the thing is I was married. Until about a year back. My wife . . . Oh, hell, she went off with this man. In the end we had a divorce. But the point is now that I care for Shakuntala. I really care for her. And yet she could be working for the outfit that had my brother killed.'

He flung his twisting hands apart in a gesture of hopelessness.

'But she is not the only possibility,' Ghote said earnestly. 'I agree that a group as well organized as India First almost certainly has an agent watching your every move. But it does not have to be Shakuntala.'

'Well, who else could it be? Look at the way it all ties up. She came along at just the right moment to have been planted on me. She took that call for me to go to meet the guy at Brabourne Stadium. She was the one who wanted to go out to Elephanta. Of course I think she's sympathetic: it's her duty to be.'

'But on the other hand,' Ghote said persuasively, 'it was perfectly reasonable for her to answer the telephone for you. And after all she was in the boat with us when it looked as if we were certain to be drowned. And there are others who are equally suspicious.'

'What others, for heaven's sake?'

'To begin with there is Miss Mira Jehangir, the receptionist at the hotel here.'

The American frowned in thought. Then his face cleared with almost comic suddenness.

'It could be,' he said. 'It certainly could be. That woman's the most darned curious female I ever met. There could be good reason for that. Do you think she was planted here to spy on me?'

'No, she was not planted,' Ghote said. 'But it is still possible that India First may have bought her. We know they do not hesitate to purchase just what they require, whether it is dacoits on the Poona road or the use of a fast launch in the harbour.'

Gregory shifted a little in his chair.

'All the same,' he said, 'you're not just producing the possibility of this Miss Jehangir – is it Jehangir? – just to confirm for me that it really is Shakuntala all along?'

'No, no,' said Ghote. 'There is even another possibility. You are knowing V. V. Dharmadhikar, the journalist?'

Again Gregory's eyes lit up.

'The guy who interviewed me,' he said. 'That certainly fits in. What do you know about him?'

'He is a journalist,' Ghote replied. 'It is his duty to interview people like you. Certainly, he seems to hang round the hotel a great deal, but that too might be through excessive loyalty to his paper. No, we must keep all three in mind.'

'All three?'

'All three.'

Gregory put his chin in his cupped hands.

'So where do we go from here?' he asked.

'There is one thing that could be done,' Ghote answered. 'I was going to tell you that the Poona police have arrested on suspicion a certain Kartar Singh. He is cousin of the leader of the dacoits, an impudent fellow who thought it would be safe to come back to his home already. I was wondering whether to go to Poona to question him myself. I think now I should go, and you should come with me.'

'Fine, if we're going to get on to the India First top brass that way.'

'Good. Now who shall we tell that we are going?'

For a moment there was a look of perplexity in the American's eyes, then he understood.

'If we make sure only one of the three knows,' he said. 'That makes sense all right, even if it does mean I have to act as a decoy duck.'

He thought for a moment.

'Can the one we tell be Shakuntala, please?' he said.

Ghote looked at him intently.

'You are sure you want?'

'Certain.'

On the way out Ghote was careful to give clear instructions to the best man in the guard party to stand by to follow Gregory Strongbow if he as much as set foot out of his suite.

Ghote, making his way through the jostling mass of people in Dadabhai Naoroji Road with Shakuntala Brown next to him and the tall form of Gregory Strongbow on her other side, looked back for the twentieth time. The high red brick arches of Victoria Terminus lay just ahead. But this might be the moment India First would choose to strike.

In the turbulent crowd, a dazzling confusion of white-shirted, dark-headed figures with here and there a turban or a Gandhi cap or the vivid splash of a sari, how could he hope to pick out one individual manoeuvring closer for the kill?

Of course there ought not to be anyone. It was not that he had not taken precautions. His men outside the Queen's Imperial Grand had been alerted in good time. If anybody lingering there had suddenly left just after they had set out themselves, he would not have been allowed to get far. Yet it was India First that he was up against. And somehow India First always seemed one jump ahead.

He turned back and glanced over at Gregory. It was almost time he fulfilled his part of their agreement. Would he bring it off? He forced the query down. It was not a particularly difficult thing to do: he must trust him.

And at that moment Gregory looked up at the ornate mass of the huge station just ahead and turned to Shakuntala with all the innocence in the world.

'You know,' he said eagerly, 'you could catch a train from there in just a few minutes' time and be in Poona in under four hours. Up in the cool, pretty good.'

He is doing it perfectly, Ghote thought. I ought to have known he would. After all, we worked it out carefully enough together.

Suddenly Gregory stopped dead just where he was.

For a moment Ghote believed the attack had begun, something he could not make out. Then he realized that it was part of the American's performance. A tiny doubt sprang up in his mind. Was it quite right that he should be able to act out something invented as well as this? But there was no time for speculation. He listened carefully. At any second he might have a part to play himself.

'It's a great idea,' Gregory was saying. 'We take off right now. We give ourselves a really good break.'

Shakuntala was looking very doubtful. Now was the moment.

'An excellent suggestion,' he said forcefully. 'It would not be a break only, it would be a very good protection for you, Gregory. To set off without a single moment of notice.'

'But . . . But we can't just go off to Poona like that,' Shakuntala said.

She seemed very much put out.

'I mean we wouldn't get there till it would be much too late to get back today.'

'We'll go to a hotel,' Gregory said cheerfully. 'That Wellesley place was OK. We could stay maybe a couple of nights. Why not?'

'But we have no clothes. Nothing. By all means let's go to Poona if you want to. It's certainly much too hot and sticky to be in Bombay unless we must. But let's go tomorrow, after we've packed a case each.'

'No, no,' said Gregory. 'It'll spoil it to make out a great schedule and everything. That train goes in a few minutes, the Madras Express. We'll just climb into it and buy some pyjamas and a toothbrush in Poona.'

'That would be perfectly possible,' Ghote slipped in. 'Certainly for one night. I would ring my headquarters when we get there.'

Shakuntala looked all round her.

'All right,' she said, 'if you both insist. But we could still get back to the hotel and pack. The train's almost bound to be a bit late leaving. If we take a taxi both ways we'll do it.'

She began searching the noisy, jerking stream of traffic for the black and yellow of a taxi.

A spasm of anxiety went through Ghote. She was almost certainly right. They had not judged the moment quite perfectly. There probably would be long enough to get to the Queen's Imperial Grand and back. And once back there, so many opportunities would arise for someone to see that they were off somewhere, that the whole plan would be riddled with holes in five minutes. If their eliminating device was to work, no one must know except Shakuntala. If she was really working for India First, she could tell them where Gregory was easily enough in Poona.

But Gregory seemed equal to the occasion.

'We'll miss the train for sure if we start trying to do that,' he said, with what appeared to be genuine feverishness. 'You can't be certain it'll leave late. When it says on the schedule that a certain train leaves at a certain time, you just have to be there if you want to get on it.'

Ghote wondered whether these were his real sentiments. They were what Americans were supposed to feel. It was possible that Gregory had succeeded in persuading himself that the situation they had contrived between them was real.

He decided that in any case he must help.

'Look at the traffic,' he said. 'A taxi might get caught up in the most deplorable jam.'

'Quite right, quite right,' Gregory said. 'Just come on.'

And by sheer force he swept them into the great station concourse, past, round, and even over the hundreds of people standing, sitting and lying there, and on to the ticket office. There at last he suffered a check as they found the end of the right queue and stood waiting while it gradually approached a tremulous and white-bearded clerk at the ticket window.

All the while Gregory kept shooting looks at the station clock as its long minute hand twitched judderingly towards their departure time. And when at last they reached the old clerk and he fumbled and dithered interminably over issuing three air-conditioned class tickets to Poona the American's impatient fury was a sight to see.

Shakuntala turned away from the ticket window.

'Really,' she said, 'you haven't any need to worry. The train is certain to leave late.'

'Then it darn well shouldn't,' Gregory snapped.

He glared like a gorgon over Shakuntala's shoulder at the white-bearded old clerk. And the old clerk simply stopped his palsied hunt for the correct tickets and blinked interestedly back.

Ghote reflected that Gregory's unshakeable attachment to the highest ideals of punctuality was certainly making this stratagem look life-like. A feeling of impatience was beginning to disturb even his own equilibrium. What if someone spotted them before they were safely out of sight aboard the train?

At last Shakuntala stepped back from the window holding the correct tickets, all in their correct form and order. Gregory heaved a gigantic sigh of relief and began striding out towards the platform where the Madras Express was waiting.

Ghote found himself almost equally relieved. In less than a couple of minutes they would be safe in the train. And then they would be out of Bombay. They would be dodging for a little the constant, ominous watchfulness of India First. Up to now, he felt, India First might have attacked Gregory in any one of a hundred ways at any moment they chose. In Poona events would be much more under his own control. Either India First would lose the scent altogether, or they would pick it up only after a warning from Shakuntala, if she was their agent. So their attack would be limited by the need to act quickly and by having to be carried out in a new area. The pressure would be off. It seemed almost too good to be true.

And this sudden move would take him out of the orbit of Colonel Mehta for a little, he reflected. No doubt the colonel would be furious at losing contact even for twenty-four hours. He was that sort of man, always wanting to be in control. But it would be worth a dose of his anger to feel free for a while now.

He would be free, too, to do some real police work. That was in a way the biggest gain of all. After these days of floating in the void without contacts of any sort, to have to deal with a simple, ordinary criminal like the man the Poona police had caught would be to eat real food again after a diet of air. He would be working on his regular routine of questioning instead of trying to decide what people completely detached from all the realities might take it into their heads to do next. It would be like coming back to life.

He marched along with brisk, short steps behind the enormously striding American.

'Professor Strongbow. Professor.'

The voice calling from behind them was unmistakably loud and clear.

11

Inspector Ghote swung round. Caught. Caught within yards of the Madras Express waiting with steam up to whisk them from under the noses of India First. Caught within minutes of getting clean away out of Bombay and the network of dangers all round them.

As he had thought from the sound of the voice that had called after them so insistently, V. V. was standing there peering from his considerable height over the heads of the crowd. When he saw they had stopped he came over to them in his usual series of long, erratic strides. And as usual he began talking while still a good distance away.

'Hallo there. So nice to bump into you.'

'You followed us,' Ghote shouted. 'You tracked us down.'

V. V.'s eyelids dropped over his unnaturally bright eyes.

'I like to know what is going on,' he said.

Ghote glared up at him.

'Why did you follow?' he said. 'I want explanation. Now. Or I would know what to do.'

'Inspector,' V. V. said, in a tone of exasperating reasonableness, 'I have a most simple explanation: Professor Strongbow is here. Professor Strongbow is a most distinguished man. What he does, where he goes, is news, Inspector.'

'Where he goes?' Ghote snapped. 'What is it to you where Professor Strongbow goes?'

'Inspector, it is item of public interest. If Professor Strongbow revisits Poona where he was staying when his brother was killed that is a matter which my readers would like to know.'

'Poona? Poona? Who said we were going to Poona?'

'Perhaps you are not, Inspector,' he said. 'But it is strange that one of your party is carrying tickets, air-conditioned class, just for Poona itself.'

But by now Ghote had recovered from his surprise and chagrin at being caught out like this.

'Yes,' he said, 'it is true we are going to Poona. I tell you that frankly. But of course off the record. Naturally the professor does not want at this time to be the subject of public curiosity.'

V. V.'s eyelids drooped once more over his prominent eyes.

'But all the same may I ask the purpose of your Poona visit, Professor?' he said.

Gregory was caught on the hop.

'Well, why shouldn't I go to Poona?' he blustered. 'It's very hot and sticky here in Bombay. Isn't that reason enough?'

V. V. smiled.

'But is it your reason, Professor?'

Gregory looked anywhere but at V. V. His eye caught the juddering minute-hand of the big station clock.

'Darn it, I won't get to Poona at all if I don't make that train this moment,' he said.

V. V. put a bony hand on his forearm. 'You are showing touching faith in the Indian railway system, sir,' he said.

But Gregory snatched his arm away, swung round and headed like a maniac for the snorting, belching Madras Express. A porter with three cardboardy-looking suitcases balanced on his head wandered into his path. Gregory brushed past at such speed that the topmost case slipped and crashed to the ground. Its tinny lock sprang open and the contents of the case disgorged themselves over the platform.

Ghote wondered whether he owed it to the unfortunate owner to apologize for the American's rudeness. He knew that he did, but decided he had better run on, or Gregory would possibly leave for Poona without him.

And as it turned out no sooner had they found three vacant seats in one of the Madras Express's air-conditioned apartments, than with a hellish shriek of steam from its whistle the train pulled out dead on time.

Shakuntala laughed.

'Well, Gregory,' she said, 'your faith in the Indian State Railways was totally justified. V. V. will be most upset.'

'V. V.? Why should he be upset?' Ghote asked.

'Didn't you hear?' said Shakuntala. 'He followed us all the way to the platform explaining the train couldn't possibly leave on time.'

'He followed us? He must be very keen to find out why we were going to Poona.'

Shakuntala settled herself in her seat.

'Well, it was a good thing anyway,' she said. 'It gave me a chance to send a message back to the receptionist at the Queen's Imperial Grand.'

Ghote stared at her.

'To the receptionist? To Miss Mira Jehangir?'

'Yes, of course. She is the one who would need to know we are only going away for a day or two. It was kind of V. V. to say he would tell her.'

Ghote sank back in his seat. So now all three of his suspects would know Gregory was going to Poona. And, worse, even if Mira Jehangir was not working for India First, she was certainly capable of retailing this bit of information to anyone who persisted in asking her about Professor Strongbow. She would expect to get some morsel of gossip in return, and that would be that.

If only they had made the trip by car. It would have been much more convenient. But the thought of driving Gregory past the very place where his brother died had been too much.

With a long dying sigh of steam the Madras Express came to a halt. Ghote looked out of the window. They had hardly left the station.

Shakuntala giggled.

For a long time nothing seemed to happen. The huge locomotive up in front was totally silent. The Goan waiters hurried along the corridors with their trays of tea, toast and jam, trying to get as much of their task done as possible before the train started swaying and rattling over the criss-cross of lines leaving the city. The group of young people taking up most of their compartment began talking in loud voices about the break they were going to have sightseeing in the mountains round Lonavla.

Suddenly there came a sharp, but deferential tapping on the carriage window. All eyes turned. The silk-suited businessman occupying the corner seat heaved himself up. He lowered the window. Balancing on the footboard outside was a shirt-tail flapping clerk. As soon as the window was down he thrust a bundle of letters into the businessman's outstretched podgy hand. Shaking his head wearily at the rigours of his life, the latter thumped back into his seat, placed the letters carefully on the flap-table in front of him and began signing away for dear life. Opposite him his wife, looking on plump and cross-legged, allowed herself just the faintest twinkle of amusement behind her gold-rimmed pince-nez.

The bulbous American Ford taxi which had brought Ghote and Gregory Strongbow from the Wellesley Hotel across the Fitzgerald Bridge and up to the massive walls of Poona Gaol came to an impressive halt. The voluminously bearded Muslim driver pressed hard on the horn button in front of the huge closed main gate.

'This was one of the gaols where Gandhiji was imprisoned,' Ghote said.

The American looked at the implacable stone walls.

'Gandhi, eh?' he said dutifully. 'All that seems a long while ago.'

He turned round to look the other way. In the distance dotted here and there on the smooth turf of the golf course parties of players, probably army officers, could be seen moving slowly from green to green.

'Yes,' Gregory said, 'I guess Gandhi is pretty well all history now.'

'History, yes,' Ghote said. 'But it is history we should not forget.'

A warder came out through the big gate. Ghote lowered the taxi window and explained what they had come for. There was a slight delay while the man checked by telephone.

Ghote found he could not help contrasting his present situation with the days of the struggle for Independence. The task of discovering whether an American visitor did or did not know the secrets of India's atomic energy establishment was far, far away from the simplicities of the mass struggle against the British. No doubt there had been dilemmas of loyalty enough then, but surely not this terrible empty world of severed links and no trust by anyone for anyone.

The warder came back out to them.

'It is Inspector Phadke who will be seeing you, Inspector,' he said with a smart salute.

The taxi rolled forward into the central courtyard of the gaol. Gregory looked round at the lowering, grim building.

'So this was where they held Gandhi,' he said. 'The very place.'

A man in the uniform of a police inspector came down a flight of stone steps to greet them. It was clear that he was far from adhering to the austere precepts of the Mahatma. His tautly plump flesh stretched the cloth of his uniform tight. Above the strained collar his face was full and rounded with prominent lips, a thick nose and luxuriant eyebrows.

In spite of his bulk, however, he ran easily down the steps and crossed over to their taxi on the balls of his feet.

'Inspector Ghote? I am Phadke. Please to come in. I take it you will want to see the prisoner right away. I will take you down myself.'

He spoke with a briskness that contrasted sharply with the softly rounded curve of his chin. Ghote thanked him and, as he got out of the taxi, explained that he had brought Gregory with him because he had been the victim of a series of unexplained attacks since his brother's death.

Inspector Phadke looked a little put out by this unexpected addition to the party. But with a slight shrug of his well-padded shoulders he led them in. They followed him along a number of high, stone corridors echoing loudly to their steps. They went through several iron-barred gates and at last down a deep and narrow stone staircase. At the bottom there ran a corridor between two ranks of cells, their outer walls consisting solely of close-set, dark-rusted iron bars running from floor to ceiling. Apathetic prisoners scarcely lifted their heads as they passed. The air was sharp-smelling.

At the end of the two ranks of cells there was another barred gate. Past it, they descended a short flight of chill stone steps and came into a little square, stone-walled room lit by a single dim electric bulb. At the far side there was a small barred door. Inspector Phadke tugged a heavy key from his pocket and with a grating squeak turned it in the lock. He stepped back and hauled the door open. In a tiny cupboard of a cell there half-stood, half-crouched an almost naked man.

'Here you are, Inspector,' Phadke said. 'Kartar Singh, or what is left of him.'

It was impossible to see more than the dull gleam of naked flesh at the back of the tiny cell.

'Out,' Phadke shouted, taking a lunge forward towards the open door.

The dimly seen figure did not budge.

'Out. Or do you want me to come and get you?'

Again the figure kept utterly still.

'All right,' Phadke said slowly, 'we will have to see what we can do to make you move.'

He took a lunging step forward towards the cell, a faint smile beginning to show itself on his full lips.

And suddenly the man in the darkness leaped forward. Phadke jumped sharply back.

Kartar Singh stood just outside his tiny cell and laughed shakily.

'You tell me to come out,' he said to Phadke.

They could see now that he was a tall man, though he still stooped as if it would be a long while before he could stand upright again. In the little cell he must have had to bend almost double.

He looked round slowly. The eyes gleamed in the gaunt face under the heavy crop of uncut Sikh hair. The jutting gush of his beard was matted and foul. But it was his naked body that attracted attention now that they could see it under the dim light of the single bulb. It was criss-crossed by dozens of heavy welts leaving hardly an inch of skin unbruised. Many were still crusted with dried blood, others had already begun to fester.

'Well, there you are, Inspector,' Phadke said. 'As nasty a dog as you could find.'

He stepped forward and thrust his heavily jowled face into the Sikh's.

'However, we are beginning to show him that insolence does not pay,' he said. 'Isn't it? Isn't it?'

Just for an instant the stooping, broad-framed, battered Sikh appeared to quail. Then he drew himself up painfully until he could look down on Phadke.

'Little inspector,' he said, 'it would take more than you to make me tell anything of my friends, more than you and all your men.'

Inspector Phadke brought the edge of his open right hand swinging up into the Sikh's face. The thud of the blow sounded like an explosion in the little, square, stone-walled room. Kartar Singh swayed from the impact. But not by the slightest sound or change of expression did he acknowledge that anything had happened.

Phadke turned away.

'Well, Inspector,' he said, 'do you think now we could be doing more?'

Ghote looked from the plump, firm figure of the Poona inspector to the gaunt, glaring-eyed Sikh.

'No, Inspector,' he said, 'I am certain you are doing your utmost.'

'Then shall we go?' Phadke said.

'Yes, by all means. I do not think there is anything I can do here.'

Ghote detected a rustle of protest from Gregory at his side. The American had been increasingly restive ever since they had seen the crouching form of Kartar Singh at the back of his cupboard of a cell with its inescapable stink and back-breaking lowness.

'Come along, Gregory,' he said quickly. 'I am sorry I had to bring you here.'

Gregory said nothing more as they followed Inspector Phadke back past the ranged cells of the other prisoners and up into the politer regions of the administrative offices. Every now and again Phadke tossed them a cheerful remark over his shoulder.

'It is better when they are a bit tough,' he said, as he opened the door of his own office. 'There is more to getting them to talk then than just one hour's work.'

'And so far you have got nothing at all from Kartar Singh?' Ghote said.

Phadke laughed sharply.

'So far nothing,' he replied. 'But do not worry yourself, my good Inspector. It will not be long now before he betrays all his friends. And in the meantime I am quite happy.'

'Inspector,' Ghote said, 'all the same I would like a word with him.'

'With Kartar Singh?'

Inspector Phadke sounded genuinely startled.

'Yes, with Kartar Singh.'

'But you have just seen.'

'I know. And now I have had time to think about him, and I would like to see again.'

'As you wish,' Phadke said with a gusty sigh.

He began to close the office door.

'No,' said Ghote. 'Up here.'

'Up here? In my office?'

'If you object, perhaps in some other room.'

Phadke looked round his office. It was a spacious and airy room, looking out on to a wide balcony where one of the prisoners squatted, naked except for a loincloth, heaving interminably at the rope of an antiquated punkah wafting in sluggish gusts of air. His services were retained apparently in spite of two large-bladed fans with their wires running, bare and unpainted, across the ceiling and down to a switch near the door. In the centre stood a large, glossy desk with a telephone and three heavy glass ashtrays on it. The chair behind was sturdy and comfortable-looking with arms curving embracingly round. To one side there was a large leather armchair with a low table placed conveniently near it and another ashtray, on a stand. Two big carpets added even more to the air of luxury. And even the harshness of the bare stone walls was softened by a pair of bright calendars hanging on either side of the big clock in places where the mortar was friable enough to take a nail.

Ghote noted that the calendars were from past years and each rivalled the other in the scantiness of the clothes its girlie wore.

'Well, if you insist, Inspector,' Phadke said. 'We can have him in here as well as anywhere else.'

'But I am wishing to see him alone,' Ghote said flatly.

'Alone? You do not—'

Inspector Phadke pulled himself up.

He laughed, tersely.

'Very well, Inspector. If that is what Bombay wants. I will have him brought up.'

He walked out through the still open door. In the corridor he stopped and turned back.

'But please, Inspector,' he said, 'do not treat him like a baby.'

'I do not think Kartar Singh is a baby,' Ghote said.

Inspector Phadke evidently decided to take this as the nearest he was likely to get to a promise. He turned and marched off down the echoing stone corridor.

Gregory Strongbow hardly waited till Ghote had pushed the door closed.

'Ganesh,' he burst out, 'this can't be allowed to go on. Why, you've only got to take one look at that Kartar Singh to see he's worth a dozen of your Inspector Phadke.'

'Yes,' Ghote answered, 'Kartar Singh is a man whose determination in not giving away his friends is most admirable.'

'But can't you do something?' Gregory said passionately. 'That Phadke, he'll kill him before long. I swear he will.'

'You are probably correct. Kartar Singh would let himself be killed rather than betray his companions.'

Gregory's eyes shone.

'Then you will do something? You can order him to be taken out of here?'

'No,' said Ghote.

A look of incredulity appeared on the American's open face.

'But . . . But, look here—'

Ghote interrupted sharply.

'Those men Kartar Singh is protecting so loyally killed your brother,' he said.

The words at least had the effect of making Gregory think. He stood in front of Ghote almost visibly preventing himself saying anything more. After a little he swung away and went to stare out of the broad window in front of the wide balcony where the punkah wallah still swung at his rope like an automaton.

'All the same,' he said, 'that man . . . Well, he is a man. Hell, I don't know.'

The sound of steps in the corridor outside stopped him saying anything more. The door opened and Inspector Phadke came in followed by Kartar Singh, held on either side by a hefty warder twisting an arm behind his back.

'Here you are then, Inspector,' Phadke said. 'Would you like these two to stay? They are most skilful at holding a man down while he is questioned.'

'That will not be necessary,' Ghote replied.

Inspector Phadke smiled.

'Very well,' he said. 'But do not think you will get anywhere by using fair words to this raper of his own sister. I know him better than that.'

He jerked a nod at the two warders. With a single concerted movement they hurled the battered, blood-stained Sikh to the ground at Ghote's feet. Then they turned and left the room. Inspector Phadke followed, still smiling.

Ghote waited in silence till the door was shut and the sound of steps on the far side had faded away. Then he looked down at Kartar Singh, who had remained where he had been flung on the floor with his head just resting on the edge of one of the big carpets.

'You can get up now,' Ghote said.

Kartar Singh moved his head a little and looked upwards suspiciously. Then in one swift movement, which still showed how lithe he must have been not long ago, he was on his feet. He stood in front of Ghote, arms folded across his chest, looking down with an expression of disdain.

'I see Inspector Phadke has been treating you roughly,' Ghote observed.

'That son of a dog could do nothing to me.'

'I think he could,' Ghote said.

'Then you are a fool.'

The Sikh infused the words with insult.

'This is what I will do,' Ghote said. 'You tell me where your cousin and the two others are hiding, and I will have you taken to Bombay out of the hands of Inspector Phadke.'

'Inspector Phadke.'

Kartar Singh spat on to the floor, missing Ghote's right shoe by little more than an inch.

Ghote, who was watching the Sikh's gaunt and battered face, heard Gregory Strongbow draw in a sharp breath. But he did not let his eyes move for an instant.

'Well, Kartar Singh, will you tell?' he said.

'You think I will tell a boy like you? I have not let out a word to that Phadke, for all he has done.'

'I think all the same you will tell me.'

The Sikh did not even reply.

'Very well,' Ghote said, 'I will come and ask you again. When shall it be?'

'I do not care when you come or when you go.'

The Sikh turned away with elaborate unconcern. He looked across at the big window. Outside the sky was pale blue and half a dozen kites were wheeling lazily across it.

12

For almost a full minute Ghote watched Kartar Singh as he looked out at the sky and the wheeling kites. Then he spoke sharply.

'That is all you have to say? That you do not care when I come again?'

Kartar Singh stiffened slightly but remained silent.

Ghote went over to the door, opened it and called along the corridor to Inspector Phadke's two warders.

'You can take him back now.'

The two men hurried in, grabbed at the Sikh with plain delight and thrust him in front of them through the door.

'I will come tomorrow at noon,' Ghote said.

He turned to find Phadke stepping in casually from the balcony.

'Well, Inspector Ghote, you did not have much success, I fear.'

'No,' Ghote replied, 'I did no better than you.'

Phadke smiled.

'But I am going to win in the end,' he said. 'And in any case I shall enjoy the struggle.'

'I expect so,' Ghote said. 'But I would like to see him once more all the same. In this office, if you would not mind. Just at noon tomorrow.'

Phadke shrugged a little.

'The requests of Bombay are our command,' he said. 'I will have him up here at the time you state. But you will not mind if I first remove the carpets?'

With the toe of his gleamingly polished brown shoe he obliterated the mark of Kartar Singh's spittle.

When Ghote and Gregory got back to the Wellesley Hotel, eager to wash and relax since they had gone up to the gaol as soon as they had reached Poona, someone was waiting for them. Sitting comfortably installed with Shakuntala at a veranda table with glasses of lime juice, looking cool and inviting, was none other than V. V.

Ghote felt a spasm of disproportionate annoyance.

He marched straight up to the gangling dark-suited journalist.

'V. V.,' he said, 'what are you doing here? How did you get to Poona so soon? We left you in Bombay. You were going back to the Queen's Imperial Grand.'

V. V. smiled.

'It is very simple,' he said. 'I did not take your message to the hotel in person. I telephoned from the station. And when I had finished I found your train still waiting at the end of the platform. So I decided to accompany. Poona is much pleasanter than Bombay just now.'

'That may be,' Ghote snapped. 'But have you no duty to your paper? Will your editor be content to know that you are up here in the cool when he must be down in the damp and heat?'

But V. V. remained undisconcerted.

'I have good reason to be here,' he said. 'Professor Strongbow is here.'

'But that is no reason for you to come,' Ghote shouted. 'What reason is that? Professor Strongbow is visitor only. If he comes to Poona when the weather is sticky and unpleasant in Bombay, is that a newspaper story?'

But V. V. only let the eyelids fall across his prominent eyes and said nothing.

'Listen,' Ghote said earnestly. 'What if I should tell you that it is specially important that Professor Strongbow should be left alone?'

V. V.'s eyes opened wide for a moment.

'It is specially important?' he said.

For a second Ghote calculated.

'Yes,' he replied. 'I will trust you and be completely frank. A matter of national security is involved.'

V. V.'s bony face looked up at Ghote.

'Inspector,' he said, 'you are telling nothing I do not know already.'

Ghote checked his rising temper.

'If you know that,' he said as icily as he could, 'then it was your patriotic duty not to have come up here, bullying and badgering.'

V. V. shook his head in disagreement.

'Inspector Ghote, you have a lot to learn,' he said. 'You must not think that you have only to pronounce the magic words "national security" to be able to do whatever you like without any attention being paid to you. That is very far from the case.'

Ghote let the temper rise, and boil over.

'How dare you say such things? When it is national security matter, it is national security matter. The Press and its stories of this and that do not count one bit any more.'

V. V. pushed himself out of his small wicker armchair.

'And who is to be judge of when it is really national security?' he asked. 'Is it to be the people who have most to cover up? Inspector, you should be glad there are newspapers in this country. Glad to the bottom of your heart.'

He stalked away along the veranda, a big, black, untidy crow of a figure. Ghote glared at him.

But for the rest of the day they saw little of V. V. and next morning Ghote, who had made sure that he was up very early, was comforted to find from a bearer he questioned that at least the journalist was still sound asleep.

When Gregory Strongbow came out of his room almost an hour later Ghote was outside waiting for him.

'Good morning,' he said to him, 'I hope you slept well.'

'Once those guys with the scooter-rickshaws had quietened down I did,' Gregory answered.

'I am sorry,' Ghote answered, 'but I had to insist you had a room at the front. At the back someone could have crept in without being once seen.'

'So that was why,' Gregory said.

'I had to take every precaution. Especially when I had deliberately brought you here to be attacked,' Ghote answered.

He would have liked to have gone on to discuss the failure of his elimination plan and what they should do about Shakuntala in consequence. But he found it difficult to broach the subject. All the way to Poona in the train the day before Shakuntala had chattered away about the wild romantic scenery of the mountains as they crept up the Western Ghats. She had been full of the ancient days when the legendary hero Shivaji and his faithful horsemen had defeated the powers of the Mogul armies in daring engagement after daring engagement. And Gregory had watched her with shining eyes.

He had laughed at her and had questioned her more extravagant assertions, like the story of how Shivaji had giant lizards at his command trained to scale perpendicular cliffs with ropes attached to them. But Ghote saw that though Gregory liked to tease her with such doubts, it might be a very different matter should anyone else doubt Shakuntala herself. He decided to wait for a little at least.

Gregory looked round about him cautiously.

'You think they'll try something today?' he asked.

'It is very probable,' Ghote replied. 'We have one advantage though. They will want to make their attack look like an accident. They would not want to have two American tourists murdered within a few days.'

'So we keep our eyes skinned for an accident happening on purpose,' Gregory said. 'Where do we begin?'

Ghote smiled.

'By having breakfast,' he said. 'We owe it to our bodies to look after their wants.'

In the dining room, where Gregory managed to evade the sternly

British breakfast in favour of pawpaw, yogurt and jasmine tea, Shakuntala soon joined them.

'Oh, I do hope we can stay here for a bit,' she said. 'There is so much more to show you, Gregory.'

The American grinned.

'Sure,' he said, 'I've heard such a lot about Poona, you know. All those old British colonels and the pukka sahibs. What was it I read on that War Memorial yesterday? Something about going forth to fight for the Empire? That's the stuff.'

'But no,' Shakuntala exclaimed passionately.

And then she realized that she had been kidded and gave Gregory a look of mock exasperation.

'For that,' she said, 'you'll spend all morning going over the ruins of the old Saturday Palace built at the height of Poona's real greatness. The gates have spikes on them to halt elephant charges, and not far away there's the street where the really big traitors had the privilege of being trampled to death.' The waiter, at that moment placing in front of her half a yellow pawpaw sprinkled with lime juice with its cluster of black seeds gleaming in the middle, suddenly gave a loud chuckle.

'You are lucky if you go there today,' he said. 'Most likely you would see an actual trampling by two elephants.'

Gregory leaned back and looked up at him.

'Oh, come now,' he said, 'I may be only a hick American tourist but you can't expect me to believe that.'

The waiter grinned till every tooth in his head was showing.

'Oh, yes, sahib,' he said, 'is perfectly true, I am assuring you.'

He adjusted the table napkin on his arm.

'Is a film unit present there today, sahib,' he said.

Gregory suddenly grinned back at him.

'You mean that? A film unit down at – where is it?'

'In the Shanwar Peth, sahib. This very morning, a.m. There will be film unit making a big filming.'

*

But when they arrived in the Shanwar quarter of the city they found they were by no means the only ones to have heard about the filming. The whole district seemed to be filled with one single-minded crowd so that even the wide streets had become impassable.

Ghote was less single-minded.

'We will never get there and back in time in all this,' he said. 'We should go somewhere else. I am told that Visram Bagh Palace should not be missed. Or in the Empress Gardens it would be nice and cool.'

'And miss the elephant trampling?' Gregory said. 'Why, that waiter would never forgive us. Come on.'

He plunged with determination into the jammed mass of white-backed figures in front of him. Shakuntala adroitly took advantage of the vacuum formed by his wide shoulders. Ghote could only follow at a distance.

But before long the American got himself entangled in one of the numerous bicycles of Poona and Ghote managed to catch up.

'Please, Gregory, listen,' he called out. 'Remember I must be back at the gaol at noon exactly. I cannot afford to be late.'

Gregory lost his expression of idleness.

'OK,' he said. 'But there ought to be time for one quick look. It's early yet.'

Ghote felt he could not deprive him of his pleasure. After all he was the victim of a tragedy. He was entitled to what passing happiness he could get.

'One look we will risk,' he said.

He hoped that as they got nearer the street where the filming was to take place the crowd would get so thick that even Gregory and Shakuntala would decide to back out. But he had reckoned without the colour of Gregory's skin. Suddenly people began to notice that they had a guest among them. The inextricable jam of humanity mysteriously opened and in no time at all they were in the very street that was being kept clear for the filming.

'Up there, up there,' Ghote heard people shouting.

'Yes, the balcony. He will see from the balcony.'

He looked up. A narrow balcony ran for most of the length of the street. Already it was packed to danger point with onlookers, but within five minutes he found himself up on it with Gregory and Shakuntala somewhere ahead of him.

He looked at his watch. Only nine o'clock. With any luck the filming would be well over before he had to set off to keep his appointment at the gaol. He began to look about him.

He could have wished Gregory had not been hustled up to the balcony ahead of him. Five yards of squeezed together spectators were separating them and even in the security given by the very density of the crowds the tall American was a vulnerable target. But he decided there was nothing he could do for the present. And in fact Gregory was probably more in danger from the frailness of the balcony than from any form of attack from a distance. The delicate structure creaked with ominous sharpness every time a new eddy of movement occurred among the dozens of people crowding its narrow length. And its filigree iron railing was already in a precarious enough state. At one point, he noticed, a whole stretch had been carried away at some already distant date. An old piece of red silken cord, the relic of heaven knew what luxurious palace at the height of the British Raj, stretched across the gap just by the spot where Gregory and Shakuntala were standing to a point about four yards farther on.

It looked as if it would stand almost no strain at all. But probably there would be some warning if it did begin to break. It would fray rather than snap, and there was a decorative iron lamp-bracket or two on the house wall to clutch on to. In any case the drop was not all that great.

Ghote looked along to the far end of the cleared street. Towering above everything else there was a pair of massive elephants, standing patiently while their mahouts arranged their heavily decorated caparisons on the directions of one of the film unit. There was a lot of shouting and argument going on. Other members of the film unit stood talking to each other or sat waiting in upright canvas chairs. Ghote wondered if any of them were stars. Raj Kapoor might be there, even. It would be something to see him act in the flesh. Or would the magic vanish? He thrust the doubt away.

It became very hot, even though the balcony was in the shade. After a while the women in the house behind began passing out refreshments of various sorts, brass tumblers of buttermilk, lengths of sugar cane, smallish mangoes cut in half. He accepted one of these. The flesh turned out to be pithy and so sharp-tasting that it set his teeth on edge. Just as he was about to drop the piece over the balcony railing he realized that one of the women was watching him from inside the house. He put the half-fruit up to his mouth again and pretended to eat.

The woman smiled to herself amusedly and he realized she had known all along that the mangoes were acid.

And still there was no sign of progress from the film unit. He looked at his watch and was startled to find it was already past ten o'clock. He began to calculate how long it would take them to get back to the Wellesley Hotel if they had to leave before the filming was over. At all costs he must not miss seeing Kartar Singh at the gaol at exactly noon.

Could he safely leave Gregory behind? What if Shakuntala was with India First? If she saw him going, would she contrive to arrange an accident herself? Or signal to an accomplice in the crowd? No, Gregory would have to come with him.

He looked at his watch again. Ten past ten.

He started to try and catch the American's eye. But it was not easy. The five yards of balcony separating them were jammed with a score and more of people, and Shakuntala was keeping Gregory busy as she pointed out with great animation various incidents among the crowd opposite. Was this some sort of plot of hers to make Gregory stay where he was?

He shook his head angrily. Fantasy was no help at all.

At last he succeeded in gaining Gregory's attention. He held up his right arm as high as he could and tapped the watch on his wrist with the index finger of his left hand. Gregory obediently looked down at his own watch. Then he twisted round to the packed crowd behind him and shrugged his shoulders helplessly.

Ghote looked along towards the film unit. To his surprise there had been a sudden spurt of progress. The two great elephants had been dressed to someone's satisfaction and were being manoeuvred into position looking down the street. A camera on a small trolley had been wheeled forward. A clapper-boy was parading up and down the empty street enjoying the laughing applause of the crowd nearby. The canvas chairs of the director and other important figures were being assiduously repositioned.

From a small, brightly painted van two men brought a floppy dummy dressed in all the glory of eighteenth-century Maratha costume with four papier-mâché iron balls bouncing and bobbing from wrists and ankles. They laid it carefully in the victim's place. There was a last flurry of shouted orders and counter-orders. The mahouts gave the tails of their animals vigorous twists. As one, the two beasts lifted up their trunks and roared.

'Sound. Cameras. Action.'

The triple yell hushed the crowd into instant, respectful silence. One more twist of the elephants' tails, another agonized double roar of protest. And the charge was on.

Shoulder to shoulder in the confined passage of the street, swaying and bumping into each other, trunks extended, enormous feet lifting and stamping, the beasts charged.

For a moment Ghote felt himself back in those more brutal days. For an instant even he shared the desperate, pounding fear that the chained and weighted victim, only days before a proud aspirant to the seat of power, must now be feeling.

And two seconds away from the moment of destruction the elephants halted. The leading beast looked at the sprawled figure. Its eyes glittered with suspicion. Slowly it reached forward with its trunk. It felt at the staring, wide-mouthed, horror-stricken face.

And with a practised jerk it tugged off a convenient morsel, conveyed it to its mouth and happily munched.

At the far end of the street the director fell into a rage which must have been a lesson and inspiration to his actors. Ghote shut his eyes tight and wished he was far, far away.

After a little he began trying to signal to Gregory again. But he and Shakuntala were completely absorbed in watching the tantrums in the distance. He tried to work out if, after all, there was a route from them along the crammed balcony and in at a window. Perhaps they could all three meet inside the house.

And it certainly seemed that beyond them there were fewer people to the square inch. Perhaps the view was less good from that angle. He saw that one man was already moving. He watched with interest. The man was young and wore dark glasses. He was bareheaded, with a rather spoilt-looking, plumpish face. When he raised both arms to work his way past a portly matron in a maroon sari, Ghote saw that he was wearing a deep-blue bush-shirt, very clean and fresh.

He seemed to be making steady progress by means of discreet shoving combined with an occasional desperate wriggle. Ghote thought that he could easily do the same. He looked over at Gregory wondering how, amid all the jabber of excitement, he could possibly attract his attention. And to his delight he saw that the big rage scene at the far end of the street had mysteriously evaporated. The director was talking earnestly to one of the mahouts while the other urged both elephants back into position for a new charge. An assistant was kneeling beside the victim rapidly moulding his face into respectability again.

Ghote once more consulted his watch.

Eleven o'clock all but two minutes. If the trampling went all right this time, with the crowd pouring away they should be able to get up to the gaol in time still.

Once more the clapper-boy paraded in front of the camera. Once more the director called for sound, camera, action. The mahouts leaped forward and jabbed their charges with short pointed sticks viciously in the rear.

Immediately the beasts let out prodigious roars of pain and disapproval. They shot forward into the empty street. Their ears were spread wide, their tusks flashed, their trunks were raised high. They trumpeted defiance and lumbered unstoppably down on their victim.

And at that moment Ghote saw the young man in the dark-blue shirt.

What distracted his sight from the overpowering spectacle of the careering elephants he never knew. Perhaps it was because the youth's arm in the crisp, blue material was the only thing moving besides the rampaging, terrified, stop-at-nothing beasts. But whatever it was, he saw what was happening up on the balcony with the concentrated clarity of a scene lifted out of a jumbled illustration by a giant magnifying glass.

The young man was hacking away at the red silk rope with a short-bladed knife.

In two seconds it was bound to snap. And the consequence was equally inevitable. The press of spectators leaning forward to see the stampeding elephants would tumble irresistibly down.

The drop was not great. Few of them would even be injured. Until the elephants reached them.

And the timing was perfect. Ghote glanced quickly towards the shrilly trumpeting beasts. They would arrive at the point where the people on the balcony would fall before anybody had even had time to pick themselves up. And Gregory was foremost among them.

'Stop. Stop.'

Ghote shouted with all the force his lungs could muster. But he knew it was useless. A mere shout was not going to stop the young, intent, plump figure sawing so concentratedly at the last strands of the red silken rope. And in all the noise from the elephants no one else was going to hear.

The short, glinting blade hacked its way through at last. With one appalling lurch the crowd on the balcony tumbled to destruction.

13

Ghote, safe himself on the part of the balcony with the iron railing, could only watch helplessly as events took their course. For a few seconds even he thought the India First man's plan was going to fail after all. Gregory, the instant he had realized what was happening, had swung round and grabbed for one of the lamp brackets on the wall behind him. He had reached it and it had taken his weight.

But then Ghote, still powerless to intervene, had seen Gregory look back and try to catch hold of Shakuntala. But she had been well beyond his grasp. And he had let go of the bracket.

Ghote even wondered whether he had seen what he thought he had. The whole sequence of events had all taken place so quickly. At one moment the old red silken cord had been intact with the blue-shirted India First agent sawing away at it. Then it had snapped. At once the crowd on the balcony had lurched forward in one slow, solid mass. Gregory had shot out an arm towards the lamp bracket, had turned almost as soon as his fingers had come in contact with it, and then had let go at once when his effort to seize Shakuntala had failed.

But whatever had happened, both of them were down in the tangle of struggling people in the street now. And the charging elephants were hardly ten yards away.

Ghote flung himself suddenly forward as the people around him, their faces shocked with fear, scrabbled wildly away from the gap in the railing.

If Gregory hopes to help down there, he thought incoherently, then I can too. I can at least try to land on my feet and get between them and the elephants.

He found himself poised to jump.

And, in a totally unexpected burst of lucidity, the whole scene seemed caught for ever just as it was at that instant. The elephants were frozen with their great front legs raised in the charge, never to descend. The tangled mass of people in front of them stayed fixed in its inextricable confusion waiting for imminent destruction through an eternity. The young assassin, slipping dexterously away from the scene of his crime, was caught in an attitude of slinking evasiveness as by a lava flow. The red silk cord he had just cut dangled, still swinging slightly, held unmoving as if it were a delicately observed detail in some huge allegorical painting.

The red silk cord.

The frozen instant passed. Ghote knelt swiftly and seized the end of the cord still attached to the railing beside him. Immediately below Gregory was rising to his feet among the chaos of limbs. Ghote shouted. He shouted with every atom of his strength.

'Grab the rope.'

At the same instant he flicked the loose end towards the tall American. And Gregory saw it. He shot out his arm and snatched it.

A moment later he had taken a good turn of it round his wrist. In another moment he had seized Shakuntala from the mêlée. He kicked his feet clear, reached up with his free hand and grabbed the rope again three feet higher up, and heaved.

Ghote, twisting a leg round the railing beside him, leaned over as far as he dared, and further. He got his hands behind Gregory's back. He tugged upwards. Gregory, with an enormous grunt of effort, propelled himself towards him and swung Shakuntala, perhaps unconscious, perhaps merely dazed, on to the balcony. A second later he was kneeling beside her. Below the elephants reached the struggling mass of people.

Ghote shut his eyes.

As if by an iron drop curtain the thought of what must be going on in the street below was shut out from his mind. And in its place came the insistent buzz of his own affairs.

He had a duty to perform. Getting Gregory to safety was only one part of it. Someone else had a claim on him too: Kartar Singh.

Up in the silence of the gaol nothing of the tumult in the Shanwar Peth would penetrate. There a different set of circumstances awaited him. With urgency.

The whole time that it took Ghote to impress on Gregory how urgent the situation was and to get him down through the house and out into the lane at the back was one confused jumble of shouting and expostulation. Sudden, unexpected, pointless questions kept presenting themselves. The American showed a tendency to wander dazedly in any direction but the right one. Could they try to revive Shakuntala, he asked. Was it really safe to leave her behind?

Ghote knew that he was snapping unnecessarily in fighting off these suggestions. Someone confronted with an experience like Gregory's in a foreign land and without friends might be expected to be in a difficult state. To counter it, he himself should have been calm and reassuring. Instead he had shouted, grown excited, been thoroughly unreliable.

Only when at last they both stood in the lane at the back of the house did he succeed in gathering himself together. Then he knew at once and clearly what he had to do. He had to get the pair of them to the gaol as quickly as possible. Nothing else at all mattered, not even setting anybody on the assassin's trail.

He looked at his watch.

It was 11.45.

They certainly could not hope to get to the gaol in fifteen minutes by foot. It was a question of how easily they could get hold of a taxi, tonga or scooter-rickshaw.

'Follow me quickly,' he said to Gregory.

The American obediently loped after him as he ran down the length of the lane, past a vermilion-coloured temple bright with profuse pictures of the gods, and out into the broad street beyond. At once Ghote realized that getting transport of any sort was going to be almost impossible. The news of the disaster with the elephants had spread like a leaping flame. People by the hundred were hurrying to the scene. Others were struggling equally furiously to get along in the other direction, either to fetch help or to avoid the unpleasantness. Together they blocked any fast progress.

And now that the crowds were involved in something more than a simple outing Gregory had lost all his foreigner's magic. No one pushed him courteously to the front any more. Instead he was someone more in the way than other people, bigger, different, more irritating.

Ghote wondered whether to abandon him.

Without him he would certainly get along faster. Wriggling and squeezing his way through alone, he might knock minutes off the time it would take him to get to the gaol. But he knew he could not do it. Gregory was in his keeping. And he had already had a sharp enough lesson about the seriousness of his danger. The young man in the blue shirt might already be aware that his plan had failed. If so, he would be doubly keen to strike again. India First were not the sort of people to take reports of failure calmly.

Ghote twisted round and dug his shoulder viciously into the gap between the two people in front of him.

Darting through and tugging the lumbering American after him, he suddenly saw just off the entrance to a nearby lane a cluster of bicycles abandoned by their owners when the filming had begun. He realized at once what they could do. They could take a machine apiece and, pedalling for all they were worth, make a wide detour beyond the crowded city centre, through the wide avenues of the Cantonment area, and round to cross the Fitzgerald Bridge at last and head for the gaol. They would have to go like the wind to do it, but with luck it should be possible.

They would also have to steal the bicycles. The policeman in Ghote rose up in protest.

He turned to Gregory.

'Out this way,' he said. 'We are going to take two of those bicycles.'

The American was quick to grasp the notion.

'Good idea,' he said. 'And we go round some back way?'

'We will have to steal the bicycles,' Ghote said.

'Come on then,' said Gregory.

The bicycles were piled up against the steps of a small square tank with a line of washing fluttering above it and a couple of buckets standing on the edge. But no one was bathing or doing the laundry at that moment. There was nothing to stop them going up to the heap of bicycles, selecting the two fastest-looking and wheeling them away. Ghote felt during every second that a uniformed constable of the Poona force ought to materialize from nowhere to stop the crime. But no one anywhere took the slightest notice.

They rode off as fast as they could go.

At the end of the lane they cut across a wide street and plunged into another passage on the far side. Here all along a row of little, open shops men were squatting beating at small brass pots with a cumulatively deafening sound. Two minutes later they emerged into a broad road much less crowded than before. They shot along it at a fine rate, swerving only occasionally to avoid a goat, another cyclist or a speeding scooter-rickshaw.

Past St Mary's Church, swing left, up through the Indian Infantry Lines, past the Polo Ground, under the railway, and they were shooting across Fitzgerald Bridge.

As they did so, Ghote held his hand as steadily as he could in front of his face and tried to read the time on his watch. Seven minutes to twelve: about a mile to go.

'We will do it,' he called back over his shoulder to Gregory.

Then a quick flutter of doubt assailed him. He turned backwards again.

'But hurry.'

As they sped along beside the golf course on a mercifully clear road, he wondered whether there would be any difficulty at the gaol gate. After all, they were criminals, bicycle thieves.

But he was also an inspector of police. The warder on duty recognized him, made no comment on his mode of transport and ushered them both in.

Again Ghote looked at his watch. They had done it easily. Three minutes to go.

At the foot of the staircase leading up to Inspector Phadke's office they met the inspector himself, standing exuding an aura of satisfied calm. Ghote was briefly conscious of how quickly his breath must still be coming after their wild ride and of how sweat-stained he must look.

'Good morning, Inspector,' he said, as cheerfully as he could. 'Is my man ready for me?'

'Of course, Inspector,' Phadke replied, with a little bow from his paunchy waist. 'Naturally a request from you would be obeyed to the letter.'

'Thank you,' Ghote replied. 'I am sorry to have troubled you.'

He began to make his way towards the stairs.

Phadke put a hand on his arm.

'One moment, Inspector,' he said. 'I would much appreciate if I could be present at your interview.'

Ghote looked back at him.

'I am very sorry, Inspector. I will not keep the man a moment. But I am convinced that if I am to get anything out of him I must do it on my own.'

Phadke's hand tightened a little on his forearm.

'Nevertheless, Inspector,' he said, 'I want to be present.'

Ghote dropped his arm sharply and swung round on the lowest step till he was facing Phadke squarely.

'I much regret,' he said, 'but I cannot agree.'

Phadke smartly climbed two steps till he stood a little higher than Ghote.

'The man is under my charge, Inspector,' he said.

'And the case is under mine,' Ghote said.

'Then we will have to see which is the most important.'

'No.'

Ghote looked at Phadke intently.

'Inspector,' he said, 'you know as well as I do that I am officer in charge for the whole business. The fact that you have custody does not affect issue.'

Phadke smiled broadly.

'Of course, of course, Inspector. But cannot we discuss in peace? Let us go into that office there and see what we can decide without unpleasantness.'

He nodded towards the open door of an office on the other side of the broad passage.

Ghote looked at his watch.

'Inspector,' he said, 'there is one minute only till noon.'

He set off up the stairs, nodded to the two warders outside Inspector Phadke's office and entered. Kartar Singh was standing looking up at the clock on the wall facing the desk.

'It is Inspector Ghote,' he said. 'You are not late.'

'Of course not,' Ghote said. 'I promised for twelve o'clock.'

The battered Sikh contrived to smile.

Then for a moment it looked as if he was going to fall, so suddenly did he sway to one side. Gregory, who had been following Ghote closely as a shadow, put out a hand to save him.

Kartar Singh shook it off.

He turned to Ghote again.

'Well, Inspectorji, since you have been such a good boy you shall have sweetmeat.'

Ghote kept utterly still.

'A temple in the Sahyadri Hills,' the Sikh said. 'You go to Peral village and take the track to Narjat. By a little lake you turn right. It is half a mile along the path.'

'You are lying,' Ghote said quickly.

Kartar Singh looked at him, stony-faced.

'You can prove. Go there.'

'We will go,' Ghote said. 'And if we find you have told the truth, I will have you transferred to Bombay straight away.'

Suddenly the Sikh seemed to choke back a sob.

'I do not care if I stay or go,' he said. 'I have sold them to you now.'

Ghote turned to Gregory.

'There is nothing to keep us here any more,' he said.

They took the bicycles to get back into the city again. It seemed the easiest thing to do. They went nearly as fast as when they had been racing to get to the gaol by noon but they rode side by side now and a few shouts of conversation were possible.

'Listen, Ganesh.'

Ghote turned his head to indicate that he could hear.

'I want to thank you again.'

'But nothing is necessary,' Ghote shouted back.

They swished on over the even surface of the road.

'It is necessary,' Gregory shouted. 'It's very necessary: I thought you were fouling up the Kartar Singh business.'

Ghote did not turn his head. There was nothing to turn for.

A moment later more shouted words came past him.

'How did you work out he'd break up like that?'

'By looking,' Ghote shouted. 'He seemed to be at his end of tether. But he is a proud man: he could not give in at once.'

'You certainly timed it right anyway. And now what?'

'To go and see if I was right. We must hire a car. But first I have to call at the police station.'

'Why is that?'

'I want a gun. They will be armed. Even for just seeing if they are really there a gun is necessary.'

'A gun?'

The shout floated into the air. They pedalled on in silence.

It was only when they were outside the police station that Gregory spoke again.

'What's the procedure for collecting this gun then?' he asked.

Ghote hurried into the building.

'I shall have to get them to telephone Bombay perhaps,' he answered. 'But it should not take long.'

'Listen,' Gregory said, catching him urgently by the elbow, 'could you fix one up for me too?'

Ghote stopped in his tracks.

'Certainly not,' he said.

Gregory looked astonished, and a little hurt.

'I can handle a gun,' he said. 'I used to captain my college pistol team as a matter of fact.'

But if he was hurt, Ghote was furious. The thoughts tumbled through his mind. Irresponsible. Playboy. Gangster. American.

He swung away.

'Absolutely impossible.'

Gregory followed him into the big, echoing entrance hall.

'I guess you're right,' he said with mildness. 'After all, I haven't done any shooting in a long while. It's somehow not considered dignified for a professor to fool around down at the range.'

As soon as they got back to the Wellesley Hotel, Ghote with a heavy Service revolver bulging his pocket and banging against his thigh, they saw Shakuntala. By association of ideas Ghote at once looked round for V. V. But for once he was nowhere in sight.

With luck, Ghote thought, we shall get away without him knowing.

In the meantime he registered the way Gregory was greeting Shakuntala. The sight of her apparently safe and sound had obviously overwhelmed him. He was fussing like a mother reunited with her lost child. Ghote left him to it and went over to the reception desk. The clerk was quick and helpful and in a couple of minutes he had arranged for a self-drive car to be brought round to the hotel entrance straight away.

Ghote went over to Gregory and told him. The American looked abruptly sheepish.

'Look, Ganesh,' he said, 'can I have a quick word with you?'

Ghote frowned slightly.

Gregory took him by the elbow and fairly pushed him across the lobby away from Shakuntala.

'It's like this,' he said in a low, urgent voice. 'Can we take Shakuntala with us? I know there may be objections, but it means a lot to me.'

A new fountain of fury swooshed up in Ghote's head. This American. Always wanting something more. Never for one instant content. If only there was not the responsibility of making sure he was safe, he would tell him to go off with the girl anywhere he liked.

And then he remembered the way the American had accepted the snub over the gun.

'All right,' he said, 'she may come, if she will do exactly as told.'

Gregory looked like a schoolboy given an unexpected half-holiday. He positively frisked across the lobby to tell Shakuntala. Following him, Ghote felt suddenly depressed.

'Hell,' Gregory said to him, 'you look as if the bottom had fallen out of the world. But we're doing all right, aren't we? We've got a pretty good idea where those guys are hiding out, and we're on our way to check. What's eating you all of a sudden?'

Ghote felt unable to explain.

'Perhaps it is those bicycles,' he said, unwilling to seem at a loss. 'I do not like to have been responsible for adding two more items to the Poona crime figures.'

Gregory and Shakuntala burst into laughter, looking at each other as if they alone could appreciate this to the full. Through the window behind them Ghote saw a little green Hindustan like the one Shakuntala had first driven Gregory in. It was drawing up outside the hotel and a man in a grease-stained shirt and a white turban was getting out.

'I think this would be our car,' Ghote said tersely.

Ghote drove. Gregory and Shakuntala had elected to sit together in the back of the little car. Nobody spoke much. Ghote was concentrating on getting along as fast as he could and on one or two private problems that were worrying him. Behind, Shakuntala and Gregory did not seem to feel the need for spoken communication.

One of the things Ghote considered, when the abruptly descending road down the wooded, crevassed slope of the Western Ghats allowed him time to think, was the matter of the assassination spot. They would have to pass it. It was only some ten miles beyond it that they would have to fork off the main road to get to the Sahyadri Hills. What would Gregory's reaction be to passing the exact place his brother had been killed?

And quite suddenly they had completed the descent. The verdant, after-monsoon woods on either side abruptly gave way to level, caramel-coloured fields. The heat took on a new steaminess. Ghote was able to push the little green Hindustan along the now straight road at a good pace without having to concentrate hard. But the opportunity for good, hard reasoning did not seem to help.

All too soon he spotted in the distance on the left the slightly rounded rise in the level ground with on top of it, standing clearly out, the huge Flame of the Forest tree under which Hector Strongbow's killers had waited so patiently. Somewhere beyond and on the other side the line of smoke from the signal fire must have risen. And now straight ahead, not far away, there were the road works. Little seemed to have been done since the time that Bholu's bullock cart had halted there, neatly blocking the whole road at just the moment Hector Strongbow had driven up so fast.

Why had he been going so fast, Ghote wondered yet again. All the driblets of information he had gathered had mounted up to that. The young, red-bearded American had been going towards Poona as if getting there was almost a matter of life and death. Why had he been in such a hurry?

Ghote looked up at the driving mirror and adjusted his position a little so that he could see Gregory's face. The serious, deep-set eyes were fixed absorbedly on the girl at his side.

Suddenly Ghote made up his mind. He would stop at the place. The vivid reminder might be just what he needed.

And then they were there. The cluster of palm-thatched huts of the little village flicked by, and a moment later the road narrowed to a single lane. Ghote pulled up.

'Hey,' Gregory said from behind him. 'Why are we . . .?'

Shakuntala leaned forward quickly.

'Do we have to stop?' she said. 'Can't we just go past?'

'I think Gregory would like to get out for a little time,' he said.

In the mirror on the top edge of the windscreen he noticed the broad-shouldered form of the American shift restlessly.

'Well, yes, Ganesh,' he said after a moment, 'of course – I mean, Hector was . . . But hadn't we better push on? There'll be other times.'

'A few minutes only,' Ghote said inexorably. 'A short rest will be a help to me. Let us get out.'

Without waiting for an answer, he opened the car door. Gregory came out a little more slowly. Shakuntala quickly followed him and he turned to her at once.

'Shall we walk to the place his car stopped?' Ghote said.

'All right,' said Gregory.

His mouth was set and he was looking straight in front of him at the neat heap of stones of the roadworks.

Ghote led the way. Gregory followed a pace or two behind. He put out his hand and Shakuntala took it. They walked in silence up to the place where Hector Strongbow's hired car had halted and where there had been that sudden volley of shots.

They stood there. Ghote watched Gregory hard out of the corner of his eye. He saw his hand was gripping Shakuntala's tightly.

Quite soon it would be the moment to take Gregory aside and ask him the question that Colonel Mehta so badly wanted the answer to. And perhaps now, in this instant of strain, his mission would be accomplished. He would hear just exactly what it had been that Hector Strongbow had said to Gregory outside V. T. Station. He would realize why Hector had been driving to Poona so fast. And he could feel that that task was over.

He felt a spurt of excitement at the thought that he could then go on, a free man, to hunt down Hector Strongbow's actual killers. He could drop back, released of all untoward responsibilities, into the familiar police routine. It would be a good moment.

Suddenly a car, coming from the direction of Bombay, pulled up just in front of them with a prolonged squeal of brakes.

Irritated, Ghote looked up. The vehicle, an oldish but still flashy-looking American convertible with its hood up, had slewed half across the road with the violence with which it had been braked. Ghote frowned. Such driving, a disgrace to the Indian motorist.

And his mouth opened in astonishment.

14

The driver's window of the flashy convertible, slewed so appallingly across the road, had been rapidly lowered and there looking out at them with an expression of wild hopefulness was Mira Jehangir.

'You,' she said. 'All of you. Here. It is a sign.'

She shot the car door open, tumbled out and came over to them at a run.

'It is a sign,' she repeated with jerky emphasis.

They looked at her in silence. None of them seemed able to think of any possible reply. At last Ghote took a step forward.

'Miss Jehangir,' he said, 'may I know what you are doing here?'

'I have run away.'

'Run away? Who from? What for?'

'He is brutal. Brutal. I could not endure one moment longer.'

Tears began to pour down her face. For a little she let them run. Then she started to brush them away with the back of her wrist so that a black smear of eye make-up spread all across one cheek.

'Please,' Ghote said with some sharpness. 'Who has been brutal? What is this? I do not understand.'

'Why, him, of course,' Mira Jehangir said impatiently. 'Mr Wadia.'

'Mr Wadia,' Gregory said. 'That's the manager of the Queen's Imperial Grand.'

'Very well,' Ghote said with calmness, 'you are running away from Mr Wadia. You state that he has been brutal. Does a question of preferring charges arise?'

'Charges? Charges? I want nothing more to do with that pig.'

Ghote received this stolidly.

'Now,' he went on, 'this matter of a sign. That is a further point I do not understand.'

Mira Jehangir gave him a look of pure scorn.

'It is a sign meeting you,' she said. 'A sign meeting Professor Strongbow.'

'Me?' said Gregory.

He was so surprised that his voice went almost squeaky.

Mira Jehangir turned her full attention on him.

'But a most wonderful sign,' she said. 'I was coming to look for you. I knew you must be somewhere in Poona. I risked everything on being able to find you. And now I have met you standing there in the road, it is a sign.'

Ghote reflected that the sign was hardly a very wonderful one. If Mira Jehangir had happened to start out a little earlier, the meeting would certainly still have occurred. Only it would have been in the commonplace setting of the Wellesley Hotel.

'And why did you want to find Professor Strongbow?' he asked.

Mira Jehangir ignored him.

'I had to warn you,' she said to Gregory. 'I had to warn you above everything else.'

'To warn me?'

Gregory sounded suddenly wary.

'You are in danger,' Mira Jehangir said passionately. 'In great danger. I have found out that much.'

Ghote marched straight up to her.

'Miss Jehangir,' he said, 'you will tell me everything you know.'

'But it is so obvious, don't you see?' she answered. 'There were those men yesterday. The ones who pretended to be from the car-hire firm. All those questions they asked about where the professor had gone. I realized at once that they were not what they seemed. And as soon as they had gone I proved it. I rang the firm. They had no such employees.'

'What questions did they ask?' Ghote demanded.

'About where he had gone. Whether he had taken all his luggage. Everything like that. Of course I told them nothing. I knew I had to put the professor's interests first.'

She turned and gave Gregory a glance of burning loyalty.

'You told them nothing? Nothing at all?' Ghote persisted.

She let him have a moment of her attention.

'Nothing,' she said. 'Not until they forced it from me. And then I knew that I had to warn the professor. Men like that do not want to know where someone is for nothing, and already his brother had been killed.'

'So you set out for Poona?' Ghote asked.

'At once. At once.'

'And this question of Mr Wadia's brutality? Where does that fit in?'

'I told you. I told you. He had made life impossible for me. I had to leave him. So I took the pig's car and set out for Poona. I knew that when I had warned the professor, he would be truly grateful to me.'

She looked at Gregory, standing there tall and reliable in his clean, well-cut tropical suit.

'I thought too you were all alone in India,' she went on. 'I thought you would need a friend.'

And suddenly her tone changed.

'But I see I am too late,' she added.

She looked pointedly downwards. Gregory was still holding Shakuntala's hand in his broad palm. He dropped it as if it was something he had picked up without realizing what he was doing. He licked his lips.

'Look, Miss Jehangir,' he said, fixing his eyes on a place just beside her. 'Look, I feel – well, I'm really more than thankful to you for telling me all this. As it so happens, it came as no surprise, but—'

'Then I have been of no help,' Mira Jehangir broke in, in a voice harsh with emotion. 'I have been of no help here. My last hope.'

'No, look,' Gregory said.

He pushed his hand into his inner pocket and brought out his wallet. 'Hell, this is difficult. But you seem to be in a jam. I mean, you may have no job to go to. I don't know what resources – well, look, I'd like you to have this.'

He stepped forward and shot out a bundle of notes towards her. Ghote could not see exactly how much was there, but there were certainly some hundred rupee notes.

Mira Jehangir looked downwards.

'No, no, I cannot,' she said. 'Or, well, it must be just a loan. A temporary loan.'

Gregory turned smiling with relief to Ghote.

'I guess we should be taking off again,' he said. 'We can't lose too much time.'

He began to walk back to where Ghote had stopped their car. Mira Jehangir drew back her shoulders.

'I too must go,' she said in an unnecessarily loud voice. 'Yes, I must go. Even though I have nowhere to go to.'

She began stalking back to her own car, or rather to Mr Wadia's.

'Well then, goodbye,' Gregory said. 'That is, goodbye for the time being.'

Shakuntala took his arm and leaning close to him whispered something energetically.

'Er – no,' Gregory said. 'I don't think so, not just at the moment.'

'But, yes,' Shakuntala said more loudly. 'You can't let her go just like that.'

Gregory looked down at her with a perplexed frown.

'I just don't see what good I could do,' he said.

'You can talk to her.'

'But, hell, I haven't anything to say.'

Gregory was beginning to sound embarrassed.

'She needs you,' Shakuntala said determinedly.

'Well, I dare say she does. But you can't go to everybody who happens to think they need you.'

Shakuntala looked up at him with eyes starting to spark.

'You must go.'

'Look,' Gregory said with some heat, 'I gave her money, didn't I? A hell of a lot of money, if you want to know. And, damn it, there's nothing else I can do.'

'You can't just let her drive away like that,' Shakuntala replied.

She was speaking loudly enough now for Mira Jehangir, sitting at the wheel of Mr Wadia's flashy convertible looking straight in front of her, to be able to hear every word.

'You Americans,' Shakuntala went on, her indignation blossoming instant by instant. 'You Americans think money solves everything. Well, let me tell you it's no substitute for ordinary, decent kindness as between one human being and another.'

'Look, I never said money cured anything. I just gave her some because she was broke, or said she was. And I did it out of kindness, pure kindness.'

Gregory was speaking quietly, but with considerable emphasis. He swung round now to Ghote.

'Come on,' he said, 'we've got a job to do.'

'You mustn't go,' Shakuntala said, as loudly as before. 'If you do, I'll stay.'

Gregory simply stood where he was, looking at Ghote enquiringly.

'Well,' Ghote said. 'We have got to hurry, of course. But perhaps a few minutes' delay, if you wanted, Gregory.'

'I don't want to stay here one single second more,' Gregory said flatly.

'All right then,' Shakuntala cut in with sudden iciness. 'I will see you later, Gregory. Somewhere or other.'

She waited for perhaps two seconds, but Gregory did nothing. Then she turned and walked over to Mira Jehangir's car. She went round the far side and got in beside her.

'For heaven's sake, let's go,' Gregory said.

Ghote followed him as he strode with enormous paces back to the hired Hindustan. They got in without a word being spoken. Ghote pulled at the starter.

They drove in steamy silence till they reached the point where they had to leave the Bombay road for the cross-country route leading to the region of the Sahyadri Hills. Here, Ghote had made up his mind, was where he would say what he had to.

So, although the side road was much less good and required constant watchfulness, he spared a moment to turn and look at Gregory. He was sitting looking straight ahead with hunched shoulders and an expression of dark sombreness.

He decided to begin with caution.

'Gregory,' he said, 'I do not think you should expect too much from this temple.'

'I'm not expecting too much,' Gregory replied morosely.

'So,' Ghote went on circuitously, 'in the event of not finding these men, or of them escaping, when we bring in men to capture them, or of them refusing in all circumstances to talk, it will be necessary then to make another approach.'

The American did not ask him what approach.

'It will be necessary then,' Ghote resumed manfully, 'to make an approach by means of Miss Brown.'

'Shakuntala?'

At least Gregory had reacted.

'Yes, you see, although it is now possible she was not responsible for the attack on you in Poona, it is still possible that she was. There is still a lot against her. Showdown will be absolutely necessary.'

'All right, all right. You're not telling me anything I don't know. Go right ahead.'

Ghote reflected dispiritedly that this was only half of what he had promised himself to say to Gregory. He took a deep breath.

'There is another matter also I would like to get cleared up,' he said.

Gregory was staring broodingly at the pot-holed road ahead.

Ghote gave a prim little cough.

'It is the matter of your talk with your late brother outside V. T. Station before you set off for Poona,' he said.

Gregory swung round towards him so violently that he gave an involuntary twist to the driving-wheel. The car swung wildly towards the edge of the road before he regained control.

'Look here,' Gregory shouted, 'I've said once and for all. What Hector told me and what I told him is a personal, family matter and of no concern to you at all. Do you get that?'

'Yes, Gregory,' Ghote said.

In even blanker silence they drove on till they reached Peral village. Here Ghote stopped and made enquiries from the small crowd that at once surrounded them. They still did not talk as they set off again along the cart track to Narjat which had been eagerly pointed out to them.

Fields gave way to jungle as they bounced along the deeply rutted track, and Ghote had plenty to think about merely keeping the floundering little car pointing in the right direction. Eventually their steady climb was interrupted by a short level stretch, and there at the end of it was the little lake Kartar Singh had spoken of. Ghote felt a sense of relief that at least so far the tortured Sikh had not misled them.

He halted the car in the shade of a giant banyan with the white-washed stone of a wayside shrine lurking in the depths of its canopy of multiple dangling roots.

'We would have to foot it from here,' he said.

They were the first words either of them had uttered to each other since Gregory's outburst. But they seemed to do nothing to break the ice.

Gregory simply grunted an acknowledgment, and Ghote locked up the little car without another word.

It was true that any question of driving was impossible. The track Kartar Singh had indicated was scarcely a yard wide, a mere trodden earth-line in the rich vegetation that now faced them.

'It would be half a mile only,' Ghote said.

He spoke cheerfully, not because he hoped to alter Gregory's mood, but because quite suddenly he had felt the need for reassurance himself. This was unknown territory to him. The close alleys of the Bombay slums where even in the full glare of midday there were patches of black darkness held few terrors any longer. Even the most lawless criminals there were within his scheme of things. He knew the way their minds worked. They were, in a way, friends. But in this jungle ahead of them now there were animals. How did their minds work? In no circumstances could they ever be friends.

'If you are ready,' he said to Gregory, 'we will go.'

'OK.'

They set off down the soft winding path. In less than two minutes it was impossible to get the slightest glimpse of the car or the huge banyan by the lake. The jungle surrounded them.

High elephant grass towered over their heads. Great trees turned the sunlight into a shimmering, darting mystery. Long creepers plunged downwards immobile and sinister. On all sides there was noise, chattering, twittering, suddenly breaking out into wild screaming. And everywhere there was sharp movement, insect-jabbing, unexplained writhings, flowers and butterflies bright, beautiful and somehow wrong.

The thought of pythons, of cobras, of deadly kraits entered into Ghote's mind and would not go. Abrupt clumps of thorn bamboo caused the path to twist and circle till all sense of direction was utterly confused. It was oppressively hot with a thick steaminess which wetted the whole body from head to foot.

Gregory, who had been forced by the narrowness of the path to drop behind, suddenly spoke loudly.

'Hey,' he said, 'when Kartar Singh told us it was half a mile, did he mean half a mile along the path or half a mile as the crow flies?'

'I do not know,' Ghote said.

A sharp-edged blade of grass swept across his forehead. The

sudden contact hurt and he put his hand up to rub the place. He saw it was streaked with blood.

Blood, he thought.

An unreasoning fear began palpitating somewhere inside him. He was smelling of blood. He was bait.

'Say, would there be tigers in jungle like this?' Gregory asked.

'No,' Ghote snapped.

He had no idea. But he could at least will that there should be no tigers.

He plunged forward. The path seemed to get even narrower till leaves were constantly brushing him on either side. And from behind after a long period of grunts and heavy breathing Gregory suddenly spoke again.

'Gee,' he said, 'I don't mind admitting it: I'm scared.'

Ghote stopped where he was and let the feeling of relief pour through him. He turned round. Gregory certainly looked very apprehensive with his face sweat-streaked, his cream-coloured suit green-smeared and dusted with layers of pollen and with a short, triangular tear on one sleeve.

'I am somewhat scared also,' Ghote said.

He smiled a little.

Gregory grinned back.

'Come on, let's push on,' he said. 'It can't be so far now.'

Ghote turned happily.

'No, I am sure you are right,' he said. 'We will see.'

He strode forward. The path took a turn round the bole of an immense sal tree. And there was the temple.

The jungle cleared ahead of them and in the middle of the small open patch the temple stood. It was not a large building and it was in a state of some neglect. But beyond doubt it was the place Kartar Singh had described.

Ghote wondered how it had got there at all. Perhaps at some time in the distant past a meteorite had fallen at this remote spot. Such an event would bring worshippers quickly enough. But with the passing of time fewer and fewer would make the long journey with the inhospitable jungle waiting at the end. You could not expect people to be faithful for ever.

And now the deserted building had been picked on as a hiding place by Hector Strongbow's killers.

Ghote felt in his pocket for the heavy, dangling revolver. Beside him Gregory parted a clump of tall elephant grass to get a better view.

'If they're there, they're inside somewhere,' he said in a low voice.

'We must creep right up,' Ghote replied. 'They cannot see us. There are no windows.'

Gregory gave him a quick smile.

'Should be easy up to there anyway,' he said.

Ghote took the gun out of his pocket. For a moment he struggled with the safety catch.

'Listen, Ganesh,' Gregory said, 'you're sure you wouldn't like me to handle that thing?'

'No thank you,' Ghote answered, with a new touch of stiffness. 'I have not served in Chicago. But during my training I passed in range practice. Sixty per cent.'

'Go ahead, go ahead. I shouldn't have spoken.'

Ghote forgave him.

'We shall go then?'

'Right away.'

They crept forward. On the soft, moist earth their shoes made no sound. They reached the beginning of the clearing. Ghote looked at the American. He looked back at the temple. All was silent there. He advanced across the short grass. No challenge came. Out of the close jungle it seemed strangely quiet without the constant buzz and hum of the insects and the callilng and twittering of the birds.

They reached the cover of the outer wall of the temple and stood with their backs to it trying to regain some calm. Some three yards away was the entrance, a square archway six feet wide and five high.

After a moment Ghote nudged Gregory. Then he dropped to all

fours and crawled along the wall till he had reached the corner of the arch. Very slowly he put his head round the jamb at ground level where a watcher inside would be less likely to realize what was happening.

When he had got his head sufficiently far round the square stone pillar of the jamb he lay still and waited till his eyes were accustomed to the gloom inside. Bit by bit he began to make out the main features of the temple interior.

There was little to discover. The building consisted apparently of one low-ceilinged hall unsupported by columns. At the far end, black against the light brownish stone of the back wall, there rose up from a low stone platform the short, round-topped, pillar-like form of a linga, carved for worship perhaps from the original meteorite which had fallen on this spot.

And this was all. Nothing else to see. No one.

He got to his feet. Gregory sidled quickly up to him, an expression of enquiry on his face.

'We had better go in,' Ghote said.

He stepped sharply through the archway. And, as he had expected, nothing happened. The temple was bare and echoing. He felt a welling sense of despondency. Having found that the temple did in fact exist, somehow he had never expected that Kartar Singh was still going to turn out to have cheated them.

'No, look,' Gregory shouted suddenly.

Seizing Ghote's arm, he dragged him helter-skelter over to one of the walls. Then he pointed.

In the darkness behind the jutting linga Ghote saw what it was Gregory had spotted. There was a second chamber to the temple. A much smaller archway, directly behind the linga, led into it. It was possible still that India First's hired thugs were waiting there.

Ghote pointed the revolver in the direction of the dark oblong of the archway and advanced. He waved Gregory to silence and crept forward on tiptoe, straining every muscle to catch the slightest sound from the darkness of the inner chamber. Step by step he approached and not the faintest noise of any sort disturbed the ancient calm around him.

Then at last he was within a pace of the squat doorway.

One sharp jump forward.

And he laughed shortly.

'Empty,' he said. 'It is hardly big enough to take all three of them.'

Gregory came up and peered in his turn into the little dark chamber.

'Well,' he said, 'I guess that Phadke was right after all. Your Kartar Singh has led us on a pretty fine wild goose chase.'

15

Inspector Ghote stared mournfully into the darkness of the little cupboard-like room behind the temple linga. Even with prolonged peering, it was still so far from the light that it was possible to make out little more than the fact that the hiding place was bare.

He slowly straightened up. He was unable to restrain a long, deeply disconsolate sigh. And then he jerked back to the short doorway.

'Wait,' he said.

He darted forward and knelt down. A moment later he got up again.

'Look at these,' he said to Gregory.

The American looked intently down at what he was holding in the palm of his hand.

'Cigarette butts,' he said. 'And a bit from a packet.'

'The sort of people who might come to worship here, if anyone does come, do not smoke factory-made cigarettes,' Ghote said. 'And touch them, Gregory.'

Obediently Gregory put out a finger.

'They're warm,' he said. 'Still warm.'

Ghote took them across towards the light coming in from the main entrance.

'Cavander's,' he said. 'They are very common, of course. But on the other hand the packets found under the Flame of the Forest where the dacoits waited were Cavander's also.'

'Heck, Ganesh, I'm sorry,' Gregory said. 'I was too quick with that wild goose stuff. Listen, those guys must have heard us coming. We weren't too quiet in all that high grass. They must have—'

'Ssssh.'

He stopped like a jammed machine at the sight of Ghote's tense, listening face.

After more than a minute he whispered very quietly into the inspector's ear.

'You're dead right. They're coming back.'

For a little they both waited, standing tautly by the temple entrance, craning to hear more. And bit by bit they did hear. The sound of the tall, dry-topped elephant grass rattling as it was parted, the noise of a body lunging through a tangle of vegetation, grunting and muttered speech.

Ghote pulled the revolver from his pocket again.

'Quickly,' he said, 'one either side of the archway.'

Gregory understood at once. He held out his hand briefly as if asking whether after all he should not have the gun. But the instant Ghote shook his head he moved quickly into position and stood poised in ambush beside the bright rectangle of vibrating sunlight that the archway presented.

The sounds of the approaching enemy grew louder and louder.

Then a distinct voice called out.

'Inspector Ghote. Inspector Ghote. You are there?'

Ghote and Gregory looked at each other.'They cannot know it is me here,' Ghote said, quite loudly. 'Those men would not know my name even.'

'Help. Help. Oh, please, help.'

The cry was agonized and pathetic.

Still pointing the gun, Ghote stepped out into the bright sunlight.

He had been ready to find himself the victim of a trap, but had not really seriously expected it. And nothing in fact occurred.

The shouts began again. He ran towards the jungle where they seemed to originate. Behind him he heard the thump of Gregory's feet. At the edge of the jungle an old peacock from the top of a dead, leafless tree let out a strident warning cry.

Ghote stopped.

'Please help.'

The cry came again. Ghote plunged down the path. And less than ten yards into the jungle he had his answer.

Of all the people, V. V. was standing there, looking wildly in every direction, the tail of his ridiculously sombre dark jacket caught firmly in a small clump of thorn bamboo.

'What the hell are you doing here?' Ghote exclaimed.

V. V.'s wild cries ceased.

'Inspector, Inspector, it is you.'

'Of course it is me. But what are you doing here?'

'Is the temple near? Did you find? You did not get lost? You were not attacked by some animal?'

The questions shot out, and the gangling journalist's huge Adam's apple jerked and bobbed with them.

Ghote took him firmly by the arm, disengaged the back of his jacket with a sharp tug and piloted him back to the path.

'The temple is just here,' he said. 'And I think you would be better out of the sun inside it.'

And, surely enough, almost as soon as he had entered the cool darkness of the deserted building, V. V. began to recover. He launched into an insistent tirade of gratitude.

Ghote cut him short.

'What are you doing here?' he barked. 'Still you have not told.'

V. V. blinked his prominent eyes.

'But, Inspector, I was about to say. It is perfectly simple. I followed you. At the Wellesley they told me you had left just that moment, by hired car. So I also hired and I took the risk of choosing the Bombay road. Perhaps I would have missed you. But luckily I encountered Miss Shakuntala Brown, and—'

Gregory Strongbow's broad hand slapped suddenly and swiftly down across the journalist's mouth and was held there hard. Ghote looked at him in astonishment. But the expression on the American's face instantly explained everything.

Someone else was approaching the temple.

Ghote listened. And this time there was a difference in the sounds which reached them in the temple interior. They were more definite, more controlled. From time to time a voice called softly and received an equally confident and quiet answer. It was plain beyond doubt that now several men were moving towards the temple, coolly ready to deal with any opposition.

And suddenly the calls took on a changed note. They ceased to be quiet instructions going from one of the oncomers to another: they became sharp shouts directed at the temple itself.

'Come out. Come out. You in there, come out. Both of you. With hands up.'

Ghote thought quickly. Then he put his mouth close to V. V.'s left ear as Gregory held him.

'You hear those men calling?' he said quietly.

He saw the whites of the journalist's eyes flick towards him.

'Those men are dacoits,' he went on, 'the dacoits who shot Hector Strongbow. And now they are coming for us. On the orders of India First.'

As he spoke he watched V. V.'s face with every atom of concentration he was capable of. And the look of understanding that came into his prominent eyes at the mention of India First was unmistakable.

Ghote decided to take a risk.

'Let him go,' he said to Gregory.

After an instant's hesitation, the American obeyed. V. V. shook his head as Gregory's grip loosened. For a moment Ghote thought he was going to call out to the advancing thugs that he too was an India First man.

But he shut his mouth again and looked at Ghote with eyes wide with curiosity.

'You know about India First then?' Ghote said.

'It was the story I was after,' V. V. replied. 'It would be the story of a lifetime.'

'You will not have any lifetime if you are not careful,' Ghote replied brusquely. 'Just listen to me.'

A new look of fear came on to V. V.'s face.

'Listen,' Ghote went on rapidly, 'those men called out just now "Both of you". They said "Come out, both of you." '

He glanced up at Gregory.

'You see what this means? They think that you and I are in here only.'

Gregory's eyes gleamed.

'You could be right,' he said.

'We must risk that I am. Now, V. V., flatten yourself by the wall just there, next to the archway. And wait. Gregory and I will run back to a little room behind the linga there. We will make as much noise as we can doing it. If we are lucky, the three of them out there will rush in after us. And then you will slip out. Do you understand?'

V. V. was looking sick with fear. But he nodded agreement.

'Very well,' Ghote said. 'If you get out without being seen, then get up that path as fast as you can. Get in your car and drive like hell along the Bombay road to Panvel. There are plenty of men in the police post there. Get them back here just as quickly as you can.'

'But will there be enough time?' V. V. said.

'It will not be easy to get us behind the linga,' Ghote said. 'We have a gun. But hurry only.'

V. V. nodded again and licked his lips.

He tiptoed over to the wall beside the archway and stood waiting. Ghote looked at Gregory.

'Are you ready?'

'OK.'

'Then, now.'

They turned together and ran towards the darkness behind the linga on its low platform. Ghote brought his heavy shoes banging down hard on the stone floor and the sound of the double set of footsteps rang out and echoed in the temple hall.

'Back. Back,' Ghote shouted. 'Get right to the back.'

Then, just as he swung round one side of the linga and Gregory swung round the other, the light coming in from the archway entrance was suddenly blotted out. He dived for the black doorway of the little chamber an instant after Gregory.

As he scrambled round he saw three figures rushing across the hall on the far side of the linga platform. He jabbed the gun in their direction and pulled the trigger.

The noise of the shot in the low-ceilinged temple was like an explosion. It halted the onrush of the thugs as if they were figures from a stopped film.

And as the echoes at last died away there was a long silence.

Gregory came and knelt close to Ghote under the low arch of the chamber entrance.

'Do you think V. V. did get away?' he whispered.

'I could not see,' Ghote answered. 'But if he stayed where he was we will know quite soon. They cannot miss seeing.'

They waited and waited. And then at last the thugs began talking to each other in low voices.

'I cannot make out what they are saying,' Ghote whispered. 'But it must mean V. V. got out. They are all three talking.'

'Pity you didn't manage to get one of them when you used the gun,' Gregory replied. 'We can't have all that much to shoot with.'

'Six rounds,' Ghote whispered back.

He felt suddenly acutely depressed. If only he had fired with less panic. If he had succeeded in putting one of the dacoits out of action, they would have been a great deal better off.

'Never mind,' Gregory said. 'At least your friend V. V. got away, and that's what's going to mean most in the end.'

'My friend? Why do you say he is my friend?'

Gregory grunted a laugh.

'You certainly trusted him if he wasn't your friend,' he said.

'I thought it was the only thing to do to take the risk,' Ghote answered.

The thought that he had taken the risk, and that it seemed to be paying off, comforted him.

'What made you think he might be safe after all?' Gregory asked.

'What he told himself: that he thought he had story of a lifetime. I thought that it might be that what had made him follow us through the jungle and everywhere was just getting story for his paper. I think it comes above everything with him.'

'You could be right,' Gregory said. 'I always felt there was something a little over-zealous about that guy. Dedicated to getting the truth in the news, eh? Well, we have 'em that way back home.'

'Let us hope we are right,' Ghote said. 'Because unless he sticks to his story now, we are going to be left here until it is too late.'

'Yes,' Gregory agreed. 'I don't think we can hold out in this little cubby hole for ever. I could do with some light for one thing.'

Ghote did not reply. There was nothing to say.

In the darkness they crouched together listening and peering out. Occasionally they heard the dacoits exchanging muttered comments. Ghote suspected that they were evolving some plan. They were certainly taking good care that nothing they said could be heard.

And then, without the least warning, the second attack came.

A shot banged out. Ghote heard the bullet smack into the wall just above the archway. It sent down a scatter of stone splinters.

Then he glimpsed a figure darting across the hall. He brought the gun up quickly and, as he did so, another bullet hit the wall over his head. It seemed to be nearer this time and the noise was deafening. The figure in the gloom was still running. He fired.

But there was only a redoubling of the booming echoes in the low hall in front of him.

'Heck,' said Gregory, 'the guy's got to the back wall here. Kind of puts us in a cross-fire if we put our heads out from the doorway.'

With a sinking heart, Ghote realized that what Gregory had said was only too true. Only by coming well out from the doorway was there a hope of getting at the man on the back wall, and coming out that far would present the other two thugs with a sitting target. The situation had turned sharply against them.

He nudged Gregory.

'Please,' he said, 'take.'

He held out the gun to him, butt foremost.

'Hell, no,' Gregory said. 'That was a pretty tricky shot you had there. Anyone might have missed it.'

'No,' Ghote said. 'There was time to have hit. I would like you to have the gun.'

'Well, I'll take it for a time anyway,' Gregory said. 'You need a rest, I guess.'

He took the revolver and waited, kneeling on one knee, as far forward into the low archway as he dared to risk going.

But it seemed the dacoits were in no hurry to exploit the advantage they had achieved. Once again they began calling out to each other. This time they had to speak more loudly because of being separated, and Ghote was able to make out what they were saying. He translated for Gregory's benefit.

'They are complaining there is not enough light.'

'They are? What about us? Still, I guess they're right. We must be pretty hard to see in the gloom here.'

'They are saying something about a torch.'

'A torch? Do they have one? If they do, it could be pretty bad.'

'They are going to fetch. One of the two by the main entrance has gone.'

'Do you think he'll be long? Maybe this is the time we ought to try a bit of action ourselves.'

'No,' Ghote said. 'It is definite we must stay here. It would be quite easy for the two of them, the moment we show our heads.'

Gregory laughed sharply.

'Guess it would be shooting a couple of sitting ducks all right,' he said. 'And those characters aren't going to stick to any sporting rules they got from the British.'

'No,' Ghote replied soberly. 'They believe in shooting to kill. That is certain.'

Once more they waited.

It was a long time till the torch arrived. But eventually it came, as Ghote had known it must. The man bringing it called out cheerfully that he was back. There was a brief discussion. And then – click – the light came on.

It was obviously ideal for the dacoits' purpose, a good, strong light sending a hard white glare right into their little hiding place.

And at almost the instant the light shone out the third attack began. Shots banged out in quick succession both from the pair near the temple entrance and from the third man on the back wall. And this time the bullets were not all smacking harmlessly into the wall above them. Some were getting right into the little chamber itself in spite of the screen which the linga and its platform gave.

And a few moments later Ghote was hit. It seemed to be a bullet that ricocheted off the wall behind him. He felt it as a sudden, totally unexpected, searing pain in his right arm. And with the shock he simply yelled out loud.

There was a shout of triumph from the dacoits. Ghote felt his head swim. Then nearer to him he heard Gregory fire.

And a few seconds later the torch went out and a long silence followed.

'You all right?' Gregory said quietly.

'I think I am.' Ghote said. 'I think it was my arm only.'

He felt at the place where the pain was with his left hand. There was a lot of blood, but the bone seemed hard and firm still.

'I think it was flesh-wound only,' he reported.

He felt braver for having used the words, and found himself able to make a confession.

'I screamed out,' he said. 'I regret. But I am not used to being wounded.'

Gregory laughed.

'It was a darn good thing you did yell,' he said. 'Those guys thought they'd finished us. They came out with a rush and I'm pretty certain I got the guy along at the back here.'

'I should have given you a gun in Poona,' Ghote said.

Gregory chuckled.

'Well, I'm in better practice than I ever thought I'd be,' he admitted.

He glanced back at Ghote.

'Look, you should try to get that shirt off,' he said. 'You're losing a hell of a lot of blood.'

'All right,' Ghote said.

He gritted his teeth and began easing his shirt past the wound. New blinding waves of pain came with every movement but he forced himself to go on.

Suddenly the two dacoits near the entrance switched the torch on again. Gregory leaned forward tensely and Ghote stopped his work on the shirt. But no attack came.

'Must be making sure we don't try creeping out,' Gregory said. 'Gives me a good light to get a bandage on you anyhow.'

Ghote went back to getting the shirt off while Gregory turned to his sentry position again. After what seemed an interminable time Ghote was able to tell Gregory that he was ready.

'You watch and I'll work,' the American said.

Ghote, whose head was beginning to swim in earnest now, managed to crawl to the chamber entrance and look out into the dim hall beyond the linga. He heard Gregory rip the shirt into strips and then felt him deftly winding them round the wound.

'Good thing I did do this,' the American said after a little. 'You're blood from here down, boy. If you'd gone on like that, you'd have been out cold before long.'

'I am feeling better already,' Ghote replied.

'That's great. Now just make a knot here, and you're OK for a bit anyhow.'

Gregory tied his knot. Then suddenly he spoke in a voice so loud that it seemed almost indecent.

'Hey, wow. Do you see that?' he said.

'What? What is it?' Ghote exclaimed.

'Gee, sorry, did I startle you? To tell you the truth I was a little startled myself. I just saw the walls of this little hidey-hole.'

Ghote looked. The walls of the little chamber were now steadily illuminated by the strong beam of the distant torch. And what neither of them had had any time to see since the torch had come on was for the first time starkly apparent: every inch of the walls' surface was covered with an exuberant foam of miniature carvings, and every one of the figures represented was in direct and unequivocal celebration of the art of love.

'Yes,' Ghote said, 'they are called mithunas. They are well known. Though these are the first I have seen, except in books when I was younger. But I had not heard of any in these parts.'

'I've read about mithunas, all right,' Gregory said. 'Most people have.'

He looked along the lines of little, sensual figures running along the wall beside him, moving determinedly from one voluptuous group to another. From time to time he stopped to take a quick, sharp glance out into the temple hall where the two dacoits waited in silence.

'Yes,' he said, 'I'd read about them. The books talk about "playful sculptures". Playful. Playful, heck.'

He went back to the archway entrance and made a long, slow survey of the hall beyond. After a little the two dacoits began talking again, but kept their voices too low for it to be possible to make out what they were saying. The light from the torch fell so steadily that Ghote decided they must have found somewhere to prop it.

Still looking outwards, Gregory spoke again.

'What do you make of them, Ganesh?' he said.

Ghote knew that it was not the dacoits that he was talking about.

'Well,' he said carefully, 'they are carvings of things we know exist only.'

'Yes. Yes, I guess so,' Gregory said thoughtfully.

He fell silent again. Ghote's head was throbbing angrily now and he was grateful for the peace. He decided he would close his eyes for a little.

'Yes, that sort of thing exists all right,' Gregory said suddenly, after what seemed to have been a long time.

Ghote kept his eyes closed.

'Yes,' Gregory went on, 'it exists. I mean, that was the trouble with Irene. My wife. My ex-wife I ought to call her.'

Again he lapsed into silence.

After a little Ghote, overcome by a sudden anxiety, opened his eyes wide. Gregory was still kneeling on one knee at the chamber entrance, looking out watchfully. To his side the torch still shone steadily on the rows of riotous little figures in their entwined, inward-looking, self-absorbed groups.

Ghote closed his eyes again.

'You wouldn't have thought she was a frigid woman,' Gregory said. 'Hell, no one in the States is allowed to look like a frigid woman. But, well, she—'

He broke off. Ghote opened his eyes again and forced himself up into a position of alertness. But there seemed to be no change in the situation.

'No,' Gregory said, with sudden firmness, 'I don't want to go around crabbing at American society. I despise people who do that.'

Ghote found he could summon up little interest. His head was throbbing with a numbing ache. His arm seemed a lot more painful. He explored the bandage with his good hand. As he expected, there was a sticky patch of blood on the outside.

He would have liked to have let himself slide away. But he knew that he must not. Gregory would need him. After all, they had only the one gun and three rounds of ammunition while the dacoits seemed to have plenty of ammunition and were alert and dangerous. Gregory would want all the help he could get.

But perhaps he could afford just two minutes' rest.

'Hey,' said Gregory.

Ghote struggled to his feet.

His head gave a screech of pain that seemed to shoot through all his body. He swayed.

'They're moving the flashlight,' Gregory said. 'What are they getting at?'

He peered forward. Behind him Ghote seemed to see the locked couples in the stonework move with the moving of the shadows.

'They're saying something out there,' Gregory went on. 'See if you can pick it up. I get the feeling they're planning something fresh.'

Ghote moved forward leadenly till he was nearer the entrance arch. Out in the temple hall the two dacoits were certainly talking, and they were moving from side to side with the torch. Just by Ghote's head now one of the little pairs of stone figures, one more ordinary than the others, seemed to start a stately little dance together.

He suddenly wished with all his heart that he could be somewhere else. Somewhere wrapped up. Safe. Cocooned. He wanted to be at home in the quiet of the night.

'What's it they're saying? For heaven's sake?'

Gregory's voice grated harshly on his ear.

He must listen. He might manage to hear something that would save Gregory. And simultaneously the other thought burgeoned in his mind. Dark. Comfort.

The torchlight wavered to and fro.

With an almost physical jerk Ghote forced himself to concentrate on the two distant voices at the far end of the hall.

'It is all right,' he said after a moment. 'They are trying to see further in only. And they have just decided that they cannot succeed.'

A merciful blackness welled up in him. He was vaguely aware that he was slumping down against the wall.

A moment later he felt Gregory gently hauling him up.

'Hey, feller, don't conk out on me.'

'I am OK,' Ghote managed to say. 'Thank you for your kind attention.'

'Now, I'll prop you up here. Then you can keep a bit of a watch-out and get some rest too.'

Gregory was handling him with great care and deftness. He gave the carnal figures on the wall opposite one last look and closed his eyes once more.

He lost count of how long he stayed where he had been propped, in a dreamy state of half-wakefulness. But suddenly he was alert again.

Someone was calling him.

'Mr Policeman. Mr Policeman.'

He started to scrabble up.

'It's OK, Ganesh,' Gregory said. 'It's just those guys. They seem to want to parley or something. Can you handle it?'

'Yes. Yes, I can,' Ghote said.

He looked at Gregory. The American was crouching in the arch-way, the gun in his right hand pointing steadily forward.

Ghote pushed himself cautiously off the supporting wall. He was conscious that the convenient handle he was using to haul himself up was the miniature carved representation of a graceful, full-figured girl curved voluptuously round her partner. It did not seem to matter.

'What do you want?' he called to the dacoits outside.

'Come out,' one of them shouted back.

'Throw your guns down and we will come,' Ghote answered.

The men laughed coarsely.

'Throw away our guns, Policemanji? When we are winning? You are wounded. We have seen that. It will not be long. But if you like, we are ready to make bargain.'

'What bargain is this?' Ghote called back.

He could not understand what possible offer the dacoits could have to make, and the effort of dealing with them seemed to be taking an unfair amount of his remaining strength.

'It is a very easy bargain, Policemanji. Tell the American to come out with you and when you come we will make sure no harm comes to yourself.'

'No.'

The dacoits did not seem put out by the refusal. The one doing the talking went cheerfully on.

'Think a little, Policemanji. What is it you have there? A foreigner only. Who is he that you should wish to die for him? He cannot even know what we are talking.'

Ghote reflected dully that this at least was true. Gregory, crouching there just beside him, had not the least notion of what was being plotted against him.

'It is very simple, Policeman. When we have dealt with the American, there is much pay for us. So we would carry you to car and drive to the Bombay road. Soon you would be in hospital and safe. In a few days only you would be at home. You have wife, Policemanji?'

And Ghote found that he was considering the offer. He was not thinking whether he should accept it, but he was turning its terms slowly over in his dulled mind. And on the face of it, they were attractive terms. All he had to do was sacrifice an unknown foreigner, who was quite likely to be killed anyway, and his own chances were automatically doubled.

He touched the bandage round his right arm. It was very heavily soaked now. He must be losing blood at a great rate. His fingers came into contact with the knot.

Gregory tied that, he thought.

'Never. Never.'

His defiant shout echoed for a long while round the temple hall. Only when it had completely died away did the dacoits' spokesman reply.

'We can wait,' he called.

When Ghote had gathered his strength again a little, he told Gregory the gist of the dacoits' proposal. Gregory did not thank him in words. But the one look he gave him showed he understood what Ghote had done, and what he could so easily have done.

'I guess we can wait too,' he said simply.

He nodded towards the running friezes of little carnal figures.

'After all, we have entertainment,' he said. 'Not that entertainment is quite what they provide,' he added after a long, thoughtful pause.

Ghote decided he was not so sure that they could wait. It would take V. V. a good time to reach Panvel and its police post. It would take a rescue party a good while to get back. They could well be too late.

And it was possible that V. V. was not going to the police at all. He might after all have been an India First spy and simply unwilling to unmask himself unnecessarily. He could safely leave the hired dacoits to do their work and creep away himself to report to his immediate superior in that chain of command Colonel Mehta had spoken of. And even if he was merely an obsessed journalist in search of a story, it was quite possible that he would consider getting to Bombay to meet a deadline more urgent than stopping in Panvel to explain things to the police.

For some time Ghote thought about all this. And then he came to the conclusion that after all he and Gregory must not just sit and wait in their little prison, with its compellingly vivid reminders of the joys of life, for death to come almost inevitably. They must make a move themselves.

After a little he told Gregory what he had in mind.

'OK, go ahead. It may work.'

Propping himself near the chamber entrance once more, Ghote called over to the dacoits. They answered quickly enough.

'You are bringing him out, Policemanji?'

'No, I am not,' Ghote called back. 'But I am going to give you good advice. There is something you do not know. There were not two but three of us in the temple. One of us got away when you ran in.'

The effort of calling this out, sentence by sentence, had exhausted him. He shut his eyes and waited listlessly to see what would happen.

The dacoits evidently thought what he had said worth thinking about. He heard them talking together in low voices. Then came their answer.

'Policemanji?'

'Yes?'

'You are lying like the dog you are. We will kill you both.'

He could not gather up enough energy to reply. Once more he shut his eyes to everything, to Gregory kneeling watchfully with the revolver resting on his thigh, to the faint sounds coming from their enemy, to the mocking little images of carefree sportiveness all around.

When he opened his eyes next it was to find the dacoits had put out their torch.

'Conserving the power, I guess,' Gregory said.

Ghote took a long, deep breath.

'There is something I must tell you,' he said.

'What's that?' Gregory answered, a little casually.

Then abruptly he put his face close to Ghote's and looked at him hard.

'Now, listen, feller,' he said, 'right now you shouldn't be telling anybody anything you don't have to. You're not looking one bit good. You just rest up while you can.'

Ghote shook his head with an effort.

'I must tell you now,' he said. 'You know that at any moment those two out there may rush us. And when our three rounds have gone, that will be that. And I want you to know this. You must know it, in case you die.'

'Hell, there's no question of anybody dying. Those guys don't realize we have so little ammunition. They're not going to risk stopping a bullet if they don't have to, and help'll be coming pretty soon. Cheer up. Cheer up.'

Ghote sighed a little impatiently.

'You are right, perhaps,' he said. 'But perhaps you are not. And I am going to tell while I am sure I have enough strength.'

'OK then. Go ahead, if it means a lot to you.'

For a few seconds Ghote sat in silence trying to arrange his thoughts. But when he did speak what he had to say came out in an unruly spate which he resented but could not control.

'It is this,' he said. 'I am not working as a policeman. I have been taken away from the CID. I am working for a Government agency, a security group. It is called the Special Investigations Agency. And Colonel Mehta, the commander, gave me one task before everything else. It is not even to protect you from India First though I have been told to do that. It is to find out just how much your brother discovered on his visit to Trombay. And you do know what he saw there, I am sure of that. That is why you have always refused to answer when I asked about what he told you before you left for Poona. But I had to keep asking. Those were my orders.'

For a moment he paused, simply to take breath.

'I wanted for you to know,' he went on. 'To know I have been trying to trick you into giving me your confidence. All this time I have been lying that this was police matter only.'

Gregory Strongbow, kneeling in the entrance of their enforced prison, still keeping an alert watch out towards where the two men with guns waited, chuckled a little.

'You certainly fooled me in the end,' he said. 'Of course, at the start I pretty well reckoned you must be from whatever the Indian equivalent of the FBI is. I expected to have a spy planted on me, perhaps even a discreet killer. But after all that we'd been through together I'd come to trust you a hundred per cent.'

'You were wrong to,' Ghote said.

Gregory chuckled again.

'Was I so wrong? You told me the truth finally. You didn't have to, not if you felt your first loyalty was to – what is it? – the Secret Investigation Agency.'

'Special Investigations.'

'Well, if you felt your first loyalty was to that, you didn't have to say a word. You could have let me die ignorant. And I reckon in any case I'm not going to die.'

'It is difficult to know which loyalty is the first,' Ghote said wearily. 'In so many directions we are tugged.'

Gregory did not reply at once. He shifted his position at the chamber mouth a little, and then glanced across at Ghote.

'Yes,' he said, 'we're tugged in a good many directions, all of us. And I think it's about time I let a different pull take over with me.'

'With you?'

'Heck, I'm just as tugged different ways as you. More even.'

'I do not understand.'

'No? Well, let me tell you something. All this while that I've been keeping Hector's big secret for him, I've been resenting him dead just as much as I disliked him alive.'

'Resenting your brother? Disliking him?'

Ghote felt his already enfeebled brain suddenly turning topsy-turvy. If there had been one point which he had taken constantly for granted ever since he had first met Gregory on the Poona road and had mistaken this unacademic figure for an American pressman, it was that Gregory was totally loyal to his brother. They had come to India together, bringing with them entwined memories of their family life, brothers friends enough to want to be with one another on a long, exciting holiday. And Hector had met violent death. That had been the picture from the very beginning. And now it had been abruptly and completely reversed.

'Sure I disliked Hector,' Gregory said. 'He wasn't a very pleasant character. He made a darn fool of himself with all that hysterical anti-Bomb stuff and got into a lot of trouble he purely deserved. And he did it out of spite that he hadn't made a bigger career. Then he ran out on his wife, who is a lovely person, with some damned beatnik girl he'd picked up. And when that blew up in his face, I thought it was just about time to take him out of the way before he did any more harm. So we fixed this good, long vacation in India. And look what a mess that got us into, thanks to my kid brother and his poking around.'

Ghote simply listened.

'Yes, that's what it was,' Gregory went on, 'plain poking around where he'd no business to be. And it just so happened that he found out something that was being kept pretty quiet over at Trombay.'

He laughed.

'Here comes what you were sent to find out,' he said. 'It's just this. India not only has the Bomb, in spite of what they all tell you, but she has had it a good long time and what's more has hit on a way of making the things at about a hundredth the cost of any previous type. So she's not only a nominal atom power, but in actual fact ready to knock hell out of practically anybody.'

He stopped and allowed himself a long, relaxed chuckle.

'Boy,' he said, 'when you gave me that stuff on the way out to Elephanta about Indians having a genius for improvisation, I couldn't have agreed with you more. And they can improvise a sight more than running repairs to an old outboard motor.'

Ghote forced himself to fight back against growing waves of weakness.

'Gregory,' he said. 'Thank you for telling.'

'Heck, I ought to have told you long ago.'

'No,' Ghote said, 'I did not trust you. I did not even trust you with a simple gun.'

He felt himself sliding sideways against the smooth stone of the pillar at his back. He struggled to get his grip on things again.

'I understand a lot more now,' he said. 'No wonder India First wanted that secret kept. I suppose Hector would not have kept quiet for long.'

'He would not,' Gregory answered. 'It was all I could do to persuade him to keep his mouth shut when we met outside that Victoria Terminus. And no doubt he was haring out to Poona to tell me he'd changed his mind about the promise he gave me. He had that much decency, I guess.'

He was silent for a little. When he spoke again, Ghote could hardly hear him because of the murmurous buzz he felt in his head.

'Ganesh,' he said. 'I've been thinking. If you weren't planted on me by the Government guys, someone was pretty certainly planted on my by India First. Listen, if we do get out of this alive, I want you to question Shakuntala, and question her till she breaks.'

'Yes,' Ghote said, 'I will do it.'

As if the words had been a signal, the dacoits' torch beam flicked on again. At Ghote's side the writhing figures of the mithunas sprang back to sensuous life.

Gregory rapidly shifted his stance in the doorway. Leaning tensely forward into the gloom, he found time for one murmured comment.

'Those damn sex-fiends,' he said. 'Won't they ever leave off?'

After that they listened in silence. Very faint scuffling sounds came from the dark temple hall.

'Damn it, what are they doing?' Gregory exploded at last.

It was impossible to make out. Ghote felt incredibly weary with even making the effort. After a long while he realized that Gregory was talking again. He forced himself to concentrate.

'This ought to do it,' the American was saying.

Ghote saw him take something from the inner pocket of his jacket. He strained to see what it was. In the sharp torchlight he eventually made it out. Something the size of a small coin, mostly white with black on it.

Hector Strongbow's CND button.

Then he saw Gregory toss the little disc carefully forward. It landed out in the hall beyond with a tiny clatter and skittled across the stones of the floor.

Two bursts of shots followed. When the echoes had died away Gregory spoke contentedly.

'I get it,' he said. 'They're trying to creep up on us. I know where they are now though, and I think I could put a shot pretty near one of them. But I'd like to save it if I can. Listen, Ganesh. Do you think you could call out to them that I've spotted them and I'm ready to shoot. If that scares them back, we've saved a bullet.'

'I would try,' Ghote whispered.

He breathed deeply. Once. Twice.

He was in real doubt whether he would be able to shout with enough force and conviction. But for Gregory's sake he was determined to try.

A last long breath.

And then he stopped. The two dacoits had begun talking to each other. Urgently and quite loudly. He caught the word 'police'. And suddenly the torch went out and there was the plain sound of feet running out of the hall.

Ghote gathered his last strength together.

'Do not go, Gregory,' he said. 'Trap.'

Then came total blackness.

16

Ghote opened his eyes and pushed himself up on his elbows. For several minutes now he had been feeling that he would be able to cope with things, and he thought that the moment had now come to see whether the curious procession of events of which he had been half-conscious had really taken place.

He looked round a little. It was as he had thought. He was lying on Gregory Strongbow's bed in his room in the Queen's Imperial Grand Hotel. Above him the seven long-bladed fans swept round and round. But about the other events that must have led to his finding himself here he would have to ask.

Gregory was standing by the tall window over which the long brocade curtains had been drawn. He was talking in a low voice to Shakuntala.

'Please,' Ghote said, 'what is the time?'

Gregory and Shakuntala wheeled round.

'You're OK?' Gregory asked.

'It's nearly midnight,' Shakuntala said. 'And you're not to worry. Everything has been taken care of.'

'It is the same day as when we went to the temple?' Ghote enquired.

'Yes, it's the same day,' Gregory said. 'A pretty long day, but a pretty good one. According to Dr Udeshi there's nothing wrong with you that some rest won't put right.'

'I feel quite well again,' Ghote said.

Gregory grinned.

'Old Udeshi gave strict instructions you weren't to move,' he said.

Ghote flopped back on the great mound of pillows behind him.

'Please, do I remember Shakuntala at the temple?' he said.

'You do,' Gregory answered. 'She was what the dacoits mistook for the police. When they heard her coming, they must have remembered what you told them about V. V. and thought the game was up. Anyway, they lit out pretty quick.'

Ghote frowned.

'But what was Shakuntala doing there at all?' he said.

'I was disobeying instructions,' Shakuntala replied with a smile. 'You know that V. V. came along while I was talking to Mira Jehangir in her car. Well, by that time I was beginning to regret I'd ever started that. She really is pretty awful.'

Grinning widely, Gregory gave her a nudge.

'Go on, tell the feller what happened,' he said.

'Well, V. V. asked where you two were, and I decided to go with him to show him. When we got to the little lake he told me to wait for him in the car whatever happened. But I began to get worried, and in the end I just disregarded what he'd said and set out to see for myself. Only I got lost.'

'Lost in the jungle?' Ghote said anxiously.

'Oh, yes,' Shakuntala answered. 'I wasn't frightened or anything, because my father was in the Forestry Service and I'm used to jungle. But I tried to be too clever and couldn't find the path again.'

'It was a pretty good thing she did,' Gregory interrupted. 'If we'd had to wait for the police it might have been too late.'

'But they came?' Ghote asked. 'V. V. did go to them?'

'Yes. We met them later, but I'm afraid they'd be too late to get the dacoits.'

'They will pick them up soon,' Ghote declared. 'The State Police are highly efficient.'

Suddenly he sat up straight on the big soft bed.

'The telephone,' he said. 'I must use the telephone.'

'Why? What is this?' Gregory asked with anxiety.

'Kartar Singh,' Ghote said. 'He told us the truth. I must arrange at once to have him brought to Bombay.'

He took the bedside telephone and asked for a number. The necessary explaining and arguing left him feeling a good deal weaker, but eventually he was able to flop back on to the mounded pillows with a sense of duty accomplished.

For some time he lay back while a bearer brought in a meal, under the personal supervision of the manager, who was looking grimly furious and was obviously missing his car, if not his receptionist.

When he had eaten his fill, Gregory looked down at him smilingly.

'You look more like your usual self now,' he said.

'I feel perfectly better,' Ghote declared.

'You're sure? You're certain?'

There seemed to be a note of undue concern in his voice. Ghote put it down to a feeling of emotional loyalty that must have grown up during their ordeal in the temple.

'Really,' he said, with a smile, 'I am quite my old self again.'

'Well, if you really are . . .'

'Yes. What is it?'

'Well, you've got some questions to ask Shakuntala, haven't you?'

The thought of what it was that he had promised Gregory to ask Shakuntala came back into his mind with unpleasant clarity. For a moment he contemplated pleading tiredness, but he felt he could hardly go back so suddenly on his protestations of a moment before, however exaggerated they had been.

He pushed himself up to a sitting position on the high bed.

'Yes,' he said, 'I have got some questions.'

Shakuntala sat down abruptly on the small, cane-seated chair near the foot of the bed. She looked up at Ghote with a suddenly strained expression. There could be no doubt she knew what it was he was going to ask.

'Miss Brown,' Ghote began, 'you told just now that you took V. V. to the lake near the temple where you knew we had gone. Why was that?'

Shakuntala looked dismayed. This was not the question she had been exactly expecting.

'I wanted him to be there in case he could help you,' she said.

'You knew Gregory's life was in danger. Was not V. V. among the most likely ones to be spying on him?'

'No. Well, yes. But—'

She stopped and looked down at her feet.

Suddenly she shook herself as if to break free from a tangle of jungle tendrils that had entrapped her. She looked straight up at Ghote.

'I knew V. V. could not be the India First spy,' she said, 'because it was me they had set to report on Gregory.'

In the far corner of the big, high-ceilinged room Ghote saw Gregory go stiff as a post.

'Yes,' Ghote said to Shakuntala, 'you were the India First spy. You were always the most likely person, even from the moment that you tried with so much force to persuade Gregory that it was all in the day's work for the dacoits to have waited all morning before deciding to attack one particular car.'

He looked down at her implacably. And saw her eyes were flashing with anger.

'Yes,' she said, 'I was an India First agent. I have worked for India First for a long time. I believed they were right. This country could take its true place in the world if its people were loyal to it as they should be, if they all worked as they should work. But understand this. I found there came a time when I had to choose between India First and something else.'

She jumped up suddenly and stood looking intently at the stock-still figure of the American in the far corner of the room.

'I found I had to choose between the country I was born in and a foreigner,' she said. 'And I found that I could not help myself but choose the foreigner. The man I once thought stood for everything I detested.'

Standing gravely in the corner, Gregory Strongbow spoke at last.

'You say you chose me. But you never said a single word to hint to me who or what you were.'

'No, I never said a single word. But all the same, from the moment I decided that my allegiance had changed I never did one single thing to help India First. I promise you that.'

'But why? Why?' Gregory said.

'I told you. For years I was with India First, heart and soul. Do you think I could change right round in the twinkling of an eye? I think more of myself than that.'

Gregory looked across at her with a perturbed frown.

'I do think I see,' he said.

'You must see,' she replied fiercely. 'You must see. All right, I had changed sides. But I still had to be loyal to what I had once believed. I was against India First. Totally, if you like. But I was still with India First in the past.'

She looked back at Gregory with utterly concentrated intentness. Ghote guessed that she had probably forgotten that he himself was in the room at all.

Gregory stood in silence. Then he took a pace forward.

'Yes,' he said, 'I see now why you let me go to find the launch at Sewri and at the same time left that message. You couldn't hound down people you'd been working with until a few days ago. I respect you for that.'

And Shakuntala fell on to the edge of the bed in floods of relieved tears.

For minutes Ghote let her weep. But he had not finished yet.

'There is one more thing,' he said eventually.

She pushed herself up from the bed and turned to him, brushing the tears away.

'Yes?'

'You told that from the moment you decided not to be loyal any longer to India First you did nothing to help them. But when was that moment?'

Shakuntala blinked at him from washed-out eyes.

'I can tell you exactly,' she said. 'It was at the moment you brought Gregory back here after he had been attacked on Marine Drive. I knew then that I could not be loyal to an organization prepared to do that to a man like Gregory, innocent and in a foreign land.'

'But it was you who sent him to that meeting on Marine Drive?'

Shakuntala hung her head.

'Yes, I admit it.'

'But you did not know an attack was planned for the Elephanta trip? I thought you were strangely confident that the launch could not be aiming for us.'

'Yes,' Shakuntala replied, 'that was a complete surprise to me. Some other agent must have watched us leave. I was sure no attack had been planned because I had heard nothing.'

Ghote nodded.

'And for the attack on Marine Drive,' he asked, 'you received orders by telephone?'

'Yes.'

'Who from?'

'I don't know. Someone high up in the organization, I think. In the ordinary way you had only one contact above you and one below. Mine were in Poona, because I was there with the Tourist Department. But it was someone else who phoned me here.'

'How did you know this man was from India First?'

'There was a code word for use in emergency.'

'I see. And you did not in any way recognize this man?'

'No. It was a man's voice, that's all.'

'And as soon as you got your instructions you acted on them?'

'Yes. At once.'

'I see,' Ghote said.

While he had been asking Shakuntala these last questions, Gregory had come up and rested his broad hands lightly on her shoulders. Now Ghote looked up at him.

'You realize what this means?' he said. 'I shall have to see Colonel Mehta immediately.'

It was about an hour later that Ghote, after making one telephone call, found himself once more making his way up the interminable flights of neglected stairs that led to Colonel Mehta's eyrie office. He had come by taxi through the now nearly deserted night streets to the back entrance of the huge, old, Gothic office block. Waiting for him there was the chowkidar, an aged Pathan, almost as much a relic of the past as the old building he guarded, wearing a turban and the traditional waistcoat and baggy trousers and armed with a crooked stick. With quavering fingers he had handed Ghote a lamp to light him on his way in the dark, silent building. It was a pathetic enough source of light, a mere tag of wick floating in coconut oil in an earthenware bowl. The little coil of thick, greasy-smelling smoke that it gave off seemed to add unduly to the stiflingly clammy heat of the old, still building.

Ghote felt a new onset of weakness as he climbed. He knew that, like Gregory earlier on, he too should have obeyed Dr Udeshi's orders and stayed in bed. He believed in doing what the doctor told him. But sometimes other things had a prior claim.

But at last he reached the top of the seemingly unending series of turning flights and there under the door with the notice saying simply 'Special Investigations Agency' was a thin line of light.

Ghote stepped forward and knocked.

'Come.'

He recognized Colonel Mehta's clipped accent. He entered, crossed the bare outer office with its embedded wall-safe, the colonel's sole concession to the need to retain any documents, and pushed at the slightly open door of the inner office.

Colonel Mehta was sitting just exactly as Ghote had seen him before, precise and upright behind the bare table with its single telephone.

'Well, Inspector,' he said briskly, 'what's all this about? I don't like holding interviews in the middle of the bloody night unless I have to, you know.'

'There are special circumstances, Colonel.'

'I should damn well hope so. Let's hear 'em then.'

'Very well.'

Ghote remained standing in front of the small, bare table, looking down a little at the spruce, seated figure of the colonel.

'Colonel, I am near the end of the whole business.'

'Near the end? And what precisely do you mean by that? You've picked up those damned dacoits, I suppose. Well, I've heard nothing of that. I was supposed to be kept bloody well informed.'

He glared round as if there might be someone in the bare room to be put immediately under close arrest.

'No,' Ghote said, 'it is not that. The dacoits have not been picked up yet. It is that I know who gave them their orders.'

'You do, do you, Inspector? I shall believe that when I hear it.'

'Very well. Then may I ask how it was that Professor Strongbow was sent to meet an apparently accidental death within minutes of my having informed you, and no one else, that he had in fact seen his brother after the Trombay visit?'

Colonel Mehta did not answer.

He looked up at Ghote from under his bristling eyebrows, steadily and hard. Then he dropped his glance and began fiddling with the button of his trimly fastened jacket. Eventually he looked up again and spoke.

'Let me get this bloody well straight, Inspector,' he said, in a voice lacking its former fieriness. 'You're saying that I was the only person who knew Professor Strongbow had learned his brother's secret, and that the orders to kill him went out so quickly that it could only have been me who gave them? Is that right? Have I got it right?'

He sounded almost humble.

'Yes,' Ghote answered, 'I am saying that the head of Special Investigations Agency is head of India First also. The simple policeman you thought would keep you ahead of any awkward enquiries has found out the truth.'

'I see. But why have you come to me with all this? Surely you should have gone higher up? It should have been a visitor from Delhi I was receiving and not a mere police inspector. Unless what you've been telling me is a mere cock-and-bull story?'

'No, it is not,' Ghote said. 'But who could I go to higher up? You know there was no one. You told me yourself it would be like that. I think no one in Delhi knew about Hector Strongbow's visit to Trombay even. I heard you telling my DSP not to breathe a word about it. Who would believe me then? And if they did, might it not be to another traitor I was talking?'

Colonel.Mehta gave a sharp grunt.

'So what have you come here to do then?' he asked.

'To arrest you, Colonel, on a charge of conspiring to murder Hector Strongbow on or about the fourth of September last.'

And Colonel Mehta laughed. A sudden splutter of mirth, as if he could not help it.

Then he slipped the heavy Service revolver from his under-arm holster and pointed it straight at Ghote.

'You bloody incompetent fool,' he said.

The shots rang out in the hot stillness of the big, deserted building like a series of minor explosions.

Gregory Strongbow came in through the slightly open door from the outer office.

'Thank you, Gregory,' Ghote said. 'I knew I could trust your shooting.'

He looked down at the body of Colonel Mehta, officer in charge of the rootless Special Investigations Agency, head of the self-centred India First group. It lay sprawled back against the bare wall of the totally bare, recordless little office.

'Unknown assailants have killed another person,' he said. 'The crime figures will be bad this month.'